THE ENCHANTER'S RISE

THE ENCHANTER'S RISE

THE NECROMANCER'S END
BOOK 2

Jack Pembroke

Podium

To Cara, Diane, Olivia, Erin, and Allen,

the bricks I am built of.

Copyright © 2025 by Jack Pembroke

Cover design by Mario Teodosio

ISBN: 978-1-0394-5919-9

Published in 2025 by Podium Publishing
www.podiumentertainment.com

Podium

THE
ENCHANTER'S
RISE

CHAPTER ONE

Failure

Inch by precious inch, Jeremiah Thorn failed. With a diamond-tipped needle, he painstakingly scratched a hairsbreadth trough into the surface of the metal plate. It needed to be perfect—perfect depth, perfect width, and perfectly in line with the spiderweb of swirling grooves he had already spent two weeks etching across the plate. The muscles in Jeremiah's back, already tight with stress, began to throb with the omen of imminent cramps.

He put the needle down and stretched, willing his aching muscles to relax. It barely helped. Gus the toad sat perfectly still on the desk, sympathetically focusing as hard as he could.

"Just one more little notch, buddy, and we'll be all done," Jeremiah whispered to his familiar. The final step was a minuscule rod of gold that needed to be placed across the line he had just carved, but it required its own tiny resting place. He chose a new needle from the leather case unrolled beside him. There were dozens of diamond-tipped steel instruments, imperceptibly but critically different from each other. He chose a size 000 rasp pick, steadied himself, and dragged it once across the line. He took his pair of tweezers and gently lifted the tiny golden rod and placed it across the whisper of a scratch he had just made. Too shallow. He scratched it one more time and placed the golden rod again. Still too shallow.

This should be easy, he thought. *This is easy.* Just a simple enchantment on a plate of metal. All he had to do was be perfect.

"Patience," he reminded Gus. "Now is where we are patient. We go extra slow, one scratch at a time, just like we were taught."

He scratched; he placed. He scratched; he placed. Hundreds of times, maybe thousands, he repeated the action. He felt the rasp wearing away at his resolve faster than it wore away the metal. After an hour he felt a stabbing pain in the joints of his finger and stopped. Rubbing the ache away he inspected his work. The notch looked no deeper now than when he had started.

Enchanting was, without a doubt, an incredible pain in the ass. The act of writing magic words, literally the physical symbols that are spoken when magic is cast, required exacting precision. Controlling the magic that flowed through the runes through slivers of material and modifying words only compounded the difficulty. His current enchantment would magically strengthen the material it was carved on if he touched a specific point. He read the somehow still incomplete enchantment.

If Contact, Strengthen

"Okay, so maybe that was overdoing it. We are still going to be patient, Gus. This is not me being impatient. But we can probably step things up a little bit, right?"

Gus wriggled and snapped his mouth open and shut.

Jeremiah stretched again, shaking out his wrists. The tiny room had seemed to close in on him in the past hour. Simple wooden walls were obscured by countless tools, piles of practice plates, and elaborate diagrams drawn in chalk. The nearly identical tools were organized in a system so convoluted that anyone would believe it to be pure chaos. But Jeremiah understood it, at least in part. That worried him.

"Patience," he repeated. "I am patient."

He scratched. He placed. Too shallow. He scratched twice; he placed. Too deep. Jeremiah froze, staring at the fleck of gold that shifted side to side in its cradle.

"Okay" was all he said, and he placed down his tools. There was a not fully ignorable urge to destroy the room and everything in it. Gus let out a single angry croak, a noise Jeremiah was tempted to echo.

Before he got to learn where his boiling frustration was taking him, he heard the slightest squeak of the door opening.

His teacher, Thurok, stood in the doorway. Small for an orc and with gray rather than greenish skin, his distinctive orcish tusks were elaborately carved with runes. Thurok was scowling at the hinges of the door, the whisper squeak seemingly capturing his displeasure above all else.

"Thorn," he said but didn't continue. Jeremiah waited as long as he could before coughing.

"Hmmm?" Thurok looked up like Jeremiah had just interrupted him. "Show your work."

Jeremiah carried the square plate of metal across the room, the result of two weeks' backbreaking effort, and held it out to Thurok like an offering. Thurok hardly glanced at it.

"Nonfunctional. Rushed and sloppy. Depth control is . . . barely improved. Focus remains terrible."

"Yes, sir," said Jeremiah. After nearly a year of similar feedback, any sense of expectation or disappointment had long since burned away. The fact that he'd said Jeremiah had improved at all should have felt like winning a blue ribbon, but, awash in an ocean of the same criticisms, it left no impression. "Any advice on how to more accurately nest the conduits and nodes?"

"Yes," said Thurok. "Do it better."

Jeremiah nodded. This was very much in line with Thurok's typical advice. "Yes, sir. Thank you, sir," he said. He didn't look at his teacher or his work but gazed somewhere beyond Thurok's left elbow.

"Enchantment is as much an art form as it is a magical discipline," Thurok said, not for the first time. "It requires absolute, singular focus. Passion is meaningless, inspiration is meaningless. Only precision matters. The sooner you understand this, the sooner you will improve beyond the simplest enchantments."

"I understand, sir. It's just . . . some precise specific guidance might help?" Jeremiah raised his gaze to Thurok's shoulder.

Thurok recoiled at the request. "You want me to do it for you? You will learn nothing. You must trust the process. It is the process that granted me the skills I have, the skills that enchanted your compatriot Allison's armor and countless other items wielded by great warriors and heroes."

"So, no?" asked Jeremiah.

"You don't want my help, your weakness wants my answers. I will give you neither and starve your weakness that much more. One day you will thank me." Thurok began to leave.

"Anything else today, sir?" asked Jeremiah. There was always more to do, even if there was nothing to do Thurok would find something. In exchange for his tuition, he worked in Thurok's enchanting workshop, helping with the menial tasks the orc considered him worthy of.

"File all receipts from today. Sharpen the picks and rasps. Sweep. Then, trace on paper ten times each the Strengthen rune, the Adhesion rune, the Decay rune, the If rune, the And rune, and the Delay rune. Once finished, you may depart."

It was another three hours and after dark before Jeremiah left Thurok the Enchanter's workshop. The shop took up the entire third floor of an expansive commercial building near the center of Dramir, the part of town that was composed of grandiose architecture and elaborate carved marble. Tonight, a late summer mist reduced the lantern lights to a soft glow.

Jeremiah enjoyed the cool moisture on his skin as he made his way toward the residential quarter. It was refreshing after being in the stuffy workshop since before sunup. After swearing off necromancy, Jeremiah had once again found himself with no appreciable talents. Enchanting had seemed like a reasonable pursuit—he could create magic equipment for his party to take on more dangerous (and lucrative) challenges, and repair or even sell gear to supplement their income.

However, it had turned out that his level of skill in enchanting fell under the opposite of talented. His 'fractured but strong' focus, which had made him such an attractive student to his necromancy teacher so long ago, was ill-suited to the intensely precise task of enchanting. When his attention and patience wavered, as they inevitably did, he'd ruin the rune and Jeremiah's status as a failure in Thurok's eyes—and his own—would be even further cemented. It was a pattern that repeated itself week after week.

Why he continued in this thankless endeavor, even he wasn't sure. Thurok allowed him to keep the small payment whenever he recharged an existing enchantment for a customer, but those jobs were rare. Perhaps the truth was that he simply did not know what else he could do. Experienced mages were few and far between, even more so the ones willing to take on a student. It was only Jeremiah's reputation for magic in Dramir that had convinced Thurok to teach him, and surely that was all that kept the orc from expelling him now.

Jeremiah passed the remains of an accountancy office that had burned down last month—not all discontent had been deterred by Vivica's defeat nearly a year ago. For a time, the immense loss of wealth among Dramir's elite following the end of the siege had served to reduce the wealth disparity between the richest and poorest of the city. The cost of goods plummeted as the nobles' need to eat overcame their businesses' need for money. There was even some social mobility, as some enterprising peasants carved opportunities out of the destabilization.

However, the movement was short-lived. Within just a few changes of the season, money once again began flowing upward, toward the pockets that were accustomed to it. In fact, the only change that seemed durable was the support for improvements in Dramir's poorest neighborhoods, many of which were being spearheaded by Delilah under Bruno's guidance. It seemed Vivica's siege had alerted many nobles to the threat of the populace within their very city, and they were keen to appear benign and charitable, at least publicly.

As Jeremiah walked, the buildings shrunk from impressive monoliths to the familiar rows of terraced homes. He exchanged a few friendly nods, and there were even some smiles sprinkled in.

"How are you doing, Mr. Thorn?" asked a human man walking with his wife. His face was weatherworn but pleasant.

"Doing fine, thank you," said Jeremiah. He didn't recognize this man. His wife pushed her husband onward with only a curt nod.

It was a roll of the dice every evening. Often it was friendly nods or hellos. Sometimes someone would call him the savior of the city. Sometimes they'd just hiss "Necromancer!" or hurl other epithets at him on their way by. Jeremiah was glad tonight was an easy one.

Home. Finally home. Jeremiah pushed open the door and the familiar smells wrapped around him like a hug. The lingering scents of Delilah's various experiments and the chemicals she used to clean them always gave Jeremiah a sensation of freshness. Allison's blade oils, which were inevitably left in the living room despite Delilah's protests. Bruno's pipe smoke mixing with whatever stew was simmering on the stove to create a rich aroma that made Jeremiah want to sink into the nearest soft surface and exist in that moment forever.

Bruno was fully absorbed in a stack of papers at the kitchen table as Jeremiah dropped his bag near the foot of the stairs and threw himself onto the sofa. As he listened to the pops of the fire and the distant tinkling of Delilah working in her alchemy lab, that knot that had been threatening his shoulders finally began to loosen.

"Jay, can you tell me what this word is?" asked Bruno.

Jeremiah extended a hand without lifting his head. "Let me see."

Bruno had recently taken charge of many of Delilah's correspondences and minor bookkeeping. He still prowled the night, but something about the last year had sparked his curiosity into the vast and exciting world of paperwork. And ever since Jay's resolution to the Vivica incident, there was more paperwork than ever.

It turned out losing most of the wealth of the nobility of Dramir below the bowels of the earth had earned Jeremiah and his friends the ire of some very well-connected people. Searching for the treasure was now a crime, and even knowledge of the direction the undead had tunneled was a state secret, so many chose to express their displeasure through a never-ending stream of lawsuits against Jeremiah and his friends. Merely resisting the legal onslaught was draining the party's resources faster than they could replace them.

Jeremiah squinted at the page Bruno handed him, angling it to read by the lantern light. "*Acquiescence*," he said. "It means—"

"No, I know what it means," said Bruno, snatching the page back. "Just couldn't read it. This guy's handwriting is so sloppy."

It looked fine to Jeremiah, but perhaps he was used to old writings at this point. It was easier than deciphering enchanting runes, at any rate.

"Where's Allison?" asked Jeremiah.

"Coming around the corner now," said Bruno.

Sure enough, Jeremiah heard Allison's voice a few moments later. Even her normal speaking voice tended to fill whatever space she was in, so it wasn't hard to make out what she was saying.

"Thank you very much for walking me home, Ophelia. I felt much safer," said Allison from outside.

"You're welcome, Miss Allday," said a small voice.

"I want you to practice your stances, okay? First and second. You can keep the trainer, and . . . Ophelia, do you need me to walk you home?"

"Yes, please, Miss Allday," said the voice.

"Okay. I'll walk you home. It's the least I can do," said Allison. Jeremiah could hear the smile in her voice.

Allison returned a few minutes later, hip checking the door open. Her arms were occupied with a variety of wooden training weapons, nicked, scarred, and pitted nearly to pieces. A suit of wooden lamellar armor, small enough to fit a child, was just as pocked with a thousand little lessons. She dropped the supplies in a heap by the door. "Okay, I've got about forty-five minutes before my next student. Just enough time to sit for a minute."

She plopped on the couch beside Jeremiah's head, her limbs going limp and her eyes falling closed.

"How's the latest warrior disciple?" asked Bruno, squinting at a new document.

Allison responded without opening her eyes. "Ophelia displays an excellent grasp of foundational tenets and a dedication to practice. She has room to improve in authoritative action and decision-making. A pleasure to teach."

"At least it pays," said Jeremiah. He reached up and squeezed Allison's shoulder.

"I kind of . . . may be . . . discounting her tuition. Just a bit," said Allison. Jeremiah felt Allison's shoulder tense.

"Would you stop doing that?" Bruno barked. "We're trying to make ends meet, Al. You and Jay are barely making a pittance combined."

"Eh, my business is my business," said Allison. She still didn't open her eyes, but her brow furrowed in defiance. "And she needs a role model. Or a big sister. Or something. She needs me."

"Well, what are you pulling in lately?" Jeremiah asked Bruno.

"What I'm 'pulling in' is intercepting all the damn assassination attempts against us," said Bruno. His eyes darted to the windows and ceiling like the very word might summon them.

"Oh no, assassins," said Allison. "I'd love an assassination attempt."

"Jay and Delilah wouldn't, I can assure you," said Bruno. "You're welcome for the ability to sleep soundly at night."

"Are you looking for us to thank you for keeping us alive?" said Allison. Her eyes popped open, the audacity of the suggestion filling her weary veins with indignant fire. Her fingers curled into fists.

"Couldn't hurt," said Bruno. He was still leaning over the papers but had gone eerily still at Allison's tone.

Jeremiah sat up and put a hand on Allison's fist, squeezing just gently enough to be felt. She exhaled, then her hand softened and opened. Then, in one smooth movement, she popped to her feet. "Come on, Jay, let's get some spear practice in!"

"Can I just die instead? Work was really rough today," said Jeremiah. The idea of moving again was torturous.

"Nope, these days are the days it's most important. You gotta hurt through the pain! Now on your feet soldier!" Allison extended a hand, Jeremiah just stared up at her with pleading eyes.

"That bad, huh?" she said. Jeremiah nodded. "All right, the habit is more important than the work sometimes. I promise we're just going to do some easy work, okay? Just to loosen you up?" She leaned toward him, her hand getting closer and closer to his face.

Jeremiah felt a day's worth of frustration boil up again, but Allison's enthusiasm and warm expression tamped it down. Slowly, reluctantly, Jeremiah reached a hand up to grab hers. Allison bounced with excitement as he got closer, then snatched his hand and yanked him on his feet.

"Attaboy! Proud of you, Jay! Let's do this!" She dragged him out in the rain, back behind the house.

Allison started him with warm-up calisthenics: jumping, hopping, jogging, and stretching. As Jeremiah breathed heavier, he started to feel a little bit better. They geared up and began some light sparring.

"So, work was that bad, huh?" she said, letting Jeremiah's wooden spear tip glance harmlessly off her shield.

"Yeah. Well, I mean no. I don't know. It just doesn't feel like he's teaching me anything anymore," said Jeremiah. He flicked the end of his short spear in a high feint, then thrust toward Allison's leg. She swatted it away with a lazy flick of her sword.

"Is he not teaching, or are you not learning?" she asked. She had been training Jeremiah in spear fighting for the better part of a year now, with some physical exercise thrown in for good measure. It also served as a great time to talk to each other.

"I guess the latter? He just tells me to 'do better' but doesn't tell me what that means or how to do it," Jeremiah tried a trio of quick stabs, shoulder hip shoulder. Nothing connected. He was never able to land even a touch on Allison unless she let him.

"Slower," she said, regarding his attacks. "You're jabbing. Remember, you poke. It's funny, that kind of teaching would probably work for me."

"What's the difference between jabbing and poking?" asked Jeremiah, though he slowed his attacks down anyway.

"Just means you're not committing to the attacks, so they're not dangerous. You ever try talking to him about his teaching style? Asking him to be more like . . . your other teacher?" Allison avoided Flusoh's name like it was a taboo. Jeremiah thought her first and only meeting with Flusoh likely spooked her.

"Oh sure, but he's not interested. He's an amazing enchanter, and I've already learned a lot just by happenstance. But I can't—"

"Balance your stance," she quickly interrupted.

"Sorry. But I can't really break through to the advanced stuff. Especially converting flat runes to curved runes. Like, over a sword blade, or on an armored plate? It's so difficult!"

They sparred in silence for a time. She pushed him into some basic defense; long loping shots or messy thrusts he had to dodge or deflect.

"Remember to counter. Otherwise, it's just free attempts to kill yo—GOOD!" she exclaimed as Jeremiah turned a deflection into a thrust. Suddenly Jeremiah was in a rhythm, defenses turned into offenses seamlessly and back into defenses as Allison herself countered.

"Yes!" she shouted and picked up the speed. "Keep it up, keep it up!" Jeremiah's heart started to pound, his mind was almost blank, letting his body and reflexes do the fighting. He realized he was experiencing muscle memory, something zombies could possess. That little thought cracked his concentration, and he began overthinking. He lost his footwork, and overcommitted to a thrust, leaning far out over his lead foot. He couldn't recover in time, and Allison swatted him with her wooden sword.

The boil of frustration that he had been nursing all day suddenly reinvigorated itself, he gritted his teeth and rubbed the sore spot on his head.

"Excellent! Jay, that was excellent!" said Allison, settling back to a neutral stance. Just like that, she banished the frustration and dragged a smile out of him.

Gods, she's such a good teacher, thought Jeremiah. She seemed to know just when and how to offer praise that kept him eager to keep going.

They took a breather, stretching out their coiled muscles.

"So . . ." she started. "Been having any nightmares lately?"

Jeremiah thought about lying, to not worry her, but it wanted to come out. "A few now and then. The uh, the man in the closet dream, sometimes. And that dream where I can feel her . . . struggling."

Allison nodded, but didn't say anything. She knew about the Vivica dreams. It had been nearly a year since he had released the undead from his control, burying Vivica somewhere far away. Hopefully forever. But even though he had never felt her struggle through his rudimentary connection with the undead, he still sometimes dreamed he could. It always woke him up feeling nauseous, as opposed to terrified like the closet dream.

"Getting better, though," said Jeremiah. "Less frequent." She just nodded again, letting him say whatever he needed. Wanting to reassure her, Jeremiah shook himself out and then pointed his spear at her in a challenge. "Wanna do something fun?" he asked with a cocky smirk.

She raised an eyebrow. "Oh? What would that be?" she twirled the sword in a flourish.

"Give me everything you've got," said Jeremiah. "All out."

"Absolutely not." Allison laughed. "That is way too dangerous. But if you're looking to get humbled . . ."

She tossed her shield and longsword off to the side and picked up a training shortsword. She held it in her off hand and tucked her other arm behind her back.

"Seriously?" said Jeremiah.

"Come to Mama," Allison dared.

Jeremiah didn't hesitate and thrust right for her chest. Allison spun like a dancer, the spearhead missing her by a hair's breadth. Facing away from Jeremiah she bent over backward into a handspring, closing the distance in a single acrobatic motion. Jeremiah tried to jump away, but Allison was already on top of him and thrust the sword into his chest.

Jeremiah sprawled backward. "What the hell was that?!" he yelled. He had never seen her move like that before.

"Improvisation and athletics. You okay?" She offered him a hand to pull him up, which he took.

Jeremiah rolled his shoulders and massaged one of his arms.

He had to admit they felt different than they used to. Harder, a little larger, some shapes he didn't recognize. In a moment of vanity, he took off his shirt and inspected himself, he felt he looked pretty good! The baby pudge he'd carried with him for the longest time was almost completely gone, and he felt an energy that he realized hadn't always been with him.

He looked up and realized Allison was present for his moment of vanity and smiling in amusement at him.

"Sorry," he said embarrassed.

"Don't be. You've worked hard. Take some pride in the results." She slapped him on his bare shoulder. "Come on in. We're done for today."

Allison collapsed into the sofa again as though time rewound itself. She patted the seat next to her, offering Jeremiah a restful moment of companionship.

Jeremiah shook his head. "Promised Delilah I'd help in the lab."

"You're *always* helping Delilah in the lab," Allison whined. Sitting with Allison after training was almost a tradition. She became relaxed, almost affectionate, after a hard bout.

"She always needs help in the lab," said Jeremiah with a shrug.

"She didn't used to," said Bruno.

"Well, she does now," said Jeremiah. "She's so busy with lawsuit stuff, she barely has time to boil a pot of water." Jeremiah peeled himself away from the couch, his muscles protesting every movement. But a promise was a promise.

CHAPTER TWO

The Burden

The stairs were a veritable mountain, but Jeremiah trudged up them one step at a time. The alchemy smells grew stronger as he reached the landing leading to the lab and his own bedroom. He knocked once on the laboratory door, and it sprung open.

Delilah stood amid a cloud of steam, her hair bound up in a great mess above goggles and a filter mask. "Toad me," she said, holding out an ungloved hand.

"Not even a hello?" asked Jeremiah, slipping past her. He grabbed his own apron and mask off the peg and put them on quickly. Whatever was in the air was starting to make his lips tingle.

"Hello, Jay. Where's Gus?" said Delilah, probing Jeremiah's body with her eyes.

"Here, here, here, calm down," said Jeremiah. He produced Gus from beneath his apron. The toad wriggled in delight at the sight of Delilah and settled to contented stillness in her hand.

Delilah stroked Gus's back. "Thaaaat's the stuff," she said, visibly relaxing. "I missed you, my little poison pal." Gus echoed the sentiment with a low chirp.

"What are we on today?" asked Jeremiah, slipping on some elbow-length gloves. He was sweating already. Delilah's lab had its own tropical climate.

"Two active decants, and one compounding," said Delilah pointing to where Jeremiah's attention was needed.

Jeremiah set to work. Delilah's lab had become a happy space for him over the months. He was glad to actually be useful instead of slaving away over stubborn metal plates that would never be good enough. Plus, she always seemed happy to see him, an experience that was notably absent from Thurok's workshop.

As Jeremiah decanted one clear liquid into another, he spotted a few papers clumped together on a rare bare spot on the wooden tables. "No paperwork in the lab," he reminded Delilah in good humor.

Delilah just grumbled in response.

"That bad, huh?" said Jeremiah.

"How's enchanting?" asked Delilah pointedly. She began to work faster, commencing several alchemical procedures at once.

"Awful. I feel like I'm not making any progress. Thurok has me practicing the same things over and over and over again," said Jeremiah. He tried to help her, but quickly retreated into his own chores, daunted by her efficient movements.

Delilah held up a flask against the light. "That is how one gets better at things."

"Yeah, but I don't think it's working," said Jeremiah. Bottle by bottle, he began to decant, slowly and carefully.

"You're not special. Practice works for everyone else in the whole wide world. It works for you too," said Delilah. She embodied her words by letting her hands work seemingly on their own, her eyes busy inspecting other experiments in progress.

Her dismissal of his frustrations stung. Everything about enchanting was hard for him. The attention to detail, the exacting nature of the work, the extreme single-mindedness of intention—it was nothing like necromancy, where his mind could flow in a hundred different directions at once and direct the great foam of bubbles.

The delay in Jeremiah's response earned him a concerned glance. "How many runes do you know at this point?" asked Delilah. She shuffled over a step closer to him, maybe sensing his hurt feelings, while remaining within an arm's reach of her work.

"I know eight runes altogether," said Jeremiah. He counted them off on his fingers. "Decay, Strengthen, Adhere, Heat, Contact, And, If, and Pause."

Delilah paused her work, furrowing her brow in surprise. "How many runes are there?" She sounded incredulous at the number.

"Dozens, I think? I have no idea how big the list actually is, Thurok won't tell me. He just says to focus on the work in front of me and . . . What was it he said? 'Don't gaze at the horizon like a filthy poet.'"

Delilah snorted and set her flasks down quickly to keep from spilling them.

"Delilah, visitor!" called Bruno from downstairs.

Delilah froze, her breath catching. Jeremiah could feel the tension radiating off her. She'd become practically traumatized by the sound of someone knocking on the door.

"Come on," said Jeremiah. "Maybe it's nothing."

"Yeah, maybe," said Delilah. She still hadn't moved.

Jeremiah put down his beaker and grinned at her. "I suppose we could hide up here forever. Just you, me, and Gus. We'll let Bruno do all the talking from now on, what do you say?"

Finally, Delilah moved, fixing him with a look halfway between pleading and amused. A weak smile twitched her lips. "Fun as that sounds, I need to always get the measure of who I'm dealing with."

"Then let's get down there before any real damage is done, shall we? I'll even let you hold Gus the whole time."

Delilah sighed and started removing her protective lab gear. "Yeah. Okay. Thanks, Jay." She unpinned her hair and swung it into Jeremiah's face on the way out with a slap.

"Like getting hit with a wet dog," Jeremiah spluttered.

A gnome, smartly dressed beneath a black umbrella, waited on their doorstep. He had a bound collection of papers tucked under one arm.

"Lady Delilah Fortune?" he asked.

"Hey, Billipop." Delilah held out her hand expectantly.

"Are you Lady Delilah Fortune?" he asked.

"You know my name, Bill."

Bill's gaze was steady. "Rules are rules."

"Yes, I am Lady Delilah Fortune," Delilah said.

"Your presence, or the presence of your attorney, is requested before the Fourth Civil Court of Dramir in three weeks' time to answer a charge of grand larceny and conspiracy." Bill thrust the bundle of papers forward.

"Did you go through my mail as well?" asked Delilah, accepting and thumbing through the bundle.

"Yes. I took the liberty of picking up your mail for you," said Billipop.

"And is this *all* of our mail?" asked Delilah. There was a deadly threat in her voice.

"I was quite thorough, Lady Fortune," said Billipop.

"Thank you," said Delilah. She turned and slammed the door in Billipop's face.

"Another lawsuit?" asked Allison, still in her spot on the couch.

"Yup," said Delilah, dropping into a chair to peruse the papers.

"Shouldn't the king be able to protect us from stuff like this?" asked Jeremiah. He could imitate Billipop's voice, he had heard it so much over the last year.

"King Hector has been instrumental in protecting us from everything he has authority over. We'd likely have been hanged long ago without his help," said Delilah. She had reached the end of the bundle and shook it as though more pages would fall out. "That's it? There isn't even a proper case here. They're just trying to force us to pay more court fees and waste our time."

"Is it working?" asked Bruno.

"Yes, dammit!" Delilah slammed the most recent delivery onto another stack of documents. "We're getting picked apart like carrion. Between legal fees, settlements, and cases we actually *lose,* we're not exactly running in the black. The money from leasing the desert fortress isn't keeping up nearly as much as I had hoped."

"I can't really pick up any more students," said Allison with a frown. She looked down at an imagined pupil with a look of sympathy.

"Thurok pays what he pays," said Jeremiah.

"I know, I know," Said Delilah. "I'm not asking you guys to do more. I just . . ." She sighed. "We need some way out from under this." She retrieved Gus from her pocket and scratched between his eyes, lost in thought.

"Hey, don't hog the toad," said Allison. She made her way from the couch and stroked Gus's back.

"One for you, Jay," said Delilah, tossing an envelope to him.

Jeremiah opened and quickly skimmed the letter. "Necromancer . . . husband sick . . . one last . . . please . . . burial . . ." He threw it into the fire. Those letters still came from time to time. Each one was a temptation, a call to the skills he possessed. A chance to help someone. There was an urge to rescue the curling and blackening paper before its plea was lost forever, but he resisted. That wasn't what he was anymore.

"What do you mean 'out from under it'?" he asked as the letter burned.

"What I mean is, it's not a matter of money." Delilah gestured at the piles. "These . . . *vultures* will just keep coming. They're probably employing people specifically to make our lives miserable. We need influence, or someone with influence on our side, to make this crap stop."

"So, again, just no help at all from the king?" said Bruno.

"Hector has a lot of constraints being an elected king," said Allison. "I mean, not a *lot* of constraints, but limitations on what he can make people do." Allison started pawing at the papers as well, sinking into the chair beside Delilah's.

Bruno shot a conspiratorial smirk at Jeremiah at Allison's use of the monarch's first name.

Jeremiah stared into the fire as they fell into silence. He felt useless in the face of the bureaucratic wrath that threatened to overwhelm them. When he was a necromancer, his name could invoke some respect, or at least fear. Now it felt like Delilah was fighting all their battles and there was nothing he could do to help.

"Wait a minute, wait a minute!" Allison leapt to her feet, a letter in hand. As she scanned the paper, a bright smile spread across her face. "How would we feel about a little adventuring?"

"Gods, yes!" said Delilah. Bruno and Jeremiah laughed at her outburst. "No, I'm serious," she said. "I am so sick of paperwork. Let's nearly die somewhere!"

"Well, you're in luck, 'cause I've got a newly discovered tomb that's claimed one life already. Due to—get this—a *trap*." Allison waved the letter enticingly.

The others oohed and aahed.

"Any other information?" asked Jeremiah.

"Just a rough location. Mountains, a few days from here. A friend of mine from the Scout Corp sent this, says it's thus far unexplored. There's no pay, but we have rights to whatever we find inside. I say we take it. Any objections?"

"Let's do it!" shouted Bruno.

"I just need to file some delay requests," said Delilah, producing a new pile of blank papers.

"I'll let Thurok know. I don't think he'll care, honestly," said Jeremiah.

There was an awkward silence. Glances were exchanged around the table, but none of them with Jeremiah.

"What?" he asked, a foreboding settling on him.

"It's just . . ." Delilah began. "Well, now that you're not a necromancer, we need to consider if it's safe to bring you adventuring." She was still holding Gus and began petting the toad again reflexively, looking to Bruno and Allison for confirmation.

"Sorry, Jay," said Bruno, "but you're a liability. You can definitely help us prepare to leave if you want."

"And you're a part of this adventuring party, so you'll still be getting a cut no matter what," Delilah quickly added.

Bruno's face screwed up at that for just a moment. "Er, yeah. I suppose so. Anyway, unless you've learned enough enchanting to actually help us raid a trapped tomb . . ."

Jeremiah tried to speak, but found he had no words. He was offended, hurt, sad, and angry all in the span of a few seconds.

Allison took a deep breath, set her jaw, and closed her eyes. "Jay is coming with us," she said. The room went deadly quiet.

"Something we need to discuss?" asked Bruno, his eyebrows raised.

"Jay is coming with us," Allison said again. Her eyes opened, bereft of any uncertainty.

Bruno scowled at her. "So, our discussion about safety? Cohesion? The whole *Jay isn't ready* conversation we had before? All of that is just, what? No longer relevant?"

"He's ready," Allison said. "We've been training his spear fighting. He's proficient. He's ready."

"Al, he's not your squire," said Bruno. "This isn't going to be practice. We'd be babysitting him." Bruno barked a laugh at the absurdity.

"If Allison says I'm ready . . ." Jeremiah started. He wasn't fully convinced himself. Combat training with Allison had been a bright spot in his days over the last year, but he still couldn't actually hit her if she didn't let him.

"Shut up, Jay, this is about not getting someone killed!" Bruno turned toward him, apparently a safer target for a raised voice than Allison, Jeremiah noted.

Delilah tried a softer tact. "Allison, I want Jay to come too. But without his necromancy, he's only a passable fighter. You said so yourself. There will be other missions."

"I can still cast acid and do the poison fog," Jeremiah said.

"Wait, why? Don't those count as necromancy?" asked Delilah.

"No magic, Jeremiah!" Allison shouted, silencing everyone. She moved in front of Jeremiah and looked him in the eye. "No casting from you at all. All those 'gray area' spells, I know where those lead."

Bruno crossed his arms. "No magic. No, Jay."

Allison glared at Bruno. "It's my operation. I say he goes," she growled.

Bruno didn't flinch. "What rank do you think you're pulling, exactly?"

Jeremiah knew he had to do something. The fracturing cohesion was more than he could stand. Tension among the party was one thing, arguing another. But this sort of fundamental difference from the party, *about* the party? It felt wrong somehow, almost taboo. He put a hand on Allison's shoulder. "It's okay, Allison. I'm not worth all this."

He might as well have tried to placate a wall. Allison didn't take her eyes off Bruno, who didn't take his eyes off her. Some secret battle of wills was going on, one which he and Delilah seemed specifically excluded from.

Bruno broke first. He glanced away and rubbed his eyes. "Fine. He comes. But if he needs to use magic, he can use magic."

"If it's life or death," said Allison, still glaring.

"It's a dungeon! It's already—" Bruno stopped himself and sighed. "Fine. Jay, no offense but don't get us killed, all right?"

"Deal," said Jeremiah.

"Great," Bruno mumbled.

"Hold up," Allison said. She outstretched her hand toward Bruno. He hesitated for a long moment, then grabbed her by the wrist. She returned the grip, and they quickly released.

"All right! This is officially an operation! We have three days to prepare. Terrain is mountainous and likely cold. Jay, I want you to secure provisions. Bruno, prep for spelunking and trap breaking. Delilah, you . . . uhh." Allison looked down at the pile of papers. "You deal with everything I don't understand!"

"Allison, please, I'm only one woman," said Delilah. She dodged Allison's swat with practiced ease.

CHAPTER THREE

The Tomb

Everyone, this is Christopher," said Jeremiah. He patted the gray donkey on the rump. His ears went flat against his head, and he let out a hateful bray. Christopher had a set of cloth saddlebags draped over his hindquarters, just a few days away from being called threadbare.

"You're not even joking," said Bruno, staring aghast at the donkey. "You really expect us to carry all of our stuff on a single donkey."

"Not at all," started Jeremiah, reaching into the saddlebags. "Due to budget constraints, everyone gets to help Christopher." He pulled out four large, empty backpacks. Each was in a similar state to the saddlebags.

"We have our own packs already," said Allison.

"Not big enough," said Jeremiah. "Everyone has to help carry food, supplies, and treasure on the way back. Hopefully."

"Is he friendly?" Delilah asked, circling the donkey. Christopher snapped his teeth at her the moment she was close enough.

"Very no," said Jeremiah. "The only donkey we could afford was one the owner was desperately trying to get rid of. Apparently, Christopher has sort of a problem with the world and everything in it."

"Jay, what the hell?" Bruno said, taking his backpack.

"Hey, you guys gave me a budget, and I stuck to it. At the very least, you each get a walking stick I found in the woods, free of charge." He presented them with four long thin sticks, mostly stripped of branch fragments.

"What are all these marks?" asked Bruno. His finger traced a swirling pattern burned into the leather of the backpack.

"That was my attempt at a Lightness rune," said Jeremiah. "It would have made the backpacks and anything inside weigh a tenth as much."

"'Would have'?" asked Allison.

Jeremiah squirmed. *Damn adventurers and their perception*, he thought. "Yes. It's, uh, nonfunctional. What it basically says is 'Lightness and Pause.'"

"But in crazy magic god language?" asked Bruno.

"In crazy magic god language, yes," said Jeremiah.

"Why *Pause*?" asked Delilah.

"To place a limiter on the magical effect," said Jeremiah. "So it just becomes lighter but doesn't fly away or set on fire from magical energy with nowhere to go. Just the right amount of magic doing just the right amount of lifting."

"Looks like it didn't work," said Bruno. He scratched some of the scorched leather, then picked out the black from under his fingernail.

"It didn't," said Jeremiah. "I don't know why. I mean, I have some guesses as to why. Somehow the enchantment isn't targeting the backpack, or maybe the Pause is too abrupt? Yeah, I think the Pause is the problem." Jeremiah sat down on the ground and began inspecting the marks. "I bet it's lighter, but only infinitesimally so," Delilah started leaning over his shoulder to help inspect. "I mean it would be lighter if it had worked. So I guess there's a problem of specificity? Or I wrote it wrong?"

"I'm seeing these tiny little tears here," muttered Delilah, poking the design.

"Tiny little tears. I'm seeing that too," Jeremiah muttered back. "I think I need to—"

"Didn't we used to have a carriage? A nice one?" interrupted Allison.

"Long since sold," said Delilah.

"Hey, if you guys wanted better provisions you wouldn't have budgeted so much to Bruno," said Jeremiah. He was grateful to move on from his failed rune.

"You don't skimp on a dungeon delve," said Bruno. "Especially not one with traps. Rather eat dry biscuits for a week than get killed by poison darts."

"Funny you should say that," said Jeremiah pulling out their designated cube of rations.

"Betrayer!" came a shout from right beside them. Jeremiah jumped away, his ears ringing. An old dwarven woman, bedraggled and flea-bitten, had crept up to Jeremiah, unnoticed by everyone else in the group, and shouted nearly in his face. "You buried that poor girl. She was to lift us up! You and your evil buried that girl alive. Do you think of her, Necromancer?! Think of dirt filling her lungs?" Jeremiah jerked back from the spitting tirade, and Allison caught him before he fell.

Delilah stepped between him and the woman, taking the full brunt of the finger wagging and cursing.

"Ma'am, I understand your frustration, but I promise that woman was only going to bring ruin to this city. No one was going to be lifted up," said Delilah.

"Says the fancy half elf, stepping out from her summer home, no doubt!" the dwarven woman looked Delilah up and down with disdain, eyes lingering on the slight points of Delilah's ears.

Bruno stepped in then, putting an arm around the woman's shoulders and turning her away. They walked a few steps together while he spoke softly. "Now, Domma Tooka, that's no way to behave. To a stranger in the street no less. Where's Ser Tooka? Young Miska and Molly? They been going to school?"

The woman's face was a mask of rage, but as she stared up at Bruno it cracked to unfathomable sorrow and she burst into tears, leaning into him. Bruno wrapped her in a hug as she wailed in Dwarvish. Jeremiah saw Bruno stiffen as she spoke. Bruno looked up and gestured for everyone to move on without him. Jeremiah, Allison, and Delilah started toward the gates of Dramir, pulling Christopher behind them.

"You okay?" Delilah asked Jeremiah.

"Yeah," he said automatically. *Dirt filling her lungs* repeated over and over in his head. He took a deep, unconscious breath.

Bruno caught up with them at the gate. Jeremiah wasn't sure, but he thought he saw the shine of tear tracks on Bruno's cheeks.

Tear tracks in blood, trapped in a closet, torn to pieces.

Jeremiah shook his head. The image had come back all at once out of nowhere.

"Friend of yours?" Allison asked Bruno.

Bruno's face was hard as stone. "Vivica didn't take nearly enough of this place down with her."

It was a long walk out of the city, west against the sun. The farther they got from the city, the farther they got from their troubles, at least that's how it felt. Farmland turned to forest, and the silent trudge turned to simple marching songs to distract them from their rapidly numbing shoulders.

Travelers grew rarer as they marched on. At first, small caravans or groups of travelers would invite them to bed down nearby. Jeremiah suspected it was for a sense of protection; they were quite generous in sharing their food.

But soon, even the travelers disappeared, and they spent their nights soaking hardtack in bean water around a fire. They were always too exhausted to do more than set up camp, the road was proving brutal. Conversation became limited to essentials, reminiscing about the carriage, and warnings when Christopher was about to bite someone.

A lone mountain appeared on the horizon. Its peak was a frequent stop for scouts to take the lay of the land. The tomb they sought was around the other side, slightly off the well-traveled path. As they approached, cold air and a slate gray sky lent the landscape an austere and barren beauty.

The climb itself wasn't arduous, even after they left the main scouts' path, but soon a ferocious wind picked up, one that sliced through the cheap winter coats they had procured for the journey. Flecks of frost sparkled on the bare rocks like scattered diamonds. The stones leeched heat from their hands and as the sun began to set, even the brief respites from the wind were of little comfort.

"Can we stop?" Delilah yelled over the gale. "It's too cold, and we still don't know where the tomb is."

"If we find the entrance we can shelter in it," said Bruno, shivering.

"Allison?" Delilah asked, looking for a decision to be made.

"We need to keep searching," said Allison. "I can feel weather coming in, and we don't have the equipment to handle a proper storm."

They split up and began combing the mountainside. Allison's contact had only given them the near useless direction of "somewhere in the middle of the mountain." Jeremiah crawled over rocks and peeked under boulders. The moisture clinging to stone was painfully cold to the touch and dampened his clothing on contact.

"Found it!" Bruno shouted from further up the mountain, the wind making him just barely audible. They converged on him to see a cave entrance settled deep into a crevasse.

"Bruno, scout it out," said Allison. Jeremiah's relief was suddenly tempered by the reminder that someone had died here recently, from a trap, of all things.

While the others huddled together for warmth, Bruno stepped away and shed his coat, transforming from shivering mountaineer to lithe adventurer. Delilah quickly snatched it up and wrapped it around herself, stealing the remaining warmth. They watched him creep along the crevasse in only his blacks and begin a slow and methodical search of the cave. He touched the ground and walls, blew into hairline cracks, and touched the roof of the cave mouth with his magic bow. Jeremiah wasn't sure how he could withstand the cold, totally exposed like that. He huddled closer to Allison and Delilah as he watched.

Finally, Bruno turned and called back to them. "Entrance is clear," he said. "Better still, there's a warm air current here."

At his proclamation, the others bustled and stumbled past each other in their mad dash to get inside. Sure enough, the moment they stepped inside the temperature jumped. It was heavenly.

"Move around and warm up," said Allison. "I'll get the gear bags."

Soon they had established a nearly comfortable camp in the tunnel. Armor and weapons of various sorts lay in neat piles. Delilah had her own area for a small mountain of bottles, boxes, bags, vials, pots, tins, flasks, syringes, and poultices. Jeremiah made himself useful by helping Allison strap her enchanted armor into place, then carefully wrapped Delilah in the tangle of leather strips that offered both protection and storage for her supplies. He smirked at her transformation from slender half elf to brown cocoon with a head sticking out.

Then it was time to don his own gear. He was the proud owner of a full set of studded leather armor, a leather cap, short spear, and round wooden shield. He hadn't worn it outside of practice with Allison, but he liked how safe it made him feel.

"How do I look?" he asked the others.

"Like a damn town guard recruit on his first patrol," said Bruno. "Al, come on. Are you sure about . . . this?" Bruno gestured toward Jeremiah and the armor suddenly felt like a costume a clown would wear.

"He'll be fine," said Allison. She was adjusting her weapons and spared barely a glance in Bruno's direction.

Bruno gave a disgusted grunt and went back to inspecting his gear. But that grunt, that single sound, was enough to call everything Jeremiah felt into question.

What am I doing here? He thought. *Bruno's right, I can't help. Without necromancy, I'm just a liability. I could get someone hurt or killed. I could get myself killed. I'm as good as a hired porter, at best. But there's nothing stopping me, not really, I could just be a necromancer again.*

The option was suddenly there, beckoning and simple. He'd be the party mage, able to reinforce their numbers with fearless undead minions, or at least able to spray acid or fill the halls with poisonous gas.

The fantasy consumed him for a moment. He'd make short work of the dungeon, and they'd return to Dramir with plenty of treasure to pay their legal fees—both current and future. His friends would agree to keep his change of heart a secret, only revealing his power when they were adventuring. He was tempted to decide right then and there, the words to announce his choice to his friends already forming in his mind.

Then, for some reason, he glanced toward Allison and found her already looking at him. Her stoic gaze reminded him of her promise and reminded him why he made it. The man in the closet had been just another enemy brutally killed by Jeremiah's minions . . . yet had also been so much more. The allies who were struck down by Jeremiah's horde when he'd made a careless mistake during a chaotic battle. No, he didn't want that power, that responsibility. It was too much.

Jeremiah tamped down his shame and doubt as hard as he could. He was an enchanter and spearman now, and even if he wasn't very good at being either, he could still help in other ways. He just had to find them.

"Are we ready?" Bruno heaved his pack onto his shoulders. It was bulging against its straps. His magic bow was slung across his back and short blades were secured all across his body. Throwing swords, Bruno had called them.

"Packed a bit extra, Bruno?" asked Jeremiah.

"A lot extra. We're going to be dealing with traps, and traps are a pain in the ass, especially in old places like this, where mechanisms and triggers will be degraded. Maybe you're lucky and it just breaks. Or maybe you're unlucky and it goes off because you disturbed the air for the first time in generations, and that was just enough to release the rotten trip wire," Said Bruno, as he pulled out and inspected each mysterious gadget.

"Is that what happened the time you took that spear fusillade right in the chest?" asked Delilah wryly.

"No, that was carelessness and stupidity," said Bruno. "Luckily it was me that set it off and that got out of the worst of it, as opposed to you, who would have probably tried to argue with the spear flying toward her."

"Remember that time I cracked my knuckles too hard and you threw up?" said Delilah, threading her fingers together with a nasty smile.

"Formation," interrupted Allison. They gathered at the entrance to the tomb. "Eyes on, everyone." Bruno squeezed two drops of Delilah's Night Eyes formula into his eyes, then handed the vial to Allison and headed into the dungeon.

Delilah took the drops after Allison and tipped Jeremiah's head back to administer them. "Are you okay?" she asked, softly enough the others wouldn't hear.

Trust Delilah to know when he was feeling off. "Yeah, I'm good. Just a little nervous." Jeremiah winced and blinked away the excess liquid from the drops. His vision swam for a minute before the shadows of the cave revealed their secrets, albeit only in black and white. Then they followed Allison into the dark.

CHAPTER FOUR

Diplomacy and Persuasion

Jeremiah stayed just behind Allison, his round shield and short spear ready to link up with her kite shield and form a solid defense at a moment's notice.

Unless I'm supposed to do something else, he thought. He tried to analyze her stance, then decided it was best not to think about it too hard. She had her spear out now. If she switched to her axe or sword he'd try to adjust accordingly.

At first glance, the tomb entrance was just a cave like any other. Dank, dark, and deceptively slippery floors where slime mold grew in patches. Then Bruno pointed out that the walls, though rough, shared a certain repeated texture, and the dimensions of the tunnels were too uniform to be natural. "Someone dug all this out," he concluded.

"That's an awful lot of work," said Jeremiah. "I wonder why . . . Oh."

Emblazoned across a wall ahead, filling the entire space from floor to ceiling, were the words:

BEYOND LIES SER GEROME FIDELIOUS
MASTER OF ORDER
KING OF CASTIGATION
KNOWER OF THE UNKNOWABLE
ENTER AND BE DAM

"'And be dam'?" read Allison.

"Do you think they meant *damned*?" asked Delilah.

Bruno shrugged, the epitaph not concerning him.

Ahead, just at the limit of his night eyes' range, Jeremiah could see Bruno creeping forward. He would occasionally stop and listen, but mostly he kept his gaze moving, sweeping their surroundings. "Trap remains," he said, indicating a shape sticking out of the floor near the wall. The party froze while he inspected it. "Clear. Set off ages ago."

They continued onwards. Jeremiah eyed the remains as he passed. A rusted iron piton had been driven into the stone, with a corroded loop near the head. It resembled a giant needle punching into solid rock. He saw another on the other side of the cave, in just as poor condition.

"Trip line," whispered Delilah. Jeremiah could see how a cord could connect both pitons but couldn't identify a mechanism beyond that.

"What'd it do?" he asked.

Delilah pointed toward the far wall of the cave. After a minute of staring, Jeremiah spotted a tiny hole drilled into the rock. It didn't tell him much.

"Got a body," Bruno called. They stopped again while Bruno searched the immediate area. "We're good. Come take a look," he said, waving them forward.

As they advanced, Jeremiah made out the unnaturally still shape of a human lying on the cave floor. It was the body of a man wearing the light leather armor of the Dramir Scout Corps and a metal cap. His cap had been smashed flat, and his neck was twisted at an unnatural angle. Dried blood and a clear fluid were crusted around his ears.

"Can anyone tell me what happened here and what we might keep an eye out for?" asked Bruno.

"Broken neck," Delilah said without hesitation. "Smashed, actually. Blow from overhead. Death would have been instant."

"Thank you, Doctor," said Bruno. "Jay, why don't *you* tell us what may have done this?" There was an edge to Bruno's voice. He wanted to prove something.

Jeremiah started to think out loud. "An overhead blow, but not much room to swing something overhead like a hammer or mace. At least, not that hard, right?"

"You tell me," said Bruno, giving him nothing.

"Bruno . . ." Allison warned.

"It's a learning experience! We're giving chances now, right? Jeremiah, tell me what killed him and where it is," said Bruno.

Jeremiah's temper flared. Whatever Bruno was trying to prove, Jeremiah wanted to prove him wrong. "All right, I don't see signs of fighting here, no blood spatter or bodies, and there are no other wounds on him. And we just saw one trap . . ."

Jeremiah started scanning the low cave ceiling, but there wasn't anything obvious. Just the normal jags of rock and lichen . . . *Wait,* he thought. In the stone, like an impossible crack, was a nearly invisible perfect circle, about a foot in diameter. It was right over the body of the dead man. He reached his spear up and wedged the tip into the crack. It betrayed just a tiny fraction of movement.

"This dropped on him, didn't it? Or maybe it moved aside, and something fell through a hole? No, the stone itself had to drop—there's nowhere for it to move. This circle thing crushed him," Jeremiah said with finality.

"Why?" asked Bruno.

That was trickier. *Why would it fall? Clearly, he set off the trap. Delilah had said death was instantaneous . . . instantaneous.* That gave him an idea. He grabbed the body by the leg and hauled it off to the side, letting it bump and drag along the ground, before giving it a little toss out of the way with the carelessness of someone far too comfortable handling dead bodies.

"Jay!" said Allison, glaring at his treatment of the body.

"What?" said Jeremiah. Beneath the body, he spotted a similar flaw in the stonework to the one in the ceiling, a matching circle. "He stepped on *this*!" he said and jabbed the circle with the butt of his spear.

The circle in the floor shifted a tiny amount, there was a click, and a column of stone dropped from the ceiling. Everyone leapt away from the deafening crash as the column smashed into the circle on the floor. It was as tall as the room and must have weighed thousands of pounds.

Bruno snatched Jeremiah's spear from his hands. "Why would you do that?!"

"Sorry!" Jeremiah held up his hands. "No one was near the trigger; I thought it'd be safe." He was somewhere between sheepish and defensive. After all, he'd been right. Whatever game Bruno was trying to play, Jeremiah had won it.

"It is *never* safe to set off a trap," Bruno said. "Whoever built the trap wants it to be triggered, and we don't give that person what they want. But yes, that's what happened to him. Good job." He returned Jeremiah's spear with some reluctance, the righteous outrage bleeding away.

Yeah, bet you had a whole speech prepared, didn't you? thought Jeremiah with satisfaction. Though he was loath to admit the satisfaction was coming from Bruno telling him he had done a good job.

As they dusted themselves off, the stone column began to slowly rise back up into the ceiling. There was a soft metal clinking that could be heard coming from the stone above.

"How the hell does this thing work?" asked Jeremiah. "What's pulling it back up? And how? Where are the mechanisms for all this? Is it a magic trap?" Jeremiah hadn't seen any signs of enchantment anywhere.

"Those are professional-level questions," said Bruno. "And what you can learn from their answers is indispensable."

"Care to enlighten us, then? I'm pretty curious myself," said Delilah.

Bruno paced as he began to lecture. "Let's look at the simplicity first. A thin column, not a gigantic block. Down, kill, up. Very efficient and yet very advanced."

"A broken neck from a rock is advanced?" asked Allison, squinting suspiciously at the ceiling.

Bruno pointed at the ceiling. "A broken neck from an ordinary rock? Not at all. But a broken neck from a rock that crawls back up into its hidey hole and waits for its next victim? That's the good stuff. Self-resetting traps take serious planning and sources of energy."

"Sources . . . of . . . energy," Delilah said, rapidly taking notes.

Jeremiah raised his hand. "What do you mean by sources of energy?" He loved these talks.

Bruno nodded at Jeremiah's raised hand. "Excellent question. We can't hear machinery. That means the mechanism is far away or magic. The column showed signs of tool work, very precise for it to be so perfectly nestled into the ceiling."

"Signs of tool work." I wouldn't have even thought about looking for that, thought Jeremiah.

Bruno continued, circling the trap and wagging a finger at it like an interrogation. "We hear the clink of chains from the hole, likely what holds up the column. So we can assume it's mechanical. Likely powered by a waterwheel of some kind. Since we're high up, that means the mechanisms likely go very far down, accessing some sort of underground river. All of that means we're in for a deep descent."

"So it could be powered by magic?" asked Jeremiah hopefully. Even Thurok would be impressed by an enchanted trap.

"Doubtful," said Bruno. "You wouldn't go through all the trouble of a magic trap just to do something mundane like drop a rock. Magic traps are awful."

"What do they do?" asked Jeremiah.

"Regrettably, anything. The nuances are beyond the scope of this lesson."

"Beyond . . . scope," said Delilah, nodding along.

"What's so indispensable about all that?" said Allison.

"We don't know *yet*," said Bruno. He knelt on the ground and extracted a thin shiv of metal from his rolled pack. He unfolded it, over and over again until it was as long as he was tall. Slipping it into the crack around the trigger, he began probing the perimeter of the circle, searching for something. He bent the shiv into a narrow arch and slipped the other end into the opposite side of the circle. For several long minutes, he continued to feed the wire around the trigger, fiddling occasionally. Jeremiah was certain the column would drop at any second to crush Bruno's hands. He managed to pass the tool entirely beneath the circular trigger, creating a loop with the two ends sticking up. Finally, he took a small box from his pack and attached it to the two ends of the tool, completing the connection.

"Lift," he said to Allison, stepping away. He retrieved a basic pry bar from his bag and waited. Allison gripped the loop in both gauntleted hands and pulled upward as hard as she could, straining against an invisible weight. The stone circle slowly rose above the floor. Only a couple of inches of stone made up the surface of the trigger, and as Allison pulled, she revealed a solid pole of rusty metal beneath. Bruno shoved the pry bar beneath the stone facade and wedged it against the metal pole. He wrenched, and the metal broke free from whatever mechanisms it was connected to below. Allison stumbled backward as the stone trigger came free, leaving a perfectly round hole in the cave floor.

"Let's go," said Bruno.

The cave began descending quickly, the slime-slick stone making for treacherous and careful climbing. Delilah and Bruno finally deployed a piton and rope to shimmy down a particularly steep slope.

"Check," Bruno said, tapping a wall. There was a sequence of long white claw marks in the stone. Everyone went on high alert, proceeding at a snail's pace. They rounded one more corner before they were hit with the smell. Jeremiah choked back a wave of nausea at the staggering stink of rot and offal. "Stay here," said Bruno and disappeared into the darkness beyond.

He wasn't gone long. "Troll up ahead. Looks like he's living here, but the cave goes deeper beyond."

"We can handle a troll," said Allison, hefting her spear. "Delilah, can you make fire or acid so we can stop it from regenerating?"

"I can, but honestly, Jay is a better source of acid," said Delilah.

"No. Magic," said Allison, focusing her disapproving glare first on Delilah, then on Bruno as well, just for good measure.

Delilah dug into her armor and produced some small clay pots, no larger than apples, and a wax paper envelope containing a white paste. "I've got five acid pots and a coating that will ignite a weapon it's applied to. But . . . can I try something?" Allison nodded for her to continue. "All right, everyone, just follow me. Take a pot and be ready to fight if this doesn't work out."

Delilah took the lead and slowly led them through the increasing stench and into a wider chamber of the cave. It had a carpet of splintered bones and a huge pile of animal skins in a corner made a bed. Jeremiah could see wriggling maggots in the bed from across the room and his stomach turned again. There was a totem of neatly arranged skulls on one side of the room, scratched into the wall above it were primitive depictions of gigantic creatures devouring smaller ones.

Sitting beside the bed, nearly blending in with the cave walls, was the troll. It was gnawing on something with only its bumpy green back exposed to them. Even sitting, it was taller than Allison by at least two heads.

Allison immediately tensed, ready to explode into action. "Bruno, sneak up and see if you can cut one of its arms off," whispered Allison. "I'll come in behind you and—"

"Ahem?" Delilah called.

The troll started, sprang to its feet, and let out a roar of outrage. It loomed twice as tall as any of them now, its bellowing mouth showing row after row of razor-sharp teeth. Its knuckles reached the ground while standing and were tipped with long, bony claws. Growling, the troll sniffed the air frantically with a long, pointed nose, pawing at the bed pile. It came away with a huge club, most of a tree trunk, really, with a wicked-looking blade of metal tied to the end, like an enormous scythe. Next it hefted a line of logs wrapped together as an improvised tower shield.

"You didn't mention it was armed," Allison growled at Bruno.

Bruno drew a pair of swords. "News to me!"

Delilah stepped forward and bellowed. "Graaaaaaaaaaguguuuuuuuuugaaaaaa!"

The troll raised its head and glared at her. It still held the weapon at the ready, but its posture relaxed ever so slightly. "Doooommuuuukaaaarrrrtoooooogaaaa," said the troll.

"You've got to be kidding me," said Bruno. Jeremiah shushed him.

Delilah continued. "Chaaaaa mmmmaaagoooo d-d-daaaaahruuuuuy. Umm, ta-taaaaaroooooofeeeefaaaaaaa!" She pointed to the exit that would lead them farther into the cave, to the group as a whole, and then to Allison's weapons. The troll gave a malicious toothy grin and began advancing on them, shield interposed and weapon held high.

"Not working!" yelled Allison, trying to force herself in front of Delilah. Delilah stopped her again and threw an acid pot at the ground by the troll's feet. The little green specks flicked onto the troll's knobby toes and singed its skin. The troll winced, immediately stopping its advance.

"Ciiiiidaaaaaaaa," said Delilah, pointing at the other pots. "Gangaganga ciiiiidaaaaaa."

The troll squinted at her, tilting its head. "Ciiiiidaaaaaa?"

"Shit," Delilah muttered. She started snapping her fingers, trying to think. "Fiiiishaaaafiss daaaaa?"

"Ciiiiiilllllddaaaaaaa?" the troll seemed to suggest.

"Ah, yes! Ciiiiilllllddaaaaaaa!" said Delilah.

The troll growled, weighing its options. Suddenly, it pointed back at the goat it had been chewing to shreds and stomped its foot, brandishing the scythe. "Bangkada ro?"

"Duro," said Delilah.

That seemed to satisfy the troll. It backed up to the wall and scooped the goat up again, never taking its eyes off the intruders. It chewed its meal as it watched them leave.

"Well, that was fascinating. You speak giant?" asked Jeremiah.

"Only enough to tell a troll we're not worth the trouble," Delilah said. "Seemed worth knowing, so I took a linguistics essentials course a few years ago. It covered things like how to turn down a gnome's dinner invitation or tell a dwarf they're wrong without offending anyone. Pretty important in diplomatic matters."

"You literally never cease to amaze me," said Jeremiah with a shake of his head.

Delilah beamed at the compliment. "Yes, well, thank you . . . Jay."

Allison glanced back toward the troll's lair. "I wonder if I could recruit him. He seemed awfully reasonable. I'd get a huge bonus for signing a war troll as a shock trooper."

"Put a pin in that, but yes, he was very reasonable," agreed Delilah.

CHAPTER FIVE

Guardians

As they continued farther down, moisture began to condense on the stone in tiny motes of water. In the motes lived even tinier fish, sparkling with a green or blue phosphorescence. It was like traveling through a tunnel of stars, albeit even more slowly than usual as Bruno took the added beauty to be a guarantee of further traps, and Delilah stopped every few feet to take samples. Jeremiah didn't mind. After the troll's lair, the air in the tunnel was fresh and pleasant. He took the time to admire the effect, wondering if the fish had been a natural part of the cave system or added by whoever installed the traps.

Even Bruno's most painstaking search yielded no hazards. They continued along the tunnel until it opened onto a huge cavern. A steep and narrow descent, like a natural staircase, led from where they stood down to to a pool of water—nearly a lake—that stretched across the cavern. No fish illuminated this place, and Jeremiah found himself missing them. The pool was of unknowable depth, its surface a dark mirror that had stood undisturbed for an age. On the far side of the cavern, an opening in the wall indicated their way forward.

"What are those things along the walls?" Bruno asked. He gestured to dozens of large stone rectangles surrounding the pool of water. They were unadorned, merely slabs of rock leaning side by side against the walls.

"Architecture?" ventured Delilah.

"No chance," said Allison. She picked a loose stone from the cave floor and hefted it in her hand for a moment, eyeing the slabs. Then with a grunt, she hurled the stone across the cavern. It landed with a *plunk* in the center of the still pool, disappearing below the surface.

Ripples from the stone spread slowly over that mirror surface, concentric rings emanating outward. Watching them filled Jeremiah with an inexplicable sense of dread.

It took nearly a minute for the first ripples to reach the slabs, tiny waves lapping against the stone. Then everything happened at once.

The cavern filled with the grinding of stone on stone. Jeremiah, his eyes fixed on the nearest slab, gasped as the front of it, which he now recognized as the lid of a coffin, slid aside to reveal a gaunt humanoid figure. Its flesh was withered and taut, and scraps of bandages hung over its limbs, long since rotted away. Around its neck was a rusted iron collar with four protruding spikes, rising like stalagmites around its face. No bandages remained on its face, only blackened skin which still held the features it had had in life. The hint of humanity remaining only made it worse when the figure raised its head with a wrench, staring blindly at Jeremiah.

"Those are mummies," said Jeremiah. He tightened his grip on his spear as his heart thudded in his chest. He was about to be in a fight without magic. He was about to entrust his life to wood and leather. His mind briefly brushed against memories of blood and dead men, but his revulsion at his own cowardice gave him focus. *I will not fail my friends again.*

The water churned as dozens of mummies lurched into the pool at once, each beginning to make their way toward the adventurers huddled at the cavern entrance.

"Is a mummy a zombie, or is there something different about these we should know?" Allison asked. She made her way to the front of the group, hoisting her shield and sword and bracing against a sturdy boulder.

"They're people who choose to become undead through ritual magic. They'll be stronger and tougher than regular zombies, and the bandages are usually alchemically treated to act as armor," said Jeremiah.

"Tips?" Bruno asked. The first mummies had reached the foot of the stone staircase and were beginning the steep climb. Aside from the splashing and shuffling of their movements, they were eerily silent.

"Cut them apart. The flesh is treated in the creation process, though, so it'll be tough," said Jeremiah.

Allison switched to her axe then turned and pointed at Jeremiah. "What do you do?"

"I poke?"

"You poke. Bruno, with me. That crap around their necks is an ancient form of armor, hopefully it'll be too rusted to help. Delilah, keep them from swarming us." The closest mummies were only a few paces away now, their eyeless gaze fixed on Allison.

"Should we retreat to the tunnel? Limit their number?" Delilah asked, rummaging through her various pockets.

"We want room to swing and maneuver," Allison answered. "I don't want us trapped in a press."

Delilah found what she was looking for and threw three glass bottles in a single motion. The bottle shattered open on the rocks nearest the water, covering the base of the stairs with pearlescent oil. The mummies that tried to climb them could find no purchase and toppled back into the water.

The first mummy reached Allison, arms outstretched. Allison swung her axe with a bellow, connecting just above the neck armor. The tines on the collar shattered but stopped the blow from cleaving the mummy's head in half. Allison swore, kicked the mummy in the chest as its hands reached for her face, sending it stumbling backward into the mummy behind it. Despite Delilah's oil hazard, the stairs were already growing crowded. The first mummy came within range of Allison again and she swung once more. This time her axe easily parted its head, and the mummy fell, limp.

Bruno darted into the opening left by the felled mummy and his swords found vulnerable targets before the creatures could react—hands, arms, and feet were severed by his twin blades, and then he was gone, flitting down the stones toward the mummies climbing out of the water, maiming as he went but never lingering long enough to be a target.

"Ready?" Delilah asked Jeremiah as several mummies closed in on their position. She shifted her grip toward the butt of her spear and stood just behind Jeremiah, who was positioned behind Allison.

"I poke," he said, like it was a holy mantra.

"Then let's poke!" Delilah thrust her longspear into the head of a mummy further down on the rocks, lodging shallow in its skull. The mummy, undeterred, tried to wrench the spear free.

"The flesh dried solid. It's like stabbing a log," growled Delilah. She braced her feet and pushed. The mummy lost balance off the side of the rocks, falling away from the spear to the water below. It disappeared briefly below the surface, then Jeremiah watched it clamber to its feet to begin the long journey anew.

"Pick it up!" yelled Allison, her frustration mounting. She swung her axe in great arcs as the mummies reached her and battered them back with shield bashes. But despite her strength, the mummies would not be felled in a single hit. Thanks to Bruno's attacks, many were missing limbs, but with the neck armor there was little he could do to thin their numbers, and they were beginning to crowd Allison.

A small group of mummies reached Allison at once. She stunned two of them in a single swing of her axe, but a third was lurking in the blind spot beneath her shield. Jeremiah spotted it, steeled himself, then raised his spear and poked.

The spear stuck barely an inch into the mummy's neck. He poked again, still to no effect. The mummy stood and swung a hardened fist into Allison's shield, denting the metal with its unnatural strength. Allison staggered from the unexpected force of the blow but managed to keep her footing.

Jeremiah poked again, but this time shoved against the mummy with all his might. It teetered for a moment, then fell backward, tumbling down the rocks.

He stared, his spear still outstretched as the mummy fell. "I did it? I did it!"

"Now do it faster and better!" Allison shouted. She hacked at one mummy while kicking another away, then brought her axe down on a third as it reached past her toward Jeremiah.

Below, Bruno struggled to continue his dance of attacks and retreats, but his options were growing limited. One heavy fist clipped his shoulder as he darted past, sending him spinning toward the pool below. He struck out mid-spin to lodge a sword into the chest of another mummy, slowing his momentum to catch his balance. The mummy didn't even notice the blow however and surged upward with its fellows, taking the sword with it.

"Al, we need to move," said Bruno, switching his remaining sword to his right hand.

"They're getting up the rocks!" yelled Jeremiah. The slippery liquid was washing away. More were closing, faster, and tighter together. Jeremiah's spear was beginning to feel perilously short.

"Right. Fall back!" Allison commanded. As she raised her shield to cover Jeremiah's and Delilah's retreat, a mummy lunged forward, seized her ankle, and pulled. Allison fell flat on the rocks as her foot was yanked out from under her. In a moment, a pile of mummies was upon her, and a dozen fists that could smash bone began hammering down. Her nonmagical shield was reduced to splinters in moments.

"Allison!" Jeremiah cried.

"I'm okay!" Allison yelled back over the din of fists pounding on metal. "The armor is too strong. They can't break it!" Blow after blow rattled her magic armor, without leaving so much as a dent. She dropped her axe—there was no room to swing it anyway—and pulled a dagger, jabbing the mummies with the weapon and raking them with her clawed gauntlets to try and create enough of an opening to escape.

"Eyes up, Jay!" Delilah's voice in his ear made Jeremiah jump. He regripped his spear and stared in horror at the horde of dozens approaching. The mummies that were not busy mauling Allison were flowing past her like water around a stone, bearing down on Jeremiah and Delilah as though spurred to fresh energy by the newly available targets.

Bruno rushed toward Allison and hacked at the mummies. His sword sliced through flesh and sinew, but they remained undeterred. Sidestepping a swipe by a passing mummy, he snatched Allison's discarded axe and retreated to Jeremiah's side. Bruno handed his remaining throwing blade to Jeremiah. "Gonna need you to do more than poke, Jay," said Bruno. He hefted the axe and swung it down onto the crown of a mummy, cracking the skull in half.

Jeremiah held Bruno's throwing sword like it was a cactus. The weight was strange, it was short, it felt clumsy in his hands. The prospect of attacking meant putting himself within reach of danger, and one of Allison's biggest lessons with the spear was to stay away from danger.

The shriek of metal on stone rang through the cavern, accompanied by Allison's shouts. Jeremiah searched for her among the mummies, and for one heart-stopping moment he couldn't spot her. But then—there, near the bottom of the stairs. They were dragging her downward and had nearly reached the water. Allison was swearing and kicking at the mummies to little effect. As her feet touched the water, she drew her longsword and heaved it toward her friends on the stairs above her. Moments later, she was sinking into the pool, dragged toward the very center, thrashing uselessly as her armor took on water. And then she was gone, disappeared beneath the surface in a riot of frothing water.

And that was the last time I saw her alive. The thought, morbid and cruel, forced its way into Jeremiah's head.

"We need a plan! Now!" Bruno shouted. He and the others retreated to the entrance of the cavern while the rest of the mummies climbed toward them. Meanwhile, the pool was already returning to its mirror-like stillness.

Delilah threw a hefty sack down onto the rocks below. It burst apart, sending thousands of metal foil strips across the surface of the water, where they began to dance and hiss white smoke like a rolling morning fog. "Knock them into the water," said Delilah. "Allison, if you can hear me—don't come up!"

No sooner had Delilah spoken than the white fog began to glow and pop with thousands of tiny flames. The hiss from the water became deafening, and despite its size, the cool cavern began to grow warmer.

Bruno closed the distance from the horde and kicked a mummy hard, sending it tumbling over the side and into the burning water. When it emerged again, the countless strips covering its body had ignited with blinding intensity. The strips burned into the mummy's preserved flesh until that too was alight, and the mummy went up in an inferno.

Jeremiah jabbed into another mummy, trying to push it off the rocks, but he was tired and sloppy. The spearhead glanced off the mummy's shoulder, and the undead surged past Jeremiah's threat range. Jeremiah shouted in panic and swung his shield like a weapon. Fingers that would have pulled the flesh from Jeremiah's face instead closed on the edge of his shield as the mummy was knocked back. The weight of the undead threatened to pull them both down, and Jeremiah fumbled at the shield's straps as he fought for balance. Delilah's arms wrapped around him as he finally managed to unlatch the buckle. The mummy fell away to the flames below, carrying Jeremiah's shield with it.

The heat was becoming intolerable now, the brilliance of the flames searing Jeremiah's vision. But the mummies kept coming. "Get back to the tunnel!" he shouted.

"We have to get Allison!" screamed Delilah. Her spear impaled a mummy, but it was buoyed by its comrades, and she couldn't push it to the edge. "Come on! Help me! Push!"

"We're getting overrun! Fall back," yelled Jeremiah. A mummy grabbed at his arm, powerful fingers closing on leather armor but mercifully missing Jeremiah's flesh. The leather came away like clay in its hands.

Reluctantly they retreated toward the tunnel, Bruno taking the rear guard with great, sweeping swings of Allison's axe. The remaining dozen mummies followed, clumping together to fit through the entrance. Bruno made his stand there, with Delilah and Jeremiah falling in to help. Killing the mummies with weapons was nearly impossible without Allison, but the three of them together could at least hold the line.

Behind the mummies, the heat in the cavern was increasing. The brilliant flames on the water grew to such heights that Jeremiah was blinded to look toward them.

Suddenly, one of the mummies' bandages was alight, and that white-hot fire crawled with ravenous speed over the dried flesh, leaping from one to two to four. With a shout, Delilah grabbed her friends and hauled them back up the tunnel as fast as she could, away from the undead.

For a moment, the mummies started to surge forward, victorious. But the triumph was short-lived. A rancid burning wind swept through the tunnel, and that flame enveloped the entire group of undead instantly. The mummies were transformed into a wall of white fire roaring like a dragon of legend.

Delilah kept pulling them away, and Jeremiah let himself be pulled. Even from a distance of fifty paces, his face burned with the heat of the fire.

"She's still in there!" said Bruno. "We've got to get through!"

"You can't!" said Delilah. "You have no idea how hot that is, it'll burn your skin off. I know, I'm sorry. But we have to wait."

Minutes passed like hours until finally the flames subsided enough to be passable. Jeremiah and his friends rushed into the cavern. It was like entering an oven. The fire over the water had burned out, and the mummies had been reduced to ashes, but Allison was nowhere to be seen.

"Get in there! Find her!" said Bruno. The three of them leapt down into the black water. Jeremiah threw himself toward the center of the pool, where he had last seen Allison go under.

The bottom of the pool, only ankle deep near the edges of the cavern, dropped out near the center. Jeremiah dove, eyes straining in the sudden darkness after so much light, reaching frantically and haphazardly. He resurfaced for air, then dove again. She had to be here. And again, he went down.

No, stupid, look! Think! Where is she? She went down here. No, here. Shit, where?! Jeremiah's thoughts were frantic and starved of both sense and oxygen. He wasn't taking the breaths he needed to keep searching. He was failing her. He had let her down. She was somewhere pale and dead under the water, and he couldn't find her or protect her or—

Jeremiah's knuckles grazed something metal, and he seized it. It was heavy, nearly impossible to move, let alone swim with. He used it to pull himself down to the bottom, wrapped his arms around the thing, screwed up all his strength, and kicked off against the floor as hard as he could toward the surface. He kicked furiously, he needed to breathe, he wouldn't let go, he was willing to drown.

Allison popped out of the water and took in a great coughing gasp of air. She started swimming to shallower waters, carrying Jeremiah now as much as he carried her. They fought the flooded metal shell that was still trying to drag Allison back down to her dignified final resting place.

"Get them! Get them!" Bruno yelled. Delilah and Bruno threw themselves at Jeremiah and Allison, swamping themselves beneath the water.

Jeremiah's foot found solid ground, *No, not solid ground, a hand!* The hand gripped his foot, and Jeremiah took as deep a breath as he could, preparing to be yanked below by some evil that had yet gone unnoticed. Instead, the hand pushed. Somewhere beneath the water Bruno was catching Jeremiah's feet as he struggled and pressed him onward until he and Allison finally clambered onto the shallow rocks, yanked along by Delilah.

"Safe now?" Allison choked. Her head spun this way and that, fist cocked with a dagger in hand.

"She yet lives!" cheered Bruno bursting from the water. He splashed toward them.

"What the—how long can you hold your breath for?" asked Jeremiah. He and Bruno wrapped Allison in a relieved hug.

"Long time," gasped Allison. "Very long time." She gulped the air greedily.

"Anyone need medical attention?" asked Delilah. She flopped into the group hug, a sodden mess.

"My eyes are killing me," said Jeremiah. He could still see white dots from staring into the blaze

"Mine too," said Bruno. "And I think I'm the first person to get a sunburn underground."

"That'll pass," breathed Delilah. "I'm so glad you're okay, hon. I was so worried," Delilah squeezed Allison tighter.

"What went wrong? Okay, I'm okay, off. What went wrong? Tell me, each of you, what went wrong." Allison shook them off, gagged up a splash of water, and found her feet again. "Bruno, you first, what went wrong."

The shift of tone was jarring, Allison gave them just a moment of comfort and then shook them back into being adventurers while they were still dripping wet.

"Too much limb-chopping," said Bruno. "I hurt them, but I didn't stop them. Would have mattered if they were alive, but . . ."

"Good, good," said Allison. She wrung out her hair. "Delilah, go."

"Uh, actually, nothing. I think I did okay," Delilah wrung her hands.

"Fair. That's an okay answer," said Allison. She looked at Jeremiah.

Should have done better, Jeremiah thought, preparing an answer. *Should have jabbed not poked. Should have been more aggressive. Should have backed you up. Should have been braver. Should have fought harder. Should have kept my shield. Should have known more about mummies.*

Her eyes flicked over his face. She took on a look of concern. "Tell me what you did right," said Allison.

"I . . . uh." Jeremiah's scrambled for an answer. The question didn't make sense. Why would she ask that? "I . . . got one," he finally said.

Allison nodded and shifted an armor plate, dumping out more water. "That's right."

CHAPTER SIX

Timing

Deeper and deeper, they descended into the mountain. At times Jeremiah thought they'd see daylight and exit out the other side by way of some as-of-yet-undiscovered cave. But each time they should have been nearing the limits of the mountain's body, they would find a switchback and go down deeper still.

"We must be below the mountain by now," said Allison.

"Just below," confirmed Delilah. "But I'm so confused about these tunnels. Clearly, they were dug out, but why is it so empty? A single trap near the entrance and nothing else?"

"I've been wondering that too," said Bruno. "From that fancy epitaph at the entrance, I thought this place would be chock full of nonsense. Instead, it's just a long, boring walk." He was, of course, making the walk even longer and more boring by continuing to diligently inspect every surface of the tunnels, despite their barrenness of any objects of interest.

More clues appeared after another hour of trudging. All at once, the roughly hewn cave walls gave way to uniform, level surfaces. Further ahead still, ceramic tile began to appear on the floor, caked with dust and grime but smooth and thoughtfully laid. The walls showed the beginnings of carved pillars and even some sketches of artistic reliefs.

They caught up to Bruno who was carefully inspecting an overhang of stone with a mirage of a grinning face carved into it. "They never finished," he said. "Looks like they dug all the way down and had just started fancying the place up. I'm guessing the farther down we go, the more finished it'll get. I suppose the trap at the beginning was just a security measure."

"That trap ever end up telling you anything?" asked Jeremiah.

"Yes, actually," said Bruno prodding at the eyes of the relief. "It says to me that we're likely done with traps. I'll keep looking, of course, but I won't bet on finding any more."

"An unfinished dungeon—is that typical?" asked Jeremiah. He traced a faint swirl carved in the wall.

"Extremely," said Delilah. "Most dungeons are either repurposed structures or naturally formed cave systems. The creation of a dungeon is a huge investment of time and resources. The expertise and labor force to create them are hard to find and maintain as well. They tend to be made at the whims of men who are averse to good investments or project planning. So it just becomes a money pit till the patron either dies or loses interest."

"So . . . why make them?" asked Jeremiah. He was becoming cognizant of the sheer amount of rock that must have been moved to reach this far into the mountain.

Delilah laughed. "'Cause they're nuts. Or they're tyrants without access to a banking system, so they need alternative security to protect their wealth."

"Tyrants don't have bank accounts, huh?" asked Bruno. He gave the relief a friendly pat on the cheek before moving on.

"Well . . . tyranny has made a lot of advances since then," said Delilah, a flicker of disapproval crossing her face.

As they continued, the decor grew increasingly ornate. One wall was dominated by a vast tile mosaic, flanked on either side by carved pillars, spiraling like twisted taffy. The mosaic depicted a scene of a woman lying supine on an altar, surrounded by six tall figures. More striking, though, was the enormous human face depicted overhead, its mouth stretched open as though preparing to swallow the scene below. The expressions of the woman and the figures were devoid of emotion.

Bruno inspected the mosaic, then reached up to press his thumbnail into the eyes of the gaping face. Out popped two small glassy stones, each the size of a pinky nail. They flashed with brilliance when Bruno held them up to lantern light. "Diamonds." From the body of the woman on the altar he popped a sizable scarlet stone. "Ruby, nice one. Whoever was bankrolling this place had some pretty lofty goals for the finished product."

"Honestly surprised that wasn't trapped," said Allison, prodding a loose mosaic tile.

"First of all, jinx," said Bruno. "Second of all, it was supposed to be." He poked at the spot where the diamonds had been remove. There was a tiny hole that disappeared deeper into the wall. "Bet if you fished around in there, you'd find a poison dart or something."

The hallway took a sharp right, leading to a T junction—the first choice of directions they'd encountered since entering the dungeon, Jeremiah realized.

"Okay, this I don't like," Bruno said, peering around the corner.

"What do you see?" asked Allison.

"Trap finding is as much about intuition as it is perception," said Bruno. He crouched in the intersecting hallway, running his hands over the large flagstones of the floor. "You begin to get a feel for where traps are going to be. You get into the head of the creator, and you just start to know where he'd put the next one. Now, see, this is weird. The floor here is too smooth, and look—it's been worn away."

Jeremiah craned his neck to see over Allison's shoulder. The center of the intersecting hallway bowed downward, as though something passing had left a smooth groove behind. "Should we look out for a giant rolling boulder?" he asked.

Bruno chuckled. "Those are a myth. Huge pain in the ass to make a rock that big into a sphere and hoist it up. You're better off just smelting an iron ball and releasing that down a ramp. Break everyone's legs in a dungeon and you've probably won."

Delilah shoved past Jeremiah and Allison. She leaned into the hall, and her ears began to move. It was subtle, but they angled and rotated just a little. Jeremiah stifled a laugh. It made her look like a cat.

"Something's coming," she said, and Jeremiah's humor evaporated. They scrambled back around the corner with the mosaic and set up for combat, Allison taking the point position. The cave rumbled. Jeremiah could feel it in his bones. The rumbling grew louder until he could make out a steady rhythm, like beats on a massive drum, so loud they rattled his teeth. His mind summoned an image of a giant marching toward them, relentless in its approach.

The footsteps became near deafening. Jeremiah clung to his spear to resist the urge to cover his ears. Louder. Closer. Nearly there.

Then, without changing tempo, they began to move away. It was almost indistinguishable at first, but gradually Jeremiah started to be able to hear his own thoughts again. After a few minutes, the footsteps faded beyond the limits of his perception.

Without speaking, Bruno slipped away from them into the dark, silent as a bird on the glide. He was gone before anyone could object.

"What do we do now?" asked Jeremiah.

"We wait. He'll be back," said Allison.

They waited, continually at the ready. The sound of their breathing grew louder as the memory of the thunder steps faded. Then, without turning his head to look at her, Jeremiah told Delilah. "You can wiggle your ears."

"Hush," she said.

"I won't. That's too cute," said Jeremiah.

"I saw too. That was super cute," said Allison. "I didn't know you could do that."

"All elves can. It's not cute; it's normal!" Delilah hissed. They went silent.

"So, do they wiggle when you're happy?" Jeremiah asked. Allison twitched and snorted, holding in a laugh.

"Shh," Delilah shushed them again, but this time they could feel the threat in it. Moments later, Jeremiah detected the same escalating rumble as before. Once again it grew to almost unbearable levels, once again it began to fade.

Bruno whipped around the corner unexpectedly and was nearly murdered by his friends. "Giant stone man," he said, hands raised at spear point. "The hallway makes a big loop, and the stone man is just following it. There's a door on the opposite side to us, halfway through the circuit. It's locked, but I think I can get it open before the stone man comes around."

"A man made of stone?" asked Allison. "Is it alive? Can we just destroy it?"

"No idea, it's covered in markings," Bruno said. He shrugged and pushed the spear tips away.

Recognition sparked in Jeremiah's brain. "Oh, it's a golem!"

"Some kind of friendly helper golem I'm sure," Allison said sarcastically.

"Nope! It's an elemental spirit bound to a body of enchanted stone. Very rare and difficult to make." Despite the danger, Jeremiah was excited to put his enchanting knowledge to use.

"Weaknesses?" asked Allison.

"Uhh, limited intuition and programming?" Jeremiah said. "Like, they will react to threats and stuff, but just by chasing and attacking. They're not going to be able to follow advanced strategies."

"I mean, can you, I don't know, turn it off or something?"

"Probably, yes," said Jeremiah. "That is, if you can convince it to lie down so I can work on it."

"Uh-huh," said Allison. She drew and hefted her mace. "How strong is this thing exactly?"

"Strong enough that your armor isn't going to help much," said Jeremiah. "The bodies of golems are magically strengthened rock. Nothing can withstand them for long."

Allison returned her mace to its holster with a sigh. "All right, then. Options?" She looked at Delilah.

"I have a few tricks, but certainly not any answers for something like that," Delilah said. She browsed her many pockets, frowning at them when no solutions appeared.

To Bruno. "Avoid it altogether," suggested Bruno. "If we're patient, I can work on the door in spurts. This thing seems stuck on a circuit. So I work when it's leaving. I move when it's approaching. Work, move, repeat. When it's unlocked, I'll come get you, and we'll all go together."

The party digested the idea. "Okay by me," said Allison finally, "but be conservative. This thing has been walking for centuries. You have all the time in the world."

They waited by the mosaic as Bruno slipped away again. The deafening footsteps continued their cycle. Half an hour passed with no sign of Bruno. Jeremiah resisted the urge to steal a peek at the magical marvel each time the golem stomped by.

At last Bruno returned, his face shining with sweat.

"All right, the door's unlocked. But I'll need everyone's help to open it. It's stone and ridiculously heavy. We should wait until it's as far away as from us as possible before we move, otherwise it's too risky it would detect you guys."

"That would mean six minutes after its passing," said Delilah. "Its loops are exactly twelve minutes each."

"You've been timing it?" asked Jeremiah. He wondered what it would be like to focus his attention on something for that long.

"Some of us have better things to do than tease others about their superior physical abilities," said Delilah. She stared at Jeremiah, and her ears flicked.

"I trust Delilah's timing," said Allison. "We follow Bruno's lead on her count."

Bruno began tightening Allison's armor while Jeremiah and Delilah walked back and forth in Bruno's direction. Bruno tilted his head as he listened. "Jay, keep on your toes. Your heels are too heavy. Delilah, you're tinkling, clicking, and, I think, clunking. Ditch whatever is doing that."

Delilah brushed a black tarry paste onto the soles of Allison's boots. It cured into a squishy film that deadened the sound of her footsteps to almost nothing. Everyone else got a lighter coating of the remnant.

Each time the golem passed, their activities would still. Six minutes after each pass, Delilah would whisper "Mark."

They finished preparing. The golem passed. The thunderous steps grew quieter and then disappeared altogether.

They waited, tense. Jeremiah became aware of the sounds of their breathing, of the sweat on his brow, of a growing ache spreading across his neck. He thought he heard Delilah take a breath, and his muscles jerked. But she didn't say anything.

They were frozen on the verge of action. The moment was coming.

"Mark," Delilah finally said, and they moved as one.

The hallway was a blur. He saw more signs of half-finished doors and hallways only one or two feet deep into the wall. The hallway was large and twisted at odd, seemingly random angles. Jeremiah imagined this creature taking up the whole of it, shoulders a hair's breadth from the wall, designed to be unavoidable.

Finally, they came to a grand stone entry. A solid stone door was ornately carved with images of a man standing before crowds of prostrate worshippers. He was wreathed in flames and flanked by impaled bodies. The door told Jeremiah everything he needed to know about the man it was built for—a man who was both life and death, to be loved and feared, worshipped and obeyed. Jeremiah despised him.

The sprout of metallic thorns on the seam of the door showed Bruno's workspace, a dozen little tools carefully arranged. Silently, they arranged to push against the heavy door. Even the slightest rasp of Allison's gauntlets made Jeremiah's heart race. He kept glancing back the way they'd come, expecting at any moment something immense and terrible would come barreling around the corner like an avalanche.

Once everyone was in position, Bruno counted them off on his fingers. Three. Two. One. They pushed.

Jeremiah chewed the insides of his cheeks to keep from making noise while straining. Their faces reddened with the effort as they strained against the immense door. Slowly, it began to move, utterly silent. The door hung perfectly balanced on invisible hinges, and as they pushed, it slowly glided open.

There was a rush of stale air from above them, Jeremiah looked up just in time to see the mouths of brass horns built into the ceiling, revealed by the moving door.

"Oh," said Bruno.

There was a blast of deafening trumpets. The door moved, and the brass horns bellowed as air rushed through them. It was a victorious announcement that the door was opening, likely audible throughout the entire dungeon.

As the echo of the trumpets faded, they could hear the footsteps, a pulsing percussion smothering the brass cry. It was fast, and growing louder, closer, like an approaching avalanche just out of sight.

"Push!" Allison screamed. They threw themselves against the door with renewed might and urgency. The blaring trumpets sounded louder and louder the faster the door opened. Jeremiah could feel the ground shivering; he didn't dare look toward the bend in the hallway.

Delilah thrust the point of her spear into the frame, levering it against the door.

Allison grabbed on with her, the spear wood bending and groaning. Jeremiah followed suit with his own, Bruno aiding him. The earthquake grew louder. Jeremiah could hear Bruno hissing through his teeth. "I didn't get us killed. I didn't get us killed. I didn't get us killed!"

A sliver of space appeared beyond the door. "Good enough—move!" yelled Allison. Her voice was almost drowned out by the rapid approach of a juggernaut.

Bruno slipped through first, followed by Jeremiah. Jeremiah felt his ribs bend near to breaking as he tried to force his way in. Bruno grabbed his arm and yanked him through. Delilah's bulky padded armor compressed as she squeezed into the gap, then stuck fast.

Jeremiah and Bruno each grabbed one of Delilah's arms and Allison pushed from behind. Then a flash of Allison's dagger and leather strips parted from her expert cut. Various glass and earthen containers fell from Delilah as Jeremiah and Bruno pulled. Jeremiah felt a pop as something gave in Delilah's wrist. Delilah screamed, but they pulled harder. They had to.

Then she was through. Allison barreled after her, armor sparking as she ground against the stone. The thudding of the golem's approach reached a crescendo, matching the wild fury of Jeremiah's panicked heart. He thought he glimpsed a shadow fall across the hallway outside, and then Allison was yelling, "Close it, close it!" and he threw himself against the door and shoved with all his might.

Jeremiah's senses were overwhelmed by thunder and panic, but somehow the door was moving. His eyes were screwed shut but he could feel the golem was right there, it was reaching for him, it was about to crush him and all his friends in a massive outstretched hand—then the door clicked shut, and everything fell utterly silent.

CHAPTER SEVEN

Once in a Lifetime

The silence rang in Jeremiah's ears. He could sense something ancient and powerful lurking on the other side of the door. Its very presence pressed against the stone slab like the sea against the belly of a ship, threatening to burst through.

"We okay?" asked Allison. She was shaking with adrenaline. They all were.

"I'm sorry," said Bruno, panting. "I thought it was clear. I didn't realize they were instruments. I thought it—"

They collectively screamed as a blow of stone on stone rattled the door, echoing thunder around them. Dust and pebbles fell from the ceiling, but the door held.

The blow came again.

Again.

Again.

As the door continued to hold, Jeremiah let out a sigh of relief. "I don't think it's getting through," he said between rolls of thunder.

"So we're trapped in here?" asked Delilah. Her armor was misshapen and lopsided, and she was cradling her hand.

"It might eventually leave," said Allison.

"Might," emphasized Bruno. He glared at the edges of the door like it had betrayed him.

"Doesn't hurt to stay positive. Focus," said Allison. "Delilah, your hand okay?"

Delilah gently touched each of her fingers to her thumb one after the other. She hissed in pain when she tried to move the middle one. "Dislocated finger, and I think something in my wrist is broken."

Bruno turned his attention from the door just in time to see Delilah yank her finger. There was a crunch as it popped back into place. The color drained from Bruno's face, but he kept steady. "S-so . . . bandages?" he asked.

"For now, yes," Delilah said. She bound her wrist with Allison's help, grunting as she pulled the dressing tight.

"This is not what I was expecting," said Jeremiah looking ahead. With imminent death no longer looming and Delilah's arm tended to, he had finally looked around the space. Beyond the elaborate vault-like door, with its damnable trumpet fanfare, the hallway continued as a blank and monotonous corridor. It was larger than the previous areas but was bereft of any sign of decorative elements.

Delilah lit their bullseye lantern and pointed it down the hall, illuminating smooth walls leading to a dead end. The beam revealed a huge stone plinth before the far wall.

"That some kind of altar?" asked Bruno.

"Get us closer and let's find out. I don't like staying here," said Allison. The blows of the stone golem's fists kept a steady rhythm against the door.

Neither trap nor ornament stood between them and the mysterious object, though Bruno's investigations of every pebble and crack grew more fastidious and frustrated the closer they got. Finally, they found themselves before the great block of marble stone. It was polished to a mirror shine all around, with elaborate gargoyle heads sneering down from the corners.

Bruno orbited the object, inspecting a relief. It depicted a great funerary procession, a score of men carrying and leading a figure in repose, with crowds of mourners following behind. The features of every single person were carved with exquisite detail, down to the anguished faces of even the most obscured mourner. It was all the more astounding given the other three sides were completely blank.

"It's a tomb," Bruno finally concluded, signaling an all clear. "This must be ol' Mr. Fidelious."

There was a pop from close behind that made Jeremiah jump. He spun to see a burning white light coming from a small sack in Delilah's hand. It cascaded white sparks in a fountain from the open drawstring top. She tossed it high up at a wall, where it stuck with a splat, casting soft light across the tomb.

"Sticky lamp, new invention," said Delilah. "Just trying it out."

The sticky lamp revealed a vaunted ceiling above them, stretching high into darkness. Etched into the walls around the tomb were the rough outlines of steps ascending up into bare rock.

Allison gestured at their newly illuminated surroundings. "What's with this place? Why is it so . . . half-finished?"

"I think it looks half-finished because it *was* half-finished," said Delilah. "Whoever this was, I'm guessing he had construction start while he was still alive. He must have made the golem too. Then he died, and the momentum of his tyranny ran out pretty fast. His followers just quit once they realized he was gone. Bad project management. Prioritization based on daily whims, so it's completely random what's finished and what's not."

"So our hopes of him being buried in a treasure vault with a king's ransom . . . ?" asked Bruno. He gazed forlornly at the big empty room, like he could just imagine great piles of treasure that should be there.

Jeremiah slapped the tomb itself. "Well, let's crack this open and see if he kept his treasures close."

Bruno chuckled. "Not even a little shy about pilfering a corpse, huh?"

Jeremiah laughed louder than he intended, but the idea was just so amusing. "Do you have any idea how many treasures and trinkets I've pulled off corpses I processed for Flusoh? I never heard a single complaint from any of them. Crack this thing open and I'll pop out his gold teeth with my bare hands."

"Ew," said Allison.

"That's just awful." Bruno grinned. "I love it. Help me push."

With a great effort, they pushed the stone lid of the tomb inch by grinding inch. When it finally crashed to the floor, dust blew around the room in an angry roiling cloud.

Together, Jeremiah and his friends peered inside. Inside lay a skeleton, doubled over on itself, one foot resting against the side of the tomb. A pair of gold bracelets and anklets hung limp on its limbs, and a thick golden crown lay adjacent to the skull.

"Looks like they just heaved him in," said Delilah.

"Not with nothin', though," said Bruno. He leaned in and pulled up a small chest, barely a footlocker, tucked in a corner at the foot of the tomb. "Jay, grab those bangles and crown, would you?"

Jeremiah climbed fully into the tomb and began wrestling the gold away from the skeleton. His focus on the treasure grew stronger, making the pounding on the door in the distance just a dull noise in his mind.

Bruno decided the chest was without traps and levered it open. A small hoard of golden coins greeted him, shimmering in the sparkling white light.

"Thaaat's what we like to see!" Bruno picked up a handful and let them tumble back into the chest with a satisfying metallic clatter. He paused, picked up a single coin, and tossed it in his hand a few times. "What the? Ah, shit. This is electrum."

Delilah and Allison groaned.

"What's that?" asked Jeremiah, as he carefully tucked the bangles into his bag.

"A silver-gold mix. It's a pain in the ass 'cause the ratio varies, so no one takes them as is. Old stuff, these were made a long time ago," said Bruno, letting the coin drop into the box with diminished glee.

"I can separate the gold," said Delilah. "It just takes a long while, and I need to get the end product certified and stamped, which eats into the profit."

Since when does money cost money? wondered Jeremiah.

"Now this is weird," said Jeremiah, holding up the crown. From a glance, it appeared to be little more than a wide band of gold meant to rest atop the wearer's head. The outside of the band itself was smooth and polished, but otherwise unadorned. The inside surface of the band, however, was studded with dark pink sapphires.

Jeremiah handed the crown to Bruno. "Why have the gems on the inside?" asked Bruno, inspecting the crown. "No one can see them, and it'd be damn uncomfortable—Oh wow! These are nice. These are *really* nice!" He held up the crown to catch the light better, peering close and hard, searching for any sign of crack or cloud in the rose-colored gemstones.

"Let me see," said Delilah. She swiped for the crown a few times before Bruno stopped dodging and let her hold it. "There's a coat of arms stamped in the gold," she said, fishing a curved lens from her robes. "It's . . . invected double fess on a kite. That's the Marquette family crest, actually. They're still around in some form or another."

"Well, they haven't been missing this stuff," Bruno said, eyeing Delilah suspiciously. He began reaching to snatch the crown away again.

"No, but . . . let's just keep an open mind," said Delilah. She stowed the crown in her robes, as opposed to the chest of coins.

Bruno and Jeremiah locked eyes. *Gone forever*, thought Jeremiah, and he knew Bruno felt the same. Delilah had plans for that crown.

Jeremiah was about to jump out of the tomb when he spotted something lumpy squashed beneath the skeleton. He shoved the bones aside to find a leather backpack, flat and cracked all over. It held the stiff form it had been in for untold years.

"Leather? That should have decayed a long time ago," said Allison.

"Might be magic," said Jeremiah. "An enchanted object is resistant to normal wear and tear. But I think the magic in this is long since spent."

Allison took the bag from him and gingerly peeked inside. "Enchantments get spent? Like, run out?" Allison asked. She unconsciously ran a hand over armor, looking nervous.

Jeremiah climbed out of the tomb and dusted himself off. "Eventually, yeah. But it tends to take a very long time, depending on how often it's used. Don't worry, your armor will probably outlive you."

"Jay, I think the tomb lid is enchanted," said Delilah. She was studying the great stone slab. It had landed upside down, revealing an underside webbed with intricate lines and designs.

Jeremiah whistled. "Looks like. Or it was, anyway."

"Dangerous?" asked Allison. She put a hand on Delilah's shoulder and pulled her back a step, interposing herself between Delilah and the stone.

Jeremiah looked it over. The diagram was wildly complicated, and he wasn't very good at reading complex enchantments yet. It was like looking at a pile of words and being asked what sentence they were supposed to make. There was a right answer, but a lot more not-quite-right answers.

"I don't *think* it's dangerous?" he finally decided. "Same situation as the bag, I think whatever magic was in here has long since run its course."

"So what's the point of it, then?" asked Bruno.

Jeremiah shrugged. "I can't be sure, but if I had to guess, it may have been an attempt to reverse death? Clearly didn't work, though."

"That would explain the trumpets," said Delilah. "It would announce to everyone that he'd returned to life to open his own tomb."

"Arrogant bastard," muttered Bruno. "Well, if that's it, are we good to go, Jay?"

But Jeremiah had frozen. Amid the web of interconnecting runes and conduits, there was one rune that looked . . . wrong.

"Jay? Talk to me," said Allison. She raised her shield. Delilah and Bruno scampered behind the tomb, taking cover.

"I don't know this rune," said Jeremiah. He reached out and traced it with a fingertip, trying to jog his memory. There were so many runes in so many patterns, each and every one of them complex and challenging in their own way. But something about this rune looked unique, in a way others didn't approach.

"Okay. Are we concerned, or is this just a professional curiosity?" asked Allison.

Jeremiah's hand began to shake. "No, you don't understand. I don't recognize this rune, not even a little. I can't say I know every rune, but this one . . . I've never seen anything like it."

"The point, Jay. What does this *mean?*" Allison demanded. Then she shot a glance back toward the entrance and the thundering blows.

Jeremiah leaned close to the writing and blew on it, dislodging a poof of dust. "It means I need paper, good paper. And a way to trace this as accurately as possible. Delilah, do you have—"

"Here," said Delilah. She handed him a gossamer thin piece of paper and a black shard of stone.

Jeremiah spread the paper over the rune. It was translucent, and even pressed against the stone he could just see the lines of the strange rune etched below. He worried the paper would tear, but it was surprisingly resilient. He closed his eyes and tried to center himself, taking deep breaths the way Thurok had taught him to prepare for exacting work. He imagined draining energy from his hand and arm to bring it to perfect stillness and control.

He let his perfectly calm arm glide over the paper. It was a small rune, but it took him several minutes to capture each facet with certainty. He held up and inspected the paper.

"All good?" asked Allison. She stole another glance toward the door and its distant thunder.

"Not yet. I need another paper, several more. Delilah, how many of these do you have?" Jeremiah rolled the page up carefully and tucked it into the reinforced pocket of his armor where he kept Gus, who croaked at the intrusion.

"Another four. You're error-proofing the copy?" said Delilah.

"Exactly," said Jeremiah. Delilah handed Jeremiah all she had, and he transcribed each one as carefully as if it were his only chance. As he completed them, he handed one each to Delilah, Bruno, and Allison, he was dimly aware of Allison walking away with her page.

With a sigh of relief, Jeremiah finished the fifth copy. "Done. Okay, I'll keep two." To the others, he said, "Keep them as safe as possible. I can't promise anything, but this might be more valuable than anything else we've found, well . . . ever."

Bruno inspected his page. "What's it say? Runes are, like, words of the gods or something, right?"

"Exactly that. When you hear me saying magical words? These are what I'm saying," said Jeremiah, pointing to the different runes around the lid.

"So what's this one say?" asked Bruno.

"No idea. It's very rare that mages have both the pronunciation and the rune for any particular word. Like, I have no idea how I'd write the rune for any of my undead spells. And I have no idea how to say any of these runes out loud, pretty sure no one does," said Jeremiah, indicating the tomb lid.

"I was really under the impression this was a thoroughly mastered craft," said Delilah.

"Yeah, aren't powerful mages supposed to be channeling arcane mysteries or something?" asked Bruno. He wiggled his fingers for emphasis.

Jeremiah scoffed. "I know we call it the language of the gods, but even the greatest mages are just babbling toddlers. Some of the babble is just barely intelligible enough to work. Same with enchanting."

"So all we need is a dictionary," said Bruno.

"That'll be all our troubles solved, guaranteed." Jeremiah's second page joined the first. "Or, come to think of it, maybe it'd make all our troubles much worse."

"Speaking of worse troubles," said Allison, returning to the group. "The door is failing."

CHAPTER EIGHT

The Hunt

A spiderweb of cracks was spreading across the door. New ones branched off like streams from rivers, cutting through mountain stone with each strike. The golem's rhythm never faltered, one strike every two seconds without fail.

"No secret exits that I can find," reported Bruno. "Just one way in and out."

Allison's face was grave as she studied the door. "You're sure we can't fight it?" she asked Jeremiah.

"I'm sure," said Jeremiah. His mind was circling a dark certainty. "These things are unstoppable. It's punching through like three feet of stone right now."

The friends were silent for a time, watching tiny chips fall from the door with each deafening slam.

"I . . . I think we're dead," said Bruno. He shrugged as he said it, and the flippancy of the gesture sent a spike of cold through Jeremiah's chest.

"Can you reinforce the door?" Jeremiah asked Delilah.

"A little, sure," she said. Not enough to make a difference." Allison nodded to her and Delilah spread a black paste over the deepest and largest cracks. The glossy texture began to fade, and the paste suddenly turned from black to bright green. If it changed anything, Jeremiah couldn't see it.

"We dead?" Bruno asked the room.

Allison sighed. "Yeah, maybe. I've got one idea, and it's a bad one."

"No such thing right now," said Delilah. Jeremiah heard the tiniest quivering hitch of fear in her voice. The cold spike in his chest bloomed into his hands and he began to shiver.

Allison pointed to the frame around the great stone entry. "The door isn't flush with the wall when it's open. Bruno unlocks the door, and we hide in the gap. Maybe it can't find us and quits, or maybe we sneak out while it's searching."

"Maybe the door crushes us when he batters it open," said Bruno.

"Maybe" was all Allison said in return.

They were quiet again. Jeremiah had brushed up against death more than once, but this felt different. This felt inevitable. The stone slab reverberated and rattled, sending more dust to the ground. He thought he heard something give inside it.

Jeremiah's breath caught as he tried to speak, but he forced out the words "I just want to say—" Allison rounded on him.

"No! No goodbyes yet! We say our goodbyes after we're dead. Stop fucking shaking, Jay. Delilah, you too. Stop it!"

"I'm not—" Delilah said.

"We act!" shouted Allison. "Get in position now. Bruno, start unlocking the door. You two get in position to hide. If it finds us, you all run and I'll keep it busy as long as I can," Allison shook them, forcing them into position. Jeremiah was slammed against the stone wall between Delilah and Allison. He squeezed himself as flat as he could.

Bruno began prying and yanking at the mechanisms holding the door shut, pausing his work with every blow against the door. Jeremiah saw the fear in every motion Bruno made, stuttering fingers and a sheen of sweat beading on his brow.

"Get ready," said Bruno. It was a meaningless statement, the only thing Jeremiah could do was hold still and not die. He looked to his left and saw Delilah's pale face, resolute and stern despite the quivering lip. To his right Allison had her eyes closed and was muttering. An oath or prayer, he did not know.

Bruno ran a metal cord from the labyrinthian lock mechanism to his place on the wall. He paused in front of Jeremiah, locking eyes with him. Bruno's gaze flicked once to Delilah and back again to Jeremiah. Jeremiah understood. *If only one, her.*

Jeremiah agreed, although he wasn't entirely sure why.

"Ready?" asked Bruno.

"Go!" Allison barked, without hesitation.

Bruno yanked the cord. There was a sound of whirring metal, a sudden catch, and a metallic shattering from the door. Not deviating from its rhythm, the golem struck the door once more. The blaring horns meant to signal a triumphant return from death bleated once in a brass shriek, and the great door burst open.

Jeremiah forced the air from his lungs and as the door careened toward him, he had time for a single thought. *At least this won't hurt.*

The deafening boom shook his bones, but the door stopped half an inch from his nose. Bruno and Delilah were untouched, though Allison would have had the visor of her helmet crushed in had she not turned her head.

There was silence, save for the sound of dust falling from the walls and ceiling. The golem did not charge blindly into the room. It was watching, observing. Searching.

A single thud as it took a step forward, then another. Silence. Jeremiah felt his breath catch as, far above his head, three stone fingers curled around the edge of the door. They were each as thick as his arm and etched in glowing blue runes. The golem was going to be thorough in its search.

Jeremiah caught the slightest shift to his left. Allison was there. He realized she was preparing to dash into the open, to turn herself into a distraction and enable their escape. She would be crushed as soon as it reached her, sacrificing herself to buy them a few precious moments to make their escape.

He wanted to shout, to grab ahold of her arm and not let go, but of course he could do neither. She tensed, about to run. About to die.

Jeremiah had no time to think, only act.

Rise.

Stretching out his will, Jeremiah touched the long-forgotten bones still heaped in the tomb. A single bubble formed in his mind. It felt like a severed limb regrowing all at once. The cold of the stone, the orientation of the bones, the sense of light, all mingled simultaneously with his own senses. It felt good. It felt like waking up a limb that had been numb, flushing away the pins and needles. The bubble felt like a little piece of him that had returned from nothingness.

The skeleton of the entombed king sprang upward, grinding the crumbling bones of its fingertips against the stone like chalk. What faint noise it made was more than enough to attract the golem's attention, and whatever loyalty it had held to the owner of those bones was long gone. The hall rang with a teeth-rattling cacophony as the massive glowing golem careened down the hall.

The instant the golem began its charge, they fled. *Evade*, Jeremiah commanded the skeleton as he ran. It had to buy them as much time as possible.

Jeremiah ran heedless of his need for breath, or of the burning in his legs. He didn't notice as they sprinted through the tiled halls or the countless switchbacks. He was dimly aware of the skeleton's efforts to evade the golem, but his present mind was fixed on the back of Allison as he willed himself to keep up with her.

The skeleton's bubble burst just as they splashed into the cavern where they had fought the mummies. The shock of cold and the sudden limitation of their speed drove the fog of panic from their minds. They staggered over to the stone stairs, collapsing as they heaved in air and let the icy water cool the burning muscles in their legs.

"G-good? We good?" Allison gasped out finally.

"S-skeleton gone . . . but good," said Jeremiah. He felt a clap on the shoulder from Bruno, directing him to a half-hearted thumbs-up.

"Let's . . . leave," said Delilah.

Together they climbed up the slippery stones to where they had made their stand. Finally back into the starry tunnel, they formed a proper marching order again. There was a question floating over the march, like a fifth party member had joined them and marched right alongside them.

"So . . . that was you, wasn't it?" Allison asked. "You made the skeleton? It didn't just pop up on its own?"

"Al, maybe now's not the time," said Bruno, glancing back at her.

Jeremiah felt immediately defensive. "The one that saved us? Yeah, that was me."

"Easy, Jay. It pains me to say it, but you made the right call."

"Oh, it's going in a different direction than I thought," muttered Bruno. He tilted his head to keep listening in.

They kept marching.

Do I say thank you? thought Jeremiah. *Or just . . . I don't know, let it go?* "Yeah," he said, confirming Allison's assessment.

More silent marching.

"Al, don't," warned Bruno.

"I just wish you didn't have to," Allison blurted out a moment after Bruno spoke.

"Dammit, Al," Bruno muttered again.

Jeremiah wanted to feel relieved, but her last comment restoked his irritation. "Sometimes you need to save everyone from certain death," he said, with a touch of attitude.

"Oh, you've got to be *fucking* kidding me!" said Delilah. Jeremiah glared at her over his shoulder, ready to defend his decision, but she was looking back down the way they had just come. He saw her ears twitch, just a little.

"Run! Run, run, run!" Delilah screamed.

The panic returned like a tsunami, carrying everyone along with it. They ran, willing their exhausted bodies onward. Jeremiah was vaguely aware of Delilah frantically shedding supplies as she ran. Vials smoked and splattered across the floor, anything that might slow their inaudible pursuer.

Jeremiah wheezed for breath as he ran. It felt like he was drowning. His friends began pulling away, even as he urged his leaden legs onward. Up ahead, Allison collided with a jutting bit of cave wall and fell in a shower of sparks. She was struggling to her knees as Jeremiah reached her, and he tried to help her up.

Allison yanked up her helmet's visor and doubled over, retching on the floor as she stumbled into a gait no faster than Jeremiah's. "Damned . . . heavy armor," she gasped.

Delilah reappeared. "Please keep running!" she said, her eyes frantic. "Please! Just a bit farther!"

Suddenly he felt it, a nearly imperceptible quiver in the bones of the very mountain around them. Rhythmic, building, and unrelenting. Jeremiah's body pulled on some last primal reserve of strength, and they surged onward.

Blue. There was a blue glow creeping in on them from behind. Crawling around the corridors and searching for them. The golem's steps merged with the pounding blood in Jeremiah's ears. He stumbled forward. Moving slowly was all he could manage, but he was moving.

Bruno doubled back to find them, seemingly unfazed by the test of endurance. His blades were drawn, and he ushered them along as they reached the bone-strewn cave of the troll. The troll stood at the ready, bearing shield and makeshift weapon and growling something in giant's tongue.

"BA . . . be ba garoo!" Delilah shouted at the troll. She waved her arms, pointing toward the blue glow. "Sha-te frista!"

The troll considered them in what Jeremiah interpreted as confusion, but it didn't advance. Jeremiah's legs gave out as he crossed the threshold of the troll's territory. Allison leaned against a wall, weapons drawn but limp with exhaustion. Delilah readied her spear, her alchemical ammunition spent. One way or another, their flight was over.

The deafening approach rattled Jeremiah's bones as the behemoth of stone at last came into view. Its body etchings glowed with an arcane blue light that sparked and flashed. The center of its head had a single cyclopean eye composed of hundreds of tiny etchings that glowed even brighter, shining a spotlight on their backs. Bearing down on them, the golem pulverized rocky outcroppings to powder, its gait neither slowing nor faltering. Titanic stone arms clawed the walls, pulling itself with a frantic tenacity even as its elephantine legs pushed its body forward. It seemed to take up the entire width of the tunnel, crushing all illusions of safety as easily as the rocks it should have.

Bruno drew his magic bow and began firing arrows at the golem, splintering them across its stony facade. "Right here! Come test me, big guy! Come chase the shadow!" he shouted.

Crazy son of a bitch is going to sacrifice himself, thought Jeremiah.

But as the golem took its first thundering step into the open space of the cave, the troll sprang into action. It moved with surprising grace, crossing the room and smashing the metal blade of its scythe into the golem with a tremendous backhand. The force of the blow exploded the makeshift weapon and stopped the unstoppable.

The golem was knocked clear off its feet, cratering the stone beneath its back. A heavy gouge marked its chest where the blade impacted. The troll was undeterred by the loss of its weapon and unconvinced of the fatality of the strike. It lifted its tower shield of logs above the golem and began driving it downward over and over again.

At least I'll see a hell of an interesting fight before I die, thought Jeremiah.

Wood was of no concern to stone. Inexorably, the golem stood, looming taller than the hunched troll. It battered the shield aside, shattering it to pieces, and gripped the troll by the shoulder. With no discernible sign of effort, it crushed the troll's arm in a firm grip and tore it away from its body.

The troll roared in pain and fury, green blood gushing from the wound for only an instant before it sealed off, and the troll's regenerative powers began growing a new arm at a rapid speed. The troll attacked again, raking across the golem's body with its claws. The golem raised its fist and crushed the troll into the floor with a blow so strong Jeremiah felt the stone beneath his feet shift.

Over and over, the golem rained blows down on the troll's body, destroying it too slowly to take it out of the fight. Jeremiah and his friends watched as the troll's regeneration rapidly repaired crushed bones, lost limbs, even decapitation. He thought of Narooka, the minotaur filled with a sea of regenerative magic, but the troll's regeneration would never run dry. And the golem seemed to possess no fire or acid.

Meanwhile, the golem was nearly invulnerable to the troll's frenzied assault. But nearly invulnerable was very different from completely invulnerable, at least when facing an enemy as tenacious as a troll defending its territory. Jeremiah realized shallow scratches were beginning to appear on the surface of the golem's body, small chips marring the edges of the reinforced stonework. It was like the weathering of a mountain that would eventually, over eons, wear it down to the ground.

Then Jeremiah was being hoisted to his feet. Delilah and Bruno each had an arm under one of his. "Come on, buddy!" said Bruno, with forced joviality. "We're going to leave this one to our new best friend."

Jeremiah's brain was not working properly. "Shouldn't we help?" he asked, as his feet tried to remember how to walk.

"You said it yourself," said Delilah. "There's no way we can take that thing on."

They limped their way to the entrance, echoes of the troll's cries of fury and pain following them through the cave. Waves of exhaustion emanated from them, and their return trip back toward the entrance took nearly as long as the first time they went through, even without Bruno sweeping for traps. Jeremiah's legs trembled with fatigue, but the knowledge of the battle behind them forced him onward.

At long last, they reached the tomb entrance and the campsite they'd made the night before. Jeremiah stumbled toward his bedroll and collapsed, certain he'd never stand again. The idea didn't bother him in the slightest.

"No, down. Down, down, down," said Allison. "We need to get some distance from this place before we rest. Grab everything now."

Their own exhaustion combined with the somewhat-careful descent gave them time to breathe again. The wide-open world felt like an ally to the enemy of the tight tunnels and looming death. Finally, they reached the forest that surrounded the mountain. They collapsed together, discarding sweaty helmets and garments. They sat in silence, still panting, the loss of adrenaline sapping their strength. All eyes were still on the mountain, a collective fear that a living avalanche would soon appear and give chase.

"What'd you say to the troll?" Jeremiah asked Delilah.

Delilah promptly threw up.

"What's that mean in giant?" Jeremiah asked. The dissipating terror had them hysterical with laughter.

They tried to make distance from the mountain with the daylight they had left but didn't get far. Exhaustion and relief at their own survival urged them to rest and sleep. Something akin to a camp was set up, armor was stripped, and meager parcels of remaining food were doled out. Christopher hadn't reappeared, and the bulk of their supplies had disappeared with him.

"So, what did you say to the troll, Delilah? I thought you only knew a few words?" asked Allison.

Delilah paused the careful organization of the strips of her armor and alchemical armaments to answer. "Kind of a mishmash of the words I did know. A familial greeting and a warning of an intruder, though far too quickly to be polite. He got the idea, though. He really is quite clever."

"Bless him. We owe him a gift or something," said Bruno. There were grunts of affirmation.

"Delilah, how's your wrist?" asked Jeremiah. She was handling things with the hand well, no signs of pain or discomfort.

"I honestly had forgotten, which is good," said Delilah. She held up her hand to inspect, and it was clearly swollen from wrist to forearm. "Broken, or severely sprained. I'll need to give a proper splint till I can see a specialist. Let me check the rest of you."

Their injuries were miraculously minor, considering what they had been through. Delilah prescribed them all bed rest with her accelerated healing potion—once they got back to Dramir, of course.

The watch schedule was set, Allison taking the first shift to keep her armor on. But an hour later Jeremiah, unable to stop reliving their ordeal, became aware no one else was sleeping either.

"Everyone still awake?" he whispered.

"Yeah."

"Yes."

"Still on watch, so yeah."

Jeremiah sat up. "I can't sleep," he said.

"Obviously. None of us can," said Bruno.

"Post-mission adrenaline," said Allison. "I'm going to take a double shift. You are all going to lie back down, close your eyes, and not stress about sleeping. Just rest."

"Isn't sleep the whole thing we're trying to accomplish?" asked Jeremiah.

"Not sleeping sucks, doesn't it?" asked Allison.

"Yeah . . ." said Jeremiah.

"Then don't try to sleep, just try to rest. All of you. No tonics Delilah, I want everyone ready to . . . break camp, if need be," said Allison. She began gathering more wood for the fire, and everyone seemed to do as she requested. Jeremiah just let himself think aimlessly, and let sleep be the furthest thing from his mind.

He awoke to screaming, he shot up and scrambled for his spear, only stopping when he saw Allison grab a screaming Delilah and hold her down.

"You're safe! You're safe! You're not in the cave; you're outside! Shhhh!" Allison shouted over Delilah's screams.

Delilah quickly calmed, her eyes frantic and darting around the campsite. "I . . . I thought I heard the golem coming. I could hear him or feel him or something. I think I was dreaming."

"I know, I know," Allison cooed.

"Let me . . . Let me go on watch," said Delilah. "I think I need to be awake for a while."

"All right, sure. Thanks Delilah. Everyone, go back to sleep."

Delilah helped Allison remove her armor, and Allison helped Delilah put her own back on. As Allison settled in, Jeremiah wiggled a little closer to her.

Allison raised an eyebrow at him. "Not sure I'm in the mood to cuddle, Jay," she said. Her eyes were bloodshot and barely open.

Jeremiah ignored the jape. "Is she okay?"

"No, but she will be. Same thing happened to you, remember?" Allison sighed and closed her eyes.

"But she must have faced death a dozen times by now, she's never reacted like that. Why now?" Jeremiah asked. He had always thought the three of them were battle-hardened, veteran adventurers. The idea that they could be affected by the same things he had shook something in him.

"We don't choose what fucks us up, Jay. She's a mortal woman, just—"

"Right, I'm sorry. I don't why it just . . . freaked me out a little," said Jeremiah.

"I get it, some part of you still sees us as heroes or something. Do me a favor?"

"Yeah?"

"Get over it—fast. I don't like the idea of being anyone's idol, especially a friend," said Allison. It was a bit brusquer than Jeremiah would have liked, but he suspected she wasn't in much of a tender mood.

"So . . . about that cuddle?" he said with a smile.

"Talk to me when you get some chest hair," said Allison.

"Kid barely survives the mountain just to be murdered at the campsite, tragic," Bruno laughed.

CHAPTER NINE

The Blade and The Bureaucrat

In the small hours of the morning, a stabbing pain in Jeremiah's back wrenched him awake. He leapt from his sleeping roll and realized the pain was within his own body—the treacherous muscles of his back were seizing up, exhaustion and dehydration spurring them on. His legs felt like lead, but he didn't want to wake anyone else, so he staggered beyond the warm ring of light cast by the embers of their fire toward the dark woods just beyond. There, he began to stretch and knead his back, trying to soothe the pain away.

"Dangerous to wander away from camp." Bruno's voice drifted from somewhere above him.

"Back spasm," Jeremiah strained to say.

"Hold still." There was a soft crush of vegetation behind him, and he was suddenly struck between the shoulder blades. The blow hurt, but the spasms instantly stopped. "Thanks," he said, rolling his shoulders. The muscle wasn't relaxed, it was just limp, paralyzed. "What was that?"

"Nerve strike," said Bruno. The sound of striking flint, and their little corner of darkness bloomed with lamp light. Jeremiah could finally see Bruno, dressed in his black leathers.

"Can you teach me that?" asked Jeremiah. It seemed like a useful trick and must have been pretty easy if Bruno could do it in the dark like that.

"Sorry, Jay. Trade secret," said Bruno, staring into the diminutive flame.

Drama queen, thought Jeremiah. "On watch?" he asked.

"Yeah. Have a seat." Bruno sat beneath a tree and patted the moss invitingly. He took off his headcover and tossed it a dozen feet away. The reinforced leather hidden inside the wrap kept it open like a bowl where it landed.

"What are the odds that golem continues to chase us?" asked Bruno, as Jeremiah settled beside him.

Jeremiah thought it over. "The golem has got one job, and it'll continue until it's done. But unless the stories about a troll's regeneration are exaggerated . . ."

"They're gonna be stuck there for a good while," finished Bruno. "The troll was making progress, though. It might take a long time, but eventually it *will* win." He began gathering acorns and small stones, making a small pile between them. "I wanted to talk to you about something."

"What's up?" Jeremiah asked.

Bruno selected an acorn off the pile and tossed it toward the headwrap. It dropped inside the hat with a satisfying *thwap*. "Was wondering if you've thought about what you're going to do."

"Going to do?" asked Jeremiah. He threw an acorn too. It bounced off the edge of the headwrap and disappeared into the dark.

"What's your plan for the future?" asked Bruno. "Lifesaving spells in a dungeon aside—thanks, by the way—you're not a necromancer anymore. You got this enchanting job, but you don't seem to like it. You don't seem to be leaning toward anything else, even though it's been a year since you were cleared of charges."

"I don't know. I guess I'm doing it day by day." Jeremiah suddenly felt angry. "Is there some kind of time limit?"

"Don't get me wrong," said Bruno. "If you keep at this enchanting thing and start giving us magic equipment, I'll make your damn bed every morning and thank you for the privilege. But it sounds like it sucks, and I'd rather you not be miserable." Bruno hit the mark with his next throw too. "Is this enchanting something you want to keep doing?"

"Not sure," said Jeremiah. He hurled a stone far past the hat. Bruno's questions were beginning to frustrate him. Was he expected to have this all worked out? It had been barely a year since he escaped a death sentence and saved the city from certain ruin. He felt he had earned a little leeway. "What about you? You had said adventuring is just what you do, or some aloof bullshit. But then I learn you're some kind of crime boss, or underworld manager, or something. That's an awful lot of responsibility for just some adventurer."

Bruno sighed. "I don't know either," he said, as he threw an acorn that bounced off the rim of the headwrap.

That wasn't what Jeremiah had been expecting. He decided to stay quiet, giving Bruno time to think. It helped Jeremiah stall for his own answer as well.

Bruno started again, his voice guarded. "I've spent a lot of the last year working with Delilah, you know? She has me deliver things, find people who are ducking her. Brings me along to lurk just behind her, make her seem dangerous. If they only knew, right?" Another acorn hit the edge of the hat and disappeared into the dark.

"If they only knew," repeated Jeremiah. He wondered how many people across her various professions knew about adventuring, or if that was some kind of secret.

"I watched Delilah write a letter once, right?" Bruno continued. "Maybe two pages, tops. She sends it off, and a school gets built in the slums. The kingdom provides money to fix a flophouse and pay a schoolteacher. Now twenty-five kids are learning to read and do numbers. She writes another letter, and now they get breakfast and lunch every day, too."

Bruno stood and began pacing. "I've done some serious shit, Jay! I've murdered, stolen, extorted, blackmailed—you name it, I've done it. I did it to create some semblance of peace and safety for people who have damn all to their names." Bruno snatched up a fistful of stones and flung them into the dark. "But I have *never* made a school, from nothing, where a bunch of kids get the chance to actually escape the hell they live in!"

Jeremiah held very still and stayed very quiet. He'd never seen Bruno like this before, being overwhelmed with emotion and frustration. It was vulnerability, or something like it.

"But Delilah . . ." Bruno pointed toward the glow of their fire pit. "She just writes a letter, says she's 'asking for Grant,' and money just appears! Who the hell is Grant?" Bruno whipped a sword from his belt and hurled it into a tree. Then he dropped back beside Jeremiah like nothing had happened. "Took her all of ten minutes."

Jeremiah waited, but Bruno seemed to have spent all his energy. "Fucking letters, man" was all he could think to say.

"Right?" said Bruno. He sighed and glanced at the sword, still quivering in the tree trunk. "I offered to stab bureaucracy for her, but she won't tell me where it lives."

Jeremiah snorted, then Bruno did too. They quietly laughed at the dark humor of a joke that wasn't entirely a joke. "If it makes you feel any better, no amount of letter writing can do what you do."

"Yeah, but no amount of what I do can accomplish what she does," said Bruno.

"No easy answers for either of us," said Jeremiah. He put a reassuring hand on Bruno's shoulder. *No answers at all in my case. I have no idea what I'm supposed to be doing,* he thought.

Bruno patted Jeremiah's hand. "Yeah, man. Thanks."

Jeremiah didn't respond, just threw another acorn toward Bruno's hat. To his surprise, it landed neatly inside. "I'm going back to bed. You need anything?"

Bruno yawned and rubbed his eyes. "Take the rest of my shift?" asked Bruno. "Should just be an hour or two."

"I'm still not allowed to take watch, remember?" Jeremiah stretched and yawned back. The sleeping bag was calling his name.

Bruno blinked and furrowed his brow, trying to understand what he had just heard. "I . . . Have you not been doing watch shifts? I thought you were between Allison and Delilah!"

"Nope, you yourself forbade me from—"

"That was forever ago. I didn't even know you!"

"From taking watches!" Jeremiah finished. "If you want to change that, you can put it to a vote in the morning. But rules are rules. Good night!"

The motion to repeal the ban on Jeremiah taking watch was introduced early the next morning, and passed with rapid, unanimous, and furious consent.

The lack of supplies turned an arduous walk back to civilization into a torturous one. Beset by dehydration induced headaches and muscle cramps, they were mercifully rescued by a trade caravan returning from the most remote communities. They traded security for transport on a wagon heaped with fresh, stinking skins and coin for food and water.

They arrived back at their Dramir home only partially enured to the stink.

"Everyone check yourself for ticks, please," said Delilah, "and do not sit—I said do *not* sit—on my couch, Bruno! Toss all clothes and armor out the back door. I'm not living with this stink for the rest of my life." She gathered up an armful of mail that had piled up inside her door.

"It's in my hair. I can feel it," said Allison.

"Yes, we're all getting baths. I'll start heating the water now. Throw on fresh clothes and sit on the floor," said Delilah. She pumped a pail of water and set it on the hearth. Banging flint and steel over tinder and kindle, Delilah quietly hissed in frustration as her exhausted hands fumbled with the tools. Jeremiah watched sympathetically. Nothing took longer than getting a fire started when you were exhausted and dying to be warm.

"First!" said Bruno and Allison simultaneously.

"No, I'm first," said Delilah. "Homeowner's privilege. You three hash out the order."

There was a silent tension as Jeremiah, Bruno, and Allison formulated a strategy. Jeremiah took first-mover advantage. "For a gold from each of you I'll take last position." A steep price and a strange strategy.

"Deal," said Allison.

"Seven silver and five coppers," Bruno countered. Jeremiah accepted the compromise as Bruno tsked Allison.

"How are you okay with going last? The water's cold by then, unless you want to heat it up all over again," asked Delilah. She was beginning to sort through her letters and toss them into a half dozen piles.

"Spent years doing corpse management. A little animal stink is nothing compared to what comes out of a—"

"Hush! I'm trying to think," said Allison. She and Bruno were staring each other down, each searching for signs of weakness.

"I'll let you go first," said Bruno, "*if* you let me use your good soap."

Allison punched the floor. "How do you know about my good soap?!"

"'Cause no normal person smells like a spring garden after a bath! They just unstink!" Bruno slapped his hands for emphasis.

Ahh, so that's what that smell has been, thought Jeremiah.

They went silent, an impasse.

Allison tried a compromise. "I have some of my old soap left. That's the old Allison smell. You can use that. It's still good."

"That the hickory smelling stuff?" asked Bruno.

Allison's mouth twisted in frustration. "And cherry wood! And plums! See, this is what I was talking about, the scent was indistinct!" Allison pivoted from Bruno to Delilah.

Delilah held her hands up. "Look, I tried, okay? Soap isn't really my thing."

"I honestly didn't think it suited you," said Jeremiah.

"Exactly! Also, shut up—you're no longer part of this negotiation! Bruno, do we have a deal or not?"

Bruno abruptly stood and began pacing. Jeremiah and Allison watched him while Delilah grumbled at a letter.

"One condition. I get to keep the soap," said Bruno, whipping a finger at Allison.

"Deal!" They shook on it. "Enjoy your barest sliver of soap," said Allison with a wicked smirk.

"Infinite bitch!" Bruno shouted.

"*Anyway.* Now that that's settled, can we talk about our take?" said Jeremiah. The electrum coins had been divided between them for transport, and the bags sat together on the table, along with the few gemstones they had recovered.

"Can we talk about our take?" said Jeremiah. The electrum coins had been divided between them for transport and now sat together on the table along with the few loose gemstones, the crown, and the magic bag.

Bruno pulled out a sampling of coins from the bag. He began tossing them to himself, almost juggling them. "Rough estimate of eighty-twenty, gold to silver."

"You can tell that just by feeling them?" asked Jeremiah.

"I've handled a lot of counterfeits," said Bruno. "You, on the other hand, are no counterfeit," he said while holding up and staring lustfully at the crown, its pink sapphires glinting with the promise of riches.

"Sorry Bruno, but that's getting returned," said Delilah. She was sorting through mail and adding the occasional letter to the infant flame in the tinder.

The coins on the table jumped as Bruno dropped his head onto the wood. "You've got to be kidding me, Delilah. The gemstones alone could—"

"Stop thinking in coins," said Delilah. "Networks and favors, that's where the real money is."

"I disagree," Bruno muttered into the table.

"We'll need to get the loose gems appraised and sold," said Allison. "The real question is this magic word, or whatever it is. You made it sound really important, Jay, exactly how valuable are we talking?"

"Oh! No promises or anything, but depending on what the word is, and assuming it's *not* a word that's already known . . . Well, pretty priceless, honestly," said Jeremiah. Two exhausting weeks of glaring at the symbol while traveling hadn't produced any new insights. Now that they were home, his excitement was returning. This kind of discovery was a once in a generation event. He gingerly extracted an etching of the rune from its reinforced pocket and stared at it.

"Priceless doesn't help us pay off lawsuits," said Bruno. "How much gold can we get for it?"

"I really don't know," said Jeremiah. "There's even something to be said for keeping it a secret. Delilah, alchemists keep some stuff secret, right? Formulas and things?"

Delilah didn't respond. She was closely reading a letter with a growing look of concern.

"Delilah?"

"Yeah. Some stuff is a secret, others we share. You share your good stuff for the prestige, you keep your best stuff a secret so no one steals it," said Delilah, still reading.

"Huh? But wouldn't . . . Uh, never mind. Anyway, we could theoretically sell the rune to another mage. Certainly name our price—whatever they can afford, anyway. Might take time, though. We'd need to find mages who could make it worth our while," said Jeremiah. His eyes flicked to the windows, and he rolled up the page again, lest an errant snooping enchanter glance the paper through the window and memorize it instantly.

Bruno grinned. "Could easily rook a bunch at once, make em all think they're getting an exclusive. Go through a few different mediums, a point a few fingers when things get interesting, a classic ten percent man loose lip swindle." Bruno's smile was relaxed and comfortable. He had it all figured out already.

"We could! But then there'd be a lot of mages angry at us, which I assume we don't want," said Jeremiah.

"Yeah, I don't want that," Allison said. She set her page onto the table, flipped it face down, then slid it further away from her. She and Jeremiah helped Bruno stack the coins into small towers, ceding conversation to the clinks of metal clattering over metal. They finished quickly, which Jeremiah thought was an ill omen.

Bruno took a count. "All right, so you two did stacks of ten. Rookie mistake, and I did stacks of five. So, it looks like we've got about . . . two hundred and forty-five coins. Assuming my ratios are correct, that makes for . . . one hundred and ninety-six gold and forty-nine silver. Not bad."

Jeremiah's head swam with a mild wave of dizziness. He still wasn't used to hearing about sums of money like that. The seventy-five gold he had received from his first adventure was still a pleasant and eerily distant memory he would occasionally dwell on. Far less concrete was when they were so rich Delilah said they had "theoretical money." That was less fun to think about.

"Minus materials for me to dissolve the coins in order to separate the metals, minus cost for having them recast and certified by a licensed goldsmith," said Delilah. Her scowl at the mail had only deepened.

Bruno deflated. "Yeah, minus those things."

Allison pushed the coins and gemstones into a single pile. "Let's not get ahead of ourselves. We can get the gems appraised while Jeremiah works on translating the rune. But first, some R and R. Two days of bed rest and light activity for everyone." She carefully toted the pile of loot to their hidden floor safe and locked it away.

Delilah sighed at her papers. "Al, why don't you go first on the bath? I need to deal with some of this."

Jeremiah and Allison shared a look of concern. "Delilah, is this really something you need to do right now?" asked Allison.

Delilah didn't respond, just carried an armful of documents into her room and closed the door.

CHAPTER TEN

The Old Ways

Jeremiah stood before a veritable monument of books, scroll cases, and steel plates. All carefully organized in a way that was indecipherable to anyone except for Thurok. In the two weeks he had been back it was the first chance he had to actually explore the collection of knowledge without Thurok being around. Thurok had been called to the palace at the request of the king, leaving Jeremiah to practice by finishing up simple lines on a shield being sent to some nobleman's son as a gift. Jeremiah recognized the enchantment, simple durability, but the fact that he was trusted with even the most rudimentary lines on an actual piece of equipment was unprecedented.

He picked a book at random, but didn't quite touch it. Thurok had personally handed him any book he intended Jeremiah to read, and that made Jeremiah nervous. A mage's library was the nerve center of their work, where rare and valuable books commingled with personal notes about the very secrets of magic. Thus, they were known to have security measures. Flusoh's security had been isolated and an ocean of undead. But Thurok's was in the middle of a city, with only a door lock between the city street and untold knowledge.

He could just ask Thurok for information, but if he explained why he needed it, he'd have to show Thurok the rune. He couldn't risk what might be the most valuable contribution he'd brought to the party in a long time.

Too risky, he thought. *All of this is too risky.*

He turned and almost walked into Thurok, who he found standing right behind him. Jeremiah froze, unsure of how Thurok was about to react. But Thurok just stared dispassionately at him.

"Sir, I, uh, I was just curious?" Jeremiah stammered, blood draining from his face.

"Curiosity kills," said Thurok. Jeremiah wasn't sure if it was a warning or a threat. Thurok reached behind himself and closed the door without looking. Thurok's library was very narrow, with little room to maneuver with just Jeremiah. Now with the door closed and Thurok standing in front of him, it might as well have been a closet.

Jeremiah's mind went back to something Bruno had once told him about lying, 'Say what they want to believe.' But what did Thurok want?

"I . . . I'm sorry. You caught me. I was being ambitious, I wanted to learn more runes to speed things up," Jeremiah said. He was gambling that, above all, Thurok wanted to be disappointed.

"You've been a slow, miserable student. Now you return from that greedy thuggery you call 'adventuring,' and now you're full of ambition?" Thurok's face revealed nothing, his gaze unflinching.

Jeremiah started to sweat. Bruno's voice whispered in his ear, *Wrap the lie in a truth, like poison in wine.*

"Sir, I was just so useless during the adventure. Without necromancy, I'm no better than . . . Well, than a thug with a spear. And until I improve my enchanting, I'm going to *remain* useless. I only know eight runes. I hoped I could look at some of your books and maybe find—"

"A shortcut," said Thurok. The venom in his voice was so powerful Jeremiah took an unconscious step back. Thurok's hand shot out and grabbed Jeremiah by the throat, holding him perfectly still.

Jeremiah waited for the grip to choke the life out of him in a rage, but it was steady. He took a cautious, shallow breath.

"Don't. Move," Thurok said. His voice had a dangerous edge to it, a warning. Jeremiah sensed something behind him, something moving closer. He heard the groan of wood straining, and the hair on his neck stood on end. Thurok's gaze rested on something behind Jeremiah.

Slowly, carefully, Thurok pulled Jeremiah forward. They swapped places and Thurok released his throat. Jeremiah dropped to one knee as air rushed into his lungs and he was overcome with a violent coughing fit. He heard the groan of wood once more, but when he looked up, all was as it had been before.

"I blame myself," said Thurok. "I should have known your laziness would drive you to such means. I'm only glad I did not return too late when my alarms were triggered. You owe me your life Thorn."

Even as Jeremiah gagged and gasped, he saw something he had never noticed, the wood grain on the floorboards. All of them, each and every one, were enchantment runes. Thousands per board, of dazzling complexity and design, flowing seamlessly even across the heads of nails. As his eyes traveled up, he followed the designs to the towering shelves that rose up above him. Jeremiah could finally see the runes, no thicker than threads of spider silk covering everything in the room. Thurok looked down at him, a master framed and surrounded by his craft.

Jeremiah stood, head bowed, but thankful he hadn't touched the books and likely gotten himself killed.

"I understand your frustration, Thorn," said Thurok.

"You do?" This was the first instance of anything approaching empathy Thurok had ever displayed. It was eerie.

"Yes. I grew up in the most savage of conditions. Born of the Flayer Clan farther south than humans and their kind travel. A place of ice and wind. I was small, weak, despised for surviving infancy. Useless." Thurok said, face blank.

"I didn't know that, sir. I'm sorry," said Jeremiah.

"What a meaningless sentence," said Thurok.

Jeremiah wasn't sure how to respond to that, so he said nothing. Awaiting further instruction or punishment.

"You may access my library, Thorn," said Thurok.

"Really? Will it be safe?" This was not at all how Jeremiah expected this conversation to go. Hell, he hadn't expected to have this conversation at all.

"Now, yes. Until I declare otherwise. Read the books, in your own time, take nothing home without my permission," said Thurok. He pressed Jeremiah to the side with the back of his hand, removing him from his path, and began to leave

"I can take them *home*?!"

Thurok whirled on him. "Only what I say you can! No book, no plate, or scroll, nor even a scrap of paper. You must ask me each and *every* time for each and *every* item. Do you understand?"

Jeremiah leaned away from Thurok, the force of his words startling. There was more in that command than simply keeping track of his books. There was danger in disobeying.

"Yes, sir," said Jeremiah.

"See to your duties then," Thurok said, leaving.

"Sir?" Thurok stopped, but didn't turn. "Can I take some scrap metal home? For rune practice?"

"Yes" was all Thurok said.

Jeremiah had set up shop across from Delilah at their dining room table. Jeremiah claimed his half of the table in a fortress of books and metal plates, which bordered on the rolling paper hills of Delilah's side. They had been working in silence, save for the occasional shuffling of papers and the quiet rasping of Jeremiah's pick on a metal plate.

"So, what are you working on?" Delilah asked. She didn't look up from her papers.

"Working on a recharge rune," said Jeremiah. He didn't look up either.

"What's that?" Delilah asked.

Jeremiah blew metal dust away from the plate, the symbols were fairly simple as far as enchanting runes were concerned. "It's a series of runes a mage can use to recharge an enchanted item."

"You mean that bag we found?"

"Mm-hmm."

They were quiet again for a while.

"So, what are you working on?" Jeremiah asked Delilah.

"Following a hunch about a legal conspiracy," said Delilah, like it was any old thing.

"Like back alley deals and secret messages?"

"More likely a bunch of lawyers in a room, smoking pipes and drinking brandy, working together to figure out the best way to ruin us," said Delilah.

"That sounds bad," said Jeremiah.

"Mm-hmm."

More silence. Delilah paused to pet Gus, who had slowly defected to her side of the table. Delilah cleared her throat.

"Yes?" said Jeremiah, looking up at her.

"I didn't say anything," said Delilah, looking back.

"Were you about to?"

"No."

"Mm-hmm," they each went back to their work.

"I, uh," Delilah started. "I did want to say that I think you did a great job in the dungeon. As just a warrior. Besides that part at the end with the necromancy," said Delilah. She paused her writing but kept her eyes on the pages.

"Oh, well, thank you," said Jeremiah.

"Mm-hmm," said Delilah.

"Mm-hmm," said Jeremiah, now smiling at his metal plate.

"It's just, you know, I'm proud of you. So's Allison. Allison and I are proud of you," said Delilah.

That was enough to pinken Jeremiah's cheeks a little. "Are you trying to score points so I'll give you the bag after it's recharged?" he said, smiling at her.

She smiled back. "No, that's just a perk." Jeremiah could sense her looking at him, or maybe he was just imagining it. But the silence was different from before. She was waiting for something.

Uh-oh. Think carefully. What is she looking for? What did I miss? thought Jeremiah.

"Thanks for supporting me," he said at last, "in the dungeon and out of it." The thanks was sincere, if just vague enough to be a nice catch-all.

He felt a light tap against his foot under the table as Delilah gently kicked him.

"Thanks," she returned.

Jeremiah tapped her foot back. "No problem."

More silence. With a pair of tweezers, Jeremiah picked up a speck of silver and lay it across a gap in the rune. It fit. He was quietly delighted.

Some of Delilah's papers—and there were many—had encroached onto Jeremiah's side of the desk. He blew them back onto her side with more force than necessary. They fluttered over what she was reading and she quickly snatched them up and added them to one pile or another.

Delilah continued her review, then reached out and pushed a corner of one of her books over to Jeremiah's side.

"Mm-hmm," said Jeremiah, freezing at the slight motion to prevent an errant scratch in the metal plate that would mean an abundance of wasted time.

"Mm-hmm," said Delilah.

"Mm-hmm," said Jeremiah.

"Mm-hmm," answered Delilah.

Delilah began scowling at her papers, rapidly flicking back and forth between several. Jeremiah began to reference design schematics in one of his books, using them as a guide and tracing a line on the plate with a piece of wax. It was a veritable flurry of activity compared to everything that came before it.

"You find out what that new rune of yours is yet?" asked Delilah when the storm had subsided.

"Not yet. Tricky stuff. It's quite literally finding the definition of a word no one knows," said Jeremiah. He had been taking books home from Thurok's by the armful.

"So how do you do it?" Delilah asked.

"Well, sometimes you can draw clues from what other known runes it looks like. You can also plug it into known enchantments and see how it changes the result. Usually, you use one technique to inform the other, back and forth, till you get it. Still, it might end up being nothing particularly useful, a synonym for a word we already have," said Jeremiah. He drew a thinner wax line inside of the first to further refine his workspace.

"Isolating your variables, I get that," said Delilah.

"Mm-hmm," said Jeremiah. He had no idea what that meant. In retribution, he pushed one of his books back onto Delilah's side.

Gus crawled on top of a page Delilah was reading, she gave him a pet then moved him back to his original spot.

The front door opened. Bruno stepped in with Allison behind him. Delilah quickly reached out and pushed Jeremiah's book back across the median.

"Hello, Jay. Hello, Deli—" Bruno started, then stopped. His eyes swept over the table as Allison navigated around him.

"The hell are you doing?" said Allison, squeezing past Bruno. "Hey, Jay. Hi, Delilah."

"Hi, Allison," Jeremiah and Delilah said in unison. Suddenly, something was wrong, but Jeremiah wasn't sure what. He felt like he had just been caught, but he hadn't done anything.

"What?" Delilah asked Bruno.

Bruno stared at Delilah for a moment before turning to Allison. "Al, can I speak with you upstairs, please?"

"Uh, sure?" said Allison. She followed him up the stairs, shrugging at Jeremiah and Delilah as she went past.

"What was that about?" Jeremiah asked Delilah.

"Dunno," she said, petting Gus and going back to her work.

They went back to silence, and soon Bruno and Allison returned. Allison grabbed a whetstone and short sword from her room and sat on the floor, a tiny pot of oil lubricating the blade as it glided across the stone with exacting strokes.

Bruno made a plate of bread, a pungent cheese, and an apple. He sat at the table with Jeremiah and Delilah. Jeremiah wasn't sure, but he thought Bruno glared at him for a moment. By the time he looked up Bruno was focusing more on his food.

"Sons of bitches . . ." Delilah said aloud. She was staring aghast at two papers, her eyes darting back and forth between them.

"Conspiracy?" asked Jeremiah.

"Conspiracy!" Delilah shouted. She slammed a packet of files on the table, rattling the dishes.

Jeremiah, Bruno, and Allison cleared away their remaining plates and books as Delilah began pulling certain pages from the pile to show them. "Look," she said.

"These are some of the first lawsuits we were served, the details of the grievances are laid out here. We were found liable for a couple, partially liable for a couple, but not liable for most of them. Then, in the *second* round of lawsuits—"

"Delilah," interrupted Allison, "you're just going to end up explaining this again to us afterward but simpler. Can we skip to that?"

"Would it kill you to—ugh! Fine." Delilah traced a line of minuscule text. "I realized there are particular turns of phrase, grammatical errors, and even spelling errors repeated between suits. Counselors reuse their writings all the time, but these were all filed by different nobles with different legal teams!"

She looked around, searching for comprehension. Jeremiah was still trying to figure out if liability was going to be important to the conclusion. Delilah sighed with impatience. "Which *means* we are not being subjected to a chaotic deluge of lawsuits from a bunch of angry nobles—this is a coordinated effort to ruin us. They sue us, the lawsuits resolve, they decide what worked and what didn't. Then they adjust new suits to be more effective and come at us again!"

"Probe the defenses for weakness," said Allison, nodding.

"Casing for the big score," said Bruno.

"I don't have an analogy, but I know what you mean," said Jeremiah. "So, remember how you said we were liable for some stuff? That was at the beginning, and they've only gotten better at it. How bad off are we?"

Bruno and Allison shared a look of concern. Delilah's frantic shuffling of papers slowed down, then stopped, then devolved into an anxious fiddling with a few pages.

"Pretty bad. The take from the dungeon might, just barely, cover our new debts. We're not broke, but only because I've been able to sell some of our debts a few times. The next round of lawsuits . . . will likely cost me the house and then some."

"And they're going to keep coming?" asked Jeremiah. Delilah nodded. She suddenly looked overwhelmed with fatigue.

"How is that legal?!" shouted Allison. She began pacing around the room, increasing the overall agitation.

"It's not," said Delilah, "but we don't have the capital to legally fight it right now, or the countersuits that would follow."

"So we automatically lose because the system is rigged against us?!" Allison yelled.

"Oh, the things we learn," Jeremiah heard Bruno mutter under his breath.

Delilah sighed and scooped the papers up, the stacks carelessly tossed together, loose pages falling away and scattering like leaves falling from a dying tree. "We can't get out from under this," she said, "so we need to find a way above it. I need to find a way to exert pressure on the people behind this. Intense pressure."

"Now we're talking!" said Bruno, his smile was ravenous with glee.

"No, we're not. We are doing no such thing. We are listening. I'm going to put out some feelers, see what I can find. Bruno, I might need your help with *some* things," she said.

Bruno's smile did not falter. "Bruno and Delilah back in the gray zone! Oh, it'll be just like the old days!"

"Jay, keep working on getting that rune translated and recharging the bag. We might end up just needing the money we can get for them, I'm sorry to say. Allison, go bat your eyelashes at King Hector—"

"For fuck's sake, Delilah."

"And explain the situation. I know he's got limitations, but what he has are friends and contacts I might be able to use. But first I'm going to go upstairs and refuel the *fucking* burners that I just realized I forgot about, that have likely ruined my reagents by now!" She snatched Gus off the table and shook the house with her footsteps.

Jeremiah had seen Delilah fired up before, but this was different. This was reckless, furious, righteous. He was only glad he wasn't going to be on the receiving end.

Jeremiah accompanied Delilah to the old quarter of Dramir. The homes here were grand but restrained, grouped together like stooped old men sharing memories. Short gates presented patinated coats of arms to signify which once-esteemed family resided within.

"Here we are," said Delilah. She stopped before the coat of arms that matched the one on the jeweled crown, currently tucked away in Delilah's professional robes. "We are expected. Now, don't—"

"Slouch, talk out of turn, make jokes, be disrespectful, fidget, fuss, complain, comment, or otherwise embarrass you," said Jeremiah. They stared at each other for a tense moment. Jeremiah slapped her hand out of the air as it jumped up to fix his hair.

"Fine! Just let me do the talking," said Delilah. She pushed, then pulled the gate with a grunt. Their arrival was announced by the metallic scream of the antique hinges.

"Why am I even here?" asked Jeremiah. He couldn't help but notice more and more signs of disrepair and neglect as they got closer. Loose stones, patches of crabgrass, a sort of malaise had settled over the grounds.

"Because I've got Bruno on another assignment and these old family patriarch types sometimes won't speak with a woman," said Delilah. They passed through an uninspired garden and Delilah rapped the lion-headed door knocker.

Jeremiah had enough time to grow bored before the door opened to a distinguished, albeit gray-looking human. He was dressed not in the typical livery of a butler but finery that had seen better days. "Might I help you?" His voice low, nearly a moan.

"Delilah Fortune, Jeremiah Thorn. We're here to see that master of the Marquette house," said Delilah with the slightest bow. "Do I have the pleasure of addressing him?"

"That would be my *father*," said the man, with a hint of distaste for the word. "I understand you have something for him? I'll see Father receives it."

"With respect sir, we would be remiss to not hand the item over ourselves," said Delilah, inching forward to make closing the door more difficult. "We have recovered a form of relic belonging to your family, one quite old, and we would like to negotiate its return."

The man sighed. "Fine. Enter then, I will alert father to your presence. With luck, he will be capable of speaking with you."

Jeremiah and Delilah entered the dusty foyer, while the scion of the household climbed the narrow, carpeted staircase.

"Father!" he bellowed from halfway up the stairs, causing Delilah to jump. "You have callers!" He turned to Delilah and Jeremiah. "Father will join us momentarily. Unless he died," he said, without a hint of humor.

"You damn well wish I was dead, you pathetic rotten wretch of a son!" came a voice. A man as frail and delicate as paper limped to the top of the staircase. He shivered uncontrollably despite the burgundy robe that wrapped him tightly. The son made no attempt to help his father as the elderly man descended, and Jeremiah saw his eyes continuously flick toward his father's feet.

"Your audience is granted," said the son with a dismissive wave, and departed.

"Lord Marquette?" asked Delilah.

"Call me Arnold," said the man, nearing the bottom of the stairs. Jeremiah stepped forward and offered a steadying arm. Arnold looked inquisitively at Jeremiah's arm before taking it and allowing himself to be helped down the final steps.

"Lord— Wait, Lord *Arnold* Marquette?" said Delilah, looking astonished.

"That's right, why the surprise?" asked Arnold, he squinted suspiciously at Delilah.

"She's just surprised you're still alive," said Jeremiah. Delilah had previously referred to Lord Arnold Marquette as a historical figure on their walk over.

Delilah's head whipped to glare at Jeremiah, her ponytail wrapping and hitting her in the face.

Arnold laughed. "You and me both! My son's been waiting for me to die for at least a decade now, lazy trash. Come to my office. You'll forgive an old man who loathes leaving his favorite robe."

"I will kill you," Delilah hissed at Jeremiah as they followed the elderly lord. "I will kill everyone who looks like you!"

Arnold Marquette's office was a small library containing a desk, a few trinkets and a thin layer of dust throughout. Whoever cleaned it came around infrequently.

"To what do I owe the visit?" asked Arnold. He produced a bottle and three small glasses from a desk drawer. The cork came loose a bit too easily. Whatever liquor was contained within had fermented long past its date. The smell overwhelmed the room in a moment.

Delilah cleared her throat. "Lord Marquette, my name is Lady Delilah Fortune, and this is my associate Jeremiah Thorn. We have—"

"The necromancer, right?" said Arnold. He poured three glasses of opaque brown liquid from the bottle.

"Enchanter nowadays," said Jeremiah.

"Cost a lot of people a lot of money, you did," said Arnold.

"I apologize," Jeremiah began, but Arnold waved a hand and passed him a glass.

"Fah, none of my money. Serves them right, with their banks and ledgers. If you're not holding your money, it's not yours." He turned toward Delilah with another glass, but she held up a declining hand. Arnold glowered at the hand and set the tumbler between himself and Jeremiah.

"Lord Marquette, we have come into possession of—" started Delilah, but Arnold interrupted her again.

"Pleasure before business," he said to Jeremiah, and they tapped their glasses together.

Jeremiah didn't give himself time to think and threw back the liquor. It could only be described as pungent. Thanks to Bruno, it was far from the worst drink he had ever had.

Arnold wiped a dribble from the corner of his mouth with his sleeve. "Now then, what's the business?" he asked Jeremiah.

Delilah cleared her throat again. "We found something belonging to your family."

"Let's have it, then," Arnold said, still speaking to Jeremiah.

Jeremiah kept darting his eyes to Delilah, trying to signal to Arnold whom to address. But Arnold either didn't understand or didn't care.

Delilah sighed, but produced the crown, holding it between Jeremiah and Arnold.

Arnold took it and flipped it over to inspect. "Hah, you were deep in the weeds when you found this! I recognize it from some old family texts. Passed down for several generations, a legacy treasure." He hefted it and dug a nail around one of the pink sapphires, as though to check if it would come loose.

"Yes. We'd like to return it," said Delilah.

"You already did," said Arnold. He inspected the sapphires closely.

Delilah closed her eyes. In a moment, her demeanor shifted. "We do require a reward for its return," she said curtly.

"There it is," said Arnold. "I've got no time for courtesies and curtsies." He set the heavy crown atop his head, his neck straining to hold it up. Then he opened a drawer and set a bag of coins onto the desk. At least a dozen gold spilled out. Jeremiah began to reach for the bag, gold in the hand was always a wonderful feeling.

"We need a favor, not money," said Delilah. Jeremiah's hand snapped back to his side.

"Oooh, she's a smart one, is she?" Arnold asked Jeremiah with a knowing smile.

"Very," said Jeremiah.

"Hurry up, what sort of favor? The house of Marquette doesn't have quite the reach it used to, but maybe I can help," said Arnold. He removed the crown and began fiddling with it again, rubbing the jewels.

"My associates and I are in some legal trouble," said Delilah. "I have reason to believe there's a conspiracy to destroy us by means of abuse of the law and its levers. We need to get out from under it."

Arnold scowled at the request, and regarded the Marquette family crest, framed on a wall. "Was a time the Marquettes would be the ones running that conspiracy.

Now we weren't even invited. There's no house built strong enough that time won't pull it down eventually."

"Your house still stands, one way or another," said Jeremiah, following Arnold's gaze to the crest.

Where do crests come from? he wondered. *What makes them so powerful? What makes them matter so much to some people?*

Arnold nodded. "So it does, so it does. Quite the feat for a line of humans. I fear it ends with my idiot son. That lazy bastard wants all the comfort and none of the responsibility. Sees me as standing in the way of whatever indolent nonsense strikes his fancy."

"Surely your house has survived incompetence in the past," said Delilah with a wince as the word 'incompetence' left her mouth.

I may have just seen Delilah faux pas for the first time, thought Jeremiah.

"Aye," said Arnold. "I'll say this, my granddaughter has the old blood in her. She'll raise us up once more, I'm sure of it. So long as her daddy doesn't whip the fire out of her." Arnold continued to nod at the coat of arms, his mood slowly improving, Jeremiah could see him imagining a stronger future.

"I've got precious few strings and contacts left to tug on," Arnold said at last, "but the ones I've got are no small-time crooks and bureaucrats. I probably can't solve this for you, but I'll see if I can put you in touch with someone who can."

Arnold started to extend a hand to Jeremiah but at the last minute turned toward Delilah. "Deal?"

"Deal," said Delilah.

The moment they shook, Arnold's face broke into a mischievous grin. "Now, forgive an old man for showing you how badly you just got had. I don't get chances like this often anymore. You're an enchanter, Mr. Thorn?"

"To a limited degree," said Jeremiah.

"Can you charge an enchanted item?" asked Arnold, the grin growing wider.

"I can . . . smaller ones anyway. Wait, is that thing . . . ?" said Jeremiah. He had studied it every which way, inspected the crown closely, and had seen no sign of enchantment at all.

Arnold cackled. "Go on, make it glow!"

Jeremiah looked at Delilah, but she just watched him, her lips a thin line of restrained annoyance at having been swindled. Jeremiah took the crown from Arnold and spoke the spell to bring an enchantment back to life.

To his surprise, there was a place for the power to go. The sapphires lit up a brilliant pink as he poured magic into them. Jeremiah staggered from the input, the sheer depth of magic the crown could contain. He let it run through him while Arnold laughed and laughed.

Finally, it was complete. Minuscule lines of enchantment glowed in convoluted patterns inside of the sapphires.

How? thought Jeremiah. *How do you inscribe enchantments* inside *of gemstones?* It made no sense. He could see lines of enchantment not just running across a flat plane but moving throughout the depth of the gem as well. *Can enchantments have depth? How? Why? What would . . . what am I even looking at?* The gulf of what he knew and what he didn't know about enchanting grew ever greater.

"Give it! Give it here!" said Arnold, grasping for the crown, frantic eagerness infusing his frail body. His withered and bony fingers snatched the treasure. With an expression of ecstatic victory, he lowered it onto his brow.

The rosy gems glowed fiercely for a moment, illuminating Arnold's pallid and delicate skin. His eyes bulged wide and glistened with renewed clarity. "My, my. I haven't felt this way for quite some time," said Lord Marquette. His voice was now measured and soft, clear and contemplative.

"Are you okay?" asked Delilah. She was trying to peer beneath the crown at the pink glow, that even now was fading.

"Indeed, Lady Fortune, quite so," said Lord Marquette. "Previous readings detailed this crown as a source of authority within our family. Supposedly, it imparted wisdom and insight to the wearer. I can see now that sometimes even legends cannot fully capture the splendor of the truth."

Lord Marquette surveyed the room, as if seeing it for the first time. His eyes found the coat of arms and hardened. "Not just yet," he whispered to himself.

"You'll keep to your end of the deal?" asked Jeremiah, unsure of exactly who he was speaking to now.

"Very much so, Mr. Thorn, and then some," said Lord Marquette. "I will ask you to take your leave. I may yet have more strings than I previously believed—I have an entire lifetime to remember."

Jeremiah and Delilah exited the manor the way they'd come. Delilah pulled, then pushed the gate shut. She glared at the front of the manor, then turned the glare to Jeremiah, placing her hands on her hips.

"There are magic items that can make you smarter," accused Delilah.

"Seems so," said Jeremiah.

"And we had one," said Delilah.

"Mm-hm," said Jeremiah.

"I'm mad at you," said Delilah.

"Fair," said Jeremiah.

CHAPTER ELEVEN

Focus

It had taken days of painstaking labor, but the recharge grid was finally complete. Without knowing what enchantment was on the bag they found in the tomb, he ran the risk of burning through his focus immediately when he attempted to recharge it. The grid was a safety net of sorts.

He had wasted four plates during the process, but now nine correctly diagrammed plates were aligned in the living room in a three-by-three grid, with the bag resting inside an etched circle on the center plate. The others had granted him all the space he needed and kept their distance lest they interrupt his progress. Jeremiah double and triple checked his work. Every rune was precisely etched, every gold bridge, silver gap spacer, and platinum repeater securely in place.

Jeremiah inspected the layout again. It was easily the most advanced enchanting he had ever attempted. If he charged the grid and something went wrong, it could destroy the diagram and send him back to Thurok for yet more plates. If it went really wrong, it could destroy the bag itself.

"Everyone," he said. He had planned to say more, but Bruno, Allison, and Delilah thundered into the room so abruptly it startled the words out of him.

"What's it do?" Allison shouted, leaning over the diagram to peer at the bag, before recoiling as though it had scalded her. The mysteries of the artifact and the runes simultaneously attracted and repelled them.

"I don't know yet," Jeremiah shooed them, and they retreated to the edges of the room. He'd have the head of anyone that disturbed the layout now. "I need to empower the runes first, then we'll find out. It's alarmingly complex. But I wanted you all here in case something . . . happens."

Bruno and Allison began a pacing contest. Delilah pulled up a chair and perched on it as though she were preparing to receive a lecture.

"What's all this say?" asked Delilah, gesturing toward the interconnected plates.

"No one knows," said Jeremiah, wishing they'd stop asking him questions he couldn't answer, "but it's what's always worked, so it's what we use. The ritual will draw magical power from me and use it to recharge the bag. Depending on what sort of enchantment is on the bag, it'll take more or less focus from me. I might end up a little loopy, like when I would do too much necromancy."

"Is there any danger?" asked Delilah.

That one he knew. "Yes. If I didn't make this correctly, I could burn out the enchantment on the bag. Or there could be an energy leak somewhere in the design that puts me into a coma. Or the bag could be damaged in a way that it does something unexpected, like explode." He resisted the urge to look over the diagram again. "I tried really hard to make sure none of those would happen."

The others nodded. There was nothing else to do but begin.

Jeremiah crouched in front of the first plate, rolling his neck and shoulders as though the process would be physically strenuous. "I'm going to charge panel one first, and once it's up to capacity it'll release into the greater rune structure. That's when the drain will happen." No one asked, but it wasn't often he enjoyed a captive audience. "The runes will direct the flow of magic, regulate it, and cut off the flow once the enchantment is activated again."

Steeling himself, Jeremiah placed his hands on the runic input marks. He took a breath to speak the ancient words, when Allison asked, "How long will it take?"

Jeremiah grunted. "Just a couple minutes. Be patient." He tuned out her reply as he refocused. Keeping his breathing slow and even, trying his best to imitate what he'd seen Thurok do, he spoke the words to initiate the flow of power from himself to the first panel.

"Is he ok?" Bruno asked. He sounded farther away than he should.

"I don't know," said Allison. "Those lines are glowing, so I think it's working. It's kind of pretty." She sounded even farther.

"I'm fine, hush," muttered Jeremiah. The runes around his hands glowed blue with energy. He was better than fine. He was charging his first ever real enchantment! His mind wandered back to how natural necromancy had felt in comparison, but he quickly refocused.

The glow of the first panel was increasing. Soon the copper plug bridging the space between this panel and the next would give way, and the full draw of magic would begin.

Jeremiah chanced a glance upward and saw perhaps the most interesting thing he'd ever see: a door. Doors are the most interesting, mostly because they're made of wood. Wood is also the most interesting because wood is small. Small is good. Dirt is small and good too. But most of all doorknobs. Clouds are definitely it. Dark is okay, but there aren't any clouds in the dark. Pass on dark. Why is it so dark? No, not dark, just indoors. Where's all the light?

Jeremiah felt like he was waking from a dream, or possibly into a dream. There was a single lantern lighting a barren room, save for a bench with a man sitting on it. The man was talking to him.

"So I said to Ginny, 'Listen, you sad excuse for a halfling, give me the diamond or I let the snakes go.' Well, Ginny doesn't give me the diamond, so I let all the snakes go, and I'm sure I don't need to explain what happened next."

"What? Who are you? Where am I?" Jeremiah only barely managed to ask these questions, as they were on par with questions about the lantern.

"Hey, he's responsive! It's Bruno, don't panic. You're in one of my safe houses," the man said, sitting up. His clothes made the most interesting sound that Jeremiah wanted to know more about.

"Bruno? Right, you're my friend Bruno. You have a knife," said Jeremiah, recalling a piece of information he had about this Bruno character.

"Generally a safe assumption, yes!" said Bruno with a laugh.

Jeremiah tried to remember. It was like assembling a puzzle that had no edges. "I was . . . with friends. Doing magic?"

"Correct, I can see why you've said mages get vulnerable with too much magic usage," said Bruno, seeming to relax a little more.

"Water!" Jeremiah shouted, he was suddenly aware of the burning in his throat, and it was the most important thing.

"There we go!" said Bruno, tossing him a corked glass bottle. Jeremiah drank it down quickly, then coughed up a gritty substance. "Finally, the dirt comes back up, wasn't sure if you were going to keep that down or not."

"What . . . happened to me?" it was all back now, but the order wasn't quite right.

"Well, you enchanted a bag, I think. Then you jumped up and ran out of the house. You were like a toddler. You became obsessed with every single thing you set your eyes on. Oh, it was all good fun for a while—hilarious, honestly—but then you started speaking those magic words. So you and I took a trip to one of my safe houses. Though I'll say this is the first time I've used a safe house to keep everyone *else* safe . . . well, maybe the second, but whatever."

Jeremiah took in his surroundings at last. Dirt was all around him. The floor was packed dirt, the walls were packed dirt, the ceiling was packed dirt. He couldn't see any doors or windows.

"How do we get out of here? How did we get in here?" he asked.

"Not for you to know sadly. I'll be black-bagging you on our way out. Not a trust thing, just a security thing, I'm sure you understand. Speaking of which . . ." Bruno stood up and slowly walked toward Jeremiah. He had a belt buckle on. It was shiny, the shiniest even. Jeremiah had never noticed before, but there were little etchings on it. Were those runes? He couldn't tell. Didn't matter; runes were boring. This belt buckle was where the action was. It must've been steel, or silver. Maybe bronze? No, those were all different colors.

"I hope we understand each other?" said Bruno. Jeremiah suddenly noticed he was closer. Had Bruno been saying something?

"Huh? Is Vivica okay?" was all he managed to say.

Bruno studied him for a moment, then laughed. "Okay, no heart-to-hearts for now, I guess. Come on, let's get you out of here and to a real doctor." Bruno snuffed the lantern, plunging them all into absolute darkness. Jeremiah heard the rustle of fabric around his head.

Jeremiah woke up in his bed. The sun was up. Gus was asleep in the water bowl, and he felt thoroughly refreshed. His thoughts turned to the day ahead, and he found a troubling emptiness.

What . . . what am I supposed to be doing? Why do my memories feel fuzzy?

He thought back. The memory of setting up the recharge grid was clear, as was beginning the ritual. Then there was a memory of not remembering anything, and now here. Jeremiah stood, breathing deep and stretching luxuriously. He changed from his bedclothes to a comfortable outfit, pocketed Gus, and headed downstairs, prepared to face whatever onslaught of ridicule he surely deserved.

"The Horse Lord has risen!" Allison declared as he came down the stairs. Bruno and Delilah were seated with her at the table eating a breakfast of oatmeal. They applauded him as he descended, and Jeremiah waved to them like an aloof noble.

"Thank you, my loyal subjects!" he said.

"Noooo, no, no, no, you don't get to lean into this," said Allison. "You don't even know what you're leaning into."

"Absolutely not!" said Delilah. "You don't get to lick my doorknobs 'in order of importance' and then roll with the consequences. You. Owe. Us. Embarrassment."

That knocked the confidence out of Jeremiah like a morning star to a leather helmet.

"Yes! That face! That's the face we are owed!" said Allison.

Jeremiah's arrogant descent down the stairs became a slouching crawl. He had no leg to stand on, time to take the bruising like a man.

"All rise for the royal dirt inspector!" shouted Bruno. "Let no dirt be different from any other dirt! Not on his watch!" Naturally, everyone stood and gave a strange salute of rubbing the backs of their hands on their foreheads.

Jeremiah, unsure of what to do, repeated the gesture back to them. This, apparently, was enough to cause a gale of laughter. Allison, unable to keep her feet, collapsed back into her chair.

"He does—he does—he does it the same way!" she choked out.

Jeremiah gave them a minute to recover. This didn't really bother him; it was actually sort of nice to see his friends laugh this hard. He hadn't seen that in a long time.

"Are we enjoying our magic bag yet?!" he asked.

"Heck no, we weren't touching that," said Bruno. Sure enough, the bag was exactly where Jeremiah remembered it, slumped innocuously in the center of the living room. "We weren't sure if it was cursed or what."

"Interesting fact: cursed magic items are usually just poorly made magic items," said Jeremiah. "It's very rare that a magic item is made to be intentionally bad. Unless it was made by Archmage Lalan. She was very mean." He hoped a display of esoteric knowledge would help him recover some standing in his friends' eyes.

"What's an archmage?" asked Allison.

Perfect, Jeremiah thought. "Excellent question. An archmage is a mage who has mastered at least two schools of magic," he said as he served himself a portion of oatmeal and sat to eat. He was ravenous.

"Or one that has gained the title through perfection of their craft by near unanimous approval of their peers," said Delilah. Jeremiah stared at her. "What? You think I wouldn't catch up on my arcane facts just because we have a mage in the fold? I live for this stuff."

Jeremiah laughed. "Yes, yes, you're very smart. Now, let's have a look at that bag!"

Delilah put a hand on him. "Hang on now, are you okay? As funny as it was watching you travel by jumping backward because 'it's faster,' I do want to know if this is permanent or anything." She looked very carefully into one of his eyes, then the other.

"I think that was just an excessive drain on my focus," said Jeremiah. "More than I've ever had before. I'm all right though, really."

How would I know, though? If my thoughts were no longer working? It was a distressing idea to consider, so Jeremiah directed everyone to the ritual panel that he had so painstakingly set up. Sure enough, the bag was right where he had left it.

The others kept their distance as Jeremiah scooped up the heavy leather bag and turned it over in his hands. He loosened the drawstring and peered inside. A glance told him all he needed to know. "Aha! Just as I suspected," he said.

Bruno, Allison, and Delilah were shoulder to shoulder, peering in greedy wonder. "What?" Jeremiah asked.

"Don't 'what' us, you asshole! What does it do?!" Allison demanded. She swatted at him from a distance, coming nowhere close but making her impatience known.

"Observe," said Jeremiah. He held up the bag and slid the entire length of his arm inside of it. His arm disappeared up to his shoulder, the bag showing no sign of disturbance beneath the surface.

"What the . . ." said Delilah. All three of them were staring in open wonder and confusion.

"It's a Giant's Bag," said Jeremiah. "Honestly, I don't know why I didn't guess that before. There's only so many enchantments people really put on bags. It contains an extradimensional space, so the inside of the bag is larger than the outside."

"How much larger?" asked Bruno.

"Let me check," Jeremiah said. "No one touch the bag while I'm doing this! Stay right there!"

He placed the open bag on the ground and stepped inside. As he wiggled like he was pulling on a tight pair of pants, the opening of the bag stretched to accommodate him, until he pulled it up over his head.

Jeremiah slowly descended into a misty abyss before touching down on an invisible surface. The light from the opening above him shone like a distant sun. He cast a simple light spell to reveal a realm of fog. He touched the floor and found no surface—his hand simply stopped moving forward. He walked with his arm outstretched, eventually reaching an invisible wall. Following the wall led him to another and another, until he had walked the perimeter of the small room. It was almost peaceful, a tiny place devoid of anything at all, wholly apart from the world. A gentle hop propelled him back toward that dim sun.

He heard a shriek as he popped his head back into the room. "Where did you go?" demanded Bruno. The three of them were collectively leaning forward, desperate to investigate but rooted by Jeremiah's warning.

"Literally nowhere," said Jeremiah, climbing out. "Inside this bag is a separate dimension, about twelve paces square. That means the bag can fit as much stuff as you'd be able to put in a room that size."

Delilah leaned toward the bag as far as she could while staying seated. "Can I go in?"

"No!" said Jeremiah, startling himself with his brusqueness. "It's too dangerous. If the bag gets damaged—look at me!—if the bag gets damaged, it breaks. If it breaks, the dimension ceases to be connected to the bag, and everything inside is—keep looking!—gone forever. I'm going to say that again: Gone. Forever. This goes for all of you, but *especially* all of you."

Jeremiah let the silence hang in the air while he glared at them, until he was sure they understood. "Okay. There's one more thing I need to demonstrate. Can one of you grab me a few things to throw in?"

"Like what?" said Bruno.

"Anything is fine, grab some silverware," said Jeremiah.

"So, like forks and knives?" asked Delilah, collecting them from the table.

"Yes, that's fine."

"But they're dirty," said Delilah.

"Just give me the things!" said Jeremiah.

"What about spoons?" Allison asked, collecting some spoons.

"I-yes! What is wrong with you people give me the silverware, this isn't a test!" Jeremiah said, rolling his eyes. "I swear, put so much as a parlor trick in front of you guys and you become skittish children." He collected the forks, knives, spoons, and single mug and threw them into the bag.

"Here." He shook the bag at the three of them. "Someone reach in while thinking of a spoon and pull out what you grab."

After a long delay, Delilah was the first to step forward. She gingerly slid her hand inside the bag, then pulled out a spoon.

"Ta-da!" said Jeremiah.

"How is that different from a normal bag?" asked Allison.

Jeremiah had to concede that one. "All right, Delilah, I want you to reach in and think about . . . I don't know, a sock. Try to pull it out." Delilah came up empty handed. "Okay, now try a bucket. Now a rock. Now try that mug." Delilah retrieved the mug.

"Wait . . . what's happening?" asked Delilah. "I thought you said it was like a whole room in there."

"It is," said Jeremiah, "but the bag knows what you're reaching for, so you'll always grab the thing you want. It's one of the main features of the bag, whatever you want is right on top, so long as it's in there," Jeremiah watched Delilah turn the mug over and over in her hands. She was thinking fiercely.

"The bag . . . knows? How does the bag know what I'm thinking?" she asked.

"Well, that's why they're called giant's bags. They were made originally by giants to carry their things. But they had such big hands they couldn't root around for stuff. So they made bags that would hand them things, essentially. At least, that's the supposed history," Jeremiah explained. He sometimes missed browsing through Flusoh's library, and wondered when he would get one himself.

"No, that's not what I asked. How does the bag *know* what I'm thinking?" Delilah asked again.

"I—uhh, I'm not sure. Magic, I suppose, right? The enchantment must be doing it," Jeremiah shrugged.

"The enchantment is doing the knowing? Or is the bag doing the knowing because of what the enchantment is doing to the bag? Jay, I'm asking you if the bag is alive and can read my mind," said Delilah, taking a step back. Bruno and Allison did the same.

"No! The bag is not alive. How the enchantment works is well beyond my expertise, but I promise this is not a nefarious bag." Delilah, Bruno, and Allison exchanged looks, seemingly unconvinced.

Bruno started, "What if I put three pieces of paper in there, one of which has an X on it, and Delilah reaches in thinking of the one with the X? But she doesn't know which one has the X."

Allison snapped her fingers. "Ooh that's a good one!"

"Come on, guys," said Jeremiah. "Think about this for a second. You can fit a whole room's worth of stuff in this bag, and whatever you want is right on top. Can we exercise our creativity for a minute?" Jeremiah was confused, were they just messing with him again?

Then he saw Delilah's eyes getting wider and wider, almost comically large as her body stiffened as the wave of possibilities hit her.

"Th-the bag is mine," she breathed.

Allison furrowed her brow. "Well now, wait a minute. I could pack every kind of weapon and have on hand whatever load-out I need for the job."

Bruno glanced at Delilah and winked at Jeremiah. "Yeah, I think it's definitely for the best that Allison gets the bag. I mean, I guess I could use it too. Allison, would you mind if I kept a few extra tools in there?"

"Stop," said Delilah. "We are not having this conversation. I carry *so* many bottles, vials, boxes, poultices, tonics, bandages, braces, bombs, salves, ointments, antitoxins, stimulants, depressants, poisons, tinctures, and salves, that I had to design an entire suit of armor for them," she moved her hands around her body, outlining the corpulent leather onion she became while adventuring. "Just to carry it all while having a modicum of protection!"

Bruno tapped his chin. "You make a good point," he said, "but you seem to be getting on just fine with the system you've got. Why mess with what already works? Allison is limited to only three weapons, and I know she'd want to carry more."

Delilah stared at him. "Do you realize how much thought goes into what I'm carrying? How selective I have to be just to be able to *move*? I am your doctor! The more I'm able to bring, the greater my contribution! This is a *game changer* for me!" Her voice was growing toward an alarming pitch.

"I hear good points all around," started Jeremiah, intending to continue the ribbing.

Delilah spun on him, face crestfallen and wounded, slightly pouting.

Oh no, he thought.

"Jeremiah . . ." Delilah said, her voice thick with grief-stricken betrayal. Jeremiah's heart wrenched, and while he was aware Allison had done something similar to him long ago, he had never developed any method to inoculate himself against this most base of techniques.

"Okay! Yes! I think Delilah should get the bag!" he said, averting his gaze from her.

"You absolute sap," said Bruno, rolling his eyes.

"Delilah, stop giving him your puppy face, of course you're getting the bag," said Allison, shaking her head at the spectacle.

"I am?" Delilah's head whipped from one person to the next, looking for any sign of dissent. Then she whooped, snatched the bag from Jeremiah's hands, and pranced around the room with it.

Jeremiah couldn't help but grin as he watched her. Her joy made him want to celebrate too.

Bruno clapped Jeremiah on the shoulder. "We probably should talk about how easily she played you," he said, shaking his head.

Jeremiah opened his mouth to reply when, like a bucket of ice water crashing over a pleasant dream, there was a knock at the door.

CHAPTER TWELVE

Metal Memories

Jeremiah filled the water pitcher and set it on the kitchen table. He wasn't sure what else to do. Billipop's latest summons dominated the room, a neat stack of papers on the table that somehow loomed over them.

"We learned some stuff while you were . . . recovering," said Allison. She stared at the summons as though it were a viper about to strike. "It's bad."

"Very bad," agreed Bruno. "We thought we were dealing with a bunch of pissed-off nobles with some revenge funds burning a hole in their pocket. Well, it is that too, but it's also something else."

"What does that mean, 'something else'?" asked Jeremiah. Bruno had a penchant for theatrics, but Jeremiah wasn't in the mood for a dramatic reveal.

"It means this is about more than money," said Delilah. She was rapidly petting Gus in her lap as she spoke. "It's a conspiracy, but one that digs deeper than I'd thought possible. There are the lawsuits, yes, but there's other stuff too. Allison's been informed there are ongoing investigations into her military past. Bruno's contacts have been turning up arrested or dead."

"Or terrified," said Bruno. "More scared of whoever is pulling strings than they are of starving without my help."

"And there have been claims against my remaining land holdings," said Delilah. "Namely this house and the Tarnothy fortress, and with that my title." Her voice was steady, but Jeremiah caught the look of fear in her eye.

"They want to erase us," said Allison. "My record is my life. There's a case moving through the military courts right now to take away several of my medals." She stared down at the table, her gaze vacant.

"I didn't even know that was possible," said Jeremiah. Besides his ignorance of military law, he hadn't known it was possible to transform his friend into the slumped, dejected woman before him.

"We're not just going to let that happen," said Delilah, patting Allison on the shoulder. "You won't have to return your medal, Allison, you earned it—"

Allison sprang to her feet, life bursting back into her all at once. "Yes, I will!" she said. "These medals are awarded at the discretion of the kingdom. If that discretion changes, for whatever reason, they can take them back."

In a moment, Allison dashed to her room and returned with a small box. "If the wrong verdict gets passed down, any of these could be forfeit." She opened the box to reveal a collection of dozens of medals, stamped pins, and badges, polished to a high shine and meticulously arranged.

Jeremiah looked from one award to the next. *Each of these is a story*, he thought. *A victory or an accomplishment or recognition.* He could understand being protective of them, little proof of who you were as a person.

Allison removed one badge, a red chevron, and held it to catch the light. "There's stuff in my record that wasn't ever supposed to see the light of day. If they manage to dig it up, whoever is doing this . . . well, let's just say a couple of medals will be the least of my concerns."

Jeremiah suppressed a chill at her words. "Who could even be doing something like this? A coordinated effort across the legal, military, and criminal worlds? And why?"

"The why is easy," said Bruno. "This is a personal vendetta—an intelligent, targeted, attack meant to undermine us each where it hurts the most."

"This is about removing our influence, systematically obliterating everything we've worked to build," said Delilah. "It goes beyond revenge. It probably ends with us dead as well, but before that, we'll be stripped of anything they can strip us of."

"And we didn't even see it until now," said Allison. She had settled heavily back into her chair, the moment of action costing her. "They keep us distracting us with lawsuits focused on maintaining our resources so we don't even notice the smaller guerrilla attacks that will destroy us. Classic strategy."

Jeremiah shifted in his chair. "Have you guys noticed them coming after me?"

The others exchanged a glance. "We looked into it," said Delilah, "but you don't really have a lot of assets to target. You already quit necromancy, and you don't really have much of a network here. Maybe targeting us is targeting you?"

Her response left Jeremiah feeling hollow. He wasn't sure if he was more bothered by the idea of someone trying to harm him through his friends, or by the idea that he was so unimportant, the conspirators didn't care enough about him to ruin his life. "Any ideas for who might be behind it?" he said, changing the subject.

"Gotta be a war veteran-turned-lawyer who chose a life of crime," said Bruno. "Who else could influence all of our spheres like this? Especially so effectively, without leaving a trace? But no, we have no idea." It was a joke, but Jeremiah could see Bruno's unease.

"We can assume the conspiracy involves multiple strata of people," said Delilah. "I've tried probing my contacts, but any string I pull just falls away without any real leads. Whoever is at the heart of it is operating so far behind the scenes they might as well be invisible." She looked dejected, her vast network had let her down.

"So what did we even learn from all this?" demanded Jeremiah. He shoved backward from the table and started pacing around the kitchen. "We've discovered there's a conspiracy to ruin us, but not just make us broke like we thought—someone out there wants to tear down everything about our lives, and we don't even know the first thing about who they are!"

"We've learned this enemy exists," said Allison. "We've learned they have reach, power, and influence, and that we can't fight them in court like we've been trying to do so far."

Jeremiah stopped pacing. "So how do we fight? What can we even do?" His hands balled into fists at his side. He'd been placed in chains, given death sentences, been used as a weapon, but he had never felt so powerless as he did right now.

Delilah appeared beside him, holding out Gus. "Here," she said. "I think you need him more than I do right now."

Jeremiah forced a weak laugh as he accepted his own familiar. Gus nuzzled his hands, and he had to admit the toad's cool skin was comforting. Or maybe it was Delilah's arm around him as she guided him back to the table.

"So, you're all caught up now, Horse Lord," said Bruno. "We're at the part where we figure out what we're going to do about it."

"I still say we go after anyone we can see," said Allison. "The lawyers, the nobles, the people whose names are on the paperwork. Become the aggressor, show them all we're not to be messed with, and suddenly whoever is pulling the strings won't have nearly as many bodies to hide behind."

"It could take us years just to get through the first layer," said Delilah. "Yes, Bruno, even with whatever awful thing you've just thought of."

"Hey, for all you know I'm planning to befriend them and win their loyalty with my charm and wit!" said Bruno, his wicked grin still in place.

"This is about influence, right?" asked Jeremiah. "Whoever's doing this has pull over people, enough to control them and keep them quiet—how do we get some of that?"

Delilah considered the question. "It takes time. I have my own network, of course, but nothing that compares with what's happening here. To be able to coordinate something on this scale would take several lifetimes."

Allison cradled her medals box. "Let's assume we don't want to wait that long."

"Lifetimes . . . wait, what about that favor from Lord Marquette?" asked Jeremiah. "He was too far gone to be involved in the conspiracy, but now he's back, and he said he might still have some strings to pull."

Delilah nodded slowly. "You're right. Marquette could be our trump card here. Granted, I don't know how he could make a difference, but old families can surprise you with their connections. I'll follow up with him. Good thinking, Jay."

Jeremiah was sure to curtail the smile spreading across his face at Delilah's praise. Her praise always felt especially nice, like it was worth more than normal praise.

She continued. "I do warn you all, though, even a favor may not be straightforward. I expect, with the levels of influence we're talking about here, a favor might just be a conversation with someone who matters. I also don't know who we may be talking to—we should all be prepared to leave Dramir at a moment's notice."

"Leave?" asked Allison. "Wouldn't that be like abandoning our position? How can we defend ourselves against the conspiracy if we're not in Dramir?"

"We can't," said Delilah. "But think of it more like a tactical retreat. We may lose some ground," she swallowed as she looked around their house, "but it's to have a chance at winning the war."

Allison slumped back again. "Never did like retreating," she grumbled. "We don't even know who we're fighting."

"Allison," said Jeremiah, looking around the table at his friends. "Everyone . . . I won't let them beat us. No matter what happens, as long as we're together, we can win this. We will win this!"

"Inspiring, yet painfully corny," said Bruno, clapping Jeremiah on the back. "I expected nothing less."

"Yeah, that was a bad one," agreed Allison.

CHAPTER THIRTEEN

Decorum

It was several weeks before anything came of Marquette's favor. But it came as a knock at Jeremiah's bedroom door.

"Whas goin' on?" mumbled Jeremiah, squinting in the light of the lantern Delilah held.

"Pack your things," said Delilah. "We're leaving."

"Tonight?" Jeremiah's mind flooded with adrenaline, stirring his dream-addled thoughts into a concise list of packing necessities he had prepared.

"Now."

Jeremiah rushed around his room, haphazardly packing his bag in the dark, and ran down the stairs after her. His heart thudded as he took in the scene. Bruno was pacing, a leather bag over his shoulder. He could hear Allison and Delilah's muffled voices from Allison's room. From the sounds of it, they were working out how much of Allison's arsenal would fit among Delilah's things in the Giant's Bag.

"What's going on?" Jeremiah asked. He looked at Bruno, hoping some pithy explanation would aid his understanding.

"Got me, this is all Delilah," said Bruno. "She won't tell us anything besides there's a carriage coming. I will say I'm not a fan of hasty jobs to desperate people, but she's got that lawyer voice going on, so I do as I'm told." He glanced up with a jerk as the door to Allison's room burst open.

"You don't need a lance. You don't even own a horse!" said Delilah. Allison stared from her room like Delilah told her to leave her head behind.

The only revelers left awake in the city at this hour were too drunk to pay the travelers any notice. Lightly leaden, their carriage rocked more than normal as they rumbled and creaked through the gates of Dramir. Most of their possessions had been placed into Delilah's Giant's Bag, minus the gear they would need in case of an ambush.

Finally, they were rolling along the quiet roads of Dramir's surrounding farmland. "All right, can we talk?" Jeremiah asked.

Delilah shook her head and pointed toward the front of the carriage, indicating the driver might be listening. Bruno opened the carriage door, leaning out over the road.

"Who's 'e pullin'?" he called up to the driver. It was some oddity of Common and Gnomish mixed together, rendered nearly incomprehensible by a thick accent of a region Jeremiah had never visited.

"Just summee gander, sir. Just a nightie," the driver called back in an accent heavy with Gnomish influence.

"Feefee Trick? That you, brother? It's Riddy Tom!" said Bruno.

Delilah crossed her arms and sighed.

"Oh, Mr. Tom! Didn't know tita too! Simpapa free, then?"

They continued back and forth in Gnomish, each using a spare hand to gesticulate wildly. Finally, Bruno returned to the carriage "Feefee's a good'un. He'll keep anything quiet."

"Do you know *everyone* in this city?" Allison asked.

"I'll put it this way—whenever someone dismisses another person's presence, I make it my business to get in good with the dismissed. I get more info from scullery maids, dung shovelers, and carriage drivers than I do from the professional skulks."

Despite Bruno's reassurance, Delilah motioned them to huddle close and spoke in a barely audible tone. "We're going to Elminia. We got a job offer, I don't know what or who for. But they demand utmost discretion and a tight timeline. From the way they're handling everything, this has to be for someone big. We can only hope they're bigger than the conspiracy."

"Elminia is a long trip," said Allison. "Two weeks by carriage, if I remember right."

"Correct," said Delilah. "We need to meet our contact at a specific street corner, at a specific time, and we get one chance to be there. If we miss it, offer's closed. And we don't have any more favors to cash in. This is Lord Marquette's doing, and whatever favor he called in, it had *reach*."

"Okay, I consider myself a bit on the naive side, but that sounds fishy even to me," said Jeremiah. Allison and Bruno grunted their agreement.

"I know! Believe me, I know. But I've checked it out in all the ways I can, and I do trust the source. I ask for your trust in turn. Don't let your guard down or anything, but let's do our best to approach this in good faith. Agreed?"

They agreed. *Not like we have any better options*, thought Jeremiah.

The boring two-week carriage ride proved a grand opportunity to focus on enchanting. Jeremiah's frenzied packing had included anything he could conceive of as being useful, which meant the books and materials Thurok had lent him had found their way into Delilah's bag. After the sun rose enough to read by, he set about his new plan to identify the unknown rune.

It was five days into their journey when the effort paid off. "It works!" Jeremiah announced, startling everyone from their travel hypnosis.

"Gods, why would you yell? Who does that?" asked Allison, resheathing the pair of daggers she had drawn from her own scabbard and Bruno's boot in one swift motion.

"Look, look, look!" said Jeremiah, holding up his plate. The glow of magic had just begun fading from the runes inscribed upon the face of the metal. He picked up a file and dragged it across the metal, leaving no sign or mark.

Bruno closed his eyes again.

"Elaborate," said Delilah, without lifting her head from its spot against the window.

"It's a Strengthen rune, I finally got it to actually work!" His friends' listlessness couldn't dampen the swell of pride Jeremiah felt. It was a glimpse into a future filled with magical equipment. "Thurok wouldn't tell me why, but it's just like the backpacks. 'Strengthen, Pause,' which I had been using, doesn't give the enchantment a chance to work. Or it does, but only for an instant."

Delilah blinked. "One rune says to strengthen the material, the other says to stop. You had them placed too close together . . . or something."

"More or less, yeah. So I expanded the diagram to go all over the place first, so it takes longer to activate the Pause rune," said Jeremiah.

Allison rubbed her eyes and peered at the plate. "Is that why it looks like two spiderwebs stacked together?"

Jeremiah nodded, patting the plate. "Pretty ingenious, I think."

"Didn't you say nodes and conduits alter the flow and properties of magic in diagrams?" questioned Delilah through a yawn. She snuggled harder into the glass window.

"Yes, that's true," said Jeremiah. The fact that she had been listening to all his sporadic ramblings on enchanting was quite gratifying.

"Could you have used one of those to slow down the magic traveling between the runes?" She mumbled, her breath fogging the glass.

Jeremiah took a breath to answer but didn't. A truth slowly broke over him, one that made his hand ache profusely and cast the last few days in a miserable light. "Yes. That is . . . also a thing . . . I could have done."

Delilah smiled peacefully. "Don't worry about it. Good job, Jay. Really. You're making progress."

Jeremiah fought back a fleck of bitterness. "You're right, I am. And this means I finally have a tool to start testing our unknown rune."

"Proud of you," crooned Bruno, without opening his eyes. "Now, don't wake me up again until it's time for magic daggers."

They rode toward gathered storm clouds on the final day of their journey. Jeremiah carved a line in his plate in the start-stop rhythm he had grown quite adept at during the journey. His tests hadn't yet elucidated the meaning of the rune, but he felt he had to be getting close. It would take some time though, as he was resorting to a guess-and-check method that he was sure Thurok would disapprove of. He brushed some metal shavings from the line and was startled when his fingertips came away blackened.

"Elminia is . . . industrious," said Allison.

Jeremiah looked at the looming clouds with new understanding. Crawling across the horizon was an atmosphere of heavy black smoke. Soon, the single immense tower of Elminia's palace appeared, wearing the smog like a thick woolen scarf. Soon the city proper came into view. With no monolithic wall to separate it from the countryside, the sprout of huts simply grew taller and denser until they formed a great labyrinth of buildings, stacked haphazardly at dangerous angles.

Their carriage rumbled past the first jagged teeth of the city. The streets were packed with carts, animals, and people. While Dramir always bustled with a pleasant vibrant life, the hum in Elminia was different. It felt dangerous and pervasive, like a hive of wasps. "This place is kind of overwhelming," Jeremiah said. He much preferred cities like Dramir that were hubs of culture and refinement.

"Oh yes!" Delilah was beaming. "Elminia is extremely resource rich, between coal, oil, and ore. It's like a great kiln where ambition is forged into success or failure. Elminia produces more technological, economic, and scientific advancements than anywhere else in the world!"

"Elminia is a chewing mouth," Bruno whispered to Jeremiah, "and if you don't have the right flavor, you get spit out into the Pit."

"What's the Pit?" Jeremiah whispered back.

"I thought the metaphor was pretty self-explanatory," said Bruno. "It's where the lowest of the low and the poorest of the poor live. It also happens to be a literal massive hole in the ground."

Delilah's enthusiasm continued unabated. "Elminia is a risk. A hundred rolls of the dice, a free spin of the wheel, a peek at the top card, but only for those brave enough to bet on themselves!" She finished her speech with a raised fist, accepting the challenge.

"Surprised you don't live here," said Jeremiah. "Sounds like you'd thrive here."

"Oh, no thanks," said Delilah, crashing back to baseline. "It smells funny here. Architecture is . . . uninspired? And there's a truly astonishing number of fires."

"Bad food, worse people, great bars, excellent steel," said Allison. "Oh, and huge guard corps! Incredibly well funded."

"It's gotten bigger since I was last here," said Bruno, his eyes darting about.

"Never stops growing," said Delilah. "The empress has been notable in her policies of unregulated expansion and construction."

The palace tower stood at the center of the city like a harpoon that pierced the earth. In addition, Jeremiah spotted little nodes of wealth. The hypnotic repetition of dirty, leaning tenements would suddenly coagulate into a fortified street of more sophisticated architecture, tiny islands of generational stability in a sea of roiling ambition.

"We're getting close," said Delilah. She leaned out the window and yelled up to the driver, "We're headed to the corner of Museus Boulevard and Tornn Avenue." Bruno glared at her. "What? Oh, umm, please and thank you, driver," she added. Jeremiah noticed she had forgotten the driver's name. Then again, he had too.

"Bruno, run ahead and make sure this isn't an ambush, yeah?" asked Allison. Bruno was out of the carriage and vanished into the crowd before she could even finish the request.

"You're sure this is a good contact?" Jeremiah asked Delilah.

She looked him square in the eye and nodded. "Absolutely. And, if it's a trap, it's overly elaborate and they deserve to get killed by us."

The carriage turned down another street, identical to many of the others. Jeremiah kept feeling compelled to crane his neck upward. Elminia's buildings all seemed to have settled into a state just shy of collapse, leaning on each other like friendly drunks. It made the city feel almost ephemeral to Jeremiah, here today but likely gone tomorrow.

Bruno leapt back into the carriage, startling them. "No ambush I can detect. I think we're in the clear."

The carriage bumped to a halt a few minutes later. "Here's we is, ma'am," called Feefee from the driver's seat. "Museus n' Tornn."

"Thank you, Mr. . . . erm . . ." Delilah glanced at Jeremiah, who shrugged. "Driver," she finished. They gathered their belongings and disembarked. With a final wave to Bruno, the carriage and driver merged into the streets of Elminia, becoming one more player in the symphony of noise.

"What now?" asked Allison.

"Now, we wait till someone—oh!" A stranger had hooked his arm in Delilah's, like a couple out for a stroll. However, the two of them hadn't taken more than a few steps before Bruno had draped a fraternal arm across the man's shoulders, an accompanying friend. Allison and Jeremiah had to press their way through the jostling crowd to keep Delilah close.

The new acquaintance was a human man dressed in finery. He was pontificating about the coal industry, audible even over the hum of the city. Bruno bantered with the man while Delilah was pulled along awkwardly. Jeremiah saw a brief glimmer of metal underneath Bruno's hand, likely a blade positioned to slip into the man's neck at a moment's notice.

"How come none of us are that slick?" Jeremiah asked Allison.

Allison's look of concentration broke into a genuine laugh. "Because it's not our job. Can you imagine two Brunos? It'd be awful!"

Jeremiah tried to imagine. "They would just stay up all night waiting for one to leave so the other could follow them," he suggested.

Snickered and bumped him with her shoulder. "Focus, this might still be a trap."

"They'd just stalk each other in circles around the house. It'd be like a dog chasing its tail!" said Jeremiah. Allison bumped him harder and shushed him, but couldn't hide a hiccup of a laugh.

Finally, the man altered course and diverted them into a hat shop. "Here we are!" he announced. An old gnome at the counter fastidiously sewed a patch onto a cap. He didn't acknowledge their arrival. "Hello, friend haberdasher!" said the well-dressed man, still tightly arm in arm with Delilah.

"Hullo," said the haberdasher.

"I'm in the market for your finest bonnet, with matching satin wings and a tulip," the man declared. This was feeling less and less like a deadly trap.

The gnome harrumphed and did not look up from his work as he waved them past the counter and toward the back rooms. Jeremiah noted as they passed that there was a small crossbow under the counter, bolt set and ready to fire.

A false wall was removed, a secret stair uncovered, and they were traversing beneath the city in a dark tunnel.

"Does every city have these?" asked Jeremiah.

"Yes," said Bruno over his shoulder.

"Off," commanded Delilah, shaking the man off his arm. As soon as Delilah was released Bruno spun the man in front of them, drawing his bow and nocking an arrow in the time it took the man to steady himself.

"Okay! Okay! Stop!" the man said, twisting in on himself and waving his hands at the arrow.

"Where are you taking us?" Delilah asked.

"To the end of this tunnel, that's all I know!" said the man.

"And what's waiting for us at the end of the tunnel?" Delilah asked again.

"A door I'm not allowed through, I don't know where it goes! Stooop!" Bruno kept tightening the string on the bow like he was about to fire. Their contact recoiled and whined every time.

"Ugh, fine whatever. Let's just go," said Delilah, moving ahead of them.

Bruno kept him at arrowpoint the entire way. The tunnel's only light came from the occasional slits of sunlight that made their way through tiny metal grates over their heads.

These must be sewer tunnels. Fancy, thought Jeremiah. Sewers were a big city luxury, though he wasn't sure if Dramir had them. *They must, right? They had everything else.*

The door at the end of the tunnel was minuscule, practically a cupboard. Their guide gave a series of complex knocks, there was a metallic clicking, and the door slowly opened. It revealed a pair of fully armored elven men, the silvery metal of their armor gilded with looping golden embellishments. Each had a spear leveled at the open doorway, but the guide seemed unconcerned.

"Code," said one of the guards. The tension in his body was evident, the spears were not leveled idly.

The guide closed his eyes, his face a mask of concentration. "Six, six, six, six, six, five, five, five, five, five, five, three, three, two, two, two, and that's it. And you say, 'That's it.'" The guards raised their spears and stepped aside. The guide gave Delilah a curt nod and disappeared back the way they'd come.

Yeah, that would have gotten me if I had only had that code by chance, thought Jeremiah. A confusing bit of wordplay for a strange code. He kind of liked it.

Jeremiah followed Delilah through the door and found himself in a hallway utterly unlike the previous. In fact, it reminded him much more of the palace in Dramir.

"Ah, shit," he heard Allison say as she emerged behind him.

"Are we . . ." Delilah trailed off as she took in the mosaic marble floors, the immense vases holding trees formed a canopy across the ceiling, the portraits depicting royal and noble figures of elven descent. "Oh my gods, we are!"

"Lady Fortune," said one of the guards, "you and your entourage are to follow us. You are to follow us at all times. Open no doors, do not stray. If any of you, any *one* of you"—the guard eyed Bruno—"disobeys an order, all of your lives will be taken immediately. Do you understand?"

Delilah nodded dutifully. "Yes, sir. Can I ask where we're going?"

"You are to meet with the empress Aubrianna. You will be respectful in the presence of the empress. You will kneel in the presence of the empress until given permission to stand."

Bruno sniffed loudly. "What if I need to—OW!" Before he could finish his remark, the guard behind Bruno pressed a spearpoint between his shoulder blades. The leading guard spun on his heel and closed the distance to Bruno in an instant, his hand darting out to close around Bruno's neck before he could react.

The guard strangled Bruno with complete dispassion, squeezing so tightly Bruno's eyes bulged. Bruno swiped at the guard's gauntlet, then spasmed as the spear point pressed again into his back. "Please do not make any jests during this meeting," said the guard. "Nor sarcastic remarks. The empress is quite busy, and we request that you respect her time."

Allison moved to break them up, but Delilah grabbed her arm, eyes glued to Bruno's face, which was turning a blotchy red. Bruno's attempts to dislodge the guard's grip became weaker until his eyes fluttered. Only then did the guard release him, letting him fall to sputter and gag on the floor.

"Your cooperation is assumed and appreciated. Come along," said the guard. The bruised outlines of armored fingers had already begun appearing around Bruno's neck.

As they followed, Delilah tended to Bruno's bleary staggering by striking him on the shoulder repeatedly. "What is wrong with you?" she hissed. "We are about to meet *Empress Aubrianna!* She's an elector for the crown of Dramir! She voted for King Hector! She's going to vote for *me* one day!" Each statement was underlined with another blow.

"Anyone else not thrilled about this revelation?" Jeremiah asked. He was noticing the lack of people in the palace. They had not passed a single servant or attendant. It all seemed quite ominous. "It shouldn't be this empty, right? We should have seen someone by now. Anyone. And that kind of makes it feel like other people aren't meant to see *us.*"

"Not thrilled," spit Allison. That was an understatement—she looked like she was walking to her own execution.

"No, hush!" said Delilah. "Listen everyone, this is the real deal. If anyone can help us escape the conspiracy in Dramir, it's Empress Aubrianna! I have no idea what she's going to ask for, but we *need* to get her on our side. We are never going to get another chance like this!"

At her words, Allison's grave expression only deepened. The knot in Jeremiah's stomach grew tighter. The secrecy, Allison's worry, their need to accept this job, whatever it was—it was all making him miss his early days as a necromancer, when he could simply skip town when things got rough. "*But I didn't have my family then,*" he reminded himself. Despite everything, this was better.

Delilah flitted and fretted over the impending meeting, somehow pacing back and forth even as they walked. They finally stopped before an unassuming door, identical to many they had passed. The guard addressed them once more, his voice never wavering from bland monotone. "Empress Aubrianna awaits through this door. You may take time to compose yourselves. Past this threshold, your lives are in the utmost jeopardy. You have never been closer to death than when you enter this room."

Jeremiah sincerely doubted that, considering they had each been at death's door more than once. But for Delilah, if for anything, he'd simply smile and nod his way through this if needed.

The guard waited for Delilah to cease her erratic primping and preening and then, with a single, passionless glance at Bruno, who paled and swallowed hard, opened the door for them.

CHAPTER FOURTEEN

Walking the Garden

Jeremiah was used to the meeting rooms of a palace being less ornate than the highly visible halls, but he did not expect the room in which they were to meet the empress of Elminia to be an empty gray cube. The walls were bereft of adornments, and the cold stone leeched the heat from their bodies. It nearly matched the interior of the Giant's Bag, save for a series of shallow steps that spanned the width of the far wall and led to a slightly raised platform.

Upon that platform, the sun rose as the radiant splendor that was the empress Aubrianna and set on the dark figure beside her. As he sank to a knee, Jeremiah tried not to stare. The empress was a sculptor's masterpiece, perfectly still as she observed Jeremiah and his friends. She wore a brilliant white gown of office, high collared and flared on the hem. Atop her head was a wicked-looking crown, spears of gold reaching toward the ceiling like stalactites and adorned with immense gemstones. While beautiful, the entire regalia threatened violence.

Another elven woman stood beside Empress Aubrianna. This one made no suggestions of violence—she promised it. Her bright red hair contrasted with black leather armor studded with silver rivets. Jeremiah realized the rivets were actually the pommels of dozens of slender knives, and when Jeremiah met her gaze entirely by accident, he knew he was looking into the eyes of a predator.

"Whoa," Bruno croaked. Jeremiah glanced over and saw Bruno was making no illusions about his opinion on the red-haired woman's appearance.

"You may rise," said the empress. Her voice was clear as a bell. "I have brought you before me to request your aid. I have heard the tale of your endeavor in Dramir. Our mutual friend inspires my confidence that you will accept my request and succeed in its completion." Her voice hurt Jeremiah's ears. She was way too loud, like she was accustomed to a larger room.

Delilah immediately filled the silence. "We are humbled to be trusted by you. Pray, though, Empress Aubrianna, we do not know the purpose for which we are summoned." Jeremiah noticed with pride that Delilah had smothered even the slightest hint of nerves.

"I have brought you here, Lady Fortune, in order to—" The red-haired woman nudged her. No words were spoken between the women, but when the empress continued, her voice was a normal speaking volume. "I have brought you here, Lady Fortune, because I have been made aware you are victims of a conspiracy in Dramir.

I wish to offer an opportunity for you to leverage your talents in exchange for the dissolution of this conspiracy."

"With all due respect, Empress, may we have the pleasure of an introduction to your attendant?" asked Bruno. He sounded strained—and not just because of his bruised throat, but because he had admirably recruited his "make fun of the nobility" voice into an "address the nobility" voice.

Another shared look between the empress and attendant. "I am Ka, royal spymaster of Empress Aubrianna," said the woman. She had addressed Bruno directly, and the two of them were now staring unabashedly at each other. It took no small amount of willpower for Jeremiah not to roll his eyes.

"Oh no, a spymaster," Allison sighed.

Delilah stiffened, but didn't falter. "A pleasure and privilege to meet you, Spymaster Ka."

"Likewise," said Ka. She didn't look away from Bruno, and Bruno didn't look away from her.

Empress Aubrianna closed her eyes. "Spymaster Ka, would you please . . . You know what, never mind. Let us just speak freely, you already made it weird." The absolutely perfect posture Empress Aubrianna maintained slipped just a little as she rubbed her eyes in annoyance.

"I did not," said Ka quietly.

A silence followed the empress's declaration. Delilah seemed at a loss to continue the conversation without formal decorum as a guide.

Then Allison broke the silence. "This is a black op, isn't it, Empress?"

Ka broke her staring contest with Bruno to reexamine Allison. "You have experience with this term, Captain Allday?"

"I do," said Allison.

"What's a black op?" Delilah asked.

"It means a job we do for the empress, that the empress will deny she requested," said Allison. Her posture had stiffened to military attention.

"Like a secret mission?" asked Jeremiah.

Allison shook her head. "Worse. They'll pretend it never happened, which means they want us to do something horrific." Allison's voice carried the slightest hint of disdain.

Delilah laughed nervously. "What Captain Allday means is that we'd like more information about your request. And maybe you can tell us exactly how you'd help with our predicament?"

Empress Aubrianna held her gaze on Allison a moment longer before answering Delilah. "Lady Fortune. Our city has seen a series of murders. These murders have been increasing in frequency and are notable in their brutality and method of execution."

"A serial killer?" asked Bruno.

"A cult," said Ka. "The killings, and their aftermath, are about spectacle."

"Targets are random?" asked Delilah.

Ka nodded. "Seemingly. My people haven't had any luck infiltrating to learn more. They're likely all known elements. Our generous reward offers have had no legitimate takers, so those involved are extremely committed." She spoke to Bruno now. Exclusively to Bruno.

"True believers," Bruno said.

"So you want us to . . . ?" Delilah said, letting the question hang.

"Fix it," Allison said. "By any means necessary, they just want us to fix it." She was trying, but the disdain was still there, lurking in her eyes and the stiffness with which she spoke.

Empress Aubrianna's posture stiffened again as she turned her eyes on Allison. "Captain Allday is correct, if curt," said Empress Aubrianna. "Captain Allday, you will *not* presume to answer questions asked of me, is that understood?" The edge of stern authority flared in her words.

"What's the method of murder?" Jeremiah asked. The conversation was happening around him, and he felt the need to be involved somehow.

"Appears to be ritual stabbing, roughly," Ka answered.

"A rough stabbing? Or like, mostly a stabbing?" Jeremiah asked.

Ka's face twisted in a facsimile of a smile. Her eyes flicked over Jeremiah, top to bottom. "I mean each murder was committed with a particular kind of knife. But given the variety of perpetrators, results are varied. Sometimes embellished."

Jeremiah could sense her answer was off. Ka and the empress were hiding something, but he wasn't sure how to probe deeper. He even felt like he *shouldn't*. He knew the palace guards were still very nearby, and he didn't want to attract their attention should he overstep.

"Resources?" asked Bruno, his face hardened now that they were talking business.

"Can't give you much, due to the nature of the mission," said Ka, her face just as hard. "Some gold, a decent safehouse, and the promise of an incompetent prosecutor if things go south."

"Wait, prosecutor?" said Delilah. She looked back and forth between Ka and the Empress.

"There would be a prosecutor because they won't acknowledge we're acting on their behalf." Allison's answer was stoic. "They won't grant us any favors. If we're caught doing something illegal, we're liable. Just like anyone else."

"Not that you need to do anything illegal," Empress Aubrianna said, "but Captain Allday is correct. Any preferential treatment would implicate us." She gave a solemn nod like that was everyone's primary concern.

Somehow that sounds worse, thought Jeremiah. The idea of an empress privately condoning immoral actions churned his stomach.

"In exchange, if you succeed, the conspiracy against you and your party will be resolved," said Empress Aubrianna.

"Resolved, Empress?" asked Delilah.

"Ended," Empress Aubrianna said.

Delilah looked at Jeremiah, concern written all over her face. What was she trying to tell him? "It sounds like you're going to have a bunch of people killed," he guessed.

Empress Aubrianna and Ka exchanged a glance. Ka nodded. "Yes," the empress said.

"It's just . . . we would probably rather you not do that," Jeremiah said. Bruno shrugged.

"Spymaster Ka, can Lady Fortune's troubles be resolved in a more diplomatic manner?" Aubrianna asked.

"Less straightforward, but yes."

"I hope that satisfies you, Mister . . ." Empress Aubrianna paused, observing at Jeremiah with an inquisitive tilt of her head, as much as the crown would allow, seeming to notice his presence for the first time. "You are Jeremiah Thorn, the necromancer, yes?"

"I was, Empress, yes."

"Was?"

"I have since given up necromancy, after the happenings in Dramir." Jeremiah knew which question was coming next.

"So, what I've heard is true. But what I've not heard yet, is why?" Aubrianna squinted, studying him.

"Too much responsibility for someone like me, Empress. My mistakes cost people their lives. It's power I do not want. The stakes are too high, the consequences too costly, and my actions weigh too heavily on my heart." It had taken Jeremiah a long time to be able to articulate why he had given up the craft, and longer still to become comfortable saying so. It was only in the last few months he'd been able to articulate an actual answer.

"I see," said Aubrianna. Another silent conversation between her and Ka, this one longer than ever.

When it was finished, Ka spoke. "The terms are set. Destroy or reveal this cult and its leaders, and your conspirators will be dealt with. In a nonlethal manner. You will receive a password with which to contact us—speak it to a palace guard only when you have information we can act on, or the cult is destroyed. Questions?"

"The gold?" asked Bruno.

"Already at the safehouse, an apartment across from the Rambling Inn. Pick the door lock to gain entry. A set of keys is inside. If you accept and are successful in this task, we will meet again upon your extraction. If you refuse or fail, we will never speak again. Good day."

"The guard's will bring you back to the tunnel from which you entered," said Empress Aubrianna. Then, to Jeremiah's shock, she added, "Mr. Thorn, I wonder if you might join me for a brief foray into the gardens after your colleagues depart."

"Um?" said Jeremiah. He heard a combination of snickers and gasps from his friends and didn't dare turn to see the look Delilah was giving him.

"This is unrelated to the mission, Mr. Thorn. My interest is entirely personal." The smile she gave him curled his toes and made his hair stand on end.

Oh shit, Jeremiah nearly said but managed to choke it into just a thought. "I would be okay with that," he said, glancing at the floor. He could feel his friends' stares boring into the back of his head.

"Mr. Thorn will be returned to you once we've had some time to talk," said the empress.

That smile again. "*This is what fish feel like when they see worms on hooks.*"

"When you're ready, Mr. Thorn," said Ka. She and Empress Aubrianna took their leave, the side door left ajar as an invitation to follow.

Suddenly Jeremiah was surrounded by Bruno, Allison, and Delilah, all competing for his ear.

"You need to tell me *everything*."

"Don't agree to anything she asks!"

"Offer your arm, but don't *take* her arm."

"No! Don't even touch her!"

"Put in a good word for me?"

"Yeah, me too."

"Just smile and nod, no matter what she says."

"Don't you *dare* kiss her!"

"What?"

"What?"

The three voices came in such a torrent that Jeremiah couldn't tell who was saying what. "Hey, back off now! She probably just wants to ask me to raise some dead guy, that's usually what people want to talk about."

Delilah crossed her arms, scowling. "Except you already told her you don't do that anymore."

"Oh yeah," said Jeremiah. He rubbed the back of his neck to relieve the growing heat of embarrassment.

"Just keep it professional," said Allison.

"No! No, absolutely not!" said Bruno, stepping between Jeremiah and the others. "Jay, don't you listen to these she-devils. You haven't so much as *glanced* at a woman since we met you. So if some empress wants you to 'explore her garden'—"

"Ew," said Allison and Delilah.

Bruno continued, "Then you go have yourself some fun. Now, I better see some swagger in your step as you walk, 'cause that tall drink of wine asked you, in front of everyone, to come attend to her personal needs. If that's not worth some cockiness I don't know what is!" He slapped Jeremiah on the back for emphasis and pushed him toward the open door.

The sting of the back slap gave Jeremiah a boost of confidence. "Can't let Allison have all the fun with royalty, right?" he said as he made his way up the stairs.

Bruno barked a laugh after him. "Attaboy, Jay!"

The space beyond the door was black as pitch. As soon as he entered it, blind and confused, the door slammed shut behind him.

"Arms up, all the way out. Spread your legs. Open your mouth, good." Rough hands shoved his limbs into position and began methodically searching him. It was Ka's voice, but he couldn't see her.

Ka's hands took significant liberties in their search that made him jump. "Is, uhh . . . is the empress going to be jealous?" said Jerelish.

The hands retracted. It was deathly quiet. Jeremiah winced and turned his head, anticipating a well-deserved slap or worse.

"You get the frog back when you're done," said Ka.

"That's my familiar!" Jeremiah protested. His hands went to Gus's pocket in his robes, but he was gone. He hadn't even felt Ka take him.

"He's a blue spine, and I'll not have him in proximity to the empress. Swallow."

Jeremiah swallowed, and something tiny that had been in his mouth without his knowledge went down his throat.

"You've just been poisoned. You get the antidote if you leave without incident. Arms out front, walk forward till you reach a door and push," commanded Ka.

"Wait, what? Poison? How long do I have? Ka?" There was no answer, she was gone.

A few hesitant steps forward and his palms pressed against a wall of cool wood. He pushed and split a beam of light around the edge of a door.

The scent of fertile soil and flower blossoms hit Jeremiah like a heady perfume as he stepped into a rainforest. Trees reached toward the gabled ceiling high above, the floor was rich with bursts of color, and flowering vines scrawled across everything like illuminated script. It was an awe-inspiring feat of gardening.

Waiting quite intentionally amid the greenery was the empress. Like marble, she stood in stark contrast against the panoply of natural colors. She smiled at Jeremiah but made no motion otherwise.

All right, time to be charming and confident, thought Jeremiah as he gingerly stepped through the foliage, *because that's what charming and confident people do: remind themselves to be charming and confident.*

There was no obvious path through the greenery, but Aubrianna waited with patient bemusement for Jeremiah to tiptoe and hop around the delicate plants as he made his way over. He assumed it was some kind of power play to make him prance around just to reach her.

In the final few steps Jeremiah chose to close beyond typical speaking distance. Close, but not too close. He took some satisfaction as her eyes widened just a little at his proximity. "Thank you for the invitation, Empress," he said. "It's quite lovely here." He ensured his eyes held hers as he said it.

Empress Aubrianna was only slightly taller than him, sans crown, but as she recovered from Jeremiah's unexpected flirtation, that authority returned, and Jeremiah found himself unsure of what to say next. *Well, it was fun while it lasted.*

"Shall I give you a tour?" the empress asked.

"Sure," said Jeremiah gratefully.

She led him through the pathless garden, pointing out particular plants of interest and sharing facts about their properties. It seemed she maintained this garden herself. Jeremiah tried to listen as he avoided crushing the more delicate plants underfoot. Empress Aubrianna had no such compulsion and simply let her feet fall where they may.

She took his divided attention as disinterest. "I apologize, you must find this quite boring," the empress said after some time. "Perhaps you would like to tell me of your adventure defeating the elven renegade that threatened Dramir?"

"Apologies, Empress. I just don't have much of a mind for plants," said Jeremiah, ignoring her question. He really didn't want to talk about that.

"Yet I watch you step so carefully. Why is that?"

It was a strange question to Jeremiah. "Because . . . I don't want to hurt the plants?"

She gave him a different sort of smile, more genuine. "Your thoughtfulness is noted. You have my permission to step where you please, I will not be offended."

"Thank you," said Jeremiah, though he still had no intention of stepping on the plants if he could help it.

"So? Your adventure?" she asked. He was about to request they skip that particular topic, but she had turned to face him directly, and it was hard to refuse, being this close to her made him want to do whatever she asked. Reluctantly, he recounted some of what had happened, leaving out some of the more personal or painful details. He was starting to feel uncomfortable in her presence.

"Ah yes, I heard about the treasures of Dramir that were lost with the renegade," the empress said, referring to the chest that went down with Vivica. A chest of incalculable value and no small number of powerful magic items. "If, perhaps, you were to tell me the location of the final resting place, we could negotiate a much more favorable solution to your dilemma. No need for clandestine quests or cloak and shadow nonsense," her arm tightened around Jeremiah's just a little.

"I'm sorry, Empress, but I swore that I would never reveal any information about what became of Vivica," said Jeremiah, loosening his arm a little. More than a few people had probed him for clues or promised shares for just a hint.

"There is no consequence I cannot protect your from Mr. Thorn, and more than a few boons that I could bestow onto you as well," Empress Aubrianna hinted with an almost wicked lilt in her voice.

"With respect, I don't know exactly where her final resting place is. Nor am I completely sure that she's at rest," said Jeremiah. He would have given anything to get off this topic.

"She's . . . alive?" asked Empress Aubrianna. The horror of the implication fractured her smile.

"I sincerely do not believe so, but I don't know for sure. I would not be surprised if she were though," said Jeremiah. He tried not to think about this as often as he could, but the idea was insidious and would ambush him from time to time.

"I apologize for my forthrightness, it was ungracious of me." She got them walking again, passing under a canopy of tropical trees Jeremiah had never seen before. "So, Mr. Thorn, what do you think of Elminia?"

Jeremiah breathed an inward sigh of relief. "It stands in sharp contrast to where we are now."

She laughed like a crystal chime, and all of Jeremiah's discomfort fled.

"Indeed. I think of Elminia as another sort of garden, one that I'm allowing to grow wild. Please understand, my lifespan is much longer than a human's, so I see far beyond the now."

"What do you see for your city so far beyond my years?" he asked.

"A long period of turmoil, sadly, as my people struggle under the weight of their choices. I have faith that, with gentle guidance, they will grow to no longer need me, or any master." Empress Aubrianna gazed serenely up at the canopy. It was difficult not to stare at her.

"Well, I guess that sounds very nice," said Jeremiah. He was certain a smarter person would have better questions than he could come up with, 'I don't understand' wasn't a question anyway.

"It will be, in time. Unfortunately, my garden seems to have attracted an invasive pest. One that I hope will be eradicated with the introduction of a predator," said the empress.

"That would be us. Empress, can you tell me anything else about this cult? Even if you're not sure it's true?" said Jeremiah. The conviction that she and Ka had been hiding something niggled at him.

Aubrianna sighed a spring breeze. "No, not about the cult. We know precious little. But . . . I fear its reach is vaster than we realize." She reached down and scooped up a handful of soil, letting it discolor her pristine hands. Just beneath the surface of the earth was a web of yellowish thin roots. The web entangled the thicker roots of surrounding plants. "Something is wrong in my garden. That's all I am truly able to say. The scent has changed, so slowly that I had overlooked it, but now I am certain."

The metaphors were becoming annoying. "So you're saying this cult might be more established than you thought?"

"I'm saying that I believe the cult has power beyond the obvious, but I cannot say what."

"*What am I supposed to do with that?*" wondered Jeremiah. He assumed her warning was only so difficult to understand because she was so much more cultured and intelligent than he was.

They had returned to the entrance. "Thank you for accompanying, Mr. Thorn." The empress gave him a gentle smile and half-lidded eyes. By all the gods, her beauty was overwhelming. There was an urge to just lean in and see what happened. He decided to choke instead.

"You're welcome," he managed. The door opened, revealing Ka standing in wait. He bowed deeply, at least confident in how to be courteous, and took his leave from the strange encounter.

Ka closed the door behind him and began leading him through empty palace halls.

"That was a really nice garden," Jeremiah said to Ka. He was aware of the dumb smile on his face but couldn't care less.

"Uh-huh" was her reply.

"She was really forthcoming, you know? Very open," said Jeremiah, continuing the one-sided conversation. He just wanted to talk to someone about it.

"Uh-huh," said Ka.

Jeremiah shook his head and laughed. "We didn't do anything, if you were worried about that."

Ka scowled at him as they walked. "What? She took you on a stroll, arm in arm, through her private garden. I watched that happen," she said.

"Well, yeah, but we didn't *do* anything," Jeremiah bared a smile at her best he could, this woman inspired a whole different kind of nerves.

They reached the hidden door in the wall, the two guards were standing on either side. "Didn't do—What is it you think—Oh! Oh gods, humans are so fucking gross! Have you no sense of romance?! Of intimacy?! You actually call an empress spending time on you *nothing*?!"

Ka waved her arms indignantly as she yelled at Jeremiah, then grabbed him and shoved him through the gap in the wall.

"Wait! You said you'd give me the antidote!" Jeremiah yelled before Ka could close the door.

"Ugh!" Ka threw a tiny pill at him that bounced down the dark hallway.

"And Gus! I'm not leaving without Gus!"

Ka looked disappointed but produced Gus from a pouch at her hip. She gave Gus a little scratch under the chin, which seemed to soothe her. She gently handed Gus back to Jeremiah and slammed the door in his face.

CHAPTER FIFTEEN

Undercover

The private meeting with Empress Aubrianna did little to alleviate Jeremiah's misgivings about the black op, but it was as Delilah had said—they were never going to get another chance like this. Allison clearly shared his concerns. She settled into a permanent bad mood as they established their new home base in Elminia.

The apartment was barren and filthy. There were two spare rooms off the main living space, more like large closets, and a fireplace that looked like a hole that had been knocked in the side of the chimney and never repaired. Dust was the primary occupant, although it shared space with its extended family dirt and grime. It took the harshest soap they could find and several hours of labor to evict the worst of the tenants. They spent another few coins on cheap furniture, already one bad day from the kindling pile.

Fortunately, the Giant's Bag meant they were very well equipped. Jeremiah laid out his enchanting gear in the room he shared with Bruno—plates, tools, long spools of gossamer-thin gold, silver, and copper, and a pile of Thurok's borrowed books that Jeremiah was wary would eventually come to life to kill him.

"I'm certain this is just as unsafe as it is ineffective," said Delilah. She had wedged a pot of stew deep into the chimney hole. The heat rising from cooking fires in the apartments below was just enough to provide a suggestion of warmth, but the smoke was choking.

Bruno swept into the room and stabbed a hunk of mysterious meat from the stew. He bit into it like an apple and spoke as he chewed. "All right, here's the plan for the next little bit. Al, I'm going to need you to try to relax, maybe go sharpen things. Jay, you're gonna keep practicing enchanting so I can have magic shoes that let me walk up walls—and magic daggers, of course. In fact, just focus on the daggers. Delilah, I'll need you to read books or something. Your most important books." Delilah gave Bruno a sharp nod.

Allison stared at him coldly. "And what will you be doing?"

"Literally everything else," said Bruno, tearing off another bite. "This is a mission to infiltrate the city's underworld, find its secrets, and expose its leadership. I'll have us out of here in a few weeks."

Delilah squeezed her eyes shut against the smoke. "What makes you think it'll be so easy? The empress's best people have already tried."

"Ah, but the empress didn't have *me*." Bruno grinned his cockiest grin. "I've done this before. Multiple times. It's kind of anticlimactic, to be honest." He started idly spinning his knife between his fingers.

Allison glared at the flashing blade of Bruno's knife. "This isn't a game. These kinds of missions can get brutal. Ugly."

Bruno's spinning knife stopped. "Oh, are you sure? You're telling me this *black operation* might be unseemly? That there might even be skulduggery or ne're-do-welling?"

Allison ignored the sarcasm. "I'm serious. These missions change people."

"Al, is there something you want to talk about?" asked Delilah. She put a hand on Allison's shoulder, but it was like reassuring a statue.

"No. It's fine," said Allison. Her jaw tightened. That door was thoroughly closed.

"See, you say that, but I'm not sure I believe you," said Jeremiah. *Knock, knock?* he thought.

"I said, it's fine!" Allison slammed her fist on the table. A long silence followed.

"Well, clearly it's not fine," said Bruno. "But places to be, and all that. I expect you all to stick to your assignments. With some luck, I'll be back before you have time to miss me." He dipped his fingers into the stew pot, scooping up some of the floating fat, and ran it through his black hair.

Delilah grimaced. "Oh, what—why did you do that?"

"Gan underco, sveeha," said Bruno, his voice adopting an accent Jeremiah couldn't place. "Needa deepa, needa natura, pe gran prof."

"You sound like someone that speaks Gnomish with a dwarven accent, trying to stumble their way through Common," said Delilah.

Bruno snapped his fingers and pointed at her. "Yas." He stepped across the room, leaning heavily on the chair to support his newly acquired trick knee. "Su see may? No see may. Yas?"

They nodded at the stranger that had evolved from their friend. One that had suffered a stroke some time ago, leaving a drooping eye and lip. The stranger strode to the door, all but barely hiding the stiffness in one leg.

"Good luck, stay safe," said Jeremiah.

"Lucka fer gennas," said the stranger. Then he spit on the floor and left, slamming the door behind him.

Allison's attitude did not improve in the days following Bruno's departure. If anything, her mood worsened, permeating their living quarters with an air of sullen misery and rebuffing any attempts to talk. Jeremiah was more than happy to close himself in his room to work on his rune. After the carriage ride, working on solid ground was a breeze.

In addition to his overly complex Strengthen plate, he had created a separate plate for each of the runes he knew that had an effect on their own: Decay, Heat, and Adhere. Unfortunately, the same strategy he'd used to delay the Strengthen diagram had not proven very useful for testing his unknown rune. Decay still caused the plate itself to rust away within minutes, Heat made the temperature of the plate increase until the metal surface warped and destroyed the rune, while Adhere made the plate stick instantly to the floor, his hands, and anything else it touched until he managed to break the enchantment.

He also created a plate containing the new rune on its own. Charging it directly hadn't seemed to change the properties of the plate in any way Jeremiah could detect, so he created a simple diagram to connect the new rune to the Strengthen plate. When he charged it in this configuration, he was disappointed to observe no difference in the Strengthen plate either—it still seemed Strengthened, but nothing else.

He looked out the window at the interminable life of Elminia that flowed just outside. He was fully prepared for the noise and anxious motion of the city to make it hard to concentrate, but if anything, it did the opposite. He was a lone island that stood in contrast to the hustle and bustle, an example of focus and calm . . . even though he couldn't actually accomplish anything with his new transcended mind.

Gus watched Jeremiah rack his brain from a comfortable water bowl. "What do you think?" Jeremiah asked his familiar. "Whatever it's doing, it should be doing it now. Unless it doesn't work on metal plates. Or on Strengthen. Or needs two runes to work, like And. Or doesn't work because the plate is already Strengthened, and I need to start from scratch."

That final possibility filled him with the most dread, so Jeremiah decided that was the one he'd start with. *Thurok would be proud,* thought Jeremiah. It was wrong—Thurok thought pride was for "gamblers and degenerates"—but still fun to think sometimes.

To his relief, the new plate took only a couple hours to complete. His hands were becoming familiar with the geometric intricacies of the Strengthen rune, and he found himself needing to reference the diagram only intermittently. He scratched the final notch in a single stroke and was pleasantly surprised when the gold rod nestled snugly inside.

"Let's give it a shot, buddy," Jeremiah said, stretching out his wrists. He connected the new plate to the mystery rune, took a moment to gather his focus, and charged the diagram.

The runes glowed softly for just a moment. Jeremiah snatched the new Strengthen plate and inspected it closely.

"Still nothing. What's this damn thing *do?*"

Jeremiah rubbed frustration and tightness from his jaw and tossed the plate onto a pile of other discards with a ringing clang.

Jeremiah stopped. Something sounded off. He picked up the plates: the old Strengthen, and the new Strengthen. He had handled hundreds of plates at this point, and his hands told him these weren't exactly equal.

He studied them side by side. Both were stronger than a normal plate, yes, but . . . With suddenly shaking hands, Jeremiah drew a rasp across the surface of each plate.

There was no doubt about it now. The new Strengthen plate was less resistant to the rasp than the old one. He tested over and over, and the rasp consistently bit deeper into the new plate than the old one.

The idea formed in his mind then, but Jeremiah forced himself to keep testing. Over the next two days, he recreated plates for Decay, Heat, and Adhere. In each case, charging them through the unknown rune lessened the effects of the main rune. Decay took hours to rust through, Heat was safe to touch for several minutes, and Adhere became only mildly inconvenient.

It was a strange feeling. This moment could prove to be his greatest contribution to the field of magic. It could be a discovery that changed the course of history. It could see him immortalized in the annals of magical history . . . but he didn't actually know what to *do* with it.

It just makes normal runes work worse. What am I supposed to do with that?

A knock at the door made him jump. "Dinner," said Allison. Then she took in the chaos of components, tools, and metal squares strewn across the floor like a game of fifty-two pickup. She cocked an eyebrow.

Jeremiah leapt to his feet, countering her gloominess with uncommon buoyancy. "Great! I've got news."

He waited until Delilah joined them at the table, though he was practically brimming over with excitement. The moment she sat, he produced the plate with the new rune with a flourish. "I think I've got it figured out!"

Delilah immediately matched his energy. "And?!" Even Allison looked more interested than she had in days.

"I think it essentially says *Gently*," said Jeremiah. "Whatever rune I attach it to, it modifies the effect to be less strong. The effect still happens, just slower or not as much."

"Wow, an adverb!" said Delilah with delight. "That sounds really useful!"

Jeremiah beamed. "Indeed, it is. Though any new word is valuable."

"Valuable how?" asked Allison. "How do we turn it into gold?" she pursed her lips at the plate in doubt.

"Um. I'm not sure, actually," said Jeremiah. "The only people I know who might want to buy it are Thurok or Flusoh, and it doesn't feel right to make them pay. Other than that, I'm not really sure how you monetize a new rune outside of just selling it."

"It's your discovery, Ja," said Delilah with a shrug. "When alchemists discover something new, they have to decide whether they're going to share it or keep it as an exclusive. But once it's out there it's out of your hands."

"I know, I know," said Jeremiah. "But this feels different to me. I want them to have it, you know? They taught me so much."

Delilah reached across the table and patted him on the arm. "You're a really good guy, you know that?"

"Yeah, and destined to be poor," said Allison. "First useful thing your enchanting turns out, and you're giving it away."

"Any money is going right out the door anyway," grumbled Delilah. "The lawsuits don't settle for cheap."

"There will be more, I promise," said Jeremiah. Still, her words stung, not least because she was right. *At least when I was a necromancer, I was worth keeping around.* He pushed the thought away, but the frustration persisted.

Being on the streets of Elminia was always awful, with the unfriendly crowds and the sense of malevolence that seemed to emanate from the city itself. Tonight, Jeremiah felt even more on edge than usual due to the two parcels tucked under his arm. Each contained a metal plate bearing the rune Gently and a letter explaining how to use it. Even if he didn't know how to sell it, he was aware that he had never held anything as valuable in his life.

He pushed through the crowds toward a jagged tooth of a building where a few youths gathered outside, wearing identical loose-fitting uniforms. As he approached, they reluctantly paused their bawdy story. The smallest among them was shoved forward to address Jeremiah.

"What do you want?" the young man asked.

"I need something delivered," said Jeremiah.

"Uh-huh, that's why you've come to the Courier's Lodge," said the young man, rolling his eyes.

Jeremiah flashed a gold coin. All at once, the young man adopted an expression of polite attention. "Listen closely," Jeremiah said, injecting as much authority as he could while whispering. "Far from here, there's a place called Throatlock Swamp . . ."

CHAPTER SIXTEEN

Wasted Potential

Jeremiah put the finishing touches on his latest enchantment diagram. It was a touch inelegant, but it was a fine proof of concept for now. He scooped up Gus. "Now comes the hard part, buddy."

He inspected the plate again, flattened out his shirt, and made the two-step journey from his bedroom to the adjacent one. He gave the door a pair of quick knocks and tucked the plate behind his back, trying to quell panic creeping up on him.

Delilah cracked the door just enough to see him. "Hey, Jay. What's up?"

"Hi, Delilah. I . . . umm." What had he meant to say? "I guess, I sort of . . . have a present for you?"

Delilah's polite expression turned into one of concern. "A gift? For me?" She retreated even further behind the door, so only half her face was visible.

Jeremiah realized he was making a mistake. This was weird. He was clearly making her uncomfortable. And worse still . . . "Okay, well, it's not exactly perfect yet, but I wanted to let you know I was working on it and maybe get an idea of if it's something you'd actually want so I don't keep working on it if you don't think it'd be useful."

In what Jeremiah could only describe as an act of intentional cruelty, Delilah just stared at him. He revealed the plate from behind his back. "This is an enchantment plate."

More silence. *No, it's an elaborate dinner plate*, he thought. Gods, why did he sound so stupid?

"Um, I mean, this is an enchantment plate that makes heat. I thought maybe it'd be useful in your lab work. Or for cooking. Or whatever else."

"That's very thoughtful Jay. Thank you." Delilah tried to take the plate from Jeremiah, but he didn't let go.

"I actually can't give it to you yet. It still overheats and breaks the enchantment. I've got to figure out how to make it only heat up to a certain point, but once I do, I'll give it to you. I just wanted to show you what I've got so far."

"Oh. Well, it looks very nice," said Delilah. She offered him a pleasant smile.

"Once I fix it, it'll always output that amount," said Jeremiah. He was starting to ramble, but he couldn't help it. "It'll just stay hot, and you can use it to boil water and stuff without making a fire."

"Huh," said Delilah. "Go on." She narrowed her eyes, her curiosity piqued.

"I—That's it," said Jeremiah. He rocked back and forth on his heels.

"How long does it last? Like, a day? A week?" She turned it over in her hands, looking at it from different angles.

"Ha! No, no, no, much longer." He forgot sometimes his friends didn't even know the basics of enchanting. Delilah was still gripping the plate. He tried to tug it back from her, but she held fast.

"How *much* longer?" Suddenly Delilah's focus and all its probing intensity shifted onto Jeremiah. She didn't look pleased or polite anymore. She looked angry.

"I—I don't know for sure?" said Jeremiah. "I'll need to figure that out. A good few years at least. It's a pretty simple enchantment."

Delilah glared at him long enough to make him profoundly uncomfortable. "Years? You estimate this would stay hot enough to boil water for years?"

"Sure, maybe a decade. But probably close to twenty years, if I tune it right."

Delilah closed her eyes. "You stupid, stupid boy."

Of all the reactions Jeremiah had imagined to his gift, this one hadn't featured. "Excuse me?"

Delilah's eyes snapped open. "I am so mad at you right now for just *handing* me this. You don't even realize what this *is*, do you?"

It was Jeremiah's turn to stare at her in stunned silence.

"Come on, Jay, think for a minute! Heat! Heat without fuel! For decades! You're supposed to be smarter than this!"

"Yes, I know it'd be useful, that's why I'm trying to make you one."

"Make me *one*? You should be trying to make hundreds. Thousands! One for every household in the world!"

At that, Jeremiah had to laugh. "That's impossible. Enchanting is a very labor-intensive process, and—"

"'Labor?!' This is lines cut into a flat metal plate! The industrial applications *alone* would—" Suddenly Delilah's face broke into a saccharine smile. "Oh Jay, this is such a thoughtful gift. Thank you!"

She pulled him into an iron-grip hug. "Now, you listen to me," she growled in his ear, a not entirely unpleasant sensation. "You're going to continue working on this. You're not going to talk about it. With *anyone*. Do you understand? Not Thurok, not Flusoh, not Allison, not me, not Bruno, not anyone. *Do you understand?*"

Jeremiah nodded, confused and terrified.

"When you get this working, you are going to knock on my door. It doesn't matter where we are nor what time it is. If I'm not home, you're to sit quietly in your room until I return. You will say it's lovely weather for a stroll, and then we will go for a walk to the patent office. Do you understand?"

Jeremiah nodded again. Pinned in a prolonged hug with Delilah was not the worst place to be.

"Good," she hissed, then returned to a normal speaking voice. "Thanks again. That was very sweet of you! Too bad it doesn't work. I have to get back to some titrations though. Bye, Jay!"

She shoved the plate back toward Jeremiah and slammed the door. Jeremiah put a reassuring hand on the pocket in his robe. Gus was holding very still. "Don't worry, buddy," Jeremiah said. "I think it's okay we don't know what just happened."

Three weeks after Bruno's departure, Allison was still in a foul mood, stomping around and snapping at innocuous questions. Jeremiah and Delilah hid in their respective bedrooms to keep as much distance between them and Allison as possible, but her anxiety seemed to bleed through the walls, made worse by her insistence that she was fine.

Jeremiah appreciated the chance to focus on his enchanting, but the expectation to hide indoors for an indefinite amount of time brought him right back to being under house arrest after his trial. It didn't help that being outside in Elminia was dreadful in its own way. Having grown up in a tiny village surrounded by pastoral countryside, the city always held a sense of wonder for Jeremiah, but Elminia was like a churning, angry cauldron. He had been cursed at, spit on, and even bitten enough times that any wonder had long since transformed into disgust.

The nearest market street comprised a cluster of food in piles or bags that occupied the center of the street and were guarded jealously by their purveyors. On one particularly dismal morning, Jeremiah selected the least damaged loaf of bread for their day's ration, paid a surly dwarf an outrageous price, and let himself be swept up in the press of bodies trudging toward home.

Jeremiah found the swirling current of heat, noise, and smells more tolerable if he turned off his brain and allowed momentum to determine his path. His mind wandered as bodies surged and jostled around him, always pushing him onwards.

Until his progress halted. Something poked against his abdomen. Jeremiah's eyes snapped up to see the tip of a knife pressed against his alchemically reinforced robes. Its wielder was a human man standing stock still directly in front of Jeremiah, sweating profusely, with eyes half-lidded in an expression of bliss.

The man hissed with excitement as Jeremiah was bumped from behind, pushing him harder against the knife. Jeremiah tried to step aside, but there was nowhere to go. Someone cursed at him and shoved him hard, and the knife tip pressed hard into Jeremiah's robes. Delilah had long since given them a chemical treatment that resisted damage and it, thankfully, held up here.

Jeremiah planted his feet and spun with force, slamming into several people who made their objections known immediately. The knife slipped off him as he was swept up once again by the stream. The man with the knife disappeared behind him. Jeremiah kept glancing back over his shoulder trying to see the man again.

Did someone just try to murder me? he thought. *No, that wasn't about me, that didn't seem to be about anyone.* He was back there somewhere, still holding the knife out, waiting for someone to impale themselves on it.

"I hate this place," he said. Gus kicked once in agreement.

Jeremiah forced his way from the stream to enter their apartment building. As always, he took a moment to enjoy the relief of escaping the dull roar of the crowd. He made his way upstairs, and, juggling the bread and other sundries, fumbled at the entrance to their apartment.

The door burst open, and a dark shape seized Jeremiah. In an instant, he was slammed against a wall, knocking the wind out of him and scattering the groceries across the floor.

A grotesque and ragged face, eyes bulging with fury, pinned Jeremiah across the chest with a forearm. The face leaned close, its breath reeking of alcohol and neglect. "Who did you *fucking* tell?!"

Jeremiah shoved at the arm, but it held fast. Where were Allison and Delilah? He wrenched his knee upward and connected with something soft. The face recoiled in pain, and Jeremiah shoved off the wall. He threw a hard elbow toward the face, twisting his body and pushing through from his feet, just like Allison had taught him.

The face shouted in pain, but recovered before Jeremiah could scramble away. In a flurry of limbs, Jeremiah was thrown face down on the floor, his arm pinned behind him. He began to speak the words that would let him exhale poisonous gas, but a greasy hand clamped over his mouth.

A crash of breaking glass. Jeremiah twisted and spotted Allison wrenching the man's head back, a broken bottle pressed to his throat.

"Hey there, dead man," she said. Her anger was cold and soft as fresh snow.

The weight vanished from Jeremiah's back. "Wait, wait, wait!" said Bruno's voice.

Allison paused, the broken bottle just starting to break the skin. "Bruno?"

Jeremiah stood, rolling his shoulder. "What the hell is wrong with you?"

"We're glad to see you, Bruno," said Delilah. She was standing in the doorway Allison had just vacated, a glass bottle in her hand as well, though hers was intact and filled with an amber liquid.

"Not thrilled, actually," said Jeremiah.

"Oh, quit whining, you milk-sipping weakling!" Bruno yelled.

Jeremiah's simmering anger burst through. "Go back outside if you want to throw a temper tantrum!"

"You little . . ." Bruno lunged toward Jeremiah. Jeremiah raised his fists, more than willing to get his ass kicked if it meant he could belt Bruno again—that had been satisfying.

He didn't get the chance. As Bruno closed the distance, Allison's hand snapped out like a viper and struck him in the throat. Bruno crumpled, clutching his windpipe as he gagged, tongue protruding.

Allison shot Jeremiah an icy glare: *Your turn.* Jeremiah held his hands up and stepped backward. His fury toward Bruno was not worth drawing Allison's ire.

Bruno's face was darkening to a deep crimson as he gasped for breath. Jeremiah's rage ebbed to concern that his friend was dying, but no one else seemed worried.

After a time, Allison squatted beside Bruno. "You okay?" she asked. Bruno nodded. "You don't ever raise a hand against anyone on this team. You know that," said Allison.

"W-was s-still in c-character," wheezed Bruno. "Tough to . . . to . . . to slip s-sometimes."

"I know," said Allison. She took Bruno by the arm and helped him to his feet. Bruno leaned on her as she ran a comforting hand over his back.

Bruno turned toward Jeremiah. The anger and hate that had been there moments ago were gone. "Sorry."

"S'all right," said Jeremiah.

While Bruno recovered, Jeremiah, Delilah, and Allison gathered up the groceries and set out a breakfast of milk and bread. They gathered around the table, dunking their bread before eating it. For a moment, aside from Bruno's filthiness and the lump swelling over his left eye, things were as they had always been.

"That hurt as much as it looked like it did?" Jeremiah asked, pointing at Bruno's throat.

"Not as much as that knee and elbow combination you gave me." He gingerly touched the bruise rising on his brow. "Allison, you should be proud of your boy, he got me good," said Bruno.

"I'm always proud of him," said Allison.

Jeremiah paid extra close attention to his bread. The mixture of pride and embarrassment at Allison's powerfully sincere approval almost hurt.

"So, what happened?" asked Delilah.

Bruno sighed heavily over his meal. "I got made." His voice cracked and for a wild moment, Jeremiah thought he might cry. The anguish on his face extinguished the last ember of anger in Jeremiah's chest.

"What does that mean?" asked Jeremiah.

"It means I'm a known element. They saw me coming, all of them did. Doesn't much matter the disguise if they're looking for you. Some of them even . . ." he swirled his cup, watching a crumb of bread slowly sink beneath the surface. "Some of them mocked me." he spoke those last words with a quiver in his voice.

Delilah tried to hide a smile. "They mocked you?"

Bruno slammed his cup down on the table. "You don't understand! I'm the Shadow of Dock Road Two. I'm both cloak and dagger. I do not make mistakes, I do not get caught, and I do *not* get made fun of. Especially not by some no-talent pickpocket squad of roustabouts."

"Everyone makes mistakes," said Allison.

"Not me. The people who make mistakes in my line of work get buried with them. My first memories are of pulling heists for bread, I *am* this work. Besides, this isn't just from a moment of carelessness. Everyone knew to be on the lookout for me, even in disguise." Bruno leaned forward, regarding each of them in turn. "Which is why I need to know—did one of you talk about what we're doing? Or that you knew me? Even in passing?"

"None of us has spoken with anyone since you've left," said Allison. "We barely left the apartment."

"Are you sure?" He absently switched Delilah's cup with his own, a behavior Jeremiah had come to think of as a nervous habit. "It's the only explanation I can think of."

"How do we know this isn't because of the empress?" asked Jeremiah. "Or her spymaster?"

"Technically it's possible, but I'm not sure why they'd do it, since they requested our presence," said Bruno. "Doesn't mean they didn't. Maybe an even better reason why they would!" Being Bruno sounded tiring. "But I should tell you, something's going on in this city. Whatever is happening here, it's happening soon."

"How do you know?" asked Delilah.

Bruno gestured all around them. "You can feel it. The pulse of the city is quickening. There's fear and desperation in the air. Everyone knows something's coming, even if they don't know they know it."

"I haven't felt anything. Have you guys?" Delilah asked Allison and Jeremiah. They shrugged, though Jeremiah's mind quickly glanced on the strange man with a knife in the street.

"Nah, nah, you wouldn't be able to feel it," said Bruno, waving away the suggestion. "You'd need to be in it. To feel the fever rising. It's not something you can just glance at."

Finally, Jeremiah asked, "So what now? Ditch the black op? Wait a while and try again?"

"Back to Dramir, back to square one," said Delilah. She leaned all the way back in her chair, letting her head hang in defeat.

"No," said Bruno. "This is still our best bet. I might need to stage my own death or look for a fall guy or—"

"I can do it," said Allison and Jeremiah at the same time. They each looked at each other in surprise.

Bruno barked a laugh. "No offense, Al, but you couldn't stop being a soldier if your life depended on it. You walk like a soldier, talk like a soldier. You even sit like a soldier." Allison shifted in her seat, then gradually returned to her rigid posture.

"What about me?" asked Delilah.

"Or me," asked Jeremiah.

"You got a money voice, Delilah," Bruno smiled as he spoke, like he was fond of it.

"What's a money voice?" asked Delilah.

"Means you talk like a rich girl who's seen the inside of too many lecture halls. Then became a doctor. And a lawyer."

"So it's me?" asked Jeremiah.

Bruno stared at him. "I don't remember going crazy with desperation, no."

"Then what else?" asked Jeremiah. "You already said Allison and Delilah can't, and you obviously can't. That just leaves me.

"I appreciate the offer, Jay," said Bruno with a good-natured smile. "I really do. But . . . I mean, you know."

Jeremiah set his jaw tight. "Enlighten me."

Bruno smirked and started to speak. Then he stopped. He looked Jeremiah up and down. "Hmm," Bruno tilted his chair back, letting it balance on the rear legs. "Well . . . it's not actually impos—"

"I won't allow it," said Allison. "He has neither the skillset nor the mindset for this. He'd get shivved in an alley."

"Al, he's not the same dough-faced boy we picked up in the woods," said Bruno. "He needs training, sure, but maybe I can work with him."

"Dough-faced?"

"You think you can pass Jay off as, what, a thug?" asked Delilah.

Bruno shook his head emphatically. "No! No, no, no!" He failed to resist a laugh creeping into his denial. "I can harden him up, but I can't take the heart out of him."

"I won't allow it," Allison said again.

"I can't help but notice none of you are talking to me," said Jeremiah. "Even though this is about me, and I'm right here."

The table went quiet. Bruno and Delilah exchanged a glance. Allison only glared at Bruno.

Jeremiah continued, "Which, I'm guessing, is because you don't think I can handle the decision of whether or not I do this."

Delilah gave him an apologetic smile. "Jay, it's not that. It's—"

"No, it's absolutely that!" Days, weeks, months of frustration were spilling forth. "I'm part of this team. I saved all your lives in that tomb. I wiped out a bandit camp for you! How long are you going to keep treating me like a child you need to protect?" Jeremiah's ire grew, the man in the closet. Fear. Loneliness.

"You're not ready for this," said Allison.

"Course he's not," said Bruno, "but I can try to get him ready. Jay, do you want to do this?"

"Yes," said Jeremiah without thinking. It was an act of pure defiance and frustration, nothing mattered more than having some modicum of control over this situation.

"It's irrelevant if he wants to!" said Allison. "I. Will not. Allow it."

Bruno crossed his arms. "No offense, Al, but you're out of your element here. I've got the expertise, and I say he's worth a shot. Should only take a few weeks. Besides, we don't exactly have a ton of options here. If I can't get him ready, I won't send him out. I promise."

Jeremiah watched Allison wage war with herself. She scowled, opened her mouth to speak, closed it, stood and paced around the room running her hands through her hair, then whirled back toward them. "Fine."

"Any other objections?" Bruno asked.

Jeremiah broke off another hunk of bread. "Nope," he chewed his piece with angry determination.

"I have reservations, I want that on the record," said Delilah like it was a point of order. Her eyes flicked up and down Jeremiah with a worried look.

Bruno nodded. "There is no record, but noted. I'm going to need help though, from both of you. Jay, you're sure you want to do this? It's not going to be pleasant."

"I handled Warlord Uuba's pain training with Flusoh, I can handle this," said Jeremiah with an affirming nod. *You're not going to scare me off this*, he thought. *I'm an adventurer through and through. I've handled far worse.*

"We'll see." Bruno reached across the table and slid Jeremiah's plate toward himself, the uneaten bread wobbling merrily.

Jeremiah frowned. "Hey, I'm hungry."

"Get used to that feeling, boy." Bruno's face broke into a humorless grin that chilled Jeremiah to the bone.

CHAPTER SEVENTEEN

The Wall

Bruno took a day to develop a training plan. According to him, Jeremiah could eventually pass for a second-story man "with a little work."

"First I need to assess your skills," said Bruno. He had cleared all of the furniture from their living room. "Climb up the wall here and traverse around the room." He patted the smooth plaster.

Jeremiah looked at the flat gray wall. He looked at the other three flat gray walls. "Just . . . hop up? And climb around the room?" asked Jeremiah. *Is this a riddle? Or some kind of test within a test?* he thought.

"Well, try anyway," said Bruno. "I don't expect you to make it the whole way around, the part near the door is going to be tricky, but let's see how far you can get." He patted the wall again. "Up, up!"

Jeremiah placed his hands against the wall. The plaster was cold and unyielding. He tried to dig his fingers in but there was nothing there save for the bumps. He placed one foot against the wall. Still no miracle appeared.

"Ambitious choice, but I approve," said Bruno. Jeremiah had no idea what he was talking about.

Lacking any other guidance, Jeremiah hopped and threw himself flat against the wall. He slapped his cheek against the plaster and dropped unceremoniously back to the ground.

Bruno chuckled. "Yeah, that was inevitable. Don't try to impress me now, keep it simple. Go ahead, try again."

Jeremiah moved over a step and bounced uselessly off the wall again.

Bruno's amusement became tinged with annoyance. "Why don't you try starting here?" He pointed to a spot in the middle of the wall that on closer inspection was . . . utterly indistinguishable from the rest.

Jeremiah braced his foot at the spot Bruno had pointed, jumped, and again splatted against the wall. Bruno just stared.

"I am *so* excited to learn the answer to this riddle," said Jeremiah sarcastically. "Is the real climb metaphorical? Do I 'climb' into a sense of—"

"I get it, you're incompetent," said Bruno, all traces of amusement gone. "You seriously can't climb this? It's basically stairs!"

"Climb this flat vertical wall? No, I'm not a bug," said Jeremiah.

Bruno nodded and gently pushed Jeremiah aside. He did exactly the same thing Jeremiah did, placing his hands and feet against the wall, but when he hopped up, he stayed aloft.

"No. How are you doing that?" asked Jeremiah. Bruno was just floating in the air.

"I'm climbing. Did you not climb trees when you were a kid?" asked Bruno.

"It was fields for miles around where I lived. But this isn't climbing, this is sticking to a wall," said Jeremiah.

"Take a closer look," said Bruno.

Jeremiah crouched to inspect. He could see, once he got close enough, that Bruno's feet were braced between two minuscule bumps in the wall. Bruno's fingertips gripped the tiniest crumbs of plaster.

"That's insane." Even seeing it, Jeremiah couldn't believe it.

"That's second-story work," said Bruno. "Climb the unclimbable. Where a normal person sees a wall, you see a ladder. Where people see a window, you see a door. You grant your people access to a whole new dimension."

"You asked me to enchant your glove to stick to walls. Why bother when you can do this? I actually started looking into how to do it," said Jeremiah. It was theoretically simple: If Contact, Adhere. He'd found instructions in one of his books about designing diagrams that would only activate when a certain rune came into contact with something. If he could weave that into a glove, all he'd have to do was slap his hand against a wall and it would stick.

"Jay, focus. Climbing, glass cutting, lock picking, burgling, all of these are complex and nuanced skills I don't have time to teach you in any depth. I just need you to *pass* as a second-story man. But that's the easy part. The hard part is I need you to pass as one of us."

"One of us?"

"The survivors." Bruno dropped off the wall and advanced on Jeremiah. "The forgotten. Street folk. Urchins. Someone that knows the struggle." He jabbed Jeremiah in the chest. "I'm going to teach you what matters."

"What is it that matters, besides climbing walls like a spider?" asked Jeremiah.

"Desperation," said Bruno. The intensity of his glare was making Jeremiah uncomfortable.

Delilah entered, and Jeremiah was grateful for the distraction until he noticed what she was holding. "Hey, guys!" She showed them a sickly yellow strip, mottled in black spots. It looked like a bad, moldy cheese. "This should take care of his teeth. Won't last forever, but he can do a reapplication if needed."

"What is that?" asked Jeremiah with dread. The very sight of it made him nauseated, speaking to a primal part of his brain that said not to touch it.

Delilah held up the strip and pointed at Jeremiah's mouth. "You took very good care of your teeth when you were younger, and I thank you for that. You have no idea how many infections I see spreading from gums to hearts. But Bruno thinks a lack of options and guidance would have been the norm for you."

Jeremiah unconsciously ran his tongue over his teeth. Whenever he'd complained about brushing as a child, his mother would lean in and smile, revealing the blackened crumbled mess inside her mouth, more like charcoal fragments than human bones. The sight had always terrified Jeremiah into obedience.

"Open," said Delilah.

Jeremiah opened his mouth.

"Don't throw up," Delilah laid one strip across his upper teeth, and one across his lower teeth. She closed his mouth for a few moments, it tasted like he had taken a swig of chunky milk, then removed the strips and inspected her work.

"Gross. Good work," said Bruno.

"I agree," said Delilah. "I thought the color depth was too far, but I'm glad I went with it."

She held up a mirror for Jeremiah, and he nearly gagged at what he saw. His teeth had been stained a multitude of yellow and orange hues, with deep pits of black settling into some of the spaces between and in the pits of the molars. "This is temporary, yeah?" he asked.

"Should be," said Delilah.

Bruno sighed. "I still think—"

"I am not removing any of his teeth!" said Delilah.

Bruno's methods of instruction turned out to be demanding one impossible task after the other. Bruno would place a tiny bell in Allison's pocket without her noticing, and it was Jeremiah's job to swipe it. But Allison's situational awareness was flawless to anyone that wasn't Bruno. Jeremiah practiced lock picking on a training lock that stabbed his fingers with a lightning-fast needle every time he messed up, which was often, and made picking the lock even harder. And he came up empty when Bruno interrogated him on the minute details of a room or location after being allowed to study it for less than a second.

Every day he asked Jeremiah to attempt to climb the wall, and every day Jeremiah failed. He had never known a vitriolic hatred toward a wall before, but this was the worst wall there had ever been.

But worse than anything was the hunger. It gnawed at him day and night, keeping him at the edge of rage. As the weeks passed, Bruno would allow him scraps here and there while the others ate normal meals at the same dinner table. "We need to get rid of the baby fat on those cheeks," Bruno had said. Jeremiah often had nothing to occupy himself besides staring and salivating at the others' plates.

He sensed the others' patience dwindling. His patience with himself was dwindling. They could not stay here forever and wait for him to achieve competence. Outwardly, they were all as encouraging as ever, but Jeremiah wasn't fooled. His chance to prove himself, to really make a difference, was running out.

A knock on the door well after dark made them all jump. Bruno peered through a crack at the visitor, then leapt to the table, draped himself onto the chair, and started shuffling cards as though he hadn't a care in the world. Allison rolled her eyes and opened the door to reveal Spymaster Ka, leaning against the wall in a mirror of Bruno's posture.

"Hey," she said.

"Hey," said Bruno. He started dealing solitaire with precise flicks of his wrist.

"Good evening, Spymaster Ka," said Delilah. "How can we help you?"

Ka thrust a bundle of envelopes toward her. "Did you have your personal mail forwarded to the palace?"

"I did, yes," said Delilah. "I have some critical correspondences to maintain." Bruno abandoned his devil-may-care routine and sighed heavily.

"Right, we're putting a stop to that," said Ka. Her gaze lingered on Bruno a beat too long before she said, "Good night," and left.

"Were you supposed to deal her in?" asked Jeremiah. Any opportunity to rib Bruno was too good to pass up—especially over the last few weeks of misery. "She looked like she wanted to play."

"She knows she's—Wait, what? Deal her into solitaire?" said Bruno, fumbling the cards in his confusion.

"Oh," said Delilah. It was a tiny squeak of a sound, almost a gasp. She held an open letter in her hand, the paper limp. Jeremiah thought he saw the tiniest quiver of her lip.

"Hon? What's going on?" Allison asked, crossing the room to see the letter.

"I, umm. I lost our house," Delilah took a halting breath. "We knew this was coming, but . . ."

"Oh, Delilah I'm so sorry," Allison gave Delilah a hug, but Delilah didn't return it.

Our house? My house? thought Jeremiah. It was a sad pain that hit him, like losing a loved one. They had lost the house where he'd spent his first night with his new family. Where he considered his home.

Allison kept up the hug with Delilah, and Jeremiah wished someone could spare him a hug as well, but none came.

When Delilah spoke again, her expression was placid. "That house was the last one my family owned. It was the house I grew up in. They'll come for the fortress next, and once I'm no longer a landowner, I'll be stripped of my title. After that, I'm sure my law and medical licenses are next. Then, assuming they aren't satisfied, I'll be placed in a debtor's prison of some sort."

"We're not going to let that happen," said Allison.

"And there is no debtor's prison that I can't get you out of," said Bruno.

"Enough," said Delilah. "None of you know how this works, this isn't your world. If you'll excuse me." She pulled away from her friends, gathered up the papers, and disappeared into her room, pulling the door closed with a soft *click* behind her.

The soft whistle of Bruno's breathing had been steady for half an hour before Jeremiah made his move. He tucked Gus into the pocket of the threadbare tunic they had chosen, slung the satchel containing a set of lockpicks and a few enchanting tools over his shoulder, and crept out of the room.

Slowly, now, he thought. *Remember all the lovely spots of this floor that creek and groan.*

The apartment was bright enough from moonlight that he could cross it without worrying about bumping into anything, but he still nearly collided with Bruno blocking the door.

"What the—how did you . . . ?" Jeremiah head swiveled back toward the bedroom where he'd been sure Bruno had been fast asleep moments before.

"Go back to bed, Jay." Bruno had his arms crossed casually as he leaned against the door.

"Let me through." Jeremiah kept his voice low to keep from waking the others. "This is happening."

"The hell it is. You're not anywhere near ready. I made a promise to Allison—do you have any idea what she'll do to me if you get yourself killed out there?"

"I don't care," Jeremiah squared his shoulders. "We're out of time and I have to try."

Bruno chuckled and shook his head. "I know you want to play at being a hero, Jay, but this isn't a game. You're not going, so just forget it."

Jeremiah's temper flared. "The only one treating this like a game is you! You failed, so you don't believe anyone else can do it. But it isn't up to you anymore, it's up to me. So let. Me. Through."

Bruno's good humor disappeared, replaced by a scowl. "You don't have what it takes. You're never going to have it. You'll quit this when the going gets tough, and it doesn't take long out there."

"Bruno, I have to do this. I can't let Delilah—can't let *all of you* lose everything because of what I did. I have to make it right, and this is the only way I can do that. So you can either help me or get out of my way."

Bruno glared at him for a long time, and Jeremiah glared right back. The silence between them was the heaviest Jeremiah had ever heard, but he refused to back down.

Finally, Bruno spoke. "You'll be on your own out there. We'll be here in the safe house if you need us, but on the ground, it'll just be you."

"I know," said Jeremiah.

"Allison's right, these missions can get real messed up. You're going to have to do stuff you don't like, stuff that'll stick with you. There will be no going back."

"I know." Was Bruno really going to let him go?

Bruno looked him square in the eye. "You promise me, right here, right now, that you'll take care of yourself, first and foremost? That you'll come home if you need to? That I won't have to go out there and recover the body of some poor kid who got in over his head?"

Jeremiah nodded once. "I promise."

"Then let's go."

CHAPTER EIGHTEEN

The Streets

Jeremiah was starving. He was sure he was actually starving. His stomach was twisted up in a knot, and the fatigue of being underfed while training kept his thoughts sluggish and his body aching. Still, he was done. The last few weeks had been a nonstop maelstrom of training, practice, education, and starvation. He now walked with Bruno in the hours where the sky took on the navy blue of the upcoming sunrise. Or it would, if Elminia wasn't belching smoke at all times day or night. They followed a narrow canal creeping its way into the city like the root of a new plant. Yellow foam built up in pockets along the banks, sticking to stony outcroppings like noxious barnacles.

"Remember the ground rules," Bruno was saying. "You're just Jay, like a million other Jays out there. You're a second-story man coming in from Shabad after a job went bad. Stay out of the Pit until you've got a crew to protect you. And don't let anyone see you cast magic; it draws way too much attention."

"I know all this, you've told me a hundred times already." Jeremiah flinched at a moving shadow cast by a tree in the wind. His nerves were getting the better of him.

"All right, then let me add something new: hurry. I don't know what's coming, I'm not sure anyone does, but things are going to get worse. Do you know what I mean?" Bruno asked sincerely.

He almost sounds scared, thought Jeremiah. *Why would it scare him if he doesn't even know what it is?* "Yes, yes, I'll hurry," said Jeremiah, waving off the concern.

You know where to find us, but only come by as a last resort," said Bruno. "Or, you know, when you're finally ready to call it. Here we are."

With a twist of his body and kick of the wall, Bruno scaled a wrought-iron fence with spikes protruding from the top to prevent that very thing. Jeremiah leapt to follow, jumping to grab the top rail. He managed to wedge his feet against the wall and scramble over the fence without sustaining any serious injury.

"Not bad, try to smooth that up a little," said Bruno.

"Bruno, my arms and legs are killing me, I'm honestly shocked I managed that," said Jeremiah. The ache of effort radiated and never stopped.

"Same," said Bruno. "I missed my calling as a teacher."

"What is this place?" asked Jeremiah. It looked like a factory and reeked of fish and rancid oil. No one was around at this hour, but the workers' tools had been haphazardly discarded, all caked with congealed fat.

"Otto's Picklery. Some of the finest pickled fish gets made here. Started as a money laundering front, but Otto was way too good at his job, and it became a legit business that outstripped the take of the gangs pressing him. Otto got enough money to get out from under their thumb, violently I might add, and expanded into fish oils in general. This city burns a lot of oil, and there's good odds it's Otto's oil," said Bruno. He patted one of the large, empty barrels lying and stopped to take a sniff. "Damn, I love that smell," he said.

"And in relation to me?" asked Jeremiah. He gave the barrel a sniff too. It was okay.

"Your point of entry. You're being smuggled into the city to avoid attention, but—so sad—you're getting caught."

An imperceptible noise caught Bruno's attention. He signaled Jeremiah, and they darted to a dark corner of the factory. Jeremiah lay still, keeping his breathing shallow. Finally, he heard the footsteps, and the glow of a lamp entered the courtyard. The light swung a few times, failed to illuminate their hiding spot, then departed.

"Ah, so Jimbo's working tonight," said Bruno. "Must be feeling better." They reached a great mountain of barrels without further issue from guards or sentries. The barrels were haphazardly stacked, reeking, empty, and falling over one another like a pile of drunks. Bruno looked through a few barrels, chose one, and rolled it up front.

"You want me to get in a barrel, don't you?" asked Jeremiah listlessly. The clothes he wore, simple and very well-worn slacks and tunic, were already dirty. Getting them covered in fish oil remnants would make them intolerable. Jeremiah hadn't realized how important clean clothes were to his sense of comfort until he no longer had them.

"I want that, yes. Very much so," said Bruno. "You're going to be trapped in here for a while, till the morning shift discovers you."

Jeremiah stepped into the barrel, cringing at the white cakey substance at the bottom of the barrel that split beneath his feet. He gingerly lowered himself in, arms tucked, desperately trying to not touch the sides of the barrel more than he needed. Even despite his disgust, he found himself wondering how the pickling remnants might taste. Gods he was hungry.

"Ready?" asked Bruno, poised to place the lid on the barrel.

"What's going to happen after I'm discovered?" Jeremiah asked.

"You'll likely come to your senses and return home," said Bruno. "We'll have a nice breakfast waiting."

"Just put the damn lid on," said Jeremiah. Nothing could make that happen. Jeremiah would not give that little smirk of Bruno's the satisfaction.

Bruno forced the lid down on the barrel, pounding it into place. The barrel suddenly tilted, and Jeremiah fell against its oily wall with a squish. There was a *thud*, and the barrel rolled once, Jeremiah rolling with it until not one single part of him was free of the fish stinking oily residue that had become a very part of the barrel like a heinous whiskey cask. The barrel righted itself, flipping Jeremiah upside down. He landed on his head, neck contorting awkwardly, as a rain of rancid white fat cakes fell over him, squishing into his hair and slipping into his mouth.

"Welcome to life on the street," said Bruno. "Try not to die."

Jeremiah grew to despise the workers of Otto's Picklery. They were lazy and slow, wasting valuable working time with idle gossip. Effie in particular needed a talking to, as every time they were about to start working, she had just one more dirty story to rile up and distract her coworkers. It wasn't until Dodric came along, gods bless him, to whip them into action that they actually started moving barrels.

The top of Jeremiah's barrel exploded with light. "Ooh, a fish!" said a scratchy voice.

Jeremiah squinted as the backlit shape formed the face of a goblin, its long, pointed ears twisting as it screeched with delight. "Man-fish, man-fish! It's been a while."

Jeremiah started to brace himself to sit up, but the lid slammed back down.

"Man-fish! Man-fish! Man-fish!" All of the workers were chanting now.

"Roast him or free him?"

"We did a fish fry on the last one, let's free this one!"

They cheered.

Given the two options, Jeremiah was relieved. Then the barrel started rolling. Over and over, he tumbled in darkness, the voices outside chanting and cheering.

The barrel tipped, the cover came away, and Jeremiah clung to its inside surface as a view of the canal greeted him below. The fish-slick wood offered no purchase, and soon he tumbled into the oily, foamy water.

The shock of the cold water stunned his cramped muscles. He reached for daylight above him, but his legs had forgotten how to work from the hours he had spent compacted in the barrel. There were shapes in the water around him, some small, and some as large as he was. The canal, he realized as he sank, was deep, far deeper than he'd thought.

Don't panic, thought Jeremiah. *Don't panic!*

He kicked his feet hard and achingly slowly began to rise back toward the sunlight. His head broke through the surface, and he filled his lungs with blessed air.

"Aw, he can swim," said one of the workers. The crowd lamented Jeremiah's survival and dispersed back to work.

Jeremiah hauled himself out of the canal and sprawled onto the bank to catch his breath. "Well, buddy, that wasn't a great start. But we're okay. Let's get to work, huh?" Gus wriggled in his pocket, happy to be wet.

Jeremiah stepped out into the streets of Elminia, a new and unknown man. Elminia took no notice.

His first order of business was food. Now that there was no Bruno preventing him from eating, he was free to get a real meal. Once he had something in his belly, he reasoned, he'd be able to think straight and figure out a plan to start learning about the cult. However, needing food meant needing money, and needing money meant needing work.

The first place Jeremiah checked for work was a squat, dingy inn called The Palm Frond. Jeremiah was greeted by the proprietor not two steps inside the door.

"Absolutely not! Get out!" shouted a Gnomish woman, laden with plates of steaming food.

"Apologies, ma'am. I'm just looking for—"

"What you're looking for isn't here!" the woman said. "No jobs, no food, no beds, no nothing. Move along!" The men at the table she was serving eyed Jeremiah threateningly.

Jeremiah and retreated back outside. "No problem, the day's just beginning. Onto the next one."

The middle and end of Jeremiah's first day as a new man in Elminia followed a similar pattern. He was shooed, shouted, and shunned from every establishment he entered with varying levels of force. As the sun set, he dodged out of the crowds and into a side alley, where he perched on a stoop to rest his throbbing feet and gather his thoughts.

All right, no luck so far. But maybe I—

"Move along," came a voice from a window above Jeremiah's head. "I'll not have you dirtying my steps!"

Jeremiah sighed and moved along, winding his way through sparser and sparser passageways until he found a spot to sit. Receded into the shadows of the buildings with just a little effort to clear away the refuse, he was no longer in anyone's way. He could finally rest.

"Don't worry, buddy, I'm sure we'll have better luck tomorrow," said Jeremiah. He caught a whiff of his clothing and gagged on the stench of river and fish fat. "That definitely doesn't help! Tomorrow we'll clean up. I guess I'll find a spot along the river. Just need to grab some soap . . ." There was a sudden block in Jeremiah's plan. He needed soap to clean up. But soap costs money. He needed a job to get the soap to get a job.

Gus pawed at him from his pocket.

"I know, I know, you're hungry too. Here, go find a snack," Jeremiah put Gus down near some trash. Gus pawed through it until he revealed a blackened heel of bread with no shortage of wriggling maggots. The toad croaked happily and began snapping them up. Jeremiah felt a touch jealous.

Doesn't look all bad. Looks like only half has bugs in it. Jeremiah shook the thought. Still hungry.

After eating his fill, Gus returned to Jeremiah's lap nestled into sleep. Jeremiah leaned his head against the wall and let his eyes close too. He was tired and very hungry. A moment's rest would—

"Oi! On your feet! Move!"

A sharp kick to Jeremiah's ribs lurched him out of sleep. A pair of people loomed over him in the dark. They wore leather breastplates and metal helms, and each had a shortsword and wooden club at their hip. City guards.

Jeremiah rubbed his eyes. His limbs felt dumb and clumsy, and his ribs ached, but he clambered to his feet. "What's that?"

"You can't sleep here," said one of the guards.

"Why not? Where can I go?" asked Jeremiah.

"Not our problem. Move!"

Jeremiah turned out onto the streets. The crowds of Elminia thinned after dark but became much meaner. He gave the people as wide a berth as he could, stumbling between alleyways. He felt much colder than he thought he should. After a few blocks, he turned down a promising new alley and curled up in a corner, tucking his arms tight against his body to ward off the cold. Tired, cold, and hungry, he slept.

"Oi! On your feet! Move!"

"Come on, leave me alone," mumbled Jeremiah.

Two guards. The *same* two guards. "No sleeping here. Keep moving," said the guard. It was only now that Jeremiah heard the boredom in the guard's voice and saw the lazy disinterest in her partner's eyes. It was rote, verbal paperwork. Jeremiah wasn't having it.

"No, I'm not causing a problem. I'm not bothering anyone. I have as much right to . . ." Jeremiah trailed off as the guard drew her wooden baton. "All right, all right, never mind."

Jeremiah had only taken a few steps when a deep, painful shock drove him to his knees. He clutched his side and retched, his vision swimming. The blow had landed right in his liver.

"You get two next time we find you," said the guard, just as bored as before. They stepped over Jeremiah and continued on their patrol. As tired as Jeremiah was, as much as he was hurt, he was confused. It was still the middle of the night, where was he supposed to go?

Another bout of wandering and Jeremiah found himself curled up on the stoop of a closed shop. He was just beginning to nod off when he heard familiar footsteps. The ache in his side throbbed, and he staggered to his feet again. All night long, he listened even as he drifted, lest he miss the footsteps that carried a warning he dared not ignore.

CHAPTER NINETEEN

Honest Work

Bleary, unwashed, and reeking of fish, Jeremiah decided on a more targeted approach a few mornings later. Days of hitting as many shops as possible had yielded exactly zero copper. Most turned him away upon sight, a couple had offered him an odd job, then laughed when he'd asked for payment afterward. When he got wise to that ploy and asked up front, doors were slammed closed in a hurry.

He had to figure out how to make himself seem valuable, and he had exactly one idea how. With an upbeat smile plastered on his face, he pushed open the door of Prim's Laundry. Aside from magic, laundry was one of the trades he actually had some skill in.

The instant he stepped inside, he was transported home. The smell, that perfect chemical smell stung his nostrils, making him think of cleanliness, his mother, and Delilah. Customer's garments were on racks or stuff sacks crowded the front room, ready to go home. No one greeted him, so he slipped toward the back, where the work was done.

A dozen great wood basins were lined up side by side, each with a pair of workers on either side. Hot coals burned beneath each basin, and Jeremiah was sweating in moments. Among the toiling launderers, he spotted an elven woman strolling from basin to basin, inspecting the work with a critical eye.

Jeremiah navigated the piles of dirty clothes of sacks to get within earshot. "Excuse me, ma'am? Are you Prim? My name is Jay, and I'm—"

"No," said Prim without sparing him a glance.

"My mother was a launderer, I know everything about it. You wouldn't need to train me or anything," said Jeremiah. That afforded him at least an appraising glance from Prim.

She was not impressed with what she saw. "I have more than enough hands for wools and linens, leave."

"I know how to handle silks," said Jeremiah. "Furs too. I can clean leather, taffeta, even brocade." His father's jeweling work had been too fastidious to hold young Jeremiah's interest, but his mother had always appreciated an extra pair of hands while she worked.

Prim studied him again, giving a suspicious look to his clothes. She sniffed, but Jeremiah knew whatever sense of smell she was supposed to have was long since gone, just like his mother's, stolen away by chemical-laden steam, lye, and harsh soaps. Enured to the smell of something as minor as rotting fish, Prim beckoned him to follow. Grinning for real now, Jeremiah trailed her through the busy room to a small yard behind the building. Clothes hung on lines in the open air, and a smaller tub of heated water occupied a corner, where two men were sat with a bundle of brushes and rags. A third man was paddling some garments out in the sun. They all eyed Jeremiah suspiciously.

Prim picked an item from the pile beside the two men. Jeremiah surmised these were the more delicate garments, finery too fragile for the work in the main basins. "What is this?" Prim asked.

Jeremiah ran his hands over the full fur coat. It was incredibly soft, but only in one direction. As he ran his hand against the grain of the fur it turned from whisper soft to stiff spines. "Dire wolf cub fur," he said. "Very rare." He had only seen it once before as a child, when a rich family's carriage had overturned near his home, unprepared for the rural roads and autumn rain, and his mother had been paid to salvage their spilled luggage.

The two men at the basin looked at each other in surprise. Prim nodded. "And what's wrong with it?"

"Not much," he said, inspecting the coat. "It's been well cared for. A bit musty, perhaps. Looks like it's been brushed correctly, no bare patches. I don't see any stretching . . . oh wait, here we are." A small patch of fur sticking up, creating an area of angry thorns. "Something spilled on it and wasn't cleaned correctly. Made the hairs clump together, which means they got twisted and sharp."

"Indeed," said Prim. She shot the two men a glare and they suddenly got back to work. "And how would you address this garment?"

"Tricky. Damage has already been done. A bottle of spirit might help, and you'd need tweezers to disentangle the hairs. Or, if 'good enough' is good enough, you can pinch and twist the hair clumps, and they'll separate over time. But you'll likely lose a few, depending on what this stuff is gumming it together." Jeremiah sniffed the patch. It had a distinctly flowery smell that he couldn't identify. He pushed the furs apart and saw the skin beneath was dry and cracked. "Ah, someone used hand soap on this spot. Apparently a floral soap?"

"Correct. This coat belongs to the friend of a valued customer. It has been sent here on referral. If I send it back to her in this condition, I will lose a potential client, and maybe even a loyal one. Here is my offer to you, if you can rejuvenate this coat to my liking, I will consider giving you a position."

Jeremiah's heart leapt, but he quickly composed his expression to match Prim's grave countenance. "I'll need tools since we're doing this the hard way." It was accepting work before payment again, but something about Prim and the smell of this place put him at ease.

A hint of a smile crossed Prim's lips. "Tools and chemicals are inside the work chest there. Take anything you need from anyone."

Jeremiah banished his hunger and fatigue through sheer force of will. This was the moment he had been waiting for. He buckled down at once, leveraging the intense attention Thurok taught him every step of the way.

Banish the thoughts, only breathe. Slow thyself. Lose yourself in the minutia of your perception.

It was all *much* easier said than done, especially with the gnawing hunger and fatigue, previously banished, working to make themselves known again.

He spent hours with a solvent and pair of tweezers until he could separate and clean, singular hairs. Even as the sun began to set, he continued his regimen of conditioning, treating, and delicate brushing, always scrutinizing his work for the slightest errant detail that Prim might notice.

He presented the coat to Prim just after closing as the last of the workers departed. "Bundle this with ground coffee beans for two days to get the smell out, and it should be all set." His hands ached and the fatigue nestled deeply behind his eyes, but he was proud of what he'd accomplished.

Prim inspected the area, holding the coat up to flickering lantern light. "Not perfect. But quite good."

The criticism didn't even faze Jeremiah. "Yeah, I think someone tried using a mild acid at some point? No idea why, but it weakened the hairs."

"A citric, yes, I suspect so as well," said Prim. She draped the coat over her arm. "I could use you. Return tomorrow, dawn. I have a collection of brocades that need attention."

"I hope you have a shady place to dry them. The yard looked far too exposed to sunlight," said Jeremiah.

She allowed a genuine smile at that, tiny but amused. "We do, yes." She reached into an inner pocket and produced five copper coins. "This will be your day's wages. Should your skills raise up my establishment, so will I raise you up as well. I am departing for the evening, hang the coat before you go."

I am on intimate speaking terms with your empress, Jeremiah wanted to brag. He appreciated her giving him a chance, but some part of him was missing the recognition of being *The Necromancer.* Instead, he thanked Prim, pocketed his coins, and took the coat out back into the yard.

"We did it, buddy! It was rough going at first, but we did it," said Jeremiah. Gus made a pathetic peeping sound. "Ah, no worries, buddy. We'll both feel better with some food." He was already salivating at the thought of the bread he could buy for dinner.

Jeremiah was trying to decide on a suitable spot for the coat, when he was punched in the face. He stumbled, his vision swimming, and someone threw him down hard. A weight settled on his chest as a man sat astride him. It was one of the men who had been washing finery.

"You think you can walk in and do my work? Take my money? Food outta my mouth? I'm a hungry man. You taking food from a hungry man?" The man pawed at Jeremiah's pockets, rifling through them, thankfully missing Gus and saving Jeremiah the difficulties of body disposal. But he did find the five copper.

"Give that back!" Jeremiah shouted. He was incensed, furious, nearly hysterical with the injustice of it.

"You did *my* work, so that's *my* money." Apparently satisfied with his take, the man stood. Jeremiah scrambled up to his feet, still facing his attacker as the man leered at him. "I won't be so polite next time I see you round these—HURK!"

Jeremiah had sunk his fist into the man's throat, sending him backward, gagging. His fury was indescribable. Allison's voice was in his ear. "*You won't win by defending. Breath is fight. Take away the breath, take away the fight.*" Jeremiah rushed the man. He drove a knee into the man's solar plexus, then smashed his nose with the palm of his hand. The man's hands went from his stomach to his bloody face. His nose blocked, his diaphragm malfunctioning, and his throat partially collapsed, he was basically suffocating. The fight was over.

Strong hands gripped Jeremiah's arms and yanked them backward while a boot was planted on his back, driving him to his knees. The two other men from earlier appeared and were now ready to interfere that their friend had been laid low. Jeremiah cursed himself for not noticing them when he'd entered the courtyard. Bruno had taught him better than that.

"Come on, Vernon, belt him good!" the man restraining Jeremiah shouted. Jeremiah struggled in vain, but Vernon was busy gasping, doubled over in pain.

"Vernon? Come on!" the man yelled again. Vernon tried to straighten but doubled over once more. He was done.

"Get the scab to the bleach," said the other man. Jeremiah kicked and struggled as they dragged him backward, struggling and failing to find purchase to resist.

They held him face up over the basin for a second, and he was able to see his adversaries' faces, ragged from years of exposure to caustic chemicals. Then they plunged him beneath the surface.

Burning bleach flooded Jeremiah's sinuses and he panicked, screaming soundlessly. An agony he had never imagined flooded his senses. He flailed, kicked out wildly, felt his foot connect with something, and the grip on him loosened.

Jeremiah hauled himself out of the bleach vat and sprinted blindly toward the corner with the water basin. As soon as he collided with it, he threw himself in headfirst. The shock of cold barely even registered as he resurfaced for more air and then plunged himself in again.

Slowly, slowly, the flames of pain began to subside. The burning did not completely fade from the sensitive tissues of his eyes, sinuses, and throat, though, and Jeremiah knew every breath would hurt for days to come.

He became aware of laughter in the yard. The men were watching his struggle with great amusement. "Nice and clean then, are yeh?" they said. "Go on, get out! Don't let us see you again!"

Shaking on his legs, Jeremiah started feeling his way toward the exit. His eyes were sore and swollen, and he kept them nearly closed. There was nothing he wanted more than to leave this yard and these men behind forever.

"No," rasped Vernon. Jeremiah's blood ran cold. Though his nose was surely broken, his throat struggled to draw breath, and his face was smeared with blood, Vernon had regained enough strength to speak. "Take him . . . round back . . . Cutter will . . . want to . . . see him."

Jeremiah tried to flee, but the men fell upon him in a moment. Their hands felt like brands on his scalded skin as they seized him.

The men dragged Jeremiah into a back lot behind a dank alley. It appeared to have once been a shop yard, but the fence had calved it away and turned it into an alley end. The lot's inhabitants, and there were many, lounged on stools and splintering chairs, piles of carpets and burlap sacks. They were surly-looking and dull. Some were talking. Some were gambling. Most were drinking.

Jeremiah's captors heaved him into the dirt, kicking up a cloud of dust that caked over his still-damp skin.

"Oooh, we got a lost little lamb!" A beady-eyed human with a patchy beard sneered down at where Jeremiah crouched in the dirt. Jeremiah noted the blade sheathed at his hip, more like a long knife than a proper sword.

The men in the lot roused to attention at the leader's proclamation. Well, some of them did. Many remained in whatever stupor they were lost in.

"Tourist come 'round taking work from honest men," said Vernon. "Prim gave him five copper for a day's work. *Five!* How's that for loyalty!"

"A tourist in Cutter's turf? Taking *Cutter's* money?" said their leader. His voice was pitchy, agitated. To Jeremiah's surprise he seemed anxious, like a new guy on his turf was some kind of threat.

"I don't want any trouble," Jeremiah said, trying to stand. The dust was like acid on his skin.

"Oh, no trouble at all," said the man Jeremiah assumed was Cutter. "We can fix this right as rain, no trouble at all."

"Sure, whatever you say," said Jeremiah, holding his hands up to show he didn't want to fight.

"Whatever I say, that's right," said Cutter. He took a step toward Jeremiah. "You took five copper from my man. I think fair's fair that you owe me . . . hmmm," He rubbed his patchy chin in deep thought. "Five silver should do it."

Jeremiah was stunned. "That's ten times what I was paid! And he took the copper back!" He thrust an accusing finger toward Vernon.

Cutter whirled on Vernon, who recoiled and coughed up the five copper. The coins disappeared into Cutter's pockets. Then he turned back to Jeremiah. "You owe me five silver, Tourist. Now pay up."

"B-but," Jeremiah stammered. The gang of men had formed a circle around them and were closing. "I need some time! I'm sure in a week—"

They jumped on him, all at once. Far too many to fend off, and Jeremiah was in no state to do so anyway. In a matter of moments, he was pinned on his back, his hands and feet held down.

Cutter crouched beside Jeremiah's left side. "You came all this way to steal my money, that's something Cutter doesn't tolerate. What's your name, Tourist?"

"J-Jay," said Jeremiah. *Stay calm*, he thought. *Nothing is going to be helped by panicking.*

"Jay, you owe me five silver." He turned Jeremiah's hand over so it was palm down in the dirt. "You know how much five silver is? Let's count together. One." Cutter stabbed the tip of the knife into the base of Jeremiah's pinky nail and twisted.

Jeremiah's body spasmed in pain. He reflexively tried to clench his hand into a fist, but it was pinned flat. Even through the pain and the fear, he was sickeningly aware he could feel his fingernail shift.

"Two," said Cutter, and moved to the next finger, repeating the process. Jeremiah felt this stab touch bone.

"Three," said Cutter. This one was slightly off target and pierced the flesh to the side of his finger, sticking into the dirt on the other side.

"Four," said Cutter. Again, off target, this one piercing through the nail directly and cracking it in half.

"Aaaand five!" Instead of a puncture, Cutter sliced the tip of the dagger along the back of Jeremiah's finger, neatly splitting the skin nearly to his wrist. The crowd Oo'd at this last one.

Jeremiah screamed. He screamed because it was all he could do.

"That's the down payment," said Cutter, sheathing the knife. "Have my money next time I see you, you little shit!"

Jeremiah nodded with his eyes shut tight, tears running down his face. Suddenly he was being pummeled and kicked as, for a few more brutal seconds, the gang beat him relentlessly. Jeremiah instinctively curled into a ball to protect Gus and guard his head and stomach against the rain of blows. Then he was thrown back to the entrance of the alley by the men as they laughed, reveling both in the torment and the fact that they hadn't been the target.

Filthy, pouring blood from his hand, Jeremiah bolted. He paid no attention to where he was going, he just knew he had to get away, far away. The air burned his damaged throat, but still he ran, dodging down alleys to avoid the still-crowded streets.

Jeremiah fled until his body failed him, then he crawled into the darkest corner he could find and made himself as small as he could. A light rain had begun to fall. Pain and exhaustion made Jeremiah's head swim, and his empty stomach heaved bile onto the dirt.

Blood continued streaming from his thumb. Jeremiah lacked even a rag to bandage the wound. His blood ran down his arm and dripped to the ground, where it mixed with his sick and flowed in a tiny rivulet toward the mouth of the alley.

"Poor lad." Jeremiah snapped awake, not sure if the voice had been a dream. But no, someone was standing over him. The little river of vomit and blood pooled around the man's shiny black shoes, but he paid it no mind as he looked down on Jeremiah's huddled form. "Poor, poor lad. Tell me, my boy, what's your name?"

CHAPTER TWENTY

Ol' Pete

You're new to town, I take it?" The man was well dressed in a tailored suit. A gold brooch of a cluster of grapes was pinned to his lapel, tiny amethysts that managed to sparkle even in their dull surroundings. The man smiled down at Jeremiah.

"Help," Jeremiah whimpered, holding up his mangled hand. "I need help."

The man sniffed the air. "Come in from Otto's, did you? Fine way to enter the city, fine indeed. Not for the faint of heart. Any luck finding work, lad?" The man ignored the bloody hand like he couldn't even see it.

"Work? Yes. No." Jeremiah was starting to feel disoriented. "Look, sir, I know you don't know me. But I really need some help w—"

"Tragic that, tragic," said the man, shaking his head. "Hands come cheap in Elminia, yes they do." The river of sick and blood continued to pool around the man's shoes, but it seemed to bother him no more than the light mist from above. "Might need your name first, lad."

"Jay from Shabad," said Jeremiah. Despite his condition, the words sprang easily to mind. His story had been drilled into him relentlessly.

"Well, Jay from Shabad, I don't suppose you have any money to pay for the kind of help you need?"

"No, I just got robbed. But I'm good for it! I can get money, I can—"

"Perish the thought! Ol' Pete doesn't deal in loans." Ol' Pete crouched down next to Jeremiah, stepping fully into the lake of fluids at his feet. "How about you just owe me a favor, hmm?"

An alarm bell sounded in Jeremiah's head. That sounded dangerous. Exceptionally dangerous. But what choice did he have? His whole body was throbbing in pain, and he was starting to shiver in the rain. He didn't need Delilah to tell him he risked illness or infection if he stayed on the streets tonight with his hand flayed open.

"Sure," said Jeremiah. "I'll owe you a favor, that's okay. Just help, please help."

Pete beamed a smile at him that was all teeth. "Of course! No trouble, Jay, no trouble at all. Clearly Elminia has given you quite the reception, as she's wont to do. Come with me, right this way."

Pete patiently waited for Jeremiah to stand on legs that quivered like a newborn foal's.

"Splendid," said Pete, retaining the smile. He put a supportive hand on Jeremiah's elbow and guided him out into the dark human rivers of Elminia. Pete navigated them with practiced ease, even with Jeremiah in tow. No curse or spit fell upon them. No shouts or shoves slowed their travel. Jeremiah could have sworn he saw people actively avoid looking at them.

They crossed into a quieter street, one of those pockets of wealth with slightly nicer, less askew townhouses. "Here we are," said Pete. He led Jay through the tiny wooden gate barricading the property from the street and rapped on the door.

"Wait, don't you live here?" asked Jeremiah. "Why are you knocking?"

The door opened to a bespectacled halfling man with a pleasant smile. "Good evening, gentlemen," he said. "What can I . . . Oh, Pete." The color drained from his face, and he retreated inside.

"Evening, Skiva," said Pete, pulling Jeremiah into the home uninvited. The door clicked shut against the torment of the streets, and Jeremiah found himself in the foyer of a home that promised warmth, safety, and comfort. He felt horribly out of place.

"Hun? Who is it?" a lightly feminine voice asked from further inside. A halfling woman in a crisp apron and bonnet peeked around a corner. There was a crack of falling pottery as she laid eyes on Pete.

"Patricia," said Pete in greeting.

"You know Pete?" hissed Skiva at his wife.

"*You* know Pete?" Patricia countered.

"Choices, choices," said Pete, looking between them. "Skiva, I'm afraid the day has come. I'll be needing use of your home."

"For . . . for how long?" asked Skiva. His eyes went to Jeremiah, and Jeremiah could read a litany of fears behind them.

Patricia came out into the entry and clasped hands with Skiva.

"Just for tonight," said Pete.

There was a skittering of feet, and a pair of young halfling girls scampered into the room to investigate the new voice in their home. They skidded to a stop at the sight of Jeremiah and hid behind their parents.

"Hello, Lucille. Lyra," said Pete. Skiva and Patricia gripped their children closer.

"Uh, I have a surprise, girls! We'll be staying in an inn tonight," said Skiva.

The children's shyness was banished, and they erupted in excited energy. "A real inn? With adventurers and mead and . . ."

"Ski, where exactly are we supposed to go? Are we just going from inn to inn asking for rooms?" said Patricia, locking down one child while the other wriggled free.

"Perish the thought!" Pete waved a hand. "Head to the Drunken Gull and tell Alexander you need a room on behalf of Ol' Pete."

Skiva and his wife looked anxiously at each other.

"Worry not," said Pete. "No favor owed. This one is on me. But I *do* need you to make your way, quickly now."

"All right kids, grab your things," said Patricia, hurrying them along. In only a few hurried minutes the family departed, tempestuous tykes in tow.

Pete turned toward Jeremiah with a wide smile. "All right, my boy. Let's take care of that hand before you bleed all over this lovely home." He led Jeremiah to the kitchen, where the furniture was miniaturized and the dishes were half-finished, and inspected the wound in the light.

Jeremiah winced as Pete dabbed his hand with a damp cloth. The older man fished in his vest and produced a length of thin wire and a hooked needle. "Wait, what are you—ARUGHHH!" Jeremiah screamed as Pete squeezed the flesh around the wound together. He tried to wrench his hand away, but Pete's grip was like iron.

"Keep still boy, keep still," murmured Pete, his face still a genial mask of patience. Once Jeremiah stopped struggling, Pete pierced the skin with a hook and began threading the wire through over and over again, stitching the wound shut while Jeremiah bit into his other hand. "There's a good lad," said Pete. His concentration was unaffected by Jeremiah's hissing and spasms of pain. Through the haze of pain, Jeremiah was even able to admire the speed of his handiwork, the flesh being knit together tightly with rapid pulls of the cord.

"There we are," said he with a smile, placing the final knot. "That'll keep the red bits on the inside, won't it? Now, why don't we scare you up a spot of dinner? There's cheese and fruit in that cupboard there, and you'll find some biscuits hidden behind the flour jar."

Jeremiah quickly overcame any misgivings about eating the halfling family's food and fell upon it with gusto. Pete didn't eat or speak, merely waited patiently on as Jeremiah devoured the offerings.

It was the most satisfying meal he had had in weeks, an easy accomplishment considering how sparse the competition was. The food sat warm in his belly, and despite the horrific events of the evening and the pain persisting all over his body, Jeremiah felt at peace. Everything was going to be all right.

He was wondering if it would stretch the hospitality of his host to return to the pantry for another round when Pete spoke. "My good lad. Jay. I truly am sorry for what happened to you." Pete's face was etched with sympathy. "You were accosted by men of ill repute, who took advantage of your isolation. Nobody deserves the cruelties visited upon you, poor boy."

The kind words nourished Jeremiah nearly as much as the food and warmth. How fortunate he was to have met this man! Who would have thought such a wretched city could deliver him such a benevolent savior as Ol' Pete.

No sooner had he thought it than an alarm bell sounded in his head. Bruno's voice came to him. "If it seems too good to be true, it definitely is." Jeremiah blinked. How did Pete know what had happened to him?

"Tell me, lad, what brings you to Elminia, so unprepared and unconnected?" Pete folded his hands on the table and leaned toward Jeremiah. It was meant to show interest, but Jeremiah found himself compelled to lean away.

"Got into some trouble in Shabad, sir," said Jeremiah. "Ran with the wrong crowd, against my better judgment. Needed to take some space away."

Pete nodded sagely. "Ah yes, plenty of opportunity for trouble in Shabad for a young lad. I've visited Shabad many a time, you know. Some of the finest fruit in the world grown in Shabad, don't you think?"

Jeremiah shrugged. "Yeah, I guess they're fine."

"I was always partial to the markets on the Road of Royals, myself," continued Pete. "Tell me, Jay, did you have any favorites? Any recommendations for my next visit?"

Okay, here we go. First test of the cover story, thought Jeremiah.

"Not really," said Jeremiah. "There are a lot of markets, and I haven't tried them all. Besides, I've heard most of them are owned by one guy who has them all competing to sell the same things." Which was actually true. Word was there was no bigger scam than becoming an independent merchant in Shabad.

Pete chuckled. "But you *must* have visited the Road of Royals, yes?"

"Of course. It's the biggest market street in the city," said Jeremiah. *This is sooo much easier than when Delilah was testing me.* Pete was probing, sure, but Delilah had a way of interrogation that switched between inquiring about facts, opinions, and emotions. Between that and her "lawyer stare" as Bruno called it, she kept him horribly off balance.

"Jay, tell me of these troubles you had in Shabad. Perhaps it's something Ol' Pete can help with! I'm known for my sympathetic ear, I am."

"Just made enemies of the wrong people. Better to get some distance for a while till things cool off," said Jeremiah.

Pete nodded again, nothing but kind understanding. "All too common a happening to a young man just trying to make his way. And what was your line of work in Shabad?"

"You could say I was a specialist in discretion." Jeremiah watched Pete's face closely for a reaction, but the other man's expression of sincerest sympathy did not so much as flicker.

"I think you'll learn to like Elminia," said Pete. "She has a wealth of opportunity for a young lad of your skills, if only you know where to look." He gave Jeremiah another winning smile. "The right friends can make all the difference there. I was born here, you see, and while I admit she takes some getting used to, you need only learn how best to twist the fortune from her."

The odd turn of phrase caught Jeremiah's ear. That's what Pete was doing right now, to Jeremiah—prodding and testing, learning how to twist him to the exact shape needed. *Need to be careful here, Pete's checking for something. I'm not sure what, but he needs to think I do*, thought Jeremiah.

Arranging his features to show what he hoped was the expected amount of gratitude, Jeremiah nodded. "Thanks for sharing some of your fortune with me. I can tell you're a useful person to know around here."

Pete bowed his head with a humble smile, and Jeremiah knew he'd hit a point of genuine pride in the man. "I only do what I can to help those less fortunate than myself," Pete said. "We all must help raise each other up here in Elminia, lest the city succumb to those ruled by baser urges."

Another odd phrase. Jeremiah didn't think Elminia was about to succumb to Cutter and his gang. Could Pete be referring to the cult? He remembered what Bruno had reported, about something coming. Maybe he could do some twisting of his own. "Pete, does the city always feel like this?"

"Mm? To what do you refer, lad?" Pete raised a questioning eyebrow, but Jeremiah thought he saw recognition underneath. Maybe even fear.

"People seem . . . strange here. Like the whole city runs hot."

Pete smiled in that way that didn't quite reach his eyes. "Elminia's always been a place that rewards ambition, we're quite well known for it."

"But this seems like more than that," Jeremiah pressed. "It's almost frantic, like . . . I don't know, like an itch or something." Jeremiah didn't know where the wording had come from, but it felt accurate.

Pete laughed, a little too loud and a little too long. "That will happen in the highest production city in the world, you know. You'll get used to the hustle and bustle in time, I'm quite sure, especially with the help of a good night's rest."

Abruptly, Pete shoved away from the table. He clasped Jeremiah's good hand in both of his own. "A pleasure to meet you, Jay. I must depart to attend other business, but please make yourself quite comfortable, and I'm sure we will be in touch soon. Mustn't forget a favor owed, after all."

With a wink, Pete departed, leaving Jeremiah alone in a stranger's home. Well, not completely alone.

He pulled out a mildly traumatized Gus, thankfully protected from the worst of Cutter's ravages. "You okay, buddy?" Gus cheeped furiously and struggled to investigate Jeremiah's wounded hand. "I'm all right I'm all right, don't worry. I'm not sure if that ended in our favor, Pete's a pretty hard guy to read. Let's just make use of this night as we can, okay?"

Gus wouldn't calm until Jeremiah let him sit on his stitches. It was calming, almost blissful, and Jeremiah ate his fill.

CHAPTER TWENTY-ONE

Progress

His body still ached and throbbed from the beating he'd endured the night before, but Jeremiah's spirits were higher than they'd been in weeks. Besides the food and rest, Jeremiah had attempted to remove the fish stink from his clothing. But each delicate soap he had found and used had only managed to mix with the fish to create something new and worse. Rotten fish was one thing, but rotten fish and florals just smelled *wrong*.

Despite a powerful desire otherwise, the only thing Jeremiah had allowed himself to take from the house was a metal pan he'd spotted in the bin. The inside was thickly laid with the lumpy remains of a blackened dinner, someone had badly burned their meal, then given up the pan as lost. The underside, however, was smooth and flat—perfect to practice enchanting. He was thankful Cutter hadn't ruined his inscribing hand.

Bruno would have chided him for getting distracted from the mission, but Jeremiah had thought of an idea last night that he just couldn't shake. Once he tried it and got it out of his head, then he'd be able to think about the mission.

Jeremiah joined the throng of Elminians, trying to move through them like Pete had, with graceful sidesteps, slipping into the smallest of gaps, and careful stride length. If anything, he was shoved and jostled more for his impudence. Nevertheless, he managed to make his way to a quiet alley. Then he left and picked another alley several more blocks away from Cutter's lot, just in case. He arranged himself to be able to see if anyone was coming and set to work.

The new diagram took him an hour to complete. As the finishing touch, he laid a length of copper wire within a long trough he had carved. The copper was not just a bridge but a conduit in itself, and one that Jeremiah hoped would slow the flow of magic considerably.

Hopefully the diagram read *Strengthen . . . Pause*. Functionally, it should have been identical to the Strengthen plate he had made on the way to Elminia but achieved with far less effort.

"I am patient," Jeremiah told himself. "I understand this will likely not work. I am okay with that."

Jeremiah placed his hands on the pan, spoke the words, and felt the magic flow from him. The runes glowed briefly. Jeremiah noticed little black flecks on the pan and wondered if they were food, then shook his head to clear the thought. It still surprised him how much more of his focus enchanting required compared to necromancy.

"Moment of truth, buddy," he said. Gus looked up from his refuse pile and croaked.

Jeremiah ran the inscription tool across the surface of the pan yet left no mar in its wake. The enchantment had worked.

"Would it have been so hard for you to just tell me that?" Jeremiah grumbled at Thurok in absentia.

It would have been easy to tell you what to do, said Thurok in his head, *but something, something, you're weak and incompetent, something, something.*

Jeremiah looked over his work and realized he had forgotten to feel proud of it. He had done it, hadn't he? Here it was, magically strengthened metal. He had made an enchantment. But the feeling never came. It was satisfying that it worked, but worthy of pride? He'd save that for the weapons.

Of course, a flat plate was one thing. Taking this same diagram and somehow resizing it and wrapping it around the blade of a sword? He had no clue how to do that.

Gus croaked again and crawled all over the pan, banging his feet on the Strengthen rune.

"What? You want me to make it even stronger than it already is?"

Gus chased a cockroach.

Jeremiah shrugged and, with considerable effort, pried the copper wire from its housing. The enchantment, now effectively doing nothing, was inert. He was about to start carving another Strengthen rune when he got another flash of inspiration.

After having been Strengthened once, carving another rune into the pan was onerous. It took Jeremiah the rest of the morning before he was able to sit back and admire his work.

The diagram now read *If Strengthen, Strengthen.*

"There, happy? Now if it's being strengthened, it will strengthen itself. And it will do that until . . . uhh . . . I guess it won't stop."

He placed his hands on the pan and charged the new diagram. Nothing seemed to change. He left no mark with the inscription tool, but that had already been true. He flipped the pan around, shook it, but if there was anything different, he couldn't detect it.

"Sorry, buddy, I don't think it—"

Jeremiah yelped as the pan shattered like glass, disintegrating into thousands of metal shards. He waited, frozen and waiting for something else to happen.

After several minutes, Jeremiah relaxed. "Okay, that was awesome," he said, "but not what I meant to do." He pondered the result. How would he explain what had happened to Delilah if she were here? He set up the enchantment to make the pan stronger and stronger—meaning, harder and harder—until . . . "Oh, I get it! It became infinitely hard and that made it infinitely brittle . . . I think."

It felt like he had solved a little mystery. Jeremiah wasn't sure if he could actually *do* anything with it, but it was certainly something he hadn't known before. He desperately wanted a new piece of metal to work on.

"Spare a copper, sir? Ma'am? Spare a copper?" In Jeremiah's mind, the act of begging was something he would resort to when all else had failed. He had not anticipated that his breaking point would be so soon into his mission. It had been a week since Prim's and he didn't dare return there, or to any business within a ten-block radius of Cutter's lot. He found himself back on the treadmill of trying to feed himself before he could manage anything else.

The supper with Pete was a memory he revisited often, though he despaired at how quickly the hunger had returned. Within a day, his ungrateful body was demanding more food. Part of him hoped Pete would reappear to repeat their exchange of help now for ephemeral future favors.

The crowds rushed by at such a pace that Jeremiah was barely noticeable to. How many such people had Jeremiah ignored, back when he'd had somewhere to go? When he'd had coin in his pocket and bread under his arm?

Jeremiah forced his thoughts back to his present situation. Fantasizing about meals he'd had was fine for helping him pass the time between guard patrols all night, but it didn't actually get him any closer to his goal. Which was food.

No! Jeremiah reminded himself. *I am infiltrating a criminal underworld, uncovering a sadistic cult, and returning information to the empress.* All this to help his friends, who were being targeted because of something *he'd* done. Jeremiah forced himself to dwell on that guilt for a minute. It dismayed him how quickly the needs of the moment overrode what he actually needed to do here.

An elven woman appeared in front of him, pulling him from his thoughts. "Now why should I give you money that I worked for when you've done no work at all?"

Jeremiah was used to this kind of question by now. The only reason anyone ever stopped was to berate him. Sometimes, he stuck up for himself, tried to explain the challenges he faced, but it never actually resulted in a coin, so most times he didn't bother. He offered the woman a bland smile. She harrumphed with satisfaction and went on her way.

"Spare a copper? No? How about you, sir? Of course not." Jeremiah glanced in all directions in case Cutter's men were nearby, and drew his feet up closer to keep them from getting crushed under the wheels of a passing carriage. The driver screamed and kicked at him as they passed, hurling obscenities at Jeremiah while nearly crushing others on the street. Jeremiah leapt to his feet and began screaming obscenities back, a moment of intense blind hatred before he sat down again. He shook his head and rubbed his eyes. He hadn't thought he had the energy for something like that.

There was an undeniable urgency in the air. Over the past week, Jeremiah had begun to see . . . something. He saw it in the way people rushed from place to place, never talking to one another. Fights were frequent, even in the middle of the day and between people who were sober.

How'd I describe it, Pete? An itch? Yeah, an itch you can't scratch. He heard someone spit, then a scream, then a knot of people formed in the middle of the street. A fight out of nowhere, and the river of people just flowed around it. Then it was over, and the knot disappeared. Jeremiah hadn't seen what happened, who had fought, or who had won. It was just a burst of violence.

But even that was unremarkable lately. There were the things that were just strange. Jeremiah didn't have any other way to categorize them. Like the man holding a knife in the crowd, he saw incidents that were somehow wrong. A businesswoman dressed in finery devouring raw beef hearts like apples outside the butcher. A suicide by a guard immolating himself in the gutter with a bottle of lamp oil. A roofer who had suddenly turned and gouged out the eyes of his colleague in the middle of the street.

Finally, there were the dreams, or rather the lack thereof. At first, Jeremiah thought he simply wasn't getting the chance to sleep deep enough to dream, but he was starting to suspect he was indeed dreaming—and forgetting. He awoke each morning as though from a nightmare, his heart racing and sweat on his skin, searching wildly for . . . something. He could never remember what, but he was certain it had just fled.

Jeremiah glanced around again, just in case. He felt exposed out here, visible on the street. Cutter's men could be anywhere, he had no idea how far their territory reached. He was in no hurry to meet the other gangs that may be around either, not after what had happened. Bruno had warned him that a man with no friends on the streets was a dead man, but Jeremiah couldn't see a way to make friends without risking becoming a victim again.

There was the Pit, of course. Bruno had warned him to stay away from the Pit without a crew to back him up, but he couldn't stay up here either, there was nothing in the way of opportunity. The gangs up here weren't really *gangs* so much as bands of thugs like Cutter's group. Surely the Pit gangs couldn't be worse than Cutter's, right? His stitches throbbed, and he shuddered at the thought.

He needed an in, and it all came back to Pete. Pete would know how to get him into the Pit. But how to get him to share what he knew, especially without owing him more favors? There was a danger to Pete that he couldn't quite understand, but he knew that Pete was not really his friend. Helpful, perhaps, if Jeremiah could play his cards right, but never safe. Then there was the possibility that Pete was part of the very cult he was trying to infiltrate.

No, thought Jeremiah. *Something about that doesn't feel right. Pete doesn't seem like a cult type. He's too self-invested. Too networked. There's a lack of devotion there that just doesn't fit.*

Besides, Jeremiah had no idea how to even find Pete. He supposed he could just start asking around, but that seemed like a good way to attract the wrong kind of attention.

Jeremiah climbed to his feet. He had wasted enough hours sitting here and feeling sorry for himself. If he hurried, maybe he could scavenge some decent scraps from behind the bake house.

He had just stepped into the flow of traffic when a hair-raising shriek pierced the din.

CHAPTER TWENTY-TWO

Payment

Jeremiah turned in the direction of the scream, earning himself a torrent of swears and shoves from the other members of the current. But the scream was echoed again and again, finally causing enough disturbance that the implacable stream of Elminia was disrupted. People began to strain their necks and look around nervously, unsure of what was happening and where the screams were coming from. But Jeremiah quickly saw when part of the stream ran backward, quickly backing away from something.

Suspended high above the crowd was a body. Even from this distance, Jeremiah could tell it was freshly killed—blood dripped onto the crowd below. The people under the deluge scrambled to get away, some being knocked to the ground and smeared in red mud.

Jeremiah fought his way toward the body, fighting against the direction of the crowd as people backed away, eyes fixed on the horrific sight. The body had been stripped naked and hoisted aloft by wires connecting it to the buildings on either side of the street, its arms fully extended. The torso was wrapped so tightly in more wire that it resembled bread rising around twine. It was as if a metal spider had captured its prey and heaved it up for all to see. The head was missing, instead only an ovoid rod of metal jutted up from the stump of the neck, creating a facsimile of a complete body, albeit with a minuscule skull.

"Did anyone see what happened?" Jeremiah called out. This had to be one of the cult murders the empress had talked about. It was ghastly and dramatic, seemingly ceremonial in the extent of the preparation. But how had it gotten all the way up there with no one noticing? No one answered his question, lost as it was in the various shouts and voices around him. "You! Call the guards!" Jeremiah isolated one man and gave him the responsibility. "And you two. Get a . . ." The looks all three of the men gave him were of distress and confusion.

I'm a vagrant, not an adventurer. Can't let that part slip out. Taking decisive control of a situation and assigning tasks wasn't something starving vagrants did. A single step back into the crowd and he was just another face.

He stared up at the body, scanning for clues to its history or killer. He could see great gouges in the flesh around the wire wrappings, but nothing fatal. It was male, human, and well muscled. A laborer of some sort? Or a soldier? Adventurer? He had put up a fight, whoever he was. Jeremiah quickly scanned the crowd for anyone with obvious injuries that might be watching their handiwork, but no one met the criteria.

"How did this happen?" Jeremiah muttered aloud. The body was pouring blood, this person was recently killed. Maybe even *just* killed. How did it get hoisted up like this in enough time for it to still be bleeding so freely?

He followed the wires to the two supporting roofs and saw they were looped around hooks that had been hammered into the masonry. That would have taken time. Jeremiah slowly closed in on an assumption—he had likely been restrained, bound to bursting in the wire that Jeremiah could see still gleamed in the sun, never used. He saw indigo bruising around the wires where they had moved while he struggled. He'd been wrapped up for a while. Jeremiah couldn't imagine how painful that must have been.

Someone finally broke away from the crowd, a man gazing up at the body in awe. He wore the apron and clothes of a baker, flour dust still on his cheeks and beneath the nails of his thick hands. Walking as if in a daze, he stepped just in front of the pouring streams of blood, looking dreamily at them. He stuck out his hand and let the blood fill his cupped palm. Then stepped fully beneath the stream, shuddering and exalting beneath the shower. Blood cascaded down his head washing away the flour and painting him red.

The crowd gasped and recoiled in disgust. The man looked up and let the blood pour into his mouth. A woman stepped out from the other side of the street. An elven woman, elegant and venerable, wearing the complex and baubled attire of aristocracy. She walked just as the man had, the crowd shifted nervously as more gasps and frightened shouts went up. She stepped in front of the man, still exalting in his baptism. He looked at her. She smiled nervously. He reached out his hand. She took it. He pulled her into a passionate embrace as they kissed furiously beneath the torrent of blood, coating each other with desperate hands.

Jeremiah stared in shock, as did everyone else. There was something so horrifyingly taboo about what he was looking at.

No, not taboo, he thought. *This is something more. Something deep.* Some part of him was appalled and fearful of the display. *No, not the display—the people. Those two, they chose this. They wanted this. How could anyone want . . . whatever this is.* Alien. That was the word. This was alien.

"Move!" someone screamed, nearly in his ear. A man shoved Jeremiah and several others aside. "He's not getting any deader! Move! Worthless gawkers! Leave it to the guards! Some of us have work to do!" The man was red-faced with fury as he crashed his way through the crowd, stomped through the empty space in the road, and crashed his way into the crowd on the opposite side. He didn't spare the spectacle even a glance, it was of no interest.

His march seemed to restore Elminia's pulse, as the crowd suddenly surged ahead again, the flow of people restored. Though it still parted, as little as possible, to avoid the flow of blood and the passionate couple.

"What in all the evils of the world is going on in this city?" said Jeremiah.

A woman bumped against him, then spat on him in response. Without thinking Jeremiah reached out and yanked her back by the hair. She screamed and snarled at him, and Jeremiah jammed a hand in her pocket and yanked out a coin, then shoved her along with an indignant shout. He ducked away from the scene, breaking off down a new street and finding a stoop to sit on.

Jeremiah fished in his pocket and found a silver coin. The coin trembled in his palm. It could be food, or safety for a night. But where had it come from again? Right, the woman.

She deserved that, thought Jeremiah. *Lucky I didn't break her face.*

"*Excuse* me?" asked Allison.

Jeremiah winced. Why had he done that? That was incredibly excessive . . . but the coin. The coin made it worthwhile.

I was defending myself anyway, he thought. *She bumped into me, then spat on me! All she had to do was* not *do that and she'd be fine. Call it a manners tax.* He held up the coin and let it catch the sunlight.

"I would be disappointed in you," said Allison.

Jeremiah suddenly felt nauseous. What had possessed him to think like that? It was so . . .

"Hello, Tourist," said Cutter.

Jeremiah tried to flee like a frightened rabbit. He hadn't seen the group of men that had formed around the stoop all at once, so engrossed in the coin he had been.

Hands grabbed onto Jeremiah and threw him back onto the stoop. Jeremiah hit the ground hard. There was laughter, familiar and cruel.

"Payment's due," said Cutter. Jeremiah scrambled to face him. A thin line of drool hung from the corner of Cutter's grin. He looked even more deranged than last time.

"Here, take it!" Jeremiah tossed the silver coin to Cutter's feet. "That's all I have." There was no defiance in him to be found, just a painful terror.

Cutter began bouncing on his toes. He seemed agitated and frantic. "Not enough, is it? Not enough! Put it in the paper! Get it! Five silver! Get it! Get it! Yeah, get it!" Cutter babbled nonsensically.

With a shriek, Cutter leapt the distance between them and swung a fist at Jeremiah's head. Jeremiah recoiled and managed to deflect the initial blow, but Cutter kept swinging, raining fists down over Jeremiah's body, head, back—anywhere he could reach. "Where's my money? Gimme my money! Put it in the paper!" Cutter yelled over and over again.

Cutter didn't even seem to notice the few strikes Jeremiah managed to land. Jeremiah realized that Cutter was on something. He was too fast, too reckless, too intent on hurting Jeremiah to notice his own pain.

Cutter clawed at his shirt and ripped it open. He tore at Jeremiah's trousers, emptying the pockets and sending enchanting tools and lock picks flying. "This is my shit now. This is all my shit now!" Cutter shouted.

Jeremiah was being robbed, stripped, in broad daylight. He was dimly aware that a crowd had gathered outside of the perimeter established by Cutter's men, yet nobody seemed interested in interfering.

Jeremiah's hand fell on his metal files. He seized it, planted his heels, and thrust the file upward toward Cutter's throat.

He missed and the file gouged the underside of Cutter's chin instead. Cutter recoiled, shouting. His face went red, and his eyes bulged. He screamed in psychotic rage, then fell upon Jeremiah with even more fury. The crowd oohed and aahed.

"I'm the big man! I'm the big man! I'm ten men tall!" Cutter screamed. His nails raked Jeremiah's exposed skin. His fists pummeled every inch they could find. When Jeremiah tried to twist away, Cutter kicked him in the teeth, snapping his head backward and filling his mouth with blood.

There was no fight to be won here. Just like he'd done a week ago, Jeremiah curled into himself, covered his head with his arms, and tried to survive.

Gradually, Cutter's drug-fueled rage slowed. His breathing grew labored, the blows becoming more intermittent until they stopped altogether. "See ya . . . tomorrow . . . tourist," Cutter panted, climbing to his feet.

"Look, guy had a frog," said one of Cutter's men. Gus was trying to hop to the relative safety of the alley refuse, having been torn away with Jeremiah's clothes.

Without a moment's hesitation Cutter screamed and ran at Gus, kicking him into a wall as hard as he could.

Jeremiah's thoughts were shredded to a thousand microscopic fragments. Consciousness fled, leaving only darkness.

He groaned before he was fully awake. Fragments of what had happened began reforming in his mind, coalescing memories of fear and pain and—Gus!

One of his eyes was swollen completely shut, the other restricted to a narrow slit. It was still daytime, and he was on the same street. Someone had dragged him to the side, out of the way of foot traffic.

"Oi, you there. On your feet, you disgrace," said a voice above him.

Jeremiah's head pounded in pain. Two guards were above him, batons drawn. Jeremiah could feel the raw stone against his skin, he had been left beaten bloody and naked.

There were people gathered in a ring around the guards, curious and amused.

"Gus, where's Gus?" Jeremiah gagged. Something was loose in his mouth. A tooth? He couldn't tell. He rolled onto his hands and knees, and realized his clothes had been shredded. The remains of his trousers hung loose on his hips. His shirt was gone.

"Where's your clothes?" the guard asked, prodding Jeremiah with the baton.

Jeremiah, as hurt as he was, still tried to cover himself. The people stared openly.

"They're there," someone in the crowd called, pointing to the pile of rags rumpled by the stoop. The guard used his baton to pick up the torn trousers and tossed them at Jeremiah. They stuck to his stomach. As Jeremiah pulled them away, he saw a long and still bleeding cut across his stomach, the tacky blood stuck to the pants.

He tried to put the pants on, but he was so dizzy. His limbs had a mind of their own, and he fell over. A few people in the crowd laughed.

"Move on!" one of the guards yelled, brandishing the baton.

The other climbed up to meet Jeremiah on the stoop, apparently no longer concerned if he was a threat. "You do this to yourself?" he asked.

"No, guy named Cutter" was all Jeremiah could say.

"You did this to a guy named Cutter?" said the guard. Jeremiah was sure he must have heard wrong.

"What? Where's Gus?" was all he managed to ask.

"Are you saying you cut a guy? Whose blood is this?" the guard asked.

Jeremiah was so confused; he tried to walk past the guard but was stopped.

"I asked you a question, who did you cut?" said the guard.

"No one," said Jeremiah. His head was starting to spin.

"You just said you cut someone," the guard declared.

"That's what I heard," said the other, drawing her baton.

Jeremiah tipped over the railing and vomited a stream of pure bile and blood.

"Gods that's disgusting," said the guard nearest him, covering his mouth with a cloth.

"I don't want to deal with this so close to lunch, June," said the other guard.

"Yeah, me neither," said June. "You can walk?" June pushed Jeremiah, causing him to stumble down the stairs. "Yeah, you can walk. Get out of here. I don't want to see you on this street again or you're going to prison."

They left him. Jeremiah stumbled up the street, still bleeding, following a painful urgency in his head.

"Gus! Where are you, buddy?" He crawled to where he had seen Gus land and pawed through the refuse. "Come on, buddy, please," he whispered.

His fingertips brushed something soft and clammy. Jeremiah gently lifted Gus's limp form from the detritus. Gus's spines were fully protruded, his color sickly and yellowed. One of his legs was turned the wrong way around. He felt heavier than Jeremiah remembered. He was limp, in a way Jeremiah had never felt before.

Jeremiah cradled Gus to his chest. "It's okay, buddy, I'm here," he choked. "I'm here, don't worry, I'm here."

People rushed past uncaring, on their way to or from, but Jeremiah knelt in the dirt, holding his entire world in his hands. "I'm so sorry, buddy." Tears streamed freely down his face. "Gods, I'm so, so sorry."

Gus peeped.

Jeremiah nearly fell from how quickly he tried to move. Holding Gus firmly against his chest, ever careful not to touch the spines, Jeremiah ran. His every muscle protested as he forced his legs to carry him, his ribs seared with every ragged breath.

Never before had he detested the crowds of Elminia as strongly as this moment. He dashed and dodged around people and carts, darted down side paths, ignored the pain that flared with every movement, ignored the abuse hurled at him by whoever he knocked down. None of that mattered. Nothing mattered except that Gus needed him.

He and his friends had agreed upon a series of procedures for how best to approach the apartment. Jeremiah ignored every one of them, slammed the building door open with his shoulder and took the steps two at a time to reach their floor. He pounded on the door, praying someone was home, and when nobody was forthcoming, he kicked it hard.

The wood around the door latch splintered. With the next kick, the door gave, and Jeremiah rushed into the apartment.

"Delilah!" he bellowed, looking around frantically.

The apartment was empty.

Jeremiah swore and tried to collect his thoughts. Delilah kept her tonics in the Giant's Bag. If he held the one he needed clearly in his mind, it should give him the right one.

He charged into Delilah and Allison's room. The Giant's Bag was sitting on Delilah's bed, and he hurried toward it. Then he noticed it was slightly open and seemed to be emitting a thin line of vapor toward the open window. Jeremiah cursed again, re-secured Gus, and climbed into the bag.

"Delilah!" Jeremiah shouted again, as he floated. As he'd suspected, Delilah was already below, working in a crammed laboratory. At his voice, she jumped and screeched in alarm.

"Jay! What's happening? Why are you—Oh no."

Without another word, she took the toad's limp form from Jeremiah's hands into her own and set to work.

CHAPTER TWENTY-THREE

Presents

There was barely any spare room to pace inside the Giant's Bag, filled as it was with laboratory equipment, but Jeremiah made do with shuffling back and forth until Delilah ordered him to stop. She worked with her back to him, hunching over her tiny patient and effectively blocking Jeremiah's view. He tried to distract himself by identifying the plentiful solutions and chemicals lining the shelves. It wasn't very effective.

Time passed. Jeremiah wished he could at least make himself useful as an assistant, but Delilah moved too quickly for him to be anything but a hindrance. As the adrenaline wore off, the pain from the beating returned, and Jeremiah started to tremble. When he rubbed his arms and realized again that he was nearly naked, he decided to wait for Gus and Delilah outside the bag.

Some new clothes helped somewhat with the shivering. Bruno and Allison still weren't back, so Jeremiah commenced pacing around the tiny apartment while he waited. It already felt so foreign to him, this warm and comfortable place he'd lived with his friends, the fresh clothing that didn't stink of fish. He missed it.

Delilah finally emerged from the bag, cradling Gus in her hands. "He's going to be okay! I think. I'm not an expert on toads."

A wave of relief and exhaustion washed over Jeremiah at her words. He sank to the floor right where he was. "Oh, thank the gods."

"You're welcome," said Delilah. She knelt to place Gus gently in Jeremiah's lap. "He suffered extensive damage to his right hind leg. I've set and splinted it as well as I could, but he may have some difficulty hopping." She smiled as Gus nuzzled Jeremiah's hand. "He's a very, very tough little animal."

"Delilah," said Jeremiah, looking at her square with his good eye. "Thank you so much. Seriously. I can never repay you for this."

Delilah's eyes widened in shock as she took in Jeremiah's appearance. "I'm just glad you got him here as soon as you did, things could have turned out much differently if you hadn't. Now let's take a look at you."

With Gus out of immediate danger, Jeremiah became aware of the pain harbored in his own body. Gentle as she was, everywhere Delilah touched seemed to highlight a new injury. "Ribs are broken. Collar bone too. Damage to the jaw and teeth, orbital bone is . . ." She prodded him, eliciting a cry from Jeremiah. "Likely fractured. Hematoma of the liver, spleen, kidneys. Follow my finger with your good eye . . . good. Can you follow my finger with your bad eye? Can you see how many fingers I'm holding up? Anything at all? All right. Ears are clear of spinal fluid, good.

Seeing signs of chemical burns in your mucosal tissue. Somebody really did a number on you."

Jeremiah let his eyes close as she examined him, trying to keep his whimpers to a minimum. Gus was safe, and that was all that mattered.

"You'll need a speed healing tonic," Delilah continued. "I'll calculate a dose for Gus too. Go on, go lie down."

Jeremiah settled on his bed. Even with the unpleasantness of the healing tonic, he was looking forward to some real sleep in a real bed. Here, nobody would hassle him. He didn't have to jump at shadows, huddle under refuse for warmth, or worry about if the weather would turn.

"Here, I'll need to monitor you and run a few tests while you're healing. I need to make sure everything is settling back where it should," said Delilah.

He took the tonic she offered him and threw it back in a single gulp. At once, the alchemical fire began its steady march throughout his body. He'd taken it only once before, after their assault on the bandit camp, it would give him a month's worth of healing in a day but ravage his body with a fever and exhaustion.

Delilah tucked Gus's water bowl on the floor beside Jeremiah's head. The last thing he saw before the fever and exhaustion overcame him was his beloved familiar, sleeping peacefully at last.

Jeremiah awoke to even worse pain than he went to sleep with. His arms and legs were being restrained by two heavy weights, and Delilah was sitting on his chest. His vision was milky and strange, like he could only half see her.

"Jay, I need to cut your eye back open so I can stitch it shut right. Otherwise, it's going to heal wrong and you're going to lose the eye. I can't give you anesthetic while you're on the healing serum 'cause you'll die. It's going to be a bit uncomfortable, you're going to feel a bit of pressure," said Delilah in a very calm, professional voice.

"Huh? Delilah? What's going on?" asked Jeremiah. He tried to move but couldn't. He looked down and saw Allison.

"You're going to be okay," said Allison in a soft, nurturing tone. "One more drop of pain in the vast ocean of life." She was wrapped around Jeremiah's legs, holding them tightly together and putting all of her weight on them.

"Embrace the suck, buddy," said Bruno. "This counts as your first tattoo." Bruno was underneath and behind Jeremiah, holding his arms tightly behind his back.

"What does? What are you doing?" asked Jeremiah. He was confused. Was he dreaming?

Calm and collected, Delilah pressed a small cloth sack against the wall next to the bed. Something burst inside and it began to emit bright light.

Jeremiah, feverish and addled, finally realized what was about to happen as Delilah produced a tiny needle and line of thread.

"N-no!" he shouted, flexing every muscle he could to try and escape, but he was weak. Bruno and Allison had no problem holding him completely fast.

"It's okay, it's okay," said Delilah. She placed one hand on his head and forced it back, forcing the eyelid into an open state. "Just a little pinch, we'll be done before you know it. It'll be faster and easier if you just hold still."

Jeremiah had never known how strong Delilah's hands were, but now he could feel the unexpected power in the pressure she exerted on him. His eye was forced open, the lid quivering in its struggle to close, his eye already pulsing with pain was now drying out as well.

The needle came closer, growing larger and larger.

"Look to your right," said Delilah.

"Get off me!" Jeremiah screamed.

"I don't *need* you to look to your right, but this will be faster and less painful if you do. Look to your right." The needle weaved and bobbed, tracking some selected point for its first penetration. "You can scream, you can yell, you can call me any horrible thing you want, but look to your right, up at the glow bag please."

"This is your fault!" Jeremiah shouted at her in anxious fear, and he looked to the right.

"There we go, good job Jay, you're okay," said Delilah. The needle got closer, then disappeared from view.

Jeremiah spasmed in pain as something gently scratched his eye, then pressed, then something gave. Jeremiah could feel hot liquid running down his cheek. He kept his good eye on the glowing bag.

Jeremiah screamed, loud and high. He cursed Delilah, he called her every name and hurtful insult he could think of as she deftly worked a whisper-thick thread into his eyeball.

"I'm gonna throw up, I'm gonna throw up," Bruno kept saying over and over again, gagging at every thread pull.

"Kick as hard as you can, Jay," said Allison. "Come on, struggle!" They encouraged him to do anything he wanted, anything he could, to distract himself.

Jeremiah was, for a moment, back beneath Cutter. Helpless, powerless, being hurt against his will, tormented even. Totally lacking control over his own body.

It went on for an eternity, intolerable and unending.

And then it lessened.

"Just a little cold," said Delilah, and a cold liquid was squirted against Jeremiah's eye. "You need to not touch your eye. If you do, you'll open your suture, and we get to do this again."

Delilah's hand finally left Jeremiah's face, allowing him to close his eye at last. He could feel something on it, just behind the eyelid, something he wasn't allowed to touch or rub.

Allison slowly let go of his legs, then backed away. Bruno whispered to Jeremiah, "I'm gonna let go too, okay? Take it easy."

Jeremiah was released and lay on the bed, feverish and exhausted. From the pounding headache to the weakness, to the pain in his eye and in every part of his body, he felt like he'd never be able to rest again. But in time the exhaustion took him, and he slipped back into a throbbing painful rest.

Jeremiah awoke feeling like he'd been run over by a carriage. It was late morning, judging by the sun, and he could hear the voices of his friends from the other room.

He tried to sit up and regretted it immediately. His ribs ached, his guts burned, and his head pounded. Gus was still fast asleep in the water bowl. "Keep resting, buddy," Jeremiah said, and made his way more carefully out of the room.

"He lives!" said Bruno, as Jeremiah shuffled into the main room. "Despite his best efforts, far as I can tell."

"Hey, Bruno," said Jeremiah, lowering himself into a chair. There was a pot of something waiting in the hot embers of the fireplace that he was eager to investigate. "New look, Al?"

Allison was clad in city guard armor. Her unruly hair had been tightly braided across her scalp. She grinned and gingerly touched her hair. "They hurt a little, but I kind of love how it looks."

Delilah gave Jeremiah another quick exam. "Wiggle your jaw? Good. Open?" She peered inside his mouth. "Ah. Hold still."

Before he could ask, she reached into his mouth and yanked out a molar, root and all. The extraction was accompanied by only a quick sting of pain.

Bruno recoiled. "*Really?!* Right here at the table?!"

"Only one, not bad," said Delilah. "I'll give you something to keep it from getting infected, Jay. How are you feeling? What hurts?"

"Everything," said Jeremiah impatiently. "Can I eat now?"

Allison set a bowl of stew before him. "It's hot, eat it slow—oh, or just drink the whole bowl, that's fine too."

Jeremiah reveled in the feeling of the food hitting his stomach, only the second proper meal he'd had in weeks. It was hot, rich, and salty. "More." Then, after a moment's consideration: "Please."

"Nope, you'll have to wait a few hours first," said Delilah. "It's a special recipe for people who've suffered malnutrition, but you can't eat too much at once."

"While you're waiting, you should open your presents," said Allison.

"Huh?" Jeremiah raised an eyebrow. The gesture made his face hurt.

Bruno sighed. "Thanks to Little Miss My Mail Is More Important Than Op Security, you got a package delivered right to our door."

"It's pronounced *Doctor*," said Delilah.

It turned out to be two packages. The first was large and bulky. He started to tear the packing paper but soon stopped. He sensed something dreadful inside. "Uh-oh. I think I know who this is from."

"Uh-oh?" asked Allison. "Why uh-oh?"

"Okay, so it's sort of a tradition that when a mage freely gives a new rune, the recipient sends a gift in return," said Jeremiah hurriedly. His hand still hovered over the paper.

Delilah nodded. "Alchemists have a tradition like that. Very common to send things to your . . . teachers." She stared down at the package and froze. "This is from Flusoh, isn't it?"

"Jay what the hell is wrong with you?" asked Bruno.

"He was my teacher! I couldn't send it to Thurok and not him," said Jeremiah.

"Yes, you could have done that very thing," said Allison. "I don't care what it is he sent you, I want it gone."

"One second," said Jeremiah. What would Flusoh send? Something good? Something bad? Jeremiah hadn't the faintest guess. He tore the rest of the paper away in a single movement.

It was a book. Its smooth, black, leather cover was embellished with gold. The edges of the pages were bright white, unblemished and unstained by use. The title, inscribed on the front, read *Flesh*.

"Kill it," said Allison.

"Wait," said Jeremiah. He cracked the book open, half expecting a blast of magical energy, but it was simple paper and pages. A quick flip through revealed dozens of highly detailed anatomical structures.

"I know some of these pictures," said Delilah. "I recognize them from medical school. They were in some of our texts, but not this detailed. And certainly not this many."

It was a strange gift. Jeremiah had already gone through extensive anatomical study with Flusoh. "Is there something else to it?" Jeremiah asked aloud.

Jeremiah opened to the back of the book, and a note fluttered to the ground.

Jerry,
When you're ready.
—F

The final page was different from the others. It was a solid but paper-thin sheet of ivory. Etched into it, rather than printed, were the diagrams, notes, guides, and everything else Jeremiah needed to perform a spell.

"It's a spell!" said Jeremiah.

"Out!" Allison declared.

No, no, no, wait, wait, wait!" said Jeremiah as Allison tried to wrest the book from him. "It's a good textbook. I don't need to learn the spell."

"If you keep it, you will. That's how these things work, Jay. It's why he sent it to you. Give it to me."

Jeremiah relented, and Allison wedged it within the pile of cooking coals. Jeremiah watched sadly as she stoked the embers into flames and waited for the edges of those perfectly white pages to char and curl.

They watched it for several minutes. "I don't think it's working," said Bruno.

He was right. When Allison fished the book out of the flames, it looked just as pristine as when Jeremiah had unwrapped it. Even the ash fell away without staining the cover.

Allison frowned. She drew a dagger and slashed it across the word *Flesh*. The blade left no mark on the book, nor on any of the paper pages. "What is going on here?"

Bruno and Delilah gathered around now. Without asking, Bruno took out a small metal file and scratched at a tiny section of the cover. Nothing. Delilah got a bottle of a clear liquid from her Giant's Bag and poured it on a random page. The liquid slid off onto the table, where it hissed and bubbled. She then tried a rubber eraser, but the text and imagery were unmarred.

Allison had lost the look of frustration and now rested her chin in her hand in quiet contemplation along with the rest of them.

"I've got some diamond-tipped cutting tools, let me get those," said Bruno.

"Yeah, let me get some stronger stuff," said Delilah.

For an hour more, all four of them tried everything they could think of to destroy the book and slowly devolved to even trying to cause a page to crease. But try everything they might, the book could not be altered or damaged in any way.

Delilah stood by an open window, wafting fumes out from her latest acid attempt. "Green slime jelly is the strongest acid I've got. If that's not doing anything, I'm out of ideas."

"Nothing," said Jeremiah looking at the book. "But you're going to need a new table." The various acids had eaten holes in most of it.

"Any guesses?" asked Bruno. He was frowning at his failed diamond-tipped drill.

"Only one, it's an artifact," said Jeremiah.

"What's that?" asked Allison. She glared at the book suspiciously.

"You know how we can use magic runes and words to affect the world? And that those words are part of an ancient language? An artifact is when someone who knows a significant amount of that language speaks an object into existence." Jeremiah riffled the pages.

"Like, they just describe it, and it appears?" asked Delilah. Her curiosity only increased, and she scrutinized the book carefully. The scary book had become the interesting book very quickly.

"Yeah, they talk it into the world. And if you're going to go through all the trouble of speaking an artifact, and I assure you it's a *lot* of trouble. You're going to make sure it's indestructible." Jeremiah opened the book fully, seeing if he could crack the spine. Nothing. That was at least satisfying.

Allison contemplated the book for a long moment. "I think I'll hang onto it for you, then," she said with a fake smile.

"I guess that's fine," said Jeremiah. After all, he didn't intend to use necromancy again. Well, *again* again. What use would he have for it? Whatever secrets it held would be of no use to him. And he had no interest in learning them. He wasn't curious about that spell. Or the detailed diagrams. Or the notes in the margins. Or even in reading the entire book in one night.

Allison disappeared into her room with the book, and Jeremiah turned his attention to the other package. This one was much smaller and lighter, but Jeremiah had an inkling of the sender. He eagerly ripped the package open.

The package contained a square of metal. It had strange ridges on it, like it had been folded into this shape. Tiny engravings spiderwebbing across the metal.

"It looks kind of like an enchanting plate," said Jeremiah. "But why would Thurok—Oh!"

Jeremiah set the plate on the ground and gestured for the others to make room.

Placing his hands on the runes, he spoke the words of enchanting. The lines on the plate hummed to life with a brilliant cerulean glow. Jeremiah's head swam but managed to stay upright.

When the plate reached capacity, he pulled away to see what would happen. But the plate just sat there, the glow fading.

"Well?" asked Delilah.

"I'm not sure," said Jeremiah. "I hope this isn't a test . . . he would do that, too." He moved to pick up the plate and it rumpled.

Jeremiah froze, the metal still bunched up around his outstretched fingers. "What the hell . . ."

The others gathered around. Jeremiah pinched the metal. It felt soft as silk. He lifted it, and the metal unfolded like a garment.

"It's . . . a shirt?" asked Bruno.

Jeremiah started to correct him, but Bruno was right. The plate had transformed into a slim tunic with long tapered sleeves. Jeremiah pulled the garment over his head. The shirt was cold and shimmered like metal, but light and flexible as cotton. It clung to his body, moving when he moved. It fit him perfectly.

"It's armor. He used my rune to make flexible metal armor!" said Jeremiah. The craftsmanship was incredible. He swung his arms around, completely uninhibited. Casting would be no problem while wearing this. Despite the pain, despite everything, he was giddy with glee.

After some experimentation, they discovered the armor had been reinforced, much like Allison's full plate. Slashing it did nothing and stabbing weapons were diminished to an uncomfortable pressure, however it only softened the blow of a bludgeoning weapon.

Jeremiah got up off the ground, clutching his stomach from Allison's most recent strike. "Okay, still going to try to avoid taking a mace to the guts."

"This is absurd," said Delilah. "You can't just change the physical properties of a material like that."

"That's literally what enchanting does," said Jeremiah. He waved his arms around again, admiring the freedom. "I can wear this under my regular clothes, and nobody will know. This is perfect for being out on the streets."

An uncomfortable silence followed Jeremiah's proclamation. He stopped waving his arms and turned to his friends. "What?"

The others exchanged a glance before Delilah spoke. "We're just . . . surprised to hear you're planning to go back out there," she said kindly.

"Yeah, especially because you've made no progress in two weeks besides getting yourself beat to absolute hell," said Bruno, less kindly.

Jeremiah gaped at them. "I'm figuring it out! I've got a plan and everything. This was just a minor setback."

Allison crossed her arms. "Nearly killed is not a minor setback."

"But nothing's changed!" Jeremiah said. "I'm still the best hope we have of getting out from under this conspiracy. I just need more time!"

"What's *changed*," said Bruno, "is that you came back here. Something you weren't supposed to do unless you had no other choice. Now I'm glad you did, really, but that means you might be compromised. Mission failure."

"I am not—Ugh." Jeremiah rolled his eyes. "I am not *compromised*. I'm a vagrant. No one gave a damn about me bleeding in the street, and no one is going to give a damn about where I went."

Delilah put her hands in a placating gesture. "Look, we've been investigating the murders from some other angles. That's why Allison's got the uniform."

"It makes it easy to get around and keep an eye on things," said Allison, get into and out of places unnoticed. Hear the gossip and such."

"Oh," said Jeremiah. It made sense that his friends were doing things without him. It made perfect sense, and it made him feel horribly lonely.

"We suspect this cult draws membership from the lower classes but is run by people higher up," said Delilah.

"And we are trying to find out who those people might be," said Allison.

"There's more to it than that, though," said Jeremiah. "This isn't just a typical cult. Like what Bruno said, you can feel it when you're living out there. You need me."

"That's just it," said Allison. "We don't. Your method was one avenue of approach, but now we have others. Ones that don't get us nearly killed and cost us a pretty alarming amount of weight loss. What are the odds that your avenue gets results that are worth the risk?"

Jeremiah growled in frustration and turned toward Bruno. "Do you agree with this?"

Bruno shifted on his feet. "We're gambling with your life, and the payout's probably not great, Jay."

Jeremiah looked from face-to-face and forced a smile. "Fine. That's just fine. Glad I won't have to deal with that anymore. Can I have more soup yet?"

The apartment was empty. Allison had left for patrol, Bruno had disappeared to who knows where, and Delilah was working inside the Giant's Bag. "See? She's doing something reckless and dangerous, and nobody cares," Jeremiah grumbled to Gus. Gus peeped in agreement from his bowl.

Jeremiah pulled his new armored shirt over his head and layered a normal tunic over it. The metal still carried a chill that ran down his spine, but it felt like cold silk. He pocketed some new lockpicks and an enchanting file and made for the window.

Gus peeped again.

"Sorry, buddy, this adventure isn't for you." Jeremiah stroked Gus between the eyes. He turned back toward the window to plan his descent.

A splash from behind. Jeremiah hadn't realized Gus was capable of indignant hopping, but that's exactly what he saw in the toad making its way toward him. Gus's bad leg still stuck out at a strange angle as he jumped, but he was making his point clear enough.

Jeremiah sighed. "Yeah, I hear it. You don't like being told you can't—"

Gus made a loud raspy belching croak.

"No, I'm agreeing with you! You're right—if I need to do this, your place is right there with me." He tucked Gus into his shirt pocket, where, for better or worse, the familiar belonged. Then he climbed through the window and, with a series of maneuvers he thought might make Bruno proud, he disappeared into the night.

CHAPTER TWENTY-FOUR

Carrots and Sticks

O kay, buddy, so I exaggerated a little when I told them I had a plan. Big deal."
Near dusk, Jeremiah had made his way up onto the rooftops near Prim's.
"Once I improvise this part, we'll be set. Oh, and I guess there's also the part where
I convince Pete to do what I tell him. But after that, we're set."

Jeremiah peered down into Cutter's lot. The winding alleys below concealed just
how near they had been to Prim's, and he had a great view of everybody. From here,
the gang of junkies looked utterly small and unthreatening, but Jeremiah's heart
still raced when he recognized Cutter among them. "*We're just gonna watch*," he
reminded himself. "*No need to go down there*."

Pete was Jeremiah's goal, but he needed a way to find him. Someone in Cutter's
gang was the key. Pete had known what had happened to Jeremiah and where to find
him just a few minutes after it had happened. Someone must have tipped him off,
Jeremiah reasoned, someone who had a deal worked out with Pete to let him know
when a poor, vulnerable soul was at their lowest. And that someone was likely among
those thugs, drinking, lounging, and gambling below.

What would Pete's informant look like? Jeremiah tried to imagine them. He
would have to relay information, so sober enough to be coherent. He may have a
little extra coin from the deal compared to his associates, which meant he'd have to
be that much smarter to hide it from Cutter.

Jeremiah inspected the men arrayed before him. He could write off entire swaths
of them, the ones too addled to even raise their heads. But among the others . . . He
observed them carefully, noting who won the most games of dice and who did the
least showboating. After hours of watching, there was no clear candidate yet.

As the night wore on, the temperature dropped. Jeremiah shivered on his roof-
top, longing for the relative protection of the alleys and wishing Thurok had thought
to line his armor shirt with something warmer. Then he got lucky.

It was an older man this time, who was dragged into the lot kicking and screaming. Jeremiah was too distant to hear what the voices were saying, but he recognized
the script just fine. Anger, threats, excitement from the gang members. That same
violent glee from Cutter.

Jeremiah's breath froze in his chest as he watched the scene play out. The man
screamed, his voice echoing futilely into the night. Jeremiah wanted to leap down
and rescue him, be the savior he'd longed for. He also wanted to flee in the other

direction, to run out of Elminia altogether, to hide where Cutter could never find him. Instead, he stayed rooted in place, sick to his stomach.

The gang members laughed and praised Cutter for his cruelty while the man sobbed. They cheered every cry of pain, took their opportunities to elicit their own, celebrated their own good fortune.

Jeremiah hated himself for letting it happen. He was letting an innocent man undergo exactly what had been done to him, because he could learn from it. He was no hero. All those fantasies of adventure and saving people he'd had as a kid had come to this—watching an act of savagery from afar, one he could have prevented, or at least helped. But no. He was letting it happen. He was no better than all those people who had stood by while Cutter beat him in broad daylight.

In fact, he was worse—he had magic and training and could actually fight these men, especially with surprise on his side. And still, he did nothing.

The man was turned loose, and like Jeremiah had, he fled. The gang members jeered him briefly, then turned back to their game and drink. The gang settled back into the exact same state that Jeremiah had already watched for several hours.

Almost. After a few minutes, one of the drinkers stood to stretch. He sauntered away from the lot, pissed against the wall they all used, and then, instead of returning to his friends, he carried on down another side street.

Jeremiah slipped after him. The man's awareness was garbage, Jeremiah realized. He followed along at a distance, sticking to shadows as Bruno had taught him, but he was sure he could have tailed him simply by following him down the middle of the street.

As they drew nearer to a main street, Jeremiah worried he risked losing the man in the night crowd and hurried to close the distance. Thankfully, the man turned at a tavern on the corner, the Ample Room, and popped inside.

Jeremiah hid himself among some trash piles and waited. Cutter's man left after only a few minutes, a new bounce in his step. Jeremiah imagined he could hear the jingle of fresh coin in his pocket. A few minutes later, the tavern door opened again, and Pete stepped out, still saying his goodbyes to someone inside.

Jeremiah nearly emerged from his hiding spot right then and there, but something stopped him. The only reason Jeremiah still had use of his thumb was because Pete had been there. The only reason he hadn't been defeated entirely by Elminia that night was because Pete had rescued him. He had already allowed a man to suffer grievously in the name of his mission—he couldn't also rob him of the closest thing to salvation this city had to offer.

Pete walked by, every bit as put-together as Jeremiah remembered, and Jeremiah kept himself hidden. Now that he knew where to find Pete, he could enact the next stage of his plan whenever he was ready. In fact, he thought as he dusted himself off, he had accomplished something noteworthy and useful tonight. He should feel great!

Too bad all he felt was a terrible knot of guilt twisting deep in his gut.

Jeremiah followed a path that took him far from Cutter's lot and found his favorite alley spot. It was at the end of the guard's patrol, so he was only roused a couple of times each night and often could skip the early morning one if the guards got lazy.

He laid his head on a pile of dirty rags that he'd squirreled away as a pillow and was annoyed when his head hit something hard. Unwrapping the pile layer by filthy layer, he soon discovered the source of his discomfort.

A black book with gold bindings. *Flesh.*

"Uh-oh," said Jeremiah.

Flesh proved impossible to be rid of. It might take minutes or hours, but no matter where he left it, eventually the book would reappear within an arm's reach. The only reprieve was when Jeremiah would place it somewhere with the intention of retrieving it. In those moments, the book seemed to understand and would wait patiently for him. However, if Jeremiah thought for a second he might finally be rid of it, it would immediately return to him.

Oh man, Allison is going to be pissed, he thought. Last she knew, the book was in her possession. With Jeremiah disappearing in the night, she'll have assumed he stole it. *No, it's mine. I didn't steal it. I just took it back.* Yet it still felt like stealing.

Jeremiah put the nuisance of the book from his mind and reminded himself to focus on the mission. He needed to learn about the cult so Empress Aubrianna would put a stop to the conspiracy working to undo his friends' lives. The cult was recruiting from the lower classes, that's what Delilah had said. That's why he was out on the streets, to see what could be learned from here. Only, it wasn't like people were just handing out pamphlets about murder cults on street corners. He had to become one of them—someone valuable enough to be recruited. And to survive long enough to do that, to make enough of a name for himself to earn the right kind of attention, he needed a crew.

That's where Pete came in. Jeremiah knew Pete had the connections he needed, but what he didn't know was how to convince Pete he was worth connecting. After spending all day racking his brain to come up a strategy, he'd realized two things— first, Pete understood how this world worked far better than Jeremiah did, and second . . . Jeremiah had no leverage whatsoever.

But neither of those things were changing anytime soon, and Jeremiah couldn't wait around for a better opportunity, so here he was the next day, waiting outside the Ample Room for Pete to arrive.

He didn't have to wait long. Pete turned up at suppertime, opened the doors like he owned the place, and disappeared inside. Jeremiah forced himself to wait ten minutes, then hurried after him.

Jeremiah reminded himself he had as much right to be there as anyone as heads turned at his entrance. He spotted Pete alone in the far corner, with a liqueur in hand and meat pie untouched in front of him. He also spotted the barman heading toward his way with a familiar glint in his eye that suggested Jeremiah was about to find his way back out of the establishment.

"Hello, Pete!" Jeremiah called, waving his hand enthusiastically, as though greeting a long-lost friend.

To his relief, Pete's confusion was quickly covered by a graceful smile, and he returned Jeremiah's wave. The barkeep harrumphed but returned to his post.

"Jay! Wonderful to see you, my lad, simply splendid," said Pete. He stood to move Jeremiah's chair as though he were buttling a fancy dinner. "What happened to your face? Oh, please excuse my impudence, you must be famished."

Pete placed the meat pie before Jeremiah as though it had been procured specially for him. The rich scents made Jeremiah's mouth water, but he resisted—something told him giving in to the urge to devour the pie would lose any advantage over Pete he had.

Instead, he said, "I'm looking for work as a second-story man."

"Charming." Pete sipped his liqueur. "Go on."

"But I'm not looking for any old work," said Jeremiah.

"Oh, no?" said Pete.

"Not picking pockets and snatching purses. Real work. Proper second-story work," said Jeremiah.

"I see," said Pete.

"And I, uh . . . I want to work with an established gang," said Jeremiah. Pete was starting to pay more attention to the liqueur than to him.

"Naturally," said Pete. "Well, lad, there's a plethora of options for someone of your skill set. I'd be happy to make some introductions of course. If we're on the understanding that I may request your services at a later time, regardless of circumstances."

This wasn't going as Jeremiah had hoped. Pete had no reason to take a risk on him. All too easily, he saw himself being handed off to the lowest rung cutthroat gang to wallow in apartment break-ins and petty theft, all while owing Pete yet another favor.

He couldn't just be another nobody in Pete's pocket. He had to prove he mattered.

"So show him who's boss," said Allison.

"No magic," said Bruno.

No excuses, thought Jeremiah.

"I'm going to be honest with you, Pete," said Jeremiah, making his voice as cold as he could. "I could kill you stone dead at this very table with a single word."

Pete's smile didn't falter, but his eyes hardened. "That's quite the statement, lad."

"Shh, shh. Just watch now," said Jeremiah. He set the tip of his dinner knife into the table. With a few quick drags, he carved the enchantment rune for *And* into the wood of the table. It was a simple rune that did nothing on its own, but it was all he needed. He placed his hand on the rune, murmured a few words, and the rune glowed a soft azure blue, nothing more.

Pete's facade of polite gentry fractured as he watched Jeremiah perform magic. *Bet you didn't see this coming, you slippery bastard.* A lifetime of struggle against society's ignorance of magic, and suddenly it was his greatest weapon. He knew stories of curses and evil witches were coming to Pete's mind now. Or perhaps stories of men who could control fire and fly. Whatever it was, it wasn't going to be comforting.

"I'm going to tell you what I want, and you're going to help me get it," said Jeremiah, in a low, even voice. "I'll take no for an answer, but you won't live to see the end of the *O*."

As quickly as Pete's courteous demeanor had broken, it returned. "Perhaps you and I have had a misunderstanding, Jay."

"Perhaps we have. Allow me to clarify the situation. I'm a second-story man from Shabad. I'm very good at my job. Here I am in Elminia, looking for a nice strong gang to put my skills to good use. With me so far?"

"Yes, I understand completely," said Pete.

Oh, it's working! thought Jeremiah. *I figured this would take longer.* This felt like tough guy stuff, something other people did. People with face scars. "I'm looking for a position of opportunity," he said. "A chance to build my reputation and be noticed by the right kind of people. Do you understand?"

"Dear lad, you must realize—"

Delilah's lessons rang through. "Maintain control of the conversation. You asked a question. He will answer it."

"Do. You. Understand," Jeremiah said.

"Yes," said Pete. He swallowed hard.

"Fantastic," said Jeremiah. He finally turned his attention to the pie. Every time he thought Pete was going to talk, Jeremiah shot him a sharp look and he quieted. There was something delightful about watching Pete squirm. For the first time in weeks, he actually had control of something. It was exciting, and he wanted more.

When he was finished eating, Jeremiah wiped his mouth on a napkin and enacted a stroke of genius that had come to him between bites. "Give me your hand, Peter."

Pete didn't move. The blood drained from his face.

"You can give it to me and keep it, or I can take it from you and leave with it," said Jeremiah. He had no idea what that threat meant, but it did the job. Pete extended a quivering hand across the table. Jeremiah took Pete's hand and dragged the tip of the knife across the back of it. He didn't press hard enough to break the skin, but left a white trail, which became a rune. The rune was Pause, which, like the And, he had carved on the table, was useless on its own, but Jeremiah bet that to Pete, it would be mysterious and frightening.

"We're going to take a little walk to the Pit, Peter. You're going to introduce me to someone of importance. You're going to recommend me highly. You're not going to mention what you saw here. Peter, shall I tell you why you're going to do all this?"

Pete stared at him, wide-eyed and silent. *Good boy*, thought Jeremiah.

"You're going to do this because I've placed a rune on your hand. And if I find the opportunity you provide me lacking, then I will simply cast a little spell, and, no matter where you are, no matter what precautions you take, your hand will detach from your body and kill you. Maybe it'll throttle you. Maybe it'll stab you. That part is up to the hand. Look at your hand, Peter, what does that rune say?"

Jeremiah raised his eyebrows, indicating Pete could answer. "I—I don't know," he said. His voice was a faint whisper.

"Pure fear breeds contempt," said Bruno. "Show him the carrot. Make him want the rewards you can offer for his loyalty. Make him decide to be your friend."

"I know you don't, Peter. I know you don't," Jeremiah gave Pete's hand a little pat and sat back in his chair. "But it's not all bad news! My little skill is going to make me very useful to the person I work with, and they are going to be *very* grateful to you for introducing us. I think favors will be owed, Peter. I think I'll insist that favors be owed to the kindly man who helped me," said Jeremiah. "I still owe you a favor, too, isn't that right? And the higher I rise, the more valuable that one favor will become. Doesn't that sound nice?"

"That . . . sounds lovely," said Pete. The congenial smile was still there, but it quivered at the edges like a leaf in the breeze. Pete was holding terribly still, frozen by fear and uncertainty. This was not a situation he was accustomed to.

"Thanks for dinner, really," said Jeremiah. He dabbed his mouth with a napkin and dropped it on the table, then fixed Pete with a mirthless stare. "Now, whenever you're feeling up to it, I say we should enjoy a nice evening stroll." *Oh man, I feel so cool right now*, he thought.

CHAPTER TWENTY-FIVE

Leverage

The Pit, true to its name, was a massive hole in the ground with long, sloping sides. It was toward what once had been the outskirts of Elminia, but as the city expanded beyond its original footprint, the Pit came to be surrounded by slums—cramped, tiny buildings, squeezing tightly together to avoid tumbling over its edge.

"'Twas a mining pit in years long since past," said Pete. "If it's said that Elminia has an infection, the Pit is the wound that delivered it." He had relaxed somewhat during their walk from the Ample Room, testing the waters with snippets of conversation, though he did keep rubbing the back of his hand.

Jeremiah and Pete stood at the end of a narrow street of the slum, gazing down into the Pit that was somehow worse. The sides were crusted with dilapidated hovels, built thoughtlessly over one another like the scales of a scab and blackened with soot that grew thicker toward the depths of the center. The sheer density of smoke and fires gave it a hellish appearance.

Yet at the Pit's center stood a stark oddity—an ornate mansion with a burnished gold roof gleaming in the light of the moon, seemingly exempt from the choking ash and plague of degradation.

Jeremiah fought to conceal his awe from Pete. He feared he was already losing his advantage over the other man since they entered a situation in which he was completely inexperienced.

They began to descend into the Pit. There were no roads. Any space that had been used by the ancient miners for transit had long since been overbuilt. Jeremiah and Pete picked their way between the haphazard buildings, trying to avoid the more disgusting hazards. Refuse was everywhere, especially near the edge, where the inhabitants of the slums above added their own waste.

Many hovels were outright destroyed, great piles of burned rubble left to rot where they fell. Through the splintered timbers and pulverized bricks of one, Jeremiah could see little flickers of firelight. People were still living in the rubble.

Pete followed his gaze. "Not much to be said for safe constructions here, I'm afraid. Landslides are not uncommon. One building knocks down another, which knocks down another and another, all the way to the bottom. Then all the rubble gets turned into new buildings. Nothing goes to waste in the Pit."

Jeremiah sidestepped a pool of putrid food waste only to land his foot in human excrement instead. "Why do people live here?"

"There's not much in the way of 'rule of law' down here," said Pete. "No guards to make a bother of those sleeping rough, or theft. Or murder, for that matter. There is a freedom here rarely afforded in what one might call "more civilized society," and I daresay the denizens of the Pit do enjoy their freedoms. Access to urban niceties paired with being beyond the reach of the law has given rise to a number of neighborhood community organizations."

The denizens Pete referred to eyed them hungrily as they passed. While Pete certainly looked out of place in his finery, he carried himself as though he hadn't a thing to worry about, and indeed the gaze of any would-be muggers seemed to linger on Jeremiah instead. He sensed that if Pete were to disappear on him, his evening stroll would meet a swift and violent end.

Pete was speaking more freely now. He seemed aware that their environment had shifted control of the situation back in his favor. "I've been giving some thought to the right place for you, lad. You don't seem like a good fit for the Bricks, unless you're interested in smash-and-grab and protection work?" Jeremiah shook his head. "I suspected not. There's also the Simmering Idiots—they're into narcotics and distribution. Quite large, friendly to the small stature races, as well, but of course not as much opportunity for a second-story man, is there?"

Bruno had coached Jeremiah extensively on the type of group he needed to join. Gangs that were too large and established wouldn't need whatever boons were offered by working alongside a cult. Too small, and they wouldn't have the reach to get noticed by one. Jeremiah needed a gang that was growing and ambitious, one that would welcome and reward a new highly skilled member.

Pete continued his rundown. "The Men of Night have been making waves recently, if assassinations aren't something you object to . . ."

"Not at all your skill set," whispered Bruno. "You'd be a miserable assassin."

"I'd rather not, hardly any challenge in it," said Jeremiah.

"Look Jay, I'm a busy man. Why don't you tell me more about what you're looking for?"

Jeremiah heard the challenge in Pete's words. He needed Pete's help, but he needed Pete's fear and respect too. "I'll already told you—I'm looking for a chance to be noticed by the *right kind of people*. And you stand to gain from this as well. You do realize that, right, Peter?"

"It's Pete, and I—"

"Peter. I asked you a question." Jeremiah stopped and glared at him. *Know your place*, thought Jeremiah. *If I say your name is Peter, then it's Peter.*

Pete gave him a practiced smile. "Jay, my lad, I'm going to make use of you one way or another. Don't you worry about Ol' Pete. I've got big plans for you."

The feeling of threat had suddenly shifted. Jeremiah tried to regain composure. "Peter, you know my request. Any opportunities that will keep me happy?"

Jeremiah noted with satisfaction that Pete unconsciously rubbed the back of his hand again. "As a matter of fact, I do indeed have a thought, and if you agree, we can make our way to meet their boss immediately. I can tell you value your time as much as I value mine."

Jeremiah nodded for him to continue.

"They're called the Stonefists, and they dabble in just about everything—theft, narcotics, intimidation. Their leader, Monty, is always on the lookout for the next foothold upward. I suspect he will take a great interest in a young lad like yourself, especially on the back of such a glowing recommendation as I am happy to provide."

Always looking for ways to move up, huh? thought Jeremiah. It sounded like Monty was exactly the kind of person he was looking for. The dabbling sounded good too. That gave him different options to stand out if second-story theft didn't work out. Not that he was trained to do anything else, but at least the option was there. "Sounds like a winner. Let's go."

Pete chuckled. "I do warn you, lad, one does not simply step into such an organization. There is decorum that must be maintained. Initiation rights, you understand. Even with my heartiest support, you should consider them quite dangerous."

"Peter." Jeremiah put a hand on Pete's shoulder. "You're talking to the most dangerous man you've ever known." Jeremiah was bluffing, but he wasn't sure he was wrong.

In the Pit there was a hole, and in that hole, there was a stair, and down those stairs was a door, and through that door was Jeremiah's destination. Pete led him through an ugly state of affairs to reach this point, and it appeared that things were only going to get uglier.

Pete rapped on the door, and a tiny slider opened. "Pete," said the eyes behind the door.

"Evening, Mardok," said Pete. "I am here to speak with Monty, and to introduce him to a sterling young man who has recently arrived in our great city." He clapped a hand on Jeremiah's shoulder.

The eyes behind the door closed, and Jeremiah heard a sigh, "Pete, after last time I'm not sure if . . . It's just that . . ."

Pete held perfectly still, not letting his gaze or smile fall away. Jeremiah could feel a tension in Pete's hand. He sensed neither anticipation nor fear though. Was it rage?

"You know what, it's fine," said the voice after a moment's hesitation, "Come on in."

"You'll find my name opens many doors," whispered Pete.

"Reluctantly opened is still open, I suppose," said Jeremiah.

"Indeed it is, lad," Pete said, leading the way inside.

The Stonefists' headquarters was stiflingly hot and reeked of cheap tobacco. The room was too small for the large cookfire at its heart, and the narrow ventilation shaft left a heady smoke to cloud the low ceiling. Surrounding the cooking area, which was cluttered with bubbling iron pots, was the body proper of the Stonefists—an amalgamation of races and demeanors, each turning to regard Pete and Jeremiah as they passed.

"Hey, Pete."

"Who's the new meat?"

"The hell you looking at?"

"'Sup, Pete."

"Keep walking, little man."

They descended further yet, a set of stairs hidden in a dark corner. Each board they stepped on begged for mercy.

At the bottom of the stairs was a narrow tunnel that Jeremiah and Pete had to stoop to traverse. Several doors led off it, but Pete led Jay confidently to one in particular. "No shoes," he said, removing his own and setting them outside the door.

Jeremiah followed suit and waited as Pete knocked, trying to feel dignified and confident while hunched barefoot in a dark tunnel.

A voice bade them enter. Illuminated by a single candle, a dwarf awaited them behind a desk. Jeremiah's first impression was that he looked like a businessman. His hair and beard were jet black, with the latter trimmed to end in a perfect point, highly waxed and stiff. He wore a simple gray tunic.

The image was ruined, however, by the dwarf's immense hands. They were easily twice the width of Jeremiah's, with forearms to match. They were folded politely on the desk, but to Jeremiah they promised a capacity for violence that made him suppress a shudder.

"Sit," said Monty. His voice was soft, deep, and surprisingly delicate.

Jeremiah looked about, but there were no chairs in the room. The tiny candle did not illuminate far enough to see the walls, and he could sense more space beyond his vision.

"I said, sit," said Monty.

Looking to Pete for guidance, Jeremiah found him already seated cross-legged on the floor. He quickly followed suit.

Oh man, this is a hell of a power move, thought Jeremiah. Sitting in the dirt was an instant subjugation, and made Monty appear larger. Even the single candle cast Monty in sharp shadows and made him the only point of focus or reference. It was like entering a little universe in which there was only Monty.

Pete cleared his throat. "Thank you for meeting with us, Monty, on this most auspicious of days. I have brought along a young man whose introduction to you I believe will be of mutual benefit. He is a lad of extraordinary talent and pedigree."

"Quite the claim coming from you, Pete," said Monty. "Who else has he met?"

"You're the first. I knew you of all people would be most discerning over such a find," said Pete.

Monty turned his attention to Jeremiah. "What am I supposed to do with you?" His voice was eerily smooth and patient, never wavering.

An odd question, it was off footing right away. Jeremiah breathed evenly to try to control his nerves. "My name is Jay. I'm a second-story man out of Shabad and I'm looking to get back at it."

"Why are you here and not there?" asked Monty.

"Ran afoul of some killers," said Jeremiah.

"Nice and vague, less is more," said Bruno.

"Why'd you bring him to me?" asked Monty, turning back to Pete. "There's no shortage of second-story men who are not lying about their origins."

Jeremiah stared at him. "I'm not lying!" he shouted. Jeremiah regretted it immediately. It sounded forced and desperate. It was.

Monty stood. He made almost no sound as he walked around his desk and stood before Jeremiah. With both incredibly large hands, he gripped Jeremiah's arm, easily closing around the entire limb. "Tell me the truth."

Jeremiah instinctively yanked his arm as Monty's hands tightened like a python's coils. "Let me go!"

"Last chance. Tell me the truth or I squeeze till the tips of your fingers burst," said Monty. Still smooth, still delicate. Jeremiah could feel monstrous strength in Monty's hands, the pressure squeezing his bones and ramping up. There was a pulsing ache in his fingers.

Jeremiah looked at Pete, his heart pounding, but Pete just watched with polite interest. He had to act. He could still cast acid with one hand, he could lob it into Monty's face. Or the gas, he could—

"Be strong," said Allison.

Jeremiah glared into Monty's deep, green eyes. They were flecked with blue starlets and looked almost gentle. "Do it, then." The words came out of nowhere. "Either believe me or don't, I don't give a shit, but finish up so I can go get paid somewhere else."

Monty didn't so much as blink. The grip loosened. "The Stonefists are organized in cells of four members each. Beneath them are subordinates, who do whatever cell members say. You will be a subordinate. Put in the time, impress us, and maybe you'll be selected to join a cell. Then, and only then, will you be a Stonefist." He returned to his desk and refolded his hands.

"Press," said Delilah.

"Not good enough," said Jeremiah. The candle flame guttered.

"I'll let you try that again," said Monty calmly. Pete subtly shifted away from Jeremiah.

"Sir, I was the best second-story man in Shabad. The best." He fixed Monty with a hard glare. "Put me in a cell or I walk."

"If I may," said Pete. He waited until Monty nodded to continue. "I have confidence in the boy's talents, but I understand you cannot simply take my word for it. Set him a test to earn his place. In the extremely unlikely event that he falls short of your expectations, I withdraw any protections my association lends, and you may do with him what you will."

Jeremiah tore his gaze from Monty to stare incredulously at Pete. Somehow the man had created himself a no-lose situation—either Jeremiah succeeded and Pete had fulfilled his end of the deal or Jeremiah failed and would be conveniently finished off by someone else, removing him as a threat entirely.

For the first time since they entered the room, Monty appeared to be thinking. He leaned back in his chair and worked the point of his beard between his massive fingers, making sure it was perfectly neat. "I'll give you a chance," he said finally, "but I'm not wasting a potential heist target on you yet. Bring me one gold."

"Easy," scoffed Jeremiah. One gold was a ludicrous amount of money to beg, borrow, or earn, but surely it wouldn't be that hard to steal. This was very good.

"You have one hour," said Monty.

This was now very bad. "One hour?" exclaimed Jeremiah.

"Raise your voice again and it'll be thirty minutes. Should you fail to place a gold on my desk by the end of the hour, I will put out a hit on you. Your time began when you walked into this room."

Monty set an hourglass on his desk; sure enough, the grains of sand within were already falling.

CHAPTER TWENTY-SIX

Old Friends

Oane hour? I haven't earned so much as half a silver in weeks!" Jeremiah kicked the closed door of the Stonefists headquarters in frustration.

Pete brushed himself off. "Quite the pickle, that."

"Pete! Pete, can you spare me a gold?"

"Hah!" Pete barked a laugh, but a strange one, in a voice Jeremiah hadn't heard before. The voice was gone as quickly as it came. "I wish you luck, Jay, I truly do."

Jeremiah calmed himself. *This is no problem*, he thought. *I can run home and get . . . Run home. Run home and ask to be saved. Run home and prove I'm worthless.*

"Pete, maybe you can help me." Jeremiah chased Pete up the stairs. "I just need a target, someplace nearby."

"I believe my help is thoroughly exhausted. Now, I have some business to attend to. If you'll excuse me." He turned to leave with haste like Jeremiah's very presence was vexing.

"Wait!" Jeremiah caught Pete's wrist. We'll split the take, how about that?" He was pleading, on the edge of begging, giving up whatever strength he had in the relationship.

Desperation he thought.

"A most generous offer, Jay, my lad, but I do think you are wasting precious time—"

"And I'll owe you a favor!" said Jeremiah.

Pete was already smiling wolfishly. "Is that so?"

"Oi, you there, what are you doing?" A guard and his partner approached Jeremiah, hands already on batons. Jeremiah stood out like a sore thumb in this part of town, a place of flower boxes and swept streets.

Jeremiah heaved the sack off his shoulder. "Afternoon, sirs. Just making a bit of money," he said, standing at respectful attention.

"Bet you is. Open the bag," said the guard. His partner was eyeing their surroundings and looking into nearby windows.

Jeremiah dutifully opened the bag for the guard. "No trouble, sirs. Have a look. I get a copper for every ten."

The guard peaked in the bag and recoiled. "You found all those round here?" His partner peaked in and sneered.

"These and more sir. Do you want me to stop? Plenty more left," said Jeremiah. *And every moment I spend speaking to you is another moment I get closer to death*, he thought.

"Nah, keep on it boy," said the guard, "just don't cause any trouble."

"Course not, sir. Just earning my bread," said Jeremiah with a servile smile.

"Good man, honest living in what you're doing, if an ignoble one," said the other guard. He gave Jeremiah a clap on the back, surprising him.

"Thank you, sir," said Jeremiah.

Jeremiah had never been stopped by the guards before like that. Harassed out of his sleeping spot, sure, every night in fact. But just . . . stopped? It was a new and strange feeling.

Granted, they were right to be suspicious, but they didn't *know* that.

Jeremiah threw the sack over the low wall and followed it to huddle behind a manicured bush. His target was two houses away, but every home in the neighborhood enjoyed a tiny walled yard, intact windows, and a reasonable number of inhabitants. Even the street was quiet, with just a handful of people out and about. The absence of furious throngs made Jeremiah feel like he'd somehow left the city.

His target was an elven woman named Lady Shasee, who enjoyed splurging on flashy jewelry, or so Pete had said. Like most elven fortunes, hers had come from a long family line, now maintained through various ancient investments.

Jeremiah felt a twinge of malice. He had spent days begging fruitlessly for single coppers just to eat—the wealth and comfort on display here were like a slap in the face.

When he opened the sack, though, he couldn't help but smile. "Hello, old friends."

The sack was filled with dead rats. Rats had not been proven hard to find in the Pit. On the contrary, it was hard *not* to find rats. Accumulating a pile of dead ones had been a simple matter of bending down and picking them up, no killing needed.

He had an hour to earn a gold. Well, more like forty minutes now. It was his first robbery, and he hadn't even been granted the time to properly case the building or make a plan. Therefore, he told himself, it was only reasonable to fall back on old habits. Just this once.

Jeremiah hesitated. His reasons for swearing off necromancy flashed through his mind—the soldiers who'd been torn apart by his zombies, the man in the closet. The countless people who had seen his power as a tool to be twisted to their own purposes. And now he was preparing to go back on his word, not for some lofty, lifesaving reason but to do a bad thing.

But is this really a bad thing? Jeremiah thought. He was stealing from a woman who had plenty, in order to get closer to uncovering a depraved murder cult—surely that balanced out to good.

The clock was ticking.

"Power justifies its own use," Flusoh said. "Come on home."

Rise.

Jeremiah hadn't anticipated how good it would feel. Back in the dungeon, when it was just a skeleton, he had been too terrified to notice, but casting the spell now felt like stretching a sore muscle. The space in his mind was vast, and the rat bubbles were so small. He reflexively stacked them together, and the tiny amount of space they took up in his head painted a terrifying picture of how many he might be able to command at a time.

He tipped the bag, spilling the rats onto the ground. They waited, primed to move at his command. "I really hope that Shasee lady isn't around, or this is going to be one hell of a nightmare," Jeremiah muttered to Gus.

Climb.

The zombified rats sprang to life and moved together like a roiling flea-infested rug. They flowed over the garden walls and scuttled up the side of the elven woman's house. Lanterns flickered downstairs, so he sent them up toward a second-story window.

Jeremiah closed his eyes and focused on the sensations. It felt amazing. Just being in this state again, sorting the bits of information and exerting his will in a myriad of directions, gave him a peace of mind he didn't realize he was missing. Why did he give this up again?

The upstairs window was closed but not locked.

Squeeze.

When alive, rats were able to squish themselves nearly flat to slip through cracks in ways that'd defy imagining. As undead, when pain and organ compression no longer mattered, they were functionally liquid. The first rats crushed their own guts out while squeezing into the seams of the window, gradually forcing it open enough that the rest of the rats could pour inside.

The rats explored the room, gradually filling in Jeremiah's sense of the place until he could be confident it was a bedroom. Since he hadn't heard any screams of horror, he assumed the room was empty.

"Uhh . . ." This part was tricky.

Take?

The trickle of information from the horde became a chaotic torrent as the rats began pilfering random objects. Jeremiah struggled to make sense of what was happening. Several rats started trying to drag something heavy toward the window, and Jeremiah had to separate their bubbles from the stack to stop them. When each seemed to have something in tow, he recalled them.

Rats started streaming out of the window, back toward Jeremiah. He hoped it was dark enough, and any passersby uninterested enough, that they would go unnoticed.

Jeremiah opened the sack expectantly as the first rats returned. They scurried inside so he could evaluate the take.

In retrospect, Jeremiah should have predicted that the objects rats would choose, even zombie rats infused with his will, would be different from what *he* would have chosen. The sack was filled with crumbs of food, dead bugs, fluff, bones from a mouse, and torn pieces of fabric. A couple coppers made it in but nowhere near enough to equate a piece of gold. Clearly the rats had seized upon whatever was nearby, likely on the floor and under furniture, when he had given the command.

Jeremiah swore. He estimated he had only about half of the time remaining, and he still had nothing to show for it. "Okay, new plan."

This time he selected a group of bubbles to form a task force of sorts, just three rats to limit the onslaught of sensory information and allow Jeremiah to direct them more specifically. He hoped, anyway. He had never attempted anything like this.

The task force rats made their way back over the wall and into the bedroom. Jeremiah tried to figure out how to command them to do what he wanted.

Climb. Search.

The rats climbed the furniture and scanned around on top while Jeremiah struggled to make sense of what they were seeing. Large, flat, soft—that had to be a bed, thankfully unoccupied. Smooth, flat, good for biting—a wooden surface of some kind. Soft, up, movement—some kind of hanging textile—maybe curtains?

Jeremiah took a breath. He had never even considered this type of necromancy, but there was no reason he couldn't figure it out. Instead of spreading his focus wide, like he was used to when performing necromancy, he had to bring it in closer. Sharper. Like with enchanting.

The information from the rats became more concrete. Dull shapes came into focus, he felt textures under his fingertips. There was a dim light from somewhere in the room, but the rats didn't register it as a dangerous light that meant people. Jeremiah sent them to investigate. It was a large vertical surface, flat and too slippery to climb. It was emitting a soft light . . . a mirror!

Jeremiah had to stop himself from shouting with triumph. The mirror was reflecting the moon from its position above a vanity table. If this was where Lady Shasee sat every morning to get ready for the day, her jewelry collection had to be close to hand.

Sure enough, the rats soon found a large box resting on top of the vanity. Opening it was surprisingly easy—it seemed the muscle memory rats retained from pilfering human stores in life applied here. They scampered over the contents, prying little hard things from their resting places. The box was filled with small nonfood objects that the rats found horridly boring.

The rats swiveled as one toward a sound from downstairs. A person was moving about, which every rat knows means danger.

Now or never! thought Jeremiah. The rest of the horde streamed back out of the sack, over the garden wall, and up to the window. The footsteps were definitely making their way up the stairs. As the rats squeezed their way through the window.

Take, return.

He held the position of the box firmly in his mind as the rats swarmed over it. "Come on, come on!" he quietly urged them. They began scurrying back toward the window with their prizes, some of them struggling to fit larger objects through the narrow opening.

The footsteps were coming down the hall now, nearly at the bedroom. Jeremiah tried not to think about what would happen if Lady Shasee discovered a robbery in progress by a horde of rats. He tried especially hard not to imagine what would happen if it were discovered that the rats were undead.

He ordered them all back, whether or not they had an object. Surely whatever they had grabbed already would be worth at least a gold piece, including the split he'd promised Pete. The rats fled, then Jeremiah remembered to send one back to close the box. It scampered across the vanity and jumped on the lid of the box just as the doorknob to the bedroom turned. Jeremiah ordered it to hide and then severed the connection.

The rest of the rats swarmed into Jeremiah's sack with their treasures. Or at least, so he hoped it was treasure—before he could check, he needed to get some distance from the scene in case Lady Shasee was about to discover she'd been robbed. He lifted the sack over her shoulder and casually exited the bush, heading back toward the Pit as though he hadn't a care in the world. As soon as he turned the corner, he broke into a sprint.

Back to the Pit. Jeremiah ducked into the corner of an abandoned hovel and knelt, not waiting to catch his breath before he opened the sack.

Out.

The rats dropped whatever they held and swarmed out of the bag, leaving only their earnings behind.

Scatter.

The rats scurried off in every direction. Jeremiah gave them a few seconds before severing the connection. Dozens of tiny bubbles burst, and he was sad to see them go. It had been like regaining his vision after being blind for over a year, but only for a moment. He missed it. He had promised he wouldn't do it again, but he still missed it.

But I did do it again, he thought. That sparked a little ember of guilt in him. *It was an emergency,* he reminded himself.

"There will always be emergencies," said Allison.

He peeked into the bag, and to his relief, discovered a respectable pile of jewelry, gemstones of various colors glittering together along with silver and pearls. This was easily worth several gold.

Gripping the sack closed, he ran straight for the Stonefists' headquarters, not daring to stop moving lest an opportunistic citizen of the Pit decide to take whatever he owned for themselves. He wasn't sure exactly how much time remained of his hour, but he knew it couldn't be much.

Pete was waiting for him in front of the entrance. "Good evening, Jay. How are you finding things?" said Pete.

"Great. Move, Pete," said Jeremiah.

"I believe we had a bargain, did we not? I'll be taking my share before you turn it all over, thank you," Pete smiled congenially, but there was a slight edge to his voice, a sliver of a threat. He was still scared of Jeremiah, but depriving him of his share would be an insult too great to suffer in silence.

"Yes, okay, fine. Just take whatever," Jeremiah held the bag open for him as they descended the stairs, out of sight of anyone that might be spying.

Pete took his time. He sat down with the bag and sorted through every piece, even producing a small magnifying glass to inspect some of the details on the precious stones. Piece by piece he sorted them into two piles.

"Can we hurry this up?!" snapped Jeremiah. There was little time left, and he was beginning to worry some had slipped by without his notice.

"Patience, patience, all in good time," said Pete, his focus completely on the split.

"Power play," said Delilah. "He's just making you sweat."

"No, this is too small-time for a power play," said Bruno, his lessons and Delilah's conflicting. "He's up to something. Maybe an unfair split."

Jeremiah was surprised to see him eschewing the more elaborate items in favor of loose stones and simple designs. Perhaps it wasn't an unfair split after all.

"Thank you, Jay. It has been a pleasure doing business with you," said Pete, collecting and pocketing his earnings. "Now, scurry along. Monty is surely waiting."

Jeremiah just about flew to Monty's office, remembering only at the last moment to kick his shoes off at the door. The dwarf sat in the light of his single candle, as if he had frozen in place when Jeremiah had looked away.

About eight minutes of sand remained in the glass as Jeremiah triumphantly emptied the contents of the sack onto Monty's desk.

Monty didn't even glance at it. "What is this?"

"You asked for a single gold, I brought you several times that," said Jeremiah. He tried to sound brash, but a sense of dread was tickling the back of his neck.

"You brought me work," said Monty. "You brought me a fence's fee. You brought me personalized pieces I can't sell. You brought me gems and metals of unknown quality, that I'll need to pay to have appraised."

"Are you serious?!" barked Jeremiah. "You're going to feed me a line of shit like that after a one-hour deadline?!" Jeremiah leaned over the table and pounded his fist into the wood, causing the treasures to jump. His heart leapt into his throat, he hadn't meant for his temper to flare, but he couldn't help it. The fatigue, the hunger, the injustice, it all swirled together to make him more volatile than he had ever been. He expected Monty to leap up and grab him with those monstrous hands and break a bone, but Monty didn't even blink.

"Have a look," said Monty, he gave Jeremiah a bemused smile. He could have been a doting uncle, indulging a child's tale of imagination.

Jeremiah swallowed and took a closer look at the treasures.

Monogrammed. Every piece of significance was monogrammed or stamped with a crest. All of it was custom. The gemstones, few that there were, were small and cloudy.

"And all of this . . . isn't worth a gold?" Try as he might, he couldn't keep the pleading out of his voice or his eyes.

Monty kept smiling. "Could be. But it's a lot of work on my part just to check, which I certainly don't owe you. So, best second-story man in Shabad, by my count, you have four minutes and forty-three seconds to produce my gold. After that, and not one second later, I offer the fine men and women upstairs—who have earned my trust the old-fashioned way—the chance to collect your head for the same price."

"I—I can't! That's not enough time!" said Jeremiah, backing toward the door.

Monty wiped his desk clean with a massive hand. The treasure clattered as it hit the floor. "Tragic."

Jeremiah ran down the stairs, his mind racing even faster. As he got to the top one of the lounging men grabbed him.

"Hang on a minute, now, hang on," said the man. His face was a patchwork of scars, with a dozen poorly cared for metal piercings in the process of making new ones. "Let me see you, let me see you." The man turned Jeremiah's face back and forth. "Oh, this'll be easy. I've got this one in the bag," said the man with a laugh.

"Hell you do, Dag," said a halfling woman cozied up with her pot of soup. "I'll have him inside an hour."

"Hey, Parga, want to team up on this one? Fifty-fifty?"

"Nah, let's make this one a good ol'-fashioned race!"

They all laughed as Jeremiah shoved the man away and made for the door. He had to think of something, but what? Run up the Pit and rob the nearest man hoping for a coin? He'd never make it back in time, even if he miraculously picked a gold from the pocket of the first man he saw.

He threw open the door and sprinted up the stairs. Maybe the head start would be enough to make some distance. A shadow loomed over him at the top of the stairs, backed by the blinding light of the setting sun.

"Need a favor, lad?" asked Pete. He was holding a gold coin in his outstretched hand.

CHAPTER TWENTY-SEVEN

Made Man

There!" Jeremiah slammed the gold coin on Monty's desk.

Monty raised one eyebrow. "You left my office all of"—he glanced at the hourglass—"two minutes ago, and in that time, you managed to find a gold?"

"Yup, just like you asked." Jeremiah massaged a stitch in his side.

"The point of the task was *steal* a gold to prove your worth as a second-story man."

"He said what he said. Press him on that fact," said Delilah.

"Ah, ah, ah! You didn't say that," said Jeremiah. "'Bring me one gold' is what you said. Here's the gold. I get to join a cell."

Monty closed his eyes and let out a groaning sigh. "While I can *only imagine* where this came from," he said, as though he knew exactly where it came from. "I said what I said. That's on me."

Jeremiah held his breath.

"You're in. Congrats. I'll add you to the register. And by the way"—Monty picked up the coin and closed it in his fist—"if it turns out you have no business being part of a cell, your exit will be far more expedient than your entrance."

Jeremiah exhaled. "Thank you, sir. Don't worry, it wasn't a fluke."

"We'll see. I still think you're lying about who you are." Monty dropped the gold back onto the desk. It wobbled where it landed, the previously flat disc was now bent in the middle. "But if you can do a good job for the Stonefists, then I suppose it doesn't much matter."

"You're Jay, right? Our new Slip?" A woman found Jay where he had been hanging around in the Stonefists headquarters. She was a gnome, with wide eyes and a small nose, standing chest high. A tight leather belt at her waist held two coils of thin rope and a scabbard for the rapier. She looked him over with a skeptical eye.

"Yeah, that's me," said Jeremiah. He was relieved—he'd missed dinner, and the company of those who'd been so recently hoping to collect a bounty on his head left something to be desired. It seemed they had been looking forward to his inevitable failure, and he had spoiled their fun by succeeding.

"Sweet Melissa. Let's go," she said.

Jeremiah followed Sweet Melissa out of the headquarters and into the still-dark shambles of the Pit. "Gotta ask about the *Sweet* part," he said. This was apparently some sort of new coworker, so he had to try to establish a bit of rapport.

"No idea," said Sweet Melissa. "Was given to me when I wasn't around. They still won't tell me."

Jeremiah snorted, and to his surprise, she flashed him a smile and laughed too. "Don't make fun," she said, and gave him a friendly push. He realized that he was thoroughly touch starved and, as a result, he was instantly smitten with her.

Ain't you a cutie? he thought. Everything about her was playful; the eyes, the smile, the little double step she had to do occasionally to keep pace with him.

"It was just a funny answer," said Jeremiah. "I wasn't making fun."

"You were gonna," said Sweet Melissa. She gave him another playful smile. "I can tell a teaser when I see one. And you, sir? I think you might be a tease."

Okay, she comes on a little strong, but that's okay, I can get behind that, thought Jeremiah. This was fun and, in a weird way, a relief. He hadn't had much of a chance to just have a nice feeling in a while, and it filled a need he wasn't aware he was wanting.

"So, I'm staying with you? In a building?" Much as he was enjoying the playfulness, the possibility of a night indoors was even more enticing.

"With me and the guys. We're Cell Four. Of course, if you've got something better lined up, by all means. But where's the fun in that?"

Jeremiah was shaking with excitement. This would change everything. He could sleep. He would feel like a person again. The night back home had only sharpened his desire for a roof and bed.

Sweet Melissa brought him to a building that perched on the very edge of the Pit, a leaning mess that looked ready to topple down and crush everything beneath it in an avalanche of dilapidation. It was beautiful.

She handed Jeremiah a key. "All you."

Jeremiah put the key in the lock and turned. With more effort than should be necessary, the deadbolt slid aside, and the door jumped open.

Sweet Melissa ushered him inside with a little curtsy. "Welcome home, Jay."

They ascended a set of rickety stairs leading to a door, upon which Sweet Melissa performed a rapid series of knocks. The room it opened into was small, to say the least, but it was moderately clean. Jeremiah was more than willing to overlook the tiny water stains beginning to form in the corners and some mysterious red tinge along some of the floorboards.

Two half orcs lounging on a couch looked Jeremiah up and down. "Well, you get what you get," sighed one.

"Don't listen to him, we're happy to have a new Slip," said the other. "I'm Shugga. This is Dronkal. We're your knockarounds."

Jeremiah waved at them, the orcs glanced at each other, and then Shugga waved back. "Hi?" said Shugga.

"I'm sorry. That was weird," said Jeremiah. Weeks of relative isolation was apparently all it took to rust up his social skills.

"Little bit," said Shugga.

"Been a rough day," said Jeremiah.

"I'm sure," said Dronkal.

"You're embarrassing us, and we're not even there," said Bruno.

"Hi," said Jeremiah. "I'm Jay."

"There we go! Good to meet you Jay," said Shugga. Dronkal sighed and rubbed the bridge of his nose. Shugga slapped Dronkal's knee. "Stop that. You know how hard it's been."

The half orcs could have been twins. Both were tall and ropy with muscle and shaved heads, and they wore matching leather armor. Their tusks were stubby, more like fangs than the tusks Jeremiah had seen on other half orcs. Each wore a pair of identical metal-capped truncheons at their hips. Knockaround meant the muscle, responsible for intimidation, they certainly seemed suited to their role.

"Jay here just skipped being a Subby," said Sweet Melissa, draping herself over an armchair. "Impressed Monty enough to get promoted right up the chain, lucky us!"

"Aw, I kinda miss the Subby days," said Shugga. "They get to get their hands dirty. We mostly just give out orders," he added for Jay's benefit.

"With a slip we can get back to some real profit work," said Dronkal. "Last Slip messed up and got himself a few years. We've mostly been collecting protections while we waited for a new one, bit of drug-trade stuff, and we've got a couple teams mugging. But it's been a while since we could do a big score. Couple of knock-arounds and a call aren't the best for the big jobs, you know?"

Jeremiah glanced around the room for another member. *I see the two knock-arounds, but where's the call?* Sweet Melissa batted her eyelashes at Jay. "Oh! *You're* the call?" said Jeremiah. Calls were killers, lethal enforcers, for when intimidation wasn't important.

"I'm your killer. Yes, sir," said Melissa proudly.

How is something so cute a killer? thought Jeremiah. He reminded himself that he had seen Delilah kill a lot of people, and that rapier at Melissa's side didn't care how cute the wielder was "So, how do we get jobs?" Jeremiah asked.

"Usually they come down from Monty," said Dronkal. "You find a lead, you can run it up the chain and if he likes it, you'll usually get it. Not always. But if you try to run a job without his say . . ."

Smack. Shugga hit his open palm with his fist. "Boss don't like that."

Jeremiah nodded. "Easy enough." He stifled a yawn. The stress of the evening was starting to get to him.

"Hey, Melissa, why don't you show Jay his room?" said Shugga.

"I have a room?" It seemed too much to hope for.

"Right up there," Shugga said, pointing. "There's also a kitchen, but you're on your own there. We don't do family meals or anything."

"Your door has a lock," said Dronkal. "No one's gonna bother you. I've been where you are right now."

"Huh?" asked Jeremiah. *Where am I, exactly?* he wondered.

"You'll see what I mean. I made a sandwich for you," continued Dronkal. "It's in your room. Head upstairs and lock the door."

Jeremiah didn't need to be asked twice. The room was unremarkable, barely more than a closet, but there was a bed in it, and a window. A window that let you look outside without actually *being* outside. In the corner was a basin of water, a cloth, and a true feast of a sandwich.

Little motes of rain were just beginning to appear on the window glass. He closed the door like he had closed a thousand doors in his life, but this time when it clicked shut the silence of the room was everything. He was alone, truly alone. He threw the bolt, and the shabby room became a fortress. They couldn't get him here. Anyone.

He placed Gus beside him. Gus was safe, still, and quiet. Total silence. There were no wild dogs, no lurking rats, no city guards. No judgmental friends and pressure and arguments.

Jeremiah ate his sandwich slowly, very slowly. He savored every bite. Something was releasing in his body. As he finished his food, his eyelids began to grow heavy.

Jeremiah stripped down and went to the basin. The water was warm, comfortably warm. There was a sliver of soap. Jeremiah washed, feeling like he was exposing skin that hadn't touched air in a long time.

The heavy eyes grew to lightheadedness. He staggered over to the bed and crawled under the sheets. The bed was as cheap as they come: a frame with a lattice of rope. It was perfect.

No one is going to get me, thought Jeremiah as he laid his head down on an actual pillow. *I can sleep. No one is going to get me.* Dronkal's words finally made sense. He had been where Jeremiah was now.

Jeremiah suddenly burst into racking, silent sobs. They were over quickly. Sleep wasn't the word for what Jeremiah fell into, it was catatonia.

Jeremiah woke with a start, heart pounding, hands already forming the movements he needed to send an acid ball at . . . what, exactly?

The previous night came back to him piece by piece as his terror subsided. It was still here, the tiny room that was all his. The lock remained secure. Sunlight and bustling sounds from the nearby slums came from the tiny window.

Jeremiah pushed himself up to sitting, and his hand landed on *Flesh*. He was unsurprised. He'd last seen the book sinking to the bottom of the canal tied to a rock, but it returned now sans rock or string. It wasn't even damp.

"I should practice some enchanting," he told the book. He had food in his belly, a safe place, and nobody was demanding he go somewhere else. It was a perfect opportunity.

Instead, he ran his fingers over the cover of *Flesh*. Books were meant to be read. He'd read a lot of books, and nothing bad had ever happened.

"It would be irresponsible of me to not to learn more about the artifact," he explained to Gus.

Gus replied with a soft croak of agreement. He plopped himself next to the book to be within petting distance.

"Flusoh made it for me as a gift, and it seems to have imprinted on me. I'm not going to be able to get rid of it anytime soon, so it would be unwise to ignore it."

"Uh-huh," said Allison.

He opened the front cover, resisting the urge to flip to the ivory page detailing the new spell. The first page of the book showed a single drawing of a nude, male human. The next page focused on dissected views of the human's arm and shoulder bones, musculature, circulatory, and nervous systems. The detail was exquisite, drawn by the hand of a master artist. Perhaps Flusoh himself.

The diagrams were engrossing, as were the margin notes reminding the reader of common anatomical variations or highlighting traits specific to humans compared to other races. He read for almost two hours before the book moved past just exploring the arm and shoulder and continued onto a section about the hand.

The detail of the hand was so incredible Jeremiah felt like he could touch it. He did, and it moved.

"Nope!" Jeremiah slammed the book shut.

What had just happened? Hallucination? Trick of the light? Brain injury born of malnutrition and blunt-force trauma?

He slowly opened the book again. It fell open to the same page with the hand. By chance or design he wasn't sure.

"I am a mage," he said out loud. "Learned and brave and other positive things."

He jabbed the illustrated hand. It was like poking a page in any book. He wiped his fingers across the drawing, and the hand followed the movement. The ink of the illustration simply bled in the direction he dragged his fingers, not leaving a trace behind. It moved like a liquid pouring across the page.

After the shock wore off, Jeremiah found the game delightful. He danced his fingers all over the page, and the drawing changed as he did so, the joints moving and the perspective rotating in response.

"Gus, you have got to take a look at this!" He made a broad gesture to demonstrate the effect to his familiar, and the illustrated hand flew off the page entirely.

Jeremiah's jaw dropped. The inky hand, in all its detail, floated in midair. It was not just a flat drawing anymore but a three-dimensional model, albeit one rendered in ink. As before, it responded to his movements, the fingers moving and rotating as he prodded it. He glanced down at the page it had come from and saw ink bleeding through to reform the drawing. No shortage, then.

Playing with the hand captivated Jeremiah for so long that Gus grew bored and took a nap. It was wondrous, one of the most miraculous things Jeremiah had ever seen, but something niggled at him.

What was the point? Why go through the enormous effort this book must have taken just for an advanced anatomy lesson? He had to be missing something.

Jeremiah flipped the book to a random page. It showed the section of the leg between the knee and ankle of an orc.

Can I . . . a fragment of an idea crossed his mind.

"Yeesss," said Flusoh's gleeful voice in his head. "Yeeeeeeessssss!"

He pulled the piece of orc leg off the page and let it float beside the human hand. With a few quick touches, he maneuvered the hand over the end of the leg, where a foot ought to go, and connected the muscles together.

The hand flopped around as Jeremiah flexed the orc calf. The leg-hand was complete.

"Oh gods, that is creepy," said Jeremiah. "This isn't just a fancy reference book, then. It's a way to experiment with building . . . *things!*"

"Abominations," said Flusoh.

Flusoh had mentioned teaching him about abominations when they'd last more than a year ago, and it seemed that his teacher had created *Flesh* as a way to impart that knowledge in his stead. Most likely, the spell at the back was the key to assembling the amalgam creatures.

"Again, abominations," said Flusoh.

"Well, I definitely don't need to learn the spell," said Jeremiah. "But I can play with the pictures. There's no harm in that."

"None at all!"

CHAPTER TWENTY-EIGHT

Heist

Jeremiah spent the entire day in his room, playing with the book and falling asleep whenever he felt like it. It was blissful.

As evening fell, Shugga knocked on Jeremiah's door. "Look sharp. Monty's coming 'round with a new job for us."

Jeremiah dressed and hurried downstairs. His three new cellmates were already gathered. Sweet Melissa was counting lengths of silken rope, sitting on Dronkal's back while the half orc did one-armed push-ups. Shugga sat quietly on the sofa, his elbows on his knees and his head bowed.

"So, uh," Jeremiah said to announce his presence.

Sweet Melissa gave Jeremiah a huge smile. "Good morning, sunshine! You must have impressed Monty an awful lot for him to be giving us a job right away."

Dronkal grunted. "Or he's trying to make you fail out early."

Jeremiah had his suspicions as to which guess was correct. "Any idea what the job is?"

As though in answer to his question, a complex rhythm rapped at the door. Sweet Melissa chirruped with excitement and skipped to answer it.

Monty wore a pitch-black tunic and pants, very similar to what Bruno would wear on a mission. He strode into the room as though he owned the place—Jeremiah supposed he did, actually—and addressed them. "I'll cut right to the chase. A few blocks up from here is a stash house for the Blackshades. They've got a shipment of Dismal set to be distributed and released tomorrow. I want it stolen."

"Joining us, boss?" asked Shugga, raising a brow at Monty's outfit.

"I am," said Monty.

"Really?" asked Jeremiah. "It's awful nice of you to look after me on my first job."

Monty looked to Jeremiah directly. "I'm here because you don't make any sense. You claim to be the best second-story man in Shabad, you complete a burglary of a target you've never seen in less than an hour, then you get fleeced by Pete right outside my door. On top of that, I have to walk you through what's fencible and what's not. So you're lying, but you maybe still know what you're on about. Tough for me to suss out. Saves me a lot of trouble if you just fail or die."

Monty grinned at the look on Jeremiah's face. "You know your letters and your numbers?"

"I do," said Jeremiah.

"See?" Monty said to the other cell members. "I'm telling you, he doesn't add up."

"We've all got secrets boss," said Shugga, waving off the suspicion. "I don't care if he's a prince, so long as he does his job and lets me do mine."

"He suits me just dandy," said Sweet Melissa. Jeremiah thought he caught a wink from her but couldn't tell.

Dronkal grumbled and gave Jeremiah a long penetrating look. "Anyway, what's the play?" he finally asked.

It took Jeremiah a moment to realize they were all looking at him, waiting for him to speak. "The play? What do you mean?"

"You're the Slip," said Shugga. "This is a Slip's job. You want us to wait here? Somewhere else? Help scout?"

"Monty too?" asked Jeremiah. With all of one robbery under his belt, a magically enhanced one at that, he did not feel ready for this.

I'm supposed to work alone, he thought. *I don't know anything about leading a heist crew.*

"I want to see you in action for myself," said Monty. "I'm sure you're *well* versed in leading a heist crew," he finished with a smirk.

"Oh . . . kay!" said Jeremiah. He tried to imagine how Allison would handle the situation. "This is officially an operation!"

"I'm thinking he's military. Or a spy. Something government related," Monty said to Dronkal.

"Undercover guard corps? Investigator?" Dronkal offered back.

"Nah, they wouldn't be bothering us. He's too small anyway," Monty crossed his arms and puzzled over Jeremiah with Dronkal.

Jeremiah turned to Monty. "So, are you actually good at anything? What do I do with you?" he couldn't let Monty get away with just blatantly harassing him in front of his new cell.

"I can do anything you need me to do, better than anyone else here," said Monty matter-of-factly.

He registered no offense from his cellmates at Monty's claim, so he suspected the dwarf wasn't exaggerating. *So true it's not even disrespectful to say out loud,* he mused. "All right, first things first. I gotta case the place. Melissa, I want you on close support. Give me space to work but be ready to come if I call you."

That prompted a big smile and salute from Melissa. "Yes, sir!"

"The rest of you fan out. Make your own way to the target, then get a vantage point to keep watch. Monty, you're up high. Shugga, Dronkal, you're backup in case things go south. Keep an ear out but don't draw attention. I'll get eyes on the situation, and we meet back here in an hour. I'll let you know how we're gonna nab the goods."

Dronkal snorted and murmured to Monty, "Nab the goods." Monty nodded sagely.

"Blades out?" asked Melissa.

I think she's asking if we bring weapons or not. Better safe than sorry, reasoned Jeremiah "I—"

"No killing unless absolutely necessary," said Monty, cutting him off.

Jeremiah raised his eyebrows. "Is this my operation or not?"

"This is your operation, and I am the leader of the Stonefists, which is my opera-tion," said Monty.

Jeremiah tried to think of a comeback but couldn't fault the logic. "Well, every-one be armed anyway."

"And you?" asked Monty. "You don't have a weapon."

"I . . . guess I don't," said Jeremiah. How had he missed that? He was so used to being able to cast magic, he hadn't even considered that someone in his position should carry a weapon. *Do I make an excuse? Say I lost it? Sold it? Oh god they're all looking at me.*

"That is just so pure," said Melissa. Jeremiah's long pause after his confession had answered all questions for him.

Monty plucked a butter knife off the table, one that would struggle valiantly against butter, and handed it to Jeremiah. "Careful, it's sharp." Shugga and Dronkal snickered.

"All right, shut it!" Jeremiah barked, tucking the knife away. "Everyone, meet back here in an hour. Melissa, let's go."

"Yes, sir!" said Sweet Melissa. She opened the door and bounded down the stairs. Then she poked her head back up. "Mm, 'sir.' I like the sound of that. You gonna get me in trouble bad, Jay." She bit her lip and batted her eyelashes at him before slipping away again.

You're gonna be a lot of fun, aren't you? thought Jeremiah wickedly. She might be exactly what he needed right now. *A damned pretty face and a literal partner in crime. Won't complain about that!*

The rest of them began to follow. Jeremiah let Shugga and Dronkal leave first, but as they left, he caught Dronkal's eye. Dronkal's expression went intensely seri-ous, his eyes wide with concern, or possibly fear. Dronkal's eyes flicked out the door, and he shook his head at Jeremiah, just a little. The entire gesture took a fraction of a second, practically instantaneous, but it conveyed such a palpable warning that Jeremiah couldn't even pretend he hadn't seen it.

Do not touch the crazy.

Sweet Melissa led Jeremiah through the slums toward the Blackshades' stash house. "Alone at last," she said.

Now that he was looking for it, there was something unmistakably preda-tory about the gnome, something that made the hairs on his arms stand on end. Something his brain knew, even if he himself didn't. "Is it normal for Monty to join you guys?" he asked, trying to divert the conversation back to business.

"Nope." Sweet Melissa started weaving close to Jeremiah. "He's taken a liking to you."

"That's what a liking looks like?" said Jeremiah. "I'd hate to get on his bad side."

"Okay, more like an interest. Monty is a very busy man. It's not unprecedented that he's taking the time to monitor you personally, but . . . well, the people he's interested in either go far or die quickly."

"Do they die because Monty kills them?" asked Jeremiah.

"Him or me," said Sweet Melissa. "And if you need to, I sure do hope it's me," she finished coquettishly.

Oh god it was right there the whole time, and he hadn't seen it. Jeremiah suppressed a shudder. "Is that the place?" They had come into view of an ugly squat building. The second floor had long since collapsed, but the bottom endured. For now. All the windows Jeremiah could see were boarded up, with candlelight peeking through the gaps.

"That's the one," said Sweet Melissa.

"All right, keep an eye out in that rubble there. Shout if something seems wrong, but don't leave. I need to know where to run to if I have to," said Jeremiah. *If trouble finds me, I sure want trouble to find you too,* he thought.

"Remember, don't run *to* me; run *past* me," said Sweet Melissa. "And don't touch any ropes." She began looping out lengths of rope from her belt, where Jeremiah realized she had dozens of spools of thin cord waiting. She climbed into the rubble of a building that Jeremiah had pointed out, leaving him alone in the shadows.

Jeremiah could hear Bruno from their lessons. "You remember what to do first?"

First, we case, thought Jeremiah.

Very slowly and keeping his distance, Jeremiah began to orbit the building, looking for any points of entry besides the front door. There were no sentries, likely to avoid standing out. *Could hop up to the second floor, see if there's a hole.*

"You could. Walk me through what would happen," said Bruno.

I get up to the second floor. Likely make a bunch of noise. Stands out, no reason for anyone to be up there. Probably isn't structurally sound, either. No go.

"Correct. Good."

Despite just being in his imagination, Jeremiah felt smart having avoided a mistake. He continued his deliberate loop of the building, listening closely.

He caught a hint of a voice from inside. *Nothing the candlelight didn't tell us,* he thought.

"No?" said Bruno. "I find most times when there's a speaker, there's a—"

Listener, right. So, more than one person.

"We're a good distance away, and you haven't heard anything else," said Bruno. "Why would a single noise carry that far?"

It was a shout. Or an exclamation. It was louder than anything else if they're talking, thought Jeremiah.

"You often shout at your friends when it's just the two of you?" asked Bruno.

No. Someone got excited . . . there's an audience, thought Jeremiah.

"Atta boy," whispered Bruno.

Windows are all boarded. Roof is a mess. Front door is . . . likely the front door. How do I get in? He considered setting the building on fire but decided it would likely burn whatever he was supposed to take. Rats were, again, an option, one that he was a little too excited for.

"There's always an excuse," said Allison

No, not this time. It was just once. We can do this correctly, he thought.

Jeremiah noticed an oddity. Part of one window near ground level allowed hardly any light at all. He took a chance and darted close.

Huddled in the shadow of the building, Jeremiah tried to squint between the wood boards, but they were pressed too tightly against one another to allow it. The shadow was still being cast against the window, unmoving. Something large and stationary was inside.

Jeremiah considered his options. A crowbar would allow him to break a board, but that would be far too loud. Unless . . .

He pulled out the table knife Monty had given him earlier. Scraping with his enchanting tools would be too noisy, but if he pressed the blade of the knife into the wood, perhaps he could indent the surface just enough for the rune to function.

Over many painstaking minutes, he imparted the rune Gently Decay into the surface of the largest board. The lines of the diagram were of uneven depth, their alignments imprecise.

Thurok would be ashamed, thought Jeremiah, frowning at the work.

"I am ashamed," said Thurok.

Oh, what else is new!

But as far as he could tell, the enchantment was complete. Jeremiah whispered the magic words to empower the diagram. The runes glowed, and a sizzling sound emanated from within the wood, like thousands of tiny bubbles popping in a glass of champagne. Shameful or not, the enchantment was working.

Jeremiah pressed his fingers into the wood. It came away in his hands like a repulsive clay, but this part was silent and most importantly, he soon had a hole that would be large enough to squeeze through.

The light was being blocked by what looked like a stack of crates. For a wild moment, Jeremiah dared to hope they contained the Dismal he was after, whatever that was, but he soon realized they were empty. Putting his hands against the bottom-most crate, he pushed the entire stack a fraction of an inch.

Jeremiah held his breath. He heard no break in the murmur of conversation inside, so he risked another push. And another.

Eventually the crates had been moved enough that Jeremiah wiggled his way inside. Flat between the wall and the crates, Jeremiah took shallow breaths. The position reminded him all too much of waiting behind the vault door for the golem to find him. He shook the memory and stepped carefully toward the edge of the crate tower to see into the room while remaining hidden.

The stash house was a large, plain room. In the center of the room was a card table, where seven people were hunched over their hands. Beneath the table was a chest, this one sporting a large padlock. His target was sighted.

Jeremiah studied the load-outs of the card players. Two of them wore metal breastplates and had greatswords on their hips. The rest were lightly armored with knives, no serious threat besides their number. Even so, altogether they made a formidable group. There was no way he'd be able to just sneak off with the chest.

He slipped back outside, no one the wiser, and reconnected with Sweet Melissa. A short walk later, they reconvened back at the house and Jeremiah described what he had seen, saying the hole in the wall was a happy coincidence.

"So, what's the plan, then?" asked Dronkal. "You're saying you can't filch it?"

Jeremiah shook his head. *How do I phrase this without sounding crazy?* "I think this situation calls for a smash-and-grab."

"We're outnumbered, outarmed, and outarmored, and you want to turn it into a fight?" asked Sweet Melissa, raising her eyebrows and bouncing a little. She sounded more impressed than anything.

"I think we can even the odds and take them by surprise," said Jeremiah. "They're just hanging around, so they're not ready for an attack, much less one that comes from inside the building."

Shugga and Dronkal exchanged a look, concern mirrored on their features. "I'm not liking there being greatswords in that room," said Shugga. "That's real hardware."

"Monty, do you think you could take two unarmored humans in a fight?" asked Jeremiah.

"Yes," said Monty without a moment's hesitation.

"And Sweet Melissa, can you make a rope snare?"

"Absolutely," said Melissa. Her hands dropped to the ropes, her fingers flicked, and like magic was a small looping knot in the cord.

Jeremiah nodded. "We snare one of the armored guys at the door. They'll be the ones answering, it's their job. At the same time, we attack from inside, in a full rush. Don't even let the others out of their chairs. If we strike hard and fast, we can overwhelm them. At the very least, I can snatch the box and run if it turns into a fair fight."

They all looked at Monty.

"You go first," Monty said to Jeremiah, "and you leave last. You try to deviate from that, I'll kill you myself."

Leading a charge was definitely not part of Jeremiah's skill set, but it would have to do. "Deal. Sweet Melissa, get your snare up. Everyone else, follow me."

The four of them, minus Sweet Melissa, waited in the shadows beside Jeremiah's ingress point. Jeremiah saw Monty run one of his massive fingers along the edge of the board where the enchanted wood had come away. The dwarf scowled, but didn't say anything.

Jeremiah started when Melissa crept up on them.

"Trap is set," she whispered, "but I need to trigger it manually. I'll rush in the front door while you rush in the back."

"Nonlethal," said Monty.

"Boss, you can't be serious," said Sweet Melissa. She looked shocked and appalled.

"They've got real steel in there," said Shugga, pointing at the building. "You can't hold us back like that!"

"Not worth risking a war with the Blackshades over Dismal, no matter how much of it they have," said Monty. "You can kill the armored ones, they're outside muscle. But no one else. If they want to run, you let them run."

"It's just the Blackshades boss," said Dronkal, a bit more measured in his response. "They don't have the muscle to hit back, even if they wanted to." The others nodded in agreement.

Monty nodded. "True. But they've been closing the noose on a lot of different smuggling routes lately. There's a future where they take dominance of the trade. If we're on their list when that happens . . ."

"We get cut out of an entire income stream," said Dronkal, nodding along with Monty now.

"Getting a stash house raided is the cost of doing business," said Monty. "Killing makes it personal."

Shugga and Melissa joined the nodding, Jeremiah realized he was nodding along with them.

The dwarf has some vision, he thought.

"Let's get this done," said Dronkal, ending the learning moment.

"We'll get in position," Jeremiah said. "We go on your signal."

Jeremiah slipped back through the hole in the wall. There wasn't room for all of them in the space behind the crates, so the others would break through as soon as they'd gone loud. Jeremiah hoped they would, at least. Charging the card table alone would be a nasty way to learn Monty was sick of him already. His heart raced with the promise of an imminent fight.

BANG! BANG! BANG!

Jeremiah heard the men at the card table jump as someone pounded on the door.

"Go see who it is. We ain't expecting nobody for another few hours," said a voice.

"Probably Dondinger. I seen that halfling scum sneaking around lately."

There was a long silence.

"Well? Go earn your pay!"

Someone grumbled and Jeremiah heard a chair moving, and the sound of a sword being unsheathed. One of the mercenaries.

Shugga reached through the hole and pried the table knife out of Jeremiah's hand. Jeremiah looked down to see the handle of a proper dagger pressed into his palm. He smiled his thanks to Shugga. The weapon failed to make him feel any safer.

"What are you going to do?" asked Allison.

Scream. Charge. Try not to die, thought Jeremiah.

"War cries are for warriors. Why don't you stick with the advantage of surprise?" said Allison.

"Silent charge," Jeremiah whispered over his shoulder. He heard Shugga pass the word back.

Allison's voice continued, "You're going first, and the most dangerous man in that room has a breastplate and broadsword. Can you kill him?"

Almost certainly not, thought Jeremiah.

"Can you take him out of the fight long enough for the others to help?"

Yeah, I can do that.

The front door opened. "Hey! You touch this door again and I'll cut you from stem to—HUAAH!"

Without a word Jeremiah slipped from behind the crates and sprinted into the room, hoping the others were following. He made no noise besides footsteps as he approached the five men wondering what had just happened at the door. They didn't see Jeremiah coming.

The armored mercenary was getting to his feet, one hand on the pommel of his sheathed sword. He looked up just in time to see Jeremiah leaping across the table toward him.

Jeremiah collided with the merc's breastplate, and they both toppled over the chair. Jeremiah wrapped the man's sword arm up in a tight embrace, then clung for dear life. The merc was big, but he wasn't strong enough to lift Jeremiah with one arm, and the sword they were so concerned about was now out of reach.

The lights dimmed as someone struck Jeremiah on the side of the head. Then, to his relief, there were shouts and thuds and grunts of pain all around him. The Stonefists had arrived.

Jeremiah chanced a glance up. Shugga and Dronkal were shoulder to shoulder, raining truncheon blows on three of the unarmored gang members, attacking and defending each other without impeding each other in an elegant and brutal dance. Monty had one huge forearm wrapped around the fourth man's neck and was gripping the face of another, his huge hands easily finding purchase on the man's jaw and throat. "Shhh, shhh," murmured Monty as he quietly strangled them both.

"Get off, you little shit!" The merc rolled on top of Jeremiah, still clinging to his arm, and began raining blows down on him. Jeremiah tried to bury his head beneath the merc's armored shoulder and willed himself to hold on.

"Haawooooooo!" Sweet Melissa leapt onto the table, rapier drawn and lasso twirling. She flicked it over the head of the mercenary grappling Jeremiah and yanked. The man gagged as the lasso cinched around his throat, his eyes popping.

Sweet Melissa pulled the merc upward. Jeremiah let him go, too addled to keep his grip, and lay on the floor in a daze. He was aware of some violence being enacted upon the merc, then the man joined his comrades in unconsciousness.

Monty appeared above Jeremiah and hauled him to his feet. The dwarf's hand engulfed Jeremiah's. "Grab the chest and the sword, that's a pricey weapon," Monty said. "We're heading to Getaway Number Three."

Jeremiah picked up a greatsword while the half orcs carried the locked chest between them. They all exited through the front door, passing by another armored woman suspended off the ground by a rope around her ankle. Her sword was lying a few paces away, and Jeremiah spent a precious moment snatching that up too. He was the best-armed beggar in the city.

They chased Monty through the streets of the slum. Jeremiah wanted to let out a cheer. It worked! Almost exactly as he'd said it would, it worked. But there was still a chance for it to unwork if the Blackshades found them, so he kept his celebration internal.

Monty brought them to a pile of rotten wood and lifted a beam, revealing a narrow tunnel leading underground. "Down."

Sweet Melissa simply scampered inside, but Jeremiah, Shugga, and Dronkal had to crawl. The tunnel led deeper and deeper into darkness. Jeremiah sensed the familiar feeling of descent.

"Drop ahead," called Sweet Melissa.

Shugga stopped in front of Jeremiah, shifted, and disappeared into the ground. Jeremiah reached a hand out and discovered a steep wooden slide. He heard a grunt from below.

"Is it safe?" he asked.

"No, come down!" said Shugga.

Jeremiah pondered that for a moment, but at Dronkal's insistent prodding behind him, he launched himself over the edge.

CHAPTER TWENTY-NINE

Little Victories

The descent down the wooden slide was quicker than he wanted, Jeremiah sucked air through his teeth as he was whisked along. Only a full five seconds of sliding, but it felt like an eternity as he sped up. It was so dark he couldn't see the bottom before he slammed into it with a dull thud.

"You all right?" asked Shugga. A hand closed on Jeremiah's shirt and brought him to his feet.

"Fine," said Jeremiah, rubbing his back. He looked around, but it was black as pitch. There was a stifling quality to his words, almost the opposite of an echo, like they surrounded him.

"Keep moving," said Monty from the dark.

"Moving where? I can't see anything," said Jeremiah.

The others groaned. "Friggin' humans," sighed Shugga, or possibly Dronkal. It was hard to tell their voices apart without being able to see them.

"Can humans not see in the dark?" asked the voice of Sweet Melissa.

"Nah, when there's no light, they're blind," said Dronkal, or possibly Shugga.

"Oh, that's terrible! No wonder they're always carrying lanterns around!"

"Quiet," said Monty. There was a scrape and a burst of sparks that illuminated everyone in an orange flash, then a torch flame sprang to life.

All around, as far as the light would reach, the cracked and dying walls of an ancient city reached into the darkness. Jeremiah stared in awe. "What is this place?"

"This is the Undercity," said Dronkal. "Built and paved over long ago."

"Good getaways and hiding spots," said Sweet Melissa. "It's a labyrinth down here."

Something tickled Jeremiah's memory. "Oh yeah. Aren't there kobolds too?"

"Not here," said Shugga. "There's another level deeper than this. That's where the kobolds live. They'll travel through here sometimes, but they'll leave you alone if you look dangerous."

Monty led them down ancient, cobbled streets, Jeremiah strayed from the group, holding the torch aloft. One house harbored the ancient remains of a collapsed bed. A stove, rusted to oblivion, sat in the corner. A door, closed but broken in half, led further into the house. Jeremiah raised his torch to see further in. The dim light illuminated a human's mummified face, peeking over the top like it had been spying on him with the brown shriveled flesh that had replaced its eyes.

Jeremiah's heart leapt in his chest. His throat tightened. He couldn't move. The man in the closet. So afraid. Trapped. Trapped in the dark.

"Jay!" shouted a nearby voice.

He was yanked away from the gaze of the peeking corpse. His breath came back all at once and he panted like he'd been drowning. "I can't . . . I can't . . ." he wheezed.

Monty walked over and put one immense hand on the side of Jeremiah's head, and two fingers against Jeremiah's throat. He pressed.

Jeremiah woke up on the ground.

"You okay?" asked Shugga.

"Yeah, I'm okay." Jeremiah struggled to his feet. "Sometimes when I see people dead like that . . . it just brings back some bad memories. Ones I have a hard time getting rid of."

"First thing you've said that I believe," said Monty. "This way, we're almost to the safe house."

They continued down the forgotten road until Monty led them inside a dilapidated building. Several rooms deep, they encountered an intact wooden door, clearly newer than anything else down here. Monty ushered them inside.

The safehouse contained a stack of bedrolls and a large metal chest. Monty closed the door behind them and barred it with an oaken plank.

"We stay the night," he said. "They'll be hunting for us now. If we're found, kill anyone that lays eyes on this door. Food and water in the chest. Bandages too."

Dronkal pulled Jeremiah to sit beside the chest. As the others began unpacking bed rolls, Dronkal pulled a poultice and some bandages from the chest of supplies. "Let's take a look at you."

He crouched beside Jeremiah, tilting his head this way and that to get a better look at the damage to Jeremiah's face. The sense that someone was caring for him seeped the adrenaline from Jeremiah's veins. "Not bad for soloing an armored merc," he said, dabbing the poultice onto some of the nastier bruises. "Bet it still smarts, though."

"Eh, not so bad," said Jeremiah. "I've seen my own guts pulled out before."

"And you . . . lived?" asked Dronkal. He was blocking Jeremiah's view of the room, but there was a distinct pause in activity.

Oops. "I'm exaggerating, I just took a cut to the guts once," said Jeremiah. That was not something survivable for the common man and, worse yet, was true. He gave a chuckle and smile to lean into the lie.

"Back to the lying," said Monty. "Much better."

After Jeremiah's face had been dressed, they turned their attention to the stolen chest. The lock stood no chance alone in a room with five thieves. Inside were four bricks of a gray, clay-like substance wrapped in a thick cloth. "Not bad," said Monty.

"This is Dismal?" asked Jeremiah. "What's it do?"

"It's a narcotic," said Melissa. "You can melt it and drizzle it over pipe weed to smoke. Makes you really sad."

"What? Why would anyone do that?" asked Jeremiah. Bruno had skipped the lesson on narcotics, summarizing it only as "Try it if it'll make people think you're cool." To which Delilah had responded, "No."

"Because afterward you feel euphoric," said Monty. "Well, for a day or so, but then the sadness comes back, and stronger. So you need more Dismal. Eventually you can only ever feel happy when you're on it, and the sadness you feel when you're off it is soul crushing. Sells great."

Hearing that made Jeremiah feel a little bit awful, but there wasn't much he could do about it. Instead, he indulged in the question he was most curious about. "So, how'd I do? I know I didn't really *steal* anything, but we got it, right?"

Monty was quiet for a long time, and while he sat silently so did the others. "Admirably," he said at last.

"Whooaaa," said Shugga, Dronkal, and Sweet Melissa.

"Really?" It had been a long time since anyone had praised Jeremiah for anything he'd done. It had been nonstop criticism from Bruno, doubts about his capabilities from Allison, and Delilah . . . Well, while she hadn't said anything *directly* critical, there was a distinct lack of support that spoke volumes. *Admirable* felt pretty damn good.

Monty nodded. "You assessed the situation. You determined your skill set wasn't the appropriate response. You used what you had available to accomplish your goal. I've known others who'd try to do it on their own out of pride. You showed discretion and vision, and I appreciate that."

Jeremiah nodded as well. Clearly, it was wisdom that carried the day, definitely not blind luck or a bumbling lack of creativity.

"So, what now?" asked Jeremiah. "Any more tests?"

Monty smiled. "Just your initiation."

The others whooped.

"Oh, that's going to be *such* a shit show," said Dronkal.

"Don't worry," said Shugga. "It's basically a bar crawl."

"Except it's more like a rampage!" said Sweet Melissa, bouncing with excitement.

"Enough," said Monty. "Bed down. Get some rest. I'll take first watch."

They settled into their sleep sacks. As the torch was doused, Jeremiah asked, "So, if you guys can all see in the dark, how do you sleep? Isn't it like there's always a light on?"

There was snickering around him. "You close your eyes," said Dronkal.

"You really can't see in the dark?" asked Sweet Melissa. "So you can't see this? No? Or this?"

Her voice had moved. She was closer.

Jeremiah started to get nervous. "Still just dark."

Something moved near him. He'd felt the still air shift. His ears strained. He could swear he heard something metallic scraping.

"Melissa," said Monty in an authoritative tone.

Jeremiah heard a sigh somewhere nearby. "Oh, relax. I wasn't *really* gonna do it."

No one spoke after that.

Jeremiah drifted and was prodded awake between the vague dreams that skirted up against memories.

"Your watch," said Shugga.

"Watch? I get to be on watch?" said Jeremiah. He was instantly alert. This was a show of trust he had not been expecting.

"Yes? I'm sure as hell not taking it," said Shugga.

"You realize I can't see?" said Jeremiah.

"You listen, then. Wake up Dronkal in a couple hours."

Taking watch in the pitch-blackness was a surreal experience for Jeremiah. Eyes open or shut didn't make a difference, so it was hard not to just let his eyes close and drift to sleep. Hell, it was hard to tell whether or not he *had* fallen asleep. But the idea that he was being trusted kept him determined and focused. To stave off boredom, he began practicing drawing enchantment diagrams in the dirt. It was another unique experience, being unable to see meant he had to trust his mind and hands without his eyes factoring in.

Was my vision just getting in the way? He thought. Granted, he couldn't see his results, but he became aware of the *feeling* of his progress. Jeremiah could feel small errors in his hands, tiny betrayals of muscle that quivered imperceptibly. *I was in the way*, he thought. *Between the image in my head and my hand, there was only me to muck things up.*

"Enchantment is perfect," said Thurok. "You are the weakness."

That's not a criticism, is it? thought Jeremiah.

"No. It is a simple truth," confirmed Thurok.

Dronkal woke up on his own, switching out with Jeremiah with only the barest acknowledgment.

They got up when Monty told them it was day. They made their way through the darkness and emerged from a trapdoor hidden in the backroom of a filthy pub; the owner came to investigate the noises, then turned pointedly away when he saw them.

Monty clapped a hand on Jeremiah's shoulder as the others continued toward home. "Good work, Jay. Keep it up."

Cloistered in his room, door locked, and toad close, Jeremiah scratched away at a piece of metal he had found outside.

If Contact And Contact Heat

The metal scrap became hot enough to burn within moments. Jeremiah dropped the plate into the empty basin where it couldn't damage his bedding, and waited for the heat to destroy the enchantment so the plate could cool again.

Alone in his room, Jeremiah had torn himself away from *Flesh* to work on Delilah's heat plate, as he thought of it. Only problem was, it still wasn't working.

He tried *If Contact And Contact Heat Gently*.

It jumped to scorching again. "Right, right, right," said Jeremiah, shaking the pain out of his hands. The runes were in the wrong order. It acted the way it had before, instantly heating the metal, which meant Gently was just sitting at the end doing nothing.

If Contact And Contact Gently Heat

The first problem was solved . . . but it had created a new one. Now it heated so slowly Jeremiah had to sit with his hands on the metal for several minutes before any change of temperature could be detected.

"At least I'm getting lots of inscribing practice," he said, scratching Gus under the chin. He was getting faster, which allowed him to test his ideas much more quickly. Unfortunately, he was down to his last three plates. He'd have to go out and scavenge more soon.

If Contact Heat If Heat Heat

Will that create an infinite loop like If Strengthen Strengthen *had?* he thought. Jeremiah briefly worried there would be an unexpected consequence of infinite heat. *No, should just break like before. Best to check, though. We're exploring, right?*

He charged the scrap and held it in front of him. The metal was charged but remained cool and would until he touched the Contact point.

Jeremiah touched the point, then threw the scrap into the basin as it entered an infinite loop of heating itself until it warped and destroyed the enchantment. It was an indistinguishable result from the usual attempts at a heating plate, unfortunately. The wood of the basin bottom was beginning to become charred.

He sighed. "I don't think I know enough enchanting to do this," he lamented to Gus. He tossed his enchanting files aside and flopped backward on the bed. *Flesh* was under his hand, like a sympathetic friend.

Jeremiah patted the book. "I just want to try one more thing first, okay? Then it's your turn."

Jay's next plate was in poorer shape than the others. In fact, he would have left it in its refuse pile if it weren't for an idea that had popped into his head after using Decay on the wooden plank during the heist. Decay wasn't a rune he used often, barely even practiced. Enchantment was all about creating things and making them better, not making them worse.

But maybe, just maybe . . .

If Contact Gently Heat and Gently Decay

The dented and pockmarked plate of metal began to warm and soften. Keeping one hand on the Contact point, Jeremiah let the plate grow warm before pressing down on it as hard as he could against the floor. The metal, softened by heat and the rune of Decay, started to flatten under his hands. Normally even such a thin metal would require much higher temperatures to reshape, far too hot to touch, but Jeremiah suspected that the Decay rune was doing the heavy lifting.

When the heat started to reach intolerable temperatures, Jeremiah lifted his hands away, inactivating the diagram. The plate held its new, flatter shape. "Hey, it worked!" Jeremiah said. Gus croaked his support.

This opened up a world of possibilities in terms of salvaging trash for enchantment practice. He looked at the plates he'd already inscribed. "Do you think we could use this"—he pointed to his newly flattened plate—"to erase those?" he asked Gus.

Gus's eyes followed Jeremiah's pointing fingers and then blinked in deep toad concentration.

"Cuts are sort of like little dents, right? What if I inscribed a Heat and Decay rune on the plate and try to smooth it blank?"

Gus let out a small unconvinced croak.

"Right, right, I'd end up turning off the Decay enchanting when I try to smooth it out."

"You did not need to inscribe the rune to know the effect," said Thurok. "Good. Enchanting begins first in the mind."

I don't think I've ever heard you say good, *but I'll take my own compliment,* thought Jeremiah.

Gus croaked again and began kicking at Jeremiah, urging him on.

"The bridges! What if we bridge two plates together?! Like the recharging diagram!" With a burst of energy, Jeremiah picked up a used discarded plate and aligned it alongside his newest creation.

"Okay, let's see if we can't link these up." He grabbed a discarded Heat plate, and his last blank. He scratched a new, and painfully complex, diagram into his last blank plate. *If Contact Gently Heat And Gently Decay and Cohesion.* "Okay, looks good. I touch the contact, it slowly gets warmer, it slowly decays, and it sticks to things," he the effect out loud to ensure he was making sense of it.

Placing a bridge was simple enough, a few precious strands of gold wire would link two plates together, letting the enchantment effect both. Cohesion would ensure they remained stable and tightly connected. "Let's see if this works."

He touched the Contact and felt the two plates adhere to each other with a *click*. He waited. Decay on its own would ruin these plates in moments. He didn't know why Thurok made him learn it—

"That only further proves your ignorance," said Thurok.

—but the Gently rune kept the process under control, if painfully slow. After almost ten minutes he reached over, keeping one hand the Contact, and rubbed his free hand across the surface of the discarded Heat plate. It was warm, but something felt . . . different. He pressed a finger down and felt the barest sense of yielding. The metal was molding under his touch. He watched in wide-eyed astonishment as the effect compounded. When next he wiped his hand across the surface of the discarded plate, all of the inscribed runes blurred and disappeared. Buffed out with just a touch. The metal was acting like clay now, softened to a similar pliability.

He removed his hand from the Contact, and the plates separated, the Cohesion rune deactivating. He held up his new creation—nothing. A blank plate, swept clean like a harvested field. Separate from the Decay rune, the metal rehardened to its normal unyielding form.

Wait, is it normal? Wouldn't Decay, like, damage the metal? he wondered. He turned the plate over in his hands, but no apparent flaws appeared. *I don't think I'd be able to tell? I'd have to talk to a metallurgist or something. Will need to be careful if I use this on armor or weapons.*

"I think this might be a big deal, buddy," said Jeremiah. Gus closed his eyes and settled in for a satisfied nap. His work here was done.

CHAPTER THIRTY

Chaff

The day of his initiation, Jeremiah's cellmates forbade him from hiding away in his room. "You'll have plenty of opportunities, don't worry," said Shugga. "What you gotta do now is rest up so you're ready for tonight."

He sat in the living room with them instead, deeply enjoying being indoors while it poured rain outside. Sweet Melissa looped a cord around Jeremiah's wrists, rapidly securing and releasing him. He watched with wonder as his freedom was summarily granted and snatched away again.

Dronkal and Shugga were practicing with their new greatswords, integrating the two-handed weapons with their cooperative fighting style. Jeremiah wished he could show Allison.

"Anyway, I heard there's a red dragon living there now," said Sweet Melissa, concluding a story about a distant trading post.

"You ever seen a dragon?" asked Shugga, his sword weaving with Dronkal's.

"Nah," said Dronkal.

"Nope," said Jeremiah. He'd love to one day.

"Just once," said Melissa. "Sea dragon or something. Didn't see the color. Was miles away on open ocean."

She tossed a loop over Jeremiah's head, and in two quick motions the rope whipped and twisted, snapping Jeremiah's hands together in a knot that Jeremiah had never seen before. With a flick of her wrist, the loop around Jeremiah's throat collapsed, hard.

Sweet Melissa rested her head on her hand and looked at him wistfully. "Just say when," she sighed.

Jeremiah gagged, the loop digging into his throat so tight it was strangling him. He reached for the rope on his neck in a panic, but for some reason, as he pulled his hands up, it further tightened the noose. His fingertips brushed the neck rope. He tried to stand, but couldn't, some rope or another ran out of slack and he couldn't move.

Darkness threatened before Sweet Melissa sighed, and tugged a loose strand, undoing the entire setup.

Jeremiah sucked in breath as the black spots were chased away. He wobbled in his chair, trying to regain full consciousness. Melissa was gazing at him with wide, pleading eyes. What they were pleading for, he didn't know. "How'd you learn so much about rope?" Jeremiah gasped. The cord practically came alive in her hands. She could tie knots at a distance and prepped many of her ropes with multiple half-finished knots for any situation.

"My dad was a sailor, a real mean one," said Sweet Melissa. "But he had all the patience in the world to teach someone knots, so I made sure I was always interested. Made him keep his hands to himself at least."

"How'd you end up out here, Jay?" Shugga asked. The greatsword blades touched with a *clink*, ceasing their weaving attack pattern, and their practice started over.

Jeremiah decided on a version of his history that was vague but true. "Dad didn't like what I was getting up to. Kicked me out. Mom didn't say anything as I was headed out the door."

"Bad home?" asked Shugga.

"Nah, they were good to me. Just didn't want what I wanted," said Jeremiah. He could still remember the 'last straw' during an argument at the dinner table, when he had implied his father would die forgotten. His father, small as he was, had raged like a hurricane.

There was an awkward silence.

"What?" asked Jeremiah. The most awkward part of the silence was that he wasn't sure why it was awkward. Melissa absently coiled her ropes, any sign of coherence or awareness gone.

"Tough to imagine walking away from that," said Dronkal.

"Yeah," said Shugga. "I would have killed for 'good to me' when I was young."

"Safe would have been fine for me," said Dronkal.

Melissa didn't chime in, but Jeremiah could hear her breathing had gone shallow and shaky.

Jeremiah himself butting up against something he wasn't comfortable with. He knew parents could be *worse* than his. In theory. It wasn't like he didn't know things could be worse. But now here he was, listening to people lamenting that they didn't have what he threw away.

Uh-oh, was I an ungrateful piece of shit? he thought. *Parents are supposed to be good to you, right? Isn't that their whole job? Bare minimum?* He had never thought of thanking his parents for what they *didn't* do . . .

Jeremiah cast around for a subject to change to. "Hey, I was wondering, what's up with that house in the Pit? The one with a gold roof? Anyone live there?"

Shugga chuckled. "Already planning your first heist? You wouldn't be the first to be taken in."

"What do you mean?" asked Jeremiah.

"The Gilded Vault is one big shiny trap," said Sweet Melissa, awakening from whatever memory she was lost in. "A guy named Cassidy Korrvas built it just to kill dumb Slips."

"Dumb anybody, really," said Dronkal. "He used to be a gangster like us, but he was one of those who made it out. One of the very, very few. As soon as he built it, he issued an open invitation to any thief or crew who thinks they're good enough to try for the personal horde of one of the greatest crime lords there's ever been."

"It's been decades now," said Shugga. "Hundreds have gone in, not a soul has walked out."

"He was a genius," said Sweet Melissa. "The stories I've heard about some of the traps in there . . ."

"How did you hear stories if no one's ever escaped?" asked Jeremiah.

"Shh!" said Sweet Melissa, batting him with a loop of rope. "Let a girl dream."

"Supposedly there's enough treasure in there to get someone set for life," said Dronkal. "But like Shug said, it's been generations, and nobody's ever gone in and lived to tell, so who knows? I think it's a bit of an eyesore myself."

"What about the guards?" Jeremiah had seen figures standing sentry on the roof.

"They won't stop you from going inside," said Shugga. "They just keep people from burning the place down and the like. You can walk in the front door or pick one of the locks all day long, but if you so much as scratch the glass, they kill on sight." He put down the greatsword, satisfied with the day's practice.

"It's been, what, two years since someone had a go?" Dronkal asked. "Come on, Shug, one more."

"Bah, fine," said Shugga.

"Two since someone made a big deal about it," said Sweet Melissa, "but people wander in to off themselves damn near weekly." She started inspecting Jeremiah's neck very closely, her head tilting this way and that.

"People kill themselves in it?" asked Jeremiah. He had a sneaking suspicion she was about to bite him, the way she was moving was like a cobra's sway.

Sweet Melissa shrugged. "Yeah, sometimes. Might as well take a chance at riches while you're at it, right?" She froze stock still, fixating on one spot.

There was a light scratching at the door.

"Cat," said Sweet Melissa, she didn't move.

"Got it," said Shugga. He cracked the door, and a small orange cat slinked inside.

"You have a cat?" asked Jeremiah. That explained the lack of rats in this immediate vicinity . . . she was still staring at his neck.

"This is Miggy, the Cell Four mascot," Dronkal said, scooping her up and aggressively cuddling her. "She's dumb, but she keeps the place clean. And she loves attention! Yes, she does! Yes, she does! My jiggle jiggle wiggle princess!"

Miggy tried to kill him, to no avail.

Jeremiah suddenly felt very alien in this space, the mundanity of their lives catching up with the lies he was presenting them with. Comfortable as it was, this wasn't his place. He had to remember that.

"Oh, before I forget," said Shugga. "We should get Jay some proper clothes for tonight. I know this great seamstress who—"

"Already done!" said Sweet Melissa, finally breaking off the stare and moving so suddenly that Jeremiah jumped.

"You bought me clothes?" asked Jeremiah, his hand went to his neck. *Did I just escape death? Why does it feel like I almost just died?* he thought.

"Without consulting me?!" gasped Shugga. "Why?! Why would you take that from me?"

"Yes, I did," said Sweet Melissa to Jeremiah. "You look like a joke, and I refuse to be seen with you."

She disappeared into her room and returned with a bundled package.

"Literally just throw it away," said Shugga. He crossed his arms and pouted.

"Consider it a welcome present. Made to measure," said Melissa, plopping it into Jeremiah's lap. She sat down across from him again, wiggling in excitement.

"How do you have my measurements?" asked Jeremiah, slowly opening the bundle.

"I'll give you one guess," said Sweet Melissa.

Jeremiah froze and glanced up at her, she was still wiggling in gleeful anticipation. "You make me profoundly uncomfortable."

She leaned close, very close. "Go on . . ." she breathed.

"Off," said Dronkal, prodding Sweet Melissa away from Jeremiah with the flat of his blade. She whimpered pitifully.

Jeremiah ran to his room and tried the clothes on immediately. A simple fitted shirt and trousers, clean, new, and of adequate quality. Everything he needed. He'd need to patch a pocket for Gus, but otherwise they were perfect.

He skipped back downstairs, feeling a new man. "How do I look?"

"Human," said Dronkal. Everyone nodded. Jeremiah wasn't sure what that meant, but he was a human, so it sounded okay.

"Definitely human," sighed Sweet Melissa. "It's really tough to get away from that with just clothes."

"It really is," said Shugga with exasperation. "If only you had a friend who lived for this kind of thing."

Jeremiah turned to Sweet Melissa. "Thank you. This means a lot." It was slightly alarming how much the gift made him want to cry.

"You can put hands in the pockets!" said Melissa.

Deep in the Pit, a gathering was in progress. The members of Cell Four walked Jeremiah down the stairs to the headquarters of the Stonefists. Jeremiah took his cue from the others and adopted a dire expression, as though he were approaching his own execution. It seemed like the right thing to do.

The headquarters were packed, and not just with the brutes that Jeremiah had seen the last time. Complete with their own distinct smell, the majority of occupants were a motley collection of weary looking men and women. They wore the battered rags Jeremiah now recognized as belonging to those who lived rough.

"Who are they?" Jeremiah whispered to Shugga.

"Subbies, our Sub cell members," Shugga whispered back.

They were, to a man, short and malnourished looking. Spindly and sallow cheeked, they looked at Jeremiah with vacant uninterested eyes.

"They're the dregs," added Sweet Melissa. "Every gang has them. The Bricks call theirs Fists, the Quick Hands call theirs Pockets, and we call ours Subbies, or Subs. Don't bother learning their names."

The Subbies kept a pointed distance from Cell Four as they waited. Jeremiah was about to ask what they were waiting for when Monty arose from the darkened stairway that led to his office.

"Up, Subs!" yelled Dronkal, calling the gathering to attention under Monty's watchful eye.

Slowly but surely the Subs heard and stood at some form of attention, to a chorus of groans and complaints.

Dronkal continued, "Subs, this is Jay. He is going to be a member of the Stonefists and a new cell member. He's proven himself to be worthy of not wallowing with your filth and incompetence."

There were angry grumbles and sneers of derision.

"He ain't look like shit to me!" one of the Subs yelled. It was a waifish human woman, with matted and greasy hair and pock-scarred face. She pointed and yelled with a wide-open mouth at full volume despite not being far. "I've been working for years to become a cell member! My son and I—"

"I got it," said Shugga. In a few quick strides he reached her, pulled his club, and thrashed her across the forehead. She bled profusely and shrieked, staggering away and cowering. The other Subs didn't react. Shugga hopped back into his position.

My son and I? thought Jeremiah, the phrase kept repeating in his head.

"Any other objections?" declared Monty. He began to walk toward the center of the room, casting his gaze left and right. Tremendous hands clasped behind his back, he was like a general addressing his troops. Where his gaze fell, the Subs cowered or looked away.

One Sub raised his hand like a school child. Like a drop of water in oil, the other Subs scattered away.

"Oh hell yeah," whispered Sweet Melissa. She bounced in excitement.

Monty nodded at the foolish Sub who spoke. "Is that something open to any of us? Can we skip being Subs and be cell members?"

"An excellent question," said Monty. "The brightest of you, the strongest of you, the most ambitious of you, or the most loyal of you, may yet escape your life of squalor and servitude. Jay has proven his skill and ambition to my satisfaction, such that I have granted him a special advancement past the rank of Sub cell member."

Shugga put a hand on his club and pointed at the Sub, looking to Monty. Monty nodded, and Shugga struck the Sub. Though, Jeremiah noted, with less enthusiasm and only across the leg. Jeremiah was a professional at this point of being beaten with clubs from his frequent run-ins with guards. The Sub yelped and favored the other leg, but no more.

Monty continued as though he hadn't been interrupted. "As always, he is stripped of status and must comply with any order, whim or suggestion from any of you, unless vetoed by a cell member, until the initiation is complete." He paused, smiling slightly. "I've decided I will be joining you, so tonight I expect you all to show me the meaning of a Stonefist party."

The Subs cheered, and Shugga clapped Jeremiah on the back. "Get ready for a wild night!"

But Jeremiah kept thinking about what that Sub had said. *My son and I.* "Hey, do a lot of Subs have kids?" he asked Dronkal and Shugga.

Shugga answered. "I think a few?"

Jeremiah looked out among them. They gambled, drank, and fought, but also laughed, joked and some seemed to be taking up a collection of sorts for one of them.

"So Subs are what to us? Nothing? Tools?" asked Jeremiah. The callousness with which Subs were regarded was starting to dawn on Jeremiah.

"Yeah, sure," said Shugga, "but who cares? The strongest and smartest of them get out and become made, proper gang members that is."

"And the rest?" asked Jeremiah, looking over the crowd.

"They stay Subs," said Dronkal. "They're too dumb or weak to be anything useful."

"Something wrong, Jay?" asked Shugga. He put an affectionate arm around Jeremiah's shoulder.

Jeremiah shrugged off the arm with a jerk. "They're still people! Being dumb or weak shouldn't matter, they deserve some amount of decency or respect, don't they? Otherwise, they're just getting used in the hopes of receiving it."

"If they really want out, they can get out," said Shugga. "Take Dronk and me. We're bigger and stronger than most of the trash out there, but definitely not the biggest."

"Definitely not the biggest," echoed Dronkal. He seemed sour about the fact.

"But I got recruited into the gang by Monty," continued Shugga. "He watched me brawl in a pub and made me a Sub. I worked my way up and eventually joined my cell. I started from nothing and here I am, a made man."

Dronkal said, "I was with the Bricks for ages, but those guys are nuts, it's all brutality with them. So I made the hard choice to break off and join the Stonefists."

Jeremiah looked around, half expecting Melissa to appear and tell her own story. Shugga apparently understood and answered the unasked question. "Sweet Melissa is . . . special?" He looked at Dronkal, who shuddered. "Yeah, a special case."

"Rare find to be sure," mumbled Dronkal.

"And what would have happened to you if Monty hadn't been in that pub?" Jeremiah asked. He couldn't quell the ember of anger in his chest.

Shugga shrugged. "No idea. Probably wouldn't be a Stonefist."

"Exactly, it was luck. Sure, you can fight, but it was for luck you got here in the first place. Same for me, I'm only here 'cause Pete found me. If he had been one street over I'd still be out there begging for coppers," said Jeremiah. He felt his voice starting to rise.

That's so very close to being me, he thought, looking out on them.

Shugga and Dronkal exchanged another look. "So, first of all," Shugga slugged

Jeremiah right across the sternum with his truncheon. It didn't hurt like getting hit on a bone, but his heart did something in his chest that scared him. "Don't presume to discount what Dronk or I went through to get here."

"Second," Shugga continued, and Dronkal rapped Jeremiah in the shin with his club, causing him to cry out in pain. "Best remember that you're not shit yet. We like you. That's why you only get a love tap. But we don't owe you anything. Understand?"

"Got it," Jeremiah hissed through clenched teeth. "Too cozy." He rubbed his shin furiously to drive out the pain.

"Anyway," said Shugga, stowing the baton, "feel free to devote your time catering to the Subs if you want. They'll cling to you like stray dogs hoping for scrap, but if one day they learn you're made of meat, they'll eat you too. You know why?"

Jeremiah shook his head, Dronkal hadn't put away his baton yet.

"Because they live day to day," said Dronkal. "They're not worried about what they can eat tomorrow, they're worried about what they can eat right now. Short sighted you see. You don't owe them anything."

Jeremiah remembered a man in a bar, a man Bruno had beaten to a pulp just to teach Jeremiah a lesson. *Val? Valen? No, that was the Colonel. Vale-something.* He couldn't remember. He remembered the fear he felt when he was about to be murdered, he remembered the disgusting drink he had been forced to try, he remembered the dull pop he heard when Bruno broke the man's jaw, but he couldn't remember the man's name.

"You owe that girl a father," Bruno had said.

Why was he thinking of that now? Why did it feel like it conflicted with what Dronkal was saying? He was too tired to make sense of any of it, but he felt like he *did* owe these people something. He wasn't sure what, and he wasn't sure how, but he felt like he did.

"Are you paying attention?" asked Vivica. "Are you listening, Thorn? Are you seeing?" Why was he thinking of her now? What did she have to do with this?

"You guys have kids?" Jeremiah asked.

"No," said Shugga.

"I have a boy somewhere," said Dronkal.

Shugga looked startled. "I didn't know that."

Dronkal nodded. "He would be about four now, Jajakal. Lives in a hamlet called Portistan, way out east by the ocean. Last I heard anyway. Lives with his mum, Beda."

"Why didn't you tell me that?" asked Shugga.

"You ever see him? Or write to him?" asked Jeremiah.

"Nah, I'll send a couple of silvers now and then. Honestly, I don't even know if they get them. But he's better off without me, no kid deserves a thug like me as a dad," said Dronkal, avoiding Shugga's question. "You got kids, Jay?"

"No, not at all," said Jeremiah. The very question was crazy to Jeremiah, he was far too young to be some child's father. Children was a question that he had never even thought to ask himself. It made him uncomfortable now that it was there.

"How come you never told me that?" Shugga asked again.

"I think it's time we get this party started," said Dronkal, standing up. "Subs! Time to move out and get *rowdy*!" There was hooting and hollering as the Subs instantly burst to life like fire touched to kindling.

"Why didn't you ever tell me?" asked Shugga.

Monty appeared then, interrupting the daggers Shugga was staring at Dronkal. "Come on gentlemen, you're holding up the festivities." He wore a genial smile, authentic and warm, that fully reached his eyes.

He fixed Jeremiah's gaze with his own, maintaining the kindly smile. "What do you say, Jay? This is your night. I want the Stonefists to feel like *home*. A place of *safety*. A place to *rest*. Where *family* lives. Where *you* live." His voice was low, almost mumbling, except for the words he stressed.

"Um," said Jeremiah. "Yeah, sure. Let's go, everyone!"

And to his surprise, there arose another cheer around him.

CHAPTER THIRTY-ONE

Fear

The Stonefists moved as a single raucous mass, cresting the edge of the Pit and inflicting themselves on proper society. Monty hung back, giving the gang room to be belligerent without his presence dampening the joviality. Jeremiah was in the center of the mass, being shoved and prodded every few steps. Shugga and Dronkal flanked Jeremiah, ensuring the Subs never became too aggressive or demanded anything out of form.

Regardless, Jeremiah crawled on all fours and brayed like a donkey, he carried multiple different Subs on his back at one point or another, he screamed obscenities at random frightened passersby and threw rocks at windows. He ate trash, ran into shops and snatched random items, and challenged powerful-looking men to fights. But consequences were few and far between. No one was willing to take him up on a fight when he traveled with an entire gang, and no shop owner was willing to cause a problem over some stolen bread or fruit with the risk of attracting more attention.

Jeremiah could feel something he hadn't felt in a long time. A lack of fear. The Stonefists were all around him, taking advantage of him and protecting him at the same time. Sure, they could force him to get into trouble, but if trouble came looking for Jeremiah, he was surrounded by a band of filthy-dangerous gang members who would keep him safe.

"Bar!" someone yelled. The horde cheered and forced their way into some unfortunate establishment. The bartender lost control of the situation, assuming he ever had it, very quickly. The Stonefists threw down money for the drinks they ordered but quickly began sneaking behind the counter to swipe bottles of their own. Jeremiah was sent to steal a bottle of brandy from the top shelf. He surprised himself by surreptitiously throwing a glass across the room, leaping the counter, grabbing the bottle, and returning before the harried bartender had even finished searching for the source of the new ominous crash.

The horde moved out just as abruptly as it had entered. Jeremiah saw Monty staying behind, speaking calmly with the bartender who raved and ranted.

Yet, as they walked, Jeremiah found himself growing more and more anxious. He kept glancing over his shoulder, expecting to see Cutter's maniacal grin, Cutter's flashing blade. The Stonefists would watch while Cutter tore into Jeremiah, laugh and wonder why he was too weak to defend himself.

"What's got you looking so jittery?" shouted Melissa, over the din of the crowd.

"Nothing, I'm just—" Jeremiah looked down at her and was surprised to see she was genuinely concerned. "Is that a real question?" he asked.

"Yeah, you look anxious. Are you okay?" she said. Being a gnome, she had to step in double time to keep up with them, but she tried her best to keep pace, while enjoying a small moat of space around her that the Subs seemed to instinctively provide.

Jeremiah knew she was some sort of sadist. Some psychopath who just might cut the organs from his body. But she was also expressing the first real concern for him that he had felt for weeks. She cared about how he was feeling. Sure, Bruno, Delilah, and Allison cared about him, but they already knew him. To Melissa, he was just another nobody who had fallen into her circle. It touched him deeply.

"I'm just . . . I'm just not *scared* anymore. It's been really scary out here, you know?" he told her, in a moment of unexpected candor. "Every day has been so uncertain. What's going to happen to me? How will I eat? Where will I sleep? Who's going to give me trouble? I know I live with you guys now, but I think it's just starting to actually hit me, you know?"

Her eyes softened. "I know. I really, really do. I know you're not *officially* a part of the Stonefists yet, not till after the initiation party, but this part is just a formality. You're in! We've got your back!"

He smiled at her, that little spider, and she smiled back up at him.

You are awfully cute, he thought. *How much trouble could you really—*

"No!" said Bruno. "The biggest no!"

Sweet Melissa's smile faded as she looked into his eyes. "What is it?" she asked.

He hadn't realized it until she asked, but there was still a tiny bit of fear in him. A modicum of trauma, living in the tightness of his shoulders or the middle of his back. "Nothing," he answered. Whatever it was wanted to stay hidden.

"Hold up!" Melissa shouted, and the horde stopped, and grew quieter to listen. With a flick of her wrist, she shot a lasso up and around his neck, yanking him down onto his knees and eye level with her. It was a *very* assertive way to regard him personally. "Jay, tell me what's wrong. Did something happen?" She put a tender hand on the side of his face.

Jeremiah's breath caught in his chest. He didn't know he was going to say it until he said it. "There was . . . this guy. Cutter. I technically owe him money. He nearly killed me. He might . . . nevermind. That's not the gang's problem. That happened before I joined." Jeremiah slammed the door on his feelings, embarrassed they came out at all. How was she dragging this out of him? It was like how Vivica had gotten him to talk in prison, or how Delilah had gotten him to break the joke about the Giant's Bag. *Did he have a weakness for a pretty face or something?* he briefly wondered.

"You have no idea," said Delilah.

With a tug, Sweet Melissa tightened the lasso. Somehow only tight enough to exert comforting pressure, and not a strangling one. "Jay, you're part of the Stonefists now. Your problems are our problems," said Melissa. "Where can we find Cutter?"

"Yeah. I know, like, four different Cutters," said Shugga. He appeared with Dronkal behind Sweet Melissa, flanking and looming behind her like colossal guardians.

"By Prim's Laundry," said Jeremiah, "but really, you don't need to do anything." It was fear talking. Part of Jeremiah wanted, on an instinctual level, to stay as far from Cutter as possible.

"Don't be dumb," said Dronkal. "No Slip of mine's going to be scared of some shitless bully too pathetic to join a real gang."

"War party, roll up!" shouted Shugga. The Subs scrambled to attention, whooping and hollering.

"What's going on?" came Monty's voice. He'd been lagging behind the horde of Stonefists, settling bar debts and keeping a watchful eye over his gang.

"We're gonna rough up some topsider who gave Jay a bad time," said Sweet Melissa. "You coming, boss?"

The Subs quieted to hear his response. "Well . . ." said Monty.

The Subs' excitement grew and grew as Monty weighed the invitation.

"Oh he's thinking about it! He's thinking about it!"

"C'mon boss when's the last time you ran the road with us?"

The Subs excitement grew and grew as Monty weighed the invitation.

"Oh, what the heck. Let's go!" said Monty with a jolly swing of his fist.

The Subs cheered. "C'mon, Jay," said Sweet Melissa. "Let's go do violence."

The tension was strong, and the Subs were restless and well lubricated. The streets had cleared out when the gang entered the area around Prim's Laundry, no one eager to catch the attention of such a mass of ne'er do wells.

"We all know the plan?" Melissa asked the group.

"What? No, what plan?" asked Jeremiah.

"Melissa, you have to tell us the plan if you think of a plan," said Shugga.

Melissa looked absolutely baffled for a moment and then shook her head. "Oh wow. I think I just had a whole conversation in my head. Okay, sorry. The plan isn't special, we run in and beat the hell out of everyone."

"Works for me," said Shugga, pulling out his truncheon.

"How do we know which one's Cutter?" Dronkal asked Jeremiah. He unsheathed his own club and tried to tap the metal cap of his weapon to the metal cap on Shugga's. Shugga pulled his club away at the last moment.

He's the one that looks like a nightmare, thought Jeremiah. Trying to remember Cutter was painful, he was gigantic in Jeremiah's memory.

"He's got a shortsword, and he's the tallest of them. I think it'll be obvious," said Jeremiah. His heart was racing, and only partially from excitement. He would be ashamed to admit out loud, but even with the backing of this entire gang with him, he was still feeling scared being this close to where Cutter had torn his hand to pieces. The fear was instinctive, a deep terror in his mind trying to assure his survival regardless of circumstances like the habits of a mad man.

"Shortsword, huh?" said Dronkal. "Boss, we going lethal?" he asked Monty.

"What's their kit like?" Monty asked Jeremiah.

"Like their weapons and armor? Shortsword was the most dangerous thing I saw. Knives, bottles, probably some clubs. No armor I could see."

Monty shrugged, "I've never heard of them, and they're outside the Pit, they'll piss themselves and run as soon as they look at us. Don't kill them unless you have to."

Melissa kicked a stone in frustration.

"Form up!" Dronkal shouted so the Subbies could hear. "If they've got a guard in that alley, I want him overrun with no hesitation. Go hard, don't stop till they know what's up!"

Jeremiah wanted Allison to meet Dronkal, or vice versa.

Real and improvised weapons began to appear in the Subs' hands. They jostled each other, riling each other up. Some seemed excited, some nervous, but none seemed as nervous as Jeremiah.

"You're leading the charge," Dronkal said to Jeremiah, pushing him closer to the alley.

"I—I am? Why?" asked Jeremiah. The instinctive fear suddenly spiked. He felt sick.

"Because this is your fight. I want you to earn this. Need a weapon?"

Jeremiah's anxiety turned to a sickening sour feeling in his stomach, and he felt like he was going to cry. It disgusted him. That part of him was supposed to be long gone. That part of him was supposed to be dead. He had dealt it a mortal blow when he fought a war, but it appeared that he needed to kill it once and for all.

"Got a wrist wrap? I think I want to do this bare-handed," he managed to choke out to Dronkal.

"Fuck yeah, I do," said Dronkal with a grin. He wrapped Jeremiah's hands in two strips of brown scrap leather, cracked and worn. Jeremiah's hands throbbed, but his fists felt like two heavy rocks at the end of his arms. They made him feel stronger.

They approached the final corner before Cutter's lot. Jeremiah's heart was pounding wildly, adrenaline supercharging the admixture of terror, bloodthirst, and exhilaration swirling through him. He bounced from foot to foot, trying to keep his energy up, trying to keep from running away.

"Attaboy," said Shugga, slapping him on the chest. Dronkal mirrored the slap on Jeremiah's back. They stung, but amped Jeremiah up more.

"You gonna get it," said Shugga. "You gonna get it!" he shouted at Jeremiah, grabbing him by the shoulders and shaking him.

"On your call," said Dronkal, jaw set, tusks protruding.

"Go! Go! Go!" Jeremiah shouted, and broke into a sprint before his legs could decide otherwise.

Blood pumped in his ears. The lot came into view, and Jeremiah saw his first targets near the entrance. One sat, fiddling with a carving knife, the other leaned against a wall. They didn't notice Jeremiah until it was too late.

"Ruin him," said Allison.

Jeremiah swung recklessly at the leaning man. The blow connected right at the tip of the chin, exactly as Allison had taught him. The man's head wrenched side-ways, but Jeremiah was already onto the next. The other man shouted in surprise and Jeremiah kicked him with the heel of his foot before he could fully stand. The man toppled over, and Jeremiah kept kicking till something caught just right and the man went limp.

Jeremiah had no time to think, he charged on, his blood pumping in his ears and filling him with a power he was certain he had lost. He turned the corner, a corner that was locked inside of his memory, a place where his hand had been torn apart and screamed of danger. In that little blank piece of the world where only something awful lived, he saw what may have been the same crowd he encountered that fateful day. They were in their repose, drunk and lounging, like they had settled back into the same position the moment Jeremiah had left and had not moved until he returned.

Cutter was there, taller than the others, larger than the others, and by far crueler than all of them. Jeremiah ran at Cutter the moment his eyes landed on him. Cutter, the demon from Jeremiah's nightmares. Cutter, the face of Elminia's cruelty. Cutter was crouched down and throwing dice with a few of his gang members. He turned to look at the intrusion just as Jeremiah collided with him, driving him to the ground and sitting on his chest. Jeremiah unleashed a flurry of punches down on Cutter's face, who swore in surprise and grabbed onto Jeremiah's shirt.

Cutter's face bled, Jeremiah felt the sweet impact of his leather-wrapped fist against flesh, but it was like striking a nightmare. No matter how hard he swung it wasn't hard enough, though he relished every wince of pain that he caused. Cutter pulled Jeremiah close, and kicked, rolling the both of them over. Cutter was bigger than Jeremiah, and certainly stronger. But what he had most of all was a lifetime of brutal experience. Jeremiah swung upward at him, the distance and position robbing his swings of most of their force. Cutter screamed like a banshee and began pummeling Jeremiah, who was instantly forced to turtle and protect his face.

Where are they? thought Jeremiah. *Where's the gang I'm a part of? Where's the support I was promised? Where's the protection I'm supposed to rely on?*

He understood. They weren't coming. He had been sent to handle this on his own. Win or lose, they wanted him to face his fear and resolve this, win or lose. *Lose it is then!* he thought. Jeremiah had no answer to Cutter from here. He couldn't dislodge him, couldn't attack him, and was forced to endure the assault. He likely would until he was beaten unconscious, then he'd be subject to whatever whims Cutter decided to implement. Jeremiah didn't care. For one glorious moment he had caused Cutter pain. He split Cutter's lip open and had the advantage. Cutter couldn't take that away from him, even if he made Jeremiah regret it.

There were shouts all around him, shouts of fear and surprise. The blank piece of the world was suddenly filled with trampling feet and the thuds of impact and screams of pain. Just a glance to the side, turning away from Cutter's fists, and Jeremiah saw a man climbing the fence to escape. A lasso whipped out of nowhere and snapped around his neck, the man gagged but completed the vault of the fence. The line went taut.

Cutter, oblivious to all of this, was yanked off Jeremiah. Jeremiah scrambled to his feet, a dozen fights played out around him, if one man being stomped by six could be called a fight. He was grabbed from behind and steadied by Shugga. He tried to shove the half orc off, but Shugga's arms enclosed Jeremiah in a bear hug, restraining him.

"Let me go!" screamed Jeremiah, he wanted to keep fighting. Even if Cutter was going to win, he wanted to hurt him just one more time.

"Nah, Slip," said Shugga. "Your man just drew the short straw."

Monty stood in front of Cutter, relaxed and waiting patiently. He was unarmed, but for those massive hands. Cutter growled, raising his fists, and Monty nodded toward Cutter's short sword, reminding him.

Cutter pulled the blade and lunged. Monty used one of his grotesquely huge forearms to deflect the blade, letting it cut into his skin without so much as a wince. He slapped Cutter with an open hand so hard it sounded like a whip crack, and Cutter spun on toes like a dancer and flopped down in the dirt.

Monty knelt alongside Cutter, who struggled to crawl away. He gripped Cutter's face with one hand, flipped him onto his back, and held him there, covering his mouth and nose.

Cutter stiffened. He clawed at Monty's hand, beat frantically at it. His eyes bulged, and all of his limbs flailed in a desperate attempt to hurt Monty. Then his struggle weakened, and a sickening quiver ran through his body.

Monty let go.

Cutter gasped for breath, coughing and sputtering. Monty returned the hand. Cutter's fight was weaker and shorter this time. He spasmed, quivered, and Monty let go.

"I couldn't beat him," murmured Jeremiah to Shugga. He felt a bubble of shame percolate in himself.

"Well, yeah," said Dronkal, coming up alongside Jeremiah to watch. "He's way bigger than you. You're a thief, you're not meant to beat up thugs."

"Kind of the whole point of gangs, Jay," said Shugga. "Him fighting you isn't a fair fight. And neither is this."

And just like that, the bubble was gone.

Jeremiah watched in awe as Monty dispassionately brought Cutter near death again and again, letting him glimpse oblivion for tiny moments, before pulling him back. Cutter's strength grew less and less with each journey, Monty always giving him back enough to fight just a little, just enough so it didn't matter.

"S-stop," Cutter gasped.

"You're asking me?" Monty looked to his left and right, as though looking for someone else.

"You b-bitch, stop," Cutter said. His eyes were just barely focused, watery and wandering.

The hand returned.

"Not sure why you're asking me," said Monty. The hand released.

"I'm done," said Cutter. "Stop." He seemed to have trouble moving his legs in his struggles.

The hand returned.

"Problem is, I don't think *he's* done." Monty pointed at Jeremiah. "See, he's the one calling the shots now. So you talk to him and let him know you want to stop."

Monty was handing Jeremiah power. He'd kill Cutter, if Jeremiah told him to. There was no question. Would that be so bad? Would the world really suffer from Cutter's loss?

The hand released. Cutter gasped again. "Stop." Still directed at Monty.

Jeremiah just watched. It was worth it. He didn't know what *it* was, but it was worth it.

The hand returned. "Why isn't there a building here? This is good real estate," said Monty, taking in the open lot.

The hand released.

"Fu—"

The hand returned.

Shugga let Jeremiah go. "Yeah, you got this, Jay," he whispered

Jeremiah approached Monty and Cutter and stood over them. He watched Cutter struggle and quiver. Monty paid Jeremiah no mind.

The hand released.

Cutter finally turned to Jeremiah. There was a dull realization in Cutter's eyes, or a recollection.

Yeah, you remember me, don't you? thought Jeremiah. He kept staring down at Jeremiah, dispassionate and cold.

"Stop," Cutter finally wheezed at Jeremiah, understanding that Monty held no mercy for him. Bruises were forming over his face where Monty gripped.

"No," said Jeremiah.

The hand returned.

"You didn't stop. Why should I?" asked Jeremiah.

The hand released.

"I'll . . . I'll kill you." Cutter glared at Jeremiah.

"That so?" said Jeremiah. He nodded at Monty

The hand returned. *His* hand returned. Jeremiah controlled the hand, the hand controlled Cutter.

His hand released.

"Doesn't give me much incentive to keep you alive, does it?" said Jeremiah.

Cutter coughed and a spurt of blood came up, something had torn in him. "I'm done, stop," said Cutter.

"Why? Why should I stop?!" demanded Jeremiah. "What reason could I possibly have?! What could I have said that would have made *you* stop? What were the magic words Cutter?"

"Please stop, you piece of shit," gagged Cutter.

His hand returned.

"Is that all? Is that all I had to say?" The more Cutter insulted, the angrier Jeremiah became. He wanted whimpering, he wanted terror, he wanted Cutter to beg and plead and see the error of his ways. Instead he was getting idiotic defiance in the face of imminent, and entirely avoidable, death.

Jeremiah wondered why he didn't feel pity. Perhaps a better man would have. All he saw was a problem to be solved. All the rest of the world was irrelevant, it was just him and Cutter. The controller and the controlled.

"What do I do with you, Cutter?" He picked up Cutter's shortsword, lying forgotten in the dirt. It was ugly and ill balanced, with rusty stains on the blade. It had not been taken care of.

His hand released.

"Weak . . ." Foamy blood ran down Cutter's cheek.

Jeremiah laughed. "Weak? Yeah, maybe. So what's a weak man to do with a problem like Cutter? I suppose a weak man would just stick you deep in the neck and be done with this problem."

He pressed the tip of the blade against Cutter's throat. A moment's pressure, and he'd never have to worry about Cutter again. A problem neatly solved, and the world none the worse for it.

"Don't do it," said the voice of everyone he had ever known and cared about, as well as his own, a young boy who wanted to be special when he was too naive to know what that meant.

"But I'm a strong man," said Jeremiah. "And a strong man knows when to forgive." He crouched down and patted Cutter on the cheek, wiping the blood in Cutter's hair. Cutter sagged in relief as Monty stepped back, no longer threatening with those gigantic hands.

"Hey, Sweet Melissa?" called Jeremiah, still hunkered down in front of Cutter.

Sweet Mellissa appeared at Jeremiah's side, practically vibrating with excitement. "Yeah, Jay?"

"I'm not going to tell you how to do your job," said Jeremiah, "but I don't want him to ever be able to make a fist again."

Melissa squealed in delight, prancing from foot to foot. "I knew you were such a good idea!"

"B-but you said . . ." Cutter gagged, looking back and forth between Jeremiah and Melissa.

"Nobody's perfect, Cutter."

CHAPTER THIRTY-TWO

Pressure

With Cutter broken, he felt there was nothing he couldn't do. Bars were open to him, alleys no longer contained monsters. Monty had given him power over Cutter, power over fear, power over life itself.

Monty rested a hand on Jeremiah's shoulder as they caroused their way back onto the street. "Well done back there. It's good to have you in the *family*." Then he pointed down a side street. "That way."

It was the first direction he'd given since they'd left, and the Subs cheered at their leader's participation. They crashed bar after bar, sometimes downing a few drinks, sometimes staying only long enough to make everyone uncomfortable. Jeremiah was buoyed by the energy, by being part of something, by having *fun*. He felt invincible.

And so, onward to anything and everything he wanted. The Stonefists gave him commands as they had the entire time, but now he took liberties of his own. He spotted a pastry in a shop window that he would have longed for in previous days. But now it was his. He opened the door, locked eyes with the proprietor, reached out, and took the pastry he wanted. The proprietor made no attempt to stop him, no objection, and even looked away with indifference.

Jeremiah had a new kind of power, different from when he was a necromancer. Then, his power had been entirely bleak; he was something to be feared, a danger to society. But now, he was a man with influence because his strength was the kind that many were familiar with: strength of arm, of peer pressure. People understood this power. He had never known that difference. He was elated to have it.

"Don't you live around here?" one of the Subs asked.

Jeremiah looked about and realized the Sub was right. This is where he had been living for a number of weeks, sleeping in dirty alleys among rats, bottles, and garbage.

"Oh yeah, I suppose so. What of it?" Jeremiah replied.

"Any good places to sleep around here?" inquired the Sub. "Got kicked out of my usual."

Jeremiah pondered his better nights. "There's a big rag pile down that alley there. They've all got a funny smell, but it seems pretty clean. There's a dog that'll challenge you for it, but he's all talk."

The Sub nodded in appreciation. Though it was a bit odd they ended up here, of all the places in the city. It didn't matter. Jeremiah could go wherever he would like. Jeremiah glanced around, looking for something to strike his fancy.

"That way," said Monty.

Monty's directions became more frequent, and more precise, dictating exactly where they would go. Jeremiah could sense Monty watching him, but he was enjoying himself too much to be concerned. What did it matter to him which bars the gang ransacked?

But Jeremiah could sense Monty's watchful eyes on him. Monty kept a close eye, observing him in bars, scrutinizing him on the streets—always following Jeremiah's gaze or watching him when he wasn't. Jeremiah was reminded of how peculiar Monty's presence felt on this journey.

What are you doing? Jeremiah thought. *What are you up to now?*

It took several streets and several bars for Jeremiah to realize something. He was getting closer to where he lived with Bruno, Allison, and Delilah. He wasn't headed directly toward it, and the risks were minimal; Allison, Delilah, and Bruno knew he wasn't to be recognized in public or acknowledged. But the proximity . . . the coincidence was unnerving.

It wasn't until they reached the Filthy Frog, that Jeremiah noticed they were spending less and less time inside any particular establishment. They'd enter, grab their alcohol, and within minutes, Monty would signal to leave. They'd vacate the bar, and Monty would pick a new direction.

"Is this normal?" Jeremiah whispered to Dronkal. "Monty coming along? Telling people where to go?"

Dronkal peeked over his shoulder. "No, Monty almost never gets involved let alone directs us. I have no idea what he's up to." Dronkal shot out a hand and steadied Shugga, who was already deep in his intoxication. "But he's not stopping us from having a good time, so it doesn't bother me."

"It doesn't bother you to talk about kids we do or do not have either," Shugga huffed, shaking off the hand in favor of the stumble.

"This way," said Monty, and the pack turned. Closer.

What just happened? The coincidence was losing credibility. Jeremiah tried to think back to what prompted the direction, but he was soon swept along to the next establishment, The Charging Bull. Jeremiah was made to take the drink of a man on a date with a pretty young woman, and down it in front of them. The couple's response, like most people's to their antics, was to quietly suffer the injustice in the face of a ferocious-looking gang.

"Let's go," said Monty, standing from his table. The Subs had only just started screaming incomprehensible drink orders at the bartender.

The Subs' jubilation was briefly stunted. "But boss, we ain't even got our drinks—" Dronkal's truncheon corrected the complaint.

They spilled back onto the street. Jeremiah looked toward Monty and found Monty looking right back at him. A dozen paces away, arms folded, observing. *I don't know how you're doing it, but I know what you're doing,* thought Jeremiah. He shook the thought as soon as he had it. *Why ruin a good time with paranoia? Monty is just having a good time in a weird dwarven way. He has no idea where my friends live.*

"That way," said Monty.

What? How?! Of all the streets they passed, all the alleys they wandered, Monty picked the one that would lead them closer to the safehouse.

Jeremiah thought back as the group pushed him on, and it became clear. *I glanced, I definitely glanced. Right in the direction I didn't want to go. No problem, I've got his measure now.*

At the next crossroad, Jeremiah gave a surreptitious glance in the opposite direction, away from the safehouse.

"This way," said Monty, indicating the correct direction.

Dang it.

Another bar, The Verbing Animal. Jeremiah found the lack of naming creativity particularly creative. Monty's behavior was different in the bar—he was no longer watching Jeremiah specifically, he now looked wherever Jeremiah was looking. Which, Jeremiah realized, was at the patrons to make sure Bruno, Delilah, or Allison weren't there.

"Drink this!" A Sub shoved a tankard into Jeremiah's hands. It swam with different hues and featured greasy film on the top and tiny mysterious particles bobbed upward before disappearing back into obscurity. The horrible drink was a blessing—if he was too drunk to realize where he was, Monty wouldn't be able to glean information from him.

"The hell is that?" asked Dronkal, peering at the drink from a distance.

"Allsorts," said the Sub. A mix of all the leftovers people don't drink."

"Veto," said Monty. He snatched the tankard from Jeremiah just before he could down it. Monty sniffed allsorts and ventured a sip. "Not bad, though."

He's keeping me sober, thought Jeremiah. *There goes that idea.*

"Let's go," said Monty.

Street by street, block by block, they closed in. Jeremiah tried every trick he could think of, to no avail. Closing his eyes, looking rapidly in all directions, trying to look the right way in the same way he had looked the opposite way didn't work, and was also difficult.

Soon, they were on the same road as the safe house.

"In here," said Monty. The Rambling Owl. They were now across the street from the safe house, in the very bar Jeremiah had stopped in himself occasionally when he lived here. It was a spacious inn, more of a restaurant with a few rooms to rent upstairs. The Subs spread out in their typical fashion while Jeremiah, his cellmates, and Monty grabbed a more central table.

Jeremiah kept his head down, worried his reaction would be obvious if he spotted one of his friends. Then he realized keeping his head down *was* an obvious reaction. Monty was watching him from across the table, the stolen tankard of allsorts still in his grip.

"Something wrong, Jay?" asked Monty.

Jeremiah panicked, *All right, stay calm. Simple question, just give the right answer.* "No," he said.

Definitely the wrong answer.

"What do you think about that girl over there?" asked Monty, gesturing with his tankard.

Jeremiah followed the motion, and it led him right to Delilah. She was seated by the window, a glass of wine and accompanying bottle her only company and reading a stack of papers. Likely more legal correspondence.

She looks sad, thought Jeremiah. Delilah was slumped on her hand. She picked up the wine glass and almost took a drink, but it didn't quite make it. She sighed and set it back down instead.

"What about her?" Jeremiah asked.

"She's pretty, ain't she?" said Monty. Dronkal and Shugga were now looking as well.

"I suppose so," said Jeremiah. *Don't have to lie about that at least.*

"Out of towner," said Monty. "Like you."

"How do you figure?" asked Jeremiah. He tried to feign the perfect balance of curiosity and disinterest.

"Skin's too light," said Monty. "She doesn't have that healthy Elminian duskiness from the soot. Stains the skin like a tattoo."

"So what?" asked Jeremiah. "Want me to steal the wine? Rob her?"

"Nah, I want you to bring her over here." Monty kept nodding in her direction, like he was agreeing with a private thought of his own.

This was bad, as bad as it got. "Doesn't look like she's in the mood to chat," said Jeremiah, trying to hide his panic.

"Convince her," said Monty.

"Get to it, Jay," said Dronkal.

"Yeah, you got the look," said Shugga. "Go charm a little."

What do I say to her? wondered Jeremiah as he approached Delilah's table. *How do I explain the situation? How do I . . .* Jeremiah caught his reflection in a mirror behind the bar. He looked good, he really did. A bruise on his face made him look daring. He was a made man now. He felt good. He flashed the mirror a winning smile. *Can't even see the missing tooth, what more could a girl want?*

Jeremiah arrived at Delilah's table, she looked up at him from her seat with the same sad and sour expression. Jeremiah pulled a chair from another table to hers.

"Now what is—"

"I don't have any money," she said. She gave no indication of anything besides wanting to be left alone.

"Wow!" said Jeremiah. He collapsed into the chair like he'd been wounded. "You went right for the kill. You didn't even hesitate. You must really want me to go away."

"Correct." The look she fixed him with was ice cold.

"Well, I came over because I thought you looked kinda miserable. We're having a nice night over there, maybe you can join us, have a few drinks on us, relax a little. Maybe get your mind off whatever has you looking so down."

"Not interested," Monotone, cold as ice.

"Of course you're not. You're by yourself with a bottle of wine. You've got papers, but you're not really reading them. Bad news, but you already know what they say. Am I right?"

Her eyes flicked down to the pages. "Yes."

She answered a question! That means we're talking! Despite the danger, this was surprisingly fun.

Jeremiah leaned across the table, tapping a finger on the papers. "Those words won't change if you keep looking at them. I think you're dwelling. Yeah, I can see it in those pretty eyes, you're definitely dwelling. So, look, you want to be sad? Be sad. You want to be alone? Be alone. Keep looking at them. But maybe, just *maybe*, you can still have a nice night. If you let yourself. So I'm inviting you to come be the center of attention for a while. I won't keep you if you want to leave. What do you say?"

Delilah just stared at him, brow furrowing, the placid disinterest replaced by curiosity and uncertainty. "No, thank you."

Jeremiah held up his hands. "No problem. Hope the wine treats you well." He left her table and returned to his own.

"Hard luck," said Dronkal.

"Half elves are a fickle lot, huh?" said Monty.

"Can't win 'em all," said Jeremiah with a shrug. *Problem solved*, he thought.

"No, you did good," said Shugga. "Just wait . . . wait for it . . . don't look . . ."

"Offer still open?" asked Delilah. She appeared behind Jeremiah and placed a hand on his shoulder.

He smiled up at her. "Just for you."

"I'm Delilah," she said, sitting.

"Beautiful name. I'm Jay, this is Dronkal, Shugga, and sourpuss over there is Monty," said Jeremiah, not waiting on the compliment for a response. He always did like her name.

"And all these?" Delilah asked, gesturing to the frenzy of Subs.

"Aspirants to a community organization," said Jeremiah.

What are you doing? he thought. *Why come over here? This could already have been over with. No, need to trust her. She of all people knows what she's doing.*

"Oi! Jay!" yelled a Sub. "Come here and—"

"Veto," said Monty. This Sub, apparently smarter than the others, immediately turned away and remained silent. At Monty's veto of a request not even completed, the Subs collectively understood something was up, and to keep their requests to themselves.

"So they're aspirants, and you're . . . ?" asked Delilah. She looked between the Subs and Jeremiah, comparing them.

"He's one of the leaders," said Dronkal. "Bit of a prodigy, really. We just had to have him."

"Very talented," said Shugga. "Real asset."

Jeremiah blushed. "Guys, relax. You're gonna embarrass me." It was already too late. That was adorable.

"Oh, you sound like you're quite the catch," said Delilah, teasing.

"Yeah, he's great," said Monty, quickly skipping past the encouragement.

"Tell us about yourself, Delilah, what brings you around here?" asked Jeremiah.

"Studying to be a defense counselor, actually," said Delilah. "Would I be wrong to assume I might see some of you or your 'aspirants' on a more professional basis someday?"

"If jail time is what it would take to see you again, it'd be worth it," said Jeremiah. She rolled her eyes but smiled at the cheesy line. "But uhh, yeah, that might be true."

"On that note, can I run something by you, Counselor?" Shugga asked. Shugga's intoxication seemed to have vanished, replaced with fierce concentration as he scooted closer to Delilah.

"Oh, I'm not a counselor yet," said Delilah, pausing the inquiry. Already a few ears were tilting in their direction.

"You'd be doing the Stonefists a service," said Monty, "and we'd be sure to remember you. Wouldn't we, Jay?" Monty's expression kept switching from genuine curiosity at Delilah to cold calculation at Jeremiah.

"She's already worth remembering," said Jeremiah. "But really, no pressure if you'd rather not."

A defense counselor? That's quite the change, thought Jeremiah.

Delilah hemmed and hawed but finally relented. "All right, what's the problem?"

Shugga scootched even closer. "Okay, so I've got a friend whose considering a plea bargain to bring an assault charge down to a breaking and entering charge. But the thing is she *did* break into the place, but she *didn't* assault the guy."

Delilah scoffed. "The prosecutor is overbidding and trying to get her to just accept the proper charge. Here's what she needs to do . . ."

It had been at least an hour, and all semblance of control had been ceded to the court of Delilah.

"No, they're bullshitting you," said Delilah. A dozen Subs were gathered around her, paying very close attention. "The guard corps is not bound to any promises they make. Only prosecution can do that."

"But they said if I don't sign, it might be months before I can see a counselor!" said the latest in a long line of worried Subs. She spoke with such fear Jeremiah felt a compulsion to help her. "My girl is at home alone. She can't take care of herself without me."

"No! They're just trying to scare you with pressure tactics. 'Might be,'" Delilah sneered into the glass of wine that had been ordered for her. "'Might be,' you hear that? They'll jerk you around with that 'maybe this, maybe that' talk all day. Never sign anything. All of you hear that? No matter what they say to you, never sign anything! They'll pin any case they want on you. And it's legal. It's all *fucking* legal!" Delilah slammed her glass, and the stem snapped, sending wine across the table. "Shit!"

A dozen hands jumped to her aid, mopping up wine with rags and sleeves before it could spill into her lap. The broken glass disappeared from her hand and was replaced by a new, full glass.

Jeremiah sat beside her still, happy to be ignored. *Was this what she was up to? Could she tell something was wrong and came to my rescue?*

Monty had been as enraptured as anyone, but he finally spoke up. "Would you be interested in work? My crew could use legal representation across the board."

"I can't, I'm not certified. Besides there are public barristers assigned to your area you can use," said Delilah.

"They're long since bought," said Monty. "I can put you through law school, and more besides. This isn't volunteer work I'm talking about. We'd keep you on a sizable retainer."

Delilah shook her head. "Sorry. I really can't, I don't know enough yet, and I couldn't actually represent anyone. There'd be no counselor protections until I'm certified. It's all a bit complicated."

Monty ceded the point with a nod. "Sure, sure, I understand. Come find me if you change your mind. So, how long have you known Jay?"

Jeremiah's heart leapt in his chest. He had been so at ease, and the question was asked so casually . . .

"A few seconds longer than I've known you," said Delilah. She gave Monty a confused look.

Right, that was never going to work on her, thought Jeremiah. "Best few seconds I ever spent," said Jeremiah.

"You don't mind coming on strong, that's for sure," Delilah said. The crowd laughed at his expense.

Jeremiah chanced a glance at Monty. He looked placid enough, politely observing, but Jeremiah could sense a frustration in his eyes.

"I just think you're worth the risk," said Jeremiah. He turned his body toward her, excluding everyone else and giving Delilah his full attention.

"Risk? What risk?" asked Delilah. She seemed genuinely puzzled.

"Risking getting embarrassed in front of all your friends. But I'd hate for pride to get between me and a girl like you." *Yeah, Delilah would be into the humble approach,* he thought.

"Oh? And what's a girl to do with a man with no pride?" She turned toward him as well, no more playing to the crowd. It was like a challenge.

And now I realize I'm not sure I know the definition of pride. Time to improvise! he thought. "Let your guard down," said Jeremiah.

She raised her eyebrows. "Let my guard down?"

The table went quiet.

"That's right. A guy who puts aside his pride for you will do what's best for you. Even at his own expense." Jeremiah hoped delivering that line with bravado would make up for it not making sense.

Delilah rewarded him with a smile. "A novel idea, I'll give you that. I deal with a lot of prideful men in my line of work."

"And tonight is certainly a night you deserve something new," said Jeremiah.

There were some snickers around the table.

"So, you think tonight is a good night for *you*, huh?" she asked.

Oh, you want to raise the stakes, do you? I can play that game, thought Jeremiah. Tonight, he was capable of anything. He leaned in close and locked eyes with her. "Absolutely," he said with intense conviction.

The playful smile dropped from her face for just a second before coming back. To Jeremiah's delight, she squirmed a bit and pushed him back. "Get outta here with that!" she laughed.

The crowd whooped and hollered.

Jeremiah felt good. Actually, he felt great. Delilah was playing her part flawlessly and was proving very fun to flirt with.

"So, Jay, how long have you known Delilah?" asked Monty suddenly.

"A few y—inutes," said Jeremiah. *Years* had almost left his mouth. Almost.

Same question twice? That felt sloppy. I think someone's getting frustrated. Jeremiah mused, choosing to ignore that it almost worked.

"You two are hitting it off well. Take her home," said Monty without a single bit of levity.

"E-excuse me?" asked Jeremiah. Shugga and Dronkal gave each other an uncomfortable look.

"Take her home," Monty repeated.

He's desperate, thought Jeremiah. *He thinks we're playacting. He's right, but he's worried it's all been for nothing.*

"I'm sorry—*you* are telling *him* to take *me* home?" asked Delilah, the look she gave Monty was pure disgust.

"That I am. And if he wants in this gang, he'll make it happen," said Monty. "He doesn't have a choice, it's an order," Monty sipped from his allsorts mug.

"Uh, boss, don't you think that's a little . . . weird?" said Shugga, looking apologetically at Delilah.

Monty's scornful look slowly melted into a sinister smile, "On the contrary, I think it makes perfect sense."

"Monty, can we talk? Privately?" said Dronkal. He stood, gesturing for Monty to join him, but Monty didn't budge.

"Rules are rules," said Monty, keeping his eyes on Delilah.

"I think we're done here," said Delilah coldly. "Good night, Jay. It was a pleasure to meet you."

"Indeed we are," said Jeremiah. "Good night, everyone." He stood up as well and made to go with her.

"Excuse me?" Delilah's voice carried a low threat, she gave him the *who do you think you are?* once-over.

"I'm at least walking you home, it's not safe out there right now," said Jeremiah plainly.

"It's actually really not." Dronkal chuckled. "So if we could all just sit back down while I—"

"I don't want any part in your *gang initiation*, or whatever this is," said Delilah, she cast a nervous glance around the room. There were a lot of Stonefists around them, and she was alone.

"You're not going to be," said Jeremiah. "Monty, if this is what you require to be inducted into the Stonefists, I want no part of it. I'll make do with some other crew."

Jeremiah saw something on Monty's face he had never seen before: uncertainty.

"Come on, boss, don't scare the talent," said a Sub.

"I—uh," Monty stuttered, uncertainty was clearly something he wasn't used to. He looked at the Subs now willing to meet his gaze, and the cell members that wouldn't. His respectability was taking a hit. "I was making a joke. I joke sometimes. It was in poor taste. My apologies, Delilah. Jay."

"I don't accept your apology, but thank you for offering it," said Delilah.

"May I still walk you home?" Jeremiah asked, offering an arm.

"You may," said Delilah, taking it.

They walked to the door arm in arm, stoic and distinguished.

"Oi fellas! Jay's gonna get him some!" screamed a Sub.

The bar erupted in a cheer and Delilah snorted in laughter at the sudden absurdity and tone deafness. That made Jeremiah laugh too. As he turned back to see who made the comment he caught one last look at Monty, who was glaring fiercely at him, before the tide of Subs departed the bar with Jay and Delilah, leaving Monty at the table.

"I . . . don't live far," said Delilah. She was trying to maintain a straight face despite the absurdity of their escort.

"I'll walk you every step of the way," said Jeremiah. The Subs were following them like ducklings, still cheering and shouting encouragement to Jay.

Delilah lead Jeremiah, arm in arm still, to the door across the street.

"Just here," she said. "Top floor."

"Every step," said Jeremiah.

A cute smile played on Delilah's lips. "All right," she said coyly.

They entered the building, the door bouncing behind them as the Subs followed them through. A continuous stream of encouragement and lewd suggestions chased them up the stairs to Delilah's door. They gathered on the landing and watched Delilah and Jar from the corner, their faces alight with anticipation.

Delilah stood with her back to the door and faced Jeremiah. "Well, here we are."

"I think we've been followed," said Jeremiah.

Delilah giggled. Had he ever heard her make that sound before?

"Seems like they're laboring under some sort of assumption," said Delilah.

"Seems like a speculation to me," said Jeremiah.

They stood quietly together for a moment, the Subs raucous noise stilling in anticipation.

Delilah started to turn. "Thanks for the—"

Jeremiah put a hand around the small of Delilah's back, pulled her in, and kissed her. It took every iota of courage he had. Worse, it felt like an awful, coercive thing to do, until he felt her kiss him back.

Suddenly it was the right thing to do, maybe the rightest thing he had ever done. Delilah was an aggressive kisser. *Very* aggressive.

The Subs went wild.

Without breaking the kiss, Jeremiah pushed her against the door. The kiss rapidly grew in intensity, becoming demanding, then frantic. He felt for the doorknob and twisted it. He and Delilah fell together through the doorway, hands too busy to arrest their fall, all while the Subs cheered and chanted his name.

As they hit the ground the intensity spiked. She bit his lip, he pinned her arm, and they both nearly jumped out of their skin when a voice said, "Ahem."

Sitting at the dinner table, the checkerboard between them forgotten, were Bruno and Allison.

"Told ya," said Bruno.

CHAPTER THIRTY-THREE

Admiration

Jeremiah and Delilah sprang apart. They scrambled to their feet, as though if they could just act natural it would be as though nothing had happened.

"So should we leave, or . . . ?" said Allison, she quickly gave the still open door a push shut, quieting the shouts from outside.

Jeremiah's head swam. His lip hurt too where Delilah had bit him, but that wasn't so bad.

"Monty tracked me here," said Jeremiah. "It's uh, it's a gang thing. I'm in a gang now. Monty is the gang leader. And there's a bunch of Subbies right outside."

Bruno's expression turned serious. "Tell me every detail."

Jeremiah described the events of the night right up until Delilah was pulled into it. Then they told their respective sides without looking at each other in halting, stunted snippets.

I fucked up, thought Jeremiah. *I fucked up so bad. That kiss was definitely not okay.* But it felt pretty okay.

"Good cover, both of you. I'm proud," said Bruno.

"Is this safehouse dark?" Allison asked.

Bruno narrowed his eyes. "How do you know that term?" When Allison pretended not to hear him, he answered, "I think we're still safe. Our cover story as renters stands up to scrutiny. I'll make sure the rumors are in our favor. Jay, you're staying here tonight, for obvious reasons."

Jeremiah chanced a glance at Delilah and caught her chancing a glance at him. Their attention both snapped to the ground.

"Allison, can I talk to you about that really important thing I need to talk to you about?" said Delilah.

"Yup." Allison had already replied before Delilah finished. They scurried into their room.

"So . . ." said Jeremiah. He had no idea what to say. Or do. Or think.

"Room is yours for tonight. Welcome home, honeypot." He grabbed his cloak and slipped out a window, leaving Jeremiah alone.

Once again, Jeremiah stood in front of Delilah's door. Once again, he was more nervous than he had ever been in doing so. It had been a difficult night of tossing, thinking, and worrying.

He raised his hand again to knock, and again he lowered it.

Had he overdone it? Yes . . . maybe. Would she ever forgive him? Obviously not.

But he had to get this over with.

He knocked.

No answer.

He had heard Allison leave early in the morning—because he had been listening for it—so either Delilah was deliberately ignoring the knock, or she was inside the Giant's Bag.

He eased the door open, and sure enough, there was only the Giant's Bag on the bed. As before, the window was wide-open to vent whatever gases might be escaping the bag. Next to the bag was the pair of goggles and fume mask she would lend him when they worked in the lab together.

Is this an invitation? he wondered. *Or does she just keep these here for when people need to speak with her?* All important questions worth standing still and pondering.

Finally, he worked up the courage to don the mask and goggles. He opened the bag further, recoiling at the blast of heat, then stuck his head in. He absently worried that some chemical gas might corrode the bag to the point of failure and cut his head off.

"Delilah? You in there?" From his vantage point, Jeremiah could see that she was indeed in there, lying a large sheet of paper over one of his enchanting metal squares. She dipped a brush in a small vial of acid and began wiping it over the paper.

"Yes?" she kept at her work.

"It's Jay," said Jeremiah.

"Yes, I . . ." she sighed. "Yes, come in."

Jeremiah clambered into the bag, imagining his shoe catching the bag's edge somehow and tearing it. No such luck.

He floated down to perch on the workbench behind her. He carefully cleared a spot and sat with his legs hanging. Technically there was room to stand next to her, but he'd be practically on top of her, like last night when—

Don't think about it, he thought.

She didn't stray from her work, which was normal. But it didn't *feel* normal.

"So . . ." said Jeremiah.

"Sew buttons," said Delilah.

Good start. Not great but good enough.

"I wanted to check in with you," said Jeremiah.

"Still here," she said.

"Good, good," said Jeremiah. *She's doing this on purpose,* he thought. *Wait, is she doing this on purpose? She's trying to gauge where I'm at. She's trying to make sure I'm okay. Well, I got here first, I'm doing the okay checking.*

"Let's talk about last night," he said, trying to sound surer of himself.

"There we go," she said. "I'm listening."

Why is it up to me to bring it up and you to listen? You were there too! No, calm, calm. She might be feeling . . . feelings. Or something. I can handle talking.

"I wanted to check how you were feeling about . . . what happened. Obviously, we were under duress, and I didn't ask for permission. I apologize if I overstepped.

I'm sure there were alternatives I could have taken, but I couldn't think of them at the time." Jeremiah congratulated himself on sounding perfectly reasonable and not at all rehearsed.

Delilah set down the beaker she'd been wiping with a *tink*. She didn't respond immediately, facing away from Jeremiah and inspecting the vials in front of her. But eventually she turned to give him an easy smile.

"I'm okay if you are. Crazy stuff happens on a mission, I'm not going to hold it against you. You did what you thought was right, and I support that."

Relief flooded through Jeremiah. So many muscles unclenched at once that he nearly slumped over. "And Bruno said he was proud of us, wasn't that gratifying?"

Delilah grinned. "That *was* gratifying! It was even unironic—he never does that." She turned back to her work.

I can just, he thought. *I can say good talk, and float back out of the bag. Maybe give her a hearty slap on the back for good measure. All I have to do is nothing, and this was just a pleasant memory . . .*

"So . . ." he said.

She didn't respond.

"Is there anything else? We need to talk about?" he asked.

"Such as?" she answered, peering into the depths of a wide-bottomed flask.

It wasn't too late. He could still do nothing.

"Well, I couldn't help but notice your response to my bit of improvisation was a little . . ." there was still time to run "enthusiastic. And I wanted to check . . . on that . . ."

TINK.

And now we wait, thought Jeremiah.

He didn't have to wait long.

"Look, Jay," said Delilah without turning around, "you know I admire you."

Uhh, what? Delilah? Admires me? thought Jeremiah.

"And . . . it may so happen . . . that . . ." She started off speaking to her vials and then slowly turned around to face him. "Maybe, over time . . . that I took the teeniest, tiniest baby step past admiration . . . and developed a sort of . . . crush . . . on you . . . aaaand the look on your face tells me saying that was a *huge* mistake! Thank you, Jay. That's quite a relief. You can see yourself out."

"No, no, no! Wait!" he waved his hands frantically to slow her down and undid whatever it was his face was doing.

"Goodbye." She turned back to her work.

"No, I'm sorry, it just caught me by surprise. I mean, you *admire* me?"

She faced him again, looking confused. "What? Of course I admire you. You're a kind man. You put your family, us, first. You're brave and considerate, and you're a great friend."

Jeremiah's instinct was to scoff. Surely, she was operating under some false pretenses he should hurry to correct. He opened his mouth to respond, but she cut him off.

"Most of all, you were a necromancer! You held power and influence in the palm of your hand, and you gave it away. You weren't exactly a player of the great game, but you were a very valuable piece. And you chose to abandon that power because you didn't feel responsible enough to wield it. You did it to keep people safe, people you didn't even know, and never would know. For no reward, and under no pressure to do so—hell, under pressure to do the opposite. And you're a *human*."

"A human?"

"Don't take it the wrong way, but humans don't tend to curb their ambition. 'Fastest way to get a human to make a fist is to put a speck of power in his palm' is the old dwarven saying. All of what you did would be a shocking decision for anyone, but for a human as well? That's just . . ." Her eyes grew wider as she spoke to him, and she became more animated, like she had been dying to say this. "Well, that's just so *interesting*!"

Jeremiah was stunned. He had never been complimented like that before, especially not by someone like Delilah.

In the silence, Delilah asked, "Do you . . . have something . . . similar? To say?"

"I—I mean no! I've never really thought about you like *that*—"

Oh, sweet gods, no. What have I done? he thought the moment the words left his mouth.

Delilah whipped back around to her vials. "That's fine."

Do something, do anything, a bad thing is happening.

"Not 'cause you aren't amazing or anything!" Jeremiah said. "You're Delilah Fortune. You're what amazing *is*. But it's like, the trees don't *want* the sun, it's too far beyond them. They're just thrilled to be in its presence."

She turned around again, this time looking annoyed. "What was that?"

Did he bad again?

"What was what?"

"That! The tree thing! And last night, with the flirting, where was all that coming from?"

"I . . . don't know?" If he squished Gus hard enough, maybe he could poison himself and die.

"Gods, would you just get out of here!" Delilah grabbed him by the shirt and pushed him upward, the low gravity propelling him all the way up to the top.

Jeremiah nearly let momentum carry him back into the bedroom, but he stopped himself. There was something here, a sort of opportunity right now. These dice needed rolling, cost be damned. He braced himself.

"Hey, Delilah. When this is all done—the mission that is—would you want to go do something? Together?"

TINK!

Delilah pressed the palms of her hands against her eyes and let out a low growl that escalated quickly into a shout. "ArghhaaAAAAH! Yes, Jay, I would like that very much! Now, get OUT!"

CHAPTER THIRTY-FOUR

Freedom

After his initiation, it seemed Jeremiah's grace period as the newest cell member was over—as soon as he got home, he was expected to start earning his keep.

"It's okay to start small," said Dronkal, petting Miggy on the couch, the orange cat stretched out as far as she could go. "I'll cover you for a bit and introduce you to our fence. But you'll need to start bringing in the goods."

"Won't Monty tell me when I need to steal something?" Jeremiah had almost been looking forward to the next challenge.

"Nah, that's just for the big jobs," said Dronkal. "You want to eat every day, you gotta get some regular work going. Our last Slip told me a few targets he never hit. You can start with those while you're getting your bearings." Miggy began furiously attacking Dronkal's hand.

"You can always come to us for help," said Shugga. "The Subbies are available to you, too. Just, for the love of the gods, don't go to Pete."

There was a murmur of agreement around the room.

"Why? What's wrong with Pete?" Jeremiah asked.

"Oh, he gets everyone at some point," said Shugga. "He can provide a solution to almost any problem, and he tends to show up when someone is at their most desperate." He went to sit on the couch, but grumbled and turned away when Miggy didn't move for him. Her claim on places to sit was apparently equal to anyone else's in the cell.

"But he's a master of trading one copper for two," said Sweet Melissa. "You'll always end up giving more than you got in the end."

"How many favors do you owe Pete?" asked Dronkal.

"I think three," said Jeremiah.

The others winced.

"What are we looking at?" asked Bruno in Jeremiah's head.

He had been lurking across a small grassy courtyard from his target for the last thirty minutes, pressed flat and out of sight among the hollyhocks.

Manor house, windows locked. The help is cleaning, going from room to room. Nice and orderly, thought Jeremiah.

"And what does orderly mean?" asked Bruno.

Predictable.

Rise.

The rat Jeremiah had obtained stirred to life. It scampered out of Jeremiah's hand, and ran for the front door, squeezing under with plenty of room to spare.

Jeremiah felt a twinge of guilt for using necromancy again after Delilah had said how interesting he was for giving it up, but this manor wasn't going to burgle itself.

"There will always be a reason," said Allison, again.

Yes, I know, I know. Just . . . stop.

Run. Evade. Squeak.

The screaming began soon after, which was understandable. It was a sizable rat, the largest one Jeremiah could find that had not yet decayed. Jeremiah dashed across the courtyard and hid behind a topiary, just below the window he intended to enter.

"What do you hear?" asked Bruno.

Jeremiah concentrated. *Multiple voices, moving. Yelling "rat" in Gnomish. It's become an all-hands-on-deck problem.*

"Is the yelling loud enough to cover the sound?"

Jeremiah tapped the window, *No, that's awfully thick glass. They'll hear it all over the house.*

"You'll need a new ingress then," said Bruno.

No time. Jeremiah pulled his inscription pick and rapidly scratched at the glass. *Decay And Decay And Decay*

Jeremiah reached up to charge the diagram, then hesitated. He added two more runes at the beginning. The diagram now read *Adhere And Decay And Decay And Decay.*

He charged the diagram and swayed on his feet, hit by sudden dizziness and fatigue. Not since the Giant's Bag recharge had he tried that many active runes simultaneously. He waited another minute, hoping the rat could keep up the chase just a little longer, then scratched out the Cohesion rune.

The window shattered, but with only a *pop* and hiss of tiny glass pellets raining down. Jeremiah pulled himself inside.

"Make sure you tell me about this in person," said Bruno.

Will do.

Screams from the other side of the house told Jeremiah the rat was still doing its job. He hurried to the living room and grabbed the elaborately decorated sword from the mantle, wrapping it in an old sheet to avoid drawing attention and cutting himself on the blade.

Jeremiah was about to leave when he saw the chests of silverware stacked near the dining table. With the entire staff distracted trying to kill a zombie rat, he risked opening one.

"Whoa, them's some fancy forks," said Bruno.

More than just silver, they were filigreed to an absurd degree. Soup spoons in the shape of clam shells, knives with sweeping and curled tips, and a half dozen different varieties of fork with tiny designs etched into them.

Bet they make the soup taste better, thought Jeremiah. He lay the sword on top and lifted three cases, huffing at the weight. With some difficulty, he swung his legs back out the window and dropped down, then took to the street where the traffic swept him toward the Subs he had recruited for the job.

"Don't let them ask, give freely as though it's a gift," whispered Delilah.

"You may not have been born with a silver spoon in your mouth, but it's not too late!" Jeremiah said as he reached the rendezvous point.

Jeremiah opened the chests with a flourish, the Subs were dumbstruck by the ridiculous cutlery.

"My kid and I ate a pigeon with our bare hands the other night, and these assholes are using knives shaped like leaves," said one.

"*Kid . . .*" The word stuck in his head, wedged firmly. Stark, yet strangely undefined.

"It's hard to think of hungry children, isn't it?" said Vivica. "But they're real. They're oh so real."

"Then consider these leaves liberated for a better cause," said Jeremiah. "Fence the sword for Cell Four and divide the silverware among yourselves."

The Subs' surprise soon evolved into excitement when they realized Jeremiah was being serious. They thanked him over and over.

It felt good.

"He's home and he's got a dog," said Jeremiah.

"Dogs are the worst," said Bruno.

Jeremiah recalled the rant Bruno would go on whenever the topic of dogs came up. *Even the littlest ones are dangerous. And regardless, they're all noisy, they're all territorial, and the big ones will actually hurt you. Oh, just kill the dog, you say? Now you're a guy that kills dogs and people get weirdly hostile. Kill a person? Big deal. Kill a dog? You're an asshole.*

Jeremiah peered down at the small double apartment rented by his next target, an ancient halfling man with a bull mastiff. Jeremiah had climbed to the roof of an adjacent apartment for a better view.

"That's a halfling war mastiff," said Allison. "The man was a rider, elite military. Those dogs are trained like soldiers. Very dangerous."

"An officer. He'll be tough to fool," said Delilah.

"So, what will you do?" they asked.

"Wait," said Jeremiah.

Over an hour passed, the sun dipping toward the horizon. But eventually, the dog went to sit by the front door. The halfling man appeared to let him outside. He strapped a saddle to the dog's back, balancing carefully, his trusty mount bearing him with great care.

"Good girl, Calliope, that's a good girl." The man's wizened voice drifted to Jeremiah's perch. "Let's take a nice walk. Where would you like to go today?"

As the dog exited with his owner, revealing its true size, Jeremiah laughed out loud. He couldn't help himself. "That—that's not a dog. That is a small bear!" The mastiff was immense and composed of solid muscle. Its head in particular was abnormally large—Jeremiah was sure it could enclose a human skill in its mouth with room to spare. He was thankful he hadn't suffered a fit of insanity and decided to enter the house while it was lurking.

Unfortunately, an evening stroll was a popular activity, so the streets were rife with potential witnesses and the occasional guard. No breaking a window or picking a lock on the ground floor without attracting attention. Jeremiah considered waiting till nightfall, but that would mean Calliope, the four-legged war machine, would be home.

"All that practice for nothing," said Bruno.

Ugh, fine, I'll do it, thought Jeremiah.

A few minutes later, Jeremiah held a rope procured for him by a Sub earlier that day. He picked up two loose, flat, cobble stones and pulled out his enchanting equipment.

Cohesion And Strengthen

"Okay, so that should stick here, yes?" He placed the stone on the roof and charged it. The rock held fast, fixed in place. "Yes!"

He tied one end of the rope to the secured brick, and one end to the brick he was still working on.

Strengthen and If Contact Pause Pause Cohesion If Cohesion Cohesion

"Buddy, help me out here," said Jeremiah. Gus wriggled awake in his clothes, ready to lend aid. Jeremiah pulled Gus out and sat him down on a roof ledge. "Okay, buddy, just need you to listen."

Gus licked his eyeball.

"So, Strengthen, pretty simple, make brick stronger. And if the contact is touched, wait, wait, then stick to stuff. Makes sense?"

Gus let out a high-pitched peep.

"Exactly! Then it goes into a cohesion loop to stick extra hard . . . I'm not sure what infinite sticky is going to do, hopefully nothing bad."

Jeremiah spent a moment admiring his work. It was easily the most complex diagram he had ever done.

Jeremiah charged the brick and wobbled a bit, his focus drained. He sat down, preparing for a period of down time, but recovered quicker than he expected. *Huh, getting better at this,* he thought. Then he touched the Contact and heaved the brick across the street. It bounced down the gentle slope of the target roof before suddenly sticking in place.

"Ha! I can't believe that worked!" Jeremiah said. "Now we just . . . Ah, dang it."

The bounce down the roof had introduced enough slack in the rope that it hung halfway down the building. A couple of quick cuts and a new knot he'd learned from Sweet Melissa, and he was back in business with a taught line connecting his roof to the target's.

I can shimmy this, he thought.

"I should hope so," said Bruno.

"Wrap your hands," said Allison.

Jeremiah shimmied inch by inch over the street, thankful for the hand wraps.

The people rushing far below thankfully kept their eyes on the road . . . save one. A young man in a fanciful hat stared up at Jeremiah from the roadside, half-eaten apple still in hand. They both froze, eyes locked, the young man mid-chew.

Jeremiah scowled at him and shook his head. The young man returned his eyes to the street and kept eating his apple.

Good man, thought Jeremiah. He finished crossing the rope and crawled up on the roof, a quick descent got him through an open second floor window.

The house was like a museum. Maps framed behind glass covered the walls, still sporting notes and scribbles from ages long past. Trophies of battle stood proudly on every surface, each one telling a story that Jeremiah couldn't hear.

"This man served an honorable life," said Allison.

"Yeah, I can see that," said Jeremiah. Knowing his friend's opinions was not always helpful.

Jeremiah's target was a uniform, which he found on a small-sized dress dummy. Carefully pressed and immaculate, it stood sentry, facing the bed like a guardian against regret. It was nearly covered in stately medals and insignia.

Allison's medal box sprang to Jeremiah's mind. "This is his legacy," said Allison. "This uniform represents the culmination of a life of hard work."

I don't like it either, said Jeremiah, unbuttoning the uniform, *but I need to do what I need to do. And I* don't *want to be here when that dog gets back.*

He bundled up the uniform, undoubtedly giving it creases that it hadn't held in a long time. But before he did, he plucked every adornment and laid them carefully on the bed. The job had requested he steal a uniform, so a uniform was all he would take.

The occupants of the illustrious smoking room screamed as Jeremiah exploded through the window, a square of wood Adhered to his forearm shielding him from the worst of the glass shards. Jeremiah snatched a framed painting off the wall and a decanter of liquor from the sideboard and dove out through another window.

"Your loyal servant returns!" Jeremiah announced, returning to headquarters after his latest conquest. The Stonefist Subs cheered. Jeremiah tossed a jewelry box and a pair of wine bottles to some waiting hands. After several weeks of thefts, during which he always made sure to nab a little something extra for the Subs, he now found plenty of eager assistants for his work, and a warm welcome anywhere Subs saw him. It was nice to give back to them, they only really worked on the promise of one day being raised above their station. It was said the Subs came and went, but he was beginning to see the same faces more than once.

Working through the list of theft targets Dronkal had given him had led Jeremiah to a bit of a reputation for retrieving specific items for interested buyers. The premium was considerable, and the objects in question tended to be less heavily guarded than money.

There were a few strange assignments thrown in, of course—twice Jeremiah had to stab a folded letter to a headboard or door with daggers. Once he had to leave a set of wet manacles at the top of a staircase. And on one occasion he wasn't required to steal anything at all, only to toss the place to make it look like someone had been unable to find what they sought.

All in all, aside from occasional stabs of guilt over stealing someone's most prized possession, he found the work varied and enjoyable—each case was a unique situation, calling upon his skillset in unexpected ways and demanding innovation. His enchanting was improving by leaps and bounds, both in designing diagrams and executing them efficiently. He was astonished at what he could accomplish. He knew so few words, but creativity in their usage meant very little could be kept safe from him. His Decay rune in particular made short work of any barrier, with his Gently rune ensuring the results could be easily controlled. With time and a surface to write on, he could Decay through most anything.

One of the Subs tapped Jeremiah on the shoulder. "Boss wants to see you."

Jeremiah immediately felt like a little boy about to be in trouble, although as far as he knew he had nothing to be worried about. He headed down to Monty's office, trying to reassure himself of that fact.

"Jay," said Monty as he entered. "Please sit."

Jeremiah settled himself on the floor. "What can I do for you, sir?"

"I've heard a rumor you've been giving gifts to the Subs," said Monty.

Jeremiah hesitated. It suddenly occurred to him that the gang boss might expect all stolen items to be subject to their usual cut. Was he about to be accused of stealing from Monty?

"I don't know if I'd call them *gifts,* boss. More like . . . extras," said Jeremiah. "Subs are people too, even if they're not officially part of the Stonefists."

"Your 'extras' have been affecting recruitment and retention," said Monty. "Subs are leaving less often, and more promising candidates are showing up. Importantly, the quality of work we're seeing from the Subs we already have is improving. You've been giving back to the gang."

"Oh," said Jeremiah. The praise made him feel uncomfortable. It reminded him of how much he was hiding.

"The strongest gangs grow from the bottom up. A stronger foundation lets the tower rise higher. What I'm saying, Jay, is thank you. You're a rare talent," said Monty.

"You're welcome, boss," said Jeremiah. He shifted, wondering if some other response was expected of him.

"I also want to apologize for the incident with the counselor," said Monty, his voice dipping ever so slightly. "That was crass and prideful of me. I was certain I had discovered some secret of yours, a folly I let guide my actions in place of wisdom. I consider myself quite adept at reading people, even if they don't want to be read. But I suppose you're of the rare type that throws me off."

"S'all right," said Jeremiah. This he had even less idea what to do with.

"I was wondering, Jay, if you would join me for a drink." Monty drew a decanter and a pair of tumblers from his desk.

"Oh! Yeah, okay."

"This is a special vintage from my youth," said Monty, pouring the whiskey. He circled to the front of the desk and handed a glass to Jeremiah. "I see myself in many of the people you're helping, Jay."

"In the Subs, boss?" asked Jeremiah, taking the glass. It was a comparison with quite the gulf.

Monty nodded. "It's where I started. Where most people start. And over years and years, I've connived, swindled, beaten, and murdered my way up the chain." He listed off the crimes with exasperation. Monty almost returned to his seat but seemed to think twice about it and instead sat down on the floor with Jeremiah.

"I guess that's just the way of things," said Jeremiah. The whiskey smelled like a wood fire.

"Indeed it is. We do what we have to do. And what we have to do, oftentimes, is just keep ourselves alive." Monty was gazing into his tumbler, letting the amber liquor swirl.

"You seem to be doing a bit better than most," said Jeremiah. This was a very strange turn of events. Why was Monty telling him this?

"Only because I stand on the backs of those I've crushed underfoot. And if any one of them"—at this he gestured upward toward the common room of the headquarters—"wants anything more out of life than the squalor they live in, they'll need to do the same."

"Kick down?" asked Jeremiah.

Monty nodded. "Kick down, aye. The Pit is a great big bucket of crabs all making sure no one gets out, 'cause that'll be one less back to stand on."

They sat quietly. Jeremiah sipped the whiskey and, despite his efforts, emitted the tiniest cough.

"I've got a way out," said Monty. "For all of us, I think."

"Out of . . . what, the Pit? The lifestyle?" asked Jeremiah.

"All of it. But it's going to require that I give more than I already have. I'm going to need your help as well, if you're the right man for the job."

Jeremiah was intrigued now. This was sounding like some sort of easy way out. A simple solution to a very complicated problem.

"No such thing," said Allison.

Exactly the sort of thing a cult would promise, thought Jeremiah.

"Desperation," said Bruno.

"I'm sure I'm up for it," said Jeremiah.

"No, you're not. Not yet. There are better thieves than you in this city, better cutthroats too. But I need someone who can see the bigger picture. Someone who understands the value of being free from all of . . . this." Monty picked up a pinch of dirt from the floor and rubbed it between his fingers, before sprinkling just a pinch into his whiskey and sipping it. "And that's where you come in. A normal Slip doesn't think past the job, or himself. He'd take those spoons, that wine, the rug, those fancy robes, all those extras you tend to nab, and sell them for himself."

"Oh, you know about all those?" Maybe he was in trouble.

"Very little escapes my notice, man-fish," said Monty with a smirk.

Jeremiah couldn't help but chuckle at that.

"Tell me, Jay," said Monty. "Why? Why are you handing that stuff directly to the Subs instead of using proper channels? Or keeping it for yourself?"

"He's already told you who he needs you to be. He's already played his . . . hand," said Bruno.

Jeremiah shrugged. "Because they deserve it? Or, I guess, because they don't deserve what they have. Some of them have kids, did you know that?"

Monty nodded. "More than a few."

"That's messed up, Monty, I—"

"Careful!" said Bruno. "You've known this all your life! Remember who you are!"

"I've never been comfortable with kids and poverty, you know? No kid should have to go through what I went through," finished Jeremiah, recovering in the nick of time.

"Same," said Monty. "Born into that hell. Helpless, scared, hungry, uncertain. The same pink babe that laughs in delight at the sight of a rat and knows no greater comfort than gentle arms slowly but surely becomes an animal." Monty stared into the dirt, his green-blue eyes shimmered with the early signs of tears, but his expression was pure rage.

Jeremiah was stunned, that was far more emotion than he was expecting from Monty. It was more than he had ever seen from him. It felt guarded, like a glimpse into something painful.

"Poor man," said Vivica. "Maybe I should have started here. He would have been an easy recruit."

"You okay?" Jeremiah asked. He lifted a hand to put it on Monty's shoulder but hesitated. This could end with a broken wrist. He risked it, trying to seem comforting without condescending.

"No Jay, I'm a damn long way away from okay," said Monty. That stare kept going, Monty was miles away, buried in some memory that he'd never been able to escape from.

"You want to give them a way out. I want that too," said Jeremiah.

"Not just a meal," said Monty. "Not just a day of comfort." The glisten of tears was hardening, the flinty intelligence returning, the rage building.

"Freedom," Confirmed Jeremiah.

"Aye, freedom," said Monty.

"Desperation," said Bruno.

"You just tell me what needs doing," said Jeremiah. This was it. Jeremiah was on the verge of something, likely exactly what he was using for.

"No," said Monty.

Jeremiah removed his hand, Monty as Jeremiah knew him, had returned. "You're gonna lead with all that and just leave me hanging?"

"I need someone exceptional," said Monty. "We get one chance. I can't waste the opportunity, and I can't waste you."

"See if you can—" Bruno or Delilah started.

"I understand," said Jeremiah. "Really. Just let me know when you can."

Monty raised his drink. "To freedom."

Jeremiah mirrored the salute. "To freedom."

CHAPTER THIRTY-FIVE

Collect

Jeremiah weaved his way through the Pit after another successful robbery, followed by distributing a box of cigars to the Subs. He had been feeling good. Great, even. Better than he had in a long time. Here, he was proficient at his work. He was trusted. Among the Subs, he was adored.

A corner mugger gave him a nod, which he returned. Jeremiah no longer worried about being targeted by random crime in the Pit. People knew he was a Stonefist, and a popular one at that. The status protected him far better than any weapon could.

The fever of the city, that ineffable sense of tension, was still building. It no longer manifested just in singular bouts of horror but was beginning to spread like a heat wave. People were disappearing, violence was becoming far more common and extreme, even casual. But even that couldn't dampen Jeremiah's mood, except to remind him he's supposed to be doing something else. He pushed the thought away. He needed some rest first, then he could think about it.

Jay climbed the stairs home and rapped out the special knock before pushing the door open. He was looking forward to collapsing onto his bed for some much-deserved rest, the last robbery had involved a long night of watching and waiting, and he was ready for bed. But almost as soon as he entered, Dronkal said, "Load up, Jay, we're leaving."

"Huh? Where are we going?" asked Jeremiah.

"We're going collecting," said Shugga. "We need to make sure you can cover for one of us if need be. Besides, it'll be good for our regulars to recognize you."

With great reluctance, Jeremiah allowed himself to be led back down the stairs. He thought of his pillow, cool and fluffy in the morning light. *I'll be back soon*, he promised.

They crossed the edge of the Pit and entered the slums. Dronkal and Shugga wore stony expressions, their greatswords and batons hanging at their hips. They walked shoulder to shoulder, and their size and pace left Jeremiah tailing awkwardly behind.

"This is our first stop," said Shugga, halting so abruptly Jeremiah collided with his backside. "You taken protection money before?"

"No. Is there going to be trouble?" asked Jeremiah.

"Doubtful," said Shugga. "Dronkal and I make sure of that. Follow our lead."

They shoved the doors open with a bang that startled the few customers, and the halfling behind the counter. The patrons took one look at the character of the men who had just entered and took their leave.

Jeremiah watched Dronkal's demeanor shift to one of outright hostility, his feet falling hard on the floor, tusks jutting and fists clenched. He stomped toward the halfling proprietor, who began to stammer. "Gentlemen! There must be some mistake, you've come far too early in the week to—oh my!"

Dronkal stepped over the halfling-sized counter, his foot connecting with the halfling's shoulder and knocking him aside. "Bird told me you've been stashin' on me, Cinta. That true?" He loomed over the tiny cheesemonger, seemingly on the verge of violence.

"No! Not at all, sir! I keep careful ledgers, I do. Your cut is here!" The halfling, shaking like a leaf, took a small pouch from the counter and held it up to Dronkal. Dronkal snatched the coin purse and peered inside.

Meanwhile, Shugga patrolled the empty shop, inspecting each wheel of cheese. They were stacked to chest height, and a thin wire for slicing had been placed delicately atop each one. Shugga gripped the edge of a wheel and ripped off a fist-sized chunk. He stuffed most of it into his mouth and chewed thoughtfully, then cut a careful wedge with the wire and stowed it.

Shugga gave Jeremiah a pointed look, and Jeremiah found his own wheel of cheese. *Was Shugga going to pay for that?* thought Jeremiah. *No, no, of course not. This is criminal stuff. We're doing criminal stuff.*

Jeremiah had never stolen anything before.

Wait, he thought. *That's not true. I've stolen lots of things in the last few days alone. I stole things at random during my initiation. Why did I even think that?* The mistake would have been comical if weren't so stark. *Why does this feel so different?*

He took the wire and sliced a piece off the pale yellow slab. The proprietor shot him a pained expression, but didn't object. Jeremiah nibbled the corner of the slice. It was okay. He tried to press the slice back into the slab. Cheese didn't work like that apparently.

"Best make sure we don't hear any more rumors," said Dronkal, satisfied with the count.

"I—I'm not sure how . . . I mean, I will! Yes, of course, sir!" said Cinta.

They left as quickly as they came, Shugga making sure to slam the door as they left.

"You saw how that went down?" Dronkal asked Jeremiah.

"I think so," said Jeremiah. "You intimidated him and got the money. Were there really rumors he was holding out?"

"Nope, none at all," said Dronkal, "but they need to be scared every time. Got that? Every single time. The moment they're not afraid of you is the moment they'll start wondering what they can get away with."

"Well, we have different philosophies," said Shugga. "I try to be a bit more friendly and let it feel like a business transaction. Really stress the 'protection' side of things."

Jeremiah nodded. "And are we actually *protecting* these people from anything?"

Dronkal shrugged. "Technically, yes, we're protecting them from other gangs who would do the same thing." He frowned. "Don't get any fantasies of noble thieves in your head, they died out long ago."

Another shop, this one selling untreated leather. Shugga took the lead and was slightly more civil to the man running the shop, but the air of threat was still there.

"Not having any problems, Gerald? Yeah? No one making payments difficult, is there?" said Shugga.

Gerald wouldn't look directly at Shugga. "No, sir, no problems. Thank you for asking."

"Well, you just let us know, all right?"

They hit up a half dozen stores, Jeremiah's mood soured like curdling cream. For some reason, he was surprised. Dronkal and Shugga seemed so nice. Brutal maybe, but they were nice to *him*. How could there be such a difference between the Dronkal and Shugga he knew and who he was seeing now?

Until it wasn't.

"You're up," said Shugga.

Jeremiah started. This was not part of the plan. "Me? You want me to do the next one?"

"Gotta learn. Go in there and tell them you're working for Dronk and Shug. Get the payment. We'll be just outside in case there's trouble, don't worry." Shugga gave him an encouraging slap on the back. There was that awful juxtaposition again, that friendliness mixed with an insistence that Jeremiah should do something awful.

It was a small blacksmith's shop set up under a shoddy overhang that bowed and bent like an old man. Everything about it was tiny—the furnace, the buckets, the hammers and anvils, everything. Jeremiah would have assumed it belonged to a gnome or halfling, but for the young human woman tapping away at a horseshoe on her anvil.

"Morning, sir!" She flashed him a smile. "What can I help you with?"

This place is small-time, thought Jeremiah. This wasn't a smith who made weapons and armor; she did nails, horseshoes and cheap knives.

"I'm here to collect," said Jeremiah, putting as much casual authority into his voice as he could, "on behalf of Dronk and Shug." He thought he sounded like a herald.

The smile slipped off the woman's face. "Got a batch of bad iron and business has been slow. Come back next week."

I really was hoping this was going to be an easy one, thought Jeremiah. He got closer to her, trying to think what would be intimidating. *'That's not my problem. You are my problem. Now, pay up.'*

The woman looked him up and down and raised an eyebrow. "That so? Then you got a mighty fine problem on your hands, don't you?" She squared up with him, gripping her small hammer hard. She definitely had some muscle on her, not enough for Jeremiah to feel cowed, not like Allison, but enough to make him awfully nervous of that hammer.

"Oh, is it time to take a stand?" said Jeremiah. "Now's your big moment?" *Please,* he silently begged, *don't make this worse.*

She didn't flinch. "Mayhap it is. I don't bring in much for you and yours. Maybe today is when I'll make myself not worth the trouble."

Jeremiah realized he'd screwed up. He had put the idea of defiance in her head like a script.

"You don't have much. It'll be real easy to take it all away," he said. It was a vague threat, nonsensical threat—and worse, as he was saying it, he flinched. His eyes flicked away from hers for just an instant, and she caught it.

"Tell you what, little man," she said with a half smile. "I'll give you two sets of horseshoes, free of charge. That's worth about what I pay to your people. We can call that square, can't we?"

Jeremiah wasn't sure. He had no idea what horseshoes cost. But if it was worth about the same then maybe it would count? "Better than nothing. Maybe they'll take it easy on you," he said.

"Oh, I sure hope so," said the woman. She grabbed eight horseshoes off a peg and handed them to Jeremiah. He bobbled them and a few clattered to the ground. "Butterfingers," she said.

He gathered them up and left.

Dronkal and Shugga were waiting around the corner. "It's just, why wouldn't you *tell* me?" Shugga was saying. "It's not weird that you have a kid, it's weird you wouldn't say anything."

"Jay! How'd we do?" said Dronkal the moment he laid eyes on him.

"She said she didn't have enough money but gave me these." Jeremiah showed the horseshoes to Dronkal and Shugga.

They burst out laughing. A flush began to rise in Jeremiah's cheeks.

"Oh, that takes me back," said Shugga, wiping a tear from his eye.

"Jay, do we own horses?" said Dronkal, still smiling, amusement sprinkled in his voice.

"No," said Jeremiah, looking at the ground like a scolded child.

"Are we in the horseshoe selling business?" Dronkal continued.

"No." It was Monty's one gold challenge all over again.

"No. She sells those at a markup. They're not even worth what she charges for them," said Dronkal.

"I love it when a Slip tries to do a thug's job," laughed Shugga. "C'mon Jay, we'll get this straightened out. You want this one Dronk?"

"Yeah, best I take this one. Jay needs to know what's up," nodded Dronkal.

Dronkal took a horseshoe from Jeremiah as he and Shugga went to visit the woman. Jeremiah reluctantly followed, his embarrassment quickly being replaced by dread.

The woman had barely entered Dronkal's line of sight when he flung the horseshoe at her. She glanced up at the sudden motion and caught the iron right in the mouth. Blood exploded from her lips, and she tumbled backward onto the floor of her shop.

"This what my name is worth to you?!" Dronkal screamed. He snatched another horseshoe from Jeremiah and threw it. The woman, curled in a ball and hands pressed to her mouth, took this next one in the kidney. She screamed through broken teeth and spasmed in pain, arching her back. "You hear my name, and you think of horseshoes?!"

Dronkal grabbed another two and hurled them, one after another. She rolled away from the first one. The second glanced off her shoulder with a sickening crunch.

Jeremiah stood frozen. The escalation of violence had locked his legs in place. Dronkal took the remaining horseshoes.

"I don't need this shit! I'll just give em back then! I'll just give em back! I'll give em *all* back! You give me what I don't need I'll give it *back!*" Dronkal continued to scream. The woman frantically produced a small metal coin box hidden beneath a table. She held it up over her head in a warding gesture. Dronkal threw the next four horseshoes regardless, three missing, one slugging her in the stomach. She curled up and waved the box desperately until Shugga snatched it out of her hands.

"Don't you ever disrespect my name again!" Dronkal spat on her broken form.

They left her there, shivering and broken. Taking her money, her dignity, and her safety in only a moment.

We're Cutter, Jeremiah realized. *We're her Cutter. We're all someone else's Cutter.*

He had to get out.

CHAPTER THIRTY-SIX

A Favor Owed

He had let himself get too comfortable. He realized that now. The sense of belonging, of being valued—he had allowed it to envelope him with warm reassurance of his own importance.

Well, no more. His cellmates were not his friends, he knew that now. His friends would never force him to do things he knew were so wrong.

Tonight, he would speak with Monty, convince him he was ready for the next step. Jeremiah was confident that that was the way to learn more about the cult. Whatever it took, he would do it—his time as a Stonefist was over.

"Let me know when you've got a lull in work," said Dronkal as Jeremiah entered the living room. "I want you out with Sweet Melissa next chance we get."

"Aww, yay!" said Sweet Melissa, looking up from the book she was reading. It was the book of *Flesh*, and she had put her own bookmark in it.

"Out with Melissa?" asked Jeremiah. "You mean like when I went with you and Shug?" his stomach dropped. He knew Melissa was a call, a killer, but the way people talked about her . . . he feared that a call was just the closest approximation to what she was.

"Yup, Monty's orders," Dronkal said. "He wants you to understand all facets of the operations. I think he might be grooming you for a cell leader position."

"Wow, that's fast," said Shugga.

"Monty seems to think there's a future for him," said Dronkal, with no small amount of pride.

"Oh, we're going to have so much fun!" said Sweet Melissa. "Just don't wear any clothes you're fond of, or rings. And nothing made of nickel if you can help it. By the way, I found this in your room. Can I borrow it?" She held up the book of *Flesh*. "It's *really* cool!"

"What were you doing in my room?" asked Jeremiah. Melissa just stared at him like it was the dumbest question she'd ever heard. "Yeah, you can borrow it."

Their secret knock was rapped on the door. The members of Cell Four exchanged looks. and drew their blades.

Dronkal went to the door. "What?" he said through the wood, foot braced against the doorframe.

"Evening Dronkal," came Pete's voice. "I'm here to see Jay of Shabad."

No one relaxed, but they opened the door to reveal Pete in his usual finery, unperturbed by the drawn weapons, holding and stroking a purring Miggy.

"Hello, Jay," said Pete. "It's time."

Despite Jeremiah's objections and fatigue, the rest of the cell had informed him, "When it's time, it's time." Apparently, he had to learn a lesson everyone in the Pit learns eventually. Pete and Jeremiah walked for nearly an hour, to an area of Elminia Jay had never been to. Pete offered no hint of what he wanted Jay to do, merely pointing out restaurants that he thought were a cut above. Jeremiah chose to remain silent.

They came at last to an entire block of apartments that had been ravaged by fire. The charred remains of all the tightly packed homes huddled together, a derelict monument to the thousands of lives that had once played out here.

All save one. At the center of the blackened field, a stone tower presided in isolation. It was short by tower standards, but the effect was intentional.

"Now then, Jay of Shabad, a favor is owed, and a favor is to be repaid," said Pete, smiling up at the tower.

"No," said Jeremiah.

"Come again?" Pete's smile persisted.

"Just no. I choose not to repay your favor," said Jeremiah. Why should he get caught up in Pete's economy? He didn't even belong here. He wasn't dependent on Pete. *I don't need to get any further involved with this life than I already am. I owe him nothing,* he thought.

"Ah that old chestnut." Pete's eyes twinkled. "You're hardly the first, you know. Every so often someone decides to thumb their nose at Ol' Pete and his silly favors. And who can blame them? But it never works out for them, lad. Do you know why?"

"I'm sure you'll enlighten me," said Jeremiah.

"Naturally, dear lad. It's because I have people killed," said Pete. He still wore that easy smile.

Jeremiah didn't flinch. "Not exactly a novel threat, Peter. And, in case you've forgotten, you're still marked." Jeremiah gestured to Pete's hand.

"Spare me, lad. The simple scratching of a rune against skin isn't enough to convey an enchantment's properties. Oh, you're surprised? Did you think I wouldn't do a little research after what you pulled? Worry not, the secret of your skill set is safe with me, and there's no hard feelings. Ol' Pete appreciates being taught a thing or two. Now as for the consequences, you'll find that certain friends may not be as willing to take the risks. New friends who do not quite have the protections you do."

Jeremiah knew he was referring to Delilah. "Bring it the fuck on," she said in his head.

"Go for it," said Jeremiah.

"Not worried about what will happen to the young lady? Cold lad, quite cold, but illuminating to say the least. How about this then—repay my favors, or I'm going to look into you a touch more than I already have."

"What do you mean?" asked Jeremiah. It was an odd threat, but it was already making Jeremiah uneasy.

"I mean, Jay from Shabad, that no one from Shabad is looking for a Jay from Shabad."

"So?"

"Mages go missing quite rarely. Powerful people like to keep track of them, you see. I suspect with a few letters, we can find out with some efficiency exactly who you are and where you're from and why you are in fact here. It'd just be a matter of determining who's missing. Perhaps we can inform your new Stonefist friends. Perhaps even the whole city—you know how gossip travels, and suddenly all the world is aware that a mage is in town and up to no good. I suspect Monty wouldn't appreciate the risk or the deception."

That did send a bolt of fear through Jeremiah. Everything would be compromised, all of his hard-won progress dashed away. No chance he'd be allowed anywhere near the cult as Jeremiah Thorn, the famous necromancer last seen commanding hordes of undead alongside the armies of Dramir and had the ear of the powers that be. He'd end up marked just like Bruno had been, a known factor. Then it'd be back to Dramir, with no home and a pile of awaiting lawsuits. The nightmare would start over, and his friends would know it was because he had done something dumb like turning to Pete.

"Well, what's the favor, first of all?" asked Jeremiah. Maybe it would be easy, some dumb smash-and-grab he could get done in just a few minutes.

"There's a good lad." He turned back to the burnt-out city block. "Now, what you see before you is the tower of Madam Furchot. Inside her bedroom is a necklace with an amber pendant. Quite gaudy, you'll know it when you see it. Fetch it for me."

"What, right now?" asked Jeremiah.

"Unfortunately, yes, I need it within the next hour. I do apologize for the time pressure, but opportunity is knocking. Ol' Pete has a chance to step up in the world, and he is obliged to take it."

"Pete, no offense, but there's better thieves than I out there. Why aren't you using them?" It was an honest question. Jeremiah had some successes under his belt, but he was no Bruno.

"Excellent question, lad. You see Madam Furchot is what's known as an evoker, and she—"

"Whoa, whoa, whoa. Wait. An actual evoker?" said Jeremiah, stopping Pete in his tracks.

Pete gave a polite nod. "Indeed, lad. That's what my sources tell me."

Jeremiah stayed silent for a moment, waiting for Pete to explain himself. But Pete just kept staring at Jeremiah's shocked expression, awaiting Jeremiah's explanation. "Do you know what that is?" Jeremiah asked.

"A mage of some sort," said Pete, waving a hand. "Who can keep track of which sort of mage does what? More importantly, it's irrelevant!"

"Evokers are mages that specialize in energy creation," said Jeremiah, pointing at the tower.

The news failed to diminish Pete's smile. "Oh?"

"They're who you think of when you think of mages. They shoot fireballs, blasts of lightning, sonic explosions, something called prismatic energy . . . Pete, is she the reason why all these buildings are burned down?"

Pete looked at the forest of blackened timber nearby with renewed curiosity. "I have heard she enjoys her solitude more than most, and this is certainly not the first time this block has burned down."

"Pete, come on," said Jeremiah. "You can't be serious. I'm probably going to get blown up before I even reach the tower! Why are you chucking *me* at this problem? I can't like, counter magic or something like that. Being a mage doesn't exactly help me against an evoker." *Being a brick wall would barely help*, he thought.

"Now, now, lad, the time for complaining has long since passed. Now is the time for action! Don't tarry, now. The night is young, and I've further work for you after this. Remember: three favors, not one." He gave Jeremiah's shoulder an encouraging squeeze Jeremiah's shoulder before departing.

Jeremiah looked up at the tower. *Maybe she's not home.*

Jeremiah scampered away from the tower's entrance. The door was so heavy and solid that it had hurt his hand to knock on it. From his hiding spot among a burnt-out building, he watched and waited for signs of activity.

The square tower had only four windows, right at the top of course, facing the directions. A crooked stove pipe jutted out from the gabled roof, seeping a wisp of smoke.

Why do mages like towers? Jeremiah wondered.

"Good views," said Flusoh. "Let's you keep an eye out for angry mobs, people asking for miracles, and thieves like you."

No movement. No lights. He could try and use enchanting to Decay through the front door, but the number of runes needed to get through such a massive slab would be considerable. Draining too much focus was a real possibility, not to mention how exposed he would be while etching them.

Jeremiah realized there would be nowhere to escape to, should she spot him. The only place to hide were the ruins of buildings she'd already proved willing to burn down.

Up we go, then, he thought.

Jeremiah darted to the foot of the tower to huddle in its shadow. He selected an ashen brick at his feet and inscribed it with the rune Cohesion. Pressing the enchanted brick against the tower left it stuck in place.

He repeated the process with another dozen bricks, each placed above the other to create a makeshift ladder. It was as he was climbing the ladder to place the tenth brick that Jeremiah encountered his first problem—he was getting tired. His training had involved a lot of climbing for sure, but the continuous up and down was starting to get to him. Likely some lost muscle from starvation too.

Craning his neck upward, Jeremiah was dismayed to realize he had covered barely a quarter of the distance to those top floor windows. His fingers and forearms ached, making even the inscribing process painful.

"Okay, buddy, we need a better plan." Gus, napping in his pocket, did not answer. Jeremiah wondered how many bricks he could carry up the ladder in a single trip. If only he didn't need to climb down the ladder, he was wasting a lot of energy in needing to get back to the ground to get more bricks.

"Huh. That's an idea."

He inscribed *If Contact, Cohesion* on two new bricks. Touching the Contact point caused the brick to adhere to the wall, releasing the Contact let the brick come free. He no longer needed to return to the ground, these two ladder rungs would take him all the way to the top.

A quick test on a wall confirmed they worked, so long as he was careful with his grip. Brushing the Contact point at the wrong moment would bring a swift end to his thieving ambitions.

Wedging the toes of his shoes between the thin seams of the stonework, Jeremiah used his climbing bricks to scale the tower. His arms ached from the work they'd already done, but the strength he'd gained working as a second-story man over the last month served him well.

He reached one of the tower windows and, praying Madam Furchot wasn't looking out the same window at that very moment, peeked inside.

The highest room of the tower was a luxurious bedroom and a storage chamber of wonders. Thick rugs were piled haphazardly, layered atop one another to cover the entire floor in a chaotic array. A four-poster bed sported a dozen pillows and a sky-blue canopy, silken and soft. Surrounding it, glass curios displayed sparkling fascinations, a thousand trinkets and treasures from the corners of the world.

Jeremiah pulled himself through the window. Crowds of intricately carved wooden masks surveyed the room, the gemstone-tipped hands of a standing clock leapt between positions seemingly at random, and an entire case of wands gleamed behind blue tinted glass.

"Steal everything," said Bruno.

No way—I don't know what this stuff is, I don't know what it does, and I want as little involvement in this woman's life as possible.

"But what if there are more of those artifact thingies in here! Or if those wands are charged and functional!"

Bruno, you don't even know what wands are, thought Jeremiah.

Jeremiah placed the bricks on the windowsill for safekeeping, then began to scan the room for the gaudy amber necklace Pete had described.

In contrast with the delicate jewels and clockwork devices that crowded the curios, the necklace was garish, sporting an oversized gem, ornate gold fittings spotted with diamonds, and a heavy layered chain. It hung on a necklace stand beside the bed.

Okay, at least this part is simple, thought Jeremiah.

He crossed the room on tip toe, senses on high alert for anything amiss.

Nothing.

He neared the necklace and inspected it for any signs of security.

Nothing.

He lifted the necklace off the stand and froze, holding his breath, waiting for something to happen.

Nothing.

"Huh," he breathed out in relief.

The floor at the center of the room exploded in a blast of flame, burning chunks of wood and carpet ricocheting like crossbow bolts. Splintered shrapnel pelted Jeremiah, who ignored the pain and dove under the bed.

"Who's in my HOUSE?!" a scream like ringing metal pierced Jeremiah's ears. From the new hole in the floor, a human woman in blazing red robes arose, held aloft by a deafening tornado of wind that whipped her gray-streaked hair in a wild frenzy.

Madam Furchot surveyed the room, teeth bared in a ferocious snarl. Blue fire smoldered around one clenched fist, while arcs of electricity sparked out from the other.

"Die in hiding then!" The flames leapt from her hand to a corner of the room, blossoming into a sphere that ignited everything it touched. Jeremiah felt the temperature rise instantly. With the other hand, she raked lightning in a circle around herself, obliterating anything it touched. The lightning caught the bed Jeremiah was hiding under, blowing the mattress to pieces, but thankfully leaving his hiding place intact. For now.

Okay, I'm screwed, thought Jeremiah.

"Consider your enemy," said Allison. "She's a mage, just like you. And she's a human, just like you."

Jeremiah seized a blasted plank of wood that had slid under the bed and inscribed on it as fast as he could.

"I'm sick of this city!" Madam Furchot was screaming. "I'm sick of the little insect people in it! I am a *god* compared to you! I will not be defied! I will burn this entire world to the ground and rule over the ashes!"

"I like her!" said Flusoh.

Let's see how willing she is to turn that fury on herself, thought Jeremiah. The diagram read *Strengthen Adhere*.

He waited for Madam Furchot to turn her attention to a yet undestroyed piece of furniture and slipped out from under the bed. Board in hand, he charged the diagram as he leapt toward her.

The sound of his incantation caught her attention. She turned just as Jeremiah reached her. He struck her on the brow with the piece of wood at the same moment she projected a bolt of lightning into his chest.

Jeremiah convulsed. His body seized with rigidity, then fell limp. His vision flashed white as he collapsed, and he became aware of falling, more pain.

"Insolent bastard!" An explosion. Jeremiah opened his eyes and found himself in a reading room. Some of the bookshelves were burning. Above him, visible through the hole in the center of the bedroom floor, Madam Furchot was trying to wrench the piece of wood off her face where Jeremiah had Adhered it.

She was blind, but no less dangerous. With a flex of her arms, the top of the tower exploded in a wave of magical force. Jeremiah could see the night sky as rubble began raining down around him. He crawled to the stairs that would take him further down the tower, his body screaming in pain at every motion.

Fire blasted downward past the staircase in a tight swirling column, coring the center of the tower. Jeremiah screamed as the flames scorched his skin, in response he threw himself down the stairs. Something high above him exploded as he reached the front door. He threw the wooden bar, pushed the door open, and fled.

The open door created a great sucking wind as air rushed into the tower to feed the fire within. Jeremiah ran as fast as he could to anywhere at all. The heat was following him, biting into every inch of his skin. He had to find a well or canal or . . .

He was yanked to the ground and doused in water. There was a hissing noise as relief settled over him.

"You were rather ablaze there, lad. No worries, all taken care of," said Pete. He continued pouring a skin of water over Jeremiah's back and head. "You seem to have upset the good Madam Furchot, she's on quite the rampage. I do believe that tower is done for. Pity that."

Jeremiah peeled his blackened shirt away from his torso. The skin underneath was blistered red, spreading from the center of his chest like a sun.

"I've a salve or two for burns," said Pete. "Remind me to grab some for you. Did you manage to retrieve the necklace?" Pete rubbed his hands together in anticipation.

"Yeah, Pete, I got it," said Jeremiah through clenched teeth. The burning wouldn't stop. In the distance, another explosion.

"Splendid! Let us depart before the good madam finishes with her tower and diverts her attention elsewhere."

CHAPTER THIRTY-SEVEN

Your Witness

This one is quite simple," said Pete. "All I need you to do is sneak into that home right there and have the man inside ingest a single drop of this tonic." He waggled a tiny bottle of a clear liquid.

"I'm drawing the line. I'm not going to poison anyone for you," said Jeremiah. "Threaten me however you want, but I'm no assassin," the burns he had received not even an hour ago were still smarting, if not getting worse.

"Hush, hush, hush! No, no, dear lad, perish the thought. Ol Pete is no assassin, heavens forbid."

"You told me you have people killed just a couple hours ago," said Jeremiah. His skin still burning from his encounter with Madam Furchot.

Pete rubbed his eyes. "Er, yes, I suppose I did. Pardon me lad, I find myself in need of rest after a harrowing few days. But no, this is no poison. It's nothing but a simple tonic that will raise the ire of the drinker. Place him in a foul mood come the morning."

"You want me to put him in a bad mood?" asked Jeremiah. There had to be simpler ways to do that. "I could just throw a rock through his window, that'd certainly put *me* in a bad mood."

"Lad, you'll forgive my impatience, but we are on a tight schedule. Suffice to say I *need* him in a bad mood. Not bravely resisting the forces out to destroy him. Now, if you please, we have one more stop after this one, and it must be timed precisely."

Jeremiah glanced at the house Pete had indicated. "Pete, he's awake. He's right there, I can literally see him working. How am I supposed to get anywhere near him?"

The man was young, in the prime of his life. A lantern illuminated the room where he bent over a reading desk. Beside him was a wine glass and half-empty bottle. He wore the same look of ardent concentration Jeremiah had seen on Delilah's face during long, challenging nights. The hour was well past midnight, but this man was awake as day, scribbling furiously.

"Counselor Berard is a hardworking man, to be sure," said Pete. "Now get to it, if you will, I have a particularly tight schedule to keep." He pressed the tonic into Jeremiah's hand and disappeared into the night.

The home was a first-floor apartment. Jeremiah was thankful for that small favor at least. His arms still ached from the tower climb.

This guy isn't going to sleep anytime soon, is he? thought Jeremiah. It would have made things easy, so there was no chance of that.

"He's likely got a court date in the morning. He's refreshing and planning his strategy," said Delilah.

So, no catnap before?

"Never!" said Delilah.

Jeremiah watched for a time, obscured by the darkness of the streets. Counselor Berard seemed completely unaware of the world outside.

Could cause a distraction and try to slip in, thought Jeremiah. It seemed risky. If Counselor Berard suspected something was amiss, he would become suspicious and watchful.

"This calls for a double bluff," said Bruno. "First, you'll need a filament thread. Then—"

No, Jeremiah silenced Bruno's teachings, for the first time in months. *This is a job for a mage.*

Jeremiah pulled out a dead rat. He carried at least one at all times now, just in case.

Rise

The tiny rat bubble sprang into existence. He had missed it. Placing the tonic bottle in the rat's mouth, he sent it to the front door, only to discover the bottle was too large to squeeze underneath. The rat scampered back to Jeremiah.

Gods forgive me for how gross this is going to be. He unscrewed the bottle and poured the entirety of the liquid into the rat's mouth, letting the muscle memory of swallowing carry it down into the rat's stomach.

The rat, now unburdened by the bottle, slipped inside.

That's step one, thought Jeremiah. It took only a little maneuvering to get the rat into the same room as the man. But how to get the liquid into the glass surreptitiously?

Climb

Jeremiah could barely make out the rat creeping up the side of the desk. Counselor Berard, engrossed in his work, didn't notice the small creature hiding behind the wine bottle.

The tonic was right there, within arm's reach of the glass. A tiny step, no larger than a gulf. The rat held perfectly still as Jeremiah thought, as only the dead can wait.

Maybe a dropper? thought Jeremiah. *Something that would fit in those little rat . . . hands . . .*

Rats had hands. Hands tipped with teeny tiny claws.

The rat touched the wine bottle with a paw. Jeremiah chastised himself. He was wasting time. There was no way to control a rat with that much precision . . . right?

He had always made an effort to make his bubbles as small as he could, requiring as little focus as possible. He'd be able to stack them into nice orderly piles, maximizing the number of bubbles he could hold without becoming overwhelmed by the space they took up. But what if he made the bubble larger? If he allowed it to take up more of his brain space, would it be more *him*?

Jeremiah concentrated on the bubble. He cut out all other distractions and gave it every ounce of his focus.

The bubble began to grow. At the same time, Jeremiah's sense of his surroundings began to fade. The tiny rat bubble was larger now than a horse, larger than when he'd raised Narooka the minotaur. It filled his mind. It was nearly as much him as he was.

He could feel the smoothness of the glass. He could feel the pressure on his sharp claws, already biting into the surface. Jeremiah raised his hand, raised his claw, and together they began to scratch. Jeremiah could hear the sound through his tiny sensitive ears; close and loud, but much too quiet for the big oafish ears of people.

Decay

Except that wasn't enough. Using a rat to scratch a rune was one thing, but there was another step he hadn't yet fit into the plan. The bubble snapped back to minuscule as Jeremiah's frustration flared again.

Stupid! I can't charge the rune without being able to touch it. I can't cast through the rat . . . can I?

Jeremiah reinflated the bubble, expanded it as large as he could. He smelled the wine, he felt the warmth of the room, the wood under his feet. Jeremiah spoke the magic words through his human mouth but placed his rat hand upon the glass.

A vast surge of energy sucked the air from his lungs. He was aware of nothing until his head smacked the cobble street. The rat's bubble snapped back to tiny as Jeremiah's consciousness tried to reassert itself. It was such a tiny enchantment, but the drain was immense. Whether casting through the rat or the distance from the target, he didn't know, but it was much harder than it should have been.

Hide

The command was weakly conveyed, but thankfully hiding was a rat's first instinct and little force of will was needed.

"Oi! On your feet! Move!"

Oh, you've got to be kidding me, thought Jeremiah.

"You think I'm having a laugh?" growled the guard. Apparently, Jeremiah had spoken aloud.

The baton struck Jeremiah in the liver, just as all the guards were trained to do. Jeremiah spasmed in pain and scrambled to his feet.

"Just fell, sirs, knocked my head," said Jeremiah pointing to where he could feel blood trickling down his jaw.

A movement caught his eye, and he glanced over just as the Counselor Berard's wine bottle exploded. The man jumped to his feet and cursed so loudly it caught the attention of the guards, who followed Jeremiah's gaze.

"A peeper, is it?" said the guard. The baton swung again, this time into Jeremiah's stomach. Jeremiah doubled over, his guts churning from the blow.

Counselor Berard left the room, likely looking for something to clean the mess.

"Climb."

"Climb? Climb what?" The guard lifted Jeremiah's chin upward with the baton.

His partner glanced up at the apartment's roof, scanning for signs of danger. "Not sure I like this one Bert, seems mouthy. Think he's making a fool of us."

The rat scaled the desk, navigating around broken shards of the wine bottle. It stood on its hind legs to reach the rim of the glass. It was imperative the rat not tip the glass—this was going to be his one and only shot. Jeremiah increased the size of the bubble, gripping the rim of the glass tightly. There was pain and his head shot back, the rat mimicking his motion as the guard yanked on his hair.

"You've picked the wrong man on the wrong night, boyo," said Bert the guard.

Jeremiah had no idea how to make a rat throw up. It wasn't something rats frequently did. He had only one idea. The bubble shrank.

"Picked the right little lady for a tummy tickle though, didn't I? What do I owe you, Berty boy?" Jeremiah wheezed out. Jeremiah had no idea what the insult meant, but the tone meant something to Bert.

The bubble grew. Now *he* was mostly in the rat again instead of the rat being mostly in *him*.

Jeremiah felt an incredible blow to his stomach, though distant and indistinct. The rat vomited the liquid contained in its stomach into the glass. The clear tonic mixed with dark red wine, along with other assortments that had been left behind when the rat expired.

Hide

The bubble shrank, and Jeremiah lay in a puddle of his own vomit, being bludgeoned mercilessly by the guards for his defiance.

When Jeremiah stopped responding to the blows, something he had learned to do very quickly, the guards relented. One of them turned Jeremiah's head with his boot. "I'm gonna take a walk around the block, and if you ain't gone by the time I get back, we're gonna wallop you again. And we'll keep walkin' and keep wallopin' till you're gone or dead. Got me?"

"Yes, sirs," whimpered Jeremiah.

The guards left. Jeremiah raised himself high enough to see into the window. Counselor Berard was holding a wine-sodden rag and looking dejectedly at the mess left behind. With a sigh, he grabbed the wine glass and downed the contents in a single gulp, then spent a few minutes gagging and drinking as much water as he could swallow.

Jeremiah leaned on Pete's shoulder as the older man hurried him along. The sky was just starting to lighten. Jeremiah's entire body ached, various contusions swelling where he had endured the worst of the beating.

"Come now, lad, come now. We mustn't dawdle, we have precious little time," said Pete. His typical air of utter control was fraying. People were starting to appear in the streets, laborers mostly, but they were still sparse and had no interest in the two of them.

"Pete, please," said Jeremiah. "I'm really beat up. Can the third favor wait? Even for a breather?" Everything hurt, everything continued to hurt. The miracle of either enchanting or necromancy he had discovered was pocketed away for when the excitement of the revelation wouldn't be marred by the concussion likely he had.

"No! We have very little time," said Pete, his pace quickening. He shot a furtive glance over his shoulder at the sliver of sun.

He pulled them up to a small townhouse home, one of many in a row. No longer were they in the presence of lawyers and men of high trade.

"Very simple," said Pete, propping Jeremiah up and smoothing his blood-slicked hair. "You are going to enter that home there and you are going to tell the man of the house to say that Darcassin Aewarin was with him for the entirety of the night in question."

"I'm just . . . delivering a message?" asked Jeremiah.

"Ah, I missed a critical component. You are going to do whatever you need to do to make sure he agrees to this, whether he likes it or not. And he won't like it," clarified Pete. "Off you go!"

"The facade is fracturing," said Delilah. "The pressure is mounting. Time is running out. He is . . . fill in the blank, Jay," said Bruno.

Desperate, he finished. "Sorry, Pete, I think I need to tap out," said Jeremiah. He slumped against Pete and let his head hang. "I'm really hurt."

"Dear lad, I truly do not have time to once again explain to you the consequences of your petulance. Now, if we can—"

"I'm sorry," Jeremiah interrupted. "You do what you need to do, but this just isn't happening." He disentangled himself from Pete and began limping home, acting defeated and broken. It was an easy role to play.

I'll let him think he pushed too hard. Let him offer a little carrot instead of all this stick. Jeremiah put a bit more sway in his limp.

"Jay, wait!" Pete ran in front of him and held him by the shoulders. "I know it's been a long night, and clearly, you've suffered, but there's just one more task ahead of you. An easy one, compared to the truly inspired performances you've managed this evening. I ask you to reach down deep, find that hidden well of strength you know you have, and repay your honest debts. One last favor and all's square. I've been good to you, haven't I? Do it for Ol' Pete."

Gotcha, thought Jeremiah.

"Sorry Pete, I just can't. I'm sure you'll be fine without this one piece of your plan. Or you can always go do it yourself, right? I'm sure you've got time."

"I don't *do* things, Jay! I . . ." Pete huffed in frustration, Jeremiah could see Pete weighing his options, then frowning at the rising sun. "All right fine, what do you want?" said Pete. Not a drop of graciousness remained in his voice.

"A favor," said Jeremiah. "Of the most serious and powerful variety. Whatever I want, whenever I want, with no limits on—"

"Yes, yes, fine! For gods' sake, boy, I'll grant you whatever your heart desires, just get in there!"

Jeremiah held out his hand for Pete to shake on the deal. Pete raised his hand and froze, staring at Jeremiah's. Something about the action was both alien to Pete and intimately familiar. There was fear in his eyes, real fear. Then Pete gritted his teeth, shook Jeremiah's hand, and pushed him toward the door.

Jeremiah turned. "Hey, actually, do you have any kind of a pick-me-up? I could really use—"

"Best the street has to offer!" declared Pete and jammed a glass bottle with an atomizer into Jeremiah's mouth, like a perfume bottle. Pete puffed it once and Jeremiah inhaled. The pain dulled, colors got brighter, the night receded just a little bit more, and he was flooded with energy.

"Woo! All right let's do this," said Jeremiah. Whatever it was in that bottle helped him concoct a foolproof plan in moments.

"This is wrong," said Delilah and Allison in regard to the plan.

I am aware, said Jeremiah.

Jeremiah knocked, and a matronly elven woman opened the door. She wore a simple apron, her hands were dusted with white flour, and her hair was pulled back in a tight bun. She smiled at Jeremiah. "Good morning, how can—"

Jeremiah punched her in the face as hard as he could. She screamed and spun away, blood shooting from her nose. Jeremiah grabbed the back of her dress and pulled her against him in a choke, pressing the blade of his dagger to her throat.

There was a loud clattering as a boy appeared. Fists balled and shaking, years away from manhood, he screeched, "Let her go! Momma, get away from him!"

"Get on the ground!" Jeremiah shouted, with as much authority as he could muster. The boy raised his hands in compliance and knelt, tears springing to his eyes.

An elven man turned the corner wielding a loaded war bow as long as Jeremiah was tall. He had all the fear of a lion facing down a mouse. "Wrong house."

"Eh, eh, eh!" Jeremiah pressed the knife harder against the woman's throat, drawing a dot of blood. "Don't do anything stupid. You loose that arrow, you might hit her." He yanked on the woman's neck, drawing her up higher between him and the arrow.

"Won't," said the man. The thick wood groaned in agony as he pulled back the bowstring.

The calmness. That terrible calmness. The prospect of shooting Jeremiah around his own bleeding and struggling wife was nothing short of boring.

Jeremiah pointed his free arm at the man's son, spoke the magic words, and launched a ball of acid on the floor just in front of the boy. The wooden floor degraded instantly, pitting and smoldering, and the boy retreated with a cry of pain as a few errant drops found his skin.

"It gets worse," said Jeremiah. "You put that bow down now or I'll whisper a word in your wife's ear and drive her insane. I've got the magic to do it." That particular detail was a rumor he had heard about himself back before he had met his friends, fresh from Flusoh's tutelage. People would believe nearly anything when it came to magic.

The man growled, like he was annoyed that magic was complicating an otherwise certain resolution, but he angled the bow away from Jeremiah. "What do you want?"

"Darcassin Aewarin was with you for the entirety of the night in question. Fill in whatever details you want, but he was with you. Do you understand?"

The man didn't answer at first, only gazed dispassionately at Jeremiah. His eyes flickered.

"He's eyeing a shot!" said Allison.

"It won't be worth it!" Jeremiah shouted. "You'll never get her back! You can still have a long and happy life together. One where your son doesn't blame you every day. Wake up from this bad dream or live an endless nightmare—it's up to you."

The man's stony facade fractured, finally really looking at his wife and son and not at a problematic target. "Fine."

"Good, good answer," said Jeremiah. "With you the whole night, understand?"

The man gave the barest of nods.

"Now, set the bow on the ground." The man didn't move. "I've got no interest in hurting this woman, but gods help me, I will break this family if you don't do as I say."

Without breaking eye contact with Jeremiah, the man slowly bent and lowered the bow to the floor.

"Kick it over here, hard."

The bow slid across the floor to Jeremiah's feet. There was a moment of silence as he and the man stared at each other.

Jeremiah whispered into the ear of the woman, "I sincerely apologize," and shoved her away. Then he fled from the house, dodging quickly into the maze of alleys in case the man decided to pursue him.

"If I knew about this, I couldn't look at you the same way ever again," said Allison and Delilah as he ran.

"They don't understand. It's okay. I would," said Bruno.

CHAPTER THIRTY-EIGHT

Boom

Jeremiah supposed he ought to feel some sense of relief for having completed all of Pete's tasks and freed himself from future expectations. Heck, he even earned himself a favor from Pete out of the deal. However, all he felt was exhaustion, bone-deep, and pain from the burns and beatings he had suffered.

Oh yeah, poor you, he thought. *Didn't even have a crazy mage break into your house and threaten to destroy your family.* He was glad that it had gone as well as it did. He might have been talking big. He'd rather eat the arrow than actually hurt that poor woman.

He trudged toward home.

No sooner had he reached the dwelling of Cell Four than the door opened and Melissa and Dronkal trooped out. "There you are!" said Sweet Melissa, hurrying toward him. "We were wondering where you'd gone off to! Come on, you and I have a surprise job today." she pranced from foot to foot.

"Please," said Jeremiah. "In the name of all that is good and holy in the world, let me rest. Pete has been kicking my ass all night with his nonsense and—"

Dronkal pushed Melissa aside and grabbed Jeremiah by the collar, pulling him up on his toes. "You listen to me," he growled. "You owe the Stonefists everything. *Everything.* If you've messed up bad enough that Pete rakes you over the coals, that's your problem. But you're a part of this cell, that means you do the cell's work. You understand?"

Jeremiah held up his hands defensively. "Okay! Okay, Dronk, relax. I'm just tired. If it's that important, I'll do it. I was just asking."

Dronkal snorted and released Jeremiah. "You don't get to 'ask.' Learn you not to fool around with Pete."

"Sorry, Jay, family comes first," said Sweet Melissa, not sounding sorry at all. "But you can go home right after this and rest, I promise."

It took every ounce of strength Jeremiah had to turn away from home to follow Sweet Melissa back toward the city, but he did. They made their way through the slums toward the nicer part of town, where morning traffic was just picking up.

It's my own fault. I threw in with Pete and that's my fault, and I tried to use that to get out of duties to my gang, thought Jeremiah.

"Your what?" said Delilah.

"You're worthy of respect Jay, even when you can justify when you're not," said Allison.

Sweet Melissa was in high spirits. "So how good are you at opening stuck jars? We don't have any jars, but it's the closest approximation to what I'm going to need you to do.

"Do you ever say, like, normal stuff?" asked Jeremiah. His limbs felt like lead. He wished he could absorb some of her bubbly energy.

She giggled. "I can tell the difference between human tendon and elf tendon by the sound it makes when you strum it. I gave up on normal a long time ago."

BOOM.

The explosion started innocuously enough, with a murmur of confusion among the pedestrians. Feet stopping, hands pointing and, as Jeremiah looked up to see what they were looking at, a tall column of earth climbing into the sky, miles away.

Like a gray flower, the column blossomed up and outward toward the apex of its trajectory. It rose, dwarfing the tallest buildings and rivaling the height of the central palace of Elminia itself. There was a granularity to it, and the gray whole slowly spread in every direction.

"It's beautiful . . ." gasped Sweet Melissa.

The dust reached them first, carried on a warm wind. Then smaller fragments moving impossibly fast, pocking the earth with little puffs.

There was a hum, and something zipped through the middle of the street, whining like a mosquito in Jeremiah's ear. Those unfortunate enough to be in its path were reduced to a red mist as their bodies disintegrated from the sheer force of whatever it was.

People began screaming. Rooftops exploded. Stones the size of oxen began to rain down, smashing buildings to smithereens. The streams of traffic were suddenly thrown to the winds of chaos as people began to scatter haphazardly, blind fear whipping them into a frenzy.

"Come on!" Jeremiah grabbed Sweet Melissa and hauled her out of the street with him. People were either running indoors or away from the source of the explosion. Jeremiah chose the former. The stores and buildings were packed to burst within moments as more debris cut through the crowd outside.

It was a lottery. There was no decision that would spare you from the rocks and boulders if it was your time to take one. People hidden beneath stalwart roofs and thick beams were crushed by the entire building. People frozen in the street were untouched as pebbles that could puncture steel missed them by a hair's breadth.

Jeremiah pulled Sweet Melissa behind an upturned market stall. He raked his inscription tools across the wood and slapped his hands against it in a matter of moments.

Strengthen

His hands worked on their own, even as his eyes darted about, there was only the image in his head being transcribed directly through his hand at previously impossible speeds. No sooner had he finished then a stone as big as a melon slammed into the wood and bounced away at an obtuse angle. Another man drew the short straw and caught it. A sequence of three more impacts cracked the magically reinforced wood. Jeremiah threw himself over Sweet Melissa, holding on to her tight as if his body could actually protect her.

For an eternity, they waited through the rain of death and pain. The screaming never ceased and was only periodically drowned out by a larger impact. Jeremiah stayed where he was, eyes squeezed shut, certain each moment would be his last.

Gradually, the rain lessened. No whizzing pebbles of death. No massive stones crashing through the sky. The screams of terror reduced to cries of pain, whimpers and moans.

Jeremiah lifted his head. The air was colored with a sepia mist of dust raised from the ground. His ears rang in the relative quiet.

They ventured out together, hand in quivering hand at the devastation that had overwhelmed the city in a single grisly, bloody moment. Jeremiah's mind struggled to comprehend the bodies, the dismemberment, the pain, the destruction. A distant part of him screamed at him to help, to do something—anything!

But it was all too much. Far too much.

Then he saw Pete.

Pete was sitting at a table outside of a café that longer existed. He sipped a cup of tea, unblemished by the universal fog of dust settling over them.

"Pete! What the hell are you—" He stopped as Pete regarded him with the usual casual smile. Jeremiah looked at the cloud of dust still rising in the distance, now mingling with the black smoke of an active fire. "Pete . . . did you do this?"

"I don't *do* anything, lad. I just set pieces where they need be and let nature take its course."

"Pete . . ." Even Jeremiah's numbness couldn't protect him from the trickle of horror and realization. "Did *I* do this?"

Pete chuckled and sipped the tea. "You're as guilty as I am, lad. That is to say, not at all. Best you divest your inquisitive nature from this moment in time. You're far more suited to be an extra set of hands for these poor people, don't you think?"

Jeremiah, his skin and clothes sticky with the dusty blood of those killed around him, grabbed Pete's unblemished collar and yanked him out of the chair. "You son of a bitch! What the hell did you do? What the hell did *I* do?!"

"Calm yourself lad," said Pete. "A very powerful woman with a very short temper encountered a string of bad luck and disrespect at a time when tempers in this city are already exceptionally short. Granted, I could never have predicted she would have such an . . . apocalyptic reaction. But, to my knowledge, you cannot control the will of others. Now, if you don't mind"—Pete pried Jeremiah's fingers open—"there are people that need your help. Off you go now."

"Hey!" said Sweet Melissa, appearing beside Jeremiah. "Come on, we've still got a job to do."

"Sweet Melissa," said Pete with a nod. Jeremiah had never heard anyone call her that to her face.

"Hi, Pete," said Sweet Melissa with a wave.

"You're right," said Jeremiah. "Can you tie tourniquets? There are some people bleeding and I can—"

"What? Jay, we have work to do," said Sweet Melissa. "Let someone else take care of all this."

Jeremiah was confused. "We need to help these people. Whatever you're doing can wait."

"Umm, no Jay, it can't. We're on a schedule here." She seemed completely oblivious to what was happening around them. The chaos, the screaming, the blood, it didn't even seem to make an impression.

"Go on without me then, I need to stay here and help," said Jeremiah. He had enough biology knowledge to at least enact some first aid.

"Hey!" Melissa whipped a lasso around Jeremiah's neck and yanked, pulling him down to a knee. "Family. Comes. First. Do you understand me? Now get your shit together, untrauma yourself, and move out."

Jeremiah grabbed the lasso cord in one hand and sliced it with a dagger blade from the other. He stood up, free from Melissa's control. "No. People need help, I'm going to help them. Go on without me."

Melissa's hand reflexively flicked and had another lasso loop tied and prepared, but she didn't use it. "See you at home," she said darkly, and disappeared into the mist of destruction.

Jeremiah helped those he could see as best he could, but there were always more. Voices begging him, or anyone, to save them. He had precious little, but was able to tear clothes for bandages, tie tourniquets, fetch water. There were others like him, trying to help, and they worked together to remove rubble and search for survivors.

The city guard was soon dispatched to start moving the dead, but precious little effort seemed to go toward saving those still living. Jeremiah saved dozens, but all he could see were the hundreds, the thousands beyond his reach.

Darkness fell again. When Jeremiah had returned home, his already stressed body was nearing its breaking point. He had spent hours pressing on wounds and dragging bodies into piles. The response from Elminia had been slow, and woefully ineffective, not that there was much to be done about many of the injured. He walked into his room and collapsed face down on the bed, a puff of dust roiling out from him.

"Hey, Jay," came Dronkal's voice from his door.

"Uh?" Jeremiah mumbled into the pillow. He felt hollow, there was just nothing left of him to care about what Dronkal had to say.

"Rough day?" There was a *thump*. "Shoo, Miggy. Daddy's working," he whispered. Jeremiah heard his door close.

"Yeah. Something exploded. Killed a lot of people. Pete had me running around all night too." Mentioning Pete caused the burns to begin aching again.

"I heard. Rattled the windows something fierce. Melissa says you skipped out on the job. That true?" Dronkal was closer, beside the bed.

"Had to. People were hurt," said Jeremiah. Despite the numbness he tightened his jaw, preparing to defend what he did.

"I gotcha, I gotcha," said Dronkal softly. "You saw people hurting and you had to act. Didn't sit right with you to walk away from that."

"Exactly," said Jeremiah. "It was the right thing to do." He relaxed, Dronkal understood.

Dronkal sat on the side of Jeremiah's bed. "I feel that. Some real shit went down today. A lot of people hurt and a lot of people dead. Sometimes a man needs to do what's right, I understand that. Melissa doesn't, but she has a hard time with stuff like that."

"I can only imagine," mumbled Jeremiah. Sleep was already creeping in, he was basically dreaming while he spoke.

Dronkal put one hand on Jeremiah's back, a gentle and reassuring pressure, then grabbed Jeremiah's arm and yanked. There was a sickening pop as the bone popped free of the socket. Jeremiah screamed into the pillow and tried to pull away from Dronkal, but he couldn't move.

"You're all right, you're all right," said Dronkal, patting him on the back. "That's a dislocation, very clean. You know who's good at fixing dislocations? Melissa. Go say you're sorry for ditching her and she'll fix that right up. Remember Jay, *we* are what's right. Family comes first."

A cheer of greeting went up from the Subs when he staggered into the Stonefists headquarters. He ignored it. He wasn't even sure where he was going until he ended up outside Monty's office. Without even bothering to knock, he opened the door.

It was dark. Empty. Jeremiah supposed Monty must be busy on a day like this. Maybe that was for the best. He curled up on the floor and slept.

A peep from Gus alerted Jeremiah a moment before the door opened. He raised his head and whimpered at the pain radiating through his body.

"Good evening, Jay," said Monty, as though this were a perfectly reasonable way to run into each other. "Tough day?"

"I did it. It was me." The words were out before Jeremiah even realized what he was saying, and then the tears choked him. His head dropped to his chest, and he wept, sobbing silently in the dark.

Monty rested a hand on Jeremiah's back and simply held it there while he cried. The kind touch made him hate himself even more, for his lies, for his violence, for his wretched power. He didn't deserve kindness. He wished Monty would strike him, throw him out of the office and even out of the gang. Let him succumb to whatever horrors were infecting Elminia.

But Monty was patient. As Jeremiah's tears exhausted themselves, he lit the candle on his desk and waited.

Finally, Jeremiah spoke. His voice was a hoarse whisper. "I want out."

"Out?" asked Monty.

"Out. Out of the Stonefists. Out of this life."

"You just got here," said Monty. "I realize you've come to enjoy certain privileges, but you still have a lot to learn."

Jeremiah shook his head. It hurt. "What you said last time, that chance to escape. Give it to me. I'm the one. I need it. Whatever escape it is that you have, I'll do whatever it takes to get it."

Cult or otherwise, I don't care at this point, thought Jeremiah.

"You are talented and resourceful," said Monty, "and shockingly naive. You may someday prove to me that you are exceptional enough to deserve that chance, that you're not going to be wasted in chasing it, when that day comes, I will happily grant it. But not today. Not yet."

Jeremiah swayed as he stood. "You want exceptional? You want to see me do what nobody else can do in this . . . this *hole* in the ground?"

Monty squinted at him, concerned but curious. "Yes. Show me."

"Abort!" said Allison.

"Don't!" said Bruno.

He drew his dagger as he approached the desk, and Monty raised an eyebrow. But Jeremiah simply set the tip of the knife against the surface and began to carve.

Strengthen And Heat

He muttered the incantation and set the runes aglow. The blue of the charge gave way to the red hot of burning wood, but only within the etched lines of the diagram. Jeremiah stepped back, letting his work speak for itself.

Monty was silent as he contemplated the glowing design. They burned brightly for several minutes, then faded.

"Pete knew, didn't he?" asked Monty, running a finger over the lines.

"Yes." Curse Pete for knowing. Curse Pete for forcing Jeremiah's power to hurt people. In whatever convoluted way he had used it, it was still Jeremiah's power that got used.

"Tell me, plainly, what this magic does," said Monty.

"It changes things," said Jeremiah. "Alters materials to be different."

"You've got this in your pocket, and you're looking for more?" Monty said. "Go live in a tower and hoard wealth with your magic scribbles."

"Not rich," said Jeremiah. "Free." He was playing the part, yes, but he was also not lying. Being beholden to others, forced to their will. He longed for freedom from servitude. Freedom from the legal oppression that had been brought onto him and his friends. Freedom that money couldn't buy.

"You can come home at any time," said Allison. "You are free."

Yes. No. I know, but not really. I want out of this life, thought Jeremiah.

"Life? What life? The fake one we made up for you?" said Delilah.

It's not . . . just that, thought Jeremiah. It was beginning to feel so confusing.

"He's in too deep," said Bruno. "He's starting to lose himself to the role."

Monty thought for a long time. Jeremiah let him. He was in no hurry.

At last Monty spoke again. "This explains a lot." He sat down heavily behind the desk. "But it changes nothing. Being able to cast magic doesn't make you exceptional."

It was Jeremiah's turn to think. There was only one possibility his mind kept returning to, no matter how forcefully he tried to push it away. "What if I bring you the treasure of Cassidy Korrvas?"

Monty laughed. The sound of it made Jeremiah's head ring. "No one could fault you with a lack of ambition! Sense, maybe. What makes you think you can conquer the Golden House, oh master thief?"

"I can do it," said Jeremiah.

"I don't want to lose a good man to foolhardiness," said Monty. "Be patient. I promise good things will come to you. You're doing good works already, such as they are, for the people of the Stonefists. Do the good you can Jay, let that be enough."

"I can do it!" Jeremiah punched Monty's desk in frustration. Why wasn't Monty letting this happen? Why was Monty forcing him to spend *more* time in this life?

Monty sighed. "Humans are all the same. You're not the first to tell me this, you know."

"I am not the same," said Jeremiah. *No, that's not it. Monty wants it to be about more than just me* or *him*, he thought. "Monty." Jeremiah softened his voice. "Give me the chance to help them. How long are you going to let them languish? If I want to throw my life away trying to build a ladder for these people, then *let* me."

Monty leaned forward, the candle throwing his lined face in sharp relief. "Jay of Shabad. If you bring me the treasure of Cassidy Korrvas . . . well, maybe the treasure will be so great we won't need to go any further. But don't. I've seen better men than you walk into that tomb. You'll die prideful just like the others."

"I won't." Jeremiah drew himself to look Monty straight in the eye. "Don't worry. I can do it."

CHAPTER THIRTY-NINE

Enchanter

Jeremiah sat on top of a poor excuse for a roof on the edge of the Pit. The embering smoke from a thousand fires glowed and sparked like tiny thunderclouds emerging from chimneys all throughout the city. Jeremiah watched the great golden mansion at the Pit's root. Its windows glowed with soft flickering light like they did every night. The exterior was illuminated by torches lit by the guards, and the entire building reflected and magnified every light the Pit created until it practically glowed. It was like a trophy for one man's victory over the inevitable.

"Hey, Bruno," said Jeremiah.

"What? Bullshit you heard me," said Bruno sitting down next to Jeremiah.

"The alternative is I just say 'Hey, Bruno' every so often in case you're nearby," said Jeremiah.

Bruno grumbled, unaware that was exactly the case.

"So, the Gilded Tomb, huh?" said Bruno.

"So you're familiar?" asked Jeremiah. He wasn't surprised.

"It's legendary in thief circles. Used to be considered the greatest challenge a rogue could face. Now it's just considered an interesting way to die," said Bruno. He produced a bottle of amber liquor and two small glasses.

"What's the occasion?" asked Jeremiah. The bottle looked fancy, the cut glass refracted what little light there was, making the bottle sparkle even at night.

"We just miss you," said Bruno. Jeremiah chuckled. "We do, really. Doesn't feel right without you around."

"How are things back home?" asked Jeremiah.

Bruno sighed and poured the pair of glasses. "Not great. The house is gone. Allison's people got our stuff out, but there's nothing left but rubble."

Jeremiah took his shot. It was woody and strong but tasted nice. He still gagged but tried to mask it as a cough.

"Wuss," said Bruno.

"Shut up," said Jeremiah.

"Guessing the Gilded Tomb is your ticket in?" said Bruno.

"Yup. All I have to do is rob a death trap and I'm in. I hope you're having better luck," said Jeremiah, coughing into his sleeve.

"Nope. This city is rife with secret societies and cults. There's one around every corner. Mostly they're filled with old, rich men that hire each other's kids and have secret handshakes," Bruno took his own shot, silently.

Jeremiah refilled his glass. He needed to redeem himself. "Not even interesting cults, huh?"

Bruno nodded. "There was one that worshipped a cockroach god. That was interesting anyway. Not surprising that they scattered the moment they were discovered."

Jeremiah laughed. "Hisspo! Yeah, it's some kind of nature spirit that manifests as a cockroach."

Bruno echoed the laugh and poured a second shot of his own. "How'd you know that?"

"It's mentioned in Flusoh's books sometimes. Hisspo's ancient," said Jeremiah. He brought the glass to his lips, but the smell made him pause. Not wanting to fail completely, he forced himself to take half a shot.

"New things every day," said Bruno absently.

They watched the Gilded Tomb together for a while, seeing the tiny men putter about, moving only inches from their perspective.

"I wanted to apologize," said Jeremiah. "I didn't realize what this whole ordeal was going to be like. I may have thought it was going to be easier than it was."

"Thought maybe you'd smarts your way out of it, huh?" asked Bruno with a smirk.

"Yeah, maybe. I just . . . I didn't realize how unfair it was going to feel, you know? It's like the ground falls out from beneath you, and you try to climb out, but it just keeps falling away and there's nothing to grab," said Jeremiah. He realized he knew that feeling. He felt that when he buried Vivica. He pursed his lips and hoped Bruno wouldn't say anything.

"Oh, I know," said Bruno.

"I guess I just want to say that I get it now," said Jeremiah.

"You get what?" asked Bruno, taking his second shot and setting the glass down. He removed a black glove from one of his hands.

"I get what it's like. To live that life. To really be a part of—" Bruno reached over and slapped him across the cheek. Not as hard as he could, but hard enough to sting.

Jeremiah put a hand to his burning cheek. "Ow?"

Bruno began putting his glove back on. "You have been out here for, what, a few months? You're tall, and have a history of being well fed. You can read, you can write, you didn't grow up stunted or damaged. And most of all, most of all, you can quit anytime you want. You can hang up your rags, come home, and people who care about you will welcome you with open arms. No one down there"—Bruno gestured at the dilapidated houses and soot choked fires—"can just walk away. They've been in it since day one, and they'll be in it till the day they die. No escape. The luckiest, smartest, and meanest of them might accomplish enough in their lives to give the kids of their kids a fighting chance to get out. But those stories are few and far between."

"All right. Sorry," said Jeremiah defensively.

"No sorry. You don't know. You can't. You're past the point of ever knowing, and you passed it decades ago," said Bruno.

They didn't say anything for a while. Bruno took another shot, and Jeremiah took that as a sign of continued friendship.

"So, how are the girls?" asked Jeremiah, hoping Bruno would take the subject change.

"Allison's worried about you every day, but I think she enjoys being a guard. Delilah isn't doing so good, always wrapped up in new mail and legal challenges she needs to navigate. She's not taking the loss of her house very well either."

"Poor girl, that's the only one she had left," said Jeremiah. Delilah's moments of sentimentality were few and far between, but they were strong. That house was where she kept her heart.

"Poor girl indeed. Clearly not in her right mind nowadays," said Bruno.

Uh-oh, thought Jeremiah. This was leading somewhere.

"So . . ." said Bruno.

"Sew buttons," said Jeremiah.

"Maybe we should have a little talk about our friend Delilah," said Bruno, filling Jeremiah's glass.

"Not sure there's much to talk about," said Jeremiah. Or at least not much he wanted to talk about.

"I disagree. I think you two may have agreed to do a little something, once this mission is over," said Bruno.

"We were literally in another dimension when we talked about that," said Jeremiah. "How could you possibly know that?" He took a full shot and embraced the gag. It made for less coughing.

"Don't need to be a fly on the wall to know what happened in there," said Bruno.

"All right, well, what about it?" asked Jeremiah. His head was starting to swim, there wasn't much of him nowadays to absorb alcohol.

Bruno put a hand on his shoulder. "You know I love you, buddy. But I think, for the sake of all that is good in the world, you should reconsider."

"For the sake of all that is good," repeated Jeremiah, the absurdity made him laugh.

"It's true! Delilah is meant to marry into a power couple that will advance her goals and, hopefully, get her into a position of real power one day. Where she can do some real good," said Bruno.

"Whoa, whoa, whoa! Marry? We just agreed on a date. Slow down, Bruno." Was he joking?

"I'm just worried. You two run at different speeds, operate on different levels. I don't want to risk the only real family I've ever known on a bad breakup, you know?" said Bruno, taking another shot. He refilled Jeremiah's.

"Yeah, that would suck," said Jeremiah. This was Jeremiah's family now too. Jeopardizing that seemed foolish.

"Also, and I know I shouldn't be saying this, but she's kind of crazy. You know she doesn't really turn off right? That ambition is ceaseless. She's still technically dating some guy from a couple of years ago."

"Technically?" asked Jeremiah. This was news.

"Well, they never broke up. She just kind of . . . forgot about him, I think. I don't want to see that happen to you."

Jeremiah looked out over the excuses for roofs of the Pit, so many lives and so many problems all playing out at once, totally isolated from each other. Was a date with an ambitious girl really such a danger?

"Thanks for worrying about us Bruno," said Jeremiah.

"You want what's best for all of us, right?" asked Bruno.

"I . . . uh . . ." Jeremiah did want that. But it was only a date, why was Bruno taking this so seriously. Unless . . .

"Bruno, do you have a . . . a thing? For Delilah?" asked Jeremiah.

Bruno sighed and fell backward, looking up at the sky. He let his legs dangle off the edge of the roof and folded his arms behind his head. "Not . . . no?" he said finally.

"That means yes," said Jeremiah.

"But not yes either. You know? She's Delilah. It's hard not to, once you've spent any time around her. She gives you that urge to keep her safe, even though she doesn't need it," said Bruno to the stars. "Like you're protecting something important, or precious, or rare, I don't know."

Jeremiah understood that feeling. It had come on strong when they encountered the stone golem. He lay back, copying Bruno. "I get that . . . she's pretty too," said Jeremiah.

"Oh yes," said Bruno.

"You going to mind if I don't look this particular gift horse in the mouth?" Even with that looming threat of disrupting the family, it felt like a particularly foolish decision to ignore the chance he had.

Bruno didn't respond for a while. Jeremiah listened to the ugly sounds of the Pit at night: arguing, screams, the sounds of crumbling buildings.

"I understand," said Bruno. "I'm happy for you. You know she's out of your league, right?"

"Oh yeah. Honestly, it's kind of a red flag that she would ever agree to a date with me."

"It really does call her common sense into question," said Bruno laughing. He poured two more glasses. They clicked them together and drank again.

"Heard what happened to Cutter," said Bruno.

Jeremiah sighed. This might not be a fun conversation. "Yup" was all he said.

"You okay? With what happened? I wouldn't take you for the type that could sleep well with that on his conscience," said Bruno.

Jeremiah didn't actually know what happened to Cutter. He had told Melissa to deal with it, and didn't stick around to see how she would interpret his instructions. "World's no worse for it," said Jeremiah.

He could see Bruno nodding out of the corner of his eye. "Good man. You're starting to learn some of those ugly truths of the world."

"You tell Delilah and Allison?" asked Jeremiah. He was a bit scared of what they might think.

"Hell no. What happens in the streets stays in the streets. They wouldn't understand what we do," said Bruno.

"We?" asked Jeremiah. That felt like being included in a very exclusive club.

"Yeah, we. Rogue types," said Bruno, like it was obvious.

Jeremiah nodded solemnly, desperately fighting the big dumb grin that threatened to take over his whole face.

"I also want to say sorry," said Bruno. His voice was barely a mumble.

"For what?" asked Jeremiah. He turned to look at Bruno. Bruno still was looking straight up, but the mirth and joviality he always wore like a second skin was gone. He looked old. Tired.

"I don't think I ever got past being compromised. Not being able to save the day doing the one thing I'm good at. I think I may even feel a bit . . . well, threatened. You're doing my job. Poorly, sure, but you're doing it."

"Had to add that 'poorly' didn't you?"

"No, you're doing a good job. Better job than I can do," said Bruno quickly. He pounded the roof with his fist in frustration. Several tiles cracked to powder and slid away.

"Ever find out how that happened? Being exposed?"

"Nah. Don't think I ever will. It could be countless different things."

"So now what?" asked Jeremiah.

"We raid a death trap dungeon," said Bruno.

"'We?'" said Jeremiah. It was a formality. He was going to ask them for help anyway. There was no way he could handle this on his own.

"Yes, we. No offense, but I've known some truly genius thieves that have never returned from the Gilded Tomb." Bruno went to fill the glasses again but decided against it.

"That bad, huh?" Jeremiah missed the drink already.

"Likely the most dangerous thing we've ever done, and that's saying something. That place serves no other purpose than to kill people that enter it," said Bruno.

"Desperate times?"

"Indeed."

"Desperate measures?"

"For certain."

"Then I'm going to need all your equipment. Delilah's and Allison's too."

Bruno sat up in an instant. "No . . ."

"I need you to secure me a place to work during the day . . ."

Bruno began bouncing with excitement. "No! You're kidding!"

"And I'm going to need all of my enchanting supplies. All of them," Jeremiah gave Bruno a cocky smile.

"Is this it?! Is this it?!" Bruno grabbed Jeremiah and began shaking him.

Jeremiah laughed. "Yeah, I think this is it. I think I'm ready to make us some magic equipm—"

"Ahahaha!" Bruno wrapped Jeremiah in a drunken hug. "We're gonna be unstoppable! Can you make me a grappling hook that crawls around like a spider?!"

"No, but remind me to show you the one I did make."

Bruno released him. "Allison and Delilah are already on board. They're champing at the bit to do anything actually; they've been cooped up too long. Just need a way to sneak us in without anyone seeing," said Bruno. "This needs to look like you took it down alone."

"Now wait a minute, is this even worth it? To save us from a bunch of lawsuits?" Jeremiah's day to day had become so all-consuming, so pressing at every moment, that the greater picture had become blurry. He hadn't forgotten, but when his stomach was taking the reins, the next copper was more important than secret cults and paper threats.

"I've been thinking about that. I've been thinking about it this whole time," said Bruno. "The fever is spiking, it's getting bad out there. Worse than it should be." Bruno looked down at the streets below, and when he looked back Jeremiah saw fear in his eyes. It was terrifying.

"Have you felt it?" asked Bruno. "The pulse of the city?"

"I think so," said Jeremiah. Something's wrong, isn't it? More than just a crime wave or more poverty. I've seen things . . . dark things. Things that go beyond desperation. It's in the people, it's in the buildings, it's in everything."

Bruno nodded. "I've seen it too. Whatever sickness this city has, it's terminal."

"Not unless we stop it," said Jeremiah.

It was a subject of heated debate, mostly Bruno arguing with himself, but eventually it was decided Jeremiah would take over the safe house bedroom for his enchantment workshop. The risk of being discovered performing magic was far too great anywhere else, and it could easily be written off as Jeremiah spending time with "that lawyer girl who was slumming it and eager to make some bad decisions."

Jeremiah was anxious to begin. The cover story of visiting Delilah would make sense if he were only gone for a few days, but more than that and they'd get suspicious. If they got suspicious, they'd come looking. And if they found him and his pile of enchanting equipment in a safehouse with other well-armed adventurers, the jig was up. The rumor mill wouldn't run in reverse, and he'd be too compromised to continue the mission.

Jeremiah demanded absolute isolation. With only a couple of days to outfit the entire party, he didn't have time to waste on anything that wasn't either enchanting or resting to be able to enchant more. He didn't have time for their company, as much as he might want it. Even Bruno was relegated to sleeping in the living room so as not to disturb him.

He arrayed the equipment before him. Every bladed weapon had been polished and sharpened to a razor's edge, as Allison had taken to the task like a woman possessed. Every garment had been cleaned, pressed, and meticulously prepared for its transformation.

It was time to put what he had learned to the test.

The bedroom had transformed from a place of rest to one of industry. Jeremiah reviewed Thurok's books, created test diagrams on bent pieces of scrap metal to ensure he would be able to navigate the various angles and materials of the three-dimensional shapes. The diagrams themselves were simpler than some that he'd used during his jobs but incorporating them into real-life objects was an entirely new challenge.

Jeremiah pulled the final thread of silver through the fingertip of the glove and knotted it. Enchanting cloth required he sew the rune into the material with metallic thread. He was no stranger to sewing, often helping his mother with basic repairs, but it was arduous work, even for just a single Adhere rune.

He snipped the thread and slipped the glove over his hand. "Okay, buddy, climbing gloves! Let's see how they feel."

Gus croaked softly.

Jeremiah spoke the magic words to charge the glove. The metallic wire glowed. He flexed his hand into a fist, feeling the wire against his skin. It was noticeable, but not troublesome. He tried wriggling his fingers to further test the comfort. His hand wouldn't open again.

"Riiiight, right, right," said Jeremiah. The glove had stuck to itself.

Jeremiah hefted Allison's favored longsword. The etchings caught the lamp light in a sparse array of lines and runes. It wasn't the sprawling spiderweb-like script of masterwork enchantment that was on Allison's magic armor or Bruno's magic bow, but even the few runes were enough to strengthen the blade and maintain its finely sharpened edge.

"This is it! My first magic weapon," he held it proudly before himself.

Gus wriggled in his bowl so violently the water splashed and bubbled.

"I agree, I did a pretty good job!" The most challenging parts, etching around the curves in the metal, had been made easier with his plate of decay, allowing him to erase mistakes, of which there had been many.

Jeremiah put his hands on the sword and prepared to charge it.

"Here we go . . ." He spoke the words, and felt magical energy rush into the blade, illuminating the tiny room in azure light.

Carefully, gently, Jeremiah lifted the sword. It felt no different than before. He swung the blade at the corner of his wooden bedframe, and with no resistance at all, the sword's edge cleaved straight through.

"Whoooooaaaaaa . . ."

If Contact Cohesion

"Okay, this should solve the sticking problem," said Jeremiah. "So long as I don't clap, but I wouldn't be doing that when I'm climbing anyway."

Gus grumbled at the gloves.

"I know, I know. But it's just like those climbing bricks, so it should work!"

Jeremiah reached up and pressed his hands against a wall, and found the gloves stuck fast.

"It works!" Jeremiah said. He jumped up, determined to scale the small wooden wall and circumnavigate the room like Bruno had once challenged him to do. His hands slid out of the gloves, and he dropped to the ground.

Jeremiah sat up, rubbing his sore behind. "So, the *gloves* are sticking to the wall. My hands are not. Noted." He looked up at the gloves, still hanging from where he had touched. "And since the Contact point is touching the wall, there's no reason for the gloves to let go, is there?"

Gus continued grumbling.

The last of Bruno's *six* enchanted throwing swords was unceremoniously thrown into the pile. His pride in the accomplishment had dwindled from the first to the sixth of them.

"I swear some of these have never even left the scabbard," said Jeremiah. He rubbed the ache from the continued focus out of his eyes.

Gus didn't respond, he was sleeping. Jeremiah yawned. It was time for him to get some rest too.

He moved to the window to let in the refreshing night breeze. The bedroom was becoming stifling with just him toiling away inside. Throwing open the shutters, he recoiled as the cheerful morning sun streamed in.

"Sonnuvabitch!" Jeremiah had apparently worked through the night and into the morning without realizing it.

"Acceptable," said Thurok.

Strengthen And If Contact Gently Cohesion

The gloves were an absolute mess of stitching. The Strengthen effect added just enough to keep the fabric from falling apart where Jeremiah had sewn in and picked out his stitches countless times.

The gloves were now, for lack of a better term, sticky. "Not exactly gloves that'll let you climb like a spider, but they're definitely gloves of climbing. And they make it harder to drop stuff!" Jeremiah said to Gus.

Gus didn't offer any new ideas, just licked one of his eyeballs. Jeremiah was beginning to associate that action with the phrase "Uh-huh."

Jeremiah smiled at the gloves. *I made a magic item*, he thought, *a real magic item. Not just a weapon or armor. But something custom, something unique.*

For the first time, he felt like an enchanter.

CHAPTER FORTY

Trap

One longsword, one longspear, *six* throwing swords, one battle-axe, two short spears, one dagger, one set of leather armor, Delilah's new breastplate, and a smattering of magical doodads.

He had a splitting headache, and his hands would never be the same. But he never stopped working over the two days, kept focused by the knowledge that this equipment stood between his friends and death.

Jeremiah inspected his final creation, a dagger especially for him. Well, he technically used a short spear too, but that was Allison's. He just borrowed it. The dagger was his.

He owned a magic weapon! The idea seemed ludicrous. Magic blades were wielded by the heroes of childhood story books, not Jeremiah. He added it to the bundle of equipment and smiled. It was time to share his work with his friends.

Emerging from the doorway, laden down with gear, Jeremiah entered the apartment to a fight already in progress. Bruno, Allison, and Delilah were slowly orbiting each other like prowling wolves in the living room, the game of cards they had been playing lay forgotten on the table.

"Absolutely not," said Allison. "You got the Giant's Bag and Bruno got his bow before that. It's *my* turn to get a magic item. I go first!"

"The Giant's Bag is a *team* item!" retorted Delilah. "We all use it, and I use it on your behalf. That's like, half a magic item at most."

"No, you're both wrong—I get the first item," said Bruno. "Jay and I have a bond, the sacred bond of the street."

"There is no bond greater than teacher and student," said Allison, pointing at Bruno like he had walked into a trap.

"Hi, guys," said Jeremiah.

"I could pay anyone to teach Jay how to jab with a spear. What I had to teach him, you can't put a price on," said Bruno.

"Pay with what money?" said Delilah. "I've juggled both of your finances for years from my house, that you all lived in. Rent free."

"Hi, guys!" said Jeremiah again with more force.

Allison whirled on Delilah. "You better not just bat your eyelashes at him and—"

"I would never! How dare you."

"It's great to see you all too. I'm fine, malnourished, splitting headache, hand cramps, the usual. Tea? No, I'm good. Food? Well, I am starving, I suppose," said

Jeremiah. Nothing broke through. He sat at the table and pulled the Giant's Bag over to himself while his friends continued to argue.

"The bag should decide!" declared Allison, pointing at the bag that Jeremiah was holding while still not noticing him.

"Elaborate immediately," said Delilah. No one noticed him.

"The bag can read his thoughts, right? So when Jay gets here, we'll have him reach in and pull out the first thing that comes to mind. Whoever's object he thinks about first will appear in his hand," explained Allison. Bruno and Delilah were nodding along with the idea.

When Jay gets here, thought Jeremiah. He thought he should be offended, but his friends were just so excited he couldn't be bothered. "Unworthy!" Jeremiah shouted.

"AAAAH!" his friends simultaneously screamed, startled by his presence. They shot together in surprise.

"Each of you are unworthy of the gifts I've come to bestow upon you!" Jeremiah stood with his hands raised overhead, his voice deep in his best impression of an angry wizard.

"How did he do that? Can Jay turn invisible?" Allison asked Delilah. Delilah shrugged and shook her head at the same time.

"He's learned so much . . ." said Bruno.

"But I suppose I am a generous mage. So, I will bestow upon thee the gifts that I have created." He put his hand in the Giant's Bag and let his gaze travel between them. He rather liked the idea of letting the bag decide.

Bruno gave Jeremiah a stern and affirming nod. One that spoke of brotherhood and shared burdens.

Allison's eyes were wide and pleading, her lip nearly quivering in eagerness. It was a look she had used before that stabbed right at his heartstrings.

Delilah batted her eyelashes at him, just once, slowly. He had no chance.

Up from the bag came a handheld metal sphere, roughly the size of a large orange. He sighed and tossed it to Delilah who screeched in delight as she caught it.

"Betrayer!" Allison and Bruno yelled, or something to that effect, Jeremiah rapidly began tossing out everything he had made to distract them from their disappointment . . . and making a comment on why it had been Delilah that got one first.

"Bruno! Quick, throw that chair at me!" shouted Allison. He threw it without hesitation, and she cleaved it in half with her new sword, the wood parting like paper.

What followed was the total destruction of every piece of furniture in the house, some used up metal plates, old pieces of armor Allison had, and some rocks they got from outside.

"This actually poses a bit of a problem," said Delilah. She was trying to yank her spear back out of the wall. It punched through much easier but didn't come out easier.

"Happy with that problem," said Allison.

"Jay! Stab me with your spear!" said Bruno, exposing his leather armored chest to Jeremiah.

Jeremiah thrust the spear into Bruno's chest, again, and just like the last few times, it left only the tiniest mar in the material. Barely a scratch.

"It's about as strong as nonmagic plate," said Jeremiah. "Delilah, your breastplate is as strong as Allison's armor, but obviously you've got a lot less armor overall, so don't get careless. A reminder: I am not as good an enchanter as Thurok. So, if your stuff gets too damaged, it might not work anymore." No one was listening.

"Tell me what this does!" Delilah yelled at the ball she had received first. It was a palm-sized metal sphere, covered in lines like a globe meant for navigation, and fit comfortably in the hand.

He was both proud of and somewhat embarrassed by this one. "I'll show you. Touch the contact point there . . . here I'll show you," Jeremiah took her hand.

"Get a room!" Bruno yelled the instant Jeremiah came into contact with Delilah.

He guided her hand to the contact point to start the enchantment, ignoring Bruno as hard as he could. "The metal will get harder and more brittle, until . . ."

Jeremiah heaved the sphere against the wall. Upon impact, the sphere shattered, sending razor-sharp metal fragments everywhere.

"They're hollow too, with a little fill valve," Jeremiah continued. "You can put whatever you want inside. They're pretty easy to make, so there's a bunch in there. I'm not sure if that's useful or good or . . ." he was suddenly feeling anxious again. Giving Delilah things was hard.

"Oh, I'm sure I can think of something," said Delilah. She picked up some of the metal fragments from the shattered ball and began to inspect it closely.

"Me! Me, me, me! What did you make for me?" Bruno raised his hand and jumped up and down.

"Besides your new armor and your *six* throwing swords, I made you these," Jeremiah held up the gloves.

Bruno snatched them before Jeremiah could blink. "What are they? Can I shoot lightning?"

"No, and I wouldn't give you gloves that shoot lightning even if I could," said Jeremiah. "They're gloves of climbing . . . sort of."

Bruno pressed a gloved hand against the wall and tried to slide it. "Oh, like grip gloves. Yeah, I've got a few pairs of these."

"Which is *why* I ended up going back to an earlier concept that helped me out of a jam once. Not as subtle, but . . ."

Jeremiah produced a refined version of the bricks he had used to scale Madam Furchot's tower. They were a pair of thin wooden squares with a curved handle protruding from the back.

"These might do the trick. If you touch here, it'll stick to just about any surface. Stop touching, and it will release. Let me show you."

He had been looking forward to this part. Jeremiah took the handles and faced his old archnemesis—the living room wall. He pressed the squares against it, touched the Contact points, and pulled himself upward. Then he released the contact point, moved his hand, and retouched the contact.

Slowly, but surely, Jeremiah began to circumnavigate the room. He reached the doorway to Allison and Delilah's room.

"Everybody watching?" he said. It was so unfair he couldn't see their faces right now. He stuck the handle to the lintel of the door frame, and hung from one hand, suspended on a handle attached to nothing. "Ta-daaa!"

"Jeremiah Thorn," said Bruno gravely. "If you do not give me those this very moment, I will kill you and steal them."

"All yours," said Jeremiah, dropping down.

Bruno grabbed the handles and launched himself at a wall. Bruno mastered the item in mere moments and began to properly scamper around the room. Hand over hand, faster and faster, incorporating longer and longer jumps and last-minute attachments to walls, Bruno swung like a monkey and stuck like a bug.

"The game has changed!" declared Bruno, before scrambling up to the ceiling. The ceiling, however, was not as convinced, and a segment of plaster detached as Bruno swung, producing a rain of particles and sending Bruno into a rolling recovery. Bruno lay there, hugging the handles to his chest and rocking back and forth. "Jay! Jay, this is so unfair! You have no idea how unfair this is!" Bruno laughed.

"I wanna turn!" said Allison.

"Yeah, I want to try!" said Delilah. She was already reaching for Bruno on the ground.

"No! Mine!" Bruno shouted, curling over to protect them.

Jeremiah looked at Allison and found her staring expectantly at him, clutching all of her weapons to her chest at once.

"Allison, I'm sorry to say I couldn't really think of anything novel or interesting to make for you. Just the enchanted axe, spear, sword, and dagger," said Jeremiah.

Allison nodded. "More than enough Jay, don't even worry. I'm so thankf—"

"Which is why I made you something a little boring."

He handed her a sharpening stone, its underside inscribed with a Strengthen enchantment. "Magic weapons are very difficult to sharpen, but this should do the trick. It's not much, but I hope you like it."

Allison took the stone and dropped to the ground instantly, beginning to silently sharpen her new magic sword in a rhythmic, almost ritualistic fashion. Her eyes were half-lidded, and she seemed to be somewhere else completely.

"Allison? Is that okay?" asked Jeremiah.

"Oh, she's in paradise right now," said Delilah, hanging from the ceiling by one of Bruno's handles. "She was honestly kind of scared she'd never get to sharpen her weapons again."

"Yeah . . . she's leagues . . . away," grunted Bruno. He experimented with climbing using only a single handle, disconnecting and reconnecting rapidly to propel himself.

Jeremiah took a moment to watch his friends play with their new toys and destroy the apartment. What was it he had been missing? What was here that wasn't at Cell Four's apartment? It was warmth, Jeremiah realized. He had a bond with Cell

Four, he really did, but it was different. It was transactional, there was an expectation. His friends here, Bruno, Allison, and Delilah—they cared about him as a person regardless of what he could provide them. He loved them for that. He knew they loved him too.

But they still had a job to do. "All right, everyone," he said. "Gather what you need. It's time to go."

Delilah, Allison, and Bruno stopped in their tracks. "Where'd *that* voice come from?" said Delilah, she arched an eyebrow and gave him a little look of admiration.

"You hear that? Jay's crackin' the whip," laughed Bruno.

"He's right," said Allison, warrior face settling in. "Let's get our heads straight. We're bringing the Giant's Bag, but keep anything critical on your person—if the bag gets destroyed, we still need to be effective."

"Don't even speak such things," said Delilah.

"Let's wreck a dungeon," said Allison.

"This is stupid," said Dronkal.

"Very," said Shugga. "You just joined. Why kill yourself now?"

"I gotta do it," said Jeremiah. He had stopped home to let his cellmates know that he was taking on the Gilded Vault. Friends or not, they had been the first source of real comfort he'd known since living on the streets. They cared about him, in their way. It seemed only fair.

Sweet Melissa pouted. "I'll miss you. We could have had a lot of fun together, you know."

Jeremiah bent to pet Miggy and she wound around his legs. "I'm . . . sure we could have. I might not die, you know."

"Yeah, there's still time for you to come to your senses," said Shugga.

"You said you have to. Why? What's making you do this?" asked Dronkal. He began pacing back and forth in the apartment.

"Just a request from Monty," said Jeremiah. Miggy bit him.

"Jay, let me talk to Monty for you," said Dronkal, moving to stand between Jeremiah and the door. "I'm sure this is just some kind of misunderstanding. He's got no reason to send you in there."

"He was clear," said Jeremiah. "This has got to get done." A lie, but not much of one. "If I don't happen to see you again, thanks. For taking care of me." Jeremiah went to leave, but Dronkal didn't move.

"You're family. You know that right?" said Dronkal.

"I know Dronk, I know," said Jeremiah.

"Try to come back." Dronkal stepped aside and let Jeremiah pass.

And then he was gone, letting the slope of the Pit carry him toward the gleaming jewel at its center. The weight of the armored shirt Thurok had made was comforting. He carried the Giant's Bag over his shoulder. He and his friends were equipped. They were experienced. They were ready.

Up close, the Gilded Vault was immense. The lustrous gold facade glared down at him, nearly blinding in the sunlight. Guards patrolling grounds and rooftops took notice of Jeremiah but remained at their posts. The nearest gave him a friendly nod.

Jeremiah had already decided that any dungeon meant to be a test of a thief's skill would punish anyone entering through the front door. Why else would Cassidy have placed all those windows? He carefully set up his ladder to access a second-story window, careful not to bump the glass, lest the aloof guards turn hostile.

"Want me to hold that?" A smiling guard had approached.

"Uhh, sure! Are you allowed to do that?" asked Jeremiah.

"Definitely! I'm just here to make sure you don't damage the house," said the guard. He took a firm grip on the ladder, holding it steady. Jeremiah climbed up to the window. This seemed too easy.

"It's unlocked," called the guard. "You can just go right in."

The window's frosted glass offered no insight as to what lay beyond. "Thanks . . . uhh . . . any idea what's in there?" asked Jeremiah. Might as well check how far this generosity went.

"No idea. But I always hear screams when people enter through the front door, so this is as good an idea as it gets."

Jeremiah took some comfort in that and examined the window, trying to look as closely for traps or alarms as Bruno would. Nothing seemed out of the ordinary.

The window slid open with silky smoothness, revealing an elegant smoking room within. There were upholstered sofas, cabinetry, plush chairs, and small tables. It appeared ready to receive guests at any moment.

Where's the spinning blades? wondered Jeremiah. *Where's the pit of spikes?* He had assumed there would be countless spikes.

The floor below the window was unremarkable, just a typical hardwood floor. Jeremiah tossed the Giant's Bag through first, then leaned through the window, scanning side to side for imminent threats.

The windowsill shifted, there was a click, and the window slammed shut on Jeremiah's back, forcing the air from his lungs. His back and ribs screamed in pain as he tried to reach back to pull the window open again but pulled his hand back wet with blood. Glancing back, he saw a wide, blade protruding along the bottom of the window sash like a guillotine. It was so sharp Jeremiah hadn't even felt it cut him.

He stretched his hand to where the Giant's Bag sat on the floor, barely reaching his fingertips inside to retrieve his enchanted dagger. Wedging it beneath the window's blade, he was able to wriggle through any further damage to his body.

Jeremiah landed on the floor in a ball, waiting for another trap to spring. Nothing happened. He inspected his wounds. His palm had sustained a shallow cut and his shirt was torn, but the armor had reduced the damage to his midsection to an angry red bruise.

He opened the Giant's Bag. "Everyone out!"

Bruno came out first, instantly dropping to the ground and scanning the room. Delilah and Allison climbed through next.

"How the hell are you already bleeding? We just got here," said Delilah. She retrieved a roll of bandages from the Giant's Bag and quickly wrapped Jeremiah's hand.

"Window trap," said Jeremiah.

Bruno sprang to the window. "Where's the trigger?"

"I think it's in the sill," said Jeremiah.

Bruno inspected the sill, the sash, and the blade itself. "Not poisoned, that's a relief."

Allison braced the window open just long enough for Jeremiah to retrieve his dagger before it slammed shut again.

"That's meant to remove fingers," said Bruno. "You're lucky you, apparently, just flopped through."

"Hush, we're on a mission," said Allison. "Bruno, you're now our guide through this nonsense."

"This is a deathtrap dungeon," said Bruno. "It exists for the sole purpose of attracting adventurers such as ourselves. They are very rare, for good reason, and tend to have fewer defenders and more traps. Many more." Bruno glanced around the room. "Granted, most deathtraps don't look like this."

"Yeah, this is rather lovely," said Delilah. A tall display case caught her eye. It contained a small library of leather-bound books with titles written in gold. Delilah stepped closer to take a better look.

"Don't!" Bruno shouted. He yanked her back just as the glass on the display case exploded. The books, which were actually expertly painted metal blocks, flew from the display case at crushing speeds. Thanks to Bruno, Delilah caught one in the upper arm instead of the face. She spun from the hit, crying out as she dropped to the floor.

Allison hauled Delilah back to the window, interposing her shield between Delilah and everything. "You okay?"

"Just a glancing hit," said Delilah. She flexed her arm, where an angry bruise was already forming. "Not broken. Thanks, Bruno."

"Don't. Touch. Anything," said Bruno, pointing at them each in turn.

"I didn't!" said Delilah.

"The trigger was under the rug, wasn't it?" asked Jeremiah.

"Yes! Go on, tell me more," said Bruno.

"Go on about what?" Jeremiah frowned. What else was there to say?

"How does that fit in with what we know?" asked Bruno. "How does it serve the dungeon's purpose? What does it tell us about the creator? We need to understand how this place works if we want to survive."

"The purpose of a dungeon is to keep people out, isn't it?" asked Allison. She kept pointing her shield at different things in the smoking room, trying to anticipate the next threat.

"It's not," said Delilah. "Cassidy invited people here, so this whole place is a trap meant to kill people."

"No, he wanted to test them," said Jeremiah. "Failing the test means you die, but his goal wasn't just to kill people."

"Correct!" said Bruno. He picked up one of the metal blocks with a grunt and heaved it onto a plush armchair. They stared as the chair snapped shut like a giant mouth, complete with serrated teeth bursting from the cushions. "That means, in some way or another, we can expect the dungeon to be fair. Cruel maybe, obtuse sure, but it needs to be fair. Otherwise, there's no way to pass the test."

"All right, Bruno, lead the way," said Allison. "I don't even want to move."

Bruno flopped onto the ground and began inspecting every fiber of the carpet. "Let's do this."

CHAPTER FORTY-ONE

Theft

"C lear," Bruno announced. He stepped onto the corner of the rug he had just been starting at and crouched to inspect the next spot.

"Bruno, that took, like, fifteen minutes," said Delilah. "Is every step going to take that long?"

"We can go faster," said Bruno. "But it will be for a very brief period of time."

An hour passed before Bruno was halfway across the smoking room. With each step, he studied not only where he would place his feet but also the room as a whole.

"He's checking to see if anything is pointed at the spot, like that bookshelf," said Jeremiah at Allison's impatient sigh.

"You guys want to see something interesting?" Bruno produced a tiny bag and tossed a pinch of bright red powder into the air. The cloud of powder coalesced in midair, taking the shape of a long, straight strand.

"Whisperwire," said Bruno. "Thinner than human hair. Love the magnetic powder, Delilah, thank you."

"Can you disarm it?" asked Delilah.

"Best not to. The less you interact with a trap, the better. There's always a chance you set it off by accident. All right, everyone, move up. Step only where I stepped."

They started to advance; Allison, Jeremiah, then Delilah, each carefully following Bruno's path. They made it two entire steps.

"Get down!" Allison shouted.

A volley of darts erupted from the walls, the ceiling, and up from beneath the carpet all at once like a swarm of wasps. Jeremiah felt something bite into the back of his ankle as he dropped.

"Who's hit?" asked Delilah, yanking a needle from her neck.

"Good!" said Allison and Bruno together.

"Hit!" said Jeremiah. He pulled the dart from his ankle and could see the small glass reservoir behind the needle, now empty.

Delilah sniffed the tip of the dart. "Gorgon toxin. Hold still." In a smooth motion, she plunged a hefty syringe into Jeremiah's thigh. He gritted his teeth as the thick needle bit deep, injecting a payload that burned in his muscle like a hot marle. She then injected herself just above the collarbone.

"We should be good, just a little numb around the injury spot. Let me know if you start to feel stiffness in your upper leg, I don't have the kit to de-petrify you."

"What the hell happened?" asked Bruno.

"I felt my helmet catch on something," said Allison. Bruno examined her helmet and pulled a now slack piece of whisperwire off the top.

"Forgot you're taller than me, especially in the armor." Bruno scowled at the wire. "Sorry." It was a very strange sorry. Begrudging, and also very nearly shameful.

"Can we just wait in the bag?" asked Allison. "Seems safer."

"No!" said Jeremiah. "If a trap so much as nicks the bag, we're dead."

"Plus, I can't monitor Bruno," said Delilah. "If he gets hurt, I need to treat him quickly."

It was another hour before they finally made it to the door of the smoking room. Bruno's inspections had become even more thorough after the dart trap. Jeremiah noted that he was starting to rub his eyes from exhaustion.

Bruno disarmed the trap on the doorknob with a deft twist of his tools, and they were finally free of the first room.

If the rest of the dungeon is like this, we might need to sleep here, thought Jeremiah.

The hallway they stepped into was mercifully free of carpet, but even grander than the smoking room. Candelabras dotted the walls at regular intervals, their candles lit and giving off a pleasant light. A rich purple wallpaper offset dark ebony wainscoting.

Delilah whistled. "This place looks expensive."

"Bruno, where are we going?" asked Jeremiah. He wasn't sure if there was a "plan of exploration" that rogues had. Or rules to stick to. *I should ask about that later*, he thought. *That sounds interesting.*

"If I had to guess," said Bruno, "I'd say the basement or the attic or the very center of the mansion."

"Bruno, that's a terrible guess," said Allison.

"You can just say you don't know," said Delilah.

"Thoughts?" Bruno asked Jeremiah.

Jeremiah was flattered. He was being consulted. "I'd say basement. You already went to the bottom of the Pit to get here, so he'd want you to go down even farther."

"Ooh he's got a thing for symbolism. I like that," said Delilah. "I feel like that tells us something about him."

"I feel bad I took us in through the second floor then," said Jeremiah.

"No, the second floor was a good choice. I can guarantee the easier the entry, the worse the traps," said Bruno, his face hovering over the floor.

Allison waved her hand over a candelabra's flame. "Bruno, how are—"

"Don't!" Bruno shouted. Everyone tensed, ready to jump, duck, or fight. Nothing happened. "I said not to touch *anything*!"

"But why are these candles here? And lit?" asked Allison, ignoring Bruno's admonishment.

"Illusion?" Bruno suggested.

Jeremiah shook his head. "Too broad an effect, and we've been interacting with it for too long. We would have noticed something off by now."

"Likely a dungeon core, then," said Bruno. He began reinspecting the floor after delivering a thorough scowling at Allison.

"What's a dungeon core?" asked Delilah, she held a small strip of paper over the flame. It turned green, then blue. She nodded at it, then put it away.

"It's a magic caretaker for the dungeon," said Bruno. "They reset traps, perform basic maintenance, stuff like that."

"It's like a golem," said Jeremiah, "but attached to a location instead of a creature. There's probably some big crystal somewhere that it's anchored to. Stronger ones can even do things like summon monsters."

Allison took a deep slow breath, apparently this revelation was frustrating for her. "Anything we can do about it?" she asked.

"We can break the crystal," said Jeremiah. But it won't just be lying around for us to find."

"All right, so we're targeting the basement," said Allison. "Let's find some stairs."

"This place seems typical of Elminian architecture, so the primary staircase will be at the center," said Delilah.

"This way, then," said Bruno. "And we'll make our way inward."

They inched down the hallway, Bruno checking everything for signs of traps. His attentions revealed a pressure plate, more whisperwire, and a suspicious candle. All were disarmed disabled or avoided. Bruno wiped the sweat from his face and forehead. "Grease me please," he said to Delilah.

She gave him a little tin of white paste. With two fingers he dabbed it across his eyebrows, nose, and lip. The paste rubbed in clear, disappearing except for a little shine on his skin.

"Sweat paste," said Delilah to Jeremiah as he leaned over her shoulder to look in the tin. "Stops you from sweating."

"What? You have that? How come we can't use it in the lab? That place is a sauna!" said Jeremiah.

"'Cause you don't *need* it in the lab. Also—"

"Stop," said Bruno. "Something just happened."

"Heard something or saw something?" asked Allison, raising her shield.

"Seen. The wood grain moved," said Bruno. He was staring harder at the grain of the floor, tense as could be.

"What does that mean?" asked Jeremiah.

"Magic trap," said Bruno. "Be ready."

"What was the trigger?" asked Jeremiah. He'd never seen a magic trap before, just mechanical ones. It had to be some form of enchanting.

"Contact!" Delilah said. Jeremiah squeezed aside as Allison ran past to form the front line.

From back the way they'd come, a strange, blurry form approached. It looked like a square of bluish translucent mist that stretched nearly to the limits of the hallway. Jeremiah would have missed it if it had not been pointed out.

"Tunnel ooze," said Allison. "They're acidic and will try to suck you into their body to digest you."

"How dangerous?" asked Bruno.

"Not especially," said Allison. "They take a while to kill, since they have no vital organs, but they're slow as molasses. You just keep backing up until . . . oh."

"Oh? What oh?" asked Jeremiah. The Tunnel Ooze crawled toward them, gliding across the floor with tiny undulating pseudopods. Jeremiah took an unconscious step back and felt his foot bump against Bruno.

"Al, I can't check our way that fast!" said Bruno.

"Oh," said Jeremiah.

"We have to take it down, quickly!" said Allison. She rushed toward the slime, Delilah followed right behind her, longspear poised over Allison's shoulder.

"Al, stop!" cried Jeremiah.

Allison heeded his warning and skidded to a stop just as she passed the door they'd come in from, the edge of known territory. She eyed the invisible boundary, and drew her axe as the ooze came within range.

Just as Allison was rearing back to strike, they heard a click from the slime's part of the hall. A line of thick metal pistons punched out from the wall. Most of the pistons thrust into the side of the slime, barely slowing its progress, but one piston caught Allison in the leg.

Allison grunted. Her armor cushioned the blow but not the torque on her knee, and she fell, twisting, just as the slime reached her. It briefly engulfed her foot, then Delilah hauled her backward, out of its reach. Whatever the ooze was made of, it left a coating of itself on Allison when she pulled away.

Allison and Delilah retreated back to where Jeremiah waited with Bruno, still frantically scanning for traps to give them space to move.

Allison clawed at her armored boot, her cries of pain escalating as a sickly scent of acid eating flesh wafted up from her. "Gods, it hurts!" Jeremiah knelt down to help, his fingertips blistering the moment he touched the ooze-covered armor.

Delilah dumped a bundle of powder on Allison's boot. Jeremiah hurried to undo the buckles.

"It's inside the armor, gods-dammit!" Allison started to scream. "Do something, come on!" She shoved Jeremiah aside to reach the buckles herself.

"It's okay," said Delilah calmly. "I got you, hang on." Another pack of powder, this one poured in the top of the boot. Allison hissed again, but her franticness lessened.

"Shit, move!" called Jeremiah. The Tunnel ooze was only a few feet away.

They leapt away, Jeremiah and Delilah stabbing into the ooze with their spears while Allison struggled to her feet. The ooze's body was surprisingly firm, it felt like stabbing a bale of hay. Their thrusts left narrow hollow indentations in the ooze that dribbled what Jeremiah assumed was blood.

Allison finally stepped between them, swinging her axe and taking great gashes out of the ooze. It did not seem to mind. Jeremiah and Delilah backed up to give her room and bumped into Bruno.

"Not ready!" he shouted. He wasn't even two paces from where they left him.

"We need to move!" Delilah yelled. She threw a packet of the anti-acid powder at the ooze, and part of it bubbled and poured away.

"Not yet!" Bruno said again.

Allison bumped into Jeremiah. "Move!"

"No!" Bruno yelled. He took a step forward, just one step, and started checking again, his eyes darting wildly.

It was only moments before they were compressed together, trapped between a flesh-eating monster and the unknown traps ahead.

"Bruno!" yelled Allison. She had to choke up on the axe to have room to swing.

"M-move!" Bruno said. They collectively jumped forward. "Drop!"

Jeremiah saw a tiny opening appear at the end of the hall, and a long iron spike fired out of it like a gigantic crossbow bolt. He dropped, Bruno dodged, the bolt missed Delilah and struck Allison in the middle of her back.

The enchanted armor saved her from being impaled, but the bolt carried enough force to send her stumbling forward, headfirst, directly into the ooze.

Jeremiah and Delilah both caught one of Allison's arms and yanked her free. Allison ripped her helmet off, and Delilah hit her in the head with another satchel of powder. Allison's skin was already an angry red.

"Move!" Bruno said again. They gained space, but not much.

"I've got an out, but I need to cavitate it," said Delilah.

"What does that mean?" asked Jeremiah. He thrust his spear into the ooze again, Delilah qualifying a solution meant there was going to be some kind of drawback.

"It's going to explode." Delilah held one of the metallic spheres Jeremiah had made and emptied a satchel inside.

"Explode?!" Jeremiah said, looking at the sphere. "There's no room for it to explode!"

"There's no room to do anything! You want to keep poking it?!"

"Cover!" cried Allison. Her shout was the only vote that mattered.

Delilah threw the metal orb into the ooze. It was sucked in but did not explode.

Oooh, this is such a bad idea, thought Jeremiah. "On it!" he shouted. Jeremiah leapt forward and thrust his spear into the ooze to strike the sphere. He saw a tiny flash of light before he was yanked to the ground. Allison threw herself on top of Jeremiah and Delilah, interposing her shield between them and the blast of burning acid that sprayed down the hallway.

The hallway was clear, the strange misty curtain transformed into a goop that now coated all surfaces. Jeremiah's ankles tingled, then stung, then burned, then felt like they were being sliced open. Some of the ooze had splashed up under the cuffs of his pants.

He drew in a breath to scream when he was engulfed in a blizzard of powder, soothing the burn back to merely painful.

They were all covered in white powder, and Delilah began another round, applying concentrated doses to specific areas.

"How much of this stuff do you have?" asked Bruno, exposing his forearms to Delilah.

"Tons. It's a standard lab safety item," said Delilah. "I don't usually carry this much, but this bag is the best thing that's ever happened to me."

"It's appreciated," Allison grimaced, as she finally removed her boot.

"Oh, sweet lord," said Bruno, gagging.

"Yep, that's a bad one," said Allison. The boot had taken some skin with it. What it left behind was weeping blood around angry red blisters.

"I can wrap and numb it," said Delilah. "More powder and anesthetic bandages all around."

Jeremiah snatched another satchel of powder from Delilah and caked it onto his ankles until it looked like a red-tinged dough. "I think I hate acid burns more than fire burns," he sighed.

"Trust me, you don't," said Allison. She hissed through her teeth and dumped more powder into her armor, some errant droplet having worked its way to her skin.

Delilah inspected Allison's face, dabbing more powder here and there. "Can't fix this though." With a finger, she reached up and wiped away one of Allison's eyebrows.

"Kinda feels like we're getting our asses kicked," said Allison. "And we've cleared one room and half a hallway."

"Do we have any potions?" asked Jeremiah.

"One," said Delilah. "Spent the last of Empress Aubrianna's gold on it, so please refrain from severe injuries."

"That's what I'm *trying* to do, if you guys would stop rushing me," said Bruno. He took a moment to rub his eyes.

"You okay, Bruno?" asked Jeremiah.

"Got some acid damage, but I'm all right. Why?" Bruno kept inspecting.

"You keep rubbing your eyes and squinting," said Delilah.

"Don't worry about it," said Bruno.

"I swear to god," Allison said. She reached into Delilah's bag and withdrew one of her poetry books. "Come here."

"Busy," said Bruno.

"Bruno. Come here," said Allison in her commander voice.

Bruno turned to face her, annoyance clear on his face.

"Read this page," said Allison. She held the book up close to his face, just past his nose.

Bruno sighed. He squinted at the page, tilting his head away. "Nor will I . . . argue it nor pray for . . . anything but . . . modesty . . . and not to be . . . angry."

"Don't lean back," said Allison.

"Can you not?" Bruno stepped away from the book.

"Oh, Bruno . . . you need glasses," said Delilah.

"I do *not* need glasses! You get glasses when you're a kid."

"Humans sometimes need glasses as they get older, it's perfectly normal," said Delilah in a very teachery voice.

"I'm not getting old, I'm fine." Bruno returned to the comfort of trap searching.

"I'm not fine," said Jeremiah. "The guy checking for traps can't see."

Suddenly they were obvious, the little signs of age on Bruno Jeremiah had never noticed. His hair was just starting to gray at the front, and there were the tini-est lines around his eyes. Bruno didn't know how old he was exactly, which wasn't uncommon, but Jeremiah had always assumed he was younger than he looked. Now Jeremiah wondered if he might be older.

"If any of you want to look for traps instead, be my guest." Bruno kept searching and moving them forward, occasionally disarming a hidden switch. He still squinted but refrained from rubbing his eyes again.

The others exchanged a look. All they could do was follow.

CHAPTER FORTY-TWO

Lessons in Dungeoneering

For such a big mansion, there aren't a lot of rooms," said Delilah. Since the smoking room, they saw no doors in the hallway besides the one they were making their way toward at the end.

"Likely a lot of the space is taken up by trap mechanisms and components," said Bruno. "They can be very space intensive."

"Do magic traps need space too?" asked Jeremiah.

"Not as much," said Bruno. "It's just a form of enchanting, like you do. Hell, *you* could probably make magic traps."

That sentence sent Jeremiah's mind reeling. A trap maker? A *magic* trap maker? That sounded so cool, but how would he even . . . *Oh! I could do a contact triggered Adhere rune to stick your foot to the floor. And then I could also super-heat it! Oh! And then I could—*

Allison snapped her fingers in front of his face. "Jay, come back to us. You can fantasize later."

"Making traps isn't very useful for adventurers anyway," said Bruno. "They're meant to protect against us."

"Not like magic items," said Delilah.

"Yeah, more of those," said Allison. "Focus on more of those."

They reached the end of the hallway at last. The door was made of strong wood reinforced with metal rivets. Etched into its surface were words in a language Jeremiah couldn't read.

"It says 'please knock' in halfling," said Bruno. "No obvious traps or mechanisms . . . This is one of those moments where knowing the man who designed the trap helps us. Is knocking an idiot test that will set off the trap? Or is it some sort of, I don't know, politeness check? What does he want from us?"

"I feel like we already failed the idiot test just be being dumb enough to come in here," said Jeremiah. "As for a politeness check? Hmm, I could see Monty making a trap like that. I say knock."

"Agreed, knock," said Delilah. "I think decorum means something to this Cassidy guy."

"All right, but back up just in case," said Bruno. Jeremiah and Delilah retreated a fair distance, but Allison stayed, shield raised.

Bruno straightened up, fixed his armor, and raised his hand to knock.

"Wait," said Allison.

Bruno went rigid, fist still poised.

"Why is it written in halfling?" asked Allison.

"Because Cassidy was a halfling, I assume," said Bruno.

"Get low and knock," said Allison. Everyone knelt down, trying to mimic a halfling's diminutive size.

From his new vantage point, Bruno gave the door three quick raps. They heard a click, and the lower half of the door opened. The upper half remained stationary.

"Ooooh, that was a good one," said Bruno.

"Damn clever, Al," said Delilah.

They crawled through the miniature door. As he passed underneath, Jeremiah saw the upper half of the door was actually a thick wooden block, presumably containing trap mechanisms. He avoided touching it.

They found themselves in a large circular room with an abnormally high ceiling. The walls were adorned with ribbons, streamers, and dozens of mirrors of all sizes, as though prepared for a wealthy child's birthday party. There was no furniture, not even carpet. Or, Jeremiah noticed, an exit.

"We should be near the center of the structure," said Delilah. "So there *should* be stairs here. Or near here or—"

On cue, the door slammed shut behind them.

"Oh, that's what that was," said Bruno.

Jeremiah stumbled as the floor beneath his feet shifted and began to rotate.

"Screw floor," said Delilah. "King Growler had one in his command chambers. Careful, it's speeding up."

Sure enough, the speed of rotation began to increase, and Jeremiah felt himself being pulled outward. At the same time, he realized they were moving downward, the celebratory decor receding overhead.

As the floor lowered, needle sharp spikes sprung up out of the walls in every direction like a hedgehog's quills. Jeremiah was suddenly aware of the deadly nature of the pull. They started small but quickly grew larger and more numerous.

The floor spun faster. Jeremiah struggled to keep his footing and avoid being thrown into the spiked wall. The others braced against the pull, leaning away and planting their feet.

"Move to the center!" said Allison. She caught his arm and helped haul him to the middle of the room.

They huddled at the center of the spinning floor. The floor continued to accelerate, however, and as they descended the spikes grew even deadlier, now sporting barbed tips.

"Hang on!" said Allison. "We'll be at the bottom soon." They gripped each other for stability, Jeremiah straining to hold on to Allison and Bruno.

"What does the trap maker want?" came Bruno's voice in Jeremiah's ear, although the real Bruno was busy bracing his feet and clinging to his friends.

A strength test? Jeremiah wondered. *No, any child knows you can't hang on forever.*

No matter how strong or agile you are. Indeed, even at the center of the room, they were subjected to dizzying speeds.

What does he want?

It dawned on him as his feet slipped the slightest inch.

"Let go!" he yelled.

"What? No, just hang on!" said Bruno.

"It's what Cassidy wants, we need to let go!" Jeremiah resigned himself to the pain and released his hold on his friends.

He was immediately pulled off balance. The difference in speed even a few feet from the center caused him to stumble. Vertigo overwhelmed his senses, and he fell, sliding along the ground, and prayed to collide with a less pointy section of wall.

Jeremiah's head slammed against brick as he hit the wall at high speed. His world continued to spin even as he became aware of pain in his leg where a spike impaled him. He braced his foot against another to take his weight as he tried not to be sick. Below, the floor continued to drop away, carrying his friends and spinning ever faster.

Jeremiah's friends huddled together in the middle, arms linked, resisting the force.

"Let go!" Jeremiah screamed. The weapons further down the wall took an increasingly crueler shape. Spikes became forks and axe heads. From his vantage point, he realized the room was a gaping maw, its teeth waiting to shred its prey.

Delilah's feet slipped out from under her, she shrieked as her grip on Allison and Bruno failed. Jeremiah watched helplessly as she was thrown, upside down, onto a barbed spike. Delilah screamed as the spike punctured her reinforced breastplate, punching into her abdomen, then she hung silently, head down.

Jeremiah wrenched his leg off the spike gouging his thigh and started climbing toward Delilah. Below, Bruno and Allison clutched each other, delaying the inevitable.

Bruno released one hand from Allison's armor, reaching for the magic climbing handles at his belt. Allison gripped him all the tighter and yelled something unintelligible. Bruno grabbed a handle and swung down to attach it to the whirling floor. He missed. Disoriented and dizzy beyond comprehension, his grip slipped, and he was pulled away from Allison and launched backward. Jeremiah watched with astonishment as Bruno twisted in midair and avoided the blades. He slammed the magic climbing handles into the wall and stood firm without a scratch.

Allison, alone in the center of the room, gripped the floor with the claws on her gauntleted fingers. The weapons lining the room changed again. No longer fearsome prongs and blades, they became needle-sharp cones with wide flaring bases. They stood out from the wall as dense and unavoidable as a hedgehog's spines, projecting a grim, efficient lethality.

The trap functioned as designed. Allison's grip failed just as the spinning floor reached its maximum velocity. She struck the spikes with a quick crunch of surrendering metal and was still. It appeared the spikes only penetrated her armor the tiniest amount.

The floor finally slotted into place with a resounding *boom*, revealing a new pair of doors set into the wall.

Jeremiah reached Delilah first. She still hung upside down. "Don't worry, we're going to get you down from here."

"Is the bag okay?" she whispered. Blood was leaking from under her armor and running down her neck. The blade had punched into her lower stomach, sneaking under the magic breastplate.

"Bag is fine," Jeremiah reassured her without checking.

Bruno arrived, the handles making the walls easy to scale. "How do we get her down?"

"Tie a rope harness. We'll push her off the spike and lower her all the way to the floor," said Jeremiah. Then to Delilah: "We're going to get you down now, okay?"

They tied the harness and started to push. Delilah screamed. "Wait! Wait, wait, something's stuck! Something inside me's stuck!"

Jeremiah inspected the puncture. At once, the anatomy knowledge sprang to his mind to make sense of the mess of the torn flesh and blood. "Delilah, I think there's a barb caught on your hip bones, right on the crest. I'm going to need to lift you up a little to unhook it."

"No, no, no, please don't!" Delilah curled up to paw at the spike in her guts before falling limp again with exhaustion.

Bruno had gone a sickly green. Jeremiah barked at him, "Hey! Look at me! I need you with me right now, got it?"

Bruno met his eyes, swallowed, and nodded.

"All right, Delilah, here we go," said Jeremiah.

"No, no, please wait. I'm not ready," Delilah sobbed.

"You can scream, you can yell, you can call me any horrible thing you want, but one, two, deep breath, three!" Jeremiah shoved, ignoring Delilah's ear-piercing scream as she slid off the spike. Whatever was caught inside her slipped free with a scraping sensation, and Bruno grunted in effort as he caught her weight, then he and Jeremiah belayed her to the floor below.

They scrambled down after her once she landed. She was already reaching for the Giant's Bag when her eyes fell on Allison, impaled on the spikes, still and silent.

Delilah pressed a small parcel of paper to her own nostrils and inhaled hard. "Gah!" She looked around with renewed vigor. "Bruno, go take a look at Allison. Jay, come here and tell me if you smell almonds." She injected herself in the neck with something.

"If I smell . . . almonds?" said Jeremiah. He leaned over the wound and sniffed but smelled only blood. "No, I don't."

"Little miracles. Okay, welcome to your first day of medical school. We're going to stitch a complex abdominal tear. I need you to inject this into my spine, between the vertebrae." She held up a massive needle, one Jeremiah had never seen before.

"You need to take the potion, I've never stitched anyone back together," said Jeremiah. He unstrapped Delilah's armor and blood poured out of the breast plate.

He deliberately looked away from the pink slimy solids that were bulging out of her stomach. He slid the needle into her back, that part was at least easy. Delilah didn't flinch.

"We'll see," said Delilah, still looking at Allison. "How is she?" she called.

"The spikes only barely punched through the armor, but she's not moving," said Bruno. "Her neck's all kinked."

"Get her down, careful as you can," said Delilah. She handed Jeremiah a strange J-shaped needle and thick thread. "You are going to sew where I tell you. I'm not going to feel it, but I can't help you either."

"Sewing. Okay, I can do that," said Jeremiah. His hands trembled with the needle, his very nature preventing him from piercing Delilah's skin.

"It's okay, I won't feel it," said Delilah in a soothing tone. "First we press the organs and tissues back into the abdominal sack using a gentle but firm pressure."

Following Delilah's instructions was somehow calming. A tiny task, one he was familiar with. The idea that he was punching a needle in and out of his friend's body sat on the sidelines, patiently waiting its turn to become a new nightmare.

Bruno finally hoisted Allison off the wall. Her armor clattered as he set her on the floor. "Rise and shine, Al, you got knocked out."

She didn't move.

"Allison?" said Bruno. He lifted her visor. "Hey, good to see you're awake . . . can you . . . Delilah! Something's wrong. Her eyes are moving, but she's not doing anything else."

"Internal decapitation," said Delilah. "Potion, now. She broke her neck."

Bruno sprinted to the bag for their one and only potion. He jammed it into Allison's mouth, forcing her jaw open with his fingers, and rubbing her throat as he emptied its contents.

For a few terrible moments, nothing happened. Then Allison gasped. Her limbs flailed out in every direction in a single great spasm.

"Oh, that was awful," she choked out. "Really awful. I've never had my neck broken before."

"Glad to have you back. Ever treat a gut wound?" asked Delilah.

"Tons," said Allison.

As Bruno vomited on the other side of the room, Jeremiah and Allison followed Delilah's guidance to stitch the hole in Delilah's abdomen back together, mostly. Allison took the lead, and didn't bat an eye at the grotesque procedure. In fact, she seemed to be almost comforted, humming pleasantly while she tended to her friend. They finished it off with a thick green paste to stem the bleeding.

As Delilah moved to tend Jeremiah's leg, Bruno asked, "Jay, how did you know what we were supposed to do?"

"Call it a hunch," said Jeremiah. "Cassidy wouldn't make a trap you could just brute force your way through, he's too tricky for that. This one was about knowing when to cut your losses and take the hit. Or something. Ouch, ow! Delilah, take it easy."

"Hush," said Delilah. "Everyone, remember, we have *no* potions now. Please, please, *please* stay sharp, and no more deadly injuries!"

"Stay sharp, huh," said Jeremiah, gazing at their spiked surroundings.

"Don't worry, Delilah," said Allison seriously. "We'll keep our heads on straight."

"Literally putting ourselves back together and you're making puns," grumbled Delilah.

CHAPTER FORTY-THREE

Cursed

As Delilah stowed her medical gear in preparation to leave the screw floor room, Allison motioned to Jeremiah. "Can I talk to you for a sec?"

There wasn't far to go, but Allison guided Jeremiah to the edge of the room where they could speak away from the others.

Jeremiah eyed the deadly spikes as though they were eavesdroppers. "What's up?" It seemed an exceedingly strange time and place for a private talk.

Allison spoke in a whisper. "I realize there's a chance I might not survive this place, I mean there's a chance none of us will but . . . look, there's something I want you to have, so I best give it to you now." She handed Jeremiah a tiny parcel, a bit of burlap tied off with string.

Jeremiah accepted the offering. It fit easily into the palm of his hand. Untying the string, he found a stringy wad of plant matter. It was thick and greasy, like a clump of roots dipped in oil. "Uh, thanks. Is this tobacco?"

"Listen," said Allison. "When you get out of here and you meet this cult, or whatever it is, they're not going to shake your hand and welcome you aboard. They're going to make you do something to prove your commitment. It won't be something you want to do. Probably it won't be something you even want to remember doing."

"You're a little late to the game Allison. The Stonefists already had me doing stuff like that," said Jeremiah. Where was this stuff when he had to go out collecting with Shugga and Dronkal?

"No, I know you think that, but . . . when it actually comes time to *use* this stuff, I want you to make sure you have it. This stuff will make it easier," she wrapped it back up in his hand, hiding it.

"Make it easier? What do you mean? And how do you know that?"

"Just easier," said Allison. "Chew it a few minutes before you have to do whatever it is. It'll taste rancid, but it's supposed to."

"I feel like I should talk the oth—"

"No. Don't tell anyone else about this. I mean it. I hope you won't need it at all, but keep it in your pocket. Just in case."

"I will," said Jeremiah, because Allison clearly needed him to just accept it. He tucked the plant away, wondering what she wasn't telling him.

Bruno was still inspecting the double doors when they returned to the group. He wiped sweat off his forehead, stood up, and began another sweep.

"Bruno, you can't keep this up," said Delilah. "We're never going to get anywhere, and besides, you're already exhausted."

"What, are you going to take a turn?" Bruno popped a crick in his neck. "No offense, but I'd rather not die immediately. If we learn enough about how Cassidy thinks, maybe I won't need to be so meticulous at every moment, but until then—"

"I have an alternative suggestion," said Allison. "What if, instead of dissecting the psychology of some long dead psychopath, we don't worry about that? What if, screw that guy?"

She drew her axe and pointed it at the wall. "Have magic axe, make magic hole."

Bruno gripped the doorknob with a cloth in his hand. There was a hiss, and a puff of green smoke leaked from the cloth, another trap disarmed.

"Bruno?" Allison asked.

"I'm thinking," said Bruno.

"I approve," said Jeremiah. "Cassidy is long dead; I can't see any reason to indulge him just because we need the loot."

"Exactly," said Allison. "I've got no stake in this. Let's just get to the end."

"I have a bad feeling about this," said Bruno. "But you might be right. Ducking the test feels like cheating the point of the dungeon but . . . I don't know, maybe that's better than beating it."

"That's the spirit!" said Allison. With that, she raised her axe and swung on the wall.

The walls in the circular room had wood paneling from top to bottom, save for the rows of spikes. But as Allison's axe tore through it, a layer of metal was revealed beneath.

"Hang on," said Jeremiah.

Decay And Decay And Decay

Jeremiah charged the diagram and stepped aside for Allison to continue her work.

The axe bit through the metal, tearing great chunks from it, the magic axe cleaving through the weakening metal. Bruno paced back and forth behind her, flinching at every swing. Finally, she cut through the metal barrier, and a whoosh of air rushed into the room.

"What, no gout of flame? No poison smog?" said Allison. "I'm disappointed."

Bruno inspected the hole. "There's a lot of mechanisms. Probably controlling traps all over the building."

"Safe to continue?" asked Allison, rolling her shoulders and hefting the axe again.

"I don't see any reason why not," said Bruno, as though he wished he did.

"Trap this, you lockpicking thug!" Allison yelled and swung her axe again. The entire house rumbled as she cleaved through its innards, each swing of her axe pulling out piles of springs, chains, levers and tie bars with steady, efficient swings.

"I think she's enjoying this," said Jeremiah.

"Allison doesn't like traps," said Delilah.

"Jay! Put an inscription on the other side and I'll hack us an exit," panted Allison.

Jeremiah poked his head into the hole. All around, he saw an endless network of delicate metal components, the nearest ones smashed to smithereens, of course. He felt a continuous flow of warm air, like the breath of the dungeon. Quickly, he wrote the same inscription on the backside of the same metallic wall.

Decay And Decay And Decay

"All you," he said, gesturing for her to continue, and Allison began hacking an exit. Even with the enchantment, the work took time, and Allison was winded by the time she waved them through.

"That's how you do a dungeon," she huffed. Bruno led them in.

They emerged in the middle of another hallway. Compared to upstairs, the ground floor was a dilapidated mess. The floor was splintery old wood, and the walls were a rough plaster. Sloppily made torches lit the space unevenly.

"The hell is this?" asked Allison.

"An aesthetic choice?" guessed Bruno. "Maybe testing your ability to handle traps in various settings."

"Oh, I'm gonna handle it," said Allison. She hefted the axe again, though she was still catching her breath.

Once again, they hacked their way through the layered wood and metal wall. By the time they exited the opposite side, Allison was sweating.

"Haven't been running enough lately," she chuckled, removing her helmet.

They were now in a serene grotto. A central fountain of marble depicted an unknown goddess with hands outstretched. Water tricked down her arms, feeding two tiny rivers that snaked through a floor of polished lapis. Lush vines with broad leaves hung from baskets affixed to the ceiling. It was like discovering a hidden oasis.

"This annoys me," said Delilah.

"The room is definitely trying to impress us," said Bruno, scowling at the goddess. "Obviously don't drink the water."

"I think it's pretty," said Jeremiah. *It'd be kind of nice to just stay here awhile,* he thought. *If I weren't convinced the statue was about to blast poison water at me.*

Allison huffed but gave a thumbs-up, agreeing with Jeremiah. She plopped against a wall and yawned deeply.

Bruno inspected the room for further nasty surprises and seemed irritated to report there were none to be found.

"Like hell the cute little peace-and-quiet room isn't trapped," said Delilah.

"I know," said Bruno, "but I've been over it twice, I can't find anything. Might just be a room to rest in?"

"Aww what a lovely spot of gamesmanship," said Jeremiah. "We're going to ignore that invite, yes?"

Allison spit and rubbed her eyes, losing the other eyebrow. "Yeah, let's keep digging."

She aligned herself with the wall she wanted gone and swung. The blue lapis tile work split, and suddenly the room was alight with violet arcs of lightning.

"You did it wrong," said Delilah.

They leapt together in a defensive formation. "Jay, what's going on?" asked Bruno. "This isn't a trap."

The lights had triggered when Allison started attacking the wall. "I think the dungeon core is angry we're cheating," said Jeremiah.

"Cheating? Oh, excuse me, I didn't know there was a rulebook. I demand a copy of the rules immediately!" Delilah shouted at the ceiling.

"What's happening?" Allison asked over the hissing and crackling of the magical energy.

"It's a summoning," said Jeremiah. "Get ready!"

The arcing strands of violet light slammed together into a tiny sphere in the center of the room. The sphere flashed, growing at incredible speeds, and took on a great bestial shape.

A monstrous bear covered in bony plates emerged from the light, becoming more distinct, like metal cooling from a forge. The bear was rippling muscle far beyond the bulk and height of even the largest normal bears. It roared in fury.

"Dire bear. Keep its focus on me and stay out of its mouth," said Allison. She swapped the axe for her short spear and banged it against her shield.

"Wisdom for the ages," said Bruno.

They scattered as Allison thrust her spear up at the bear's nose to keep its attention. The magic spear pierced the bear's nostril, and it roared so loud the air shook. It lunged toward Allison, mouth agape, baring teeth as long as Jeremiah's hand.

Allison dodged to the side and stabbed the spear into the bear's neck, its bony plates cracking at the impact. At the same time, Delilah thrust her spear into the bear's side, pushing hard to penetrate the thick hide and muscle. Bruno slashed at the backs of the bear's feet.

Jeremiah thrust at a flank with his own spear, but lacking the magic weapons of his friends, it was like stabbing a raw steak with a dull knife.

The bear swung a monstrous claw at Allison and knocked her flying across the room. She collided with the goddess statue, letting it catch her in the open arms.

"You all right, Al?" called Bruno.

"F-fine," Allison wheezed. She stood, but something was clearly wrong in the way she moved. With effort, she raised her weapons and staggered toward the bear again. Banging her shield once to draw its attention, she thrust her spear into its neck.

Azure blood gushed from the wound, but the bear was unperturbed. It batted Allison to the side again, then turned toward Delilah.

"C'mere, big guy, time to slow you down," said Bruno. In a flurry of blades, he tore through the tough sinews of the bear's back leg.

The bear toppled onto its side, and they lay into it, swinging and stabbing at whatever spots they could reach.

Jeremiah realized Allison was not among them. She was a few feet away, hunched over and panting.

"Al, toss me the spear!" called Bruno. Allison heaved the spear toward Bruno like it as made of lead rather than throw it and dropped her shield as well in the process.

The bear clambered back to its feet. "Jay, get this thing over!" Bruno yelled. He was dancing just beyond the bear's reach, Allison's spear at the ready.

Jeremiah cast a ball of acid at the bear's feet. It pooled under the bear's paws, burning through the sensitive pads. The bear growled and retreated from the pool, roaring in pain as its injured legs gave way again.

Bruno rushed in with a ferocious scream, ramming the spear into the bear's underside. He shoved hard, spinning away from the bear's raking claws, only to return and shove the spear deeper.

With one last hard push, the spear reached the bear's heart. The animal shuddered and spasmed, its limbs a flurry of claws, then lay still.

"Health check!" Delilah called.

"Good!" said Jeremiah.

"Good," said Bruno.

"G-g-good," wheezed Allison.

"Textbook work, everyone," said Bruno.

Delilah was rushing to Allison's side. "Hon, what's going on?"

"F-fine," said Allison. She was sweating profusely, her face growing pale.

"I've seen her work harder than that," said Jeremiah. "Something's wrong, she shouldn't be breathing this hard."

"Respiratory," mumbled Delilah. "Anyone else feeling anything?" Everyone was at normal levels of exhaustion.

Delilah touched Allison's face and asked if she could feel it. Then shook her left arm around.

"She get hurt fighting the bear?" asked Bruno. He was slowly backing away from Allison, not quite looking at her.

"Maybe. Could be a heart attack?" said Delilah. She gave Allison an injection that Jeremiah recognized as a blood thinner, to no immediate effect.

"It started earlier than that," said Jeremiah. "She was out of breath after the first wall she hacked through."

Delilah shook her head. "Can't be a gas. We would have smelled or seen it, or my detectors would have—Oh no."

"What?" asked Jeremiah.

"I left my detectors in the bag!" Delilah dashed to the hole in the wall they'd entered through. She pulled a metal ring from the Giant's Bag with dozens of small slips of white paper threaded onto it. She flipped through them until she found one tiny page that was pitch-black.

"Oh no. Oh no, no, no . . ." Delilah drew a small tin box from the bag. She broke the wax seal around the lip of the box and revealed a second ring of paper slips. She waved them at the hole, and one of the slips turned from white to black in seconds.

"Get her in the bag!" Delilah screamed.

"What? What's going on?" asked Bruno. He and Jeremiah were already helping Allison to her feet. Her legs wobbled beneath her.

"It's Furnace Curse. Jay, I need your help inside. Bruno, stay out here and guard us."

"Delilah, I'm fine, I'm not cursed." Allison tried to shake off Bruno and Jeremiah with a weak shrug.

"I did not go to medical school for eight years for *you* to tell *me* you're fine! You are suffocating, and we need to improvise a solution."

The three of them manhandled Allison into the bag. Jeremiah leapt down after, floating down to a chaotic scene as Delilah cast aside piles of lab equipment to make room to lay Allison down.

"Here to help," said Jeremiah. "What's Furnace Curse and how do we stop it?"

Delilah spoke quickly, snatching chemicals and lighting burners. "It's not a curse, it's a gas, odorless and invisible. It makes you suffocate. This place was built on top of a coal deposit, and there's probably small fires burning underground all the time. That's why the walls were pressurized. It's like a natural trap."

"I can breathe just fine," said Allison.

"I swear to all that is holy, stop arguing with me," said Delilah. "You are dying. You are dying and I have very little in the way of options to save you. Jay, grab those bottles there and the bag of—the *other* bottles, Jay, are you trying to get us killed?!"

Jeremiah jumped when she shouted and grabbed what he hoped were the correct bottles. "We can try to get out, find a potion," he said. "I'm sure we can get one on credit, or steal it, or something."

"Potions won't work. She's not injured. I have to pump her full of breathable air, put her in a coma, and then pressurize the inside of the bag."

"Whoa, what? Put me in a coma?" Allison turned to Jeremiah with a face full of confusion.

"Ahh, I have no time to explain, just trust me!" said Delilah. "Jay, inside that box you'll find a bunch of syringes. Give me the one labeled *Allison*."

Jeremiah opened the box she'd indicated. It was full of syringes, and each was labeled with a name—Bruno, Allison, Delilah, Jeremiah, and several he didn't recognize. He grabbed the requested needle and handed it to Delilah.

"Say good night, Allison," said Delilah, plunging the needle into Allison's neck before she could react.

"I never—" Allison slumped over.

Delilah continued setting various chemicals to heating and separating, her hands a blur over the equipment.

"Is she going to be okay? Are we?" asked Jeremiah. He was desperate for reassurance that everything was going to be perfectly fine.

"Doubtful, but I'm going to try. She was the only one wheezing. If you start feeling sleepy . . . well, we can cross that bridge when we come to it." Delilah affixed a tight leather mask around Allison's mouth and nose and connected a thin tube between the mask and a glass pipette.

"Head up," said Delilah. "I need you to seal the bag and not open it again. I'll open it from my side when it's safe."

"Okay, I'll have Bruno get us out of here," said Jeremiah.

"Makes no difference, she'll fare no better outside the dungeon than she will inside of it. If you can get out, do it. If you can get what we came for, do that."

Jeremiah could see beneath the frantic energy a twisted anxiety. He could see it in her gritted teeth, the way she dug her nails into everything, and the barely perceptible shine in her eyes. "Hey, Delilah, it's going to be okay. It's not your fau—"

"Then whose fault is it, Jay?!" Delilah screamed. Proper screamed louder than he'd ever heard her before. Most disturbing was how she didn't falter in her preparations for even a moment. "Who was in charge of the gas detectors?! Who forgot them in the bag? Who made the mistake?! Who lost our house?!"

She grabbed at anything on the table, a rack of glass tubes, and threw it against a shelf. She balled up her hands in her hair and screamed, eyes tightly shut and tears finally running down her cheeks.

It was terrifying to see her like this. Jeremiah reached out a hand to comfort her, but Delilah suddenly sprang back into action again like nothing had happened.

"Leave," she said softly.

CHAPTER FORTY-FOUR

Principles

Jeremiah emerged back into the oasis room to find Bruno touching a blank wall. "Bad news," he said. "The holes Allison hacked open just closed up. Wall grew back over it like a damn scab."

"Worse news," said Jeremiah. "Allison and Delilah are out of action for now. Maybe for . . . well, for now." There didn't seem any reason to panic Bruno about how sick Allison really was. Besides, he didn't really understand it himself. "No bag either, Delilah says we need to keep it shut."

They were quiet for a moment. There was a surreal quality to the situation. Two adventurers down, they were at half strength. No fighter, no doctor. Jeremiah felt horribly exposed. "What now?"

"We carry on," said Bruno. "Through the wall?"

Jeremiah shook his head. "That's what got Allison sick. And I don't think the dungeon liked it either, that's why the bear was summoned."

Bruno nodded. "Want to take a guess why we got beared trying to hack through this wall, and not when we went through the last two walls?"

Jeremiah thought for a minute. "It didn't react until Allison hit the wall again. Summoning something so large must take a huge amount of energy. We're close to something important, aren't we?"

"You're learning quick. I think it tipped its hand with that one."

"So we press on?" asked Jeremiah. "Even though we're down two people?"

"To sound only the exact proper amount of cocky, we still have the most important person for this place," said Bruno. "Let's get what we came for." Jeremiah shouldered the Giant's Bag gently, almost tenderly, like he might disturb the people inside.

They tried the door leading what should be further into the dungeon. The short hallway beyond was reminiscent of an undersea cave, with blue glowing crystals hanging from the ceiling and shells dotting the walls. There was no exit.

"Ugh, tacky," said Bruno, scowling in disgust at a glowing conch shell.

"Why would there be a dead end?" asked Jeremiah. "Space seems to be at such a premium here, it's just a waste." He thought of all the gizmos packed into the walls. Committing a hallway to nothing seemed like a poor design idea.

"Good point, what does that mean?" said Bruno nodding. Jeremiah was beginning to notice a little stillness that would come over Bruno when he was administering a test. Like he was being careful not to give away an answer with an errant glance.

"That means . . . it's not a dead end, is it? It also means it'd be weird for that last room to only exist as a nice place to rest."

As Bruno busied himself checking the new hallway for traps, Jeremiah contemplated the inconsistency. He pushed away the thoughts about Allison that kept bubbling up. Delilah was doing her job, and she was relying on him to do his.

Bruno had already searched the oasis room more thoroughly than Jeremiah ever could, and he hadn't spotted anything notable.

"What's with these theme-y rooms?" Jeremiah asked. "One big centerpiece to draw your attention—that's got to have something to do with it, right?"

"Isn't it awful?" said Bruno. "Where's the subtlety? I'm expecting a basement with skeletons chained to the walls next."

Jeremiah contemplated the statue. It had been damaged during the battle with the dire bear, and now the goddess looked up to arms that ended in stumps. Water still bubbled forth from them, flowing down to feed the twin rivulets on the floor.

Rivulets that continued into the dead-end hallway before disappearing into the floor. "Huh," said Jeremiah.

The spray from the water was ice cold. When the statue had been whole, the water seeped gently from the palms, so he would have had to raise his hands in a near-embrace of the statue to reach the outflow. In its broken state, water burbled up from the statue's stumps, spilling onto Jeremiah's shoes.

"Oh, I get it!" Jeremiah pressed his palms into the smooth marble of the broken stumps, firmly enough to block the flow of water. After a moment, he heard a *click*, and the wall blocking the dead-end hallway slid away, revealing a new passage.

"Not bad!" said Bruno, giving Jeremiah a politely quiet round of applause. "Good reasoning. You should have let me check the water lines for traps, though."

"Thank you for the almost compliment," said Jeremiah, humbly accepting it as absolutely a compliment.

"You almost earned it. Now step aside and let's get this hallway checked out."

Bruno kept Jeremiah close and began testing him. Asking him to pick out oddities that might signal a trap, feeling for aberrations in air flow and temperature that could mean a seam in a trigger.

"Luckily, disarming most traps is just a matter of breaking them," said Bruno. He snaked a metal hook under a pressure plate, gripped it, and yanked. Something snapped underneath the stone floor. "And breaking anything is easy. Oh sure, there's some that are set off by breaking them. But they're less common, out of your expertise for now."

"Gotcha," said Jeremiah.

"Of course, there's traps that are so convoluted that you only think you're breaking them. Those are called Rats Nest designs. You'll learn that there are different designations of traps and triggers," Bruno continued to ramble on, pressing a cork into a concealed hole in the wall.

"Uh-huh," said Jeremiah.

"Now, there's also Shark Fin structures, and those date back—"

"You trying not to worry about Allison?" Interrupted Jeremiah.

"Yes, please don't disrupt my cope," said Bruno. "Anyway, a Shark Fin is an anti-tool component—"

Jeremiah just let Bruno talk; listening was proving to be an effective coping tool as well.

Eventually they reached the end of the underwater themed hallway. The aquamarine stones became odd chaotic gray bricks, stacked haphazardly along either side of them like a long-abandoned tunnel. It reminded Jeremiah of the first dungeon he had entered with his friends, some old cellar of a great castle. Glowing crystals became oily torches, and the hall descended down stone stairs into darkness below.

They followed the underwater themed hallway until it reached an abrupt end as a spiral stone staircase with flagstone steps. It was even lined with oily torches, evoking a dingy old castle. Jeremiah found it eerily similar to the fortress in Nosirin.

"I hate this guy," said Bruno. "And I hate stairs."

"You're not that old yet," said Jeremiah.

"Not because I can't climb them, you ass," said Bruno. "It's because traps are a lot easier to hide on stairs. They're also harder to access safely, especially when going down them. Harder to dodge without jumping down and risking more traps, and a lot easier to get tagged by something and knocked down the stairs onto more traps."

"That's exactly what's going to happen," said Jeremiah suddenly, his eyes going wide with the epiphany.

"What? How do you know?" asked Bruno, he eyed Jeremiah suspiciously.

"Think about it. What was the whole point of that Tunnel Ooze? Allison said it wasn't a difficult fight, but it forced you into setting off traps. The door with a message written in halfling? What's the point of the warning? This Cassidy guy wants you to set off his traps," said Jeremiah.

"Of course he does, that's the point of traps," said Bruno.

"No, it's more than that," said Jeremiah, turning Bruno to look him hard in the eyes. "These rooms have ridiculous themes. For whom? The traps are convoluted and weird. Why? The Dungeon Core and the Furnace Curse gas stops you from getting through walls. Hell, even the guards outside are paid to stop people from getting into the house in a way that isn't right."

Bruno smiled at Jeremiah, shaking his head in disbelief. "It's pride. Cassidy is damn proud of his little house of traps. He wants to show it to us. He wants us to see the traps, the decor, all of it."

Jeremiah slapped him on the shoulder. "Exactly! He may have thought he was building a test for thieves, but what he was really doing was—"

"Building a shrine to his own sense of pride," finished Bruno. "Look at how clever I am. Look at my impeccable taste, learn my important lessons, admire my deadly traps, but most especially, don't avoid them . . . which is why something is going to force us down the stairs faster than we want."

"So we can set off more traps," said Jeremiah, laughing at Bruno's depiction of Cassidy.

"But why do that if the admirers are going to be killed?" Bruno asked.

"Does it matter?" answered Jeremiah with a shrug.

"Hah! You weren't born for this kind of work Jay, but you're certainly a talented amateur. That being said, I'm going to need you to acid splash the ceiling. I've got a hunch now."

Jeremiah adjusted the Giant's Bag and tried not to think about his friends inside. The bag felt far too light on his shoulders for the importance it carried. Taking careful aim, Jeremiah fired several balls of acid against the gray stone ceiling where Bruno had indicated. The acid hissed, and as it dripped away, a distinct rectangular outline appeared—a large trapdoor about the width of the passageway.

"Allow me." Bruno leapt onto the wall, clinging to the smooth stone with one of the magic handles, and pried into the gap with a throwing sword. After a few stiff jabs and a wrenching motion, the trap door sprang open. A massive round boulder fell onto the stairs and began rolling down with the deafening sound of stone on stone. As it went, darts, spears, and swinging blades stabbed at its wake. They heard it roll around and around the spiral stairs before settling somewhere far below.

"Giant rolling boulder," said Bruno. "Figures."

They descended the stairs together, navigating the discarded trap elements. The boulder had done a better job than they ever could have.

"Boulder chases you down the steps into all the other traps, which end up slowing you down enough that the boulder hits you," said Bruno.

"Just like the tunnel ooze," said Jeremiah. He picked up one of the spears that had thrust down from the ceiling. It was solid, but horribly balanced. Purely industrial.

"A rushed trap is a dangerous trap," said Bruno, he picked his way over a barbed let that lay on the stairs.

Click

"What was that? What did you step on?" asked Bruno. He crouched, preparing to leap to safety.

Jeremiah whipped his head around frantically. "Nothing, I didn't step on any—"

There was a thunderous boom, and a familiar sound began above them. A rumbling angry growl that grew louder and louder. A second boulder.

"Oh, you gotta be kidding me!" shouted Bruno.

Bruno shoved Jeremiah to the outside of the staircase and yanked him to the ground. The edge of the stone flagons bit into Jeremiah's back and shoulders as Bruno yanked his arms up over his head, stretching him out long and thin as possible in the corner where the stairs met the wall.

The boulder shook the stairs like an earthquake. All that kept Jeremiah from sprinting down the stairs was the trust he had in Bruno. Bruno threw his swords as fast as a bird's wings beat, the magic blades biting deep into the stairs above them and wedging there.

The sight of the boulder rolling toward them caused Jeremiah to shrink even further back into his corner. The boulder struck Bruno's blades, altering its course by the slightest amounts away from Jeremiah and toward the inner wall.

Bruno leapt with an acrobat's grace, springing off the wall diving through the narrow gap between boulder and ceiling.

Jeremiah remembered seeing Bruno jump, and the distinct texture of the surface of the boulder. Then he was looking up at his friend's concerned face.

"Jay? Jay, can you hear me?" Bruno leaned close, putting his ear to Jeremiah's mouth. "I can feel you breathing, so you're not—"

Darkness.

"Wake up, Jay, come on!" Bruno was doing something to Jeremiah that made his body jerk, and his chest hurt.

Jeremiah's lungs screamed for air. He obliged them, prompting something awful to shift in his chest.

"There he is!" cried Bruno.

"Am I okay?" said Jeremiah.

"You're alive," said Bruno. "But you're hurt. Your nose is messed up, and uh . . . your foot is, uh . . . b-broken." He swallowed hard.

Jeremiah pushed himself up and waited for the agony. It never came. He looked at his foot. It was crumpled strangely—his toes and the front half pointed straight up toward his head, as though someone had tried to roll up his foot like a sleeping mat. It didn't hurt.

He touched it. Still nothing. He grabbed the injured part with both hands.

"Oh no, please don't!" Bruno said.

Jeremiah unrolled his foot with a long sinewy crunch. It didn't hurt. Bruno puked with enthusiasm. Jeremiah felt his nose and found it flattened against his face.

"We weren't going to outrun that boulder, were we?" asked Jeremiah. His voice sounded nasally and unfamiliar.

"No." Bruno gagged. "You can never outrun the rolling boulder."

"Thanks, then, for not letting me try," said Jeremiah. "Get your swords, let's get off the stairs before another one of those things shows up."

The stairs opened to a massive underground room. Jeremiah half expected it to be stacked high with bodies, like the crypt King Growler had prepared for him. Instead, this one was stylized like a gigantic dungeon cell, complete with skeletons in the final stage of decay shackled to the wall.

The pair of boulders nestled at a holding space at the bottom of the staircase. Jeremiah eyed them as he limped past, half expecting them to leap up somehow to finish the job. He was able to walk if he was careful about placing his weight on the heel of his foot, but an ache was starting to grow. He didn't exactly miss Delilah's gigantic needles yet, but he suspected he would soon.

"There won't be any traps in this room, I reckon," said Bruno. "Cassidy wouldn't want to distract from his grand finale." He crossed the room with confidence to inspect a great vault door on the far side. It was monolithic and depicted a host of angels in dramatic poses cavorting and playing trumpets and harps. They clustered tighter and tighter as they approached the center of the door, but at its center was a large devil's head with curled horns and a wide-open mouth. The angels kept a respectable distance from the face that looked outward with a look of mild surprise.

Bruno had traveled the room unmolested, but as Jeremiah moved to follow, the ache in his foot flared and blossomed. He gasped, trying not to scream, and then gave up and screamed as loud as he could. The pain spread from his foot to his hips and ribs to his smashed-up face, building like a house fire until it became a raging inferno consuming everything in its path.

Then it was as bad as it was going to get. Jeremiah's screams faded to whimpers, then he was panting. The inferno still burned through him, but he could handle it, could master it and set it aside. At least enough to continue.

Bruno had been following Jeremiah's progress patiently, letting Jeremiah scream himself out. "Caught up with you, huh?"

"Yes, yes it did," Jeremiah growled. "What's up with the door?"

Bruno looked at the masterpiece of metal and sighed. "Cassidy and I wouldn't have gotten along based on taste alone. Sad. I need to take my time here. Wait further back for me. I don't want you anywhere near this thing."

Leaning on his short spear as a crutch, Jeremiah took his distance and let Bruno work.

"This room reminds me of the dungeon in Nosirin. Remember that?" asked Jeremiah.

"With the bodies?" asked Bruno, prodding at the eyes of an angel.

"Yeah, hundreds of them," said Jeremiah. His memory stacked them up again, piles and piles in neat rows.

"Yup, just for you," said Bruno absently.

Jeremiah remembered with a jolt that they'd executed prisoners in preparation for his arrival. People had been ordered to death because a necromancer was coming to help, and he'd need material to work with. *Just for you,* he repeated in his mind. *Just for me . . .*

How far a cry Nosirin had been from where he was now, he realized. From blindly commanding hundreds of undead to manipulating a single rat with unimaginable precision. Even casting magic through it—that was a sign of mastery he'd never known was possible. He felt a swell of pride at the achievement.

"Tell me of your achievements," said Allison.

His pride snuffed out as suddenly as an extinguished candle. The Tragedy had only happened because of his achievement. His supposed mastery had led to pain and death and suffering on an unprecedented scale. Without him, it wouldn't have been possible.

"It wasn't my fault," said Jeremiah. "Pete said—"

"What did Pete say?" said Allison. "What was it Pete said that forced you to obey him?"

If Jeremiah had only failed or even refused, thousands of shattered lives would still be whole.

He saw it now, clearer than he'd ever allowed himself before. If he'd kept his promise to quit necromancy, none of that day would have happened. He wouldn't have been able to join the Stonefists, he wouldn't have been a successful thief, he wouldn't have been able to poison the wine. Maybe he and his friends would have been poor forever, maybe they would have had their lives ruined. But how many would have survived?

"There will always be a reason," said Allison.

"Always," said Flusoh.

"All right, I got the gist of it," said Bruno. "This head here is a countdown mechanism. Let me show you." He twisted the head of one of the angels, one with a more menacing disposition and holding a subtle knife behind its back. As the head turned away from the devil face, an aperture in the center opened to reveal a deep fist-sized hole in the devil's mouth.

Bruno released the angel. Jeremiah heard a faint ticking sound as the head gradually rotated back toward its original position.

"Obviously, this hole in the middle is the mechanism to open it, which you access by activating the timer. It's a classic timed lockpicking challenge, with just one wrinkle."

At Bruno's words, the timer ran down and the aperture slammed shut. "Ah," said Jeremiah. "Failure means dismemberment, huh?"

"So it would seem," said Bruno. "I've had a poke around inside with the tools, but it's too deep for *just* the tools. I'll need to get in there manually, which I am very loath to do."

Bruno wiggled his fingers. "Fortunately, Cassidy's cheesy design sensibility has left plenty of spares around. Jay, if you would?" He gestured to the nearest skeleton shackled to the wall.

"I can't." Jeremiah was almost as surprised as Bruno to hear the words leave his lips.

"Can't? You okay?" Bruno looked Jeremiah up and down.

Jeremiah licked his lips. "I won't. I won't raise the dead anymore. I keep hurting people. People ask me to do necromancy, and when I do, terrible things happen," he took a deep breath, steeling himself to make a hard decision. "People get executed. People get killed by accident." The man in the closet could see him. "*I* kill people. By accident. I don't even see them die, or feel it, but it still happens because of me."

"There's that accountability we were looking for," said Vivica.

"I don't want to be that monster anymore. I *won't* be that monster anymore . . . really, this time."

Bruno nodded along until Jeremiah finished. "Okay, okay. But consider the following—what the fuck are you talking about? We're in a dungeon. Our lives and *our friends' lives*—you didn't forget about them, did you?—are at stake here. So quit philosophizing and get the damn job done."

"No." It was scary to say with Bruno scowling at him, but Jeremiah was resolute. "We do it the old-fashioned way."

"'We,' he says," muttered Bruno, rolling his eyes and turning back to the lock. "Gets a spine now he does, when it's not his ass on the line," Bruno spared Jeremiah a sneer of disgust. "Bet your tune would be different if *you* were the one sticking your hand in here."

"It wouldn't," said Jeremiah.

"Shut up!" Bruno barked. "Let me concentrate."

Bruno reset the timer and prodded the mechanism inside the angel's neck with his tools. The angel's gaze now frozen, the aperture permanently revealed.

Finally, flexing his fingers and taking a breath, Bruno plunged his hand into the hole. The timer only sporadically twitched as he worked, face screwed up in concentration.

Jeremiah watched confidently. Bruno could handle this lock, just like the countless others Jeremiah had watched him conquer with ease. So why was something tickling the back of his mind? Not a memory or an idea, more like a vibration. Like the answer was whispered to him by the angels on the door.

This was the end of the dungeon, the final task of Cassidy's monument. The culmination of his life's work, to be passed on to the right person. What would he plan for this moment, right when you're about to best his dungeon and usurp his crown? To make him second best and undo all that pride . . .

"Juuuust about there," said Bruno.

"I want to be remembered," said Cassidy.

Jeremiah understood. "Bruno, wait!" he shouted.

But it was too late. "Got it!" Bruno announced with triumph. There was a loud bang from inside the door, and the head of every angel turned to stare down at him.

CHAPTER FORTY-FIVE

Mementos

Bruno's face contorted in a silent scream. He yanked on his arm to no avail. A low groan escaped him, the sound building in volume to a shout, a roar, a howl of fury.

"Bruno! Bruno what happened?!" Jeremiah hobbled over to him, but he had no idea what to do.

"Something just went through my arm!" Bruno shouted. "It was the primary bolt. It shouldn't have done that! Why did it do that?!" Bruno yanked again and screamed.

"Because that's what it was designed to do. Cassidy wants to be remembered, he wants you to leave something behind," said Jeremiah.

"Oh no, no, no." Bruno started to shake. "Oh come on, no. I can't lose an arm. I can't lose an arm."

"Can you get yourself out?" said Jeremiah.

"Yeah, yeah, I can do that," said Bruno. With his free hand Bruno began sliding a paper-thin shim between his arm and the hole. He took deep breaths and closed his eyes, probing with the shiv.

"*Bruno will get out of this*," he thought. "*He'll just pop the trap open and free himself. Any second now.*"

Bruno began tugging on his arm, closing his eyes and attempting to maneuver something inside the hole that Jeremiah couldn't see.

Jeremiah was surprised to hear Thurok's voice come to the forefront of his mind. "*This is not a test. This is a debt to be paid. You must understand sacrifice.*"

"The bolt feels loose," Bruno mumbled, wincing as he pulled. "Like it's not attached to anything." There was a metallic clatter ringing from inside the door.

"It might not be," suggested Jeremiah.

Bruno scoffed. "W-what's the point of that? Then it'd just be stuck! That makes no sense. M-maybe it broke, hang on . . ."

"Bruno, I think it might be working as intended," said Jeremiah softly. He put a hand on Bruno's shoulder.

Bruno suddenly swung his free hand at Jeremiah in an awkward attack. It glanced off Jeremiah's head as he ducked out of the way, falling to the ground when he tried to stand on his broken foot.

"You sonnuvabitch!" Bruno screamed at him. "This is your fault! One skeleton would have been enough! You selfish bastard!" Bruno kicked at him, and Jeremiah scrambled away, just out of his reach.

"All that power and you're worried about you! You'll save your own skin time and time again but when it's not you on the line you're suddenly trying to be a better person?! Bullshit Jay! You think it's some noble deed that you won't use necromancy? Because you're not responsible enough?! Because you might screw up? We keep swords away from children because they're not responsible, Jay! You're a man! A sorry excuse of a coward of a man!"

Bruno raged and yanked his arm so hard Jeremiah thought it would tear free. But he was transfixed, no one had ever spoken to him about his decision like that.

"Bruno, I'm doing the right thing. I—"

"Oh, you piece of shit. You absolute—" Bruno kicked at him again. "You like the little pats on the head you get? You like that everyone congratulates you for being weak? That's what they're doing Jay! You're telling them you're too weak to handle it, and they pat you on the head and call you a good boy for being honest with yourself! You're treated like a damn child, and you love it! Because it's safe! Because it's easy!" Bruno's face was a mask of fury and disgust. "You're pathetic, Jay! You really are pathetic!" Bruno kept screaming. "You think you're so noble, giving up your power? You're weak! You try to hide it behind your moral arguments, but you're just a frightened little boy!"

His fervor echoed around the chamber. Jeremiah stared, stunned into silence.

"It's wasted on you." Bruno's voice was low now, venomous. Jeremiah was afraid to listen. "All that power, wasted on someone too scared to use it. You could do so much more, could *be* so much more than you are."

Bruno rested his head against the door, his breathing ragged. Jeremiah, in contrast, held his breath. He was terrified Bruno would start up again.

"I'm sorry," said Jeremiah, and in that moment he was. In that moment, all of his moral questions and debates and fear fell away, and he saw himself exactly as Bruno had described—too overwhelmed and too afraid to wield the power he'd once craved. Or, more accurately, too afraid of the responsibility it demanded. "You're right. I'm sorry."

Bruno remained motionless. His breathing slowed, though still pulled through clenched teeth. Blood seeped from the hole, pooling on the floor below.

"Get a rope," Bruno said again, "and make some heat. I'm going to need you to cauterize . . ." He swallowed. "Something."

Jeremiah started on the heating surface first, etching a simple Heat rune into an enchanting plate. His hands moved with practiced efficiency, even though the rest of him was trembling. He charged the plate, bringing it to blue-hot before the enchantment broke, and set it by Bruno's feet.

He tied the first rope around Bruno's trapped arm, as close as possible to the door. The rope cut into his forearm, and Bruno hissed in pain as Jeremiah winched the windlass as tight as he could. He added the second rope around Bruno's upper arm, hoping to reduce the blood flow as much as possible.

"You ready?" asked Bruno, nodding toward the sword.

"Are you?" asked Jeremiah.

"No," said Bruno.

Jeremiah picked up the sword.

"Okay, just . . . try to get as much on this side of the door as you can, okay?" said Bruno. He grabbed a few scraps of his ruined leather armor and put them between his teeth.

"Okay, here we go," said Jeremiah, raising the sword over his head with two hands. It felt so strange; the sword, the situation, what he was about to do.

"Do it!" shouted Bruno.

"You ready?!" Jeremiah shouted back.

"Do it!"

Bruno screamed. Jeremiah screamed. Jeremiah brought the sword down. The cut wasn't perfect, but the enchantment did enough of the work to get the job done in a single swing.

Bruno was free. Bruno dropped and slammed the stump of his arm onto the burning hot metal plate at his feet. Jeremiah jumped down onto him and helped press. Bruno just kept screaming, his body convulsing in pain. The hiss of boiling blood and stink of cooking flesh filled Jeremiah's senses with the white cloud of steam that rose up.

"Hold it! Hold it!" Jeremiah shouted at Bruno. He didn't know much about burning wounds shut, but he knew you had to keep it there till the job was done.

Bruno suddenly went limp in his arms, and Jeremiah struggled to hold him up. Eventually, Jeremiah shoved Bruno off. No further parts of Bruno's arm came off, save for a blackened circle of blood on the plate.

Jeremiah wrapped the medical bandages around as much of Bruno's arm as he could. He was acting on instinct, his mind blank, he was only observing his hands at work. He wrapped and wrapped until there were no bandages left. Bruno remained unconscious, or dead.

Jeremiah fell backward when he was finished, laying on the floor of the dungeon, exhaustion suddenly overwhelming him. He felt dizzy, he felt sick. He had hacked apart his friend's arm like an amateur butcher. He closed his eyes. It wasn't sleep taking him. It was something else, some part of him that just wanted everything to stop.

"You die?" Bruno's voice woke Jeremiah out of whatever stupor he had been in.

"Huh? Bruno? You okay?" Jeremiah tried to sit up, but just couldn't bring himself to do it, he felt too weak.

"Lost an arm and burned it shut. Nah, I'm not okay. You okay?" said Bruno. He was laying where Jeremiah had left him.

"Cut my friend's arm off and . . . coming to terms with the fact that I might be a coward," said Jeremiah. "Also, Allison might be dead, and my foot broke in half."

"Big day," said Bruno.

"Big day," confirmed Jeremiah.

They lay like that for a while longer, basking in their various pains.

"I can still feel my arm," said Bruno.

"Oh yeah?" said Jeremiah.

"Yeah. Hurts," said Bruno.

More quiet suffering.

"Want to see the fabled treasure?" asked Jeremiah.

"Yeah . . . Yeah, I do," said Bruno. They finally managed to sit up together. Jeremiah couldn't help but look at Bruno's red-stained stump. Bruno was doing the same.

"Can a potion fix this?" asked Bruno.

"No, can't regrow pieces," said Jeremiah, "but maybe we can get your arm out of there and put it back on."

Looking at the hole, Jeremiah could see the bloody stump of Bruno's arm sticking out, the tiny white circles of bone just barely visible. He took the spear and touched the severed arm. As soon as he did, a metal plate snapped down, covering the hole. There was a mechanical chunk sound from inside the door, and a dull grinding noise.

"I think the door ate your arm," said Jeremiah.

"Oh yeah?" asked Bruno.

"Yeah," said Jeremiah.

They stared at the door together.

"Sure, why not? Let's just get out of here," said Bruno.

The vault door opened now without resistance, sliding smoothly along a track. The treasure room within could have contained a small house, but it was empty save for a black marble writing desk in the very center.

Atop the desk were two stacks of papers and a large orange crystal, streaked with blue. As they approached, the colors of the crystal swirled and twisted.

Jeremiah hadn't expected Cassidy's fabled treasure to be a pile of gold and jewels—he hadn't known what to expect, at this point—but a pile of paperwork was still a surprise. He picked up a stack and leafed through it.

"These are all legal documents . . . I'm seeing land deeds, contractual agreements for farming subsidies, credit for agricultural companies. Business licenses and identification papers, too."

"It's a new life," said Bruno, looking through his own stack. "A real way out. There's a new identity, a new purpose—everything the enterprising street urchin could need, all prepped in advance. True freedom in another life."

"Not for us, though," said Jeremiah. "The treasure's just a means to an end for me. Besides," he turned to the crystal. "That's the dungeon core. It's the most interesting thing here."

The tiny motes of blue pulsed at Jeremiah's words.

"Valuable?" asked Bruno.

"No idea," said Jeremiah. The crystal was the size of his palm, but when he moved to pick it up, he found it stuck fast. Further inspection revealed it was built into the marble of the desk.

"Let's just smash it," said Bruno. He gestured the motion with his missing hand, and grimaced.

"Nah, hang on," Jeremiah had a different idea. With his enchanting tools, he etched the runes Gently Decay into the marble surface around the crystal. Once charged, he began to rub the marble, and the affected section of the massive desk eroded under his hands, revealing more and more of the crystal.

The dungeon core was larger than it had seemed, plunging below the surface of the desk. Jeremiah needed both hands to lift it from its place, and it rang discordantly when he did, intoning like a warped bell. The colors swirled in a frenzied tempest.

"I think it's panicking," said Jeremiah, holding the dungeon core up to torchlight to watch the colors race.

"Good. I'm still deciding on whether I'd rather break it." Bruno's missing hand reached for the hilt of his sword.

"Let's keep it for now. But if either of us so much as stumbles on our way out"—he raised his voice to speak to the crystal directly—"we bust it on the nearest rock."

They gathered the paperwork bundles. It felt like a light haul for besting a dungeon of legend, but Jeremiah reminded himself that words on a page could be more valuable than any monetary prize—he knew that better than most. He suspected Monty would agree.

"Exit's this way," said Bruno. He pulled a lever that had been camouflaged to match the stone wall and revealed a cramped hallway. "Wouldn't want to be seen leaving back out the way we came in. That'd defeat the whole purpose of a new life."

The tunnel felt interminable on Jeremiah's mangled foot. Draped over Bruno and leaning on his spear wasn't enough to avoid the occasional errant, and agonizing, bump on the floor. They emerged well outside the city in a patch of arid and dusty land that looked like it had never seen a plant. Jeremiah's face was already swollen into an unrecognizable mess, so Bruno did not require them to take any extreme measures to return to the safe house.

Unfortunately, the nonextreme measures were still extensive. Six hours after they escaped the dungeon they arrived back at the apartment, and Jeremiah was on the verge of collapse. As soon as they arrived, Bruno disappeared into the bedroom. Jeremiah thought it tactful to allow him space. He set the Giant's Bag on the floor and lay down beside it, letting anxiety and exhaustion quarrel over whether or not he should sleep.

A rustling sound jerked him out of an uneasy slumber. The Giant's Bag was opening.

At once, Jeremiah was fully awake, on his feet—well, foot—and helping Delilah as she crawled out, hand over hand, to collapse on the floor. She was panting, pale, and sweaty despite having stripped down to her smallclothes. Her hands were red and raw.

"Alive," she gasped in answer to Jeremiah's unspoken question. "She's alive. I don't know how. I swear, nothing can kill that woman. She's the toughest thing I've ever seen."

The fear gripping Jeremiah's heart released, and he sank to the floor. "I can't . . . Thank you, Delilah. Thank you." The words felt like empty offerings to the spent husk of a woman before him, but they were all he had.

"Welcome." Delilah spoke to the ceiling, eyes half-lidded. "How'd you guys fare? Get the treasure?"

"We got the treasure," said Jeremiah. "But we had to cut off Bruno's hand. It's okay though, we burned it shut."

Without looking away from the ceiling, Delilah closed her eyes and began to cry.

CHAPTER FORTY-SIX

The Fever

One upside of everyone assuming Jeremiah was dead was that there was no particular rush to return Cassidy's prize to Monty. Until he reappeared, he was just the latest cocksure thief to throw his life away in the name of avarice. In fact, he and his friends didn't even think about the treasure for a week as they focused their energy on recovering from the ordeal.

Allison remained Delilah's top priority. It was several more days before Delilah let her be moved from the Giant's Bag to the apartment proper, where she continued to fuss over her like an anxious mother bird.

At least Allison had stopped resisting treatment—while she could remember only snatches of the dungeon leading up to her poisoning, even she was not stubborn enough to deny the tremors and shortness of breath that still lingered. Thus, she submitted to Delilah's attention and insistence with only minor complaints.

Bruno was much less cooperative, especially when Delilah proposed he may have to lose more of his arm, depending on the state of things. It was only after she pointed out that putting off a proper exam could result in amputating the entire limb or even death that he acquiesced, looking pointedly away as she removed the bandages and inspected the mutilated flesh beneath.

"How this didn't throw a clot and kill him I'll never know," said Delilah.

Her professional opinion was to cut away more of the arm and create a less complex injury, to which Bruno graciously and gently disagreed as loudly as he could.

Only after the others had been stabilized and Delilah herself took a day to rest did she turn her attention to Jeremiah. He did his best not to protest—she had no sympathy left to offer—and bore the readjustments of his foot and nose as stoically as he could. It was a relief to be sent to bed with a healing tonic, where nothing would be asked of him for a few precious hours.

Most of his dreams were lost in a feverish haze as he faded in and out of sleep, but one image kept finding its way back to the forefront of his mind. Jeremiah was collecting rocks on a mountain face and piling them on one spot to build a cairn. The pile rose higher and higher, until he realized that all the rocks were skulls, and they began babbling ceaselessly, a thousand voices screaming, their words crawling into his ears like a swarm of bees and carrying away his brain, piece by piece.

When he emerged again, it was morning. Bruno sat alone at the table, Allison and her guard uniform were gone, Delilah nowhere to be seen—working in the lab or, Jeremiah hoped, resting.

Bruno greeted him with a nod and kicked out a chair. Jeremiah sat. He was grateful for the invitation, but words escaped him. He averted his gaze from Bruno dealing himself cards one-handed. It was all too surreal, and all too scary.

The old chair creaked as Bruno leaned backward, stretching and rolling his neck. When Jeremiah still kept his eyes fixed on the table, he said, "You're gonna have to look at me eventually, you know. We live together."

"That's a good point," said Jeremiah. "I should probably move out."

"Well, we've got a lovely selection of farm holdings for you to choose from, picked fresh from the deathtrap dungeon. Fancy places too. Cost an arm and a leg."

Jeremiah smiled. "Actually, my leg is feeling much better now."

"Oh? Just an arm, then. Heck of a deal, if you ask me."

"Sorry Bruno, you're just not that good a salesman." Jeremiah finally forced his gaze from the table and took in his friend as he was. Bruno was studying him in his casual manner. His sleeve was pinned loosely over the stump. Jeremiah could still see those little signs of age he'd first noticed in the dungeon, seeming ever so slightly more pronounced.

"Ah, bummer. I was thinking of going into real estate now that I'm taking an early retirement from roguing. Not going to be much of a lockpicker now. Or trap disarmer." Bruno tried riffling the deck and scattered cards all over the table and floor. "Or card dealer, for that matter."

Jeremiah bent under the table to help pick up cards. "I really am sorry, Bruno. I should never have let it happen."

Bruno smirked like he was going to crack a joke, then shook his head. "Nah, you shouldn't have. But if you learn something from it, maybe it'll be worth it, you know? I'd gladly trade the hand of a rogue past his prime for you to become the mage you're supposed to be."

Jeremiah nodded. "I was so focused on taking responsibility for what I might do, I never considered my responsibility for what I don't do. I won't make that mistake again."

"Good. Frees you up to make some real mistakes. That's important too, you know."

"'The mistakes of great men are just as great as their accomplishments,'" said Jeremiah. "Colonel Valen told me that once."

"Ignoring the fact that you just referred to yourself as a great man, and how loath I am to agree with Valen, he's right." Bruno had gathered the deck and began to shuffle again. This time, the cards riffled into a neat stack, just as they were supposed to. "Allison's going to be pissed," he added, looking longingly at the cards.

"I know," said Jeremiah, "but it's not up to her, is it? No more than it's up to me where she swings her sword. I need to own this. And if that doesn't make her happy . . . well . . . I hope she can get past it someday." He was certain there was a more empathetic conclusion he could come to, but he wasn't sure what that was yet. "Does it hurt?" asked Jeremiah.

"More than I can explain. And it's itchy, that's the worst part. I was ready for pain, but I didn't expect that."

Jeremiah watched Bruno's fingers practice their unfamiliar dance. "Do you really think you're past your prime?"

Bruno sighed. "Every day, a little bit of sand gets put in my pockets, and I can't take it out. I can fight it, I can rage against it, but I can't stop it." He flexed the fingers of his remaining hand. "My body doesn't move quite as fast as I remember. And yeah, it's harder to see the markings on the cards than it used to be."

"I guess you're going to need to learn how t—hey, that deck is marked?" Jeremiah lunged for it, but Bruno yanked them just out of reach. "We played for money with those cards!"

"Weren't we just talking about learning from our mistakes?" Bruno riffled the cards with one hand in the air, still beyond Jeremiah's grasp. "Now you know never to play with someone else's deck, especially with a known cheat!"

Jeremiah laughed as Bruno effortlessly held him off with one foot. It felt good to laugh, a glimpse of normalcy he hadn't even realized how badly he'd needed. For a brief, healing moment, everything was going to be okay.

Then the moment passed. Bruno's face grew serious again. "Are you going to be ready to head back out soon? Things are getting bad out there. Allison reported there have been riots without any purpose or goal, just random riots."

"Shit," said Jeremiah. "Has Delilah had a chance to look over the paperwork? Anything there I shouldn't just give over to Monty?"

"If you're okay with handing this guy the means of escape for himself, and maybe a good chunk of his gang, if he's the type to share. Do you think there's any risk he skips out on your deal, and you never see him again?"

Jeremiah considered what he knew about Monty. "Not a chance."

"Then it's yours," said Bruno. "Delilah says the monetary value wouldn't help our situation nearly as much as getting you in with the cult. Whatever we gain they're just going to take till Aubrianna tells them to stop. Are you ready to do this?"

A thrill of fear ran down Jeremiah's spine. It all came down to this. The culmination of months of work and suffering was nearly at an end, one way or another. His friends, the empress, and the entire city were depending on him getting this right.

Jeremiah took a deep breath and looked Bruno square in the eye. "I'm ready."

"The key to a better life," said Monty. "That's what they all said, about the Gilded Vault. I guess I didn't imagine it would be so literal."

"Cassidy was a fan of subverting expectations," said Jeremiah. They were in Monty's office, reading by the light of that single candle, the claustrophobic darkness crowding them like a smothering fog.

"'Cassidy?' You're on a first name basis with him, huh?"

Jeremiah chuckled. "After what he put me through, I know him better than I know myself."

"What was it like?" asked Monty, looking away from the papers he had been studying so earnestly.

"Intense," said Jeremiah, looking over Monty's head. "A lot of traps. Magic ones too. And themed rooms."

"Themed rooms?" asked Monty, cocking an eyebrow.

Jeremiah nodded. "Theme rooms."

Monty sighed audibly. "Allow me to offer you advice: If anyone asks, you never entered the vault. It's much easier to believe and you won't nearly be the target you would be otherwise," said Monty.

Monty read over the papers again. Jumping back and forth between particular pages, his brow furrowed with concentration. He began taking notes and touching his quill to certain words and letters.

"I'm going to need to talk this over with some people, see how I can best use it to help the Stonefists . . . assuming I'm not discovering a code." More checks back and forth between pages, punctuated with curious grumbling.

"I didn't see anything that looked like a code," said Jeremiah. He meant Delilah, but he'd still be surprised if she had missed something like that.

"You don't know the Cant, you wouldn't know how to look for it," said Monty, trailing off again. He evaluated Jeremiah, as though seeing him for the first time. "I'll be honest, I was not expecting to hear from you again. You have proven yourself, more than I ever would have dreamed when I first laid eyes on you. You must know, there is freedom in what you've handed me. You've more than earned it for yourself, if you prefer."

Jeremiah nodded. "I know, but let it be for those who don't have any other option. I do. Also, I have no interest in farming. Assuming your offer is still valid, of course?"

"Of course." Monty spoke in a low voice, nearly to himself. "A mage that bested the Gilded Vault. That will get their attention, without a doubt." Then to Jeremiah: "It will take me the day to make contact and arrange the meeting, return here this evening and we will go there together. I advise you to take the time to ready yourself in any way you deem appropriate—I know nothing of what happens past the moment of introduction. Be prepared for anything."

His words reminded Jeremiah of what Allison had said back in the dungeon. *"They're going to make you do something to prove your commitment. It won't be something you want to do."* His fingers brushed the burlap parcel which was still nestled deep in his pocket, and he nodded. "I will be."

Jeremiah considered parading his victory over the Gilded Vault around the Stonefists and basking in glory but soon realized nothing about it sounded appealing. In fact, imagining their laudations and excited questions when all he could feel was shame for letting Bruno down made him sick to his stomach, so he spent his time outside the Pit.

He soon realized what Bruno had meant when he'd said things were getting bad. Much of the rubble from the Tragedy had been cleared, but the destruction remained—homes and shops were simply gone, and the people had nowhere to go. People of all races, classes, and ages huddled in alleys or wandered aimlessly. Even the fevered rush of traffic that had once been the lifeblood of the city had been thinned, becoming meandering and unfocused, except for the wagons that headed for the cemeteries, laden down with the dead.

One thing that hadn't changed, though, was the malice underlying Elminia. If anything, it was worse. The loss of routine and basic security for so many people at once, the pain of bodily injury or the death of loved ones—Jeremiah could imagine a city where such an event would unify those remaining, let them come together and rebuild. But here, people seemed to have grown even meaner.

People gripped whatever they could and guarded it jealously. Temporary constructions on the ruins of buildings quickly became the targets of squabbles and violence until they collapsed. Jeremiah watched two women nearly kill each other over a scrap of bread, ceasing their fight only when one had been hobbled, left unable to fight or fend for herself. She was quickly robbed of what little remained in her pockets by others who had been watching the fight. The edges of the Pit seemed to be creeping further outward, swallowing those who previously had sure footing and safe distance.

The cutthroat ambition of Elminia was alive as well. The remaining businesses jockeyed for position among themselves, charging a premium for whatever goods they managed to procure. Jeremiah could only imagine the furious scramble that had to be going on behind the scenes for newly available property.

The city guard seemed to have returned to business as usual, albeit with many more homeless to harass from the corners. When he thought about it, Jeremiah supposed it wasn't surprising that Empress Aubrianna was allowing the city to recover with so little oversight. He guessed she might describe it as a wildfire, burning through overgrowth so that new life may thrive.

Something was certainly thriving in the aftermath of the Tragedy. It was pulsing, reveling in the chaos, tightening its grip over Elminia. It was the same presence he'd felt seeing the headless man suspended over the city, the same lingering dread, half remembered from his dreams.

Whatever it was, it was closer than it had ever been, an invisible predator stalking an entire populace. Jeremiah steeled himself to face it.

He prayed he would be enough.

CHAPTER FORTY-SEVEN

Blasphemy

The night was theirs, two more hooded figures going about their unseemly business in the shadows of the Pit, where the darkness only grew deeper.

"All I know is where to go and what to say," said Monty. "I don't know what we'll find there. I was instructed to bring someone 'exceptional,' and that if my companion was found lacking, there would be no second chance."

"You think I'll be enough for them?" asked Jeremiah.

"I'm betting my life on it," said Monty. "You have provided the Stonefists a remarkable service. I hope that what we are doing tonight will go a small way toward repaying you."

Monty stopped short, halting Jeremiah with a hand on his shoulder. He took a deep breath, closing his eyes and carefully considering his words. Jeremiah gave him the time. "Look. The Stonefists are the only family I've ever known. Raising them up, giving any of them a chance for a better life—that's everything I've been working for. And then I find you, and you hand it to me on a plate. I might have thought I'd begrudge you for making it look so easy, but I don't. I thank you, Jay, with every ounce of gratitude I can muster."

The outpouring of appreciation took Jeremiah by surprise. "You're welcome. I'm glad it'll go toward the cell members, they'll appreciate it more than me."

"I don't fault you for not grasping the whole of it. The Stonefists now have something to offer no one else can. We'll attract and retain the best talent, and the only way any other gang can compete is to offer something similar. I welcome them to do it."

Monty led them to a nondescript decrepit shack, of which there were thousands in the Pit. It sat dark, like all the others, seemingly abandoned, like all the others.

But something about the shack was off. Looking at it bothered Jeremiah in a way he couldn't describe. The sloppy angles, an architectural staple in the Pit, seemed intentional, like they existed to offend the sensible eye. It looked like something Jeremiah would see in a nightmare, plucked out and transplanted into the real world.

"I've cased this place more than once," said Monty, squinting at the face of the shack. "I can't make sense of it. It's hard to remember, somehow."

"You feel it too, then?" Jeremiah shivered. "It's like it doesn't belong here." He realized he'd never come to this part of the Pit before. Even now, he felt an urge to turn and flee, call the whole thing off.

"There's another thing, too," said Monty. He pointed at the ground. "What do you see?"

Jeremiah looked, frowning at the bare ground. There wasn't anything *to* see where Monty had pointed. Then he realized. "There's no rats here. Anywhere." That was its own kind of eerie. Rats and the Pit were synonymous. To see them exclude a location made it feel like it was somewhere . . . else.

Monty nodded. "I've never seen a living thing come here voluntarily. Once again, are you sure you want to do this?"

No, Jeremiah wanted to say. No, and you're too good a man to be wrapped up in all this. Instead, he said, "I'm sure. Let's do it."

"Time to get this over with, then," Monty said.

Stepping over the threshold of the shack turned the air in their lungs rancid, as though something inside them had rotted. The walls were pocked and scaling, and the normally packed earthen floor was strangely damp and crusty. Jeremiah drew his dagger in anticipation of danger. Monty balled up his gargantuan fists.

A staircase led them downward, toward the faint glow of a lantern. Jeremiah did not expect light to improve the situation much. The deeper they went the more the building began to feel hostile, like the very beams of wood were infused with malice.

Once as a child, Jeremiah caught a baby rabbit, upturned by the neighbor's dog. He still remembered how the rabbit's heart had felt against his palm, rapid and light, as though ready to take flight at any moment. His heart now hammered the same tattoo against his ribs as they descended deeper and deeper.

Finally, they found the source of the glow—a small oil lamp sat beside an immense bloated man, grotesquely swollen and nude. The man's skin was mottled and split with decay, his eyes were glassy, and his mouth contorted into a bloody harlequin grin.

Jeremiah knew the man was dead, so he nearly jumped out of his skin when the corpse spoke. "You've come to feast!" The head jerked and twisted.

"Steady," Monty murmured to Jeremiah. Then he said to the body, "I've come and brought an exceptional specimen, as is required."

At first there was nothing, but then the corpse stirred. Something in the swollen gut twisted and writhed against the skin. Then a split appeared, ragged and puckered, running from the corpse's belly button down to its crotch and beyond. The corpse's gut surged, and a man's head pushed through the breach. The man was slick with congealing blood and began wailing like an infant as he forced his way from the body. He was nude as well, a full-grown adult, and he deposited himself onto the dirty floor in a festering pool.

Jeremiah's heart was pounding in his chest from the horror. "Gods curse this place," whispered Monty, backing away from the ghastly sight.

The man—an elf, Jeremiah could see now—ceased his childish wailing and placed a thumb in his mouth before standing up before them.

"Name yourselves," he gurgled around his thumb.

"I am Monty, leader of the Stonefists"

"I am Jay, of Shabad."

"I am Nascent," said the elf, his voice was a high falsetto. "We shall start with the dwarf. Boy, make yourself comfortable in the next room, the amenities are at your disposal. No peeking."

Jeremiah looked to Monty for confirmation. He was ready to fill this building with poison gas at a moment's notice.

"It's all right, go," said Monty.

Jeremiah left the room through a door indicated by Nascent. The next room was no different than the others, save for a figure bound on the floor. It was a humanoid shape, wrapped so tightly in black leather its gender or race couldn't be determined. Its arms were bound behind its back, and its knees against its chest. The face was covered, and Jeremiah had no idea how it could breathe.

In front of the restrained form was an unrolled pack of butcher's tools. These were the amenities. Jeremiah grabbed a delicate looking filet knife and carefully sliced at the leather surrounding the forms face.

"Stay calm, I'll get you out of here. I can—"

"Cut me!" The figure shouted. Jeremiah scrambled back in surprise as the bound form wriggled in excitement, only its mouth freed from the bindings. "Cut me! Use me! Butcher me how you want! Ahahaha, I'm your little calf! Who wants my delicacies?"

The figure's tongue slid out of its mouth and flopped about like the feeler of a probing insect.

Jeremiah felt his grip on calm sanity slipping, this was all too much. He covered his ears to the ramblings of the bound figure that continued to writhe as much as it could.

Do I free this thing? thought Jeremiah. *Does it want to be freed? Does it know any better? What is this place? What's happening?*

He jumped at a tap on his shoulder. Monty was standing over him, scowling at the amenities. "You're up. Keep it together," said Monty.

The only thing that stopped Jeremiah from running out of the room was the knowledge he'd be running into one just as bad.

"It's okay to be scared," said Allison. "It's not okay to lose yourself in fear."

Jeremiah closed his eyes and stood up slowly and calmly. He had a job to do.

"Come in, seeker of freedom," said Nascent.

Jeremiah found Nascent drinking from his water bowl, tipping it back over his face in a clumsy soppy manner. The biological muck that washed off his face and neck revealed pruning and pale skin. Nascent had been inside that corpse for a long time.

"How did you find me?" Nascent asked directly.

"I followed Monty," said Jeremiah. He didn't want to give out even a modicum of information more than was asked.

"Yes, yes, quite the boring dwarf. Do you know why he brought you, Jay of Shabad?"

"He said he needed someone exceptional," said Jeremiah, his tone flat and businesslike.

Nascent put his thumb back into his mouth and toddled toward Jeremiah. It was an intentional mockery of walking, unsteady and with rapid tiny steps.

Suddenly Nascent toppled forward. Jeremiah instinctively caught him but shoved him away almost as fast. The brief contact had left a mucus-like film on Jeremiah's robes.

"Oops, I fall down!" said Nascent. He giggled and cooed at his own antics.

"Touch me again and I'll kill you," said Jeremiah. Truthfully, he would just run, but he didn't want to be this thing's source of fun.

Nascent popped the thumb out of his mouth and straightened, disappointed in not finding a receptive partner. "What makes you deserving of true freedom? Why were you chosen as exceptional?" asked Nascent.

"I'm a mage," said Jeremiah. "An enchanter, to be specific."

"Oooh, that is special," said Nascent. He began crawling up the deflated torso of the corpse. "We would be pleased to have you, yes we would. But all have to prove their sincerity." Nascent reached up and pried open the mouth of the dead man. Something was glittering in the back of his throat. Nascent reached in and pulled out a long golden shiv. It looked like a gigantic sewing needle, as big as a dagger.

"You're not going to ask me why I want to join? Or tell me about what it is you do?" This was moving too fast. He didn't want to know what a giant sewing needle was going to be used for.

"It matters not," said Nascent. "Your desire to join is the only thing that matters. Your desire to taste freedom. If you sought to join, only because you wanted to destroy us all, you would be welcome."

Fancy that, thought Jeremiah. No reason to affirm or deny anything.

Nascent held out the needle toward Jeremiah. At first Jeremiah was afraid he was supposed to pierce himself with it or let Nascent do it. But it was being offered, and Jeremiah took it.

The needle was heavy, solid steel with a gold plating, and incredibly pointy.

"You must make us an offering," said Nascent. "Only the truly exceptional may enter. All must come to us as a pair, but only one is ever admitted. You have until sunrise, no lollygagging, you must be sure."

Nascent curled up on the chest of the corpse and took one of its distended breasts into his mouth. Jeremiah tried not to vomit as Nascent's throat worked noisily, and something went down his throat.

"You . . . want me to kill Monty?" asked Jeremiah.

"I want for nothing," said Nascent, popping his mouth off the corpse. "Simply bring me his head by morning. With his heart stuffed into his mouth if you please. Now, unless you'd like to join me . . ." Nascent hefted the other breast, shaking it toward Jeremiah.

Jeremiah gagged and spun out of the room, stowing the needle blade beneath his belt. He almost ran into Monty who was leaving the waiting room.

"We done here?" asked Monty.

Jeremiah nodded. Over Monty's shoulder he could see the bound figure was still now, clearly dead. The knives had not been disturbed.

CHAPTER FORTY-EIGHT

Easy

His head. *Bring the dwarf's head.*

The words echoed in Jeremiah's ears. Even the ashen-tainted air of the Pit was crisp and fresh compared to the air inside that house of horrors, but Jeremiah was still back in that awful room, hearing those words again and again.

"Talk to him," whispered Delilah. "You can figure something out together."

"Don't be stupid," said Bruno. "You'd be giving away your only advantage. He's not your friend. He's likely going to kill you. Either he kills you and you don't get into the cult or you don't kill him and you don't get into the cult."

"Come on," said Monty. "Let's get you out of here." He gripped under Jeremiah's elbow and pulled him along, and Jeremiah realized he'd barely been walking.

"What do you mean, get me out of here?" he asked.

"Whatever that was, it wasn't for you," said Monty. "It wasn't for any of us. You don't have to tell me; it's written all over your face. So we're getting you out of here. Somewhere beyond their reach. You've started a new life once, Jay of Shabad, get ready to do it again."

"Wait, hang on." Jeremiah pulled his arm free. "We're just walking away? After all I've done, you're telling me no?" Was this a trick? Maybe Monty had been given the reverse of the instruction Jeremiah received—Was Monty going to lead him to some quiet shadow and strangle him?

"Jay, I'm not stupid. I know you're not either. I know exactly what they asked you to do." Monty spoke matter-of-factly, as though discussing the weather. "But you're not a killer, and whatever's going on in there is beyond anything we need to be involved with. So we're getting you out of here. No one gets a glimpse and walks away, least that's what I've heard."

"Hang on," said Jeremiah again. He stopped walking. "What about you? You can't just walk away from everything. If you think they'll come after me, they'll come after you too." Monty was talking nonsense. He was just going to throw his hands up and abandon the entire endeavor. He'd asked Jeremiah to defeat an unbeatable dungeon, and suddenly it was too scary?

"Does he look scared?" said Allison.

"I have no intention of leaving anything. Don't worry about me, I can protect myself more than well enough for *their* kind. But I can't protect you to the same degree, not while you're in Elminia. So, if you would kindly stop dawdling, I'm trying to save your life."

"What kind is *their* kind that the Stonefists can't protect me?" asked Jeremiah, standing his ground.

"I don't know," said Monty, which was strange enough on its own. "But I can feel it. I can tell. Something's not right with them, they're more than just a particularly ruthless gang. More than just some damn secret society of killers. They're something worse."

"Lead the way," muttered Jeremiah, feeling intimidated at the description and Monty's certainty.

He followed Monty out of the Pit. In the meantime, his mind raced. There had to be a way out of this. Maybe he could bring another head? There were plenty of bodies around these days, maybe any old dwarf would do—it wasn't like the corpse in there had been taking a close look, right?

If he told Monty what he needed, to infiltrate this cult, maybe Monty could help him think of something. But that would lose him the only advantage he had, which was that Monty assumed he wouldn't do it.

"Unless he's about to do the same to you," said Bruno.

His own thoughts felt like an angry swarm of insects, swirling, buzzing, and overwhelming. A cold sweat beaded up on the back of his neck. He felt cold all over.

They crested the lip of the Pit, moving from shadow to shadow. Monty moved more like a hunter in the dark than a sneaking thief.

"The world isn't going to miss one gangster," said Bruno.

He's not just a gangster. He's trying to protect me. He's trying to protect his family.

"You knew you'd have to do things you didn't want to do," said Allison. "This is why I didn't want you out here."

But I am out here. I accepted the mission.

The mission. How important was the mission? Was it worth a good man's life? Was it worth a good man's blood on Jeremiah's hands?

Was a single man's life worth throwing away everything? He and his friends would flee Elminia, back to the conspiracy they left, only made worse in their absence? They would abandon the empress and the city to whatever fate was threatening to swallow it whole?

Was everything he'd done until now a waste? Cutter, Gus, Allison, and Bruno—all that pain and suffering would just be thrown away because Jeremiah was too much of a coward to do the hard thing.

"You'll never be able to take this back," said Delilah.

He couldn't.

He had to.

"Then take every advantage you can get," said Allison.

"You don't owe anyone a fair fight," said Bruno.

Jeremiah felt for the little burlap parcel. It was nestled snug in his pocket, waiting for him.

"It will make it easier," said Allison.

"Is easier what you want?" asked Delilah.

Easier is what I need.

With trembling hands, Jeremiah unwrapped the piece of burlap. The oily wad shined in the moonlight.

"You chew?" Monty asked.

Jeremiah nearly dropped the parcel. "Uh, yeah. Sometimes."

"Bad habit," said Monty. "Come this way, there's a getaway man we can use up ahead. He'll get you out of Elminia unseen."

Jeremiah tucked the clump into his cheek. It tasted like a leather treatment chemical and rotting meat. He gagged and nearly spat it in the dirt. His mouth was bone dry, but he forced his jaw to work the vile wad, feeling the oily juices slip down his throat.

Jeremiah's gums ached. The cold in his body began to drain away. He wasn't feeling warmer exactly, just a lack of cold.

Okay, that's a good start, he thought. *I'm starting to feel less nervous. Now I can think more clearly.*

"Here," said Monty. In an instant he was gone, slipped between the rotted beams of a collapsed house, a space just barely big enough to fit through.

"Remember . . . useful . . . for," whispered Bruno as Jeremiah followed Monty into the dark. He was sure what Bruno had taught him would be useful here, but he was struggling to remember. It was becoming difficult to remember Bruno at all.

The tunnel was pitch-black. Monty lit a torch for Jeremiah's benefit. Jeremiah realized they were in one of the tunnels like he had taken to the palace when he'd first arrived in Elminia. It felt like several lifetimes ago. Had he been with anyone else during that visit? The detail seemed unimportant.

"We're almost there," said Monty.

Jeremiah followed dutifully. He realized he couldn't taste the clump of plant anymore. His mouth felt numb.

"He can't . . . could . . . ask . . .," said someone's voice in his head. A strange, errant thought. Jeremiah shook it off.

Jeremiah considered his options. A spell would take too long, be too obvious and would not guarantee a kill.

"Wait, hang on." The thought floated across his head, unanchored and unfamiliar. *"I'm not ready to murder someone in cold blood!"*

Was that his own voice? It seemed very far away, strange and irrelevant.

"Keep a lookout here," said Monty. "I'm going to check ahead."

The big needle dagger Nascent gave wasn't the only one, he realized. He had the magic one. That would make all of this even easier. All he had to do was choose the right target.

The lungs? No, a mortal wound was too difficult and slow. He didn't want Monty to be able to react.

The brain? Dwarven vertebrae were particularly thick and durable. The possibility for an instant kill was there, but that was a tiny target. A miss would mean a flesh wound at best.

"We're clear, come on," said the old dwarf. Jeremiah followed.

That left the heart. Dwarven hearts were more centrally located compared to human hearts and buried in muscle from the front. But from behind and below there was very little protection.

"Just a few more blocks," the dwarf was saying. "The last-minute passenger will be expensive, but . . ." he trailed off as he looked at Jeremiah.

"Hm?" asked Jeremiah.

"You all right?" asked the dwarf. "You look . . . calm."

"I feel calm," said Jeremiah. "Surprisingly so."

"I see. Better than panicking, I suppose. Don't worry, we'll have you safely on your way soon."

"Okay," said Jeremiah.

The old dwarf continued to talk as it walked. Talking was good. The words were irrelevant, but talking meant distracted.

Jeremiah leaned back, eyeing his target's back, visualizing the vulnerable paths to his beating heart. He needed to start the blade low and thrust it upward to go under the ribs.

"*I . . . how . . . stop!*" That voice again. It wasn't helpful now, so Jeremiah ignored it.

The target was still talking. It turned and put a hand on Jeremiah's shoulder. It seemed to be expecting some sort of response, so Jeremiah nodded, once, the target turned its back again.

Jeremiah shuffled, masking the drawing of his dagger. The target didn't notice. He thrust the weapon into the target's body, just as he'd planned. Yes, that was correct. He'd pierced the heart. The blood told him as much. Fortunate that the target wore no armor. Now was it a twist? No, that'd be needed for a normal blade, but for a magic one he could just wrench. There we go.

There was a rapid series of impacts as something from the target slammed back into Jeremiah's stomach, but the flexible armor beneath his robes protected him.

Now where was that connection point? He really wanted to make sure the heart was fully disconnected. *Upper left should be—No, this is from behind, it's mirrored. Ah yes, the dwarven aorta branches off the right first, unlike the human aorta which goes down.*

That should do. The target toppled, and Jeremiah withdrew the blade. He flipped it onto its back, and it smiled at him for some reason. The target placed one of its massive hands on Jeremiah's cheek and said something soft, nearly inaudible. But words didn't matter. What mattered was that it could still reach him with those huge, dangerous hands. It was still a threat.

Jeremiah slashed the target's throat open, and winced as the blood stung his eyes.

"*No . . .*" said a voice in his head. He had no idea whose, nor did he care.

"On to the hard part," he said.

Even with a magic dagger it was grueling work. The target's musculature was dense, and a dagger was a poor tool for the job. But eventually, the head came free. He set it aside to drain.

"Oh darn, I don't have a bag." Jeremiah sighed. What a pain.

Fortunately, a sack of refuse was always within easy reach. He decided not to empty it, the objects within would help absorb any leaking blood.

As he stuffed the head into the bag, he felt movement in his robes. The frog that lived in his pocket was trembling.

"Is there a problem?" he asked, then smiled at his own foolishness. Frogs couldn't talk. If it became too bothersome, he'd just leave it somewhere.

"You . . . won't ever . . . time," said someone.

He retraced his steps, leaving the corpse where it lay. It no longer mattered. All things considered he had completed his task in good time. A bit messy, sure, but alas it was messy work.

Jeremiah enjoyed the night air as he walked back in the direction they had come, bag slung over his shoulder. But he began to feel off as he walked. He couldn't put his finger on it. Something niggled at him, some sort of concern or problem.

He checked the bag, worried he'd forgotten something. But no, the head was still in there.

The head.

That bothersome feeling him gnawed at him, growing worse as he walked.

Did that . . . How could I . . . How? thought Jeremiah.

He was starting to feel cold. He shivered, rubbing his arms as he walked. And he was starting to shake again. He became aware of something in his mouth and spit out a dried-up wad of plant matter. What had that been for again?

"To make things easier," came the answer.

Things? What things? Had he done something bad? He did what needed doing, wasn't that right? There was an important job to be done, and he had done it. He wished Bruno were here, Bruno would understand. Or maybe Allison, she might too. Delilah . . . No, she wouldn't. She'd have some sort of problem with it. Likely a long-winded problem.

Delilah. He could hear her now. *"Your hands were tied? You had no other option? Think now, there was* nothing *you could do?"*

Jeremiah took a minute to rest on a darkened stoop. He should keep going, it wasn't safe to just hang about. But he just needed to sit down, at least until he stopped shaking.

His breathing was starting to speed up, his heart was pounding. Why? Had he forgotten something? Was there a mistake he had made? Some instruction he had neglected? Oh, he had needed to put the heart in . . .

Oh no, he thought. *Oh shit, oh shit. What did I . . . did I?*

The bag. There was something in the bag, something bad. It was like he was holding something he had plucked from a dream, the details of its origin hazy and indistinct. With growing dread, he lifted the flap and looked inside.

The blue-flecked green of Monty's eyes staring back at him, the light long since gone. Jeremiah gasped and closed the bag.

"I killed him," he said. "Oh gods, I killed him."

But the words didn't feel real. The memory was fuzzy, distant, like a story he had heard from someone else.

The drug made it easier, he thought, *just like she said.*

He waited for the impact of his actions to crush him. He wanted to throw up, or scream, or cry, or anything. But it never came. It was too distant; the association was too weak to hit him the way it should. The way Monty deserved. The way *he* deserved. Something was missing, something indescribable.

"Buddy? Are you okay?" he asked Gus, peering into his pocket. Gus was curled up tiny but reached out just a little to snap at Jeremiah's finger, before curling back up. "I'm sorry, buddy. I did a real bad thing."

He waited again for the impact, but again there was only that terrible absence. Was this what Allison was giving him? Was this what easier meant?

He had to get home. His friends would know how to help. He grabbed the bag and started to walk, then stopped.

Help do what? he thought. *They can't unkill him. It'll be dawn soon. I have to get back, or everything will be wasted. I did exactly what I was supposed to do. I don't even know what I'm scared of. Shit, I killed him. I cut his whole fucking head off! He said something, and I didn't even care what. I didn't care about anything.*

Jeremiah turned toward the Pit and kept walking. He tried to ignore the dreadful weight in his bag, bouncing against him with every step.

CHAPTER FORTY-NINE

Descent

Jeremiah returned to that nightmarish shack without thought for Monty, the mission, or anything at all. His feet carried him while he tried desperately to think of anything else at all.

His thoughts kept returning to home—his first home, where he'd grown up. There had been a creek near there that the local boys swam in every summer. After the rains, it would swell, the waters rising and rushing past in a dizzying current. The other boys, tanned and strong from their work on the farms, would goad each other into swimming across at ever wider, more dangerous points, daring one another to stare death in the face and emerge victorious.

Jeremiah's family worked no land. His hands were soft and uncalloused, more accustomed to holding garments and books than the sturdy tools of his peers. As the boys jeered at each other to test their mettle, the taunts were never directed toward Jeremiah.

But one day, the pain of being overlooked had grown more cutting than his fear. The waters were high and terrifying, sweeping debris past the banks faster than the boys had ever seen. Their whooping and hollering bravado barely concealed the dread of the scene. They jostled one another and joked, but even the older boys didn't dare shove anyone in today, as they sometimes did.

Jeremiah, among them but not with them, had felt that familiar ache growing in his chest for so long now. And as the boys turned away from the creek to head home, the ache flared into desperation—to be noticed, to belong. To matter.

Much like during his walk back to the Pit his legs had carried him to that shoreline before his brain could comprehend it. His knees flexed and launched him toward those dark, rushing waters, flinging his body as far as possible toward that distant shore.

As he flew, he'd felt elated, free—unbound by being different, weaker, more afraid. It was a moment of unbridled joy that seemed to stretch to the horizons.

Then he hit the water. Cold and shocking, his boots became weights in an instant, and the current seized him, even stronger than it had looked. Water washed over his head even as he clawed for the sky. Invisible masses collided with him and forced him down or spun him dizzy.

Jeremiah had time to realize that he was about to die, even if his body refused to accept it. He flailed and kicked away those treacherous boots and was swept downstream anyway, at the mercy of the creek. His bids for air were awash with lungfuls of water as waves crashed over him again and again.

And then he was being dragged. Someone hauled him up onto the shore and struck his back until he coughed up water. A cheer went up, and the boys thronged around Jeremiah's rescuer, a broad-shouldered boy with sandy hair. They thumped him on the back, adulation mixed with banter, and Jeremiah was left on the ground, coughing and drawing ragged breath, while they celebrated their hero.

Why was he thinking of this now? Jeremiah's bag thudded against his legs as he descended the stairs of the shack. Thud. Thud. Thud. He had wanted to be a hero, to be someone who mattered, and he'd learned what that cost. Thud. Thud. Thud. Then he'd tried to put that childish dream behind him, and that had cost him too.

What now? What would young Jeremiah have thought of him now, descending now toward the horrors that awaited with the blood of a good man on his hands? What did he think of himself now?

"You did what you had to do," said Allison.

"There's always another way," said Delilah.

Jeremiah arrived before the corpse. It regarded him with the same unseeing eyes.

Nascent slithered out from his rotten cocoon again. "Have you brought what I asked for?" he hissed.

"I think so," mumbled Jeremiah. The entire walk back to this house of horrors had been in a daze. He was trying to come to terms with what he had done, but it was like trying to take responsibility for the actions of something nonsensical you did in your dreams.

There was horror, but it was a vague and distant horror.

"Show me," said Nascent.

Jeremiah reached into the bag without looking, hoping that maybe his hands would close on nothing. But they found the tacky wet clump of hair that was Monty's blood-soaked beard. The contact made it real, and the breath left his lungs as he felt the weight of the head when he pulled it out of the bag.

He looked away, he couldn't fathom the risk of seeing Monty's yes looking back at him. Accusing him of being a murderer, maybe even a kin slayer, according to Monty. They were a family, after all.

"And the heart?" said Nascent.

"In the bag," said Jeremiah. He gagged, remembering something thick and vague.

"I requested it be in the dwarf's mouth," said Nascent. He was drawing closer to Jeremiah, smiling.

"I've got the heart. Isn't that enough?!" Jeremiah barked at him.

"No," said Nascent. "Put it in his mouth."

There was no going back. Nascent held all the cards and was going to pay them one by one. Jeremiah set Monty's head down on the ground and crouched beside it, still not looking.

Please, just let this end, he thought.

He had handled hearts before, and heads. Hundreds even. All part of Flusoh's processing. But these were his. He knew this heart, and he knew this head.

He fished around in the bag for the heart and had to peel it away from the burlap lining. He had almost retrieved it when it jumped in his hands, one last errant pulse. It had performed hundreds of thousands in its living days, why not one more?

Jeremiah gasped in shock as the heart pumped once in his hand, jumping back into the bag and squirting cooling blood between his fingers.

"Freshhhh," hissed Nascent with satisfaction.

Again, Jeremiah pulled it out. Luckily, that one thump was all it had left. A final bit of revenge from Monty.

"See?" said Jeremiah, holding it out for Nascent to inspect. It was heavy, very heavy. Dwarf hearts were huge compared to human hearts, and had an entire extra fifth chamber that Jeremiah had never been able to determine the purpose of.

"The mouth!" Nascent hissed. "In the mouth!" He was quivering with excitement and had started running his hands over his nude body.

Jeremiah stifled a sob. This was sadism, pure twisted sadism. But he had to.

"You don't have to," said Delilah. "There's always another way."

"Except sometimes there isn't," said Bruno and Allison.

Jeremiah was forced to look at Monty's face. He had been so dignified in life, so self-assured and strong. Now his face was slack and pale. The tension, having completely left him, made his face appear soft and melting. Rigor mortis would set in soon, but for now the head was still fresh enough to be limp. There were scraps of discarded vegetable peelings on his face, brown rot wiping off on his beard and nose.

"You were a liar," whispered Monty. "I knew it all along. You pleaded and begged and manipulated me. Just to stab me in the back. I wanted to keep my people safe. That included you."

Shut up, thought Jeremiah. *You would have done the same to me.*

"At least you'll still have money," said Monty mockingly. "At least you won't be poor. What a tragedy that would be."

Jeremiah opened Monty's slack jaw with two trembling fingers. The teeth came apart with a sucking sound. He picked up the heart and placed it against Monty's lips like a red apple.

"It doesn't fit," Jeremiah whispered to Nascent.

"Make it fit!" Nascent squealed at him. Nascent was beside himself with anticipation.

Jeremiah held his breath and pushed, cinching his eyes shut. There were cracks, there were pops, the heart compressed and oozed out captive blood.

"Yes, yesssss," hissed Nascent eagerly.

Something gave, something split, and Jeremiah's hand came into contact with Monty's mouth. It was done. He held up Monty's head, now just a bit heavier, for Nascent to inspect.

"Perfect, that was perfect Jay of Shabad," sighed Nascent. His ecstatic quivering had become a languid calmness.

"Am I done?" asked Jeremiah. He was dizzy, so many horrific sensations were playing out in his mind and hands over and over again.

"Yes, Jay. You are done," said Nascent. "You are worthy of true freedom. We are all too pleased to have you. Our leader will receive you, a most auspicious honor."

With surprising ease, Nascent rolled the humongous corpse onto its side. It sloshed over like a sack of water, revealing a stairway beneath that led down into darkness.

"Descend, Jay of Shabad," said Nascent. "Descend and discover your birthright."

Nascent took Monty's head from Jeremiah, and Jeremiah began to descend the stairs.

Jeremiah had traveled fewer than a dozen steps before the light above him was blotted out, plunging him into darkness. Nascent must have rolled the body back over the opening. Jeremiah kept a hand on both walls and felt each step carefully before committing his weight. It was slow going, leaving Jeremiah far too much time with his own thoughts.

"Not even the dignity of a burial," said Monty. "Leaving me with that freak."

"Sorry, boss."

"You murdered Monty because a sadist told you to," said Delilah. "Because you're on some sort of mission. Who are you, Jeremiah Thorn? What else are you capable of?"

He was terrified of himself. He was terrified of how easy it was to convince himself what he did was necessary.

The air in the stairwell grew chilled and damp.

Flashes of the murder came to him. They remained murky and indistinct, but insistent, as though some part of him was desperate to cling to the scraps. His mind filled Monty's last words with limitless possibilities—in some renditions, Monty forgave him, or was proud of him, in others he cursed him, promised he'd have revenge in hell.

Selfishly, Jeremiah found himself wishing the old dwarf were with him. Monty's presence had been so reassuring, in its way. He wondered what would happen to the Stonefists now. Was there a succession plan? With a start, Jeremiah realized that was probably meant to be him. Did anybody else know about Cassidy's treasure? What would happen to Sweet Melissa, Dronkal, and Shugga?

"I would have taken care of you, too," said Monty. "We could have figured it out together."

"You couldn't risk it," said Allison. "You did what you had to do."

He'd tried to fight back, Jeremiah remembered. Monty had understood Jeremiah's betrayal in an instant and tried to defend himself. Probably would have succeeded if not for the hidden armor, one more secret kept from the man who was laying down his life to project Jeremiah.

"Stay focused," said Bruno. "You're almost there."

But that was impossible. Jeremiah hurried down the pitch-black stairs, faster and faster. Monty giving him power over Cutter. Monty apologizing for Delilah. Monty begging him not to throw away his life in the Golden Vault. Monty telling him something, something Jeremiah would never hear, with his last breath in this world.

Jeremiah's foot slipped. He lurched forward in the dark and threw his arms out to catch himself. His palms slammed into the walls on either side, and he held there, half suspended over empty air. His breathing was ragged, his mouth dry.

He missed his friends. He missed his cellmates. He missed Monty. Allison had been right. He never should have been out here. He never should have leapt from the shore, unheeding the tumultuous waters below.

But he had, and this time nobody was here to pull him out. With shaky breaths, he pushed himself backward, finding the stone steps with his feet. He took one more step. And one more. One more. Just keep going.

After an age in darkness, an almost imperceptible brightening began to appear. With each step, Jeremiah became surer of it, until finally the final landing of the staircase came into view.

A lantern hung beside a simple iron door. Folded neatly on a stool was a dark red robe, and atop it rested a beautifully carved ivory and gilded gold mask. The mask showed a blank face with only two slots for eyes. It was pristine, as if it had been newly created just for him.

Jeremiah understood the request. He donned the robe over his clothes and felt lost in the billowing fabric. It was unadorned, but of good quality. He slipped the mask over his face and buckled the sturdy leather strap behind his head. Then he turned to the door.

He smelled the rust, felt the cold, unyielding metal beneath his palm. On the other side of this door was whatever it was that Monty had died for. He touched the door ring. It was strangely warm. He pulled, and the door screeched on its hinges.

Light flooded into Jeremiah's world, blinding him. He squinted and just made out a robed figure waiting on the other side.

This figure wore the same robes, but his mask was decorated with a mother of pearl luster and a circle of sapphires on the forehead. The figure was slightly smaller than Jeremiah, just as lost in the robes as Jeremiah felt. It stepped forward without hesitation and threw its arms around Jeremiah in a tight hug.

"You did it," said the figure, a male voice. "You made it. It's all over now. You can finally be free." He emphasized the last word with a tightening of the hug.

Jeremiah indulged his feelings of abject isolation and nerve-breaking stress by wrapping the man up in his own hug, squeezing just as tight. It felt good. For a moment he forgot all the horror and fully embraced the lie.

"I know, friend, I know," said the man. He rubbed Jeremiah's back affectionately. "You've been through a lot to get here."

The embrace was everything Jeremiah's body longed for. The isolation, the horror, for just a moment it was blotted out by the kind gesture of another. Tears leapt to his eyes. He leaned into the hug, feeling weakness flooding his body as the stranger supported his weight.

Jeremiah would have liked to stay in that moment for the rest of his life, to never again need to think about what had gotten him there or face whatever fresh hardship awaited. To let his worries fade into obscurity while someone cared for him.

But he still had work to do.

Jeremiah released the embrace, and the stranger let him step away. "Thanks."

"Not at all, friend, not at all. We all understand the pain of shedding our old lives for a better one. Not to mention you came to us via Nascent, not easy." His voice was gregarious and charming.

"You can call me Lyle," said the man. I know your name is Jay, but if you'd prefer to be called anything else, just let me know."

"Jay is fine," said Jeremiah. This man was, somehow, stranger than anything else thus far. "You're the leader here?"

The man shrugged. "I like to think of myself as a guide. But, if there were anything like a true leader here, I suppose it would be me. But come on in, there's lots to show you."

Lyle brought Jeremiah to the next door, turned and began fussing with Jeremiah's robes, straightening and smoothing out rumples. It was strangely similar to something he had seen Delilah do before.

You've got a sense of propriety, thought Jeremiah. *Or experience and concern with refinement.*

"Look at him, it's natural," said Delilah. "He comes from my circles."

"Now don't be nervous," said Lyle. "It's going to be a lot to take in, but I promise most everyone here is very friendly, if not private."

The primping complete, Lyle put his hand on the door. "Ready?" he asked. Jeremiah could hear the anticipation and delight in his voice.

"Ready," said Jeremiah.

"Welcome home, Jay," said Lyle, and threw the door open.

Jeremiah took in his surroundings. They stood in a subterranean city, similar to the one he had passed through with Monty and his cellmates, but this one was obviously lived in. Great crystal lights, set to glow by magic, adorned huge stone columns. Ancient buildings of crumbling stone had been fitted with warm, homey tapestries. Rather than the cramped ruins of the city Jeremiah had seen, this place enjoyed wide, expansive spaces. He could see other robed figures moving about.

We must be beneath the second city, he thought. *The place nobody goes because it's overrun by kobolds. Well, I don't see any kobolds around here.*

He started forward and nearly fell. Lyle caught him, a supportive arm under his elbow. His legs were trembling, he realized. In fact, his entire body felt on the verge of collapse.

Lyle pulled him back upright. "Yeah, those stairs are awful. May I make an offer? There's a lovely little inn nearby. Very nice. I'll cover your stay. We can save your orientation for tomorrow."

"Orientation?" asked Jeremiah.

Lyle laughed with genuine amusement. "I really don't know what else to call it. Initiation sounds far too dire. I just want to give you the tour, help you find your feet. But I suspect I will find you a far more attentive audience if I allow you some time to rest first. You've been through a lot today."

"That . . . would be nice," said Jeremiah.

"I insist even," said Lyle, his voice as soothing as aloe. "Take some time to rest. The whole world will be here waiting for you when you get back."

The inn was indeed what passed for lovely down here, the crumbling walls updated with fresh plaster and new wood doors. Jeremiah's room featured heavy curtains over the windows, three locks on the door, and a rug.

Jeremiah dropped onto the bed. "We're okay, buddy. We're okay." Details of the murder drifted across his mind, sometimes in sharp focus, sometimes barely recognizable. Gus didn't respond. Tears threatened again, then nausea, but mostly he was overwhelmingly exhausted.

"We're okay."

Somewhere between blinks, he fell asleep.

CHAPTER FIFTY

Orientation

Jeremiah had no idea how long he slept. Underground, there was no clear indication of the passing of time. It took him a moment to remember where he was, and why everything was bathed in a soft blue ambient light.

"We're almost through this," he whispered to Gus. "Just some recon, get the lay of the land, learn what we can. Then we can head home and this whole thing can be someone else's problem." Gus gave him a weary chirp.

The murder threatened to push its way back into his thoughts, but Jeremiah closed his mind to it. It was done, and he had to live with that for the rest of this life—no point agonizing over it now, when there was so much still at stake.

"Atta boy," said Allison. "Get the job done and come on home."

Jeremiah left his room and headed downstairs. Lyle was speaking with the innkeeper, and somehow conveyed delight through his mask as Jeremiah entered the room.

"Jay! Wonderful to see you, did you rest well? So glad to hear it. Come, let me show you around. There's a wonderful café just this way, you must be famished." He ushered Jeremiah out of the inn with a gentle guiding arm.

"Now don't be nervous," said Lyle. "It's going to be a lot to take in, but I promise most everyone in the flock is very friendly."

A passerby waved to Lyle, and he returned the greeting. "First things first—robes are optional, masks are not. We don't really have rules here per se, in fact that's kind of the whole point of this place, but the masks are for everyone's mutual protection and safety. We won't force you to wear it of course, but don't be surprised if you get . . . er . . . reprimanded for going without one."

They passed a handful of individuals who had eschewed robes for typical clothing, and a group who walked completely nude together, save for their masks.

Lyle led Jeremiah down the magically illuminated streets, stopping only to offer greetings when someone acknowledged him. Jeremiah could see that once it became clear he was performing an orientation, the others let him be.

"The main point of our little community is freedom," said Lyle. "You'll find no guards down here, only the law you can enforce yourself. Anything you want to do, you can."

As they passed one building, Jeremiah heard a chorus of passionate moans and gasps coming from inside. No, more than a chorus—it was a swarm.

"So when you say I can do anything . . ." Jeremiah began.

"Anything!" exclaimed Lyle, gesturing emphatically. "This is the last great bastion of true freedom. I want you to shake off that feeling of looking over your shoulder you had topside. It'll take time, I know. But down here, you are well and truly free."

"Isn't that dangerous?" asked Jeremiah. He imagined a serial killer would have quite the time down here.

"It can be, but no more dangerous than topside, really. I ask you, how many crimes do guards truly prevent? More likely they just harass honest men. The law is just an illusion of security. Down here, we've stripped away the illusion. Down here there is true equality in—no, wait," Lyle held up his hands. "I promised I was going to stop proselytizing to new people. I get too excited and can't stop myself. That café is right this way."

They sat down together at a small table outside a small café that would have looked at home on the streets far above. Jeremiah poked a small flower decorating a window box. "I thought this whole area had been overrun by kobolds."

"Ah, yes. It was, until we took it over and put up some barriers. I recommend you stay away from any small holes in the perimeter walls. The kobolds don't venture here much anymore, but anything outside of our territory is theirs. We'll show you all the safe ways in and out, don't worry." He waved a hand, and a small figure arrived with a pair of coffees.

"Hey, Lyle," said the young woman. She wore durable work wear, and a mask was decorated with painted orange flames curling around the eyes.

"Hello, Madella," said Lyle. They leaned in and tapped their masks together in a facsimile of a cheek kiss. "How's the roast today?"

"Well, enough, not sure I let the beans breathe as long as I should have though. Give a test?" asked Madella.

Lyle tipped his mask back to slip the cup underneath.

"Male, shaved, no scars, strong chin, younger," Jeremiah noted what features he could see in that brief moment.

"Hm," said Lyle. "Touch bitter."

"'Fraid of that," said Madella. "By the way, I could use some new copper piping for the stills. You know someone for that?"

"I do, but we can talk later. I'm working right now." Lyle nodded toward Jeremiah.

"Oh!" Madella turned toward Jeremiah. "So sorry, I didn't even notice. Welcome!" Jeremiah could hear the smile in her voice.

"Thank you," said Jeremiah. The presence of something as mundane as a café down here was distressing.

"He got the new-guy blues?" Madella asked, eyeing Jeremiah. "Who'd he come down with?"

"Nascent, I believe," said Lyle.

"Oof," said Madella, recoiling at the name. She rested a hand on Jeremiah's shoulder. "You're here now, hon. I promise it's worth it! Come by and see us anytime, till you find your feet." With a comforting squeeze, she left them to their coffee.

"Ah, another tip for you. Make friends! People down here have a lot of proclivities. Some stranger than others, but we all have them. So we generally are willing to help each other fulfill those desires and are helped in turn. It's never too early to network, Jay. Networking is very important down here. Don't be afraid to just say hi."

"Of course. Do you know a guy who calls himself Ol' Pete?" Jeremiah asked.

Lyle almost spat out his coffee. "Yes, I'm sorry to say. That vulture had been orbiting us for a while, trying to circumvent the proper channels. If you, or any of your friends, happen to kill him, I will consider it a personal favor. One I will pay back in *spades*."

"That bad, huh?"

"I used to try and keep tabs on who owes him what, but it's impossible. By the way, you don't get to admit anyone. We have people for that. You can point them in the right direction, but discovering us for yourself is part of the journey. And the test."

"And the test . . ." Jeremiah's head dropped to his chest as a wave of emotion washed over him. He'd killed Monty in cold blood, stabbed him when his back was turned. Snuffed out his life with a few quick strokes.

"Steady," said Allison.

Lyle reached across the table and put a hand on Jeremiah's. "You did what you had to do to get here. You earned your freedom. Same as anyone else down here. You're not alone."

Jeremiah could barely hear him. Those fragments rushed back, flashing before him. "He didn't see it coming. He trusted me."

"Hey, look at me, Jay." Lyle lifted Jeremiah's chin. "You did what you had to do. That's all there is to it. It's harder for some of us than for others, but it's what brings us together. You're free now."

"Keep it together Jay, there's still work to be done," said Allison.

"You didn't have to—" started Delilah.

"Later," insisted Allison.

But I— thought Jeremiah.

"Later!" said Allison. "We mourn the losses later. Losses of comrades or losses of ourselves. We mourn later. Keep fighting, soldier."

Gradually, the wave receded. "I'm all right." He took some deep breaths. "I'm all right."

"You will be," said Lyle. "Drink some coffee, you'll feel better."

Jeremiah sipped his coffee. The heat helped center him. "You're talking about ultimate freedom. So I could just, for example, up and kill Madella, and no one would stop me?"

Lyle nodded. "If that were your desire, by all means. Of course, someone might stop you. She might stop you. You might get killed for it after the fact. With Madella, I guarantee it. But you have the freedom to do whatever you like, and the people around you, in turn, have it as well."

"How is that different from topside?"

"Excellent question!" Lyle's eyes weren't visible behind his mask, but Jeremiah imagined they were shining with excitement. "Have you ever found yourself powerless before those who were simply born richer, or stronger, or luckier than you?"

Jeremiah thought of the countless people rushing past him, too disinterested to toss him a copper so he could eat. He thought of the long march from sleeping spot to sleeping spot, always moving for the sake of keeping the guard's boots out of his ribs. He thought of his fate being handed down by a court who had already decided he was to be enslaved. "Yeah, I have."

Lyle's voice softened. "Topside, you are bound by unjust laws, by societal taboos whose purpose is to control you. People are thrust into their station in life with little means to escape, entire lives are spent toiling in service of those above."

Jeremiah found himself nodding, in spite of himself. He added a lump of sugar to his cup, stirring it as he thought. His spoon rode the ridge of the cup for just a second, eliciting a shrill ceramic screech.

"Ah," said Lyle, flinching hard at the sound, fingers curling and head tilting. His cringe was apparent even beneath the mask. "Sorry, that noise cuts right through me." Jeremiah laid his spoon down with apology and Lyle relaxed. "Down here," he continued, "there is no judgment, no arbitrary power differences. There is only the freedom to live your life as you see fit." Lyle tapped his coffee cup to Jeremiah's in a forced cheer.

"So, this girl," said Jeremiah, gesturing to Madella, "killed someone so she could run a café?"

Lyle laughed into his coffee, "So to speak. To run a café free of taxation, regulation, and certainly at a greater profit. Ask her to put some whiskey in your coffee and she'll do it. Topside she'd need to be registered as a bar, and pay greater taxes, for a simple favor of spiking a morning coffee at their customer's request."

"So she killed someone," said Jeremiah, pressing the issue.

"Not everyone has the same requirement of entry, and it's not my place to discuss hers," said Lyle, quashing the inquiry.

Jeremiah looked around the café, taking in the ambience in the silence. Decorated as it was with colorful tapestries, cushions for seats, and tiny pillows abound, it was still an ancient building. He could see signs of old graffiti scratched onto the walls, some still just legible.

Gorrus makes . . . The rest was scratched out, but beneath that, replacing the original message was *My daddy . . . 'cause he can't.* Part of the replacement text was illegible as well.

Jeremiah was beginning to grow uncomfortable. After Nascent, he'd been expecting more of . . . of whatever Nascent was, not this social commentary that he kept finding himself on the verge of agreeing with. He drained his cup and set it onto the table. "Can we keep walking? I want to see for myself."

Lyle nodded and placed a gold coin on the table as they left, a gesture Jeremiah was certain had been for his benefit.

The little utopia was roughly a dozen city blocks to a side. Robes and masks aside, it was remarkably similar to a stroll in any other city. As they headed toward an open market square, they began passing more and more people, as well as stalls advertising food, drugs, weapons, animals, sexual favors, and stolen goods of all varieties.

Jeremiah observed that money exchanged hands most times, but not every time—some transactions seemed to fall in the realm of barter, and at least once he spotted a small-statured woman simply take what she wanted with no effort to conceal her theft, and there was no clear response from the merchants. For her, a hard glare was apparently payment enough.

The same woman gave Jeremiah and Lyle a cheery "Hullo!" as she passed. Everyone seemed remarkably friendly, a far cry from the attitudes he'd grown accustomed to on the streets of Elminia. Jeremiah had to assume walking by Lyle's side came with certain privileges.

He had to admit it was more pleasant to be here than up above. There was no furious rush of traffic, no beggars to be kicked or overlooked, no guards ready to beat anyone who chose the wrong stoop to take a rest. People seemed . . . happy.

"It's a delusion," said Delilah. "Society's laws exist to protect us from people like this. You're looking at a congregation of predators."

"How many people are down here?" he asked. "Do they all get a personal tour from the man in charge?"

"Down here right now or in total? I want to say around twelve hundred total? But at any one time, who knows? Plenty of people coming and going. We have many members who only stop by now and then."

"And the tour?"

Lyle chuckled. "No, not everyone gets a personal tour, I admit, though I do try to meet new people when I can. I was informed you might have some talents that could be uniquely valuable to us as an organization."

"Because I'm a mage?" asked Jeremiah.

"That very thing."

An alarm bell sounded in Jeremiah's head. After all that talk about freedom, of course Lyle intended to manipulate Jeremiah for his own purposes. But he smiled and followed, just another willing member of the flock.

"Dismal!" one man called out to Jeremiah. His robes were full to bursting, and his mask was pockmarked with gold leaf and had two tiny stylized horns on top. "We've got the purest Dismal here! Corruption paste as well, eyebite, poppy juice, you name it we got it!" Jeremiah had accidentally made eye contact and was now being hawked directly. "New guy! I've got what you need! Amnesiatics of every flavor! First taste is free with me!"

"Need anything?" asked Lyle.

"Let me have a look," said Jeremiah. He had spotted the resiny weed that Allison had given him among the various troughs and bottles of drugs. "What's this one here?" he asked.

The shopkeeper told him.

"I see," said Jeremiah. "Thank you."

"It's okay, in case you're wondering, you won't get in any trouble down here," said Lyle, stopping to give Jeremiah time to view dazzling selection, tastefully organized by color and implement of application. There were purple needles, gray bricks, green salves, red waxy weeds, vials of clear liquid, and more.

"No, I get it. I'm all right," Jeremiah said again, apologizing to the vendor.

"You come by anytime, new guy, Papa's here for you!" said the vendor. He went back to calling his wares to the crowd.

"Ah, here's someone you should know," said Lyle. He led them toward a raised stage and waved to a man with a mask that had been painted fully forest green with thin purple lines coming down from the eyes. The man grasped a leather-wrapped mace in his left hand and a bundle of ropes in his right, each of which led to a collar around the neck of a person. The collared individuals wore rags over their emaciated bodies and burlap hoods over their heads. One of them was clearly a child.

"See?" said Delilah. "Predators."

Ah, thought Jeremiah.

"Morning, Lyle," said the man. "New blood today?"

"Good morning, Cocar," said Lyle. "Yes, this is Jay. He's new to our ranks and has a bright future ahead. I imagine he'll be able to make excellent use of your services after he finds his footing."

"Wonderful! Pleasure to meet you, Jay. Feel free to reach out with requests anytime." He inclined his head toward Jeremiah before bringing his wards up onto the stage.

"I feel compelled to ask about what appear to be slaves, among all this freedom," said Jeremiah as Cocar began to show his wards off to the crowd, pulling the hoods off their heads with a flourish.

"Slaves is a legal term," said Lyle. The first was a human woman, staring around herself with wide terrified eyes.

Here we go, thought Jeremiah. The second was an older Gnomish man. Cocar held up his delicate fingers as evidence of a skilled worker.

"You may find it hard to believe, but many of Cocar's indentures come to him willingly. They choose indenture contracts to secure food and to pay off debts that might otherwise be life-threatening."

The third hood, the child's, came free to reveal a human boy, perhaps eight years old, with hollow cheeks and bulging yellow eyes that darted from face-to-face, finding only cold porcelain masks turned back toward him.

"So, they just freedom themselves into lifelong bondage," said Jeremiah. He felt sick.

"Some do, yes," said Lyle. "Others' contracts are temporary. But, as I said, they are often the result of a voluntary exchange. It was a choice. Sometimes people regret their choices, but that's the price of freedom."

Jeremiah cast his gaze around the market square. He spotted more people wearing collars, ropes, or chains among the crowd, but unlike the true members of the flock, the slaves wore no masks.

"Remember," said Lyle, "you're under no obligation to use indentures yourself. Just because you can doesn't mean you must. Most of us adopt a *live and let live* philosophy. I'm sure you wouldn't want your fellows to impede your personal freedoms? Extending them the same courtesy is simply being a good neighbor."

"Of course," said Jeremiah. Cocar was now bent to negotiate with shoppers, ordering the slaves to demonstrate whichever actions the potential buyer was interested in. "Wouldn't want to impose my will over anyone else."

"My thoughts exactly!" said Lyle. "Now, if you'll step this way—there is something I have been really looking forward to showing you."

CHAPTER FIFTY-ONE

The Circle

Lyle's chatter increased as they walked, and Jeremiah realized Lyle's excitement was undercut with a growing nervousness. About what, though, he had no idea.

They didn't have far to go, Lyle led Jeremiah to a building unlike the others around the back of the market square. It was recently built, constructed of heavy stone blocks, and featured no windows. A pair of stone doors at the top of a grand set of stairs. As they approached, Jeremiah spotted tiny enchanting runes engraved upon the doors' surfaces.

"Now," said Lyle, standing between Jeremiah and the door, "we face an important moment. If you're really a mage, great. We can do a lot with that. But if you can open this door . . . well, we're going to need to have a very important talk."

Jeremiah studied the door. The etchings were an unpowered enchantment diagram. It was complex and some runes were unfamiliar to him, but nothing seemed out of the ordinary.

"This hedonistic wretch lives a life devoid of discipline," said Thurok. "There will be some sort of childish trick to overcome, nothing that demands true expertise."

"First thing's first," said Jeremiah. He placed his hands on the door and spoke the words to charge the diagram.

Lyle clapped his hands in excitement. "Oh, that's already more than I dared hope!"

The diagram stayed dark, however, the door sealed. Jeremiah frowned and traced the intricate lines. After a few minutes, he discovered a break where several lines should intersect. There was an indentation there, as though a small circular chunk of the surface had been removed.

He tapped the spot. "Here's the problem. The diagram isn't complete until these lines link up. It looks like a piece is supposed to fit in there."

"Something like this?" Lyle produced an amulet on a chain from his robes. It was a pendant of the same dark stone the building was made from, with several intricate lines crisscrossing the center.

"Such pedantic idiocy," said Thurok.

"Probably that exact thing, yes," said Jeremiah, trying to keep the annoyance out of his voice.

"Go ahead, take it," said Lyle, offering the pendant. Jeremiah could hear his smug smile.

Jeremiah took Lyle's pendant and pressed it into place, aligning it with the points of the runes. Sure enough, it slotted in perfectly. Jeremiah incanted again, and the door glowed briefly before the gap between the doors yawned open, like the mouth of a lazy beast.

"We have so much to discuss," said Lyle. He took the pendant from Jeremiah and ushered him inside.

It was darker in the building, and Jeremiah's eyes needed a moment to adjust. Details emerged slowly—the room was circular, with a few plain doors around the perimeter. They stood upon a polished black metal floor. Enchanting implements were hung on one wall, but otherwise the room was empty.

"What do you think?" asked Lyle, arms outstretched.

Jeremiah looked around, wondering what Lyle was referring to. Finally, he realized it was beneath their feet—incalculable tiny lines swarmed the floor, spreading in all directions like cracks in a frozen lake. It was by far the largest enchantment diagram he had ever seen. Jeremiah recognized the material as adamantine, a very rare, very resilient metal. His father had sparingly used pieces of adamantine the size of a fingernail in his jewelry work, and here was a circle that spanned an entire room.

He began to walk the perimeter, admiring the intricate details. "What is this? Did you engrave it?" If so, then he had vastly underestimated Lyle—this diagram was the work of a master.

"This is the great project," said Lyle. "The culmination of generations of work. Well, a piece of it anyway. I'm the sole custodian in Elminia. I maintain it, charge it, and occasionally improve upon the design. And if you're interested, I'd like you to join me."

Jeremiah realized this was why Lyle had been nervous—he didn't want the help, he needed it.

"Pull back," said Bruno. "Make him chase you."

"Umm." Jeremiah ran a finger over one node, as though inspecting its craftsmanship. "I'll think about it, okay?"

"Don't act like you're not impressed!" Lyle cackled. "This is the rarest opportunity, the chance to work on a true masterwork. And the pay is great, if you know what I mean."

Something was off about Lyle in this place. The veneer was cracking, Lyle was becoming more erratic.

"Reel him in," said Delilah.

"Actually, I have no idea what you mean. Speak plainly—what exactly are you offering?"

Lyle was silent for a time. When he next spoke, the erratic nature was gone, his voice was measured, colder than Jeremiah had yet heard. "Whatever it is that brought you here, we can procure it, in ways you've never even thought of. An entire army working to satisfy your every whim. We have members here from the lowest serial killers to the upper ranks of the regency. Join me in this work, and you may command them all."

This was different than anything Lyle had said before. It was frightening. "You make it sound almost like a shadow government," said Jeremiah.

"There's a form of shadow government in Elminia," said Lyle, "and we control that too. Every single soul of consequence that harbors secret desires knows our touch, is beholden to the pursuit of that need." Lyle knelt down to inspect an inscription closely.

Something else was going on here. The flock was much more than a cult of hedonistic indulgence.

"Sole custodian, but also said 'we,'" said Delilah.

"This isn't the only diagram, is it?" asked Jeremiah.

Lyle looked at Jeremiah. Through the masks, they held each other's gaze. Jeremiah tensed. His life was being weighed at this very moment. The other man had given no hint of threat, but Jeremiah could feel it, plain as day.

"It is not," said Lyle.

"Careful!" said Allison. "No one knows where you are. If you die down here, you'll just disappear."

"No, press," said Delilah. "He brought you here because he needs you."

Jeremiah snapped his fingers, trying to bring his own levity into the conversation. "The cult serves the enchantment, doesn't it? This place had to have come first. The work of generations, you said? That means the cult formed around it."

"Correct," said Lyle. Still cold, but with a hint of a smile in his tone.

"But," Jeremiah began, pacing as he talked, "there's always been someone to steward the enchantment, someone like you. You're not an old man. You're not just looking to pass on the task to someone when you die. No, something is changing."

It all made sense. The fever in Elminia was peaking, everyone knew something was coming and nobody knew what. But this was it, the something was in this room with him right now.

"Perhaps," said Lyle.

Jeremiah stopped pacing. "Lyle, what does this enchantment do?"

Lyle hesitated. Too long.

"He wants to trust you," said Bruno. "Let him."

Jeremiah crossed the space between them and spoke in a low whisper. "Let's pretend I didn't come down here just to get high. Let's pretend I'm looking for something more interesting. More meaningful. I know you've carried this alone for a long time. I also know there's nobody else like me coming along again anytime soon."

It was Jeremiah's turn to put a reassuring hand on Lyle's shoulder. Lyle stared at him, but Jeremiah couldn't read anything from his face or posture. Lyle could have been weeping, or smiling, or preparing to kill him. He had no way of knowing.

Lyle was still as if he'd been carved from marble. When he spoke, his voice was a whisper. "Do you believe in the power of true freedom? Truly believe?"

Jeremiah exhaled, filling himself with Lyle's worldview, forcing himself to accept the other man's reality, just for a moment. "I do."

Another moment's silence passed as Lyle scrutinized him. For what, Jeremiah had no idea.

Then Lyle spoke, quickly and harshly, like a confession. "I need someone to help control them."

"Control people?" Jeremiah frowned behind the mask. "That doesn't make any sense, I thought this whole thing was about freedom?"

"Not the people," said Lyle.

The air chilled. "What . . . uh . . . what do you mean, 'not the people'?" Jeremiah suddenly felt very alone, save for a terrible truth lurking just beyond his comprehension.

"The people need help," said Lyle, with dreadful composure. "It's not their fault. It's just their nature." He began walking toward the center of the diagram, one arm outstretched, reaching for something Jeremiah couldn't see. "They need help grasping the possibilities. All of the possibilities."

Lyle reached the center, and his hand was warped as though it were reflected in a deformed mirror. There was something in this room. Something wrong.

"The curtain has worn so thin, for so long," said Lyle, letting his hand twist and split in the wrongness of space. "And the people weaken the curtain as well as they give in to their needs. The thinner the curtain, the more they give in. It's beautiful."

"Lyle, is this some kind of mind control?" asked Jeremiah.

"No! The exact opposite. We are liberating them. We will shine a light on their very souls, and they will reach a transcendence of true self-awareness." Lyle caressed the split of wrongness. "All people, everywhere, will truly know themselves, will finally be able to reach past society's boundaries to seize exactly what they need.

"But for such a miracle, we need help . . ." He raised his gaze to Jeremiah, formed a fist in the air, and yanked.

Something tore, something in the world.

Jeremiah looked into the tear, and his mind was blasted with a riotous torrent of concepts pouring forth and crashing against the brick-and-mortar bulwark of reality. Jeremiah became aware of concepts for which there were no words, concepts of pain beyond pain, the texture of loneliness, the taste of despair, the stretching sensation of unbound chaos that would scatter your body and soul at the slightest breeze. His mind reeled at an infinite number of memories of torment and indulgence. But there was also a calling, one that pierced deep into the animal part of his brain and gave him permission to ride any impulse that came to him. To be an impulse. Freedom from himself, from his doubts, from his fears, anxieties, regrets, temptations, weaknesses, flaws, everything.

"You are a microcosm of perfection," it said. "Embrace thyself."

"But I fear," Jeremiah's mind spoke back.

"Then fear without limit," it said.

"I don't want to fear."

"Then fear nothing. All you do, all you feel, all you think, is perfection. You are the paragon of you."

He was of limitless potential. Nothing could stand in his way.

It was bliss.

Jeremiah's mind recrystallized, scabbing over the blind insanity that had threatened the very boundaries of his sense of self.

"You're okay! You're okay!" Lyle was saying.

"What . . . what was I?" Jeremiah asked. It was the right question but also made no sense. He was lying in a heap on that black mirror floor, his head ringing. The wrong-space was once again invisible.

Lyle was by his side, helping him sit up. "I'm so sorry, I should have eased you into that."

"What was it?" asked Jeremiah.

"That was a glimpse into another world," said Lyle proudly. "One that's now so very close to ours. The thinness of the veil helps the people of this city to understand themselves and their true needs."

"It felt . . . chaotic," said Jeremiah. It was as close a word as he could muster.

Lyle chuckled. "Yeah, first time is quite the hit."

"It also felt, well, evil," said Jeremiah.

"Capital-*E* Evil, even!" said Flusoh.

"That's just the shock," said Lyle. "You'll get used to it."

"Lyle, was that Hell?" asked Jeremiah.

"Absolutely not," said Lyle. "Hell is a plane of pure tyranny and wickedness. It's what our world is becoming, with its relentless laws and bureaucracy."

"Check the other one," said Flusoh.

"Was it the Abyss?" asked Jeremiah.

Lyle sighed. "The name of the plane doesn't matter. What matters is that it will free our people—all people—from the chains that bind them. Both internal and external."

"Yeah, it's the Abyss. Gross," said Flusoh.

Jeremiah had learned about the other planes of existence during his studies with Flusoh. Hell and the Abyss were indeed two distinct versions of damnation, though to a normal person the difference would be pedantic.

Hell was a world of torment and ironclad hierarchy, where the very concepts of law and order were woven into the fabric of existence. It was populated by creatures called devils, monsters most known for striking deals with mortals in exchange for their souls.

The Abyss, on the other hand, was pure chaotic evil. Any semblance of order was only built upon one's ability to enforce it. It was populated by demons, nightmarish creatures of limitless variety.

"You're trying to bring demons into the world?" asked Jeremiah.

Lyle held up a finger. "No, no! Simply pulling a demon into the world is easy. Any mage who knows conjuring can do it. What we're doing here is bringing a blessed other plane to our realm, making them coterminous with each other."

"And how is that different?" asked Jeremiah.

"It's about the influence of the Abyss itself! The thinning of the barrier has already been affecting this city for generations. Why do you think Elminia is so wealthy and successful? People take chances here. They bet long, they pursue their dreams with reckless abandon and fight for them tooth and nail. You must have felt it. It drives you to greatness."

That rising fever. Jeremiah shuddered. All those horrific things he'd witnessed and experienced flashed through his mind. Cutter. Monty. The Tragedy. Selfishness and suffering run rampant.

But if Lyle's words were true, all that was simply another side of Jeremiah's success. Conquering the Gilded Vault, daring to kiss Delilah—he didn't want to believe it. How could something so wonderful be linked to something so evil?

Lyle was watching him closely. "The power is within you, within all of us," he said. "All we're doing is setting it free."

"I . . . I understand," said Jeremiah. In truth, his thoughts were a maelstrom. He wanted to be great, not evil. He wanted that power but feared the responsibility. Were they really so entwined?

A sense of urgency was rising in Jeremiah's chest. He was standing on that stormy shore again, rushing darkness below. He hoped he was strong enough this time. "What do you need from me?"

Lyle took Jeremiah's hands in his own and spoke in a low voice. "We are close. The fabric between worlds is nearly worn through. You are to become an expert in this most wonderous enchantment. It is carved in adamantine, and cannot be marred by common tools, but I will show you how to maintain it.

"And when the time comes, and it is coming soon, you will help me control the emissaries of the Abyss, to protect our people while the purveyors of infernal power guide us all in a journey of self-discovery."

"Emissaries?" Jeremiah asked. "You mean the demons. That's what you're talking about. You're going to be in control of the demons."

"Yes. With our combined power, we will bind their wills to ours, and bring true freedom to our people." Lyle's hand fell to the amulet as he spoke. "We will be the vanguard of a new, better world, one where we may live unfettered. When you falter, I will aid you. When I stumble, I will have faith in you to catch me. Will you join me in this great project, brother?"

"I am with you." Jeremiah heard his own voice as though it had come from far away.

Lyle gripped Jeremiah's forearm and pulled him into an embrace. "Then at last, true freedom is at hand."

CHAPTER FIFTY-TWO

Screaming

Jeremiah took a deep breath, tasting the dust in the air. Every step he took away from the stone building and the wrong-space inside helped restore some of himself. Gradually, he came to feel more anchored, less adrift.

Taking his leave from Lyle had been as easy as saying he needed to rest, which wasn't a lie at all. The other man had seemed to understand without reservation, waving him toward the door with a promise to find him later to begin teaching him about the enchantment.

The city was bustling with more activity than earlier. It seemed people were returning after a day of topside life. Likely getting off work and headed to their hedonistic reprieve. Jeremiah's feet carried him smoothly past the market crowds, nodding automatically in response to the friendly greetings people offered upon seeing his clean, white mask.

"We're scouting, Gus," he muttered. "Defensive structures, weapons, militia organization. We're going to note anything of note, and then we're going to leave."

Gus didn't respond. He had remained huddled and still since Jeremiah had glimpsed the Abyss. Or was it for longer?

Jeremiah walked the city, but his mind was back in that room, the adamantine diagram under his feet.

"*You are perfection*," said the call of the Abyss.

Jeremiah shook his head and realized he had no idea where he was. He had taken no note of his surroundings or their defensive capabilities. His heart was racing, and all he could think about was the enchantment and what was coming.

He had to get out of here before Lyle showed him the Abyss again. The prospect evoked dread and longing in equal measure. What would happen if he listened to that voice once more? What would he be capable of? The question tantalized and terrified him.

"You're on edge," said Delilah. "Focus on the mission."

"We'll take care of it," said Allison. "Follow the plan. Follow the orders."

Yeah, they would take care of it. His friends, or the empress, or anyone else at all. He wouldn't need to enter that room ever again.

"*You are perfection.*"

"I am human," said Jeremiah out loud. "I am fallible. I can't forget that, or people die." A passerby nodded sympathetically.

The desire-fear still burned like a small ember in his heart, but Jeremiah forced himself to continue walking. He tried to put the question of how his friends would deal with an ancient, nearly indestructible adamantine enchantment out of his head to focus on the task at hand.

"Just gather information," said Delilah. "Just enough to convince the empress we've fulfilled our side of the deal, and you can be done."

That did sound nice. Jeremiah imagined shrugging off the mantle of deceit and returning to his old life—a burgeoning enchanter, surrounded by friends who cared about him. That wouldn't be so bad, right? That could be good enough.

Jeremiah noted that in a city of absolute freedom, nobody seemed interested in guard duty. Many denizens carried weapons, but few wore armor, and each was focused on their own immediate surroundings. Nobody was keeping an eye out for trouble generally, the way a patrolling city guard might.

"All this freedom may leave them vulnerable," said Jeremiah. "No organization, no structure, likely no plan."

"No discipline," Allison chimed in. "No hierarchy, no command structure, absolutely no reliability. This is awful."

As he assessed the intersection of organized defense and total freedom, he noticed bells were hung high on the street corners, with long hanging ropes. Nobody paid them any mind. Jeremiah surmised they may be part of an alarm system, although it wasn't clear who would respond to the alert. Disabling all of them would be quite an effort, possibly worth it? Jeremiah filed the information away.

He used his newcomer privilege to learn where the other entrances were—nobody appeared to use the staircase at the bottom of the Pit like he did, if they could help it. Three more-popular ones were accessible from Elminia proper, converging underground to form a main entrance tunnel, meaning access points were relatively limited. The main entrance landed in the underground city with a grand doorway, framed with huge stone chains carved directly into the stone, depicted with the links cracked and broken.

Jeremiah rolled his eyes at the cliché symbolism. He was tempted to follow the tunnels back up and learn where they emerged, but he worried he would not be able to bring himself to return if he did. *Or do I just not want to leave?* The thought slipped through him and was gone in a moment.

Structurally, the city gave cult members an advantage. The hodgepodge of buildings in various states of repair meant people familiar with them could move from place to place unseen by an assaulting force. Lots of places to hide. Perhaps a smaller team could use the same architecture to its advantage.

This was helping. Focusing on the mission made it easier to ignore the tickle at the back of his mind, the one he couldn't ignore now that he had a name for it. The Abyss spoke to him beyond his hearing, a faint whisper on the back of his neck wherever he went.

A sizable force could get in through that main thoroughfare, thought Jeremiah.

"It's a choke point," said Allison. "Easy to defend, one would assume there'd be some kind of defense or alarm."

"Definitely," said Bruno. "Traps or alarms at the very least."

"Better idea," said Delilah. "We can get infiltrators in by shadowing the exits. Pressuring people who can."

Jeremiah sensed the body before he saw it, a familiar empty pull of necromantic potential drawing his gaze before he even realized what he was looking for.

There. A dead woman by the side of the street.

The masked denizens of the flock just stepped around the body, save for a few who prodded it with a foot, then moved on as though dissatisfied with the quality. The dead woman also wore robes and a mask, although the mask had been cracked by one of the dozens of stab wounds that marked her face and body. A puddle of blood was pooling beneath her. The murder was fresh.

Someone had enjoyed their freedom. Someone had heeded an urge to indulge, and it had led to the violence arrayed before him. The whisper in his mind grew stronger for a moment, as he took in the scene. Jeremiah could almost sense the ecstasy the murderer felt.

"Yours?" someone asked.

Jeremiah jumped. A woman was standing beside him, tall enough to be of orcish descent and wearing deep purple robes. Her mask was a chaotic swirl of colors. Trailing behind her, a pair of collared halflings stood close, looking away from the body.

"Um, no," said Jeremiah. "I didn't do this."

The woman waved a hand. "I meant, are you claiming it? Or do you just want a piece?"

Jeremiah shook his head. "Just looking," he muttered.

The woman snapped her fingers, and the two halflings moved to the corpse and hauled it between them.

"Her own fault," the woman said as her slaves struggled to lift the body. "Walking around down here without situational awareness. Something like this would never happen to me."

"I wonder if she thought the same thing," said Jeremiah.

"Psh! If she did, she was clearly wrong," said the woman. "C'mon, let's get this thing moving." She left, the slaves following with the body.

That doesn't concern you," said Allison.

"You're on edge as it is, focus on the mission," said Delilah.

Jeremiah watched the woman leave, and no one was giving her a second glance.

What's one more atrocity? thought Jeremiah. He had to know. He didn't know why he had to know, but he did. He looked down and saw some of the woman's skin flaps had been left behind on the ground by whoever had cut them away. This had happened in view of everyone.

"It's a deep dark hole, kid," said Flusoh. "They chose this. They all chose this."

"You're right, they all chose this. They chose everything that happens here," said Jeremiah, surprising himself. The memory of the man in the closet. He was here. He was everywhere down here. What did that mean?

But Jeremiah watched them go. No one else gave them a second glance. His hands hurt, and he realized he had been digging his nails into his palms.

"The people weaken the curtain when they give in to their needs," Lyle had said. "The thinner the curtain, the more they give in."

What lay at the juncture between humanity and absolute freedom?

Ignoring the chorus of voices in his head telling him to let it go, Jeremiah began to follow the woman. He had to know.

Toward the edge of the city, illuminated by only the barest remnants of that soft blue glow, the woman's slaves hauled her prize.

Jeremiah followed from a moderate distance, noting that the woman's situational awareness was . . . mediocre at best. When they reached a wide low building, she held the door open for her slaves to drag the corpse inside. A simple sign above the door read "Butcher."

"Whatever is in there, you don't need to see it," said Allison.

"Oh, but you do," said Flusoh.

He shoved open the swinging double doors and found himself on the customer side of a butcher's counter. A glass case displayed cuts of meat and sausage. Jeremiah did a double take on the stack of human legs alongside the more typical cuts of meat.

The corpse was already up on the butcher's block while an enormous human cut away its robes, revealing the naked and torn flesh beneath. The orcish woman stood by and watched him work.

"Ah, Kelthris has been at this." The butcher's voice was thick and deep. He had eschewed his robes for a thick leather apron and wore a bloodred mask with a wet, reflective sheen. "He took his choices and was happy. Wasteful to be honest, but to each his due." The butcher pointed to some sections of missing skin.

"Thought he was off the girls?" said the woman.

"Switched again. Some bloke made him sick and put him off. She's in good shape though, give you six silver."

"Oh, feeling generous, Gurg?" said the woman. "This is as fresh as they come, you know."

Gurg and the woman haggled for a few minutes before she accepted a price. Coins in hand and slaves in tow, she swept out of the shop. "Help you?" Gurg asked Jeremiah, beginning to work on the corpse.

Jeremiah finally raised his face from the dead woman. Upon seeing the pristine condition of his mask, Gurg's demeanor changed instantly. "Ah, welcome! Finding your feet?" the butcher asked.

They just love *new people. Why is that?* wondered Jeremiah.

"You make them feel better about their decisions," said Delilah.

"You're a potential new asset," said Bruno. "Or product. Or victim."

"Stop getting distracted!" said Allison. "Scout and leave."

"Yes, I'm just getting the lay of the land, so to speak," said Jeremiah. The polite joviality tasted like sand in his mouth.

The man laid down his knife to introduce himself. "I'm Gurg, and I'm something of a staple down here. Storage is my game mostly, but I dabble in meats as well, as you can see, and procurement. Odds and ends. If you need it, I can get it for you."

"Weapons?" asked Jeremiah. "Armor? Potions?"

Gurg nodded. "Exactly what I'm talking about, real product! Yessir, I've got the lot. I'm the supplier for the militia down here."

This was the good stuff. This was what he was here for. "Oh, there's a militia? That's a little surprising," said Jeremiah.

"Collective defense, very important. If the call goes out that there's real trouble, militia members grab their gear and muster. People have fun with it, to be honest. Breaks up the day."

"Have trouble often?" asked Jeremiah.

"Eh, no, not really. Once in a while adventurers stumble in, or the kobolds get restless and make a raid. There are bells stationed all over, so if you see a kobold, just give a ring."

Gurg brought out his cleaver. Jeremiah tried not to flinch as he brought it down on the woman over and over, separating the cuts that were of interest to him. The woman's limbs and torso were expertly sectioned. He collected the blood runoff in a bucket placed under his block. Certain organs—the liver, heart, and pancreas—he placed carefully aside and wrapped in paper before dropping the rest into a large barrel with a fleshy *splat*.

The head Gurg left intact. He displayed it on the counter, setting the broken mask aside and pulling the hair back away from the face so the woman's limp face and blank eyes greeted anyone who walked through the doors. Satisfied, he salted the limbs and torso sections, then bundled them up for storage.

"I'm going to head down to the warehouse, if you're interested in the tour," Gurg said. "There's lots of inventory I don't have space for up here. Fresh stuff, too. And you can see the storage facility on offer."

"Okay," said Jeremiah. "I'd like to see what else you have." His blood pounded in his ears. He may have been a necromancer, but he had never witnessed such disregard for a lost life, much less one that had been a member of the community a mere hour prior.

"Great, you can give me a hand with this, then." Gurg handed Jeremiah a few packaged pieces of the woman and bade him follow.

Jeremiah had handled thousands of bodies in his life. The packages he carried now felt different. Heavier. He could still feel the warmth of life through the white paper.

Gurg led him down a short hallway before they arrived at an iron door sealed with a trio of locks. This door was properly secured, reinforced with several layers of bolted plates. "Gets a little loud in there," he said.

He undid one lock, and Jeremiah heard a low murmur from beyond the door.

The second lock clicked, and the murmur turned to a roar.

With the third lock, the voices began to scream.

Gurg threw the door open, and a chorus of wailing assaulted them. "Let me know if you see anything you like, I offer good discounts for newcomers," he called over the din.

The walls of the warehouse were lined with row upon row of cages, and in nearly every one was a living person. Jeremiah saw men and women of every age and race staring back at him. Some were silent, but most screamed, their voices blurring into a continuous cacophony of inconceivable despair and terror. The screams filled Jeremiah's ears, his head, his lungs. He could feel it in his teeth and in his hair.

"Right over here, please," shouted Gurg. He led Jeremiah past the cages toward an area where a dozen bodies hung by their ankles, chest cavities hollowed out. Another blood-stained butcher's block stood nearby, as well as a row of shelves bearing similar white paper packages.

"Weapons and gear are all down that way, but as you can see, we have the means to store plenty of live bodies until you need them. Good security, and the cost covers food and water."

"Oh, that's nice," said Jeremiah. The smell. The screams were so overwhelming he hadn't noticed the stench. It was indeterminate, organic, and it set off every instinctive alarm in his brain.

"Come on home," said Allison. "You don't need to be here; you have enough information."

"I do processing and dressing too, if that's what you're looking for. Detonguings, blindings, full amputation. Stuff like that."

"Oh good," said Jeremiah. The screams weren't stopping.

"You've done enough, come home," said Delilah.

"I sell wholesale too, if you're not intending on bringing your own."

"Oh yeah," said Jeremiah. The screams weren't stopping.

"Come home, let us take care of this," said Bruno.

"Sure enough. Got a fine selection to be sure—"

The screams weren't stopping.

"Got the standards, of course, men and women—"

The screams weren't stopping.

"Got 'em younger, too, of course—"

The screams weren't stopping.

"Oh, you eat children," said Jeremiah.

"Aww, yeah! Come on *home*, kid!" said Flusoh.

The screams weren't stopping.

"Wha? Me? Never. Cannibalism is barbaric. I just sell what people are buying."

"Ah, of course," said a man who wasn't as Jeremiah as he used to be.

"If you've got the coin I can get you the real veal specials as well."

The man in the closet screamed at him from every cage.

"Oh yeah?"

"Sure. Women with child are hard to come by in the wild. But if you're patient we can—"

Rise.

CHAPTER FIFTY-THREE

Rise

Move your fucking arm!" Jeremiah screamed down at Gurg. Jeremiah's magic dagger plunged down over and over again, sending great lashes of blood across the empty open floor in the room like a crimson whip.

Gurg screamed as Jeremiah's blade bit deep, but kept his arm raised to protect his face. Two hooked zombies were pulling him in opposite directions, raising him up off the ground.

The screams escalated around them and Jeremiah's blade fell again and again. Sharper than any surgeon's scalpel, the dagger sliced through muscle and sinew, and as Gurg's screams joined the others, it shattered Gurg's mask to hack at the face below.

Jeremiah kept stabbing even after Gurg's voice had fallen silent and his body sagged in the grip of the two zombies holding him. Cold fury pumped through his veins along with disgust at every atrocity the butcher represented.

When Jeremiah finally stopped, he was drenched in sweat as well as blood. The screams of the caged people had never ceased throughout the act of violence, but when he ripped off his mask and robes, they faded. Jeremiah's ears rang in the quiet. He became aware of a hundred faces turned toward him as he panted, wearing only his simple trousers and magic armor.

"Hey. Hey, let us out!" someone shouted. Others began to clamor as well, pleading for Jeremiah's mercy.

"Stay where you are!" said Jeremiah. The voices fell silent as the faces watched him fearfully, unsure if he was to be their savior or the harbinger of yet more horror.

Little did they know. Jeremiah turned back to the butcher's block, to where the book of *Flesh* awaited him patiently. It had been there when he walked in, it had always been there. He opened the tome to the ivory sheet, the page containing the instructions for the spell of abominations he had forbidden himself from learning, and read.

The knowledge poured into his mind, taking up space in his memory. The spell was his now, known and mastered, a small miracle bestowed upon him by the powers of the book. Magical energy pulsed in his fingertips, radiating through him and begging to be used.

Jeremiah breathed deeply. The putrid air was ripe with possibility. His mind was calm, quiet for the first time in many months. No more deceit, no more confusion, no more fear. Walking away from the cult now to report what he'd learned would just let more innocents die, would allow more chances for others to interfere with what he knew must happen. What he had the power to accomplish.

He would deny his power no longer.

The yawning sense of death drew him toward a heavy door at the far end of the room of cages. The door creaked on rusted hinges, and Jeremiah had to throw his bodyweight against it to force it open.

The light from the door illuminated a mountain of bodies, bones, organs, and dismembered parts. Man and animal alike reposed in various states of decay, stacked and neatly oriented like cordwood. The pile was several times taller than he was, nearly reaching the ceiling, and longer than it was tall. Barrels lined the walls, and a monstrous grinder at one side of the room denoted its purpose of reducing all waste to slurry.

Jeremiah wasted no time. His fingers tingled with power, and he thrust his hands into the pile.

The words came to him as though he'd known them all his life. His sense of touch expanded outward, encompassing the entire pile. Cold, wet flesh became clay under his will. In a singular force of will, he compressed it all, and the pile became a single mass, one colossal and horrible corpse melted together like a thousand wax candles. His creation was ready.

Rise.

Jeremiah's knees buckled as he pumped magical necromantic energy into the immense corpse thing. Greater than the sum of its parts, more complex and more chaotic, it filled his mind like a massive solid object, no fragile bubble to be finessed and toyed with.

The great bulk heaved as hundreds of hands and arms and feet stirred to life, contorted and rearranged within the mass, drawing upon the knowledge in Jeremiah's mind to form a great network of muscles. With an awful convulsion, it reared back and reached the ceiling, a tower of death, a hundred-handed giant.

"Good enough," said Jeremiah.

The back wall of the warehouse exploded as the abomination crashed through, lurching its way forward like a millipede on a multitude of scrabbling arms, legs, hooves, and claws. Dozens more limbs thrashed and grasped at nothing, hundreds of yawning mouths and protruding heads lolled and moaned in a dull roar.

The screaming began again. Jeremiah ignored it, and sent the giant through the next wall, where Gurg had indicated weapons were stored. Despite its mass, the giant moved with dizzying speed.

The warehouse armory contained hundreds of spears, axes, hammers, swords, and crossbows. The giant crashed into the displays and seemed to absorb the weapons into itself, passing them from hand to hand until it was like a grotesque army unto itself.

Jeremiah took one spear of his own. A lifetime ago, he had failed to kill a man with a spear just like this. He would fail no more.

The hundred-handed giant tore its way free of the warehouse, splintering and shattering the facade with ease. "I'll be back for you!" Jeremiah said to the caged people. He couldn't be sure if they heard him over their own wails, or whether his words sounded like a promise or a threat, but he had work to do.

Following the train of destruction out to the city, Jeremiah soon found one of the alarm bells. He yanked the rope hard, ringing the bell five times. Then he turned toward his abomination. In the larger space, it reared back to its full height, easily as tall as a two-story building, and bristled with weapons.

The abomination waited for him, quivering with anticipation, and Jeremiah climbed, the protruding limbs carrying him aloft. Atop his monstrous steed, he rode toward the nexus of the city.

The first militia members rounded a corner, weapons drawn to respond to the source of the alarm. Dozens of masked men and women skidded to a stop as their eyes fell upon the horror.

The hundred-handed giant reared back, brandishing its weapons. A hundred mouths gnashed their teeth and moaned, a sickly chorus emanating from deep within the creature as the militia members looked on in stunned horror.

Jeremiah looked down at their cowering from atop of his giant and was disgusted. "You wanted freedom? I am free! I am everything you've ever wanted!"

The abomination surged forward. The hundred-handed giant tore across the ground faster than a man could sprint. The militia members screamed and scattered.

Most were crushed beneath the abomination's bulk, while those that fled were slaughtered by the press of weapons that it wielded. Jeremiah sent acid balls toward the few that managed to retreat, taking grim satisfaction in their cries of pain. "I am your victory! Rejoice, my will be done!"

Rise.

From the bodies of the militia, he raised a swarm of skeletons and zombies, stacking bubbles into the space remaining in his mind. The abomination was soon thronged by the undead, like flies around livestock.

Kill.

The horde began to move.

Wait.

Atop his titanic steed of corpses, Jeremiah stayed his hand, for just a moment. There were slaves here. Innocents. There had to be a way to protect them.

They would use them as shields, of course they would, and Jeremiah knew he couldn't distinguish between them through his thin connection with the undead.

He looked down, frustration mounting. Was this it? Was he already shackled? He saw the faint lines traced in his armor, the perfect examples of control. Unknowable words, organized by a master's hand.

No, he wasn't done yet.

Jeremiah closed his eyes, focusing on his connection with the undead, and the expertise of enchanting that lived in his mind.

Search. If masks, kill. Otherwise ignore.

It was like writing in his mind, a script of intention born of the words he inscribed on metal and wood. They weren't words he knew in terms of enchanting, but he understood how to express them.

The undead began to move. They felt his intent. They *were* his intent.

Buildings shook as the giant barreled onward. They were reaching more populated areas now. The first unsuspecting people were dashed to pieces before they even had a chance to comprehend what they were seeing. Jeremiah raised those bodies intact enough to become undead and sent them to join the horde.

The alarm bells began ringing again. Jeremiah welcomed it. "Run! Hide! Fight! It makes no difference!" he bellowed over the bells.

The screams were rising now as Jeremiah sent the giant careening through the city streets, targeting the densest knots to trample and slashing at the rest.

Then the skeletons and zombies came. They sought out the hiders, the errant runners, and the cowards. Pulling them into the light and devouring them. Jeremiah watched in satisfaction as a zombie shoved aside a trio of slaves who had been interposed to protect their master. The zombie fell upon him as he screamed for aid, until his voice cut short when the zombies tore off his lower jaw. He died afraid, he died alone, and as the slaves ran, Jeremiah smiled.

Rise.

The bells clanged all over the city now. Jeremiah directed the giant toward the main entrance, where so many had already gathered in their attempt to escape. The hundred-handed giant careened not into the tunnel, but against the wall around it. Smashing the chains to smithereens and sending great rocks tumbling down onto the people escaping. The giant whipped its bulk into the walls over and over again, Jeremiah hanging on for dear life, until the tunnel gave way and collapsed completely.

The market square now bustled with a very different energy as people fled before the giant's approach. Jeremiah urged it forward, crushing market stalls and cult members. He saw his undead struggling to breach a barricaded building. The giant reared up and threw itself down onto the roof, collapsing the building completely.

There was no escape.

Checking in with his undead, Jeremiah realized they were now encountering more unmasked people than not. Perhaps the number of cult members was truly dwindling, or perhaps some were catching onto the fact that only masked people were being targeted. If so, there was a simple enough solution.

If no masks, bring here.

Dozens of people were carried, escorted and dragged to the square. Any that tried to flee were run down and dragged back again. Satisfied, Jeremiah dismounted the giant, bringing the spear with him. The giant would continue to rampage on its own. Jeremiah had other concerns.

CHAPTER FIFTY-FOUR

Denial

The heavy-dark-stone building sat silent, untouched by the death and chaos surrounding it. Jeremiah selected an escort of three skeletons to accompany him. He had yet to see any sign of Lyle, and if the man was still anywhere in the city, he'd be here.

The enchanted stone door awaited him, as before. Jeremiah withdrew his enchanting tools as he reached it and etched the missing lines into the stone with a few quick strokes. Adjusting for the circular indentation in the surface was hardly a challenge after working with the challenging geometry of gloves, armor, and weapons. With a quick charge of the diagram, the doors yielded to admit him.

Jeremiah started through, then reconsidered. His escort stood sentinel as a group of skeletons chased down some cult members down the street. The air filled with their screams as the skeletons overtook them.

Strengthen. If Strengthen, Strengthen

The runes fit easily alongside the locking diagram on the stone door. He charged them, locking the stone into an infinite loop, and walked through. He threw the doors shut behind him, the infinite hardness and infinite brittleness causing them to explode, stone shards flowing like rain down the stairs.

"Lyle!" shouted Jeremiah as he strode inside. "Get out here and take what's coming to you!"

But all that greeted him when he entered that circular room with the polished metal floor was that wrong-space of the Abyss, suspended in the center of the room, invisible yet as real as the hard adamantine beneath his feet. Its presence and its approval filled Jeremiah's mind for a moment, threatening to overwhelm him.

"Conquer, slay, lay waste," said the Abyss. *"You are beautiful in your fury."*

Jeremiah gritted his teeth and tried to close his mind to its influence. Alien thoughts that were equal parts his own and foreign. "I'll deal with you soon." He turned his attention instead to the three doors set around the perimeter of the room.

Leaving one skeleton in the main chamber to alert him if Lyle attempted to escape, Jeremiah tried the first door. It led to a torture chamber, because of course it did. Barbed instruments of torment adorned the walls, and a brazier of coals containing pokers and brands still glowed with heat.

At the center of the room, the remains of the most recent victim were still lashed to a large wooden rack. It was a half-elven girl, drawn and quartered, face still twisted in agony. Her skin bore evidence of the pain she'd endured in her last hours, puckered burns and lacerations still oozing fluids.

Jeremiah wondered what he'd been doing when she'd died. Having coffee with Lyle? Taking a nice rest at the hotel?

His disgust at himself flared, then receded. He didn't commit this atrocity. Her fate wasn't his fault. Walking away from the cult, doing nothing and allowing things to continue—that would have been a failure.

Jeremiah released the manacles that still held the girl's wrists and ankles and arranged her limbs in place beside her torso. He rested his hands gently against her marred skin and cast his new spell again. The body melded back together, once again whole.

Rise. Follow.

He would have use for her later.

There was still no sign of Lyle, so Jeremiah continued onto the second door. This one featured a lock so basic even Jeremiah could pick it in a matter of minutes— clearly Lyle had relied on the stone outer doors for security.

With a *click*, the door gave way to reveal a treasure vault. Tiny chests were neatly arranged along shelves around the room, and a larger chest sat in the center of the floor. Jeremiah opened several of the smaller chests to find piles of silver and copper coins, with a few odd gold thrown in.

The larger chest held the true treasure. Jeremiah heaved the lid open to discover gold and platinum trade bars, rolls of gold coins, tiny boxes containing gemstones and, sitting at the center of the chest, a familiar wicked-looking crown.

Jeremiah withdrew the crown to inspect. Spears of gold reached upward; large gemstones twinkled in the torchlight. He had seen this crown once before, upon the head of Empress Aubrianna. In his hands was either the genuine item or a perfect copy of it. Lacking Bruno's expertise in appraising jewels, he couldn't be certain which he held, but he had a hard time imagining Lyle locking up a fake.

He summoned a handful of zombies from outside to raid the treasury, stacking the smaller chests to be carried together and ordering two zombies to transport the larger chest between them. When he was ready, they would help him bring the riches to the surface.

That left only one more room, and the last possibility of finding Lyle. Jeremiah gripped his spear as he turned the knob, prepared to thrust it into the other man's chest should the opportunity arise. His skeletons waited, similarly poised.

He steeled himself and threw the door open with a shout, rushing into the room— yet Lyle was not there. Jeremiah lowered the weapon to take in his surroundings.

These were Lyle's personal quarters, without a doubt. The room was small but lavishly adorned, velvet tapestries and soft linens offsetting the austere stone architecture. It was a space that spoke of homeyness.

Jeremiah confirmed that Lyle was not hiding anywhere in the room before turning his attention to the contents of the space. A corner bookshelf was stuffed full to bursting with arcane tomes, histories of Elminia and her noble families, and books on demonology. A worn, overstuffed chair suggested the countless evenings Lyle may have spent poring over the books.

Something about the bookshelf caught Jeremiah's eye. There, the light dust that coated the books was missing in one spot, an area frequently disturbed. Jeremiah reached between *Heraldries Through the Ages* and *Summoning Vol. 1: Souls and Spirits*. He half expected to find a trigger for a secret staircase, but instead he withdrew a tiny black leather-bound journal.

Jeremiah flipped open the journal. It was handwritten in a text Jeremiah couldn't decipher, long passages in either an unknown language or code. He did recognize enchantment runes, however, diagram designs with inscrutable notes scribbled in the margins. Jeremiah tucked the notebook away to peruse later.

He returned to the main chamber. Lyle may have escaped, but there was still a critical task before him. The skeletons' feet clattered across the adamantine floor as Jeremiah swept through to grab one of the specialized tools from the wall. It was a simple inscription knife made of the same black metal, designed for intricate work. He recognized a small strengthening rune on the blade.

Jeremiah knew he had to inscribe close to the center, or as close as he could bear. As he approached, the whispers of Abyssal power became manifest, a voice speaking directly into his mind.

"Jeremiah Thorn. Necromancer. A slave in all but name. We can see the mountain of chains that burden you. Poor Jeremiah, poor scared Jeremiah. So scared, so strong. We have such sights to show you."

The whisper carried with it promises of boundless freedom and power. And happiness.

Jeremiah stopped in his tracks, stymied by the wave of wholesome indulgence it imparted on his psyche. Wisdom, love, fulfillment, the smallest tastes brushed tantalizingly against his mind.

"It's boundless, Jeremiah Thorn. The wretches use their freedom for acts of greed and wickedness. But within the infinite expanses of the Abyss, peace and tranquility can be found. Everything can be found."

"It's . . . it's all in there?" asked Jeremiah. He didn't even know what "it" was, only that it was anything and everything he'd ever wanted. His hand drifted toward the wrong-space, moving of its own accord.

"It is, Jeremiah Thorn. You need only enter the rift. We will find it together. Everything you want, everything you ever will want. Everything forever."

Jeremiah's fingers brushed it, the wrong-space, and the call became overwhelming. It was the satisfaction of every desire, it was assurance, it was affirmation of everything he'd ever wanted to believe about himself. His eyes fell closed as he basked in its glory. He needed this. He deserved it.

Something thumped, hard, against his chest. He heard an angry croak. A tiny bastion of thought somewhere deep in his mind spoke up. It was him, and it was not him, and though the Abyss filled his mind with the truest most enticing concepts it could know, one piece remained inviolate.

Jeremiah withdrew his hand. "I want to destroy you."

"Thy will be done," said the Abyss.

Jeremiah dropped to his knees and scratched the adamantine floor. The entire surface was already covered in runes, and Jeremiah had to move the knife in deft, sure strokes to create his tiny additions, linking them through the lines of the existing diagram.

It wasn't enough to simply mar the surface. That much could be fixed—even he could do that. He had to destroy it entirely.

Strengthen. If Strengthen, Strengthen

He etched the runes just prior to the terminal components near the rift. Jeremiah charged it, making it a part of the diagram. The same unconceivable power that was maintaining the wrong-space now flowed through his runes as well. Infinitely hard, infinitely brittle.

Jeremiah faced the wrong-space and raised his spear overhead. The Abyss sang to him, praised him, and welcomed him still. It . . . wasn't too late, Jeremiah realized. He could still have all he desired, everything this life had denied him. The loneliness, the hate he had endured, the feelings of worthlessness—all could be erased.

But they are part of me, Jeremiah thought. *Just as my friends and my magic and my decisions and my mistakes are part of me. This life is mine, and I desire no escape from it.*

He thrust the spear point downward.

The entire floor exploded like a pane of glass. The work of generations, meticulously cared for hundreds of years, shattered at the affront of a single moment of self-denial.

Jeremiah winced as metal shrapnel sliced his legs. The wrong-space buckled and twisted, becoming momentarily visible as it writhed, then faded as reality slowly subsumed the flaw in its fabric.

His ears rang from the explosion. He could feel blood dripping from where he'd been hit by the chunks of adamantine that now littered the ground. Jeremiah listened for the whisper of the Abyss worming into his thoughts. But there was only him now, and his undead, waiting in utter stillness.

CHAPTER FIFTY-FIVE

Pay for it

Jeremiah mentally checked in with his undead. Absent targets, the abomination patrolled, only occasionally breaking from its route to trample a foolish cult member who underestimated its speed. The zombies and skeletons continued combing through the city, now rarely encountering any living beings. Whatever remained of the cult and their slaves awaited him in the market square.

Using some blankets from Lyle's room, Jeremiah rigged up some sacks for his treasure-hauling zombies and began to fill them with as much adamantine they could carry. The skeletons kept a watchful eye, and the newly animated half elf girl simply stood by, carrying an iron poker in each hand, awaiting her purpose.

The city was nearly silent by the time Jeremiah left to make his way back to the market square. He spotted the hundred-handed giant first, as tall as a building and eerily still. Rounding the corner, he spotted the knot of huddled survivors in the center of the square, surrounded by their undead guard.

A murmur swelled as Jeremiah entered the square. Every eye was fixed on him, conveying equal parts hope and fear.

The undead parted so Jeremiah could survey the group. The survivors held their breath before Jeremiah's judgment. Whether consciously or not, they had clumped themselves into two distinct groups. The larger group was obviously comprised of slaves, dressed in rags and flinching away from Jeremiah's gaze. A small contingent, however, wore more refined attire and watched Jeremiah warily. Even without the masks, the members of the cult wore their status plainly.

Lyle was not among them, not that Jeremiah had expected he would be. He addressed the larger group. "Indentures, if any among your number was in fact a member of the flock, identify them now." The slaves glanced at each other, but none spoke.

That was good enough for Jeremiah. He turned toward the smaller group. Half a dozen faces looked back at him, terror now plainly written on them.

One Gnomish woman broke rank, throwing herself at Jeremiah's feet. "Please! I've done nothing wrong!" Tears streaked down her face, dripping onto her red robes. "I was just selling coffee. I never did the bad stuff!"

Jeremiah recognized the voice of Madella, the owner of the café he'd visited with Lyle. "You were just running a business, right?"

Madella nodded emphatically. "Yes! I was just here to make a little money. I never took slaves or hurt anyone, I swear!"

Come.

The half elf girl appeared beside him. Her body still bore the evidence of the torture she had endured in life. In fact, if it weren't for the vacant expression on her face, she could have passed for living.

"All you did was turn a blind eye while innocents were kidnapped, enslaved, tortured, and killed," said Jeremiah. "Living your peaceful little life at the expense of countless others."

The terror returned to Madella's eyes. "No! It wasn't me! I would never—"

"You can explain yourself to her." Jeremiah stepped back, allowing the half elf girl to take his place. She raised the pokers she'd been carrying over her head.

Kill.

The iron cudgels fell, and Madella screamed. The others cowered, retreating from the barbarism but finding nowhere to go. Jeremiah watched impassively as the execution was carried out, and when Madella's screams finally ceased, he raised her.

Rise.

Kill.

The half elf girl and Madella turned on the rest of the cult members as the zombie guards closed in. Their deaths were brutal but swift, a luxury many—even most—of their victims had not enjoyed, Jeremiah reminded himself. He did not relish the violence, but he took some satisfaction in a job complete.

Jeremiah turned back toward the slaves. They scrambled over themselves to get away from him, but Jeremiah dispersed the zombie guards to give them space. "There are others in Gurg's warehouse. Free them and bring them here."

At his words, it was as though a dam broke and released a torrent of voices, the slaves all talking at once.

"Please don't kill us!"

"Are we your slaves now?"

"That was amazing!"

"My contract says—"

Jeremiah held up his hands to stem the chatter. "We're leaving. All indentures are void."

"But in the event of my master's death, my contract passes to—"

"Any who wishes to contest the specifics of their contract can speak to that thing," said Jeremiah, pointing to the hundred-handed giant standing sentry over the square. There were no further questions.

As a handful of slaves went to fetch Gurg's prisoners, Jeremiah took the time to walk the streets. They were a bloody mess of bodies, crushed by the abomination or torn apart by the undead. He took in the carnage with grim satisfaction, pleased his horde had been able to carry out his more detailed commands.

Until.

Amid the corpses and destruction littering the streets, Jeremiah spotted an all-too-familiar configuration—three corpses, chained together. Their heads were covered by burlap sacks.

"Masks. Not specific enough," Jeremiah thought. The undead had not discerned between the masks of the cultists and the bags. Here, chained together, were the bodies of those who could not escape. It appeared they had suffered from the weapons of the abomination, hacked and smashed to pieces.

And there was the boy. His tiny body lay among the others, still masked, a gaping hole in his chest.

Cocar the slaver was nowhere to be seen, but even so, the people bound by chain had had no hope of escape.

He knelt beside the bodies, cursing under his breath. He'd forgotten them, allowed them to be caught in his tidal wave of destruction. It was a mistake, one that had cost three innocents their lives.

There lay the boy, still masked, his tiny body among the others with a gaping hole in his chest. Jeremiah pulled the bag off his head and revealed the man in the closet, eyes wide and unseeing.

His heart raced, his breath caught in his tightening chest, and Jeremiah quelled it. Not with rage or apathy but acceptance. *No. This boy suffered his own tragedy*, thought Jeremiah. *Don't let your pain overshadow his loss.*

He blinked, and the boy stared back at him, eyes yellowed and bulging in a frightened confusion that came alongside his final moments.

"I'm sorry," said Jeremiah. "I made a mistake. You died because of me. I'm sorry." The boy didn't answer.

"Come on, let's get you out of here. This is no place for children," Jeremiah said to the boy.

Jeremiah lifted the boy. He waited for the crushing shame of his error, but it didn't come. The boy had died because Jeremiah had been willing to do what needed to be done, what only Jeremiah could do. His death was a consequence of Jeremiah's actions, one he bore responsibility for, but his actions weren't wrong.

The boy was all too light, small to begin with and now missing the weight of his own lifeblood. Jeremiah had handled countless corpses in his day, but this one was different. He gently cradled the boy to his chest as he walked, wondering at his newfound capacity for sorrow without regret.

The slaves and prisoners had gathered in the market square. Nearly a hundred eager faces looked up as Jeremiah returned, now with expectant hope rather than fear. They could have left at any time—the undead now stood inert, waiting—but they seemed to be waiting for their savior to lead them out of hell.

"We're leaving. Stay with me," said Jeremiah. The crowd eyed the boy Jeremiah carried with sadness and despair, but they followed.

They walked through the grisly city together, still bathed in that pale blue light and eerily silent. The undead stood motionless as the living passed, save for the treasure-bearing zombies that followed. Jeremiah cast one final look back at the hundred-handed giant, barely visible over the buildings, before mounting the stairs that would lead them back up to the Pit.

He felt strangely at peace. He still carried the boy, and as Jeremiah's body began to complain about the burden, the labor felt an appropriate penance for his deeds. The low voices of the slaves and prisoners behind him were comforting as he climbed, reassuring him that, in spite of the sorrows he would bear for the rest of his life, he had done the right thing.

The procession through darkness paused as Jeremiah sensed a trapdoor above. His muscles ached, but he had strength enough for one more death. He reached his will just beyond the trapdoor.

Rise.

The slaves gasped at Nascent's screams, but Jeremiah smiled. He waited until the immense corpse that Nascent inhabited finished tearing him to pieces, then shifted its bulk away from the exit.

The exodus of slaves was a slow and painful one. There were so many stairs, and the slaves were so weak, but with patience and the help of the stronger slaves, they all were eventually able to reach the surface.

The sun had risen. It felt glorious on Jeremiah's skin, like it was burning away the cruelty and evil he had been awash in. He could finally release all the undead under his command, save those hauling treasure that still followed their group. The bubbles of the zombies and skeletons popped easily enough, but the solid block that was the abomination clung to its existence. Instead of simply removing his will, he had to focus on it, chip away at the block until it was gone.

The space in his mind was his again. He carried the boy despite the desperation in his body to set him down, and led the people through the Pit, ignoring the open-mouthed stares. The survivors followed him without question. He was their hero, after all.

Near the crest leading to the slums, Jeremiah turned to the crowd. "I don't have any answers for you," he said. "I don't know how you got here, and I don't know where you should go from here. All I can do is give you another shot. There's enough here for all of you to get a fresh start."

He called forward the zombies carrying the coin chests and had them face the survivors.

Dump it.

In one motion, the zombies overturned the small chests, emptying their contents into the dirt. The survivors looked at the pile of coins, looked at Jeremiah, then tentatively began crowding around

"You've all been through the same hell together. Try to remember that," Jeremiah said as the survivors filled their pockets. Then he left, trailed by the two zombies carrying the adamantine shards and the larger chest between them.

Jeremiah clutched the boy as he made his way through the streets toward home. The mindless river of people dammed and parted, the sight of a dead child enough to break their ceaseless pace. Where Jeremiah walked, a change seemed to spread. To set eyes on the dead boy came with a cost, an understanding. Suddenly no longer able to ignore what so many people had known as only a concept.

You know he dies, thought Jeremiah, *but here he is. Right in front of you.* Some of the people looked away or hid their eyes. Part of Jeremiah wanted to shout at them, to force them to see and look into the eyes of a dead boy who had no one. But he knew it was a fool's errand, they did not wish to see, and so could not be shown.

Allison was leaning against the wall of their building, cutting slices off an apple. She saw the boy in Jeremiah's arms, the zombies in their robes and masks, and the chest they carried, and gave Jeremiah a sad smile. "You okay?"

"It's over," he said.

"I guess so. You want to take him upstairs?" said Allison, gesturing to the boy.

"I do. I—" He choked on his words.

"I know. It's okay," said Allison.

Jeremiah carried the boy up the stairs. Each step felt arduous now, during the journey the boy's frail body had become intolerably heavy. He staggered at the final landing and caught himself, panting from exertion. His grip was slipping. The last thing he wanted was to let the body fall. It would be shameful, or disrespectful. He wasn't sure, he just couldn't let it happen.

Allison was there with him. "Just a few more steps. Let it hurt. Pay for it." She moved ahead to hold the apartment door open for him.

Jeremiah gritted his teeth and pushed the pain from his mind. He forced his legs to move, squeezed his muscles till they seized, but didn't let go. He entered the apartment and knelt down, using the truly last vestiges of strength he had to lay the boy down gently.

Bruno and Delilah were there, taking the chest and sack from the zombies. Allison knelt next to Jeremiah and put her arm around his shoulders.

"I know what it's like," she said. "I'm going to take you to your room, okay? You need to rest. We'll talk about it when you're ready."

Jeremiah wanted to protest. He was sure he didn't deserve to rest right now. But he was tired, so very tired.

He didn't bother to undress, merely placed Gus in his bowl and collapsed onto the bed. Sleep took him the moment his head hit the pillow, black and thankfully dreamless.

CHAPTER FIFTY-SIX

Not Okay

When he awoke again, his mind reeled to process everything that had happened over the last day. The sun was setting, he was still tired, but it was time to put everything in its place.

Delilah, Allison, and Bruno were all home, seemingly waiting for him. The crown, or its duplicate, rested in the middle of the dining room table between them.

Where was the boy?

Jeremiah spotted him. He had been laid to the side of the room, wrapped tightly in a white sheet. A part of him took offense that his friends were paying attention to a treasure while there was a dead child in their midst. His part was done, he reminded himself.

"I can't wait to hear this one," said Bruno, nodding at the crown.

Delilah jabbed him with her elbow.

"Oh, yeah, sorry. You okay, Jay? With, you know"—Bruno glanced at the covered body—"everything?"

"Yeah, I'm okay. Have a seat. This is a long one," said Jeremiah.

Jeremiah told them what happened after he left with Cassidy's treasure. When he got to the part about killing Monty, he avoided mentioning Allison's drug. It was something between them, something she had shared in confidence. The look on her face told him she understood anyway.

"You stabbed him?" gasped Delilah. "Just stabbed him? In the back? And then you... Oh, Jay. I—I don't know how . . ."

Bruno came immediately to his defense. "What choice did he have?"

"I—I don't know, but . . ." Delilah trailed off, looking at Jeremiah as though with new eyes.

"Maybe there was another choice," said Jeremiah. "If there was, I couldn't think of it. I did what I did, and I have to live with that."

Allison nodded. "It's always easy to pick apart what the best course of action would have been after the fact, but it's different when you're the man in the field. I trust Jay made the best decision he could have."

With her vote of confidence, Jeremiah plunged ahead in the story, telling them about Nascent and Lyle. When he started describing the city, Delilah pulled out a paper to begin taking notes. "Tell us everything you can remember," she said. "Let's start with numbers. Approximate is fine. We can do layout and orientation next."

Allison pulled out a long roll of paper. "I want you to give us a map if you can as well. Ingress points, chokes, defenses—things like that. Bruno, can you write to Ka so we can get a strike team together? She can give us a force disposition to work with."

"Ah, wait, hang on," said Jeremiah. "There's no need for that; they're all dead."

His friends stared at him, then at each other.

"What?" he asked. "I told Allison it was over."

"I thought you meant you got the information we needed!" said Allison, letting her map snap shut into a paper tube once again.

"I didn't say I *finished*. I said it's over! What else would that mean?!" said Jeremiah.

"Al, you did not tell us he said it's over," said Bruno. "That is very different than what you said."

"You wiped out the whole cult?" asked Delilah. She slid her papers off the table and leaned closer to Jeremiah, utter confusion and doubt clouding her face.

"Not quite," said Jeremiah. "I wasn't able to find Lyle. It's possible I missed him dying in the attack, but I doubt it. No doubt there are cultists who weren't down there at the time, and some who escaped. But I took care of the entire reason the cult existed."

He told them about the adamantine enchantment diagram, doing his best to describe the effect the Abyss had on him. Delilah and Allison looked confused, but Bruno was nodding along.

"That explains it, then, the rising fever," said Bruno. "Good to know it was just a transdimensional demon gateway and nothing too serious."

"Lyle said there are others, too," said Jeremiah. "He didn't say where. I have his notebook, but it's in code—we might be able to decipher it. I don't think they're in Elminia though. That's just a gut feeling, but our best bet for learning more would be to track him down. He was gone by the time I got back there with the hundred-handed giant."

Delilah closed her eyes and massaged her temples. "And what in all the hells is a hundred-handed giant?"

Jeremiah found the final part of the story the easiest to recount. He told them matter-of-factly about Gurg and the prisoners, about killing the butcher and creating the abomination. His friends' expressions ranged from glee to horror as he described the destruction he wrought through the city. Only when he reached the part about finding the boy did he falter.

"They were . . . he was . . . they never stood a chance," he said. A fresh wave of emotion threatened to overwhelm him until Allison put a hand on his arm.

"It wasn't your fault," she said. "Not really."

"Yes, it was," said Jeremiah emphatically. "It was a consequence of my choice, my mistake." He sighed. "I still think taking out the cult was the right thing to do, but his death—all their deaths were my responsibility. I need to be able to accept that."

His friends exchanged worried glances. "And you're okay with that?" asked Allison. "I kind of thought you might take it a bit harder."

Jeremiah nodded. "It's like you said—I had to make a choice. I could have come back, reported what I'd found, and maybe, eventually, the empress would have done something. But Lyle said they had people at the highest levels. I think it was well within the realm of possibility that any attack would be stopped, or at least stalled until it was too late."

"Definitely," said Delilah. "This cult was a lot bigger than we thought, and conventional methods had already failed. It's why Empress Aubrianna decided on a black operation in the first place."

"You made a choice," said Bruno. "You chose to act. With everything you had."

"I had to," said Jeremiah. "What chance did they have without me?"

"Jay, I want to ask again," said Delilah. "Are you okay?" She scootched her chair a bit closer to Jeremiah.

"Yeah," said Jeremiah. "I'm okay. Not great, but I'm okay. It's just the way of things."

"You don't have to be okay," said Delilah softly. She put a hand on his shoulder, and Jeremiah felt his throat constrict.

"Really, I'm okay," he said.

Delilah stood up and wrapped her arms around his head, pulling him against her chest. "You don't have to be okay," she whispered.

It hit all at once. The guilt, the fear, the sadness, the regret, the disgust at what he'd seen. Jeremiah exploded into sobs against her, full body shaking sobs. He clutched her as tight as he could. He heard her hiss through her teeth as he clutched too hard, but she squeezed back harder to tell him it was all right. The whole time she continued to whisper, but Jeremiah couldn't hear her.

Jeremiah felt Allison wrap her arms around him from the opposite side.

He felt Bruno put a firm hand on his shoulder.

"H-he didn't even have a chance to be a kid," Jeremiah sobbed. "He was just a kid, and I killed him. I killed a kid. I killed a kid. I killed a little boy!"

"Shhh, you're okay. You're okay," whispered Delilah.

Jeremiah couldn't stop. "I've killed so many people! I've killed so many people!" he sobbed uncontrollably and lost himself in his grief. He cried shamelessly until his lungs ached and his nose ran. Until there was nothing left in him.

"I don't regret it," he said, finally pulling away from Delilah. Bruno and Allison moved away as well. "I don't regret what I did. I would do it again. I just . . . I just wish I didn't have to." He looked at the covered body again. "I'm sorry kid, I'm really sorry."

"You don't have—er, what I mean is, you did the right. Uh . . ." Bruno started to say, but it fell apart. Delilah nodded toward the door. "Yeah, I need to get ahead of this," said Bruno.

"Ahead of what?" asked Jeremiah.

"Monty's dead, and you were seen with him last. I don't want anyone gunning for you." Bruno tried to grab his bag with his missing hand, then switched and slung it over his shoulder. "Good work, Jay."

Delilah reached out and touched Jeremiah on the shoulder, her face troubled. Then she left, leaving only Allison and Jeremiah.

Jeremiah let out his breath. It was all out in the open now, and his friends didn't hate him, not even Delilah. Probably.

"Just one more order of business, then," said Allison, gesturing toward the boy's body. "Come on, I know a place."

Despite the fatigue still residing in his body, Jeremiah insisted on carrying the boy to his final resting place. Allison walked beside him in her guard's regalia, spade in hand, and nobody spared them a second glance.

They walked beyond Elminia proper, past the factories that thronged her, until they reached unclaimed wild fields. Jeremiah chose the crest of a small hill, where a light breeze played through the tall grass, and began to dig.

A proper grave was backbreaking work, Jeremiah soon discovered. He finally accepted Allison's help, if only to finish before dark. As she took over, he sought out a suitable headstone.

The rock he chose was large and flat. Using his enchanter's tools, he etched an epitaph into the stone.

"That should do it," said Allison. She panted from the exertion of digging but hoisted herself smoothly out of the grave.

The boy looked extra small to Jeremiah's eye, lying in his final resting place, wrapped tightly in the white sheets. Like burying a single grain of rice. He put the stone at the head of the grave.

"'Remembered,'" read Allison. "Fitting."

Jeremiah nodded. He couldn't take his eyes off the tiny form at the bottom of the grave.

"Are you okay?" Allison asked.

"No," said Jeremiah. "And that's all right."

Then he picked up the shovel to finish burying the boy, knowing he'd carry the sorrow for the rest of his life. He was glad for it.

CHAPTER FIFTY-SEVEN

Meetings

Another meeting? Is this going to happen every time?" asked Jeremiah.

Delilah had just returned home from filing their report with Spymaster Ka. "Of course," she said. "After serious events, there will always be meetings to discuss them. They're very important, and I don't understand why you guys don't like them. Is it a human thing? Like, meetings take up a significant portion of your total life expectancy?"

"Shit, that might be it," said Bruno. He was seated at the table, truncated arm extended as Allison fitted a new prosthetic over it.

"I don't like it because I don't trust it," said Allison. She pulled a buckle tight around Bruno's bicep and tucked the leather end. "We're either getting a pat on the head or tied off."

"Tied off?" asked Jeremiah.

"Sometimes a black op needs to be fully darked," said Allison. "That means leaving no one with any knowledge of what really happened, no loose threads. How's that feel, Bruno?"

"Weird," said Bruno, flexing his arm. The prosthetic was an L-shaped hook sporting a hinge and spring.

"Don't be ridiculous, Al," said Delilah. "They have no reason to kill us off."

"No reason you know of," Allison retorted. "Who knows how far the influence of this cult reached? Some very important people might be very angry. If the empress herself enters the room, we can relax. But until she does, we're going with full combat readiness, or we're not going at all. Hence the hardware. Give it a try?"

She handed Bruno his magic bow, and he used the hook to draw the string back toward his chin. The hook popped open with a *clack,* releasing the bow string, but too early in the pull.

"Sit down, let me calibrate that spring," said Allison. "Let's get it to a tension you're comfortable with."

"An archer . . ." said Bruno. "All those years of dagger throwing, lock picking, pick pocketing, trap disarming—and now I'm just an archer. *Twang.*" He somehow made the sound of firing a bow sarcastically.

"Don't worry, you'll adapt," said Allison. "I've known some great warriors with a limb difference. And there's more specialized equipment than just an archer's hook too. Maybe someday you'll have a whole arsenal, just like me! But for now, let's just focus on getting you ready for this meeting. Try that?"

Bruno drew the bowstring again. This time he managed a full draw and held it. It released with its typical musical hum. "It's gonna take some getting used to, that little extra pull when I want to shoot. But at least I'll be able to help if shit goes sideways. You sure I can't have it regrown or something? Like, with magic?"

"That magic does exist," said Jeremiah, "or at least it has in the past. But magic that powerful is . . . well, the stuff of legends."

"Archers are invaluable," said Allison. "That's why they always get the best prosthetics. Delilah can help you with caring for any heat rash or blisters."

Bruno frowned at the hook, Jeremiah could see him trying to flex his fingers, but the hook remained still."

Jeremiah had never felt comfortable in the trappings of luxury at the best of times, but after the last few months, it just seemed disgusting. The meeting room was large and ornate, with tapestries on each wall depicting great moments of history that Jeremiah lacked the context to understand. His friends were seated at a large round table, scattered among the cabinet members and prominent businesspeople.

Most of the two dozen seats were filled, with the attendees chatting among themselves as they waited for the meeting to begin. Delilah spoke with anyone who could hear her, while Bruno and Allison remained silent and tense. Jeremiah had thought having other people at the meeting was a sign of safety, but Bruno and Allison weren't convinced. They didn't give an explanation.

Seated across and conspiring with a dwarven woman was Pete, vibrant in a stylish new suit. What had he said? *"Ol' Pete has a chance to step up in the world, and he is obliged to take it."*

How many people died just for you to have a seat at this table? thought Jeremiah darkly. He was, in some way, responsible for Pete being here. The Tragedy was, in some way, a part of Pete being here. What had Pete promised, and to whom, that was worth up-jumping a street-level favor dealer into an attendee at the empress's table? Pete had only given Jeremiah notice with a wink when he arrived and otherwise pretended not to know him.

Where to now, Pete? thought Jeremiah. *Is this the top? Or just another rung on the ladder?*

He continued to glare as teas and wines were distributed among the guests from discreet servants, accepting a coffee for himself. One way or another, he suspected he'd need the energy boost.

A footwoman stepped into the room, interrupting Jeremiah's rumination. "Presenting her eminence, Empress Aubrianna of Elminia."

Allison released a breath she had been holding.

Everyone in the room stood and straightened to attention as, like the sun cresting the horizon, Empress Aubrianna swept into the room. In her wake were two columns of the golden armored royal guard that took up positions around the perimeter of the room.

Jeremiah swallowed. He had been through a lot, but the empress remained an oppressively attractive person. She took one of the remaining chairs. Ka followed her like a shadow, eyes darting about as they entered.

"Good evening," In this room, Empress Aubrianna's voice was appropriately booming. "I thank you all for making the time to attend this meeting on such short notice. We have learned information that has a bearing on every sector of Elminia. Spymaster Ka?"

Ka launched into a sanitized report of Jeremiah's findings, never citing Jeremiah as the source, referring to the cult as a "fortunate discovery by a group of intrepid adventurers." There were gasps, and grumbles of concern, and as soon as she finished came the questions of causality, fault, logistics, and spin.

Jeremiah receded into his thoughts as the discussion of countless horrors turned to political jockeying. *All of these important people, and they still bicker like children. Why does Pete even want to be a part of this? He can schmooze, sure, but he's got nothing to actually offer them. He's just building a network or something.* Jeremiah sipped his coffee, not quite as good as Madella's. *Just a big ol network of people, the most important people. La dee da. Doing their most important things and saying their most important thoughts . . .*

Important people.

The most important people.

Jeremiah glanced around the room with new attention. This meeting was attended by the most high-ranking citizens of Elminia, a congregation of influence, power, and wealth.

"We have members here from the highest ranks of government to the lowest serial killers," Lyle had said. "Nothing happens without our knowledge and without our consent."

You're here, aren't you? thought Jeremiah. *You'd have to be. Where else, if not at the beating heart of it all? Making sure every little thing goes just as it should.*

He had to be sure.

Jeremiah's gaze slid across the faces in attendance, crawling over their features, searching for something, anything, that might indicate which of these smarmy aristocrats was actually a sadistic cult leader.

Lyle was younger, remembered Jeremiah, mentally eliminating some of the truly venerable members.

He was male—Jeremiah eliminated the women.

Human, elven, or half-elven eliminated the smaller races.

Shaven, with a strong chin, no scars. That eliminated only a couple.

Half a dozen men fitting the description remained. How could he identify if Lyle was among them?

Jeremiah began to stir his coffee, letting his spoon scratch the edge of the cup. *Screeeeeech* went the teacup, that distinct ceramic on ceramic grind. The harsh sound was light but audible even through the argument ramping up at the table.

One of them, a middle-aged man, some sort of merchant or industrialist, gave the slightest flinch at the sound.

Screeeech.

"Jay, what are you doing? Stop that," hissed Delilah.

Jeremiah kept his eyes on the merchant and pressed the spoon into the side of the cup hard. *Scr-scr-scr.* The spoon moved just slightly, grinding into the cup. The merchant twitched with each noise, even as he tried to focus on the discussion among his fellows.

Jeremiah tightened his grip on the cup. He turned the spoon, just slightly, to catch the edge.

SCREECH.

The merchant shuddered and nearly gagged, his nails biting into the table surface before balling into fists as he recomposed himself.

Got you, thought Jeremiah.

Jeremiah looked up and found Ka staring directly at him, eyes hard as steel, trying to pierce deep into his mind.

Jeremiah stared back and gave the slightest nod.

Ka calmly took hold of a tiny metal stud on her armor. She pulled the stud away easily and pressed it against the unsuspecting empress's neck. There was a blue flash, a rush of air, and the empress was gone.

Every guard in the room slammed the butts of their spears to the ground and leveled the blades at the table attendees. Allison leapt to her feet and drew her sword and shield in a single fluid motion.

The room was silent as the grave, the guests stunned into terrified silence.

Ka stood, and all eyes fell upon her. "Mr. Thorn. You have the order."

Jeremiah stood and pointed at the merchant. The moment he did, guards swarmed the other attendees, grabbing them from their chairs and evacuating them out of the room. In a moment, the merchant was alone and terrified, raising his hands to ward off the spears leveled at him.

"What is going on here?" the merchant shouted. "I demand an explanation!"

"Hi, Lyle," said Jeremiah, standing.

The merchant stared at him in confusion. "Listen here, you ignorant thug, I am Phillipe DeMarquoix, honorable citizen of Elminia and owner of the PDM Shipping corporation. You will address me with the respect I am due, as a special consultant to the empress!"

"Jay, you sure about this?" Allison asked.

"Not yet," said Jeremiah, making his way around the table. There were plenty of people in the world who didn't like that sound. But after all the others were eliminated, in the beating heart of the empire, for there to be just one who shared that reaction . . . it was just too perfect to be a coincidence.

Bruno stood as Jeremiah passed. "What's the game?" he whispered.

"Desperation," Jeremiah whispered back.

Jeremiah marched up to Phillipe and spun the man's chair around, to stand over him. "This is the leader of the demonic cult."

"Preposterous!" laughed Phillipe. "Surely you're joking?"

"No, it's you," said Jeremiah. "I recognize your voice." That would be easy enough to disguise, of course, but he didn't need to be accurate. This wasn't a court of law. All he needed was fear.

"Oh yeah, that's definitely him," said Bruno from behind Jeremiah. "I seen him before."

"Bag," Jeremiah said to Delilah, and she tossed the Giant's Bag to him. Jeremiah pulled out Lyle's journal and its encrypted writings. "We have evidence that this journal from the leader's quarters matches your handwriting." Another lie, but he saw panic flicker in the merchant's eyes.

"I demand to see my counselor!" Phillipe shouted. He tried to stand, but Jeremiah grabbed his shoulder and forcibly sat him back down.

"I think traitors to the city don't get to see their counselors," said Jeremiah. "Counselor Fortune, cover your ears, please."

Delilah put her hands over her ears and turned around. Phillipe paled, a sweat breaking on his brow. The act of a counselor, someone beholden to truth, averting their senses evoked real terror. "This is completely illegal," he whimpered. "I am entitled to legal representation."

"Normally, yes," said Jeremiah. "But capturing the head of the cult would be a real boon and would make the empress very happy. Live would be best, of course, but unfortunately, you tried to kill me and escape justice once your secret was discovered."

Jeremiah grabbed Phillipe by the wrist and forced a special dagger into his hand—the long needle-shaped dagger that Nascent had given to him. "And this weapon will undoubtedly match the wounds found on previous victims of the cult's violence." He wrapped his own hand over Phillipe's, forcing him to grip the dagger.

"That's insane! This is a conspiracy!" Phillipe was openly panicking now. He looked at the remaining two guards who stared back stoically, spears leveled toward him.

"Look, he had another one of those books on him!" said Bruno, pulling a book seemingly from Phillipe's robes. Jeremiah didn't know when Bruno had snuck one from the bag, but it was a very impressive bit of sleight of hand.

"That's not mine!" yelled Phillipe. He recoiled from the book in shock.

Jeremiah pulled Phillipe's close, pressing the tip of the needle dagger into his own shoulder. He gritted his teeth at the pain as the blade dug into his flesh, splattering blood onto Phillipe's face. "Most importantly," Jeremiah growled. "I *want* this."

Phillipe's expression of panic shattered into one of manic rage. Instead of resisting Jeremiah's grip on his hand, he leaned into it, driving the dagger deeper into Jeremiah's shoulder, before springing backward onto the table.

"You don't even understand what you've done," sneered Phillipe—Lyle. He crouched low on the table and exhaled. A deep purple smoke emanated from his lungs, soon enveloping him in a billowing opaque cloud.

"Form up!" shouted Allison, and the guards scrambled together into a defensive position. She grabbed Jeremiah and yanked him backward, away from the growing cloud.

Ka caught Bruno's eye, nodded once, and then disappeared in the same blue flash as the empress. Lyle laughed from within the smoke as Jeremiah and his friends joined the assembled guards, weapons drawn, and braced themselves.

CHAPTER FIFTY-EIGHT

Meeting Adjourned

The smoke cloud continued to billow outward to envelop the room, momentarily blocking out the lights but causing no harm to the assembled combatants. The smoke was so thick, it obscured Bruno and Delilah, although they stood less than an arm's length away from Jeremiah.

He heard Lyle incanting in a low voice, then a ripple went through the smoke, and he felt a pulse of familiar *wrongness*. "He summoned something!" he shouted.

A rush of wind pushed the heavy smoke backward. Delilah was holding the end of a hose emitting a constant powerful airstream, the other end of which snaked back inside the Giant's Bag. The heavy cloud resisted the wind, but gradually Delilah cleared the space around them, pushing the smoke back against the walls, where it smeared and stained the fabric of the tapestries like it was more floating oil than smoke born from flame.

The wind also revealed a trio of demons, and Lyle nowhere in sight.

The first demon scuttled up the wall the moment the smoke cleared. It had the shape of a huge spider, but its limbs were made of barbed chains. The chains bulged and writhed, dribbling blood from between the twisting links. Over the grinding of metal, Jeremiah heard muffled screams from within it.

The spider demon reached the corner of the ceiling and screeched, then launched a single chain link, red with heat, at the assembled group. The link landed at Allison's feet and exploded against her armor, sending her stumbling backward and the others diving for cover.

The next demon had not moved from where it stood at the center of the room. The ram-headed beast with its violet flame surveyed the group, raising its open hands in a welcoming gesture, but Jeremiah didn't have time to contemplate its desires, because at that moment, the third demon sprang into action.

With an ear-splitting roar, the demon, which had the form of an immense ape as large as a troll, crossed the room in a single bound. Its head was grotesquely oversized and misshapen, with a distended lower jaw that wobbled and swung as it charged. With one swipe of a massive paw, it sent the guards flying.

"A Gorgugon demon," said Flusoh's voice in Jeremiah's mind. "Big brute, quite straightforward."

Delilah raised her longspear and charged the ape, gouging the spear head deep into its thigh. It swatted her aside with the back of its hand. She grunted from the impact but rolled across the floor with an agile turn.

"Regroup on me!" cried Allison. More royal guards were pouring into the room. She dodged another explosion from the spider demon and hurled herself toward the ape's legs.

There was no response from the guards to Allison's order, no sound of acknowledgment nor stomping of armored feet. Jeremiah poked his head around the toppled chair he crouched behind, and spotted them, surrounding and attacking the ram demon, who continued to stand, statuesque, in the center of the room. Their non-magical weapons seemed unable to break the demon's hide.

"A Baphocyst, neat!" said Flusoh. "A mesmerizer, have fun with that one."

As Jeremiah watched, one guard fell to his knees. "Glory! Glory to the true horned god! My blood for you, my bones for you!" Tears of rapturous joy streamed down his face.

"Elwin, what the hell are you doing?" said another guard. "Get up!"

"He's gone mad!" said another. "He thinks he's worthy of the horned one's gaze! The arrogance! None are worthy lest he deem it!"

"I'll not have one of my men turning traitor against the empress!" the head guard turned his spear on the supplicant, skewering him through the neck.

"Oh, come on!" Allison shouted in frustration at the guards.

The mote of flame pulsed brighter. Jeremiah glanced at it, and in an instant, everything made sense.

There was only one being worthy of power in the universe: Baphomet. It was just true. A simple and beautiful truth, something you could be sure about, truly sure about. How could you not strive to be held in Baphomet's regard? It made no sense to do anything else.

Gus kicked hard in his robes. The little bastion of himself that was Gus flushed the magical control from his mind.

"Don't look at the flame!" Jeremiah shouted.

At that moment, Jeremiah's chair exploded. In his rapture, he'd forgotten the spider demon. His arms were lacerated by burning splinters, but at least the ram's mesmerism over him seemed to be broken.

The guards' squabbling began to turn violent. They raised sword and spear against another, the ram forgotten, barely even slowed by another explosion in their midst.

Bruno loosed an arrow at the spider. "Jay, we have to stop that chain thing! It's ruining the rightful worship of the He Who Dwells!" The spider hissed, its rasping voice mingled with distant screams and began firing projectiles toward Bruno instead, forcing him to run for cover.

"I said don't look at the flame!" Jeremiah yelled at Bruno's cover. "It's hypnotic!"

"Well, you said not to, so I did. Happy?!" came Bruno's voice from somewhere in the room. "Why were you trying to keep me from the greatest knowledge that's ever been?!"

Allison's roar of anger drew Jeremiah's attention. The ape gripped her around the torso and held her aloft even as it roared in annoyance at Delilah's darting spear jabs.

"Let me go!" Allison punctuated her words with axe gouges into the ape's fingers. She wrenched the axe and one of the ape's fingers was severed. The ape roared with fury, and shook her, whipping her back and forth through the air. When the shaking stopped, Allison hung limp in its fist.

"Allison!" cried Jeremiah. He cast an acid ball and launched it at the ape. It sizzled and burned away layers of fur and skin, sending globs of acid down toward Delilah who was trying to pierce its knee.

In one smooth motion, the ape hurled Allison at Jeremiah and seized Delilah. Allison's armored form collided with Jeremiah like a ballista bolt, knocking them both backward.

"Al, wake up!" he gasped, trying to wriggle free. "Al you're so much heavier than you look, get off!"

Allison didn't respond.

Jeremiah finally worked a hand free and flipped her visor up. "Allison!"

With a start, Allison came to. Her eyes focused on Jeremiah, and she rolled to the side. "Sit rep!"

Blessed air rushed back into Jeremiah's lungs. Some of his ribs were bruised, but he couldn't worry about that now. "Help Delilah!"

Allison spotted the ape hooting and waving Delilah around like a rag doll and rushed to help. Jeremiah clambered to his feet, clutching his side, and spotted Bruno, now loosing arrow after arrow at the remaining guards, still trying to murder each other amid the explosions.

"Bruno! What are you doing?" cried Jeremiah, reaching to lower his bow.

"They are unworthy, they are all unworthy of His promise." The magic bowstring sang as the mechanism of Bruno's prosthetic released again and again. "Hey, this thing's great!" he said to Jeremiah with a smile, enjoying the prosthetic. Another guard fell, a fountain of blood erupting around Bruno's arrow lodged in his throat.

"Stop!" Jeremiah swiped at the bow, but Bruno twirled out of reach. "You're mesmerized, snap out of it!" *Oh, please let that be enough*, he thought. Bruno on the wrong side of this fight was almost as bad as it could get.

The last guard fell to Bruno's arrow, falling atop the pile of at least a dozen dead elves with an arrow through the eye. With a roar of triumph, Bruno turned toward Jeremiah, who immediately abandoned his attempts and leapt for cover. Bruno's bow sang and an arrow grazed the back of Jeremiah's calf.

"Don't worry Jay, there's a place for you with Him! I just gotta send you there, I'll grab Al and Delilah next. We can vouch for them."

"Delilah, lay down some smoke!" Jeremiah called.

Delilah had at some point been discarded by the enraged ape. She lay stunned one leg crumpled beneath her, as the ape grabbed with both hands at the frantically evading Allison. At Jeremiah's word, she nodded weakly and pulled a flask from the Giant's Bag.

An explosion rocked her as she'd cocked her arm to throw, sending her and the flask tumbling and releasing the cloud of gray smokescreen around her. The ape finally caught Allison again and stuffed her into its hanging mouth. The dangling lower jaw suddenly snapped upward like a sprung trap, the teeth sparking and denting the magic armor.

"Bruno! Try to—" Jeremiah screamed on reflex, only to duck his head back down as an arrow sailed through the space his head had occupied. "Oh, right," He stretched his senses toward one of the fallen guards.

Rise.

Three of the guards littering the floor surrounding the ram climbed to their feet and charged toward Bruno. As Bruno pivoted to evade them, Jeremiah dashed out of cover and made for Delilah's smoke cloud.

The cloud was so thick, Jeremiah was instantly blinded. Thankfully, Delilah caught his arm before he could collide with her. "Bruno or Allison?" she asked.

The cloud was so thick, Jeremiah couldn't see her face, but he was nonetheless grateful for her presence. "Allison," he said. "We need her to take down the goat thing."

"Baphocyst," Flusoh reminded him.

"Okay," said Delilah. "I can get her free, but I need you to cover me."

At once, Jeremiah raised the rest of the fallen guards and ordered them to attack the ape. Delilah didn't say a word, but Jeremiah felt her move away. Mere moments later, he became aware of his zombies being torn asunder. He hoped Delilah had had the time to do whatever she was going to do.

Another explosion went off far too close, and Jeremiah's smoke cloud was dispersed. His ears ringing, he barely heard the twang of Bruno's bow just before an arrow buried deep into his shoulder. "Arghhh!"

"Accept the Lord of the Deep or perish." Bruno loosed another arrow as Jeremiah flung himself to the side, deliberately choosing to fall on his injured shoulder. He grunted with both pain and satisfaction as Bruno's arrow went wide, anticipating a dodge in the other direction. "Look I appreciate the gamesmanship Jay, but I need to be the one that kills you or it doesn't count as a sacrifice!"

There was a roar of rage behind him, and Jeremiah whirled to see Allison drop to the ground, her armor sporting new dents from its time in the ape's jaws but otherwise unharmed. Delilah's longspear jutting from the ape's cheek and a riot of smoke and sparks erupting inside its mouth.

"I'll slow down Bruno," Delilah said, reaching into the Giant's Bag. "You guys take down that goat!"

"Don't look at the flames," huffed Jeremiah as he and Allison sprinted toward the ram centaur. Allison nodded once and turned her head to the side, regarding their target with her peripheral vision.

"Your blood is fit to sate His—oh god no not again!" Bruno broke off with a yelp as a pouch smashed against his armor, releasing a whimsical poof of pink dust. He began scratching at himself, dropping his bow to frantically claw at the gaps in his armor in a mad jig.

"Yeah, you remember the itching powder, don't you?!" Delilah shouted to him.

"Renounce what's-his-name and you get the antidote!" she held up another sachet with a tantalizing bob, blue dust flurrying out beneath it.

With a battle cry, Allison leapt the final few yards to the ram and slashed her axe across its flank, body checking its bulk to stay beneath the sight of its mesmerizing flame.

The ram did not react, except to turn its head slowly toward Allison. No blood sprung from the wound. The blow was accompanied by an odd tearing sound, like a stack of paper being ripped in half.

Jeremiah reached the ram and began hacking at it with his magic dagger. Whereas the mundane weapons of the guards had failed to penetrate its hide, the magically enhanced weapon sliced through easily. He slashed at it again and again, watching as the violet skin parted to reveal a strange papery flesh that tore and crumbled away from his knife.

"Jay, look out!" yelled Allison.

With a shout, Jeremiah fell backward from a dark, angry cloud that spewed forth from the ram's wounds. With a menacing buzz, the cloud streamed into the air, pulsing and undulating, before diving back down toward him.

It enveloped him, and suddenly he was within a hurricane of buzzing, angry wasps. Their tiny heads were those of people, all moaning and wailing as they stung with long razor stingers. Jeremiah was being covered in searing red welts as the cloud swirled around him.

"Oh, lookit that!" said Flusoh. "The Baphocyst was a hellwasp nest this whole time! Very interesting species. Invasive to the Abyss, actually. Quite the ecological problem down there."

With the concentration born only through Flusoh's brutal pain training, Jeremiah shoved the incredible pain aside and focused. He spoke the words, exhaled his own cloud, a sickly poisonous gas that soon enveloped the swarm surrounding him. He held his breath as the stings slowed so as not to breathe in his own poison.

The insects were falling all around him, but it wasn't fast enough. Jeremiah swayed on his feet. Only then did he notice the welts all over his body were tinged with green, creeping poison making its way into his veins.

The angry cloud around him was gone now, but its damage had been done. Jeremiah watched the scene before him as though in slow motion—Allison tearing through the body of the ram, which seemed to crumble as more and more wasps swarmed out of it.

Bruno, with a fresh coat of blue powder, picked his bow back up and was exchanging volleys with the spider demon, leaping constantly from point to point to evade the explosions. "Apologies all around!" he shouted.

More gas . . . Need to make more gas. Still too many wasps, Jeremiah thought as he watched the rest of the hellwasps coalesce into a new swarm and dive toward Allison. He muttered the magic words as hellwasp poison gathered darkness in his eyes and prepared to cast.

Another sting on the back of his neck, and Jeremiah nearly breathed poison gas directly into Delilah's face. She retracted the needle and said something to him, but all he could hear was his own pulse as whatever she had injected him with fought off the poison and set his heart beating in double time.

She grew clearer, and the graying world rushed with color. Jeremiah gasped as all the noise he'd missed slammed into his eardrums at once and his heart raced.

"No time to explain," Delilah was saying. "Need you to take care of—ah!"

She was yanked off her feet mid-sentence, back in the grasp of the enraged ape. The spear was gone from its cheek, leaving a purple bloody mess behind. Delilah screamed as the ape tilted back its head and raised her over his mouth.

"Shit, shit, shit!" Allison charged the ape, hellwasp swarm following right behind her. It didn't seem concerned about Allison's axe biting into its legs, but when the swarm began to sting his flesh as well, it yowled and squealed in pain, turning away from the half-elven morsel and swatting at the source of its agony.

A nearby explosion interrupted Jeremiah's calculations, and Bruno dashed past, twisting to avoid another projectile. "Can you give me a hand with this damn chain-spider thing?!" he asked. "All my arrows do is annoy it!"

Jeremiah opened his mouth to try and cast an acid ball, when he heard Flusoh's voice again.

"It's a Chain Sepulchre. Technically not a demon, but only demons know how to make one. Buncha souls crammed in there. Look for a blood red chain link—it's the one that never moves. Break that and the whole thing falls apart."

Jeremiah relayed the information to Bruno.

"How the hell do you know that?!" Bruno yelled back, scurrying between the Chain Sepulchre's legs and using its own body for cover.

Wait, how do I know that? thought Jeremiah. *How do I know any of this?*

He knew some things about demons. But names? Weaknesses? He'd never studied them that much in detail.

F-Flusoh? thought Jeremiah.

"What?" answered Flusoh.

Flusoh, are you talking to me right now?! thought Jeremiah.

"Obviously?" said Flusoh.

Since when?! How long have you been doing that? Can you read my thoughts?

"How is this surprising? You can hear me, can't you? I've been helping you for weeks."

Well, yeah, I mean, sort of. It just feels like thoughts I'm thinking.

"What did you think telepathy sounded like? You weren't going to hear me with your ears. What sense would that make?"

But I didn't—

"Focus!"

Jeremiah ducked another explosion. The ape seemed to have decided the hell-wasps were Allison's fault, and had seized her again, roaring as the stings peppered his hands and face, swinging both her and Delilah through the swarm like fly swatters.

"Goddammit stop picking me up!" Allison laid into the ape, switching to her sword and sliding the blade up into its wrist, popping tendons with a meaty *twang*. Enough of the ape's fingers went limp that it dropped her but immediately started grasping for her again.

Struck by sudden inspiration, Jeremiah rushed toward them. He picked a tile just beyond the current melee, and rapidly inscribed *If Contact, Adhere* into its surface, and charged it. It was the fastest he had ever inscribed anything in his life, and it was perfect. *Thurok would actually be proud,* he thought in the moments between motions.

"Allison, stand here!" Jeremiah pointed to his diagram, then scrambled out of the way as his friend leapt toward it.

She stomped her foot into the tile and the magic surged. Delilah still in its other fist, the ape swiped to grab her again.

This time Allison didn't budge and began hacking at the ape's wrist. It barked in outrage, and pulled on her harder, straining to lift the warrior. Jeremiah feared Allison's leg would be pulled off, but fortunately the armor was taking the pressure.

The ape, in mounting rage, spiked Delilah into the ground. She bounced and went stiff as a board, hands curling up and eyes rolling back in her head. It seized Allison with both hands, ignoring even the attacks of the hellwasps, so fixated it was on failing to lift Allison. "Put your back into it!" she yelled.

Jeremiah ran to where Delilah had landed. Jeremiah jammed his hand in the Giant's Bag. *That thing she waves under people's noses when they're knocked out,* he thought. In his hand appeared that exact item: a small corked vial. He waved it under her nose, and she gasped, startling back to consciousness.

"It has a heart!" she gasped out. "I could feel its pulse, it has an axillary artery, the layout is similar to a human's, find my spear!"

It hurt his soul to leave her, but he did, turning to survey the room. All furniture had been reduced to splinters and debris, around which Bruno continued to leap and twist, arrow after arrow searching for the key link. Jeremiah shut out the distraction of Allison's tussle with the ape and the near constant explosions from the spider and focused.

There! The haft of the longspear was the only unbroken piece of wood in a pile of crushed chairs, its magical properties protecting it.

As Jeremiah hurried to retrieve the weapon, Bruno let out a whoop of triumph. "Gotcha, you leggy sonnuvabitch!" The tortured screams that had been backdrop to the battle rose to a trembling fever pitch, then the Chain Sepulchre exploded, flecks of metal ricocheting hard enough to shatter stone.

Absent the constant tattoo of explosions, the only sounds were Allison and the ape screaming at each other. "Bruno, help me with this," said Jeremiah, hefting the longspear.

The ape paid them no mind as they approached with the weapon but continued roaring in fury and yanking on Allison while she cut its arms to ribbons. Jeremiah thrust the spear as deep as he could into the ape's back, under the ribs and upward. Bruno gripped the haft behind him, and together they drove the spear into the demon. The demon's dense muscle resisted the killing blow until Delilah grabbed ahold as well.

"Push with your legs, haft close to the body, power from the ground," she instructed. They obeyed, Jeremiah trying to press his heels through the stone floor, and something in the ape's body gave. The spear slid deep.

With a final agonized roar, the ape shuddered and collapsed. Jeremiah quickly cast his poison breath to relieve Allison from the hellwasp swarm and broke the enchantment holding her in place. Delilah limped over to check her for injuries but froze when a hysterical laugh echoed around the chamber, making his blood run cold.

"My, my. Quite the show," came Lyle's voice. "I have to say, that was much more entertaining than the usual cabinet meeting." The space above the table began to distort and change color like the air itself were bleeding. Lyle stepped from the warped distortion, coalescing from the mix of colors.

"Face us, coward," growled Allison.

Jeremiah's entire body throbbed with pain, but the thought of taking down Lyle made all of that seem irrelevant.

"It's been a long time since I've encountered such a fun group," said Lyle thoughtfully. He broke into a crooked grin, one that was somehow too big for his face, and continued in a voice quite unlike his own. "You know what? I think I will."

CHAPTER FIFTY-NINE

Brawl

W hat else you got?" Allison shouted with limitless bravado.

Lyle spoke words of magic while forming quick precise hand gestures, and oily black tentacles oozed out from a hole in reality in front of him. They snaked around his body, coiling and wrapping him, then hardened and snapped, leaving Lyle in a form of black full plate armor.

"Jay! Give us some pointers here, how do we get to this guy?" said Delilah. Bruno was circling the table that Lyle stood upon, trying to find an opening for his arrows, but he wasn't able to penetrate the armor.

"He's powerful, but he's still just a mage. He needs to concentrate to cast spells," said Jeremiah. "Keep him off balance. Break his concentration."

Jeremiah was struck by a flurry of violet lights fired from Lyle's outstretched hand. It was like being struck by clubs over and over again.

"Bruno, keep his attention!" Allison yelled.

"He doesn't give a shit about me! I can't hurt him!" Bruno shouted back. As if to demonstrate, Bruno darted in and slashed with the one blade he could wield. Lyle took the blow on the armor, then the armor attacked back. A spine of metal split off and shot into Bruno's ribs, penetrating deep into his body like a splinter.

Bruno stumbled back, coughing and gasping for air.

Allison took the opportunity to shield charge Lyle, but an inky pool of shadow swept out from beneath Lyle's feet and snagged Allison's legs in a black tentacle. She slashed at it, slivers burning away but was thoroughly restrained.

"Bruno's got a punctured lung. Jay, get in there while I treat him," said Delilah.

She threw a smoke bomb down at Bruno's feet and disappeared into it.

"No," said Lyle. He gestured at the smoke screen and blew it away with a gust of wind. "I want to watch when it *wriggles.*"

Bruno suddenly spasmed in agony, mouth open in a wordless scream.

"And you, burn," said Lyle. He pointed at Delilah and a trio of bright beams of flame shot into her. The raking flames blackened the skin on one side of her face and ignited her hair. The clothing around her armor caught fire. Delilah screamed and spun away, swatting the flames on her clothes and scalp. Her normally unflappable nature burned away as she panicked from the pain.

"Yes, feel the skin bubble! Feel it pop!" Lyle was giddy with excitement.

"You son of a bitch!" Allison yelled, more black tentacles had wrapped around her arms and body.

"Pathetic," said Lyle. "Your turn, Jay. Would you like to throw acid? Breathe the poison gas? Go on, surprise me."

Jeremiah drew his dagger and tried to think of a strategy. If he could—

"Too late, banished," said Lyle. With a gesture and a word, Lyle seemed to fall away from Jeremiah. The entire room seemed to fall away, stretching out like seeing infinity through a keyhole, blackness surrounding the edge of everything.

And then Jeremiah was sitting in a chair. It was a brown leather chair, upholstered and comfortable. The remnant throbbing of the hellwasp stings had stopped, all pain and discomfort stopped. He wasn't breathing. He didn't need to. He was alone in an endless expanse of white all around him.

And then he wasn't alone.

"Hello, Jeremiah Thorn." A man appeared before Jeremiah. He was a human, wearing a solid black suit with a single heavy diamond at his collar. His hair was short, featherlight, and black as pitch. He was incredibly handsome, all hard, masculine angles, but with perfect supple skin and kind brown eyes.

"What—what happened? Where am I? Who are you?" Jeremiah shot up from the chair. Had he died? His hand went to his pocket, and he found Gus curled up defensively.

"You were banished," said the man matter-of-factly. "Sent away. Kicked to another dimension by a demonologist. Can you guess which dimension?" The man's voice was playful and raspy, he began pacing a lazy circle around Jeremiah.

"The Abyss? This is the Abyss?" said Jeremiah. Through some magic Jeremiah couldn't even conceive up, Lyle had sent him bodily to one of the domains of the afterlife. Though it was just a white space with a chair. He had been expecting . . . anything else.

"Ha! No, no. I caught you on your way down. This place isn't meant for mortal eyes," said the man. "I can give you a glimpse of the real deal if you don't believe me. It's just behind all this whiteness. You'll probably claw your own eyes out, but I've seen worse decisions."

"Send me back!" Jeremiah shouted at him. His friends were fighting Lyle right now, their lives at stake, and they were losing.

"Keep it together," said the man. "Time flows funny here. This is all taking place between heartbeats. I just wanna talk."

"Who are you?" asked Jeremiah. "Are you the Abyss? Are you the voice I spoke with before?" This didn't sound exactly like the presence he had encountered at the center of the cult's circle, but it wasn't exactly not either.

The man chuckled. "Call me B. And no, we haven't spoken before, not directly. Oh sure, the Abyss runs through me, just like it runs through everyone down here. From the lowliest imp to the double hyena headed nut job that runs everything, we're all cut from the same cloth."

Jeremiah's shock instantly gave way to irritation. "So interesting!" he said sarcastically. "The B obviously stands for Baphomet, one of the demon princes of the Abyss. You want something. Out with it."

B whistled. "Got a little pepper in you, huh? I like it! As for what the *B* stands for, I find a little mystery—"

"Lyle summoned a Baphocyst," Jeremiah interrupted.

Baphomet nodded. "Yup, that's one of mine, got me there. Spoil sport. Clever boy though, I'll give you that. As for what I want? You got it backward, I want to know what *you* want."

"Pass," said Jeremiah. *Can I kill him? Probably not, right?* thought Jeremiah.

Baphomet laughed and waved him to sit. "Relax, Jeremiah! So jumpy. I'm not here to screw you over or trick you or whatever else you're thinking. I'm trying to give you a gift."

"In exchange for my soul or deals or favors or something," said Jeremiah, trying to speed things along.

"Wrong!" shouted Baphomet triumphantly, thrusting a finger at Jeremiah. "In exchange for nothing. You ask, I give. Free of charge. No strings. No promises."

Jeremiah was taken aback by Baphomet's offer. "I don't want any of your crooked deals or cursed wishes or whatever you're planning. You're a demon. I have no reason to even consider this," said Jeremiah.

Baphomet threw his hands up. "Bah! That's all devil talk. Contracts and souls and twisted wishes. Those guys give us all a bad name. Jay, I can give you more power than you'll know what to do with, and I don't ask for anything. I just want you to have it."

"Why?" asked Jeremiah pointedly.

"Why? Why?! Because you *get* it, Jay! Because you really get it. You understand. This guy here . . ." Baphomet waved his arm, and an image appeared before Jeremiah, floating and insubstantial. It was a moment, frozen in time, of Jeremiah riding his hundred-handed giant. "This guy here? He gets it," said Baphomet. He leaned in and kissed the image of Jeremiah.

"I am free! I am everything you've ever wanted!" shouted the Jeremiah in the image. Jeremiah didn't even remember saying those words.

"Oh, as sweet as sweet music," said Baphomet with a shiver.

Get what? thought Jeremiah. He looked at himself in the image. He couldn't remember the emotion he felt then, not really. *A demon prince valued me in that moment. That can't be good.*

"So, if I ask you to give me the power to kill Lyle and save my friends?" asked Jeremiah. There was no reason to trust this demon, but his interest was piqued. If he was telling the truth. Which he certainly wasn't.

"I will give you that very thing," said Baphomet. "You just tell me how you want it. You want new spells? I can teach you spells that you've never dreamed of. Magic words that have never been heard by human ears. Words that haven't been heard since . . . well, for a very long time. I've got enchantment runes too. Runes that would make Thurok prance with glee. Runes that will change the very course of history. Would you like that, Jay? Would you like to change the course of history?"

"You know Thurok?" said Jeremiah. He didn't know why that's what stood out to him, it just felt so personal.

"Thurok and your mom and dad and friends, blah, blah, blah. A single mortal's story isn't exactly privileged information. But don't get hung up here, Jay, just tell me what you want."

"What exactly can you give me? Specifically?" asked Jeremiah. New magic and runes were an enticing offer, especially if it really was free. And saving his friends . . . that was worth any price.

"Anything. Everything," declared Baphomet with a broad grin. "Just say it. Say it out loud and it's yours. All I ask . . ."

Here it comes, thought Jeremiah.

"Is that you do whatever you want with it," finished Baphomet. His smile widened at Jeremiah's continued surprise and confusion. "Anything you want at all."

Jeremiah glared at Baphomet. "I'm going to use it to protect people," said Jeremiah. "I'd use it to help people. To give them a better life."

"Yes! Good!" said Baphomet.

"I'll fight evil with it. I'll find these other circles and destroy them, and the cults protecting them," said Jeremiah, louder and angrier that his defiance wasn't being rewarded.

"Absolutely! Blast the whole organization to pieces!" said Baphomet with mounting enthusiasm.

Jeremiah stared at Baphomet in confusion. How did this make any sense?

"Why?"

The smile dropped from Baphomet's face. He took a deep, centering breath and looked at Jeremiah with genuine pain. "Because the world needs to see it, Jay. The world needs to know and understand the strength of one man. That the power resides in each and every one of them. They only need to seize it."

"I . . . I'm sorry what? You're saying this is for the *good* of people?" This was not headed in the direction he was expecting.

"Yes! You realize Jay, that that flower pruning tight ass empress has more 'power' than you ever will? And you could kill her with your bare hands? And she rules over thousands, where's the justice in that? You've seen what happens when people control other people. What they do to each other . . ."

Another wave of the hand, and images of a thousand atrocities over a thousand generations committed by a thousand rulers flashed around Jeremiah, a dizzying number, a riot of grotesque images and sounds. All at once they stopped.

"I believe in you, Jay," said Baphomet, the grin returning. "I think you might believe in you too. I think you might have found the will to do what needs to be done. To make those decisions. You just need the strength to make them. And I'm willing to invest in *you*."

"To change the world . . ." said Jeremiah. He could save everyone. He could set everything right. Free the people from their cycle of poverty. Stop the waste of life from wars. Wipe out the demon cults. He could do it all, he might be the only person that could. He'd owe Baphomet nothing, he could stop whenever he wanted, he could dodge the pitfalls of power that had claimed so many others.

"That's right Jay. It's all for you, and only you. Lyle doesn't get this deal. Lyle doesn't understand, not really. Jay, I want to send you back in a blaze of glory. You'll blow Lyle to pieces, save your friends. Maybe even get the girl, eh?" Baphomet winked at him. "And you'll not worry a thing about lawyers and courts taking away what matters to you ever again."

"And if I say no?" asked Jeremiah.

"I'll be sad," said Baphomet with an exaggerated pout. "And that's all. I can't force it on you. Well, I can, but that's just a curse. No Jay, you have to want it. You have to choose it. Only you can do that."

Jeremiah could imagine saying yes. Jeremiah desperately wanted to say yes. And why not? He'd been subjected to all manners of unfairness, legal and otherwise. Great powers sought to ruin his life via paperwork and court orders. How is that fair of someone who can raise armies of the dead?

"I can see it," said Baphomet with a knowing smile. "It's hitting you. You're feeling it. The oppression of man starts with restraining the strong. It's time Jay, it's time to become ungovernable. It's time to become the paragon of the individual. Just ask . . ."

"No strings?" asked Jeremiah.

"Not a one," confirmed Baphomet. "Not even a handshake."

Jeremiah ran his hands through his hair and let out a growl of frustration. *This is stupid. This is the stupidest thing I've ever done. I* know *this is the wrong thing to do, but I have to do it,* he thought. "Gonna have to turn you down," said Jeremiah.

Baphomet nodded, seemingly not surprised. "Tell me why."

"'Cause I don't honestly think I know better than anyone else," said Jeremiah.

Baphomet nodded again. "You're sure? You're sure you want to turn down the power to shape the world as you like it, with no strings attached?"

"I'm sure," said Jeremiah. He had made countless mistakes, he never seemed to stop making them. Incredible power he hadn't earned was only going to result in mistakes he couldn't handle. He had only now learned to handle the death of a single child. What would more power do to him? Who would suffer from that shortcut? He didn't know, and that was the problem.

"Then this is one of those rare occasions where I've misjudged someone," said Baphomet, with a hardy shrug. "You'd just end up under someone's thumb all over again, and they'd be the ones controlling these gifts, gifts I'm only offering to you. Think of me, Jay, when Lyle is peeling off Delilah's periosteum and eating it, I want you to think of me. Just so you know you could have stopped it but chose not to."

Baphomet and the chair vanished in a flash of black fire. The whiteness of the room began to stain and deform with color and space. Gargled sounds like underwater screams began to fade into reality, and Jeremiah hit the ground of the palace's meeting room, skidding to a stop.

Bruno was spasming in agony, Delilah was screaming in pain and smoldering, and Allison was fighting a losing battles against black tentacles that were beginning to twist her limbs backward.

Lyle had not noticed Jeremiah's return. More palace guards were pouring into the room, and Lyle was obliterating them just as fast as they could enter, laughing at their hopelessness.

"Thought we lost you for a minute there, Jeremy," said Flusoh. "Are you ready to make some abominations?"

Abominations? With what? The dead palace guards—they were everywhere. His mind raced with potential, there was so much to work with.

"Wait for it, wait for it . . ." said Flusoh.

Jeremiah's eyes scanned over the bodies, mentally building a refined version of the hundred-handed giant, until his gaze settled on the demon corpses. *Oh!* thought Jeremiah.

"Yes. Yeeeeeeessss," said Flusoh gleefully.

Did it work the same for demons? Did they react to necromancy? Were there dangers? Jeremiah briefly pondered until he saw Delilah dumping a resiny liquid on her burned face and scalp, while jamming a needle into Bruno's neck. There was no time to worry.

He cast the spell of Flesh, and as fast as possible, began to work.

The Gorgugon made an excellent pallet, having so much bulk and musculature. Jeremiah slapped the clawed arms of the Baphocyst underneath the Gorgugon's. There were dead guards as well, and Jeremiah dragged their bodies one by one onto the creation. He cast the spell of Flesh and replaced the Gorgugon's fingers with human arms, sloughing them away from their previous owners, some still clutching spears.

"Foolish, foolish!" Said Lyle. He stretched out his hand and began pouring flames through the door into the column of guards that were arrayed in a tight phalanx. The flames rolled over and through their shields and they began to scream. "Yes, let me hear that sweet music," Lyle hissed. He turned his attention to Allison, still struggling against the black shadowy limbs. "Now, let's wrench that neck. Not too much, just enough." Slowly, Allison's head began to twist as the shadows wrenched at her. She gritted her teeth and tried to resist, but the turning was slow and steady. "That little crunch. Let's hear that soft little crunch, like leaves underfoot," said Lyle.

Not done yet, not enough time, need to distract him, thought Jeremiah. "You're just a cheap sadist!" Jeremiah yelled. "You don't care about freedom for anyone, you just want to hurt people and need an excuse to do it!"

Lyle whirled on Jeremiah, shocked, confused, and absolutely appalled at the words. The black limbs ceased twisting Allison's head. "Freedom is *all* that I care about! The freedom for all, to do anything they want!"

"You hid underground because you feared the bigger fish that could tell you no. You're the entitled child of entitled children, throwing a generations-long temper tantrum."

Just a few more connections . . .

"You were never worthy of freedom!" shouted Lyle. A new pulse of wrongness, stronger, sickening, one that rolled out from Lyle like a wave of heat. Jags of purple light coursed out from Lyle's fingertips and punctured the air like glass, scattering images of their surroundings through the air in a mad refraction.

Now or never.

Rise.

In Jeremiah's mind there appeared a malformed and oily blob. It twisted and wormed, grew and shrank, quivered and froze. It was sickening to his thoughts, but it was still his to control.

Kill.

The Gorgugon lurched up, demonic flesh charged with undead magic. Each finger was the muscular arm of a dead guard, and at the end of each was a hand holding a spear. It leapt toward Lyle in a single bound, slamming into him and interrupting whatever horrid spell he was planning on casting. The multitude of spears drove Lyle into the ground and slashed at him while the ape demon tried to crush him with both hands.

Lyle hit the ground with a grunt of pain, but the spears couldn't penetrate the strange demonic armor surrounding him. The abomination squeezed with all its might, but it couldn't crack Lyle's shell.

"Fruitless! A waste of a beautiful creature," declared Lyle. The armor began splintering off and growing like a black vine up inside of the abomination, new branches bursting through the skin and severing limbs as it grew. While powerful, and immune to pain, the abomination could not counter the mystic armor.

Jeremiah was in motion while Lyle was preoccupied. He reached Allison and slashed at the shadow tentacles with his dagger, freeing one of her arms. "I've got this, get Delilah," said Allison. With her sword arm free she was able to start pruning away the shadow. With Lyle distracted the tentacles were no longer actively engaging her.

Delilah was shivering uncontrollably and seemingly oblivious to what was happening around them.

"I—I can't move," she said. "In shock. Need stim—stim—stimulant c-compound four." Even as she spoke the burned flesh on her face split and wept blood.

"I'm here. Stay down," said Jeremiah. He reached into her Giant's Bag and grabbed what she needed, pressing the needle into her neck. He felt the oily blob in his mind quiver and begin to dissipate. He looked back in shock to see his new creation being split into pieces by the black vines of armor that had fully infested the abomination. Lyle laughed as they retracted and the ape demon fell over, destroyed.

That was all he had. If a giant monster made of demon and mortal flesh wasn't going to be enough, what chance did he have?

"Pathetic!" Declared Lyle, standing back up. He eyed Jeremiah administering aid to the shivering Delilah. "I will strip the periosteum from her bones and make you watch," he giggled in wicked glee. It was eerily reminiscent of the sounds Nascent had made, nearly childish, giddy.

The little laugh twisted something in Jeremiah, something angry and hateful. He lay Delilah back down gently, then turned his attention on Lyle, eyes burning with rage. "Step up you pompous little bitch," said Jeremiah. He charged.

Lyle opened his arms wide. "Yes, come to me. Rend yourself upon me."

Mid-stride, Jeremiah pulled his armored shirt up over his head and, with a flick, wrapped it around his fist. He raked one of his adamantine inscription tools at just the right spot on the enchantment written into the armor, and the flexible silken metal solidified. Lyle was still cackling when Jeremiah threw a steel-wrapped fist in a full haymaker punch into the side of his head.

Jeremiah had seen how impenetrable Lyle's was. He had also seen, on many occasions, Allison getting her brains scrambled by a vicious hit that knocked her skull around.

Lyle collapsed and covered his head with his arms, trying to ward off the blows. Jeremiah straddled him and rained punches down, bouncing Lyle's head off the floor or striking it left and right. Lyle kicked his feet helplessly, unable to dislodge his mounted attacker. Jeremiah felt spikes of armor detaching and inserting into his flesh. It hurt, but all it did was hurt.

"Come on! Get knocked out!" Jeremiah growled at Lyle. Lyle's defending arms started losing their strength as Jeremiah scrambled Lyle's brain like shaking an egg in a jar. Lyle tried to cast a spell, but his concentration failed him.

Bang. Bang . . . Bang . . . Bang . . . Bang . . . Bang.

Jeremiah was exhausted, he was panting, sweating, and Lyle still wasn't knocked out. Lyle's arms floated up at Jeremiah, weak and drifting aimlessly. His legs had stopped kicking. Was he concussed? Definitely. Was he conscious? Technically. And that wasn't good enough.

"Let me help you with that," said Allison. She had appeared beside Jeremiah.

Allison reached down and grabbed Lyle by the waist, Jeremiah rolling off. She lifted Lyle bodily off the ground, tossing him up on her shoulder. Lyle struggled meekly, still dizzy from the pounding Jeremiah had given him. Allison gripped Lyle's legs and whipped him forward in a high arc, Lyle's head snapping into the table so hard the wood split. Lyle's arms and legs suddenly went absolutely rigid, and his body curled slightly inward. Jeremiah could hear a sputtering sound from inside the helmet.

"Is he dead?" Allison asked Jeremiah.

"I don't know," he panted. "Maybe?"

Allison hoisted Lyle up again, stiff and unconscious, and whipped him into the table again. The stiffness disappeared in an instant and Lyle went completely limp.

"How about now?"

"That did it," gasped Bruno. "The thing in my ribs just stopped moving."

Jeremiah took the needlelike cultist dagger and placed the tip into the eyehole of Lyle's helmet.

"What are you doing?" asked Bruno, gingerly reaching into Delilah's bag.

"Not leaving anything to chance," said Jeremiah. He stomped down on the pommel.

CHAPTER SIXTY

More Meetings

S eriously? We seriously have to do this again?" asked Bruno. He drummed his
fingers on a table identical to the one they'd sat at mere hours earlier.

It was later the same night. The four of them were battered, bruised, and
exhausted, and they were seated in the exact same meeting room, although this
time the other seats were empty. It had taken a team of palace servants three hours
to remove the bodies and debris, to scrub blood out of the carpet and tapestries, to
replace the furniture, and figure out how to remove the abomination. There was still
evidence of the battle in damage to the drywall and textiles, but at least it was clean.

"Yes!" said Delilah. "This is one of those important events I was talking about,
and we need to discuss it with the stakeholders." Lyle's flames had burned the hair
off one side of her head, and the healing potions supplied by Empress Aubrianna
couldn't regrow it. Still, Jeremiah thought it looked pretty good on her.

"Hey," whispered Bruno, giving Jeremiah a nudge. "I don't know if I said this
before, but doin' Lyle like that, while he was unconscious? Just to be sure? That was
hard man. Really hard."

"It was surprisingly easy," said Jeremiah. There had been no doubt in his mind,
assuring Lyle's death was paramount.

"No, I mean—Dammit, Jay, don't be lame now—It was cold. You know? Real
killer stuff," said Bruno. He gave Jeremiah a severe face and approving nod.

"Thanks?" He had killed a lot of people and wasn't entirely sure why this one
was special to Bruno.

"It's just, you know, I'm sorry," said Bruno. Jeremiah wasn't sure what for, but he
took the apology. They were seldom offered by Bruno, and trying to get more details
would jeopardize the moment.

"No worries, it's what we do," said Jeremiah, returning the severe nod.

"That it is," said Burno, giving yet another severe nod, but this one while looking away from Jeremiah. That made it feel special, like it was now a given that they
were on the same page and didn't need to acknowledge each other.

A footwoman stepped into the room in an uncanny repeat from earlier in the
evening. "Presenting her eminence, Empress Aubrianna of Elminia."

This time, at least, instead of sweeping elegance the empress simply stomped in
and took a seat. She looked drained, but not nearly so much as her spymaster. Ka
dropped into her seat without so much as a glance toward Bruno, her face drawn
with stress.

"Thanks for still being here," said Empress Aubrianna. "I hope you don't mind if we dispense with formalities. Good. The security of this meeting room has been confirmed thrice by Ka, so we can speak freely. If I may begin—what the hell was that?"

"That was Lyle, the cult leader," said Jeremiah. "A valued member of your inner circle, it would seem, but also a man hellbent on bridging this world with the Abyss. The entire cult was in service of that goal."

"Mm-hmm," said the empress. "And if Counselor Fortune's report is to be believed, you single handedly infiltrated *and destroyed* this cult?"

"That's correct," said Jeremiah. "If you follow the directions Delilah provided, you can go to the undercity and see the evidence for yourself."

Ka cleared her throat. "Um, I wouldn't recommend that, actually. The team I sent to investigate just returned, and apparently there's some sort of massive amalgamation of body parts roaming around that doesn't take kindly to visitors. One of yours, necromancer?"

That was news to Jeremiah. He quickly scanned his mind any remnants of that solid block that had been the hundred-handed giant had required but found not a pebble remaining. "Uhh, I mean, it *was*. I'm sorry to say. It's rare for an undead to remain active after release, but this might be one of those moments."

He glanced at his friends. Allison looked horror-struck, but Delilah spoke up quickly. "I would take this opportunity to point out that, per our agreement to destroy the cult or procure information relating to it, we are under no obligation to make the area safe and therefore any remaining undead, monsters, or kobolds are beyond the scope of our mission."

Ka scowled, and Jeremiah continued before she could retort. "There's another thing you should know." He reached into the Giant's Bag and withdrew the empress's crown. "I recovered this from the cult's treasure vault."

Empress Aubrianna's expression remained neutral as she gingerly accepted the crown. She removed the identical one she had been wearing and inspected them side by side. Then she placed the new crown atop her head and turned to Ka. "You're in trouble."

To Jeremiah's surprise, Ka dropped her head to her hands, flushing a deep red that nearly matched her hair. He felt a surge of sympathy—it was a rough night to be the empress's head of security.

"So, we're done, right?" asked Bruno. "We destroyed the cult, returned your stolen crown—which you didn't even know was gone—revealed one of your inner circle is a demon summoning traitor and saved your city? We good?"

Delilah winced and closed her eyes. "I swear to god why do I even bring you to these?"

But the empress merely nodded. "You may rest assured the empire settles its debts amicably. You have indeed accomplished the task set before you, and thus the conspiracy in Dramir will be resolved."

"Without bloodshed," Jeremiah reminded her.

The empress regarded him with a raised eyebrow and a faint smile. "Of course. We wouldn't want you to suffer the guilt of *violence* on your conscience."

"Thank you," said Jeremiah, pretending not to hear her sarcasm.

"Finally, allow me to present to you all a token of gratitude," said Empress Aubrianna.

Ka stood and approached Delilah with a small medal box. She opened it, but as Delilah reached toward it, she cleared her throat loudly, interrupting the motion.

"It's a black ops award, you only get to see it," whispered Allison. "You take pride in knowing you were awarded one." Ka continued around the table to allow Allison to view the medal. Allison gazed at it thoughtfully for a moment, then nodded, and Ka continued.

"B-but . . . I want a medal," said Delilah. Her eyes followed Ka around the table.

Jeremiah peered into the box. Lying within was a silver disc threaded on white ribbon. They lacked engravings or decorative elements. He followed Allison's lead, observing the medal for what seemed an appropriate amount of time, then nodded for Ka to continue on.

"You military types are so weird," said Bruno, after completing his turn in the ritual. "So, are we done here?"

"Oh-my-god-stop-talking-for-two-seconds," breathed Delilah.

"Nearly," said Empress Aubrianna. "Before we conclude, however, I wanted to extend my personal appreciation. Mr. Thorn, you and your friends have performed admirably under a range of situations. Would you have any interest in joining the employ of my regime? I am confident we would be able to make use of your abilities in a variety of missions."

He could see Delilah preparing to respond, but Jeremiah decided to speak up first. "Thanks, but no thanks. With all due respect, I've done enough in service of crowns—both yours and that of Dramir. Let us know if you need us in the future and maybe we can negotiate a deal then, but otherwise, we have our own lives to rebuild."

The empress nodded. "I understand. In that case, thank you all for what you have done here, and for your indefinite continued discretion." Her gaze traveled over their faces again, one by one, lingering just a second longer on Jeremiah's. "You are dismissed."

It was a strange feeling to have nothing he should be doing. His things were packed, a trivial task since he'd been carrying most of his worldly possessions in his pockets for the last several months. Bruno, Allison, and Delilah were out tying up loose ends with their respective positions and cover stories, leaving him to try to remember how to relax.

The apartment was quiet. The entire city had felt quiet, somehow, in the week since he'd destroyed the enchantment circle. That feverish hum had dissipated, and Elminia seemed to feel just as lost for what to do as Jeremiah did now. Of course people still went through the motions that momentum gave them, work and bustle and the like, but that desperate energy had gone out of it.

Jeremiah rolled over on his mattress and pet Gus. He supposed he could visit his old cellmates, say his final goodbyes. Bruno had easily sold the idea that the cult had killed him. The thought made his stomach turn. Monty was gone, and now that the events of the underground had had time to settle in his mind, he kept drifting back to his memories of the murder. Or rather, the lack of memories—try as he might to grasp what had happened, the further he got from that night, the more his recollection was reduced to the facts, rather than the lived experience.

"I killed Monty," he said out loud, trying to feel the horror he knew he should. Gus shivered at his words, but Jeremiah himself felt numb to it. That numbness disturbed him. Committing a cold-blooded murder should not be a comfortable, forgettable affair. His lack of feeling felt wrong.

Jeremiah sat up in bed and grabbed his enchanting gear. He had to distract himself, and if he wanted to start pulling his weight as an enchanter back in Dramir, he had better keep his skills sharp.

The enchanting tools were comfortable in his hand, the plates inviting, with their smooth, flat surfaces. It was child's play to etch the runes, he hardly had to think to connect them together. He filled the surface of the plate in a matter of minutes, drawing quick, confident lines to form the minuscule runes.

Heat and Pause and Pause and Pause and Pause and Pause and Pause and Heat

Would it really be that simple? Jeremiah looped the enchantment back on itself. Never before had he managed to cram so many runes onto a single plate. He was doing so much more with the same amount of space, just by keeping his runes neat and organized.

He dropped the plate on the floor and charged the diagram. The temperature of the metal increased rapidly, then stopped. Jeremiah could feel the heat radiating off it, the Pauses interrupting the Heat command just before it grew hot enough to deform the runes, then the temperature spiked again as the enchantment looped around and continued running.

"Huh," said Jeremiah. Gus repeated the sound in a toad's croak. This would work. He could adjust the number of Pause and Heat runes to calibrate the stability or even change the maximum temperature of the plate. And of course, a different material would be able to withstand much higher temperatures before destroying the enchantment.

"Dammit is that all I had to do?! That's stupid! That better not really be the answer!"

Gus hopped into his lap and went to sleep.

CHAPTER SIXTY-ONE

Intervention

The night before their departure for Dramir, Jeremiah paced in front of Allison's door. Bruno and Delilah were out on errands, and there was one more crucial question that he needed to answer. He highly suspected it was going to get ugly, but he had learned that sometimes ugly things needed to get done.

After strengthening his resolve one last time, he rapped quickly on Allison's door. She answered.

"Hey, J—"

"What did you give me?" Jeremiah asked, his voice steady and strong.

"A combat drug, one we used in the military," Allison answered right away.

"Is it permanent? Did it make me do what I did?" asked Jeremiah.

"No. It doesn't last long, least not with the amount I gave you. It only gave you a little edge to do what you needed to do with Monty, it would have long worn off by the time you were underground," said Allison. She leaned away from Jeremiah.

"You use it, don't you?" asked Jeremiah.

"I have. And maybe, yes, I use it from time to time," said Allison.

"I need you to promise me you won't use it again," said Jeremiah.

Allison's look of confusion broke into a half smile, waiting to see if Jeremiah was going to reveal what he was saying as a joke. "I'm not going to do that Jay. Sometimes it's something I need."

"It's cowardly," said Jeremiah.

Allison's eyebrows rose, and her jaw set. "I understand that you've been through a lot, Jay, so I'm not going to dignify that with the response typical of calling a fighter a coward."

"I need to know that people matter to you," said Jeremiah. "I need to know that we're not just a resource to you."

"Jay, how can you say that?" said Allison. The chair screeched as she stood.

"You've done black ops before. You told Bruno that you've killed people in their sleep, back when we attacked the bandit camp—"

"Jay, stop," said Allison.

"—and that you could do it again. You kicked a man off the wall in Dramir for refusing to fight, to set an example. Were you on that drug then? Answer me now."

"That is none of your business!" Allison shouted at him.

Jeremiah didn't wilt in the face of her anger. "I need to know if you keep that stuff on you! Do you have some on you right now? I need to know if you're just a fist full of that stuff from becoming like the cultists, capable of anything without remorse!"

"You're a civilian Jay! You don't know what it means to serve, okay?! To do the work that needs to be done for something greater than yourself! Just stop!" Allison shouted. She was loud, damn loud when she wanted to be.

Jeremiah stepped around her and went into Delilah and Allison's room, grabbing the Giant's Bag.

"What are you doing? Put that down!" Allison yelled, moving toward him.

But before she could stop him, he stuck his hand in the bag and pulled out a fistful of the same resiny weed that Allison had given him. It was at least thrice as much as she had given him.

Allison clenched her fists at him and growled, "Jay, of course I have some! And it *was* in a box!"

"I don't want you to have this," said Jeremiah. "I barely remember killing Monty. Am I wrong to assume it helps you not remember what you do as well?"

Allison's face of rage fractured and downgraded into frustration. "Yes, that is another thing that it's good for. Better than trying to forget with booze or . . . other stuff."

"I need you to remember. I need you to be able to face what you've done. With a face full of tears. Till you can't do it anymore, if that's what happens," said Jeremiah.

"Jay, you are not going to lecture me on this," said Allison. She stepped into the room and began advancing on him as she spoke. "Congrats on killing your *first* child, but until you've walked the path of service you do not get to tell what I need to do! I have fought, and killed, and butchered, and sabotaged, and terrorized, all in the name of my kingdom. I do what I need to do to survive. Do you understand me?!"

"What's the name of the drug?" asked Jeremiah, unflinching in the face of her wrath.

"What?" asked Allison, surprised at the sudden question.

"What. Is the name. Of the drug," Jeremiah asked again.

Allison's nostrils flared and she stopped her advance. A hand went up to fiddle with her hair and was quickly put down again.

"S-Soulrot. It's called Soulrot," said Allison, deflating.

"Are the effects permanent if you abuse it?" asked Jeremiah.

"It gets . . . Jay, this isn't—" She stopped when she met his gaze, unflinching but sympathetic. "It can take a long time to get back to normal. After a while. Maybe the ceiling lowers a little. Just a little," said Allison.

"Enough that you've noticed," said Jeremiah. He put the clump of weed back in the bag.

"Yeah, maybe," murmured Allison.

Jeremiah cautiously approached her and took her hands in his. "Listen, Al, I'm not saying this because I'm angry. I'm saying this because I want what's best for you, okay? And that stuff isn't what's best for you."

She yanked her hands away and sat down on the bed with a thump. "You don't know what's best for me Jay. I chose a life of sacrifice and service when I joined the military. I believed in it so much that I was chosen for certain missions. Ones normal soldiers can't handle."

"The black ops," said Jeremiah.

"Well, we'd call them special operations, but yeah," said Allison. "It was an honor to be trusted by my kingdom for such duties."

Jeremiah let the conversation rest for a moment. He sat down next to her and leaned against her a little, she returned the lean.

"You've done some stuff, huh?" said Jeremiah.

"Yeah," whispered Allison.

"I'm sorry."

"Don't be. I made choices, same as you."

But were they? Were they the same choices? thought Jeremiah. He dashed the thoughts away, that way lay judgment.

"Do you want to talk about it?" asked Jeremiah.

Allison chuckled. "You don't have that kind of time."

"I'd make time for you. You know that," said Jeremiah.

Allison tilted her head to rest it on Jeremiah's despite being taller. "Yeah, I know. But the legend of the Hungry Dark isn't something I'm ready to talk about now, if ever."

"The Hungry Dark?" said Jeremiah.

"Heh, yeah, we don't get to choose our names," said Allison.

They continued to lean against each other for a while, letting the silence and weight of what they had discussed percolate.

"Will the nightmares come back?" Jeremiah asked Allison. He was really hoping they wouldn't.

"Oh yeah," said Allison. "But they'll feel different. Usually. Hey, Jay?"

"Yeah?"

"If you ever imply I'm a coward again, I will actually kick the shit out of you in public. In front of God and everyone."

"Yeah, sorry about that. I still want you to stop taking that stuff," said Jeremiah.

"The next time I think I need it, I'll remember that. But no promises, it's a combat drug, not recreational. A girl's gotta do," said Allison.

"I understand," said Jeremiah.

"Glad you're home, Jay."

"Me too, Al."

The spires of the palace of Elminia sank out of sight, leaving only her dusky clouds of smoke smeared across the horizon. The scene was in some ways eerily similar to the way they'd arrived, rumbling along the country road toward Dramir in a horse-drawn carriage, but instead of the tension and anticipation of the unknown mission ahead, they were heading home.

Or at least, whatever counted as home now. "So where exactly are we staying?" asked Jeremiah.

"I found us a place to stay in the merchant's quarter," said Delilah. "It's just a few blocks from where the house was, hopefully it'll be a nice place to stay while the empress undoes whatever damage she can."

"Still bugs me that we never did find out who was behind it all," said Bruno.

"Me too," said Allison. "What's to stop them from starting everything back up as soon as the attention from the empress dies down?"

"Spymaster Ka assures me it will be taken care of in a *permanent*, nonlethal manner," said Delilah. "Although she did still seem annoyed about the nonlethal part."

Bruno chuckled. "Yeah, well, she's had a tough week. Probably would have been nice to take out her frustrations on some frumped-up foreign nobles. Although I will say she did give me some good ideas for getting into her line of work."

"Considering becoming a spymaster?" asked Allison.

"Seems like a cushy job," said Bruno. "I just run my usual information operation with the biggest strongarm the kingdom has to offer."

Delilah beamed at him. "That's a wonderful idea! You'd have such an important impact as part of King Hector's cabinet."

"It might take a while to achieve, of course," said Bruno. "I'm not even sure Dramir *has* a spymaster."

"No one's sure," said Delilah.

"Well, I've been thinking about creating a training hall," said Allison. "One specializing in fighting giant monsters. Turns out I hate getting picked up. I really, *really* hate getting picked up."

"Ah, so we're not exactly going to be raking it in, is what I'm hearing," said Bruno. "Guess I shouldn't hang up my adventuring gear just yet."

Delilah counted off on her fingers. "A bureaucrat, a teacher, and a newly licensed defense attorney probably won't be rolling in wealth, even without the conspiracy draining us," she said. "Unless Jay is about to announce his new career enchanting things for the crown?"

"I—Wait, is that a real job?" Jeremiah asked.

"Court mage is a job," said Delilah. "But it's definitely more about politicking than magicking. You interested?"

"Hard pass," said Jeremiah. "I've had enough politicking at this point to last several lifetimes. What I was thinking was taking a stab at some real enchanting. Not just working for Thurok and churning out the same diagrams everyone always wants."

"Ugh, he's an artist now," groaned Bruno. "Glad you got some practice starving, Jay, you're gonna need it."

"You never know, the weather might get nice enough for a stroll," said Delilah.

The others looked at her with confusion, but she stared out the window and pretended not to notice. Something niggled at the back of Jeremiah's brain, like what she said was important, but he couldn't remember why.

"Anyway," he said, deciding whatever it was could wait till later. "I want to see what I can learn from Lyle's journal. If he's right that there's more circles out there, we may have a much bigger problem on our hands than anyone realizes."

"Ah," said Bruno. "So adventuring gear very much still on, got it."

"About that," said Allison. "We need a crash course in mage killing. I didn't like how easily Lyle was able to take us out."

"Uhh," said Jeremiah. "My own training didn't exactly cover how to murder people like me."

"Not a problem, we'll develop a curriculum together," said Allison.

"And I don't suppose it matters how deeply uncomfortable that makes me?"

"Not at all."

Jeremiah leaned his head back against the carriage wall and let his friends' voices wash over him as they launched into a detailed discussion of how they personally would go about disarming, restraining, dismembering or otherwise incapacitating him. It was good to be home.

EPILOGUE

The sun was rising over Dramir. Despite the cramped quarters of their new, hopefully temporary, apartment, it did have a balcony, with an excellent view of the sunrise. Jeremiah gave a pat to the dungeon core, pulsing gently on the tiny table where it had been keeping him company during his enchanting, and turned to watch the sun come up, leaning on the railing to stretch. He had been out there for a long time.

"Made any progress understanding that thing?" asked Delilah.

"The dungeon core? Kind of. I can tell the broad strokes of how it feels now. But I think it really needs a place of its own to be able to settle in. The Gilded Tomb might be hard to beat.

"I can relate," said Delilah. "This place just isn't home."

"Yeah, I miss our old place too," said Jeremiah. He'd found himself avoiding the part of town that had once been home.

They stared at the sunrise together for a while.

"So that Abyss stuff," said Delilah. "Do you think one of those circles could be here in Dramir?"

"If so, it's not nearly as active as the one in Elminia," said Jeremiah. "It's almost hard to remember now, right? That madness enveloping everyone. Impulsivity, making decisions we normally wouldn't . . . it's almost hard to know what was us and what was the Abyss, you know?"

Delilah nodded. "Yeah, I understand. It's okay. I'm not going to hold you to anything you said then. You weren't in your right mind."

Jeremiah stared hard at the rising sun, trying to puzzle out what she meant. "Well, no. I'm not going to hold *you* to anything you said. Because *you* weren't in *your* right mind."

Delilah glared at him. "What? How dare you say I wasn't in my right mind? I was perfectly in control of my faculties. You were the one going on crazy missions on your own and taking needless risks."

"All my risks made perfect sense!" said Jeremiah. "Wait, are you saying you meant everything you said while we were in Elminia?"

"Yes, of course, I always mean what I say." Delilah was starting to look flustered. "But you're saying you still meant the things *you* said?"

"Yes, obviously," said Jeremiah. "So, you still want to go . . . you know, do something? Together?"

"Yes, obviously!" said Delilah.

Jeremiah turned back to the sunrise. Somehow this outcome had failed to enter into his plan for this conversation.

"So . . ." said Delilah.

"Sew buttons," said Jeremiah. He glanced over and found her looking at him. Her soft smile, glowing in the warm hues of a rising sun, stole the air from his lungs. "You wear the sunrise nicely."

Delilah's smile widened into a grin for a moment, then she compressed it down into pursed lips, though the grin still threatened to escape. She turned back to the balcony. "Again with that. Why do you have to be so corny?"

"'Cause you like it," said Jeremiah.

"Ugh, I know. That's easily the worst part," said Delilah.

"So, even though I did all that stuff. Even though I'm a necromancer again, you're still . . . interested?" asked Jeremiah.

"Why would that matter?" asked Delilah.

"It's just that last time we talked, you said that me choosing *not* to be a necromancer was a big part of how you felt."

"I did say that," said Delilah. "Being a human that turned down power made you interesting. But honestly—accepting the responsibility and consequences of your power? That makes you *attractive*."

"I guess being a necromancer has its perks," said Jeremiah. Now he was trying to restrain his own dumb smile.

"And you're okay with all the stuff I did?" asked Delilah.

Huh? What had she done, exactly? Jeremiah racked his brain for a long moment, during which time Delilah kept fidgeting, which was so cute it was almost an incentive to keep thinking. But she was clearly suffering, so he relented. "Okay, I'm stumped. What have you done?"

She stared at him like he was stupid. "I lost our house? All our money? I got you mutilated on the streets? I nearly got Allison killed by Furnace Curse and because of that I got Bruno's hand cut off?"

"Uhh . . ." said Jeremiah. *We're going to need to revisit this, aren't we?* he thought. "I forgive you."

Delilah sagged with relief, rubbing her palms into her eyes. "You have no idea how happy I am to hear that."

"Oh, by the way, I have a little gift for you," said Jeremiah.

"So, you're the spoiling type, huh?" said Delilah with a cautious smile.

"Well, it's nothing new exactly, but I've been working on it all night," said Jeremiah. He picked the plate off the table and held it behind his back as he turned toward her. "And I finally got it to . . . Whoa."

Delilah was backlit by the sunrise now, posing casually against the rail. She looked actually radiant. "What's wrong?"

Jeremiah had never considered that a woman might know how to pose on purpose. Delilah was teaching him a valuable lesson. "Nothing. So, uh. Here." He held out an enchanting plate toward her.

"Feels like we've been here before." Delilah stepped toward him. "But something's missing . . ."

"Yeah, but it, uh, I got it to . . ." He trailed off as she moved to stand in front of him, smooth and languid and bathed in golden sunlight, she looked like a gentle flame. The plate wasn't holding her attention.

"Got it to . . . ?" Delilah, leaning toward him. Her eyes fluttered, her head tilted.

Jeremiah felt himself drawn toward her like she had a gravity all her own. "To . . . work . . ."

"What!" she shouted in his face, making him jump and nearly drop the plate. "The hot plate? It works?"

"Yes, yes, I got it to work, it holds a stable temperature and everything," said Jeremiah rapidly. "Now, where were we?"

"Dammit, Jay, I gave you one instruction! You only had to do one thing when you got it to work!" Delilah snatched the plate from his hands and shoved past him. "It's-lovely-weather-for-a-stroll-let's-go-for-a-walk-right-now!"

"Okay, okay! Just let me get—"

"Now!"

Simultaneously flustered, confused, and oddly pleased with himself, Jeremiah walked with Delilah into the light of a new day.

ABOUT THE AUTHOR

Jack Pembroke is the author of the Necromancer's End series, originally released on Royal Road. He brings his twenty-five years as a Dungeon Master to the page in stories of adventure and kinship featuring strong characters. He believes in struggle as a primary source of drama and that weaknesses make characters (like humans) more believable. Pembroke also has a dog; he's a good boy.

JOIN THE FELLOWSHIP
follow us on our socials

 podiumentertainment.com

 @podiumentertainment

 /podiumentertainment

 @podium_ent

 @podiumentertainment